RESURRECTION

ILLUSTRATED WITH WOOD ENGRAVINGS BY

FRITZ EICHENBERG

RESURRECTION

A NOVEL IN THREE PARTS

by LEO TOLSTOY

THE TRANSLATION BY LEO WIENER REVISED AND
EDITED FOR THIS EDITION BY F. D. REEVE
WITH AN INTRODUCTION BY ERNEST J. SIMMONS
AND ILLUSTRATED WITH WOOD ENGRAVINGS BY
FRITZ EICHENBERG

THE HERITAGE PRESS · NEW YORK

INTRODUCTION

DURING THE SECOND HALF OF 1899 the atmosphere of the Tolstoy household was tense over the mighty effort to complete *Resurrection*, which was then appearing serially in a magazine. Racing against time in the face of anguished telegrams from the editor for the next week's copy, the seventy-one-year-old author, deserting his family, shut himself up in his study for days on end, taking his meals at odd hours, and refusing to see visitors. Always the exacting artist, he kept mangling successive sets of proofs, repeatedly rewriting whole sections, and hurrying off last-minute changes for an installment just about to go to press. Fresh manuscript chapters in his almost illegible handwriting were cleanly copied by members of the family and their guests. Duplicate sets of corrected proof had to be prepared for translators for foreign publication. Urgent cablegrams and letters from abroad offered huge sums for first publishing rights. Finally, on December 18, Tolstoy noted in his diary: "Completed *Resurrection*. Not good, uncorrected, hurried, but it is done with and I'm no longer interested."

Tolstoy's sense of relief may be partly attributed to the fact that he had been working away intermittently on this novel for more than ten years. The theme had been supplied by his good friend, the eminent jurist and writer, A. F. Koni. He told Tolstoy the story of a man who had come to him for legal aid. As a youth this man had seduced a pretty orphan girl of sixteen who had been taken into the home of a relative of the young man when her parents had died. Once her benefactress observed the girl's pregnant condition, she drove her away. Abandoned by her seducer, the girl, after hopeless attempts to earn an honest livelihood, became a prostitute. Detected in stealing money from one of her drunken "guests" in a brothel, the girl was arrested. On the jury that tried the case, fate placed her seducer. His conscience awakened to the injustice of his behavior, he decided to marry the girl, who was sentenced to four months in prison. Koni concluded his story by relating that the couple did actually marry, but shortly after her sentence expired, the girl died from typhus.

The tale deeply moved Tolstoy, and its effect may well have been connected with an acute stirring of conscience. For shortly before his death he told his biographer of two seductions in his own life which he could somehow never forget. "The second," he said, "was the crime I committed with the servant Masha in my aunt's house. She was a virgin. I seduced her, and she was dismissed and perished."

Over the years, however, Tolstoy's efforts to cast this story of real life into literary form were repeatedly interrupted by the manifold activities and extensive polemical writings growing out of his spiritual revelation. Only with some reluctance did he devote his few free hours to the creation of fiction, and it is possible that *Resurrection* might never have been finished if it had not been for a special set of circumstances. The government's cruel persecution of the Dukhobors, a peasant sect that practiced a form of Christian communism not far removed from Tolstoy's own preaching, and among other things rejected military service, had reached a crucial stage. For several years Tolstoy and his followers had been aiding the Dukhobors. Now it was decided that the most practical remedy for their misfortunes was to have them emigrate. The Russian government was willing and Canada agreed to accept them pretty much on their own terms. The problem was to obtain money to transport and settle in Canada some twelve thousand Dukhobors. Tolstoy helped to organize a campaign to raise funds. Although he had surrendered the copyrights of all his works written since his spiritual change and allowed anyone to publish them free, he now decided to sell a novel and devote the proceeds to the fund to aid the emigration of the Dukhobors. Going over his portfolio of unfinished manuscripts, he settled upon *Resurrection* as the one calculated to earn the most money, and he set to work with a will to complete this long novel.

Tolstoy had calculated correctly. The first full-length novel in twenty years from the celebrated author of *War and Peace* and *Anna Karenina*, a man now universally known also as a great religious reformer and moral thinker, was an event of keen international interest. While *Resurrection* was appearing serially in Russia, simultaneous publication in translation was arranged in England, France, Germany, and the United States. Partly because of the previous renunciation of his copyright privileges, much pirating went on; this caused Tolstoy a great deal of embarrassment in the light of the first publication rights he had sold to various firms in an effort to realize the maximum income on behalf of the Dukhobors. Pirated copies of the novel quickly appeared in Russia; twelve different translations came out in German alone in 1900; and fifteen editions, under several authorized and unauthorized imprints, accumulated in France during 1899 and 1900. Extreme liberties were often taken in these foreign versions. When the French readers of the serialized translation in *Echo de Paris* complained that the love scenes, which they relished, were too infrequent, the businesslike editor had no scruples about omitting the next regular installment and substituting for it one in which the hero and heroine were again occupied with each other. On the other hand the editor of *Cosmopolitan*, which had bought the first serial rights in the United States, did not hesitate to tone down or delete love passages which he thought might offend the sensibilities of this magazine's respectable middle-class readers.

The Russian censor caused additional trouble and not a little anguish to Tolstoy, who in some instances protested the deletions of this high executioner of words. The censor, however, could hardly be expected in those days to tolerate the author's sacrilegious barbs against the church or his exposure of the way prisoners were treated in Siberia. In fact, very few of the many chapters of the novel escaped the censor's dreaded blue pencil, and it is estimated that he made 497 separate alterations or deletions in the text. Not until 1936 did the complete and unaltered text of *Resurrection* appear in Russian, in the huge Jubilee Edition of Tolstoy's works.

In the course of writing the novel Tolstoy did considerable research, reading many books and articles—he read six books on prostitution alone—and he consulted experts on legal procedure, visited jails and talked with convicts. Once he got fairly into the work it absorbed him completely and he told his wife that since *War and Peace* he had never been so powerfully gripped by the creative urge. Koni's slender tale served only as the initial inspiration for the erection of a huge, complex superstructure; and as in the case of Tolstoy's other two large novels, the story element grew to formidable length, with numerous ramifications. There were several quite different beginnings, and again and again he cast out themes and introduced entirely new ones. Even such a small detail as the description of the external appearance of the heroine exists in as many as twenty variants. There were six separate drafts of *Resurrection*, and before Tolstoy had finished his extensive revisions, he had piled up enough rejected material to fill a volume almost as large as the novel itself.

As in Tolstoy's previous full-length novels, there is a great deal of autobiographical matter in *Resurrection*. In many respects the hero, Dmítri Nekhlyúdov, resembles his creator, and a number of the other characters are plainly modeled on people Tolstoy knew. For example, Topórov is a thinly disguised and unflattering portrait of the sinister and celebrated Procurator of the Holy Synod, K. P. Pobedonóstsev. Some of the autobiographical aspects are curiously stressed in an interesting passage in the diary of Tolstoy's wife. While wearing her eyes out over recopying his labyrinthine manuscript, she vented her spleen against *Resurrection* largely because her husband had refused first publishing rights for her edition of his works—he had previously signed over to her the right to publish for money anything he wrote before his spiritual revelation, that is, before 1881. "I torment myself," she wrote, "over the fact that Leo Nikolayevich, a seventy-year-old man, describes the scene of fornication between the serving girl and the officer with the peculiar relish of a gastronome eating something tasty. I know, because he himself told me about this in detail, that in this scene he is describing his own intimate relations with his sister's serving-girl. . . . I'm also tormented by the fact that I see in the hero, Nekhlyúdov, portrayed as progressing from his downfall to his moral resurrection, Leo Nikolayevich, who thinks this very thing about himself."

Abroad, especially in England and the United States, *Resurrection* was enthusiastically received and enjoyed a larger sale than any other work by Tolstoy up to that time. Though some conservative foreign critics expressed indignation over what seemed like excessively frank and un-Victorian treatment of sex and over the novelist's contemptuous regard for the conventions of law and order and the sacredness of the church, progressive critics showered praises on perhaps the only man in Russia at that time who had the courage to expose in fiction the evils that beset his country. In Russia the publication of *Resurrection* was an event transcending its artistic significance. Something of the widespread excitement aroused by the novel as it appeared serially is reflected in a letter to Tolstoy by his friend V. V. Stasov, a distinguished art critic: "How all of us here rejoiced when we learned that the chapters of *Resurrection* will not be 60 or 80 but 100 or more! Without exception all are saying on every side: 'Ah, there will be more, more will be added! May God grant that there will be more and more!'"

II

Resurrection has naturally forced comparison with those supreme works *War and Peace* and *Anna Karenina*, and it must be admitted that it falls below the lofty artistic achievements of these earlier novels. However, its best things, artistically speaking, belong to the narrative method of Tolstoy's earlier fiction rather than to the compressed, direct, and stylistically unadorned manner of the later period after *What Is Art?* was published. In *Resurrection* there is that same wealth of precise, realistic detail which conveys the appearance of indubitable actuality to imagined situations, as well as a roundness, a completeness, and the vitality of life to his characters. In its enchanting setting the account of the first pure love of Nekhlyúdov and Katyúsha Máslova, certainly the finest section of the novel, is all compounded of that same wonderful, elusive quality that transformed the girlish loves of Natasha in *War and Peace* into the uncommunicable poetry of youthful dreams. Tolstoy never did anything more delightfully infectious in fiction than the scene of the Easter service in the village church where the young hero and heroine, after the traditional Russian greeting, "Christ is risen," exchange kisses with the carefree rapture of mingled religious exaltation and dawning affinity for each other.

There is much of the old master also in Tolstoy's handling of the trial scene, in the portrayal of high society in both Moscow and St. Petersburg, and in the re- markably realistic treatment of the brutal march of the convicts to Siberia. In this area, however, the satirical representations of society are much less objective, and more grim and didactically purposeful than in *War and Peace* and *Anna Karenina*. Herein, indeed, lies the major artistic fault of Tolstoy's last full-length novel.

While he was writing *War and Peace*, Tolstoy, troubled by the thought that the radical critics would attack him for failing to expose the faults of the privileged classes and the dark misery of the peasantry in his work, wrote to a friend to defend his avoidance of social problems: "The aims of art are incommensurable (as they say in mathematics) with social aims. The aim of an artist is not to resolve a question irrefutably, but to compel one to love life in all its manifestations, and these are inexhaustible. If I were told that I could write a novel in which I could indisputably establish as true my point of view on all social questions, I would not dedicate two hours to such a work; but if I were told that what I wrote would be read twenty years from now by those who are children today, and that they would weep and laugh over it and fall in love with the life in it, then I would dedicate all my existence and all my powers to it."

Some thirty years later Tolstoy turned his back on this admirable credo of relative objectivity in art in writing *Resurrection*—an unashamedly purpose novel. To be sure, most great novels are in one sense or another purpose novels, but the purpose is sublimated in a depiction of life free of any special pleading that distorts the essential artistic unity of the whole. In *Resurrection* Tolstoy's purpose of con- demning the violence of government, the injustice of man-made laws, and the hypocrisy of the church, and of pleading the Biblical injunction to judge not that you be not judged, obtrudes in a rather scholastic manner throughout the novel.

In fact, *Resurrection* is in many respects an amazingly accurate portrayal of the spiritual biography of Tolstoy, and though this may detract from it as an artistic performance, it provides rich and authoritative material for all who wish to understand the tremendous moral and religious struggle of one of the foremost thinkers in the latter half of the nineteenth century. For the essence of much that Tolstoy thought and suffered during and after his spiritual travail is condensed in the pages of this novel.

Nekhlyúdov's youthful idealism, forgotten in a subsequent period of debauchery in the army and in high society, which in turn is followed by a spiritual crisis, moral suffering, and an intense search for the meaning of life, is a pattern of development that Tolstoy himself experienced. Although there are certain autobiographical elements in the immediate cause of the crisis, the soul-searing confrontation of Nekhlyúdov with the prostitute Katyúsha Máslova at her trial for robbery and murder, ten years after he seduced her as a pure young girl, is based on the stuff of Koni's real-life story. But the handling of the theme from this point on is done entirely in terms of the religious, moral, and social convictions that Tolstoy eventually arrived at after his own conversion.

Despite this rather doctrinaire approach, the resolution of the future relations between Nekhlyúdov and Katyúsha is worked out with considerable psychological subtlety. The hero recognizes, as does Katyúsha after being unjustly convicted, that his initial determination to follow her to Siberia and marry her is simply an effort of self-sacrifice to atone for having started her on her wayward path. Before this action can come from the heart, before it can be purged of every aspect of self-interest, sentimentality, and conscious do-goodism, he must undergo his own Golgotha on the way to achieving a new faith where practice of the Golden Rule is instinctive and not calculated. His example and patient ministrations also begin to work a moral change in Katyúsha, and this transformation is completed by her harsh prison experiences in the course of which she learns from some of her fellow convicts, especially among the political prisoners, the true dignity of man. Katyúsha's original pure love for Nekhlyúdov is restored. Here, in the struggle between the truth of the moralist and the truth of the artist in Tolstoy, the artist prevails, and he makes no concession to the conventional happy ending of virtue rewarded. Sensing that she will only be a hindrance to the work that Nekhlyúdov must do in the world in living according to his new faith, Katyúsha gives up this happiness by deciding to share in marriage the life of one of her fellow prisoners who loves her with an entirely platonic love. Sex, indeed, is the inevitable victim of the higher synthesis of the Tolstoyan life of the spirit.

In the many scenes, often brilliantly realized, in the courts, the prisons, in Nekhlyúdov's dealings with his peasants, and in the homes of high society, rarely is the moralizing element unadorned by abundant trappings of real life. However, these scenes, through which Nekhlyúdov sometimes moves like a somnambulist, often appear to be contrived indictments of various aspects of Russian society designed to explain and justify the hero's spiritual resurrection. For every abuse revealed and for every moral corrective administered, chapter and verse may be found in the various controversial books and articles that Tolstoy had already written on these subjects. The positions taken are argued with all his consummate skill, and irony and paradox are employed most effectively. Yet, in some of these passages, Tolstoy, either as the omniscient author or through the mouths of his characters, seems to be searching for absolutes in a world of incomplete knowledge and imperfect men. Occasionally there are lapses of taste, as in the blasphemously satiric account of the Russian Orthodox Church service, and at least once he fails to grasp the historic significance and political thinking of a whole group of characters he introduces—the revolutionary intelligentsia.

Among the scores of secondary characters in *Resurrection*, hardly any lack that baffling artistic touch of definition and individualization which dazzled readers and critics alike in the great novels of Tolstoy's earlier period. However fleeting their roles may be, the judges and jurymen at the trial, the amazing women inmates of Katyúsha's cell, and the various political prisoners are brought to life with a few deft strokes of description and psychological observation. And still more memorably characterized are those creatures of high society and official Moscow and St. Petersburg life—the Korchágin family, especially the mother and her daughter Missy, who hopes to marry Nekhlyúdov; the cynical advocate Fanárin, who symbolizes the irrelevance of justice in the courts of law; the Vice-Governor Máslennikov, whose official duties are regarded as mere appendages to social climbing; and the General's pretty wife Mariette, whose delicate suggestions of a liaison with Nekhlyúdov he regarded as a more reprehensible and much less honest approach than that of the streetwalker who accosted him.

The story of *Resurrection*, however, is overwhelmingly the story of Nekhlyúdov, who is imbued with his creator's instinct to discover the purpose of life. In the first part of the novel the hero emerges as a rather fascinating man of action who engages our sympathies in his developing personality. As a member of the gentry, Tolstoy's own class which he knew so well, Nekhlyúdov has many of the appealing traits found in Prince Andréi in *War and Peace* and Levin and Vronsky in *Anna Karenina*.

But unlike these characters, Nekhlyúdov is soon confronted by a crisis that transforms him into an intellectual Tolstoyan, a development that seems false to his nature, and more dictated by the author than by life. In the remainder of the novel he is more acted upon than active in a series of situations patently designed to aid him in his search for the meaning of life. And he finds it in the end, very much as Tolstoy did, in the Sermon on the Mount. "With that night there began for Nekhlyúdov an entirely new life," the novel concludes, "not so much because he entered it under new conditions, as because everything which happened to him after that assumed an entirely new meaning. The future will show how this new period of his life will end."

This hint at a sequel to the novel has some basis in fact, for shortly after he finished it, Tolstoy wrote in his diary: "I want terribly to write an artistic, not a dramatic, but an epic continuation of *Resurrection*: the peasant life of Nekhlyúdov." Apparently in his new existence the hero was to play the part of a peasant, perhaps a successful Tolstoyan peasant, which would have been unique in either fiction or life. But Tolstoy never lived to complete this grand design.

According to Tolstoy's principal criterion of real art, namely, infectiousness, which he developed in his treatise *What Is Art?*, *Resurrection* holds up quite well. That is, the novel deals with feelings profoundly expressed by the author and re-enacted so that they infect readers and cause them to share these feelings with him and with each other. And certainly more than any of his other novels, *Resurrection* fulfils Tolstoy's definition of the best art, for it evokes in us feelings of brotherly love and of the common purpose of the life of all humanity—a striving to achieve spiritual and moral perfection through service to others.

ERNEST J. SIMMONS

TABLE OF CONTENTS

BOOK THREE

THE CHIEF CHARACTERS

Prince Dmítri Ivánovich Nekhlyúdov (Mítenka)

Ekaterína Mikháylov[n]a Máslova (Katyúsha, Lyubóv, Lyúbka)

Simón Petróv Kartínkin ⎫
Evfímiya Ivánov[n]a Bóchkova ⎬ *co-defendants*

Ferapónt Emilyánovich Smyelkóv, *a merchant*

Pyótr Gerásimovich, *a schoolteacher*

Karolína Albértovna Kitáeva, *a madam*

Sófya Ivánovna ⎫
Mar[í]ya Ivánovna ⎬ *Nekhlyúdov's aunts*

Matryóna Pávlovna ⎫
Tíkhon ⎬ *their servants*

Agraféna Petróvna ⎫
Kornéi ⎬ *Nekhlyúdov's servants*

Prince Korchágin

Princess Sófya Vasílevna

Princess Mar[í]ya (Missy)

Shénbok, *a fellow-officer*

Natálya Ivánovna Ragózhinskaya (Natásha), *Nekhlyúdov's sister*

Ignáti Nikíforovich Ragózhinski, *her husband*

Máslennikov, *a government official*

Bogodúkhovskaya ⎫   ⎧ Márya Pávlovna Shchetínina
Shústova   ⎪   ⎪ Emíliya Rántseva
Koroblyóva   ⎬ *prisoners* ⎨ Markél Kondrátev
Kryltsóv   ⎪   ⎪ Novodvórov
Simonsón   ⎭   ⎩ Makár Dyévkin

PRONUNCIATION

The accent mark indicates the stressed syllable. Vowels have approximately the Continental value. A Y before a vowel is always pronounced like the Y in English YET; thus the hero's name, *Nekhlyúdov*, sounds roughly like NYECK-*lyou*-DUF, the sound of the middle syllable approximating that of the italicized part of WIL*l you*.

"Then came Peter to him, and said, Lord, how oft shall my brother sin against me, and I forgive him? till seven times?

"Jesus saith unto him, I say not unto thee, Until seven times; but, Until seventy times seven." (Matt. xviii. 21–22.)

"And why beholdest thou the mote that is in thy brother's eye, but considerest not the beam that is in thine own eye?" (Matt. vii. 3.)

"He that is without sin among you, let him first cast a stone at her." (John viii. 7.)

"The disciple is not above his master: but every one that is perfect shall be as his master." (Luke vi. 40.)

RESURRECTION

BOOK ONE

NO MATTER HOW PEOPLE, CONGREGATING IN ONE small spot to the number of several hundred thousand, tried to disfigure the ground on which they were crowded; how they paved the ground with stones, so that nothing would grow on it; how they weeded out every sprouting blade; how they smoked up the air with coal and naphtha; how they lopped the trees and drove away all animals and birds—spring was spring, even in the town. The sun gave warmth; the grass, reviving, grew strong and lush wherever it had not been scraped away, not only on the strips of lawn of the boulevards, but also between the flag-stones; and the birches, the poplars, and the bird-cherries had unfolded their sticky, fragrant leaves, and the lindens had swelled their bursting buds; jackdaws, sparrows, and pigeons were joyfully preparing their nests as they do each spring, and flies, warmed by the sun, were buzzing along the walls. And the plants, and the birds, and the insects, and the children all were gay. But the people—the big, the grown-up men and women—did not stop cheating and tormenting themselves and each other. People regarded as sacred and important not this spring morning, nor this beauty of God's world, given to all creatures to enjoy—a beauty which disposes to peace, concord, and love—but that which they themselves had invented in order to dominate each other.

Thus, in the office of the provincial prison, what they regarded as sacred and important was not that the blissfulness and joy of spring had been given to all animals and to all people, but that a registered document, bearing a registered seal and a heading, had been received the day before, ordering that at nine o'clock in the morning of this, the twenty-eighth day of April, three prisoners, two women and one man, who were kept in the prison subject to a judicial inquest, should be brought to the court-house. One of these women, being the chief criminal, was to be delivered separately.

So now, on the basis of this order, at eight o'clock in the morning of the twenty-eighth of April, the chief warden entered the dark, stinking corridor of the women's department. He was followed by a woman with a careworn face and curling gray hair, wearing a jacket with purled sleeves, and a belt with blue piping around her waist. This was the matron.

"Do you want Máslova?" she asked, going up with the warden on duty to one of the cell doors which opened into the corridor.

The warden, rattling his keys, turned the lock and, opening the door of the cell from which burst forth an even greater stench than there was in the corridor, called out:

"Máslova, to Court!" and again closed the door, waiting for her to come.

Even in the prison yard there was the brisk, vivifying air of the fields, wafted to town by the wind. But in the corridor there was a depressing, typhus-laden atmosphere, saturated by the odour of excrements, tar, and decay, which immediately cast a gloom of sadness on every newcomer. The matron, who had just arrived from the yard, felt this herself, despite being accustomed to the foul air. Having entered the corridor she suddenly felt tired, and she wanted to go to sleep.

In the cell there was bustling about, women's voices, and the steps of bare feet.

"Livelier there, hurry up, Máslova, I'm telling you!" shouted the chief warden through the door of the cell.

About two minutes later, a short, full-breasted young woman, in a gray cloak, thrown over a white jacket and a white skirt, walked briskly out of the door, swiftly turned around, and stopped near the warden. The woman's feet were clad in linen stockings, and over them she wore the prison shoes; her head was wrapped in a white kerchief, underneath which, apparently intentionally, protruded ringlets of curly black hair. The woman's whole face had that peculiar whiteness which is found on the faces of persons who have lived a long time in seclusion, and which reminds one of potato sprouts in a cellar. Her small, broad hands, and her white, full neck, visible from behind the large collar of the cloak, were the same. What was striking in this face, especially against its dull pallor, were her jet-black, sparkling, slightly swollen, but very lively eyes, one of which had a slight squint. She carried herself very erect, extending her full bosom. Having come out into the corridor, her head thrown back a little, she looked the warden straight in the eye and stood ready to execute anything that might be demanded of her. The warden was about to lock the door, when the pale, austere, wrinkled face of a gray-headed old woman emerged from it. The old woman began to tell Máslova something. But the warden pressed the door against the old woman's head, and the head disappeared. In the cell a woman's voice burst out laughing. Máslova also smiled, and turned toward the little barred window of the door. The old woman pressed her face against the little window from the other side and said in a hoarse voice:

"Above all, don't say nothing extra; stick to the same story, and let that be the end of it!"

"Just so it's over one way or another, it can't be any worse," said Máslova, shaking her head.

"Of course, there's just one; there's no two ways about it," said the chief warden, with superior confidence in his own wit. "Follow me, march!"

The eye of the old woman, visible through the window, disappeared, and Máslova stepped into the middle of the corridor, and with rapid, mincing steps walked behind the chief warden. They descended the stone staircase, passed by the men's cells, even more stinking and noisy than the women's, from which they were everywhere followed by eyes at the holes in the doors, and entered the office, where two armed soldier-escorts were already waiting. A clerk sitting there handed one of the soldiers a document, reeking of tobacco smoke, and, pointing to the prisoner, said, "Take her!" The soldier, a Nízhni-Nóvgorod peasant, with a red, pock-marked face, stuck the paper into the rolled-up sleeve of his overcoat, and, smiling, winked to his companion, a high-cheeked Chuvásh, in order to direct his attention to the prisoner. The soldiers, with the prisoner between them, descended the staircase, and went to the main exit.

A small gate opened in the door of the main exit, and, stepping across the threshold of the gate into the yard, the soldiers, with the prisoner, walked out of the enclosure and proceeded through the town along the middle of the paved streets.

Cabmen, shopkeepers, cooks, workmen, and officials stopped and looked at the prisoner with curiosity; some shook their heads and thought, "This is what bad behaviour, not our behaviour, leads to." Children looked at the robber in terror, being reassured only because she was accompanied by soldiers and could not do anything now. A village peasant, who had sold some coal and had drunk some tea in the tavern, went up to her, made the sign of the cross, and gave her a kopek. The prisoner blushed, bent her head, and muttered something.

Feeling the looks directed toward her, the prisoner imperceptibly, without turning her head, cast side glances at those who were gazing at her, and the attention which she attracted cheered her. She was also cheered by the spring air, which was pure in comparison with that in the jail; but walking on the stones hurt her feet, unaccustomed to walking and shod in clumsy prison shoes; and she kept looking down where she was going and trying to step as lightly as possible. As she passed near a flour shop, in front of which pigeons were strutting, unmolested by anybody, the prisoner almost stepped on a gray-blue one; the pigeon fluttered up, and flapping its wings, flew right past the prisoner's ear, fanning the air against her. The prisoner smiled, and then sighed deeply, having remembered her position.

CHAPTER II

MÁSLOVA'S STORY

The story of prisoner Máslova's life was a very common one. Máslova was the daughter of an unmarried menial servant-woman who had been living with her dairy-maid mother in the estate village of two maiden landowner sisters. This unmarried woman had a baby every year, and, as usually happens in the country, the baby was baptized, but then the mother did not nurse the child—unwanted, appearing unasked-for, and interfering with her work—and it soon died of starvation.

Thus five children had died. They had all been baptized, then they were not fed, and then died. The sixth, begotten by an itinerant gipsy, was a girl, and her fate would have been the same, if it had not happened that one of the old maiden ladies went into the stable to scold the dairy-maids about the cream, which smelled of the cows. In the stable lay the mother with her pretty, healthy, new-born baby. The old lady scolded them for the cream and for having let a woman who had just given birth into the stable, and was about to leave, when, having caught sight of the child, she took pity on it, and offered to become its godmother. She had the girl baptized, and, feeling sorry for her godchild, gave the mother milk and money, and the girl lived. The old maiden ladies called her "the saved one."

The child was three years old when her mother fell ill and died. The old stable-woman, her grandmother, was harassed by her grandchild, and so the ladies took the girl to the house. The black-eyed girl grew to be exceedingly vivacious and charming, and the old maiden ladies took delight in her.

There were two maiden ladies: the younger, Sófya Ivánovna, who had had the child baptized, was the kinder of the two, and the older, Maríya Ivánovna, was the more austere. Sófya Ivánovna dressed the girl, taught her to read, and wanted to make her her ward. Maríya Ivánovna, however, said that she ought to be brought up as a working girl—a good chambermaid—and consequently was exacting, and punished and even struck her, when not in a good humour. Thus, between these two influences, the girl grew.up as partly a ward and partly a chambermaid. She was even called by an in-between name—not Kátka or Kátenka, but Katyúsha. She did the sewing, tidied up the rooms, cleaned the icons with chalk, cooked, did the grinding, served the coffee, did light washing, and sometimes sat with the ladies and read to them.

Several men sued for her hand, but she did not wish to marry, feeling that a life with those working people, her suitors, would be hard for her, who had been spoiled by the comforts of the manor.

Thus she lived until her sixteenth year. She had just passed her sixteenth birthday, when the ladies were visited by their student-nephew, a rich prince, and Katyúsha, not daring to acknowledge the fact to him or even to herself, fell in love with him. Two years later, this same nephew called on his aunts on his way to war and stayed four days with them, and on the day before he left, seduced Katyúsha and, pressing a hundred-rouble bill into her hand on their last day, departed. Five months after his visit she knew for sure that she was pregnant.

After that everything seemed hateful to her, and she thought of nothing else but of a means for freeing herself from the shame which awaited her; she not only began to serve the ladies reluctantly and badly, but once, not knowing herself how it happened, her patience gave way: she said some rude things to them, which she herself regretted later, and asked for her dismissal.

The ladies, who had been very much dissatisfied with her, let her go. She then accepted the position of chambermaid at the house of a police officer, but she could stay there only three months, because the police officer, a man of fifty, began to annoy her; once, when he had become unusually persistent, she grew excited, called him a fool and an old devil, and dealt him such a blow in the chest that he fell down. She was sent away for her rudeness. It was useless to take another place, for the child was soon to be born, and so she went to live with a widow, who was a country midwife and trafficked in liquor. She had an easy childbirth, but the midwife, who had delivered a sick woman in the village, infected Katyúsha with puerperal fever, and the child, a boy, was taken to the foundling house, where, according to the story of the old woman who had carried him there, he died soon after his arrival.

When Katyúsha moved into the midwife's, she had in all 127 roubles, twenty-seven of which she had earned, and one hundred roubles which her seducer had given her. When she came away from that house, all she had left was six roubles.

She did not know how to save money, and spent it on herself, and gave it away to all who asked for some. The midwife took for the two months' board—for the food and the tea—forty roubles; twenty-five roubles went for placing the child; forty roubles the midwife borrowed to buy a cow with; and twenty roubles were spent for clothes and for presents, so that there was no money left when Katyúsha got well again and had to look for a place. She found one at a forester's. The forester was a married man, but, just like the police officer before him, he began to pester Katyúsha the very first day. He was hateful to her, and she tried to evade him. But he was more experienced and cunning than she; above all, he was her master, who could send her wherever he pleased, and, having waited for an opportune moment, he seduced her. His wife found it out, and, discovering her husband alone in a room with Katyúsha, she began beating her. Katyúsha defended herself, and a fight ensued, in consequence of which she was expelled from the house, without getting her wages. Then Katyúsha went to the city and stayed there with her aunt. Her aunt's husband was a bookbinder, who used to make a good living but now had lost all his customers and was given to drinking, spending everything that came into his hands.

Her aunt had a small laundry establishment, and thus supported herself and her children and her good-for-nothing husband. She offered Máslova a place in her laundry; but, seeing the hard life which the laundresses at her aunt's were leading, Máslova hesitated and went to the employment offices to look for a place as a maid.

She found such a place with a lady who lived with her two sons, students at the gymnasium. A week after she had started work, the elder boy, with sprouting moustaches, a sixth-form student, quit working and gave Máslova no rest, importuning her with his attentions. The mother blamed Máslova for everything and discharged her. She could not find another job; but it so happened that once, when Máslova went to an employment office, she there met a lady with rings and bracelets on her plump bare hands. Having learned of Máslova's plight, how she was searching for a place, the lady gave her her address and invited her to her house. Máslova went there. The lady received her kindly, treated her to pastry and sweet wine, and sent her chambermaid somewhere with a note. In the evening a tall man with long grayish hair and gray beard entered the room; the old man at once sat down near Máslova and began, with gleaming eyes, and smiling, to look her over and to jest with her. The landlady called him out into another room, and Máslova heard her say: "She is fresh, straight from the country!" Then the landlady called out Máslova and told her that this man was an author, who had much money and who would not be stingy with it, if he took a liking to her. She pleased the author, who gave her twenty-five roubles, promising to see her often. The money was soon spent in paying her aunt for board, and on a new dress, a hat, and ribbons. A few days later the author sent for her again. She went. He again gave her twenty-five roubles, and proposed that she find herself a separate apartment.

While living in the apartment which the author had rented for her, Máslova fell in love with a merry clerk, who was living in the same building. She herself told the author about it and moved to another, smaller apartment. The clerk, who had promised to marry her, left for Nízhni-Nóvgorod without saying a word to her and obviously abandoning her, and she was left alone. She wanted to stay in the apartment by herself but was not permitted to do so. The inspector of police told her that she could continue to live there only by getting the yellow card and subjecting herself to examination. So she went back to her aunt's. Her aunt, seeing her fashionable dress, her cape, and her hat, received her respectfully, and did not dare offer her a laundress's place, since she regarded her as having risen to a higher level in life. For Máslova the question whether she had better become a laundress or not no longer existed. She now looked with compassion at that life of enforced labour in the front rooms, which the pale laundresses, with their lean arms—some of them were consumptive—were leading, washing and ironing in ninety-degree soapy steam, the windows remaining open winter and summer—and she shuddered at the thought that she, too, might be reduced to such a harsh life. And just at this time, which was exceedingly hard for Máslova, as she could not find a single patron, she was approached by a procuress, who furnished houses of prostitution with girls.

Máslova had started smoking long before and, toward the end of her affair with the clerk and ever since he had abandoned her, had been drinking more and more. Wine attracted her, not only because it tasted good, but more especially because it made her forget all the oppressive things of the past, and because it gave her ease and confidence in her own worth, which she did not have without it. Without wine she always felt sad and ashamed.

The procuress treated her aunt to dainties and, having given wine to Máslova, proposed that she should enter the best establishment in the city, representing to her all the advantages and privileges of such a position. Máslova had the choice: either the humiliating position of a servant, where there would certainly be persecution by the men and secret, temporary adultery, or a secure, quiet, legalized condition and open, legitimate, and well-paid constant adultery—and she chose the latter. Besides, by this she meant to pay back the wrong done her by her seducer and the clerk and all the other people who had treated her shamefully. She was also enticed by the words of the procuress—and this was one of the causes that led to her final decision—that she could order any dresses she wished, of velvet, of faille, of silk, or ball-dresses with bare shoulders and arms. And when Máslova imagined herself in a bright-yellow silk dress with black velvet trimmings—décolleté—she could not withstand the temptation, and surrendered her passport. On that same evening the procuress called a cab and took her to Kitáeva's well-known establishment.

From that time there began for Máslova that life of chronic transgression of divine and human laws which is led by hundreds and hundreds of thousands of women, not only by permission, but under the protection of the government caring for the well-being of its citizens: that life which ends for nine out of every ten women in agonizing disease, premature old age, and death.

In the morning and in the afternoon—slumber after the orgies of the night. At three or four o'clock—a tired waking in an unclean bed, seltzer to counteract the effects of immoderate drinking, coffee, indolent strolling through the rooms in dressing-gowns, jackets or wrappers, looking behind the curtain through the windows, a lazy exchange of angry words; then ablutions, pomading, perfuming of the body and the hair, the trying-on of dresses, quarrels with the madam on account of these clothes, surveying oneself in the mirror, painting the face, the eyebrows, eating sweet, rich food; then putting on a bright silk dress revealing the body; then coming out into a bright, gaily illuminated parlour: the arrival of guests; music, dances, candy, wine, smoking, and adultery with youths, middle-aged men, semi-children, and desperate old men; with bachelors, married men, merchants, clerks, Armenians, Jews, Tartars; with men who were rich, poor, healthy, sick, drunk, sober, coarse, tender; with officers, private citizens, students, schoolboys—of all conditions, ages and characters. And shouts, and jokes, and quarrels, and music, and tobacco and wine, and wine and tobacco, and music, from evening to daybreak. And only in the morning liberation and heavy slumber. And the same thing every day, the whole week. At the end of the week—a drive to a government institution, the police station, where officers in government service, the doctors, men who sometimes seriously and austerely, and sometimes with playful mirth, examined these women, annihilating that very sense of shame which has been given by Nature not only to men, but also to animals, in order to put a check on transgressions; then they would hand them a license for the continuation of these transgressions of which they and their partners had been guilty during the past week. And again such a week. And thus every day—in summer and winter, on week-days and on holidays.

Máslova spent seven years like this. During that time she changed houses twice and was in a hospital once. In the seventh year of her sojourn in a house of prostitution, and in the eighth since her first fall, when she was twenty-six years old, there happened to her that for which she was imprisoned and for which she was now being led to the court-house after six months in jail with murderers and thieves.

CHAPTER III

THE MORNING OF
PRINCE NEKHLYÚDOV

At the same time that Máslova, worn out by the long march, reached, with the soldiers of the guard, the building of the circuit court, that very nephew of her maiden ladies, Prince Dmítri Ivánovich Nekhlyúdov, who had seduced her, was lying on his high, rumpled spring bed, with its feather mattress, and, unbuttoning the collar of his clean holland night-shirt with its ironed gussets, was smoking a cigarette. He was gazing in front of him with motionless eyes and thinking of what he would have to do that day and of what had happened the day before.

As he recalled the previous evening, which he had passed at the house of the Korchágins, rich and distinguished people whose daughter, so all were convinced, he was going to marry, he drew a sigh, and, throwing away his finished cigarette, was on the point of taking another out of his silver cigarette-holder; but he changed his mind, and, letting down from the bed his smooth white feet, found his way into his slippers; he threw over his full shoulders a silk dressing-gown, and, striding rapidly and heavily, walked into the adjoining dressing-room, which was saturated with the artificial odours of elixirs, eau de Cologne, pomatum, and perfumes. There, with a special powder, he cleaned his teeth, which had many fillings, rinsed them with perfumed mouthwash, and then began to wash his body all over and to dry himself with various towels. He washed his hands with scented soap, carefully cleaned his long nails with a brush, and rinsed his face and fat neck in the large marble wash-stand; then he walked into a third room, near the bed-room, where a shower was ready for him. There he washed his muscular, plump, white body with cold water and rubbed himself off with a rough towel; then he put on clean, freshly ironed linen and his shoes, which shone like mirrors, and sat down in front of a dressing-table to brush his short, black, curly beard and the curly hair on his head, which was rather scanty in front.

All the things which he used, all the appurtenances of his toilet—the linen, the garments, the shoes, the ties, the pins, the cuff-buttons—were of the best, of the most expensive kind; they were unobtrusive, simple, durable, and costly.

Having selected from a dozen ties and pins those which he happened to pick up first—at one time, choosing had been new and amusing, but now it made no difference to him—Nekhlyúdov put on his well-brushed clothes, which were lying on a chair, and, clean and perfumed, though not feeling very fresh, proceeded to the long dining-room, the parquet of which had been waxed on the previous day by three peasants; here stood an immense oak sideboard and an equally large extension table, which had a certain solemn appearance on account of its broadly outstretched carved legs in the shape of lion-paws. On this table, covered with a fine starched cloth with large monograms, stood a silver coffee-pot with fragrant coffee, a sugar-bowl of similar design, a cream-pitcher with boiled cream, and a bread-basket with fresh rolls, toast, and biscuits. Near the service lay the latest mail, the papers, and a new number of the *Revue des Deux Mondes*. Nekhlyúdov was about to sit down to his mail, when the door from the corridor opened and a plump, elderly woman in mourning and with a lace head-dress, which covered the widened parting of her hair, glided into the room. This was Agraféna Petróvna, the chamber-maid of Nekhlyúdov's mother, who had but lately died in this very house, now staying on with the son as housekeeper.

Agraféna Petróvna had at various times been abroad with Nekhlyúdov's mother and had the looks and manner of a lady. She had lived in Nekhylúdov's house since her childhood and had known Dmítri Ivánovich when he was a boy and when they called him Mítenka.

"Good morning, Dmítri Ivánovich."

"Good morning, Agraféna Petróvna. What is the news?" asked Nekhlyúdov, jestingly.

"A letter from the princess, or from her daughter. The chambermaid brought it long ago; she is waiting in my room," said Agraféna Petróvna, handing him the letter, and smiling significantly.

"Very well, in a minute," said Nekhlyúdov, taking the letter and frowning, as he noticed Agraféna Petróvna's smile.

Agraféna Petróvna's smile meant that the letter was from the young Princess Korchágin, whom, in Agraféna Petróvna's opinion, Nekhlyúdov was going to marry.

"Then I will tell her to wait," and Agraféna Petróvna, picking up the crumb-brush, which was out of place, and putting it away, glided out of the dining-room.

Nekhlyúdov broke the seal of the perfumed letter, which Agraféna Petróvna had given him, and began to read:

"In fulfilment of my self-assumed duty to act as your memory," so ran the letter on a sheet of thick gray paper with uneven margins, in a sharp, broad hand, "I remind you that to-day, the twenty-eighth of April, you are to serve on a jury and consequently can by no means drive out with Kólosov and us to look at the pictures, as yesterday, with your characteristic thoughtlessness, you promised us you would; *à moins que vous ne soyez disposé à payer à la cour d'assises les 300 roubles d'amende que vous refusez pour votre cheval* for not having appeared in time. I thought of it yesterday the moment you left. So don't forget it.

"Princess M. Korchágin."

On the back was the following addition:

"*Maman vous fait dire que votre couvert vous attendra jusqu'à la nuit. Venez absolument à quelle heure que cela soit.*

"M. K."

Nekhlyúdov frowned. The note was a continuation of that artifice which the young Princess Korchágin had been practising on him for the last two months, and which consisted in tying him ever closer to herself by invisible threads. However, Nekhlyúdov had, in addition to the usual indecision before marriage which all people have who are past their first youth and are not passionately in love, another important reason which kept him from proposing at once, even if he had made up his mind to do so. This reason was not that he had ten years before seduced and abandoned Katyúsha—this he had entirely forgotten and did not regard as an impediment to his marriage; the real cause was that at that time he was having an affair with a married woman, which, though he had broken off, had not yet been acknowledged as broken by her.

Nekhlyúdov was very shy with women, and it was this very timidity which had provoked a desire in that married woman to subdue him. She was the wife of the marshal of the nobility of the district to which Nekhlyúdov used to go for the elections. This woman had drawn him into the affair, which from day to day had become more binding on him and at the same time more repulsive. At first, Nekhlyúdov could not withstand her seductive charms; then, feeling himself guilty toward her, he was not able to break off the affair without her agreement. This was the reason why Nekhlyúdov felt that he had no right to propose to Princess Korchágin, even if he wished to do so.

On the table just now there was a letter from that woman's husband. Upon noticing the handwriting and postmark, Nekhlyúdov blushed and immediately experienced an onrush of energy, which always came over him at the approach of danger. But his agitation was pointless: her husband, the marshal of the nobility in that very district where the more important estates of Nekhlyúdov were located, informed him that at the end of May there would be an extra session of the County Council and asked him to be sure and come in order to *donner un coup d'épaule* in the important County Council questions concerning schools and roads to which it was expected that the reactionary party would put up strong opposition.

The marshal was a liberal, and with several who thought as he did was engaged in struggling against the reaction which had set in during the reign of Alexander III; he was busily occupied with this struggle and knew nothing of his unfortunate family life.

Nekhlyúdov recalled all the painful minutes which he had passed in connection with this man: he recalled how once he had thought that her husband had found out and how he had prepared himself to fight a duel at which he had intended to shoot into the air, and he recalled that terrible scene with her, when in despair she had rushed out into the garden ready to drown herself in the pond, and how he had run after her to find her. "I cannot go there or undertake anything, until I hear from her," thought Nekhlyúdov. The week before he had written her a decisive letter in which he had confessed his guilt and had declared himself ready for any atonement; but, nevertheless, for her own good, he regarded their relations as forever ended. He was expecting an answer to this very letter but had not received one. That there was no answer he considered partly a good sign. If she had not agreed to break off, she would have written him long ago or would have come to see him, as she had done on previous occasions. Nekhlyúdov had heard that there was a certain officer there who was courting her, and this made him jealous and at the same time filled him with the hope of being free of the lie which was harassing him.

Another letter was from the superintendent of his estates. The superintendent wrote Nekhlyúdov that he would have to come down himself, in order to be confirmed in the rights of inheritance and, besides, to decide the question of how the estates were to continue to be managed; whether as they had been under the late princess, or, as he had proposed to her and now was again proposing to the young prince, by increasing the inventory and himself working the land, which had been parcelled out to the peasants. The superintendent wrote that such use would be much more profitable. At the same time he excused himself for being late in sending the three thousand roubles which were due on the first. The money would be sent by the next post. The reason for this delay was that he had been absolutely unable to collect from the peasants, who had gone so far in their dishonesty that it became necessary to turn to the authorities to compel them to pay their debts. This letter was both pleasant and unpleasant to Nekhlyúdov. It was pleasant for him to feel his power over his extensive possessions, and unpleasant, because in his first youth he had been an enthusiastic follower of Herbert Spencer and, being himself a *large* landed proprietor, had been particularly struck by the position in *Social Statics* that justice did not permit the private ownership of land. With the directness and determination of youth he maintained that land could not form the object of private ownership, and he not only wrote a thesis on the subject while at the university, but also at that time really distributed to the peasants a small part of the land (which did not belong to his mother, but which by inheritance from his father belonged to him personally) so as not to be possessed of land, contrary to his convictions. Having now become a large landed proprietor by inheritance, he had to do one of two things: either renounce his possessions, as he had done ten years before in connection with the 500 acres of his paternal estate, or by his silent consent acknowledge all his former ideas faulty and false.

He could not do the former, because he had no other means of subsistence but the land. He did not wish to serve in a government capacity and in the meantime had acquired luxurious habits of life, from which he considered it impossible to depart. Nor was there any reason why he should, since he no longer had that force of conviction nor that determination nor that ambition and desire to surprise people which had actuated him in his youth. Similarly he was quite incapable of doing the second, of recanting those clear and undeniable proofs of the illegality of private ownership of land which he had once found in Spencer's *Social Statics* and the brilliant confirmation of which he had found later, much later, in the works of Henry George.

For this reason the superintendent's letter did not please him.

CHAPTER IV

HIS THOUGHTS ABOUT THE MARRIAGE

Having finished his coffee, Nekhlyúdov went into his study to find out from the summons at what time he was to be at court and to write the princess an answer. The study was reached through the studio. Here stood an easel with an upside-down, unfinished picture, and sketches were hanging on the wall. The sight of this picture, on which he had vainly worked for two years, and of the sketches and of the whole studio reminded him of his recently particularly strong feeling of impotence to advance farther in painting. He explained this feeling as coming from a too highly developed æsthetic feeling, but still the consciousness of it was exceedingly disagreeable to him.

Seven years before, he had given up his government position, having decided that he had a calling for painting, and from the height of his artistic activity he looked down somewhat contemptuously on all other activities. Now it turned out that he had no ground for that, and thus every reminder of it was unpleasant. He looked with a heavy heart at all this luxurious equipment in his studio, and in an unhappy frame of mind entered his study. The study was a very large and high room, with all kinds of adornments, appliances, and comforts.

He immediately found in the drawer of his immense desk, under the division "Urgent," the summons which said that he had to be at court at eleven o'clock. He sat down and wrote a note to the princess, thanking her for the invitation and promising to try to come to dinner. But after he had written this note, he tore it up:

it was too personal; he wrote another—and it was cold, almost offensive. He again tore it up, and pressed a button on the wall. An elderly, morose, cleanly shaven lackey with sideburns, in a gray calico apron, came to the door.

"Please send for a cab."

"Yes, sir."

"And tell her—there is somebody here from the Korchágins waiting for an answer—tell her that I am much obliged and that I shall try to be there."

"Yes, sir."

"It is impolite, but I cannot write. I shall see her to-day, anyway," thought Nekhlyúdov and went away to dress himself.

When, all dressed, he appeared on the porch, his familiar cab with the rubber tires was already waiting for him.

"Yesterday, the moment after you had left Prince Korchágin," said the cabman, half turning around his powerful, sunburnt neck in a white shirt collar, "I got there, but the porter told me, 'He has just left.'"

"Even the cabmen know of my relations with the Korchágins," thought Nekhlyúdov, and the unsolved question, which had of late constantly preoccupied him —whether he should marry Princess Korchágin or not—rose before him, and, as happened to him with the majority of questions which presented themselves to him at that time, he was unable to solve it one way or the other.

In favour of marriage there was, in general, first of all, the fact that marriage, in addition to supplying him with a domestic hearth, would remove the irregularities of sexual life and would make it possible for him to lead a moral existence; secondly, and most importantly, Nekhlyúdov hoped that a family and children would give a meaning to his empty life. This was for marriage, in general. Against marriage, in general, was, in the first place, the fear of losing his liberty, a fear which is common to all old bachelors, and in the second, an unconscious dread before the mysterious being of a woman.

In favour of his marrying Missy in particular (Princess Korchágin's name was Maríya, but, as in all families of a certain circle, she had a nickname) was, in the first place, her breeding, for in everything, from her wearing-apparel to her manner of speaking, walking, and laughing, she stood out from common people, not by any special features, but by her general "decency"—he could not think of any other expression for this quality which he esteemed highly; and in the second place, because she respected him above all other men, consequently, according to his conceptions, she understood him. And it was this understanding of him, that is, the acknowledgment of his high worth, which testified in Nekhlyúdov's opinion to her good mind and correct judgment. Against his marrying Missy in particular was, first, that it was quite possible that he should find a girl who would possess an even greater number of desirable qualities than Missy had and who consequently would be worthier of him; and, secondly, the fact that she was twenty-seven years old and, therefore, must have been in love before—and this thought tormented Nekhlyúdov. His pride could not make peace with the thought that at any time, even though it be in the past, she could have loved anybody but him. Of course, she could not have foreseen that she would meet him, but the very idea that she could have been in love with some one else offended him.

Thus there were as many arguments in favour of marrying as against it; at least all these arguments were equally strong, and Nekhlyúdov, laughing at himself, called himself "Buridan's ass." And he remained one, for he could not make up his mind to which bundle to turn.

"However, since I have received no answer from Márya Vasílevna (the marshal's wife), and have not completely settled that affair, I cannot begin anything," he said to himself.

The consciousness that he could and should delay his decision was agreeable to him. "However, I will consider all this later," he said to himself as his carriage soundlessly drove over the asphalt driveway of the court-house.

"Now I must act conscientiously, as I always execute and always should execute my public duties. Besides, they are frequently interesting," he said to himself, passing by the doorkeeper into the vestibule of the court-house.

CHAPTER V

IN THE JURORS' ROOM

In the corridors of the court-house there was already animated motion when Nekhlyúdov entered.

The guards were either walking rapidly or even running, without lifting their feet off the floor but shuffling them and, out of breath, carrying orders and documents back and forth. The bailiffs, the lawyers, and the judges went from one place to another; the plaintiffs, and the defendants who were not under guard, morosely paced back and forth along the walls or sat waiting their turn.

"Where is the circuit court?" Nekhlyúdov asked one of the guards.

"Which? There's a civil division, and a trial court."

"I'm a juror."

"Criminal division. You ought to have said so. Here, to the right, then to the left, second door."

Nekhlyúdov followed his directions.

At the door indicated two men stood waiting for something. The one was a tall, fat merchant, a good-hearted man who had evidently had something to drink and eat and was in a very happy frame of mind; the other was a clerk, of Jewish extraction. They were talking about the price of wool when Nekhlyúdov walked over to them and asked them whether this was the jury-room.

"Here, sir, here. Are you one of us, a juryman?" the good-natured merchant asked, winking merrily. "Well, we'll all work together," he continued, upon Nekhlyúdov's affirmative answer. "Baklashóv, of the second guild," he said, extending his soft, broad, flabby hand. "We'll have to work. With whom have I the honour?"

Nekhlyúdov gave his name and went into the jury-room.

In the small jury-room there were some ten men of all sorts. They had all just arrived, and some were seated, while others walked about, looking each other over and getting acquainted. There was an ex-officer in his uniform; the others wore long or short coats, and only one was clad in a sleeveless peasant coat.

Though many of those present had been taken away from their work and complained that this was a tiresome business, they all showed a certain pleasure at knowing they were performing an important public duty.

The jurors, some having become acquainted with each other and others having merely guessed who was who, were talking about the weather, about the early spring, and about the work before them. Those who did not know Nekhlyúdov hastened to become acquainted with him, obviously regarding this as a special honour. Nekhlyúdov took this as something due him, as he always did among strangers. If he had been asked why he regarded himself superior to most people, he would not have been able to answer the question, because no part of his life was distinguished by any particular qualities. The fact that he spoke English, French, and German correctly, and that his linen, his attire, his ties, and his cuff-buttons came from the top purveyors of these articles, could not have served at all, so he knew himself, as a reason for supposing his superiority. And yet, he unquestioningly assumed this superiority and received expressions of respect as something due him and felt offended whenever they were not forthcoming. In the jurors' room he had occasion to experience the disagreeable sensation arising from an expression of disrespect. Among the jurymen was an acquaintance of Nekhlyúdov's. This was Pyótr Gerásimovich (Nekhlyúdov never had known his family name and even boasted of this fact), who had formerly been a teacher of his sister's children. This Pyótr Gerásimovich had finished studying at the university and now was a school-teacher. Nekhlyúdov never could bear him on account of his familiarity and his self-satisfied laughter—in general, on account of his "vulgarity," as Nekhlyúdov's sister used to put it.

"Ah, you are caught, too," Pyótr Gerásimovich met Nekhlyúdov with a guffaw. "You could not wriggle out of it?"

"I did not even intend wriggling out," Nekhlyúdov said, austerely and gloomily.

"Well, that is a citizen's virtue. Just wait, when you get hungry and they won't let you sleep, you will sing a different song!" Pyótr Gerásimovich shouted, laughing louder still.

"This priest's son will soon be saying 'thou' to me," thought Nekhlyúdov, and with a face expressive of a sadness which would have been natural only if he had suddenly received the news of the death of all his relatives, he went away from him and joined the group which had formed itself around a tall, cleanly shaven, stately gentleman animatedly telling a story. The gentleman was telling about the lawsuit which was being tried in the civil department, as if it were something he knew well; he called all the judges and famous lawyers by their first names and patronymics. He was expatiating on the wonderful turn which a famous lawyer had given it, as a result of which one of the contesting parties, an old lady, though entirely in the right, would have to pay an immense sum to the other party.

"A brilliant lawyer!" he said.

He was listened to with respect, and some tried to put in a word of their own, but he interrupted them all, as though he were the only one who could really know anything.

Although Nekhlyúdov had arrived late, he had to wait for a long time. The case was delayed by one of the members of the court who had not yet arrived.

CHAPTER VI

THE JUDGES AND
THE PROSECUTOR

The presiding judge had come early. He was a tall, stout man, with long, grayish side-whiskers. He was married, but led a very dissolute life, and so did his wife. They did not interfere with each other. On that morning he had received a note from the Swiss governess, who lived in their house in the summer and now was on her way to St. Petersburg, that she would wait for him in town, in the Hotel Italy, between five and six p.m. And so he was anxious to begin and end the sitting of the court as early as possible, in order to get a chance of visiting this red-haired Klára Vasílevna, with whom he had begun a love-affair the summer before in the country.

Upon entering his chambers, he bolted the door, took out a pair of dumb-bells from the lowest shelf of the cupboard with the documents, and twenty times moved them up, forward, sidewise, and downward, and then three times squatted lightly, holding the dumb-bells above his head.

"Nothing keeps up a man's physique so well as washing with cold water and gymnastic exercises," he thought, feeling with his left hand, a gold ring on its ring-finger, the swelling biceps of his right arm. He had still to do the windmill, for he always did these two exercises before a long session, when the door was shaken. Somebody was trying to come in. The presiding judge hurriedly put the dumb-bells away and opened the door.

Tolstoy
Resurrection
page 20

"Sorry," he said.

Into the room stepped one of the members of the court in gold-rimmed spectacles; he was short, with raised shoulders and a frowning face.

"Again Matvyéy Nikítich isn't here," said the member with displeasure.

"Not yet," replied the presiding judge, donning his uniform. "He is eternally late."

"I wonder he is not ashamed of himself," said the member, and angrily sat down and took his cigarettes out of his pocket.

This member, who was a very punctilious man, had had an unpleasant encounter with his wife that morning, because she had already spent the money which was to have lasted her the whole month. She had asked for some more in advance, but he insisted that he would not depart from his rules. A scene ensued. His wife said that if he insisted upon this there would be no dinner—and that he had better not expect any. Thereupon he left, fearing that she would keep her word, for she was capable of anything. "So this is what you get for living a good, moral life," he thought, looking at the shining, healthy, gay, and good-hearted presiding judge, who, spreading wide his elbows, with his beautiful white hands was smoothing his thick and long grayish side-whiskers on both sides of his embroidered collar. "He is always happy and content, but I suffer."

The secretary entered, bringing some papers.

"Very much obliged to you," said the presiding judge, lighting a cigar. "Which case shall we launch first?"

"I suppose the poisoning case," the secretary said, seemingly with indifference.

"Very well, let it be the poisoning case," said the presiding judge, reflecting that it was a case that might be ended by four o'clock, whereupon he could leave. "Has Matvyéy Nikítich not yet come?"

"Not yet."

"And is Bréve here?"

"He is," answered the secretary.

"Tell him, then, if you see him, that we shall begin with the poisoning case."

Bréve was the assistant prosecuting attorney who was to prosecute at the present sitting.

Entering the corridor, the secretary ran into Bréve. His shoulders high, he was almost running along the corridor; his uniform was unbuttoned, and he carried his briefcase under one arm; he continually clicked his heels on the floor and swung his free arm in such a manner that the palm of his hand was perpendicular to the direction of his walk.

"Mikhaíl Petróvich wants to know whether you are ready?" the secretary asked him.

"Of course, I always am," said the assistant prosecuting attorney. "Which case comes first?"

"The poisoning case."

"Very well," said the assistant prosecuting attorney; but he did not think it well at all, for he had not slept the whole night. There had been a farewell party, where they had drunk and played cards until two o'clock in the morning; then they all called on the women in the very house where Máslova had been six months ago, so that he had not had any time whatsoever to read up the brief; he hoped to be able to do so now. The secretary, who knew that he had not yet read up the poisoning case, had purposely advised the presiding judge to start with it. The secretary was a man of liberal, nay, even radical views. Bréve, on the contrary, was a conservative and, like all Germans in Russian service, a devout Orthodox; the secretary did not like him and envied him his place.

"Well, how about the Skoptsy sect?" asked the secretary.

"I said I could not," said the assistant prosecuting attorney. "For want of witnesses —I shall so report to the court."

"But, all the same—"

"I cannot," said the assistant prosecuting attorney, and, swaying his arm as before, ran into his study.

He delayed the case of the sectarians on account of the absence of an absolutely unimportant witness who was not at all needed, and his reason for doing this was just because the case was to be heard in a court where the jury were an intelligent set and where it might easily end in acquittal. By agreement with the presiding judge, this case was to be transferred to the session in a district town where there would be more peasants on the jury and a better chance for conviction.

The movement in the corridor was becoming more animated. Most people were gathered near the hall of the civil division, where they were trying the case about which the stately gentleman, the lover of lawsuits, had been telling the jurors. During an intermission, there emerged from that court-room the old woman whose property the brilliant lawyer had succeeded in wrenching away in favour of a pettifogger who did not have the slightest claim to it. The judges knew that, and the plaintiff and his attorney knew it even better; but the case had been conducted in such a manner that it was impossible not to take the property away from the old woman and give it to the pettifogger. The old woman was a stout lady in holiday clothes and with enormous flowers on her hat. Upon coming out the door, she stopped in the corridor and, spreading her plump short arms, kept repeating as she turned to her lawyer: "What does it all mean? I ask you, now! What does it mean?" The lawyer was looking at the flowers on her hat and, not listening to her, was thinking about something else.

Tolstoy
Resurrection
page 22

Behind the old woman, hurrying out of the civil division court-room, re-splendent in his wide-open vest, and with a self-satisfied expression, came that same famous attorney who had fixed matters in such a way that the old woman with the flowers was left penniless, while the pettifogger, who gave him a fee of ten thousand roubles, received more than one hundred thousand roubles. All eyes were turned to the lawyer, and he was conscious of it, so that his whole countenance seemed to be saying, "Please, no expressions of respect," as he rapidly passed by everybody.

CHAPTER VII

ASSEMBLING THE JURORS

Finally Matvyéy Nikítich arrived, and a bailiff, a spare man with a long neck and sidling gait, and also a lower lip that protruded sidewise, entered the jury-room.

This bailiff was an honest man, who had received a university education, but was not able to keep a place any length of time because he drank like a fish. Three months before, a countess, his wife's patroness, had got this place for him, and he had so far been able to hold it, which made him feel happy.

"Well, gentlemen, are you all here?" he said, putting on his pince-nez and look-ing over the top of it.

"Everybody, I think," said the merry merchant.

"Let us see," said the bailiff, and drawing a list from his pocket, he began to call out the names, looking now through his pince-nez and now over them.

"Councillor of State I. M. Nikíforov."

"Here," said the stately gentleman, who knew about all legal matters.

"Retired Colonel Iván Semyónovich Ivánov."

"Here," said a thin man in the uniform of a retired officer.

"The Merchant of the second guild, Pyótr Baklashóv."

"Here," said the good-hearted merchant, smiling widely. "Ready!"

"Lieutenant of the Guards Prince Dmítri Nekhlyúdov."

"Here," answered Nekhlyúdov.

The bailiff, looking with an expression of pleasurable politeness above his glasses, made a bow, as if to honour him above the rest.

"Captain Yúri Dmítrievich Dánchenko, Merchant Grigóri Efímovich Kuleshóv," and so on.

All but two were present.

"Now, gentlemen, please proceed to the court-room," said the bailiff, pointing to the door with a polite gesture.

They started, and, each pausing to let another pass through the door before going out himself, went into the corridor and from there into the court-room.

The court-room was a large, long room. One end of it was taken up by a platform, which was reached by three steps. In the middle of this platform stood a table which was covered with a green cloth, bordered by a green fringe of a darker shade. Behind the table stood three chairs with very high carved oak backs, and behind the chairs hung a bright life-sized picture of the emperor in the uniform of a general, with a sash; he was represented with one foot forward and his hand resting on his sabre. In the right-hand corner there hung a shrine with an icon of Christ crowned with thorns and there stood a lectern, and on the right side was the desk of the prosecuting attorney. On the left, opposite the desk, was the secretary's table, set back against the wall; and nearer the spectators was a carved oak railing, and back of it the unoccupied bench of the defendants. On the right side of the platform stood two rows of chairs, also with high backs, for the jurors, and below them were the tables for the lawyers. All this was in the front part of the hall, which was divided by the railing into two parts. The back half was occupied by benches, which, rising one behind the other, went as far as the back wall. In the front benches sat four women, either factory girls or chambermaids, and two men, also labourers, evidently overwhelmed by the splendour of the room's interior and therefore speaking to each other in a whisper.

Soon after the jurors had entered, the bailiff went with his sidling gait to the middle of the room and shouted in a loud voice, as though he wished to frighten somebody:

"The Court is coming!"

Everybody rose, and the judges walked out on the platform. First came the presiding judge, with his muscles and beautiful whiskers. Then came the gloomy member of the court, in gold-rimmed spectacles, who now was even more gloomy, because just before the session began he had seen his brother-in-law, a candidate for a judicial position, who had informed him that he had just been at his sister's, and that she had told him that there would be no dinner.

"Well, I suppose we shall have to go to an inn," said the brother-in-law, smiling.

"There is nothing funny in that," replied the gloomy member of the court and grew gloomier still.

And, finally, the third member of the court, that same Matvyéy Nikítich, who was always late. He was a bearded man, with large, drooping, kindly eyes. This member suffered from a gastral catarrh; on his doctor's advice he had begun a new regimen that morning, and it was this new regimen which had detained him at home longer than usual. Now, as he was ascending the platform, he had a concentrated look, because he was in the habit of making every possible sort of guess to solve those questions he set himself. Just now he had made up his mind that if the number of steps from the door of the chambers to the chair should be divisible by three, without a remainder, the new regimen would cure him of the catarrh, but if it did not divide exactly, the regimen would be a failure. There were in all twenty-six steps, but he doubled one, and thus reached the chair with his twenty-seventh step.

The figures of the presiding judge and of the members of the court, as they ascended the platform in their uniforms with the collars embroidered in gold lace, were very impressive. They were conscious of this themselves, and all three, as though embarrassed by their grandeur, swiftly and modestly lowering their eyes, sat down in their carved chairs, back of the table with the green cloth, on which towered a triangular Mirror of Law with an eagle and a glass vase such as is used on sideboards for confectionery; there was also an inkstand there, pens, clean paper, and newly sharpened pencils of all sizes. The assistant prosecuting attorney had come in at the same time as the judges. He at once walked up to his place near the window just as hurriedly, with his briefcase under his arm, and waving his hand in the same manner as before, at once buried himself in reading and examining the papers, utilizing every minute to prepare himself for the case. This was the fourth time he had had a case to prosecute. He was very ambitious and had firmly determined to make a career, therefore he regarded it as necessary that the cases should go against the defendant every time he prosecuted. He was acquainted with the chief points in the poisoning case and had even formed a plan of attack, but he needed a few more data and was now hurriedly reading the briefs and copying out the necessary points.

The secretary was seated at the opposite end of the platform and, having arranged all the documents that might be needed, was looking over a proscribed article, which he had obtained and read the day before. He was anxious to talk about this article to the member of the court with the long beard, who shared his views, and was trying to become familiar with its contents before he spoke to him about it.

CHAPTER VIII

SWEARING IN THE JURY

The presiding judge looked through the papers, put a few questions to the bailiff and the secretary, and, having received affirmative answers, gave the order to bring in the defendants. The door back of the railing was immediately thrown open, and two gendarmes in caps and with unsheathed swords entered and were followed by the defendants—by a red-haired, freckled man and two women. The man was clad in a prison cloak, which was much too broad and too long for him. As he entered the court-room, he held his hands with their outstretched fingers down his legs, thus keeping the long sleeves back in place. He did not glance at the judges or the spectators, but gazed at the bench around which he was walking. Having reached the other end, he let the women sit down first and himself carefully sat on the very edge; gazing fixedly at the presiding judge, he began to move the muscles of his cheeks, as though whispering something. Behind him came a young woman, also dressed in a prison cloak. Her head was wrapped in a prison kerchief; her face was ash-white, without eyebrows or lashes, but with red eyes. This woman seemed very calm. As she was going up to her seat, her cloak caught on something, but she carefully, without any undue haste, freed it and sat down.

The third defendant was Máslova.

The moment she entered, the eyes of all the men who were in the court-room turned to her and for a long time were riveted on her white face, with its black, sparkling eyes, and her full bosom underneath her cloak. Even the gendarme near whom she passed gazed at her uninterruptedly, until she had gone beyond him and sat down; then when she had sat down, he quickly looked away, as if conscious of his guilt, and, straightening up, fixed his eyes on the window in front of him.

The presiding judge waited until the defendants had taken their seats and, the moment Máslova sat down, turned to the secretary.

Then began the usual procedure: the roll-call of jurors, the discussion about those who had failed to make their appearance and the imposition of fines upon them, the decision in regard to those who wished to be excused, and the completion of the required number from the reserve jurors. Then the presiding judge folded some slips of paper, placed them in the glass vase, and, rolling the embroidered sleeves of his uniform up a little and baring his hirsute arms, began, with the gestures of a magician, to take out one slip at a time; these he unrolled and read. Then the presiding judge adjusted his sleeves and ordered the priest to swear in the jurors.

The old priest, with a swollen, sallow face, in a cinnamon-coloured vestment, with a gold cross on his breast and a small decoration pinned to his vestment, slowly moving his swollen legs under his garment, went up to the lectern which stood under the icon.

The jurymen rose and in a crowd moved up to the desk.

"Please, come up," said the priest, touching the cross on his chest with his swollen hand and waiting for the approach of all the jurors.

This priest had taken orders forty-six years before and was preparing himself to celebrate his jubilee in three years in the same manner in which the cathedral priest had lately celebrated his. He had served in the circuit court since the opening of the courts and was very proud of the fact that he had sworn in several tens of thousands of people, and that at his advanced age he continued to labour for the good of the Church, of his country, and of his family, to whom he would leave a house and a capital of not less than thirty thousand roubles in bonds. It had never occurred to him that his work in the court-room, which consisted in having people take an oath over the Gospel, in which swearing of oaths is directly prohibited, was not good; he did not worry about this but, on the contrary, liked it very much, often having an opportunity to get acquainted with fine gentlemen. He had just had the pleasure of meeting the famous lawyer, who inspired him with great respect because he had received a fee of ten thousand roubles for nothing more than the case of the old woman with the immense flowers.

When the jurors had walked up the steps of the platform, the priest, bending his bald, gray head to one side, stuck it through the greasy opening of the scapulary, and, arranging his scanty hair, addressed the jurors.

"Raise your right hands and put your fingers together like this," he said, in the deliberate voice of an old man, lifting his plump hand with dimples beneath every finger and putting three fingers together. "Now repeat after me," he said, and began, "I promise and swear by Almighty God, before His Holy Gospel and before the Life-giving Rood of the Lord, that in the case, in which—" he said, making a pause after every phrase. "Don't drop your hand, but hold it like this," he addressed a young man, who had dropped his hand—"that in the case, in which—"

Tolstoy
Resurrection
page 26

The stately gentleman with the whiskers, the colonel, the merchant, and others held their fingers as the priest had ordered them to do; some of these held them high and very precisely, as though this gave them special pleasure; others held them reluctantly and carelessly. Some repeated the words too loudly, as though with undue zeal and with an expression which said, "I'm going to talk and keep on talking"; others only whispered and fell behind the words of the priest and then, as if frightened, hastened belatedly to catch up with him; some held their three skinny fingers tightly together and flaunted them, as if afraid of letting something fall from their hands; others kept spreading them and again closing them up. All felt awkward, and only the old priest was firmly convinced that he was performing useful work. After the oath had been administered, the presiding judge told the jurors to elect a foreman. The jurymen arose, and, crowding together, went into the deliberation room, where almost all immediately took out cigarettes and began to smoke. Somebody proposed the stately gentleman for a foreman; he was chosen by unanimous consent, and, throwing away and extinguishing the cigarette butts, they returned to the court-room. The stately gentleman announced to the presiding judge that he had been chosen foreman, and, stepping over each others' feet, they sat down in two rows, on the chairs with the high backs.

Everything went without a hitch, and not without solemnity, and this regularity, order and solemnity afforded all the participants pleasure, for it confirmed them in their conviction that they were performing a serious and important public duty. Nekhlyúdov, too, felt this.

The moment the jurors had taken their seats, the presiding judge made a speech to them about their rights, their duties, and their responsibilities. While delivering his speech, the judge kept changing his pose: he leaned now on his right arm, now on his left, now on the back and now on the arm of his chair; he smoothed out the edges of the papers, or he stroked the paper-knife, or fingered a pencil.

Their rights consisted, according to what he said, in being permitted to ask questions of the defendants through the presiding judge, in having pencil and paper, and in being allowed to inspect the exhibits. Their duty consisted in judging justly and not falsely. And their responsibility was this: if they did not keep their consultations secret, or if they established any communication with the outside world, they would be subject to punishment.

Everybody listened with respectful attention. The merchant, smelling strongly of liquor and restraining himself from loud belching, approvingly nodded his head at every sentence.

CHAPTER IX

EXAMINATION OF THE DEFENDANTS

Having finished his speech, the judge turned to the defendants.

"Simón Kartínkin, rise!" he said.

Simón got up with a jerk, and the muscles of his cheeks moved more rapidly.

"Your name?"

"Simón Petróv Kartínkin," he answered rapidly, in a crackling voice, evidently having prepared his answer in advance.

"Your status?"

"Peasant."

"What province and district?"

"From Túla Province, Krapívensky District, Kupyánsky parish, village of Bórki."

"How old are you?"

"Going on thirty-four; born in one thousand eight hundred—"

"What is your religion?"

"I am a Russian, an Orthodox."

"Married?"

"Not at all, Sir."

"What is your occupation?"

"I worked in the corridor of the Hotel Mauritania."

"Have you been in court before?"

"I have never been tried before, because I used to live—"

"You have not been tried before?"

"So help me God, never."

"Have you received a copy of the indictment?"

"I have."

"Take your seat! Evfímiya Ivánova Bóchkova," the presiding judge addressed the next defendant.

But Simón continued standing, and Bóchkova could not be seen behind his back.

"Kartínkin, sit down."

Kartínkin continued to stand.

"Kartínkin, sit down!"

But Kartínkin still stood up; he sat down only when the bailiff ran up, and, bending his head down, and opening his eyes unnaturally, said to him in a tragic whisper: "Sit down, sit down!"

Kartínkin dropped as fast into his seat as he had shot up before and, wrapping himself in his cloak, began once more silently to move his cheeks.

"Your name?" the judge addressed the second defendant with a sigh of fatigue, without looking at her, and looking up something in the document which was lying before him. The presiding judge was so used to his cases that, in order to expedite matters, he was able to attend to two things at the same time.

Bóchkova was forty-three years old; her status, a lower middle-class woman from Kolómna; her occupation, corridor maid in the same Hotel Mauritania. She had not been under trial before, and had received the indictment. She answered all the questions extremely boldly, and with such intonations as if adding to each answer: "Yes, Evfímiya, and Bóchkova, got the copy, and am proud of it, and allow nobody to laugh at me." She did not wait to be told to be seated but sat down the moment the last question was answered.

"Your name?" the woman-loving presiding judge exceedingly politely addressed the third defendant. "You must stand up!" he added, softly and kindly, noticing that Máslova was sitting.

Máslova started up with a swift motion and with an expression of readiness, thrusting forward her full bosom, looked, without answering, at the face of the judge with her smiling and slightly squinting black eyes.

"What is your name?"

"Lyubóv," she quickly replied.

In the meantime, Nekhlyúdov, who had put on his pince-nez, was watching the defendants as they were being questioned. "It can't be," he thought, riveting his eyes on the defendant. "But how can it be Lyubóv?" he thought, upon hearing her answer.

The judge wanted to continue his questions, but the member of the court in the spectacles, saying something angrily under his breath, stopped him. The judge nodded consent, and again turned to the defendant.

"Lyubóv?" he said. "You're not down here as that."

The defendant remained silent.

"I ask what your real name is?"

"By what name were you baptized?" the angry member of the court asked.

"Formerly I was called Katerína."

"It is impossible," Nekhlyúdov kept saying to himself, and meanwhile he knew beyond any doubt that it was she, the same girl, half-ward, half-chambermaid, with whom he had once been in love, precisely, in love, but whom he had seduced during an uncontrollable transport and then had abandoned, and whom he later never thought of, because that recollection would have been too painful to him and would have too clearly condemned him; it would have proved that he, who was so proud of his "decency," not only was not decent, but had simply treated this woman foully.

Yes, it was she. He now saw clearly that exclusive and mysterious individuality which separates one face from another and makes it exclusive, unique, and unrepeated. Beneath the unnatural pallor and plumpness of her face, this individuality, this sweet, exceptional individuality, was in her face, her lips, her slightly squinting eyes, and, above all else, in her naïve, smiling glance, and in that expression of readiness, not only in her face, but in her whole figure.

"You ought to have said so," the judge said, still very softly. "Your patronymic?"

"I am illegitimate," said Máslova.

"How were you called by your godfather?"

"Mikháylova."

"What could her crime be?" Nekhlyúdov continued to think, breathing with difficulty.

"Your family name?" continued the judge.

"Máslova, by my mother."

"Status?"

"Lower middle-class."

"Orthodox?"

"Yes."

"Occupation? What was your occupation?"

Máslova was silent.

"What was your occupation?" repeated the judge.

"I was in an establishment," she said.

"In what kind of an establishment?" angrily asked the member in the spectacles.

"You know yourself in what kind," said Máslova, smiling, and, immediately turning around, she again fixed her eyes on the presiding judge.

There was something so unusual in the expression of her face, and something so terrible and pitiable in the meaning of the words which she had uttered, in her smile, and in that rapid glance which she then cast on the whole court-room, that the presiding judge lost his composure, and for a moment there ensued a complete silence in the room. The silence was broken by the laughter of one of the spectators. Somebody else cried, "Hush!" The presiding judge raised his head and continued the questions.

"Have you ever been tried or under judicial inquest before?"

"No," softly said Máslova, with a sigh.

"Have you received the indictment?"

"I have."

"Take your seat," said the presiding judge.

The defendant lifted her skirt with a motion with which dressed-up women adjust their train, and sat down, folding her small white hands in the sleeve of the cloak, without taking her eyes off the presiding judge.

Then began the roll-call of the witnesses, and the removal of witnesses, and the selection of a medical expert, and his call to the court-room. Then the secretary rose and began to read the indictment. He read with clear and loud enunciation but so rapidly that his voice, with its incorrectly articulated r's and l's, merged into one uninterrupted, soporific din. The judges leaned now on one arm of the chair, now on the other, now on the table, or against the back, and now closed their eyes or opened them and whispered to each other. One gendarme several times repressed an incipient convulsive yawn.

Among the defendants, Kartínkin never stopped moving his cheeks. Bóchkova sat very quietly and erect, occasionally scratching her head underneath her kerchief.

Máslova sat motionlessly, listening to the reader and looking at him; now and then she shuddered, as though wishing to contradict, blushed, and drew deep sighs; she changed the position of her hands, looked around her, and again riveted her eyes on the reader.

Nekhlyúdov sat in the first row, on his high chair, the second from the end; he did not take off his pince-nez, and gazed at Máslova, while his soul was in complicated and painful toil.

CHAPTER X

THE INDICTMENT

The indictment ran as follows:

"On the 17th of January 188—, Ferapónt Emilyánovich Smyelkóv, a Second Guild merchant from the town of Kurgán, died suddenly in the Hotel Mauritania.

"The local police doctor of the fourth district certified that death was due to rupture of the heart, caused by the excessive use of alcoholic liquids. The body of Smyelkóv was interred.

"A few days later the Siberian merchant Timókhin, a friend and fellow-townsman of Smyelkóv, returned from a trip to Petersburg, and on hearing of the circumstances attending Smyelkóv's death, announced his suspicion that Smyelkóv had been poisoned for the purpose of stealing the money he had with him.

"His suspicion was confirmed by a preliminary investigation, which established:

"1) That just before his death Smyelkóv had received 3,800 roubles from his bank, but the inventory taken of the possessions of the deceased revealed only 312 roubles 16 kopeks.

"2) That Smyelkóv had spent the whole day and night preceding his death with the prostitute Lyúbka (Ekaterína Máslova) in the brothel and in the Hotel Mauritania, to which, at his request and in his absence, Ekaterína Máslova went from the brothel with the purpose of fetching money. In the presence of Evfímiya Bóchkova and Simón Kartínkin, both servants at the hotel, Máslova unlocked and then locked the suitcase containing the money with a key given her by Smyelkóv himself. When the suitcase was open Bóchkova and Kartínkin testify to having seen packs of hundred-rouble banknotes therein.

"3) That on returning to the Hotel Mauritania from the brothel, Smyelkóv was accompanied by the prostitute Lyúbka, who, on the advice of Kartínkin, sprinkled a white powder supplied to her by Kartínkin into a glass of brandy which was then given to Smyelkóv to drink.

"4) That on the following morning Lyúbka (Ekaterína Máslova) sold to her mistress (witness Kitáeva, owner of the brothel) a diamond ring which Máslova claimed had been presented to her by Smyelkóv.

"5) That the chambermaid, Evfímiya Bóchkova, deposited 1,800 roubles on current account at the bank on the day following Smyelkóv's death.

"A medical examination of Smyelkóv's body, a port-mortem, and a chemical analysis of the contents of Smyelkóv's digestive organs, revealed the presence of poison, which fact led to the conclusion that death had come as a result of poisoning.

"The accused Máslova, Bóchkova, and Kartínkin all pleaded not guilty. Máslova stated that while the merchant Smyelkóv was in the brothel were she 'works,' as she expresses it, she was actually sent by the merchant to the Hotel Mauritania to get him some money, and that, having unlocked the suitcase with a key given her by the merchant, she took out forty roubles, as she was told to do, but had taken nothing more; that Bóchkova and Kartínkin, in whose presence she unlocked and locked the suitcase and took the money, could testify to the truth of her statement. She further said that when she came to the hotel for the second time, she did, at the instigation of Kartínkin, give Smyelkóv some kind of powder, which she thought was an opiate, in a glass of brandy, hoping he would fall asleep and that she would be able to get away from him. As for the ring, Smyelkóv, having beaten her, himself gave it to her when she cried and threatened to go away.

"Evfímiya Bóchkova stated that she knew nothing about the missing money, that she had not even gone into Smyelkóv's room, but that Lyúbka had been busy there all by herself; that if anything had been stolen, it must have been by Lyúbka when she came with the merchant's key to get his money."

At this point Máslova gave a start, opened her mouth, and looked at Bóchkova.

"When," continued the secretary, "the receipt for one thousand eight hundred roubles from the bank was shown to Bóchkova, and she was asked where she obtained such a sum, she said that it was her own earnings for twelve years, and those of Simón, whom she was going to marry. Simón Kartínkin, in turn, in his first statement, confessed that he and Bóchkova, at the instigation of Máslova, who had come with the key from the brothel, had stolen the money and divided it equally among themselves and Máslova." At this, Máslova gave another start, and even rose, blushing scarlet, and began to speak, but the bailiff stopped her. "At last," the secretary went on reading, "Kartínkin confessed to having supplied the powder in order to get Smyelkóv to sleep. When examined the second time, he denied having had anything to do either with stealing the money or giving Máslova the powder, accusing her of having done it alone. Concerning the money placed in the bank by Bóchkova, he said the same as she—that is, that the money was given to them both in tips by guests during twelve years' service."

Then followed an account of the examination of the prisoners when they were confronted, the depositions of the witnesses, and the opinions of experts. The indictment concluded:

"In consequence of the aforesaid, the peasant of the village Bórki, Simón Kartín-kin, thirty-three years of age; the lower middle-class woman Evfímiya Ivánova Bóchkova, forty-three years of age; and the lower middle-class woman Ekaterína Mikháylova Máslova, twenty-seven years of age, are charged with having, on the 17th of January 188—, conspired together to steal from the merchant Smyelkóv, money and a ring to the value of two thousand five hundred roubles, and of having given the merchant, Smyelkóv, poison to drink, with intent to deprive him of life, from which his, Smyelkóv's, death resulted.

"This crime comes under Section 4 and 5 of Article 1453 of the Penal Code. Therefore, and in accordance with Article 201 of the Criminal Court Procedure, the peasant Simón Kartínkin and the lower middle-class women Evfímiya Bóch-kova and Ekaterína Máslova are subject to the jurisdiction of the District Court and are to be tried by jury."

Thus the secretary ended the reading of his long indictment and, putting away the documents, sat down in his seat, passing both his hands through his hair. Everybody drew a sigh of relief with the pleasant conviction that now the examination would begin, when everything would be cleared up, and justice would be done. Nekhlyúdov alone did not experience that sensation: he was all absorbed in contemplation of the terrible charges brought against Máslova, whom he had known as an innocent and charming girl ten years before.

CHAPTER XI

INTERROGATION OF THE DEFENDANTS

When the reading of the indictment was ended, the presiding judge, having consulted with the members, turned to Kartínkin with an expression which manifestly said that now they would most surely ascertain all the details of the case.

"Peasant Simón Kartínkin," he began, leaning to his left.

Simón Kartínkin got up, holding his hands close at his sides, bending forward with his whole body, and continuing to move his cheeks inaudibly.

"You are accused of having, on January 17, 188—, in company with Evfímiya Bóchkova and Ekaterína Máslova, stolen Smyelkóv's money from his suitcase, and then of having brought arsenic and of having persuaded Ekaterína Máslova to give it to the merchant Smyelkóv to drink in wine, from which his death ensued. Do you plead guilty?" he said, leaning to his right.

"It is absolutely impossible, because it is our duty to serve the guests—"

"You will tell that later. Do you plead guilty?"

"Not at all. I only—"

"You will say that later. Do you plead guilty?" the presiding judge repeated calmly, but firmly.

"I can't do that because—"

Again the bailiff ran up to Simón Kartínkin and stopped him in a tragic whisper.

The presiding judge, with an expression on his face as if this matter had been settled, changed the position of the elbow of the arm in the hand of which he was holding a paper, and addressed Evfímiya Bóchkova.

"Evfímiya Bóchkova, you are accused of having taken on January 17, 188—, in company with Simón Kartínkin and Ekaterína Máslova, from the merchant Smyelkóv's suitcase, his money and ring, and after dividing the property up among yourselves, of having tried to conceal your crime by giving the merchant Smyelkóv poison, from which his death ensued. Do you plead guilty?"

"I am guilty of nothing," the defendant spoke boldly and firmly. "I did not even go into his room—. And as this lewd one went in there, she did it."

"You will tell that later," the presiding judge said again, just as gently and firmly as before. "So you do not plead guilty?"

"I did not take the money, and I did not give him anything to drink, and I was not in his room. If I had been in there, I would have kicked her out."

"You do not plead guilty?"

"Never."

"Very well."

"Ekaterína Máslova," began the presiding judge, addressing the third defendant, "you are accused of having come from the house of prostitution to a room in the Hotel Mauritania with the key to the merchant Smyelkóv's suitcase, and of having taken from that suitcase money and a ring," he said, as though reciting a lesson learned by rote, bending his ear to the member of the court on his left, who was telling him that according to the list of the exhibits a certain vial was missing, "of having taken from that suitcase money and a ring," repeated the judge, "and, after having divided up the stolen property, and having arrived with the merchant Smyelkóv at the Hotel Mauritania, of having offered Smyelkóv poisoned wine to drink, from the effects of which he died. Do you plead guilty?"

"I am not guilty of anything," she spoke rapidly. "As I have said before, so I say now: I did not take it, I did not, I did not, I took nothing; and the ring he gave me himself."

"You do not plead guilty to the charge of having taken the twenty-five hundred roubles?" said the presiding judge.

"I say I took nothing but the forty roubles."

"Do you plead guilty to having put some powders into the wine of the merchant Smyelkóv?"

"I do. Only I thought that they were sleeping-powders, as they told me, and that nothing would happen to him from them. I had no intentions of doing wrong. I say before God, I did not wish his death," she said.

"And so you do not plead guilty to having taken the money and ring of the merchant Smyelkóv," said the presiding judge. "But you do plead guilty to the charge of having administered the powders?"

"I plead guilty to this, only I thought they were sleeping-powders. I gave them to him to put him to sleep; I had no other intention."

"Very well," said the presiding judge, evidently satisfied with the result. "Tell, then, how it all happened," he said, leaning against the back of the chair, and placing both his hands on the table. "Tell everything as it happened. You may be able to improve your position by a frank confession."

Máslova continued to gaze at the presiding judge and to keep silent.

"Tell how it all happened."

"How it happened?" Máslova suddenly began, in a hurried voice. "I arrived at the hotel; I was taken to his room, and *he* was already there, very drunk." She pronounced the word "he" with a peculiar expression of terror, opening her eyes wide. "I wanted to drive home, but he would not let me."

She stopped, as though having suddenly lost the thread of what she was saying, or recalling something else.

"Well, and then?"

"And then? I stayed there, and then drove home."

At that point the assistant prosecuting attorney half raised himself, leaning unnaturally on one elbow.

"Do you wish to ask a question?" said the presiding judge, and, on the assistant prosecuting attorney's affirmative answer, he indicated by a gesture that he could put the question.

"I would like to ask whether the defendant had been acquainted with Simón Kartínkin before that," said the assistant prosecuting attorney without looking at Máslova.

Having put the question, he compressed his lips and frowned.

The judge repeated the question. Máslova gazed frightened at the assistant prosecuting attorney.

"With Simón? Yes," she said.

"I would like to know in what way the defendant was acquainted with Kartínkin, and whether they frequently met."

"In what way we were acquainted? He used to ask me to come to the guests, but there was no other acquaintance," replied Máslova, restlessly turning her eyes from the assistant prosecuting attorney to the presiding judge and back again.

"I would like to know why Kartínkin used to ask Máslova exclusively, and no other girls?" said the assistant prosecuting attorney, half-closing his eyes and with a light Mephistophelian smile.

"I do not know. How can I know?" replied Máslova, casting a frightened look all around her, and for a moment resting her eyes on Nekhlyúdov. "He asked whom he pleased."

"Has she recognized me?" Nekhlyúdov thought in terror, feeling all his blood rush to his face; but Máslova did not separate him from the rest and, turning immediately away from him, riveted her eyes on the assistant prosecuting attorney, with an expression of terror on her face.

"The defendant, then, denies having had any close relations with Kartínkin? Very well. I have nothing else to ask."

And the assistant prosecuting attorney immediately removed his elbow from the desk and began to write something down. In reality he was not writing anything at all, but only running his pen over the letters of his brief, but he pretended to imitate the prosecuting attorneys and lawyers who, after a clever question, make a note in their speeches that are to crush their opponents.

The presiding judge did not at once turn to the defendant, because he was just then asking the member of the court in the spectacles whether he agreed to his asking questions previously prepared and noted down.

"What happened next?" the presiding judge continued his inquiry.

"I came back home," continued Máslova, looking more boldly at the judge, "and gave the money to the madam and went to bed. I had barely fallen asleep when one of our girls, Bérta, woke me up with 'Go, your merchant has come again!' I did not want to go out, but the madam told me to go. In the meantime, *he*," she again uttered this word with manifest terror, "he had been all the time treating our girls; then he wanted to send for some more wine, but his money was all gone. The madam did not trust him. So he sent me to his room; and he told me where his money was, and how much I should take. So I went."

The presiding judge was whispering something to the member on the left and did not hear what Máslova was saying, but to show that he was listening, he repeated her last words.

"You went. Well, and then?" he said.

"I went there and did as he had ordered me to do. I went to his room. I did not go by myself, but called Simón Mikháylovich, and her," she said, pointing to Bóchkova.

"She is lying; I did not put my foot in there—" began Evfímiya Bóchkova, but she was stopped.

"I took out four red bills in their presence," Máslova continued, frowning, and without glancing at Bóchkova.

"Well, did not the defendant notice how much money there was in it, while she was taking the forty roubles?" again asked the assistant prosecuting attorney.

Máslova shuddered the moment the assistant prosecutor addressed her. She did not know how to explain her feeling, but she was sure he meant her harm. "I did not count, but I saw there were some hundred-rouble bills there."

"The defendant saw hundred-rouble bills—I have nothing else to ask."

"Well, so you brought the money?" the presiding judge went on to ask, looking at his watch.

"I did."

"Well, and then?" asked the presiding judge.

"Then he took me with him once more," said Máslova.

"And how did you give him the wine with the powder?" asked the judge.

"How? I poured it into the wine and gave it to him."

"Why did you give it to him?"

Without answering the question, she heaved a deep and heavy sigh.

"He would not let me go," she said, after a moment's silence. "I got tired of him, so I went into the corridor, and said to Simón Mikháylovich, 'If he'd only let me go —I am so tired.' And Simón Mikháylovich said, 'We are tired of him, too. Let us give him some sleeping-powders; that will put him to sleep, and then you will get away.' And I said, 'Very well!' I thought it was a harmless powder. He gave me a paper. I went in, and he was lying behind a screen, and asked me at once to let him have some cognac. I took from the table a bottle of liqueur brandy, filled two glasses—one for myself, and one for him—and poured the powder into his glass. I would never have given it if I had known what it was."

"Well, how did you get possession of the ring?" asked the presiding judge.

"He himself had made me a present of it."

"When did he give it to you?"

"When we came to his room, I wanted to leave, and he struck me on the head and broke my comb. I grew angry and started to go away. He took the ring off his finger and gave it to me, asking me to stay," she said.

Just then the assistant prosecuting attorney half-raised himself, and, with the same feignedly naïve look, asked the judge's permission to put a few more questions.

His request being granted, he bent his head over his embroidered collar and asked:

"I would like to know how long the defendant remained in the merchant Smyelkóv's room."

Again Máslova was overcome by terror and, her eyes restlessly flitting from the assistant prosecuting attorney to the presiding judge, she muttered, hurriedly:

"I do not remember how long."

"Well, does the defendant remember whether she called elsewhere in the hotel upon coming out of the merchant Smyelkóv's room?"

Máslova thought a while.

"I went into the adjoining room—it was unoccupied," she said.

"Why did you step in there?" said the assistant prosecuting attorney, carried away, and addressing her directly.

"I went in to fix myself, and to wait for a cab."

"And was Kartínkin in the room with the defendant, or not?"

"He came in, too."

"What did he come in for?"

"There was some of the merchant's cognac left, so we drank it together."

"Ah, you drank it together. Very well. And did the defendant have any conversation with Simón?"

Máslova suddenly frowned, grew red in her face, and rapidly said: "What I said? Nothing. I have told everything that took place. I know nothing else. Do with me what you please. I am not guilty, and that's all."

"I have nothing else," the prosecuting attorney said to the presiding judge and, unnaturally raising his shoulders, began swiftly to note down in the brief of his speech the confession of the defendant that she had been in an unoccupied room with Simón.

There ensued a moment's silence.

"Have you nothing else to say?"

"I have said everything," she declared with a sigh and sat down again.

Thereupon the presiding judge made a note of something and, having listened to a communication which the member of the court on his left had made to him in a whisper, he announced a recess of ten minutes in the session and hurriedly rose and left the room. The consultation between the presiding judge and the member on his left, the tall, bearded man, with the large, kindly eyes, consisted in the latter's information that his stomach was slightly out of order and that he wished to massage himself a little and swallow some drops. It was this that he had told the presiding judge, and the judge acceded to his request and granted a ten minutes' recess.

Right after the judges rose the jurors, the lawyers, and the witnesses, and, with the pleasurable sensation of having performed a part of an important duty, they moved to and fro.

Nekhlyúdov went into the jurors' room and there sat down at the window.

CHAPTER XII

NEKHLYÚDOV'S FIRST MEETING WITH KATYÚSHA

Yes, this was Katyúsha.

Nekhlyúdov's relations with Katyúsha had been like this:

Nekhlyúdov saw Katyúsha for the first time when, as a third-year student at the university, he passed the summer with his aunts, working on his essay about the ownership of land. His vacations he usually passed with his mother and sister on his mother's suburban estate near Moscow; but in that particular year his sister was married and his mother went abroad to a spa. Nekhlyúdov had to work on his essay, and so he decided to spend the summer with his aunts. There, in the depth of the country, it was quiet and there were no distractions; and the aunts tenderly loved their nephew and heir, and he loved them and their old-fashioned ways and simplicity of life.

During that summer Nekhlyúdov experienced that rapturous mood which comes over a youth when he for the first time discovers, not by the indications of others, but from within, all the beauty and significance of life and all the importance of the work which is to be performed in it by each man, when he sees the possibility of endless perfectibility of himself and of the whole universe; and when he devotes himself to that perfectibility not only with the hope but with the full conviction of being able to attain the perfection of which he has been dreaming. During that year, while attending his lectures, he had had a chance of reading Spencer's *Social Statics*, and Spencer's reflections on the ownership of land had made a strong impression on him, especially since he himself was the son of a large landowner. His father had not been rich, but his mother had received about twenty-five thousand acres of land as a dowry. It was then the first time that he had perceived the cruelty and injustice of private ownership, and, being one of those men to whom a sacrifice in the name. of moral demands affords the highest spiritual enjoyment, he had decided not to make use of his right of the ownership of land and had given away to the peasants the land which he had inherited from his father. And it was on this subject that he was writing his essay.

His life on the estate of his aunts, during that summer, ran like this: he rose very early, sometimes at three o'clock, and before sunrise, frequently before the morning mist had lifted, went to bathe in the river at the foot of a hill and returned home while the dew was still on the grass and the flowers. At times, he sat down, soon after drinking his coffee, to work on his essay or to read up the sources for it, but very frequently, instead of reading or writing, he went away from the house and wandered across the fields and through the woods. Before dinner he fell asleep somewhere in the shade of the garden; then, at table, he entertained his aunts and made them laugh by his gaiety; then he went horseback riding or rowing, and in the evening he read again or sat with his aunts playing patience. Frequently he could not sleep during the night, especially when the moon was shining, because he was overflowing with an excited joy of life, and so, instead of sleeping, he would stroll through the garden, dreaming and thinking.

Thus he had quietly and happily passed the first month of his life with his aunts, without paying the slightest attention to the half-chambermaid, half-ward, black-eyed, light-footed Katyúsha.

At that time, Nekhlyúdov, who had been brought up under his mother's wing, though nineteen years of age was an entirely innocent youth. He dreamed of women only as a wife. But all the women who, according to his opinion, could not be his wife were people and not women. But on Ascension Day of that summer a neighbour happened to call with her children, two young ladies and a schoolboy, and a young artist of peasant origin who was staying at their house.

After tea they began to play "widow-catch" in front of the house, on the lawn which had already been mowed. Katyúsha was included. After several changes of places Nekhlyúdov had to run with Katyúsha. It was always pleasant for Nekhlyúdov to see Katyúsha, but it had never occurred to him that there could be any special relations between them.

"Well, I won't be able to catch them," said the cheerful artist, very swift on his short and crooked but strong peasant legs, who was now "it," "unless they stumble!"

"You!... Not catch us?"

"One, two, three!"

They clapped their hands three times. With difficulty restraining her laughter, Katyúsha rapidly exchanged places with Nekhlyúdov, and, with her strong, rough little hand pressing his large hand, she started running to the left, rustling her starched skirt.

Nekhlyúdov was running fast, and, as he did not wish to be caught by the artist, he raced as fast as his legs would carry him. As he looked around he saw the artist close at Katyúsha's heels, and she, moving her lithe young legs, did not let herself be caught, but got away to his left. In front was a clump of lilac bushes behind which no one was running, and Katyúsha, looking back at Nekhlyúdov, made a sign with her head to him to join her behind the bushes. He understood her and ran back of the clump. But here, back of the lilac bushes, there was a small ditch overgrown with nettles which he did not know about; he stumbled into it, and in his fall stung his hands on the nettles and wet them in the evening dew; but he immediately got up, laughing at himself, and ran out into a clear spot.

Katyúsha, smiling brightly and her eyes as black as moist blackberries, was running toward him. They met and clasped each other's hands.

"You got stung, I think," she said, adjusting her braid with her free hand; she breathed heavily and, smiling, looked straight at him with her upturned eyes.

"I did not know there was a ditch there," he said, himself smiling and not letting her hand go.

She moved closer to him, and he, himself not knowing how it all happened, moved his face toward her; she did not turn away, and he pressed her hand more firmly, and kissed her on the lips.

"Oh, my!" she muttered, and, with a swift motion freeing her hand, ran away from him.

She ran up to the lilac bushes, picked off two branches of white lilacs from which the blossoms were already starting to fall, and fanning her heated face with them and looking around at him, swinging her arms freely, went back to the players.

From that time on the relations between Nekhlyúdov and Katyúsha were changed, and there arose those other relations which are established between an innocent young man and an equally innocent young girl who are attracted to each other.

The moment Katyúsha entered the room, or if he saw her white apron from a distance, everything seemed to him as though illuminated by the sunlight, everything became more interesting, more cheerful, more significant, and life was more joyful. She experienced the same. It was not merely Katyúsha's presence and nearness that produced that effect upon Nekhlyúdov; it was also produced by the mere consciousness that there was a Katyúsha, just as she was affected by consciousness of his existence. If Nekhlyúdov received an unpleasant letter from his mother, or if his essay did not proceed satisfactorily, or if he felt an inexplicable youthful sadness —it was enough for him to think of Katyúsha's existence and that he would see her for all that to be dispersed.

Katyúsha had many household cares, but she generally did them all in time and in her leisure she read books; Nekhlyúdov gave her the works of Dostoévski and of Turgénev, which he himself had just finished reading. Nothing gave her so much pleasure as Turgénev's *A Quiet Spot.* They conversed with each other in fits and snatches, while meeting in the corridor, in the balcony, in the yard, and sometimes in the room of the aunts' old chambermaid, Matryóna Pávlovna, with whom Katyúsha was living and to whose room Nekhlyúdov used to go to drink tea. The conversations which took place in the presence of Matryóna Pávlovna were very enjoyable. It was much worse when they talked to each other alone. Their eyes at once began to say something different, something much more important than what the lips were saying; the lips pursed, and they felt uneasy, and hastened to get away from each other.

These relations existed between Nekhlyúdov and Katyúsha during the whole time of his first visit at his aunts'. The aunts noticed these relations, were frightened, and even wrote about them abroad to Princess Eléna Ivánovna, Nekhlyúdov's mother. Aunt Maríya Ivánovna was afraid lest Dmítri should have an affair with Katyúsha. But her fears were groundless: Nekhlyúdov, without knowing it, loved Katyúsha as only innocent people love, and his love was his main shield against his fall, and against hers. He not only had no desire to possess her physically, but was even terrified at the thought of such a possibility. The fears of the poetical Sófya Ivánovna, that Dmítri, with his uncompromising and determined character, being in love with the girl, might make her his wife without paying any attention to her origin and position, were much better founded.

If Nekhlyúdov had then clearly been conscious of his love for Katyúsha, and especially if they had tried to convince him that he could not and should not by any means unite his fate with that of the girl, it might have easily happened that he, with his customary directness in everything, would have decided that there were no urgent reasons against marrying a girl, whoever she might be, if he loved her. But his aunts did not tell him their fears, and so he departed without confessing his love to the girl.

He was convinced that his feeling for Katyúsha was only one of the manifestations of those feelings of the joy of living, which at that time filled all his being, and which was also shared by that sweet, gay girl. As he was leaving, and Katyúsha, standing on the porch with his aunts, saw him off with her black, slightly squinting eyes full of tears, he was conscious of leaving behind him something beautiful and dear, which would never be repeated. And he felt very sad.

"Good-bye, Katyúsha, I thank you for everything," he said over Sófya Ivánovna's cap, seating himself in the carriage.

"Good-bye, Dmítri Ivánovich," she said in her pleasant, affectionate voice and, restraining the tears which filled her eyes, ran into the vestibule, where she could weep at her ease.

CHAPTER XIII

ANOTHER VISIT TO HIS AUNTS

After that Nekhlyúdov did not see Katyúsha for three years. And he saw her only when, having become an officer, he, on his way to join his unit, stopped to see his aunts, a completely different man from what he had been three years before.

At that time he had been an honest, self-sacrificing young man, ready to devote himself to any good cause; but now he was a dissolute, refined egotist, who loved only his own pleasure. Then, God's world had presented itself to him as a mystery, which he had joyfully and rapturously tried to solve; but now, in his new life, everything was simple and clear and was defined by those conditions in which he happened to be. Then, he had regarded as necessary and important a communion with Nature and with men before him who had lived, thought, and felt (philosophy, poetry); now human institutions and dealings with friends were the necessary and important things. Then, woman had presented herself to him as a mysterious and enchanting creature—enchanting by dint of her very mysteriousness; now, the significance of woman, of every woman except those in his family or the wives of his friends, was quite definite; woman was one of the best instruments of the pleasure that was his. Then, money had not been needed and less than a third of the money offered him by his mother had sufficed, and he had been able to re- nounce the land left him by his father and give it to the peasants; now, the fifteen hundred roubles given him every month by his mother were not enough, and he had had some unpleasant encounters with her over money. Then, he had regarded his spiritual being as his real ego; now, he regarded his healthy, virile, animal ego as his actual personality.

All this terrible change had taken place in him only because he had quit trusting himself and had begun to believe others. The reason he had quit trusting himself and had begun believing others was because he had found it hard to live by trusting himself: while trusting himself, every question had to be solved not in favour of his own animal ego in search of frivolous enjoyments, but nearly always against himself; whereas believing others, there was nothing to solve—everything had been solved before and not in favour of the spiritual, but of the animal ego. More than that: while he trusted himself, he was constantly subjected to the judgment of others; while believing others, he met the approval of those who surrounded him.

Formerly, when Nekhlyúdov had been thinking, reading, and speaking about God, about truth, about wealth, about poverty—all his neighbours had considered this out of place and even ridiculous, and his mother and his aunt had called him *"notre cher philosophe"* with good-natured irony; but when he read novels, told nasty anecdotes, went to the French theatre to witness ridiculous vaudevilles and gaily narrated them, he was praised and applauded by everybody. When he had regarded it as necessary to limit his needs and had worn an old overcoat and not drunk liquor, everybody had considered this an odd and boastful originality; but when he spent large sums on hunting, or on re-doing his extremely luxurious study, everybody praised his good taste and gave him expensive things. When he had been chaste and had intended to remain so until his marriage, his relatives had been afraid for his health, and even his mother was not grieved, but, on the contrary, rejoiced, when she heard that he was a real man and had won a certain French woman away from his friend. But the princess could not think without horror of the incident with Katyúsha—namely, that it might have occurred to him to marry her.

Similarly, when Nekhlyúdov, upon having reached his majority, had given the peasants the small estate inherited from his father, because he had considered the ownership of land an injustice, his action had horrified his mother and his relatives and formed a constant subject of reproach and ridicule for all his kin. They never stopped telling him that the peasants who had received the land had not only not become any richer, but that, on the contrary, they had been impoverished through the establishment of three taverns and from having stopped working. But when Nekhlyúdov, upon entering the Guards, had gambled away so much money in the company of distinguished comrades that Eléna Ivánovna was compelled to draw on her capital, she was hardly grieved, for she considered it natural and even good to have this virus inoculated early in youth and in good society.

At first Nekhlyúdov had struggled, but it was a hard struggle, because everything which he had considered good while trusting himself, was regarded as bad by others, and, vice versa, everything which he, trusting himself, had regarded as bad, was considered good by all the people who surrounded him. The end of it was that Nekhlyúdov succumbed, ceased trusting himself and began to believe others. At first this renunciation of self had been unpleasant, but this disagreeable sensation lasted a very short time, and soon Nekhlyúdov, who in the meantime had begun to smoke and drink, no longer experienced this unpleasant sensation, but rather a great relief.

Nekhlyúdov surrendered himself, with all the passion of his nature, to this new life, which was approved by all around him, and drowned that voice in himself that demanded something quite different. This had begun after his arrival in St. Petersburg and became an accomplished fact by his entrance into military service.

Military service in general corrupts people by putting those who enter it in a condition of complete indolence, that is, by giving them no intelligent and useful work to do, and by excusing them from common human obligations, in place of which it substitutes the conventional honour of regiment, uniform, and flag, and by investing them, on the one hand, with an unlimited power over other people, and, on the other, by subjecting them to servile humility before their superiors.

But when to this corruption of the military service in general, with its honour of uniform and flag, and its legalization of violence and murder, is added the seduction of wealth and close connection with the imperial family, as is the case in the select regiments of the Guards, in which only rich and aristocratic officers serve, this corruption reaches, in the people who are under its influence, a condition of absolute insanity of egotism. Nekhlyúdov was in such an insanity of egotism from the time when he entered the military service and began to live as his comrades did.

There was nothing to do but to wear a uniform which had been beautifully made and brushed, not by himself, but by others, and a helmet and weapons, which had also been made and burnished and handed to him by others; to ride on a beautiful horse, which somebody else had brought up, exercised, and groomed; to go thus to instruction or to parade, with people similarly accoutred, and to gallop, and brandish his sword, to shoot, and teach others to shoot. There was nothing else to do, and the most distinguished dignitaries, young and old men, and the Tsar and his suite, not only approved of this occupation, but even praised and rewarded it. After doing this it was regarded as good and important, squandering money which came from one knew not where, to come together in the officers' clubs or in the most expensive restaurants to eat, or, more particularly, to drink; then to go to the theatre, to balls, and to women, and then again riding, brandishing sabres, galloping, and again squandering money, and wine, cards, and women.

Such a life has a peculiarly corrupting influence upon the military, because if any man, not belonging to the army, should lead such an existence, he could not help but feel ashamed of it to the bottom of his heart. But military people think that it cannot be otherwise, and brag and are proud of such a life, particularly during war time, just as was the case with Nekhlyúdov, who had entered the army immediately after the declaration of the war with Turkey. "We are ready to sacrifice our lives in war, and therefore such a careless, gay life is not only permissible, but even necessary for us. And we do live such a life."

Such were the thoughts which Nekhlyúdov dimly thought during that period of his life; during that time he felt the rapture of liberation from moral barriers, which he had erected for himself before, and he continuously remained in a chronic state of egotistical insanity.

He was in that condition when, three years later, he visited his aunts.

CHAPTER XIV

A NEW IMPRESSION
OF KATYÚSHA

Tolstoy

Resurrection

page 46

Nekhlyúdov called on his aunts because their estate was on the way to the regiment, which was in advance of him, and because they had earnestly asked him to, but chiefly, now, in order to see Katyúsha. Maybe in the bottom of his heart he already had evil intentions in regard to Katyúsha, which his unfettered animal man kept whispering to him, but he was not conscious of this and simply wanted to visit the places where he had been so happy before and to see his somewhat funny, but dear and good-hearted aunts, who always surrounded him with an invisible atmosphere of love and delight, and to look at sweet Katyúsha, of whom he had such an agreeable recollection.

He arrived at the end of March, on Good Friday, at a time when the roads were thawing and the rain was pouring down, so that he arrived wet to the skin and chilled, but brisk and wide awake, as he always was during that time. "I wonder whether she is still here!" he thought, as he drove into his aunts' familiar snow-covered old country courtyard with its brick wall. He expected her to come running out on the porch upon hearing the tinkling of his bell, but on the servants' porch there came out only two barefooted old women with their dresses tucked up and buckets in their hands, evidently busy washing floors. Nor was she at the main entrance; none came out but lackey Tíkhon, in an apron, who, no doubt, was also busy cleaning up. In the ante-chamber he met Sófya Ivánovna, in a silk dress and a cap.

"Now, it is nice that you have come!" said Sófya Ivánovna, kissing him. "Máshenka is somewhat ill; she was tired out in church. We have been to communion."

"I congratulate you, Aunt Sófya," said Nekhlyúdov, kissing Sófya Ivánovna's hands. "Forgive me for having wet you."

"Go to your room. You are wet through, and even your moustache— Katyúsha! Katyúsha! Quick, bring him some coffee."

"Right away!" the familiar, pleasant voice was heard from the corridor.

Nekhlyúdov's heart gave a joyful leap. "She is here!" And he felt as though the sun had come out from behind the clouds. Nekhlyúdov merrily followed Tíkhon to his old room to change his clothes.

Nekhlyúdov wanted to ask Tíkhon about Katyúsha—how she was, and whether she was going to marry soon. But Tíkhon was so respectful and, at the same time, so stern, and so firmly insisted upon pouring water from the pitcher upon Nekhlyúdov's hands, that he did not have the courage to ask him about Katyúsha, and inquired only about his grandchildren, about the old stallion, and about the watch-dog, Polkán. All were alive and well, except Polkán, who had gotten rabies the year before.

He had barely thrown off his damp clothes and was dressing himself, when he heard hurried steps, and somebody knocked at the door. Nekhlyúdov recognized the steps and the knock at the door. Nobody walked or knocked that way but she.

He threw his damp overcoat on and went up to the door.

"Come in!"

It was she, Katyúsha. Still the same Katyúsha, even more charming than before. Her smiling, naïve, slightly squinting, black eyes were as upturned as before. She wore, as formerly, a clean white apron. She brought from his aunts a cake of scented soap, fresh from the wrapper, and two towels, one a large Russian towel, and the other a terry-cloth one. The untouched soap, with the letters distinctly marked upon it, and the towels, and she herself—everything was equally clean, fresh, un-touched, agreeable. On seeing him, her sweet, firm, red lips pursed as before from uncontrollable joy.

"Welcome, Dmítri Ivánovich!" she uttered with difficulty, and her face blushed all over.

"I greet thee—you," he did not know whether to say "thou" or "you" to her, and he blushed, just like her. "Are you alive and well?"

"Thank God. Your aunt has sent you your favourite pink soap," she said, placing the soap on the table, and the towels over the back of an armchair.

"He has his own," said Tíkhon, defending his guest's independence and pointing proudly to Nekhlyúdov's large open toilet bag, with its silver lids and an immense mass of bottles, brushes, pomatums, perfumes, and all kinds of toilet articles.

"Thank my aunt for me. I am so glad I have come," said Nekhlyúdov, feeling that there was the same light and gentleness in his heart that used to be there in former days.

She only smiled in reply to these words and went out.

His aunts, who had always loved Nekhlyúdov, this time met him with even greater joy than usual. Dmítri was going to the war, where he might be wounded or killed. This touched his aunts.

Nekhlyúdov had so arranged his journey as to be able to spend only one day with his aunts, but, upon seeing Katyúsha, he agreed to stay until through Easter which was two days away, and telegraphed his friend and comrade Shénbok, whom he was to have met in Odessa, also to come to his aunts'.

Nekhlyúdov felt the old feeling toward Katyúsha from the first day he saw her. Just as formerly, he was still unable to look at Katyúsha's white apron without be-ing excited; to restrain his joy when he heard her steps, her voice, her laugh; without a feeling of tenderness to look in her eyes, which were as dark as blackberries, especially when she smiled; nor, above all, could he help seeing with embarrassment that she blushed every time she met him. He felt that he was in love, but not as formerly, when this love had been a mystery to him and he did not dare acknowledge that he was in love, and when he had been convinced that it was possible to love only once; now he was consciously in love and glad of it; he had a dim idea what this love was, though he concealed it from himself, and what might come of it.

In Nekhlyúdov, as in all people, there were two men; one the spiritual man, who sought his well-being in such matters only as would be other people's, too, and the other, the animal man, who was looking only for his own well-being, ready to sacrifice the well-being of the whole world to it. During that period of his insanity of egotism, provoked by his Petersburg and military life, the animal man was ruling within him and had completely suppressed the spiritual man. But, upon seeing Katyúsha and again feeling the same feeling which he had had for her before, the spiritual man raised his head and began to assert his rights. During the two days preceding Easter an internal struggle, though unconscious on his part, agitated him incessantly.

In the depth of his soul he knew that he ought to depart, that there was no reason why he should stay at his aunts' any longer, and that nothing good would come of it, but it was so gay and pleasant that he did not even say it to himself, and stayed.

On the Saturday evening preceding Easter Sunday, the priest, with the deacon and the sexton, having, as they told it, with difficulty journeyed in a sleigh over puddles and dirt in order to make the three versts which separated the church from the house of his aunts, arrived to serve the matins.

During the matins, which were attended by Nekhlyúdov, his aunts, and the servants, he did not take his eyes off Katyúsha, who was standing at the door and handing in the censers; then he gave the Easter kiss to the priest and his aunts, and was on the point of retiring, when he saw in the corridor Matryóna Pávlovna, Maríya Ivánovna's old chambermaid, and Katyúsha getting ready to drive to church, in order to get the bread and Easter cakes blessed. "I will go with them," he thought.

The road to the church was passable neither for wheel carriages nor for sleighs, and so Nekhlyúdov, who ordered things at his aunts' as though he were at home, told them to saddle the horse for him, the so-called "old stallion," and, instead of going to bed, dressed himself in his gorgeous uniform with the tightly fitting riding breeches, threw his overcoat over his shoulders, and rode on the overfed, stout old stallion, that did not stop neighing, in the darkness, through puddles and snow, to church.

CHAPTER XV

THE EASTER SERVICE

For the rest of Nekhlyúdov's life this matin remained one of his brightest and strongest memories.

The service had already begun, when, having groped through the dense darkness, lighted up occasionally by patches of snow, and having splashed through the water, he rode into the yard of the church on the stallion that kept pricking his ears at the sight of the little street-lamps that were burning all around the church.

Having recognized Maríya Ivánovna's nephew, the peasants took him to a dry place where he could dismount, tied his horse, and led him into the church. The church was full of people celebrating the holiday.

On the right were the men: old men in home-made caftans and bast shoes and clean white leg-rags, and young men, in new cloth caftans, girded with brightly coloured belts, and in boots. On the left were the women, in bright silk kerchiefs, plush sleeveless jackets, with brilliant red shirt-sleeves and blue, green, red, and motley-coloured skirts, and small boots with steel heel-plates. The modest old women, in white kerchiefs, gray caftans, old skirts, and leather or new bast shoes, were standing in back of them. Here and there, on both sides, stood the dressed-up children, with slicked-down hair. The peasants were crossing themselves and bowing, tossing their heads; the women, especially the old women, riveting their faded eyes upon one icon with its tapers, firmly pressed their joined fingers against kerchief, shoulders, and stomach, and, saying something under their breath, were standing and making low obeisances, or were kneeling. The children, imitating their elders, prayed attentively, as long as they were watched. The gold iconostasis was resplendent from the gilt spirals that on all sides surrounded the large candles. The candelabrum was aglow with its candles; from the choir loft were heard the joyous voices of the amateur choristers, with the roaring basses and the descants of the boys.

Nekhlyúdov went to the front. In the middle stood the aristocracy: a landowner, with his wife and his son in a sailor blouse, the police officer, the telegraphist, a merchant in top-boots, the village elder with a decoration, and to the right of the ambo, back of the landowner's wife, Matryóna Pávlovna, in a short lilac dress and white fringed shawl, and Katyúsha, in a white dress with tucks, blue belt, and red ribbon on her black hair.

Everything was holiday-like, solemn, cheerful, and beautiful: the priests in their bright silver chasubles, with their golden crosses, and the deacon and sextons in their gala silver and gold copes, and the dressed-up amateur choristers, with their plastered-down hair, and the gay dancing tunes of the holiday songs, and the continuous blessing of the people by the clergy with their triple, flower-bedecked candles, with the ever-repeated exclamations, "Christ is risen! Christ is risen!"—everything was beautiful, but best of all was Katyúsha in her white dress and blue belt with the red ribbon on her head and with her sparkling, rapturous eyes.

Nekhlyúdov was conscious of her seeing him, though she did not turn around. He noticed that, as he passed by her, up to the altar. He had nothing to say to her, but he made up something and said, when abreast of her:

"My aunt said that she would break her fast after the late mass."

Her young blood, as always at the sight of him, flushed her sweet face, and her black eyes, smiling and rejoicing, looked naïvely upwards and rested on Nekhlyúdov.

"I know," she said, smiling.

Just then a sexton with a brass pot, making his way through the crowd, came past Katyúsha, and without looking at her, brushed her with the skirt of his cope. The sexton had done this evidently in his attempt to express his respect for Nekhlyúdov by making a circle around him. Nekhlyúdov was amazed that he, this sexton, did not comprehend that everything that was there, or anywhere else in the world, existed only for Katyúsha, and that he could disregard anything else in the world but her, because she was the centre of everything. The gold of the iconostasis gleamed for her and all these candles burned in the candelabrum and in the candlesticks; the joyous refrains, "Behold the Passover of the Lord! Rejoice, O ye People!" were for her. Everything good that was in the world was only for her. And Katyúsha understood, so he thought, that it was all for her. So it seemed to Nekhlyúdov, as he looked at her stately figure in the white dress with its pleats, and at her concentrated, joyful face, by the expression of which he could see that what was singing in his heart was singing also in hers.

In the interval between the early and late mass, Nekhlyúdov went out of the church. The people stepped aside before him and bowed. Some recognized him, and some asked, "Who is he?" He stopped on the parvis. Beggars surrounded him: he distributed the small change which he had in his purse and walked down the steps of the porch.

It was now sufficiently light to distinguish objects, but the sun was not yet up. The people were seated on the churchyard graves. Katyúsha had remained in the church, and Nekhlyúdov stopped, waiting for her.

The people still kept coming out, and, clattering with their hobnails on the flagstones, walked down the steps and scattered in the yard and cemetery.

A decrepit old man, Maríya Ivánovna's pastry-baker, with trembling head, stopped Nekhlyúdov to give him the Easter greeting, and his old wife, with

wrinkled neck beneath her silk kerchief, took a saffron-yellow egg out of a handkerchief and gave it to him. At this point a young, muscular peasant, in a new sleeveless coat and green belt also came up.

"Christ is risen!" he said, with laughing eyes, and, moving toward Nekhlyúdov, enveloped him with an agreeable peasant odour and, tickling him with his curly beard, three times kissed him in the middle of his mouth with his own strong, fresh lips.

While Nekhlyúdov was kissing the peasant and receiving from him a dark brown egg, there appeared the lilac dress of Matryóna Pávlovna and the sweet black head with the red ribbon.

She espied him above the heads of those who were walking in front of her, and he saw her face gleaming with joy.

Matryóna Pávlovna and Katyúsha stopped before the door to give alms to the beggars. A beggar with a healed-over scar in place of a nose went up to Katyúsha. She took something out of her handkerchief, gave it to him, and, without expressing the least disgust—on the contrary, with the same joyful sparkle in her eyes—kissed him three times. While she was giving the beggar the Easter kiss, her eyes met Nekhlyúdov's glance. Her eyes seemed to ask: "Am I doing right?"

"Yes, yes, my dear, everything is good, everything is beautiful, I love you."

They walked down the steps, and he walked over to her. He did not mean to exchange the Easter kiss with her, but only to be closer to her.

"Christ is risen!" said Matryóna Pávlovna, bending her head and smiling, with an intonation which said that on that day all were equal, and, wiping her mouth with her rolled-up handkerchief, offered him her lips.

"He is risen indeed!" replied Nekhlyúdov, kissing her.

He looked around at Katyúsha. She burst into a blush and immediately went up to him.

"Christ is risen, Dmítri Ivánovich!"

"He is risen indeed!" he said. They kissed twice and stopped, as though considering whether it was necessary to proceed, and having decided in the affirmative, kissed for the third time, and both smiled.

"You will not go to the priest?" asked Nekhlyúdov.

"No, Dmítri Ivánovich, we shall stay here," said Katyúsha, breathing with her full breast, as though after a labour of joy, and looking straight at him with her submissive, chaste, loving, slightly squinting eyes.

In the love between a man and a woman there is always a minute when that love reaches its zenith, when there is nothing conscious, rational, or sensual. Such a moment for Nekhlyúdov was the night preceding Easter Sunday. As he now recalled Katyúsha, this moment alone, of all the situations in which he had seen her, loomed up and effaced all the others: her black, smooth, shining little head, her white dress with the pleats, chastely embracing her graceful figure and girlish bosom, and that blush, and those tender, sparkling eyes, and in her whole being two main characteristics—the purity of the chastity of love, not only toward him, he knew that, but of her love for everyone and everything, not only for the good that there was in the world, but even for the beggar, whom she had kissed.

Tolstoy
Resurrection
page 52

He knew that she had that love, because he was conscious of it in himself that night and that morning, as he was conscious that in that love he became one with her.

Ah, if all that had stopped at the feeling which he had experienced that night! "Yes, all that terrible business was done after that night of Easter Sunday!" he now thought, sitting at the window in the jury-room.

CHAPTER XVI

THE TRIUMPH OF THE ANIMAL

After returning from church, Nekhlyúdov broke his fast with his aunts, and, to brace himself, followed the habit which he had acquired in the army, and drank some brandy and wine, and went to his room, where he fell asleep in his clothes. He was awakened by a knock at the door. Knowing by the knock that it was she, he arose, rubbing his eyes and stretching.

"Katyúsha, is it you? Come in," he said, rising.

She half-opened the door.

"Dinner is served," she said.

She was in the same white dress, but without the ribbon in her hair. As she glanced into his eyes, she beamed, as if she were announcing something very joyful to him.

"I shall be right there," he said, taking up the comb to comb his hair.

She stood there for a minute. He noticed it and, throwing away the comb, moved toward her. But she immediately turned around and walked with her customary light, rapid gait over the corridor carpet-strip.

"What a fool I am!" Nekhlyúdov said to himself, "Why did I not stop her?"

And he ran after her through the corridor.

He himself did not know what it was he wanted of her; but it seemed to him that when she had entered his room he ought to have done what everybody does under such circumstances, but he had not done it.

"Katyúsha, wait," he said.

She looked back.

"What do you want?" she said, stopping.

"Nothing, only—"

And making an effort, remembering what other men in his position would do in such a situation, he put his arm around Katyúsha's waist.

She stopped and looked him in the eyes.

"Don't do that, Dmítri Ivánovich—don't do that," she muttered, blushing and with tears, and with her rough, strong hand pushed away the embracing arm.

Nekhlyúdov let her go and for a moment felt not only uneasy and ashamed, but disgusted with himself. He ought to have trusted himself, but he did not understand that this uneasiness and shame were the best qualities of his soul begging to be freed, though he, on the contrary, thought that it was his stupidity that was speaking within him, and that it was necessary to do as everybody else did.

He caught up with her a second time, again embraced her and kissed her on the neck. This kiss was not at all like those first two kisses: the first, the unconscious kiss behind the lilac bush, and the other, in the morning, at church. This kiss was terrible, and she felt it.

"What are you doing?" she cried in such a voice as if he had irretrievably broken something endlessly valuable, and ran away from him at full speed.

He arrived in the dining-room. The dressed-up aunts, the doctor, and a lady from the neighbourhood were standing by the hors d'oeuvres. Everything was as usual, but in Nekhlyúdov's soul there was a storm. He did not understand a word of what was said to him, answered questions haphazardly, and thought only of Katyúsha, recalling the sensation of that last kiss, when he had caught up with her in the corridor. He was not able to think of anything else. Whenever she would enter the room, he, without looking at her, was with all his being conscious of her presence and had to make an effort over himself not to look at her.

After dinner he at once went back to his room and long paced up and down in the greatest agitation, listening to all the sounds in the house and waiting to hear her steps. The animal man which was dwelling within him not only raised his head, but had trampled underfoot the spiritual man which he had been during his first visit and even on that morning while at church; and now that terrible animal man ruled all alone in his soul. Though Nekhlyúdov was always on the watch for Katyúsha, he did not succeed in seeing her alone once that day. She probably was avoiding him. But toward evening it so happened that she had to go into the room adjoining the one which he occupied. The doctor was staying overnight, and Katyúsha had to make the bed for him. Hearing her steps, Nekhlyúdov, stepping lightly and holding his breath, as though getting ready to commit a crime, walked up behind her.

Having put both her hands into a pillow-case and holding the corners of a pillow, she looked back at him and smiled, not a gay and joyful smile as before, but a smile of fear and pity. This smile seemed to tell him that what he was doing was bad. He stopped for a moment. A struggle was still possible. Though feebly, the voice of genuine love for her was still audible in him, which told him about *her*, about *her* feelings, *her* life, but another voice kept saying to him, "Look out, or you will lose *your* pleasure, *your* happiness." And this second voice drowned the first. He went up to her decisively. And a terrible, uncontrollable, animal feeling took possession of him.

Without letting her out of his embrace, Nekhlyúdov seated her on the bed, and, feeling that something else had to be done, sat down near her.

"Dmítri Ivánovich, dear, please let me go," she said in a pitiful voice. "Matryóna Pávlovna is coming!" she cried, tearing herself away; there was, indeed, some one coming toward the door.

"Then I will come to you in the night," he muttered. "You are alone?"

"What are you saying? Never! You must not." She spoke with her lips only, but her whole agitated, embarrassed being spoke something quite different.

The person who came to the door was indeed Matryóna Pávlovna. She entered the door with a blanket over her arm, and, looking reproachfully at Nekhlyúdov, angrily upbraided Katyúsha for having taken the wrong blanket.

Nekhlyúdov went away in silence. He did not even feel ashamed. He saw, by Matryóna Pávlovna's expression, that she blamed him, and knew that she was right in blaming him, just as he knew that what he was doing was bad; but the animal feeling, which had come up from under the former feeling of genuine love for her, took possession of him and reigned all alone, to the exclusion of everything else. He now knew what had to be done to satisfy his feeling, and he was looking for a way of doing it.

During the whole evening he was beside himself: he now went in to see his aunts, now went away from them to his room or out onto the porch, and kept thinking of nothing else but how he might see her alone; but she avoided him, and Matryóna Pávlovna tried not to let her out of her sight.

CHAPTER XVII

NEKHLYÚDOV AND KATYÚSHA

And so the whole evening passed, and night fell. The doctor retired. The aunts went to bed. Nekhlyúdov knew that Matryóna Pávlovna was now in the aunts' sleeping-room, and that Katyúsha was alone in the maids' sitting-room. He again went out on the porch. The air was dark, damp, and warm, and filled with that white mist which in spring dispels the last snow, or itself rises from the melting snow. From the river, which was within one hundred steps of the house, down a hill, came strange sounds: the ice was breaking.

Nekhlyúdov descended from the porch and, walking over the puddles on the crusted snow, went up to the window of the maids' room. His heart beat so strongly in his breast that he could hear it; his breath now stopped, now burst forth in a deep sigh. In the maids' sitting-room a small lamp was burning; Katyúsha was sitting at the table alone and looking in front of her, lost in thought. Nekhlyúdov long did not stir, looking at her and wondering what she would do when unconscious of anybody's presence. For a couple of minutes she sat motionlessly, then raised her eyes, smiled, shook her head as though reproachfully at herself, and, changing her position, abruptly placed both her hands in front of her on the table and stared ahead of her.

He stood and looked at her, and at the same time heard the beating of his own heart and the strange sounds that came from the river. There, on the river in the mist, a continuous slow work was going on, and now something crashed, or cracked, or rushed down, and now the ice-floes tinkled like glass.

He stood and looked at the pensive face of Katyúsha, which was tormented by an inward struggle, and he was sorry for her, but, strange to say, that pity only intensified his passion for her.

The passion took complete possession of him.

He tapped at the window. She quivered with her whole body, as though from an electric shock, and terror was expressed in her face. Then she sprang up, went up to the window, and pressed her face to the window pane. Nor did the expression of terror leave her face when, upon screening it with the palms of her hands, she recognized him. Her face was unusually serious, such as he had never seen it before. She smiled only when he did, only as though submitting to him, but in her soul there was no smile, but terror. He motioned to her with his hand, calling her out into the yard to him; but she shook her head to say, No, she wouldn't come out, and remained standing at the window. He put his face once more to the window, intending to cry to her to come out, but just then she turned to the door—evidently somebody had called her. Nekhlyúdov went away from the window. The mist was so heavy that, walking back five steps from the house it was not possible to see the windows but only a black mass, from which the red, seemingly enormous light of the lamp shone brightly. On the river there was the same strange crashing, rustling, crackling, and tinkling of the ice. Near by, through the mist, crowed a cock, and others near him answered, and then far away from the village came intermingling cockcrows, finally joining into one. Everything else around, except the river, was absolutely quiet. This was at second cockcrow.

After having walked a couple of times around the corner of the house and having several times stepped into a puddle, Nekhlyúdov once more went up to the window of the maids' room. The lamp was still burning, and Katyúsha was again sitting at the table alone, as if in indecision. The moment he came up to the window, she looked up at him. He knocked. And, without watching to see who it was that had knocked, she ran out of the maids' room, and he heard the back door snap open and creak. He was already waiting for her near the entrance and immediately embraced her in silence. She pressed close to him, raised her head, and with her lips met his kiss. They were standing behind the corner of the entrance on a spot from which the ice had melted, and he was full of a tormenting, unsatisfied desire. Suddenly the back door again snapped open and creaked in the same manner, and Matryóna Pávlovna's angry voice was heard:

"Katyúsha!"

She tore herself away from him and returned to the maids' room. He heard the latch being fastened. Soon after that all grew silent; the red eye of the window disappeared, and nothing was left but the fog and the noise on the river.

Nekhlyúdov went up to the window, but no one was to be seen. He knocked, but there was no answer. Nekhlyúdov returned to the house by the main entrance but did not go to sleep. He took off his boots, and went barefooted along the corridor to her door which was the one adjoining Matryóna Pávlovna's room. At first he heard Matryóna Pávlovna's quiet snoring and was on the point of entering, when suddenly she began to cough, and turned around on her creaking bed. He stood as though petrified for five minutes in one spot. When everything again grew silent and the quiet snoring was heard again, he, walking on the deals that did not creak, came right up to her door. Everything was quiet. Evidently she was not asleep, for he could not hear her breathing. But the moment he whispered, "Katyúsha!" she leaped up, went to the door, and angrily, so he thought, began to persuade him to go away.

"That's not right! How can you! Your aunts will hear you," said her lips, but her whole being said: "I am all yours!"

And it was only *this* which Nekhlyúdov understood.

"Just for a moment, please open. I implore you," he uttered the meaningless words.

She grew silent: then he heard the rustling of her hand as it groped for the latch. The latch clicked, and he slipped in through the opened door.

He seized her, as she was, in her coarse, rough shirt with her bare arms, lifted her up, and carried her away.

"Ah! What are you doing?" she whispered.

But he paid no attention to her words, carrying her to his room.

"Ah, you must not—let me go—" she said, all the time clinging to him.

When she, trembling and silent, without saying a word, went away from him, he came out on the porch and stood there, trying to reflect on the meaning of all that had taken place.

It was now lighter outside; down below, on the river, the crackling and ringing and crashing of the floes was stronger than before, and to it was now added the sound of the rippling water. The mist was settling, and behind the wall of the mist the waning moon appeared, dimly illuminating something black and terrible.

"What is this? Has a great happiness or a great misfortune come on me?" he asked himself. "It is always like this, it's like this for everybody," he said to himself, and went to sleep.

CHAPTER XVIII

DEPARTURE

On the following day, brilliant, cheerful Shénbok came to the aunts' to fetch Nekhlyúdov, and he completely fascinated them with his elegance, kindness, gaiety, generosity, and love for Dmítri. His generosity very much pleased the aunts, but it baffled them somewhat by its extremes. To some blind beggars who came to the house he gave a rouble; in gratuities he spent about fifteen roubles; and when Suzette, Sófya Ivánovna's lap-dog, in his presence had so scratched her leg that the blood began to flow, he offered to dress her wound, and, without a moment's hesitation, tore up his cambric lace-edged handkerchief (Sófya Ivánovna knew that such handkerchiefs cost not less than fifteen roubles a dozen), and made bandages of it for Suzette. The aunts had never before seen such gentlemen and did not know that this Shénbok owed some two hundred thousand roubles, which, he knew full well, would never be paid, and that therefore twenty-five roubles more or less made no difference to him.

Shénbok stayed only one day, and on the following night drove off with Nekhlyúdov. They could not stay any longer because it was the last day to report back to their regiment.

On this last day of Nekhlyúdov's stay at his aunts', while the memory of the night was still fresh, two feelings rose and struggled in his soul: one, the burning, sensual recollections of animal love, even though it had grossly failed to give him what it had promised, and a certain self-satisfaction of having reached a goal; the other, the consciousness that he had done something very bad, and that that evil had to be mended, not for her sake, but for his.

In this condition of his insanity of egotism, in which he now found himself, Nekhlyúdov thought only of himself—of whether he would be criticized, and how much he would be criticized, if it were found out how he had acted toward her, and not of what she was experiencing or what would become of her.

He thought that Shénbok guessed at his relations with Katyúsha, and that flattered his vanity.

"I now see what has made you so suddenly fall in love with your aunts," Shénbok said to him, when he saw Katyúsha, "and why you have passed a week with them. If I were in your place, I would not leave myself. Charming!"

He also thought that although it was a shame to leave at once, without having had the full enjoyment of his love, the peremptory call to duty was advantageous in that it broke the relations at once, which otherwise it would have been difficult to sustain. He also thought that it was necessary to give her money, not for her sake, not because the money might be useful to her, but because it was customary to do so, and he would have been regarded as a dishonest man, if, after taking advantage of her, he did not pay her. And so he gave her money—as much as he thought proper according to their respective positions.

On the day of his departure, after dinner, he waited for her in the entrance until she came. Her face flushed when she saw him, and she wanted to pass by him, indicating with her eyes the open door into the maids' room, but he kept her back.

"I wanted to bid you good-bye," he said, in his hand crumpling the envelope with the hundred-rouble bill. "I—"

She guessed what it was, frowned, shook her head, and pushed his hand away.

"Do take it," he mumbled, putting the envelope in her bosom, and ran back to his room, frowning and groaning, as if he had burnt himself.

Afterwards, he paced his room for a long time, and crouched, and even leaped and groaned aloud, as though from physical pain, every time he thought of that scene.

Tolstoy
Resurrection
page 58

But what could a man do? It is always like that. It was like that with Shénbok and the governess, of whom he had told him; it had been like that with Uncle Grísha; and it had been like that with his father, when he was living in the country, and when that illegitimate son, Mítenka, alive still, was born to a peasant woman. And if all do like that, it must be right. Thus he tried to console himself, but could not in any way. The memory of it burned his conscience.

In the depth, way down in the depth of his soul, he knew that he had acted so meanly, so contemptibly, and so cruelly that with the consciousness of this deed he not only could not criticize any one, but even could not look straight into people's eyes, and that he certainly could not regard himself as a fine, noble, magnanimous young man, such as he considered himself to be. And yet he had to continue in that opinion of himself, if he wished to lead the same free and happy life as before. For this there was but one means: not to think of it. And that is what he did.

The life which he now entered upon—the new places, comrades, and the war—helped him do this. The longer he lived, the more he forgot, until, at last, he had completely forgotten.

Only once, when, after the war, he visited his aunts with the hope of seeing her, and when he found out that Katyúsha was no longer there, that soon after his departure she had left them to give birth to a child, that she had given birth somewhere, and that, so the aunts had heard, she had been completely ruined—his heart gave him a painful twinge. To judge from the time of the child's birth, it might have been his, and yet it might have been somebody else's. The aunts said that she had turned bad and had become just such a dissolute character as her mother. This criticism by his aunts gave him pleasure, because it in a certain way justified him. At first he intended to look up Katyúsha and the child, but then, since in the depth of his soul he was too much ashamed and pained to think of it, he did not make the necessary efforts to locate her, and still more forgot his sin and ceased thinking of it.

And just now this amazing coincidence reminded him of everything and demanded the confession of his heartlessness, cruelty, and meanness, which had made it possible for him to live for ten years with such a sin on his conscience. But he was still very far from such a confession, and now he was thinking only that all might be found out, that she or her counsel would bring out the facts and would put him to shame in front of every one.

CHAPTER XIX

THE COURT RESUMES

Nekhlyúdov was in this frame of mind when he left the court-room for the jurors' room. He sat at the window, listening to the conversations that took place about him, and smoking incessantly.

The gay merchant obviously sympathized with the merchant Smyelkóv's pastime with all his heart.

"Well, he was a great carouser, in Siberian fashion. He knew a thing or two, when he selected such a girl to love up."

The foreman was expatiating on the importance of the expert testimony. Pyotr

Gerásimovich was jesting with the Jewish clerk, and they were both laughing about something. Nekhlyúdov answered in monosyllables to all the questions which were addressed to him and wished only to be left alone.

When the bailiff, with his sidling gait, again called the jurors to the court-room, Nekhlyúdov experienced a sensation of terror, as though he were going not to give a verdict but to be tried. In the depth of his soul he felt that he was a scoundrel who ought to be ashamed to look people in the eye, and yet he, by force of habit, ascended the platform with his usual self-confident gait and sat down in his seat, the second from the foreman's, and, crossing his legs, began to play with his glasses.

The defendants had been removed and now were being brought back.

In the court-room there were new faces—the witnesses—and Nekhlyúdov noticed that Máslova several times looked up, as though she could not take her eyes off a fat woman, all dressed up in silk and velvet, who, in a tall hat with a large ribbon and with an elegant reticule on her arm, which was bare up to the elbow, was sitting in the first row, next to the railing. This was, as he later found out, the madam of the establishment in which Máslova had lived.

Then the examination of the witnesses began: their names, religion, and so forth. Then, after the sides had been consulted as to whether the witnesses should be examined under oath or not, the same old priest, with difficulty moving his legs, and in the same manner adjusting the gold cross on his silk vestment, with the same calm and conviction that he was performing an exceedingly useful and important work, administered the oath to the witnesses and to the expert. When the oath was finished, all the witnesses were led away, and only one, namely, Kitáeva, the proprietress of the house of prostitution, was allowed to remain. She was asked what she knew of the affair. Kitáeva, with a feigned smile, ducking her head with its big hat at every phrase, told, with a German accent, everything in detail and coherently:

At first the hotel servant Simón, whom she well knew, had come to get a girl for a rich Siberian merchant. She sent Lyubásha. After a while Lyubásha returned with the merchant.

"The merchant was already in raptures," Kitáeva said, with a slight smile, "and at our place continued to drink and treat the girls, but as his money gave out, he sent that same Lyubásha, for whom he felt 'predilection,'" she said, glancing at the defendant.

It seemed to Nekhlyúdov that at these words Máslova smiled, and this smile seemed disgusting to him. A strange, indefinable feeling of loathing, mingled with compassion, arose in him.

"And what has your opinion been of Máslova?" timidly asked the blushing candidate for a judicial place who had been appointed by the court to be Máslova's counsel.

"The very best," answered Kitáeva. "An educated girl and chic. Educated in good family, and could read the French. At times drank a little too much, but never went too far. Very good girl."

Katyúsha looked at the proprietress, and then suddenly transferred her eyes to the jurors, and rested them on Nehklyúdov, and her face became serious and even stern. One of her stern eyes squinted. For quite a while these two strange-looking eyes were turned upon Nekhlyúdov, and, in spite of the terror which took possession of him, he was unable to turn his glance away from these squinting eyes with the bright whites around them. He recalled that terrible night with the breaking ice, with its mist, and, above all, with that upturned waning moon, which rose before daybreak and illuminated something black and terrible. These two black eyes, which gazed at him and past him, reminded him of that black and terrible something.

"She has recognized me," he thought. And Nekhlyúdov seemed to crouch, as though expecting a blow. She calmly heaved a sigh, and once more began to look at the presiding judge. Nekhlyúdov, too, sighed. "Oh, if only it were over," he thought. He now experienced a sensation like that which he had experienced before, out hunting, when he had to pick up a wounded bird—he felt disgust, and pity, and annoyance. The wounded bird would flutter in his game-bag, and he would feel loathing and pity, and would like to kill it and forget.

It was such a mixed feeling that Nekhlyúdov was now experiencing as he listened to the interrogation of the witnesses.

CHAPTER XX

THE CORONER'S REPORT

As if to spite him, the case was drawn out long: after the examination of the witnesses and the expert, one after the other, and after the assistant prosecuting attorney and the lawyers for the defense had, with significant looks, asked a number of useless questions, the presiding judge told the jurors to inspect the exhibits, which consisted of a ring of enormous size, with a setting of rose-diamonds, which evidently fitted on the stoutest of forefingers, and of a vial in which the poison had been analyzed. These things were sealed, and there were small labels upon them.

The jurors were just getting ready to inspect these objects when the assistant prosecuting attorney again raised himself in his seat and demanded that the medical examination of the corpse be read before passing to the inspection of the exhibits.

The presiding judge, who was hurrying the case as fast as possible in order to get to his Swiss woman, was well convinced that the reading of that document could have no other effect than causing boredom and delaying dinner, and that the assistant prosecuting attorney had requested it only because he knew he had the right to make such a request; still, he could not refuse, and so ordered it to be read. The secretary got the document and again in his monotonous voice, with his guttural *l* and *r*, began to read.

Tolstoy
Resurrection
page 62

"The external investigation showed that:

"(1) Ferapónt Smyelkóv's height was two arshíns and twelve vershóks[1]."

"I declare, he was a strapping fellow," the merchant, with concern, whispered into Nekhlyúdov's ear.

"(2) His age was from external appearances fixed as approximately forty.

"(3) The body had a bloated appearance.

"(4) The colour of the integuments was greenish, here and there tinged with darker spots.

"(5) The skin on the surface of the body had risen in pustules of different size, and in places had come off and was hanging in the shape of large flaps.

"(6) His hair was dark blond, thick, and easily came out at a touch.

"(7) The eyes stood out of their sockets, and the cornea was dimmed.

"(8) From the apertures of the nose, of both ears, and of the cavity of the mouth a lathery, foamy, serous liquid was discharged, and the mouth was half open.

"(9) There was no perceptible neck, on account of the bloated condition of the face and chest."

And so on, and so on.

Four pages contained twenty-seven points of such kind of a description of all the details revealed at the external examination of the terrible, immense, fat and swollen, decomposing body of the merchant who had been carousing in the city. The sensation of indefinable loathing, which Nekhlyúdov had been experiencing, was intensified at the reading of this description of the corpse. Katyúsha's life and the serous liquid which issued from his nostrils, and the eyes standing out from their sockets, and his treatment of her, seemed to him to be things of the same order, and he was on all sides surrounded and absorbed by these things. When, at last, the reading of the external investigation was over, the presiding judge heaved a deep sigh and raised his head, hoping that all was ended, but the secretary immediately proceeded to the reading of the internal investigation.

The presiding judge once more lowered his head, and, leaning on his arm, closed his eyes. The merchant, who was sitting next to Nekhlyúdov, with difficulty kept himself from falling asleep and now and then swayed to and fro; the defendants and the gendarmes behind them sat motionless.

[1]An arshín equals twenty-eight inches, and a vershók equals one and three-quarters inches.

"The internal investigation showed that:

"(1) The cranial integuments easily separated from the cranial bones, and suffusion was nowhere noticeable.

"(2) The cranial bones were of medium thickness and sound.

"(3) On the dura mater two small pigmented spots were observed; they were approximately four lines in size; the dura mater itself was of a pale white hue," and so on, and so on, through thirteen points.

Then followed the names of the coroner's jury, the signatures, and then the conclusion of the medical examiner, from which it was clear that the modifications which had taken place in the stomach, and partly in the intestines and kidneys, as discovered at the inquest and as mentioned in the official report, gave a right to conclude, *with a great degree of probability*, that Smyelkóv's death had been caused by poison which had found its way into the stomach with the wine. From the modification in the stomach and intestines, which were at hand, it was difficult to determine what kind of poison it was that had been introduced into the stomach; but that it found its way into the stomach with the wine must be surmised from the fact that a large quantity of wine was discovered in Smyelkóv's stomach.

"Evidently he was a great hand at drinking," again whispered the merchant, waking up.

But the reading of this official report, which lasted nearly an hour, did not satisfy the assistant prosecuting attorney. When it was over, the presiding judge turned to him:

"I suppose it would be superfluous to read the document referring to the investigation of the internal organs."

"I should like to ask to have this examination read," sternly said the assistant prosecuting attorney, without looking at the presiding judge, raising himself with a sidewise motion and giving the judge to feel, by the intonation of his voice, that the request for this reading constituted one of his privileges and that he would not relinquish this right, and that a refusal would serve as a ground for appeal.

The member of the court with the long beard and the kindly, drooping eyes, who was suffering from the catarrh, feeling himself very weak, turned to the presiding judge:

"What is the use of reading it? It only delays matters. These new brooms sweep longer but no cleaner."

The member in the gold spectacles did not say anything and looked gloomily and with determination in front of him, expecting nothing good from his wife, or from life in general.

The reading of the document began:

"On February 15, 188–, I, the undersigned, at the request of the medical department, as given in writing in No. 638," the secretary, who had such a soporific effect upon all persons present, began in a determined tone, raising the pitch of his voice, as if to dispel sleep, "in presence of the assistant medical inspector, have made the following examination of the internal organs:

"(1) Of the right lung and of the heart (in a six-pound glass jar).

"(2) Of the contents of the stomach (in a six-pound glass jar).

"(3) Of the stomach itself (in a six-pound glass jar).

"(4) Of the liver, the spleen, and the kidneys (in a three-pound glass jar).

"(5) Of the intestines (in a six-pound earthenware jar)."

The presiding judge in the beginning of the reading bent down to one of the members and whispered something to him; then to the other and, having received an affirmative answer, interrupted the reading at this point.

"The court finds the reading of the document superfluous," he said. The secretary stopped and picked up his papers. The assistant prosecuting attorney angrily made a note of something.

"The jurors may examine the exhibits," said the presiding judge.

The foreman and a few of the jurymen arose and, embarrassed as to the disposition of their hands, went up to the table and in turns looked at the ring, the jars, and the vial. The merchant even tried the ring on his finger.

"Well, he had a good-sized finger," he said, upon returning to his seat. "As big as a cucumber," he added, obviously enjoying the heroic conception which he had formed of the poisoned merchant.

CHAPTER XXI

THE LAWYERS AND
THE DEFENDANTS

When the examination of the exhibits was ended, the presiding judge declared the judicial inquest closed and, without any interruption, wishing to get through as soon as possible, asked the prosecutor to begin his address, in the hope that he, too, wishing both to smoke and to have dinner, would have pity on them. But the assistant prosecuting attorney pitied neither himself nor them. The assistant prosecuting attorney was by nature very stupid, but he had the additional misfortune of having graduated from the gymnasium with a gold medal, and of having received a reward at the university for his thesis on the servitudes of the Roman law, which made him exceedingly self-confident and self-satisfied (which was still more increased by his success with the ladies), and consequently he was extremely stupid.

When given the floor, he slowly rose, displaying his whole graceful figure in an embroidered uniform and, placing both his hands on the desk and slightly inclining his head, glanced over the whole room, avoiding only the defendants, and began:

"The case which is before you, gentlemen of the jury," he began his speech, which he had prepared during the reading of the official report and coroner's inquest, "is, if I may so express myself, a characteristic crime."

The address of an assistant prosecuting attorney, according to his opinion, ought to have a public significance, like those famous speeches which had been delivered by those who later became famous lawyers. True, among the spectators there were only three women, a seamstress, a cook, and Simón's sister, and one coachman, but that did not matter. Even the celebrities had begun in the same way. It was a rule of the assistant prosecuting attorney always to be on top of his situation, that is, to penetrate to the depth of the psychological significance of the crime and to lay bare the sores of society.

"You see before you, gentlemen of the jury, if one may so express oneself, a characteristic crime of the end of the century, bearing upon itself, so to speak, the specific characteristics of that melancholy phenomenon of decomposition, to which, in our day, are subjected those elements of society that, so to speak, are under the ultra-burning rays of that process—"

The assistant prosecuting attorney spoke a very long time, on the one hand trying to recall all those clever things which he had thought of, and, on the other—and this was most important—endeavouring not to stop for a moment but to let his speech flow uninterruptedly for an hour and a quarter. He did stop only once, and for a while kept swallowing his saliva, but he soon found his bearings and made up for the interruption by his intensified eloquence. He spoke sometimes in a tender, insinuating voice, shifting from one foot to the other and looking at the jurors, and sometimes in a quiet, businesslike tone, glancing at his notes, and sometimes in a loud, condemnatory voice, addressing now the spectators, now the jurors. He did not look once at the defendants, however, who had riveted their eyes upon him. In his speech were all the latest points which had become fashionable in his circle and which had been accepted as the latest word of scientific wisdom. Here were heredity, and inborn criminality, and Lombroso, and Tarde, and evolution, and struggle for existence, and hypnotism, and suggestion, and Charcot, and decadence.

The merchant Smyelkóv, according to the definition of the assistant prosecuting attorney, was a type of a mighty, unspoiled Russian, with his broad nature, who, on account of his confidence and magnanimity, had fallen victim to deeply perverted persons into whose power he had come.

Simón Kartínkin was an atavistic production of serfdom, a crushed man, without education, without principles, even without religion. Evfímiya was his mistress and a victim of heredity. In her all the characteristics of a degenerate personality could be observed. But the chief mainspring of the crime was Máslova, who represented the phenomenon of decadence in its lowest form.

"This woman," so said the assistant prosecuting attorney without looking at her, "has received an education, as we have learned here in court from the evidence of her proprietress. She not only can read and write but can also speak French; she is an orphan, who no doubt bears in herself the germs of criminality; she has been educated in a family of cultured gentlefolk and could have lived by honest labour; but she left her benefactors, abandoned herself to her passions, and, to satisfy them, entered a house of prostitution, where she stood out from among her companions by her education, and, above everything else, as we have heard here from her proprietress, gentlemen of the jury, by her ability to influence the visitors by that mysterious quality, which has of late been investigated by science, especially by the school of Charcot, and which is known by the name of hypnotic suggestion. By means of just that quality she took possession of a Russian hero, that good-natured, trustful Sádko, the rich merchant, and used that confidence, first to rob him, and then pitilessly to deprive him of life."

"He is getting dreadfully off on a tangent," said the presiding judge, smiling, leaning down to the austere member.

"He's a terrible blockhead," said the austere member.

"Gentlemen of the jury," the assistant prosecuting attorney continued in the meantime, gracefully bending his lithe form, "the fate of these persons is in your power, but, to a certain extent, the fate of society, which you influence by your sentence, is in your power. Carefully consider the meaning of this crime, the danger to which society is subjected by such pathological individuals, if I may so express myself, as Máslova, and guard it against contagion, guard the innocent, strong elements of society against contagion, and, often, against destruction."

As though himself crushed by the importance of the impending decision, the assistant prosecuting attorney, evidently highly enraptured with his own address, fell back in his chair.

The essence of his address, outside of the flowers of eloquence, was that Máslova had hypnotized the merchant, by insinuating herself into his confidence and, having arrived in the room with the key, in order to fetch the money, had intended to take it all for herself, but, having been caught by Simón and Evfímiya, had been compelled to share the booty with them. Later, intending to conceal the traces of her crime, she came back to the hotel with the merchant where she poisoned him.

After the assistant prosecuting attorney's address there rose from the lawyers' bench a middle-aged man in a dress coat with the broad semicircular white starched shirt front, and with animation defended Kartínkin and Bóchkova. He was the attorney who had been employed by them for three hundred roubles. He justified their actions and put all the guilt on Máslova's shoulders.

He refuted Máslova's testimony that Bóchkova and Kartínkin had been with her when she took the money, pointing out the fact that her testimony, as that of an established poisoner, could have no weight. The money—the twenty-five hundred roubles—said the lawyer, could have been earned by two industrious and honest people, who received as much as three and five roubles a day in gratuities. The merchant's money had been stolen by Máslova and had been given to somebody, or probably lost, since she was not normal. The poisoning was done by Máslova alone.

Therefore he asked the jury to declare Kartínkin and Bóchkova not guilty of the robbery of the money, or, if they did declare them guilty of robbery, to return a verdict of no participation in the poisoning and of no premeditation.

In conclusion, the lawyer, to sting the assistant prosecuting attorney, remarked that the eloquent reflections of the assistant prosecuting attorney explained the scientific questions of heredity, but were irrelevant in this case, since Bóchkova was the child of unknown parents.

The assistant prosecuting attorney, as though growling, angrily made a note and with contemptuous surprise shrugged his shoulders.

Then Máslova's counsel arose and timidly, hesitantly made the defence. Without denying the fact that Máslova had taken part in the robbery, he insisted that she had had no intention of poisoning Smyelkóv and had given him the powder merely to put him to sleep. He wanted to make a display of eloquence, by surveying Máslova's past, how she had been drawn to a life of debauch by a man who remained unpunished, while she had to bear the whole brunt of her fall, but this excursus into the field of psychology was a perfect failure, so that all felt sorry for him. As he was muttering about the cruelty of men and the helplessness of women, the presiding judge, wishing to help him out, asked him to keep closer to the essentials of the case.

After this defence, the assistant prosecuting attorney rose again and defended his position about heredity against the first defence counsel by saying that the fact that Bóchkova was the daughter of unknown parents did not in the least invalidate the doctrine of heredity, because the law of heredity was so firmly established by science that we not only could deduce a crime from heredity, but also heredity from a crime. As to the supposition of the defence that Máslova had been corrupted by an imaginary seducer (he dwelt with particular sarcasm on the word "imaginary"), all the data seemed to point to the fact that she had been the seducer of many, very many victims who had passed through her hands. Having said this, he sat down victoriously.

Then the defendants were asked to say something in their own justification.

Evfímiya Bóchkova repeated that she knew nothing, that she had not taken part in anything, and stubbornly pointed to Máslova as the only culprit. Simón repeated several times:

"Do as you please, only I am not guilty, it's all wrong."

Máslova did not say anything. To the presiding judge's invitation to say something in her defence, she only looked up at him, glanced at everybody, like a hunted deer, and immediately lowered her eyes and burst out into loud sobs.

"What is the matter with you?" asked the merchant who was sitting next to Nekhlyúdov upon hearing a strange sound, which Nekhlyúdov suddenly let out. It sounded like a checked sob.

Nekhlyúdov did not yet grasp the full significance of his position and ascribed the restrained sobs and the tears, which had come out in his eyes, to the weakness of his nerves. He put on his pince-nez in order to conceal them, then drew his handkerchief from his pocket and began to blow his nose.

The dread of the disgrace with which he would cover himself if all in the courtroom should learn of his act, drowned everything going on inside him. This dread was strongest of all in this initial period.

CHAPTER XXII

THE COURT SUMS UP

After these words of the defendants and consultation between the two sides about the form of the questions to the jury, which lasted for quite a while, the questions were put, and the presiding judge began his résumé.

Before recapitulating the case, he, with a pleasant, familiar intonation, explained to the jury at length that burglary was burglary and theft was theft, and robbery from a place under lock was robbery from a place under lock, and robbery from an unlocked place was robbery from an unlocked place. While giving this explanation, he very frequently glanced over to Nekhlyúdov, as though anxious to impress him in particular with this important fact, in the hope that he, comprehending its whole import, would be able to explain it to his fellow jurors. Then surmising that the jury was sufficiently instructed in this truth, he began to expatiate on another truth, namely, that murder was an act from which ensues the death of a man, and that, therefore, poisoning was also murder. When this truth, too, had, in his opinion, been absorbed by the jury, he explained to them that when theft and murder are committed at the same time, then the crime constitutes both theft and murder.

Notwithstanding the fact that he wanted to get through as soon as possible and that the Swiss girl was waiting for him, he was so accustomed to his occupation that, having begun to speak, he could not check himself, and so he minutely instructed the jury that if they found the defendants guilty, they had a right to give a verdict of guilty, and that if they found them not guilty, they were empowered to pass a verdict of not guilty; but if they found them guilty of one thing and not guilty of another, they could declare them guilty of one thing and not guilty of another. Then he explained to them that, although they had such a right, they must use it with discretion. He also wished to instruct them that if they gave an affirmative answer to a given question, they therewith accepted the question in its entirety, and if they did not accept it in its entirety, they ought to specify what it was they excluded. But upon looking at his watch and seeing that it was five minutes to three, he decided to pass at once to the review of the case.

"The circumstances of the case are as follows," he began, and repeated all that had previously been said by the defence, and the assistant prosecuting attorney, and the witnesses.

The presiding judge spoke, and the members on both sides listened to him with a thoughtful expression and occasionally looked at the clock, finding his speech very beautiful, that is, such as it ought to be, but rather long. Of the same opinion were the assistant prosecuting attorney and all the court attendants and all the spectators in the court-room. The presiding judge finished his résumé.

It seemed that everything had been said. But the presiding judge could not part with his privilege of speaking—it gave him such pleasure to listen to the impressive intonations of his own voice—and he found it necessary to add a few words on the importance of the right which was granted to the jurors and how attentively and cautiously they ought to make use of that right and not misuse it, on the fact that they were under oath and that they were the public conscience, and that the secrecy of the jury-room must be kept sacred, and so on, and so on.

From the time that the presiding judge began to speak, Máslova did not take her eyes away from him, as though fearing to lose each word, and therefore Nekhlyúdov was not afraid of meeting her glance and uninterruptedly looked at her. And in his imagination there occurred the common phenomenon that the long-missed face of a beloved person, at first striking one by the external changes which have taken place during the period of absence, suddenly becomes precisely like what it was many years ago: all the changes disappear, and before the spiritual eyes there arises only that essential expression of an exclusive, unrepeated, spiritual personality.

Precisely this took place in Nekhlyúdov.

In spite of the prison cloak and the heavier body and swelling bosom, in spite of the broadened lower part of her face, the wrinkles on her brow and temples, and the somewhat swollen eyes, it was unquestionably that same Katyúsha who on that Easter night had so innocently looked up at him, the man beloved by her, with her loving eyes, smiling with joy and with the fullness of life.

"Such an amazing coincidence! How wonderful that this case should come up during my turn as a juror, that after ten years I should meet her here, on the defendants' bench! And how will all this end? Ah, if it only would all end soon!"

He still did not submit to that feeling of repentance which was beginning to speak within him. It appeared to him as a coincidence which would pass by without disturbing his life. He felt himself in the condition of the pup who, having misbehaved indoors, is taken by his master by the back of his neck and has his nose stuck into the mess he has made. The pup whines and pulls back, in order to get away as far as possible from the consequences of what he has done and to forget them, but the inexorable master does not let him go. Just so Nekhlyúdov was conscious of the mess he had made, was conscious of the mighty hand of the master; but he still did not understand the significance of what he had done and did not acknowledge the master himself. He kept wanting not to believe that what was facing him was his business. But an inexorable, invisible hand held him, and he felt that he would never wring himself away from it. He still kept a bold expression and, by force of habit, his legs crossed, carelessly played with his pince-nez and sat in a self-satisfied attitude in the second chair of the first row. In the meantime he was conscious, in the depth of his soul, of all the cruelty, meanness, and rascality, not only of what he had done, but also of his whole indolent, dissolute, cruel, and self-satisfied life; and that terrible curtain, which as if by some miracle had for twelve years concealed from him that crime and all his consequent life, was already swaying, and he could briefly glimpse behind it.

CHAPTER XXIII

THE JURY DELIBERATES

Finally, the presiding judge finished his speech and with a graceful motion raising the question-sheet, handed it to the foreman, who had walked over to him. The jury rose, glad to get away, and, not knowing what to do with their hands, as though ashamed of something, went into the consultation-room one after another. The moment the door was closed behind them, a gendarme went up to the door and, unsheathing his sabre and shouldering it, took up a position near it. The judges arose and walked out. The defendants, too, were led away.

Upon reaching the jury-room, the jurors, as before, immediately took out their cigarettes and began to smoke. The unnaturalness and falseness of their situation, which they all had been conscious of in a greater or lesser degree while seated in the court-room, passed the moment they entered the jury-room and began to smoke, and, with a feeling of relief, they made themselves at home and began to converse in an animated manner.

"The girl is not guilty, she is just tangled up," said the good-natured merchant. "We must be indulgent with her!"

"This we shall consider later," said the foreman. "We must not be misled by our personal impressions."

"The presiding judge made a fine résumé," remarked the colonel.

"Very fine indeed! I almost fell asleep."

"The main thing is that the servants could not have known about the money, if Máslova had not been in a conspiracy with them," said the Jewish clerk.

"Well, did she steal it, in your opinion?" asked one of the jurors.

"You can't make me believe it," cried the good-natured merchant. "The red-eyed wench did it all."

"They are every one of them a nice lot," said the colonel.

"She says she never went inside the room."

"Yes, you believe her. I won't believe that slut for anything in the world."

"But what of it if you won't?" said the clerk.

"She had the key."

"What of it if she did have it?" retorted the merchant.

"And the ring?"

"She told about it," again shouted the merchant. "The merchant had a temper and had been drinking and walloping her. And then, of course, he was sorry for what he had done. 'Take this, and don't cry!' From what I heard, he must have been a strapping fellow, two and twelve, and weighing some three hundred pounds."

"This has nothing to do with the case," Pyótr Gerásimovich interrupted him. "The question is, whether she did it all and persuaded the others, or whether the servants took the initiative."

"The servants could not have done it by themselves, for she had the key."

The disconnected conversation lasted quite a while.

"Please, gentlemen," said the foreman. "Let us sit down at the table, and consider the case. Please," he said, sitting down in the foreman's chair.

"Those girls are contemptible," said the clerk, and, in confirmation of his opinion that Máslova was the chief culprit, he told how one of these girls had stolen a watch from a friend of his on the boulevard.

This gave the colonel an opportunity of relating a more outstanding theft of a silver samovar.

"Gentlemen, let us take up the questions in order," said the foreman, tapping his pencil on the table.

All grew quiet. The questions were expressed as follows:

(1) Is Simón Petróv Kartínkin, a peasant of the village of Bórki, Krapívensk District, thirty-three years of age, guilty of having conspired on January 17, 188–, in the city of N——, to deprive the merchant Smyelkóv of his life, for the purpose of robbing him, in company with others, by administering to him poison in cognac, from which ensued Smyelkóv's death, and of having stolen from him about 2,500 roubles and a diamond ring?

(2) Is the lower middle-class woman Evfímiya Ivánova Bóchkova, forty-three years of age, guilty of the crime described in the first question?

(3) Is the lower middle-class woman Ekaterína Mikháylova Máslova, twenty-seven years of age, guilty of the crime described in the first question?

(4) If the defendant, Evfímiya Bóchkova, is not guilty according to the first question, may she not be guilty of having, on January 17, 188–, in the city of N——, while a servant in the Hotel Mauritania, secretly stolen from the locked suitcase of a hotel guest, the merchant Smyelkóv, which was in his room, the sum of 2,500 roubles, having for this purpose opened the suitcase with a false key?

The foreman read the first question.

"Well, gentlemen?"

To this question, the reply was readily made. All agreed to answer, "Yes, guilty," finding him guilty of participation, both in the poisoning and in the robbery. The only one who would not agree to finding Kartínkin guilty was an old artisan, who answered all questions with a view to acquittal.

The foreman thought that he did not understand and explained to him that there was no possible doubt of Kartínkin's and Bóchkova's guilt, but the artisan replied that he understood it all, but that it would be better to exercise mercy. "We ourselves are no saints," he said, and stuck to his opinion.

To the second question about Bóchkova, they replied, after long discussions and elucidations, "Not guilty," because there was no clear proof of her participation in the poisoning, upon which her lawyer had dwelt so emphatically.

The merchant, wishing to acquit Máslova, insisted that Bóchkova was the chief instigator of the whole thing. Many jurors agreed with him, but the foreman, trying to be strictly legal, said that there was no ground for finding her guilty of participation in the poisoning. After many discussions, the foreman's opinion prevailed.

To the fourth question, about Bóchkova, they replied, "Yes, guilty," but, since the artisan insisted upon it, they added, "but with a recommendation of mercy."

The question about Máslova brought forth violent arguments. The foreman insisted that she was guilty both of the poisoning and of the robbery, but the merchant did not agree with him, and he was joined by the colonel, the clerk and the artisan; the others seemed to waver, but the opinion of the foreman began to prevail, especially since all the jurors were tired and eagerly accepted the opinion which was more likely to unite all and therefore to free them.

From everything that had taken place at the inquest, and from what Nekhlyúdov knew of Máslova, he was convinced that she was not guilty either of the robbery or of the poisoning and at first was certain that all would find it so, but when he saw that, on account of the merchant's awkward defence, which was based on the fact that Máslova pleased him in a physical way, a fact of which he made no secret, and on account of the opposition of the foreman for that very reason, and, especially, on account of the fatigue of everyone, the verdict was turning toward finding her guilty, he wanted to retort, but he felt terrible about saying anything in regard to Máslova—it seemed to him that everybody would at once discover his relations with her. At the same time he felt that he could not leave the case as it was but that he had to retort. He blushed and grew pale by turns and was on the point of saying something, when Pyótr Gerásimovich, who had remained silent until then, evidently provoked by the foreman's authoritative tone, suddenly began to oppose him and to say the very thing Nekhlyúdov had intended to bring out.

"If you please," he said, "you say that she is guilty of the robbery because she had a key; could not the hotel servants have later opened the suitcase with a false key?"

"That's it, that's it," the merchant seconded him.

"It was not possible for her to take the money, because in her situation she could not dispose of it."

"That's what I say," the merchant confirmed him.

"It is more likely that her arrival gave the servants the idea, and they made use of the opportunity and then shoved everything into her lap."

Pyótr Gerásimovich spoke in an irritated manner. His irritation was communicated to the foreman, who, for that very reason, began with greater stubbornness to insist upon his own, opposite views; but Pyótr Gerásimovich spoke so convincingly that the majority agreed with him, finding that Máslova had not taken part in the robbery of the money and ring, and that the ring had been given to her. When the discussion about her part in the poisoning began, her warm defender, the merchant, said that she ought to be found not guilty, because she had no reason for poisoning him. But the foreman said that they could not help finding her guilty because she had herself confessed to administering the powder to him.

"She gave it to him, but she thought it was opium," said the merchant.

"She could have deprived him of life with opium," said the colonel, who was fond of digressions, and began to tell that his brother-in-law's wife had poisoned herself with opium, and that she would certainly have died if a doctor had not been near, and if the proper measures had not been taken in time. The colonel spoke so persuasively, self-confidently, and with such dignity, that nobody had the courage to interrupt him. Only the clerk, infected by his example, decided to interrupt him in order to tell his own story.

"Some get so used to it," he began, "that they can take forty drops. A relative of mine—"

But the colonel did not permit himself to be interrupted and continued his story about the effect of the opium on the wife of his brother-in-law.

"Gentlemen, it is already past four," said one of the jurors.

"How is it, then, gentlemen?" the foreman addressed them. "Let us find her guilty without premeditated robbery, and without seizing any property. Is that all right?"

Pyótr Gerásimovich, satisfied with his victory, agreed to this.

"But deserves mercy," added the merchant.

All consented to this, only the artisan insisted upon saying "Not guilty."

"That's what it amounts to," explained the foreman, "without premeditated robbery, and without seizing any property. This makes her not guilty."

"Put it down: 'and deserves mercy.' That means clearing off the whole matter," merrily said the merchant.

Everybody was so tired and so confused by their discussions that it did not occur to any one to add to the answer: "*Yes, but without the intention of killing.*"

Nekhlyúdov was so agitated that he did not notice that. In this form the answers were written down and taken back to the court-room.

Rabelais tells of a jurist, to whom people had come in a lawsuit, and who, after having pointed out all kinds of laws, and having read twenty pages of senseless juridical Latin, proposed to the contending parties to cast dice: if they fell even, the plaintiff was right; if odd, the defendant was right.

Thus it happened here. This or that verdict had been accepted, not because all had agreed to it, but, in the first place, because the presiding judge, who had made such a long résumé, had forgotten upon that occasion to say what he always said, namely, that they might answer the question: "Yes, guilty, but without the intention of killing"; secondly, because the colonel had told a long and tiresome story about his brother-in-law's wife; thirdly, because Nekhlyúdov had been so agitated that he did not notice the omission of the clause about the absence of any intention to kill, and because he thought that the clause, "without any intention of robbery," annulled the accusation; fourthly, because Pyótr Gerásimovich did not happen to be in the room—he had gone out—when the foreman reread the questions and answers; and, chiefly, because everybody was tired, and all wanted to be free as soon as possible, and therefore agreed to a verdict which would bring everything to an end.

The jury rang the bell. The gendarme, who was standing at the door with the unsheathed sword, put it back into the scabbard and stepped aside. The judges took their seats, and the jurors filed out from the room.

The foreman carried the sheet with a solemn look. He went up to the presiding judge, and gave it to him. The presiding judge read it and, evidently surprised, threw up his hands and turned to his colleagues to consult with them. The presiding judge was surprised to find that the jury had modified the first condition by making it, "Without the intention of robbing," while they had not equally modified the second by saying, "Without the intention of killing." It now turned out by the jury's decision that Máslova had not stolen, not robbed, and yet had poisoned a man without any evident cause.

"See what absurdity they have brought here," he said to the member on the left. "This means hard labour, and she is not guilty."

"Why not guilty?" said the stern member.

"Simply not guilty. In my opinion this case is provided for in Article 818." (Article 818 says that if a court finds the accusation unjust, it may set aside the jury's verdict.)

"What do you think?" said the presiding judge, turning to the kind member.

The kind member did not answer at once. He looked at the number of the document which was lying before him, and it would not divide by three. He had made up his mind that he should be with him if the number would be divisible; notwithstanding this, he, out of the goodness of his heart, agreed with him.

"I myself think this ought to be done," he said.

"And you?" the judge turned to the angry member.

"On no condition," he answered, firmly. "The papers are saying, as it is, that the juries acquit the criminals. I won't agree to it under any circumstances."

The presiding judge looked at his watch.

"I am sorry, but what is to be done?" and he handed the list to the foreman to read.

All arose, and the foreman, shifting from foot to foot, cleared his throat, and read the questions and answers. All the members of the court, the secretary, the lawyers, even the assistant prosecuting attorney, expressed their surprise.

The defendants sat unperturbed, obviously not understanding the purport of the answers. Again, all sat down, and the presiding judge asked the assistant prosecutor to what punishment he proposed to subject the defendants.

The assistant prosecutor, delighted at the unexpected turn which Máslova's case had taken, and ascribing this success to his eloquence, looked up some points, rose, and said:

"Simón Kartínkin ought to be subjected to punishment on the basis of Article 1452 and paragraph four of Article 1453; Evfímiya Bóchkova on the basis of Article 1659; and Katerína Máslova on the basis of Article 1454."

All these punishments were the severest which it was possible to mete out.

"The court will withdraw for the purpose of arriving at a sentence," said the presiding judge, rising.

All arose at the same time, and, with relief and the agreeable sensation of a well-performed good work, began to leave the room or to move up and down.

"My friend, we have done a shameful piece of business," said Pyótr Gerásimovich, walking up to Nekhlyúdov, to whom the foreman was telling something. "We have sent her to hard labour."

"You don't say?" cried Nekhlyúdov, this time not taking notice at all of the teacher's disagreeable familiarity.

"Precisely so," he said. "We did not put down in the answer, 'Guilty, but without the intention of killing.' The secretary has just told me that the prosecuting attorney is giving her fifteen years of hard labour."

"That's the way we gave the verdict," said the foreman.

Pyótr Gerásimovich began to argue with him, saying that it was self-evident that if she did not steal the money, she could not have had the intention of killing him.

"But did I not read the answers before coming out?" the foreman justified himself. "Nobody contradicted."

"I was not in the room at that time," said Pyótr Gerásimovich. "But how did you miss it?"

"I did not think it was that way," said Nekhlyúdov.

"This comes from not thinking."

"But this can be corrected," said Nekhlyúdov.

"No, now everything is finished."

Nekhlyúdov looked at the defendants. They, whose fate was being decided, sat just as motionless behind the railing in front of the soldiers. Máslova was smiling at something. A rotten feeling began to stir in Nekhlyúdov's breast. Before this, anticipating her acquittal and sojourn in the city, he had been undecided as to how to act toward her. In any case, his relations with her would have been difficult; but now, the hard labour and Siberia at once destroyed every possibility of any relations with her. The wounded bird would stop fluttering in the game-bag and reminding him of itself.

CHAPTER XXIV

THE SENTENCING

Pyótr Gerásimovich's suppositions were correct.

Upon returning from the consultation-room, the presiding judge picked up a document and read:

"On April 28, 188–, by order of his Imperial Highness, the Criminal Division of the Circuit Court, by virtue of the jury's verdict, and on the basis of par. 3, art. 771, par. 3, art. 776, and art. 777 of the Code of Criminal Procedure, has decreed: Peasant Simón Kartínkin, thirty-three years of age, and the lower middle-class woman Ekaterína Máslova, twenty-seven years of age, to be deprived of all civil rights and to be sent to hard labour: Kartínkin for the period of eight years, and Máslova for four years, with the consequences incident thereupon according to art. 25 of the Statutes. But the lower middle-class woman Evfímiya Bóchkova, forty-three years of age, to be deprived of all special rights, both personal and civil, and of all privileges, to be incarcerated in prison for a period of three years, with the consequences incident thereupon according to art. 48 of the Statutes. The expenses of the court incurred in this case to be borne in equal parts by all the defendants, and in case of their inability to meet them to be paid by the Crown.

"The exhibits presented in the case to be sold, the ring to be returned, and the jars to be destroyed."

Kartínkin stood as erect as before, holding his hands with their spreading fingers down his sides and moving his cheeks. Bóchkova seemed to be quite calm. Upon hearing her sentence, Máslova grew red in the face.

"I am not guilty, I am not guilty!" she suddenly shouted through the court-room. "This is a sin. I am not guilty. I had no intention, no thought of doing wrong. I am telling the truth! The truth!" And, letting herself down on the bench, she sobbed out aloud.

When Kartínkin and Bóchkova left, she still remained sitting in one spot and weeping, so that the gendarme had to touch her by the elbow of her cloak.

"No, it is impossible to leave it like this," Nekhlyúdov said to himself, entirely forgetful of his rotten feeling, and, without knowing why, rushing out into the corridor, in order to get another glimpse of her. Through the door pressed the animated throng of the jurors and lawyers, satisfied with the result of the case, so that he was kept for several minutes near the door. When he came out into the corridor, she was far away. With rapid steps, and without thinking of the attention which he was attracting, he caught up with her, and, going past, he stopped. She had ceased weeping, and only sobbed fitfully, wiping her flushed face with the end of the kerchief; she passed beyond him, without looking around. Having let her go by, he hurriedly went back, in order to see the presiding judge, but the judge had just left.

Nekhlyúdov caught up to him only in the vestibule.

"Judge," said Nekhlyúdov, approaching him just as he had donned his light-coloured overcoat and had taken from the porter his silver-knobbed cane, "may I speak with you about the case which has just been tried? I was one of the jurors."

"Yes, certainly, Prince Nekhlyúdov! Very happy, we have met before," said the presiding judge, shaking Nekhlyúdov's hand at the pleasant recollection of how well and gaily and how much better than many a young man he had danced on the evening of his first meeting with Nekhlyúdov. "What can I do for you?"

"There was a misunderstanding in the answer in regard to Máslova. She is not guilty of poisoning, and yet she has been sentenced to hard labour," Nekhlyúdov said, with a concentrated and gloomy look.

"The court has passed sentence according to the answers which you have handed in," said the presiding judge, moving toward the entrance door, "even though the answers seemed to the court not to be relevant to the case."

He recalled that he had intended to explain to the jury that their answer, "Yes, guilty," without a specific denial of intention to murder, only confirmed premeditated murder, but that, in his hurry, he had forgotten to do so.

"Yes, but cannot the error be corrected?"

"A cause for appeal may always be found. One must consult the lawyers," said the presiding judge, putting on his hat somewhat jauntily and moving toward the door.

"But this is terrible."

"You see, one of two things could have happened to Máslova," said the presiding judge, wishing to be as agreeable and polite to Nekhlyúdov as possible; he straightened out all his whiskers above the collar of his overcoat, and, lightly taking Nekhlyúdov's elbow, continued on his way to the door: "You are going out, are you not?"

"Yes," said Nekhlyúdov, swiftly putting on his coat and going out with him.

They came out into the bright, cheering sun, and it became necessary to speak louder, in order to be heard above the rattling of the wheels on the pavement.

"The situation, you see, is a strange one," continued the presiding judge, raising his voice. "One of two things could have happened to her, I mean to Máslova: either almost an acquittal, with incarceration in a prison, from which might have been deducted the time already passed in jail, or merely an arrest, or otherwise hard labour—there was nothing between these two. If you had added the words, 'but without the intention of causing death,' she would have been acquitted."

"It is inexcusable that I omitted them," said Nekhlyúdov.

"That's where the whole trouble is," said the presiding judge, smiling and looking at his watch.

There were only forty-five minutes left to the latest hour appointed by Klára.

"If you want to, ask a lawyer for help. You must find cause for appeal. It is always possible to find such. To the Dvoryánskaya," he said to a cabman; "thirty kopeks—I never pay more than that."

"If you please, your Excellency."

"My regards to you. If I can be useful to you, call at Dvórnikov's house, on the Dvoryánskaya—it's easy to remember."

And, bowing graciously, he drove off.

CHAPTER XXV

A CONVERSATION WITH
A LAWYER

The conversation with the presiding judge and the fresh air somewhat calmed Nekhlyúdov. He now thought that the sensation he had experienced was exaggerated by his having passed the whole morning under such unaccustomed circumstances.

"Of course, it is a remarkable and striking coincidence! I must do everything in my power to alleviate her condition, and I must do so at the earliest possible moment—at once. I must find out in the court-house where Fanárin or Mikíshin lives." He recalled the names of these two well-known lawyers.

Nekhlyúdov returned to the court-house, took off his overcoat, and went upstairs. He met Fanárin in the first corridor. He stopped him and told him that he had some business with him. Fanárin knew him by sight and by name and said that he would be happy to be of service to him.

"Although I am tired—but if it will not take you long, tell me your business—come this way."

Fanárin led Nekhlyúdov into a room, very likely the private chambers of some judge. They sat down at the table.

"Well, what is it about?"

"First of all I shall ask you," said Nekhlyúdov, "not to let anybody know that I am taking any interest in this matter."

"That goes without saying. So—"

"I served on the jury to-day, and we sentenced an innocent woman to hard labour. This torments me."

Nekhlyúdov blushed, quite unexpectedly to himself, and hesitated. Fanárin flashed his eyes on him and again lowered them and listened.

"Well?" was all he said.

"We have sentenced an innocent woman, and I should like to have the judgment annulled and carried to a higher court."

"To the Senate," Fanárin corrected him.

"And so I ask you to take the case."

Nekhlyúdov wanted to get over the most difficult point as soon as possible, and so he said, blushing:

"I shall bear the expenses in this case, whatever they may be."

"Well, we shall come to an understanding about that," said the lawyer, with a smile of condescension at his inexperience.

"What case is it?"

Nekhlyúdov told him.

"Very well, I will take it up to-morrow, and look it over. And the day after to-morrow—no, on Thursday, come to see me at six o'clock, and I shall have an answer for you. Is that all right? Come, let us go, I have to make some inquiries yet."

Nekhlyúdov said good-bye to him and went away.

His conversation with the lawyer and the fact that he had taken measures for Máslova's defence calmed him still more. He went out. The weather was beautiful, and it gave him pleasure to breathe the spring air. The cabmen offered him their services, but he went on foot. A whole swarm of thoughts and recollections in regard to Katyúsha and to his treatment of her at once began to whirl around in his head, and he felt melancholy, and everything looked gloomy. "No, I will consider that later," he said to himself, "but now I must divert my mind from these heavy impressions."

He thought of the dinner at the Korchágins' and looked at his watch. It was not yet late, and he could get there in time. A tramway car was tinkling past him. He ran and caught it. At the square he leaped down and took a good cab, and ten minutes later he was at the entrance of the large house of the Korchágins.

CHAPTER XXVI

DINNER AT THE KORCHÁGINS'

"Please, your Excellency! They are expecting you," said the kindly, stout porter of the large house of the Korchágins, opening the oak door of the entrance, which moved noiselessly on its English hinges. "They are at dinner, but I was ordered to ask you to come in."

The porter went up to the staircase and rang a bell.

"Is anybody there?" asked Nekhlyúdov, taking off his overcoat.

"Mr. Kólosov and Mikhaíl Sergyéevich, and the family," answered the porter.

A fine-looking lackey, in dress coat and white gloves, looked down-stairs.

"Please, your Excellency," he said, "I am to ask you in."

Nekhlyúdov ascended the staircase and passed to the dining-room through the familiar, luxurious, and spacious parlour. Here the whole family was sitting at the table, excepting the mother, Princess Sófya Vasílevna, who never left her study. At the head of the table sat the elder Korchágin; next to him, to the left, was the doctor; to the right, a guest, Iván Ivánovich Kólosov, formerly the provincial marshal of the nobility and now a director of a bank, a liberal comrade of Korchágin's; then, on the left, Miss Rheder, the governess of Missy's little sister, and the little four-year-old girl herself; on the right, exactly opposite, was Missy's brother, the only son of the Korchágins, a schoolboy of the sixth form, Pétya, for whose sake the whole family was still staying in the city, waiting for his examinations, and his tutor; then, on the left, Katerína Aleksyéevna, an old maid forty years of age, who was a Slavophile; opposite her, Mikhaíl Sergyéevich, or Mísha Telyégin, Missy's cousin, and at the lower end of the table, Missy herself, and, beside her, an empty place.

"Now, that's fine. Sit down—we are just at the fish," said the elder Korchágin, carefully and with difficulty chewing with his false teeth, and raising his bloodshot, apparently lidless eyes.

"Stepán," he turned, with his mouth full, to the stout, majestic butler, indicating with his eyes the empty plate. Although Nekhlyúdov was well acquainted with old Korchágin and had often seen him, especially at dinner, he never before had been so disagreeably impressed by his red face with its sensual, smacking lips above his napkin stuck into his vest, and by his fat neck—above all, by his whole pampered figure. Nekhlyúdov involuntarily recalled everything he had heard of the cruelty of this man, who, God knows why—for he was rich and of distinguished birth and did not need to earn recognition by zealous service—had had people flogged and even hanged when he had been the commanding officer of a territory.

Book One

Resurrection

page 81

"He will be served at once, your Excellency," said Stepán, taking from the buffet, which was filled with silver vases, a large soup-ladle and nodding to the fine-looking lackey with the whiskers; the lackey at once arranged the untouched place near Missy, on which lay a quaintly folded starched napkin with a huge coat of arms.

Nekhlyúdov walked all around the table, shaking everybody's hand. All but old Korchágin and the ladies rose when he came to them. On that evening walking around the table and shaking the hands of everybody present, though with some of them he never exchanged any words, seemed to him particularly disagreeable and ridiculous. He excused himself for being so late and was on the point of seating himself on the unoccupied chair between Missy and Katerína Aleksyéevna, when old Korchágin insisted that, even if he did not take any brandy, he should take an appetizer from the table on which stood lobsters, caviar, various kinds of cheese, and herrings. Nekhlyúdov did not know he was so hungry, but when he started on a piece of cheese sandwich he could not stop and ate avidly.

"Well, have you loosened the foundations?" said Kólosov, ironically quoting an expression of a reactionary paper which was opposed to trial by jury. "Have you acquitted the guilty and sentenced the innocent? Yes?"

"Loosened the foundations—loosened the foundations—" laughingly repeated the prince, who had an unbounded confidence in the wit and learning of his liberal comrade and friend.

Nekhlyúdov, at the risk of being impolite, did not answer Kólosov, and, sitting down to the plate of steaming soup which had been served to him, continued to munch his sandwich.

"Let him eat," Missy said, smiling; she used the pronoun "him" in order to point out her intimacy with him.

Kólosov, in the meantime, proceeded, in a loud and brisk voice, to give the contents of the article attacking trial by jury which had so exasperated him. Mikhaíl Sergyéevich, the nephew, agreed with him, and gave the contents of another article in the same paper.

Missy was very *distinguée*, as always, and well, unostentatiously well, dressed.

"You must be dreadfully tired and hungry," she said to Nekhlyúdov, when he had finished chewing.

"No, not very. And you? Did you go to see the pictures?" he asked.

"No, we put it off. We were out playing lawn-tennis with the Salamántovs. Really, Mr. Crooks plays a marvellous game."

Nekhlyúdov had come here to be diverted; it was always pleasant for him in the house, not only on account of that good taste in luxury which agreeably affected his feelings, but also on account of that atmosphere of insinuating kindness with which he was imperceptibly surrounded here. But, strange to say, on that evening everything in the house was distasteful to him, everything, beginning with the porter, the broad staircase, the flowers, the lackeys, the setting of the table, to Missy herself, who now appeared unattractive and unnatural to him. He was also disgusted with Kólosov's self-confident, mean, liberalizing tone; he was disgusted with the ox-like, self-confident, sensual figure of old Korchágin; he was disgusted with the French phrases of the Slavophile Katerína Aleksyéevna; he was disgusted with the repressed countenances of the governess and the tutor; and he was particularly disgusted with the pronoun "him," which had been used in regard to himself. Nekhlyúdov always wavered between two attitudes toward Missy: sometimes he saw her as though with squinting eyes and as if in moonlight, saw everything beautiful in her; she seemed to him fresh, and beautiful, and clever, and natural. Then again, he saw her as though in the bright sunshine, and he could not help noticing her defects. That evening was just such an occasion. He now saw all the wrinkles on her face; he knew that her hair was artificially puffed up; he saw the angularity of her elbows, and, above everything else, observed the wide nail of her thumb, which reminded him of her father's thumbnails.

"It is an exceedingly dull game," Kólosov remarked about the tennis. "The *laptá* we used to play in our childhood was much more fun."

"No, you never tried it. It is awfully much fun," retorted Missy, pronouncing with particular unnaturalness the word "awfully," so Nekhlyúdov thought.

And then began an argument in which Mikhaíl Sergyéevich and Katerína Aleksyéevna, also, took part. Only the governess, the tutor, and the children were silent and, obviously, were bored.

"Quarrelling all the time!" exclaimed old Korchágin, bursting out into a guffaw; he took the napkin out from his vest and, rattling his chair, which the lackey immediately took away, rose from table. All the others got up after him and went up to a small table, where stood the finger-bowls, filled with warm scented water; they wiped their mouths and continued the conversation, which did not interest anybody.

"Am I not right?" Missy turned to Nekhlyúdov, trying to elicit a confirmation of her opinion that a man's character is nowhere manifested so well as in a game. She had noticed in his face that concentrated and, as she thought, condemnatory expression of which she was afraid and wanted to know what it was that had caused it.

"Really, I do not know; I have never thought about it," replied Nekhlyúdov.

"Will you go to see mamma?" asked Missy.

"Yes, yes," he said, taking out a cigarette, and in a tone which manifestly meant that he would prefer not to go.

She looked at him in silence, with a questioning glance, and he felt ashamed. "How mean! To call on people in order to make them feel bad," he thought about himself, and, trying to say something agreeable, announced that it would give him pleasure to go, if the princess would receive him.

"Yes, yes, mamma will be happy. You may smoke there. Iván Ivánovich is there, too."

The lady of the house, Princess Sófya Vasílevna, was bedridden. For the last eight years she had received her guests while lying in bed, amidst laces and ribbons, amidst velvet, gold tinsel, ivory, bronze, lacquer, and flowers; she did not go out and received only her "own friends," as she expressed herself; that is, all such people as, in her opinion, stood out from the crowd. Nekhlyúdov was among these friends, because she regarded him as a clever young man, because he and his mother were close friends of the house, and because it would be well if Missy married him.

Princess Sófya Vasílevna's room was beyond the large and small drawing-rooms. In the large drawing-room, Missy, who preceded Nekhlyúdov, suddenly stopped and, holding on to the back of a gilt chair, looked straight at him.

Missy was very anxious to get married, and Nekhlyúdov was a good match. Besides, she liked him and had accustomed herself to the idea that he would belong to her (not that she would belong to him, but he to her), and she reached out for her goal with unconscious, but persistent cunning, such as the insane are possessed of. She said something to him in order to elicit a declaration from him.

"I see that something has happened to you," she said. "What is the matter with you?"

He recalled the incident in the court-room, frowned, and blushed.

"Yes, something has happened," he said, trying to be truthful, "a strange, unusual, and important thing."

"What is it? Can't you tell it?"

"Not now. Forgive my not talking about it. Something has happened which I have not yet had time to think over," he said, and his face became even redder.

"And you will not tell me?" A muscle on her face quivered, and she moved the chair to which she was holding on.

"No, I cannot," he answered, feeling that in answering her thus he was answering himself and confessing that really something important had happened to him.

"Well, let us go."

She tossed her head, as if to drive away unnecessary thoughts, and walked on with faster steps than usual.

It appeared to him that she compressed her lips in an unnatural manner, as though to keep back tears. He felt ashamed and pained at having grieved her, but he knew that the least weakness would ruin him, that is, it would bind him. And on that evening he was afraid of it more than ever, and so he reached the princess's cabinet with her in silence.

CHAPTER XXVII

IN PRINCESS KORCHÁGINA'S BOUDOIR

Princess Sófya Vasílevna had finished her very refined and nourishing dinner, which she was in the habit of eating all alone, in order that she might not be seen at that unpoetical function. Near her lounge stood a small table with coffee, and she was smoking a *pajitos*-cigarette. Princess Sófya Vasílevna was a lean, tall brunette, with large teeth and big black eyes, who was still trying to look young.

There was a rumor about her relations with her doctor. On previous occasions Nekhlyúdov generally forgot about this; on that evening he not only thought of it, but, when he saw the doctor near her chair, with his pomaded, shining forked beard, he was overcome by loathing.

At Sófya Vasílevna's side, on a soft low armchair, Kólosov sat by the table, stirring his coffee. On the table stood a glass with liqueur.

Missy entered with Nekhlyúdov but did not remain in the room.

"When mamma gets tired and drives you away, come to me," she said, turning to Kólosov and Nekhlyúdov in such a tone as though nothing had happened between them and, with a merry smile, inaudibly stepping over the heavy rug, went out of the room.

"Good evening, my friend! Sit down and tell me all about it," said Princess Sófya Vasílevna with her artificial, feigned smile, which remarkably resembled a real smile, and showing her beautiful large teeth, which were as artistically made as though they were natural. "I am told that you have come from court in a very gloomy mood. This must be very hard for people with a heart," she said in French.

"Yes, that is so," said Nekhlyúdov. "One often feels his in— One feels that one has no right to sit in judgment."

"*Comme c'est vrai,*" she exclaimed, as though struck by the truth of his remark and, as always, artfully flattering the person she was talking to.

"Well, how is your picture getting on?— It interests me very much," she added. "If it were not for my ailment, I should have gone to see it long ago."

"I have given it up altogether," dryly replied Nekhlyúdov, to whom the insincerity of her flattery was now as obvious as her old age, which she was trying to conceal. He was absolutely unable to make himself be pleasant.

"What a pity! Do you know, Répin himself told me that he has real talent," she said, turning to Kólosov.

"How shamelessly she lies," thought Nekhlyúdov, frowning.

Book One

Resurrection

page 85

Having convinced herself that Nekhlyúdov was not in a good humour and that it was not possible to draw him into a pleasant and clever conversation, Sófya Vasílevna turned to Kólosov, asking for his opinion about the latest drama, in such a tone as though Kólosov's opinion was to solve all doubts, and as though every word of that opinion was to be eternalized. Kólosov criticized the drama and used this opportunity to expatiate on his conceptions of art. Princess Sófya Vasílevna was taken aback by the correctness of his views, tried to defend the author of the drama, but immediately gave in or found some compromise. Nekhlyúdov was looking and hearing, but he saw and heard something completely different from what was going on in front of him.

Listening sometimes to Sófya Vasílevna, sometimes to Kólosov, Nekhlyúdov observed, first, that neither Sófya Vasílevna nor Kólosov had the least interest in the drama or in each other, and that they were conversing only to satisfy a physiological necessity of moving the muscles of the mouth and throat after dinner; secondly, that Kólosov, having drunk vodka, wine, and liqueur, was a little intoxicated—not as intoxicated as peasants are who drink at rare intervals, but as people are who make a habit of drinking wine. He did not sway, nor say foolish things, but was in an abnormal, excitedly self-satisfied condition; in the third place, Nekhlyúdov noticed that Princess Sófya Vasílevna during the conversation restlessly looked at the window, through which fell the slanting rays of the sun upon her, fearing that too strong a light might be shed on her old age.

"How true that is," she said about a remark of Kólosov's and pressed a button in the wall near the lounge.

Just then the doctor arose and, being a familiar friend, went out of the room without saying a word. Sófya Vasílevna followed him with her eyes, continuing to speak.

"Please, Filípp, let down this curtain," she said, indicating with her eyes the curtain of the window, when the fine-looking lackey had come in in answer to the bell.

"You may say what you like, but there is something mystical in him, and without mysticism there can be no poetry," she said with one black eye angrily watching the movement of the lackey who was fixing the curtain.

"Mysticism without poetry is superstition, and poetry without mysticism is prose," she said, sadly smiling and not letting out of sight the lackey, who was still busy with the curtain.

"Filípp, not that curtain—the one at the large window," Sófya Vasílevna muttered, with the tone of a sufferer, evidently regretting the effort which she had to make in order to pronouce these words, and immediately, to soothe her nerves, putting the fragrant, smoking cigarette to her mouth with her ring-covered hand.

Broad-chested, muscular, handsome Filípp made a slight bow, as though to excuse himself, and, stepping softly over the rug with his strong, well-shaped legs, humbly and silently went up to the other window and, carefully watching the princess, so arranged the curtain that not one single ray could fall upon her. But here he again did not do exactly right, and again exhausted Sófya Vasílevna was compelled to interrupt her conversation about mysticism and to correct Filípp, who was hard of understanding and who pitilessly tormented her. For a moment there was a flash in Filípp's eyes.

"Who the hell knows what you want, no doubt is what he said to himself," thought Nekhlyúdov, who was watching the whole game. But handsome, strong Filípp at once concealed his motion of impatience and began calmly to carry out the order of exhausted, powerless, false Princess Sófya Vasílevna.

"Of course, there is a larger grain of truth in Darwin's teachings," said Kólosov, throwing himself back in the low armchair and looking with sleepy eyes at Princess Sófya Vasílevna, "but he oversteps the boundary. Yes."

"And do you believe in heredity?" Princess Sófya Vasílevna asked Nekhlyúdov, vexed by his silence.

"In heredity?" Nekhlyúdov repeated her question. "No, I do not," he said, being at that moment all absorbed in the strange pictures which for some reason were rising in his imagination. By the side of strong, handsome Filípp, whom he imagined to be an artist's model, he saw Kólosov naked, with a belly in the shape of a water-melon, and a bald head, and thin, twig-like arms. Just as disconsolately he thought of Sófya Vasílevna's shoulders, which now were covered with silk and velvet; he imagined them in their natural state, but this image was so terrible that he tried to dispel it.

Sófya Vasílevna measured him with her eyes.

"I think Missy is waiting for you," she said. "Go to her; she wanted to play you a new piece by Schumann—it is very interesting."

"She did not want to play anything. The woman is just lying for some reason," thought Nekhlyúdov, rising and shaking Sófya Vasílevna's translucent, bony hand, covered with rings.

In the drawing-room he was met by Katerína Aleksyéevna, who at once began to speak to him.

"I see the duties of a juror have a depressing effect on you," she said, speaking, as always, in French.

"Forgive me, I am not in a good humour to-day, and I have no right to make others feel bad," said Nekhlyúdov.

"Why are you out of humour?"

"Please excuse my not telling you why," he said, trying to find his hat.

"Do you remember how you told us that one must always tell the truth, and how you then told us such cruel truths? Why, then, do you not want to tell it now? Do you remember, Missy?" Katerína Aleksyéevna turned to Missy, who had come out to them.

"Because that was a game," Nekhlyúdov answered seriously. "In a game it's all right, but in reality we are so bad, that is, I am so bad, that I, at least, am not able to tell the truth."

"Don't correct yourself but, rather, tell us why we are so bad," said Katerína Aleksyéevna, playing with words and seeming not to notice Nekhlyúdov's seriousness.

"There is nothing worse than to confess that you are out of humour," said Missy. "I never acknowledge such a feeling in myself, and so I am always in a happy frame of mind. Well, let's go to my room. We will try to dispel your *mauvaise humeur*."

Nekhlyúdov experienced a sensation such as a horse must when it is being patted in order to be bridled and hitched. But on that evening it was harder for him to pull than at any previous time. He excused himself, saying that he had to go home, and began to say good-bye. Missy held his hand longer than usual.

"Remember that what is important to you is also important to your friends," she said. "Will you be here to-morrow?"

"Hardly," said Nekhlyúdov, and, feeling ashamed (he did not know whether for himself or for her), he blushed and hurriedly went out.

"What is it? *Comme cela m'intrigue*," said Katerína Aleksyéevna, when Nekhlyúdov had gone. "I must find out. Some *affaire d'amour-propre—il est très susceptible, notre cher* Mítya."

"*Plutôt une affaire d'amour sale*," Missy was about to say but restrained herself, with a dimmed expression which was quite different from the one her face had when speaking with him; she did not tell that bad pun to Katerína Aleksyéevna, but merely remarked:

"We all have good and bad days."

"I wonder whether he, too, will deceive me," she thought. "After all that has happened, it would be very bad of him."

If Missy had been asked to explain what she understood by the words, "after all that has happened," she would not have been able to say anything definite, and yet she knew beyond any doubt that he had not only given her hope, but had almost promised her. All this had been done not by any specific words, but by glances, smiles, insinuations, and reticence. Nevertheless, she regarded him as her own, and it would have been hard for her to lose him.

CHAPTER XXVIII

NEKHLYÚDOV "CLEANSES HIS SOUL"

"Disgraceful and disgusting, disgusting and disgraceful," Nekhlyúdov thought in the meantime, walking home through familiar streets. The heavy feeling which he had experienced during his conversation with Missy did not leave him. He felt that formally, if one may so express oneself, he was in the right with regard to her; he had said nothing to her that would bind him, had made no proposal to her, but basically he was conscious of having bound himself, of having made a promise to her, and yet to-day he felt with his whole being that he could not marry her. "Disgraceful and disgusting, disgusting and disgraceful," he repeated to himself, not only in reference to his relations with Missy, but to everything. "Everything is disgusting and disgraceful," he repeated to himself as he ascended the porch of his house.

"I won't eat any supper," he said to Kornéi, who followed him into the dining-room where the table was set and the tea was ready. "You may go."

"Yes, sir," said Kornéi; he did not leave, but began to clear the table. Nekh-lyúdov looked at Kornéi and was overcome by a hostile feeling toward him. He wanted to be left alone, but it seemed to him that everybody was pestering him, as though on purpose. When Kornéi had left with the place settings, Nekhlyúdov started over to the samovar in order to make some tea, but, hearing Agraféna Petróvna's steps, he hurriedly went into the drawing-room in order not to be seen and closed the door behind him. This room—the drawing-room—was the one in which his mother had died three months before. Now, upon entering this room, which was illuminated by two lamps with their reflectors—one near his father's picture, the other near his mother's portrait—he recalled his last relations with his mother, and they seemed to him unnatural and repulsive. And this, too, was dis-graceful and disgusting. He recalled how, during her last illness, he had simply wanted her to die. He had said to himself that he wished it in order to see her liberated from her sufferings, but in reality he had wished himself to be freed from the sight of her agony.

Wishing to evoke a good memory of her, he looked at her portrait, which had been painted by a famous painter for five thousand roubles. She was portrayed in a low-necked black velvet gown. The painter had evidently made a special effort in painting the bosom, the space between her breasts, and the shoulders and neck, dazzling in their beauty. This was absolutely disgraceful and disgusting. There was something loathsome and blasphemous in this portrait of his mother as a half-naked beauty, the more loathsome, since three months ago this very woman had been lying there, dried up like a mummy, and yet filling not only the room, but even the whole house with a painfully oppressive odour which it was impossible to overcome. He thought he could scent it even now. And he recalled how the day before her death she had taken his strong, white hand into her bony, discoloured little one, had looked him in the eye, and had said: "Do not judge me, Mítya, if I have not done right," and in her eyes, faded from suffering, stood tears. "How disgusting!" he said once more to himself, looking at the half-bare woman with her superb marble shoulders and arms and with her victorious smile. The nudity of the bosom in the portrait reminded him of another young woman, whom he had also seen décolletée a few days before. It was Missy, who had found an excuse to invite him to the house, in order that she might appear before him in the evening dress in which she was going to a ball. He thought with disgust of her beautiful shoulders and arms. And that coarse animal father, with his past, his cruelty, and that *bel esprit* mother, with her doubtful reputation! Disgraceful and disgusting, disgusting and disgraceful!

"No, no," he thought, "I must free myself; I must free myself from all these false relations with the Korchágins, with Maríya Vasílevna, with the inheritance, and with everything else—Yes, I must breathe freely. Abroad—to Rome, to work on my picture." He recalled his doubts in regard to his talent. "What of it? If only to breathe freely. First to Constantinople, then to Rome, only to get rid of all jury service. And I must arrange that matter with the lawyer."

And suddenly the prisoner, with her black squinting eyes, arose in his imagination with extraordinary vividness. How she did weep during the last words said by the defendants! He hurriedly extinguished his finished cigarette and crushed it in the ash-tray, lighted another, and began to pace up and down in the room. And one after another the moments which he had passed with her rose in his imagination. He recalled his last meeting with her, that animal passion which then had taken possession of him, and the disenchantment which he had experienced when his passion was satisfied. He recalled the white dress with the blue ribbon, and the morning mass. "I did love her, did sincerely love her with a good and pure love during that night: I had loved her even before, when I had passed my first summer with my aunts, and had been writing my essay!" And he remembered himself as he had been then. That freshness, youth, and fulness of life was wafted upon him, and he felt painfully sad.

The difference between what he had been then and what he was now was enormous; it was just as great, if not greater than the difference that existed between Katyúsha at church and that prostitute who had caroused with the merchant and who had been sentenced on that very day. Then he had been a vigorous, free man, before whom endless possibilities had been open; now he was conscious of being on all sides caught in the snare of a foolish, empty, aimless, and worthless life, from which he saw no way out, and from which, for the most part, he did not wish to get out. He recalled how, formerly, he had prided himself on his straightforwardness; how he had made it his rule always to tell the truth and how he had done that; and how he now was all entangled in a lie, in a most terrible lie, a lie which all the people who surrounded him regarded as the truth. And there was no way of getting out from this lie—at least he did not see any way. And he was sunk deep in it—was used to it, and pampered himself by it.

How was he to break off those relations with Maríya Vasílevna and with her husband in such a way that he should not be ashamed to look into his eyes and into the eyes of his children? How was he to unravel his relations with Missy without lying? How was he to extricate himself from the contradiction between the acknowledgment of the illegality of the ownership of land and the possession of his maternal inheritance? How was he to atone for his sin before Katyúsha? He certainly could not leave it as it was. "I cannot abandon a woman whom I have loved and be satisfied with paying a lawyer and freeing her from hard labour, which she does not deserve —that is, settle the whole matter by giving money, just as I thought then I was doing what I ought by giving her money!"

And he vividly remembered the minute when he had caught up with her in the corridor and put the money in her bosom and had run away again. "Ah, that money!" he recalled that instant with the same terror and disgust that had overcome him then. "Ah, ah! how contemptible!" he said aloud, just as then. "Only a rascal, a scoundrel, could have done that! And I am that rascal, that scoundrel!" he again said aloud. "And am I really," he stopped in his walk, "am I really such a scoundrel? If not I, who is?" he replied to his own question. "And is this all?" he continued to upbraid himself. "Are not your relations with Maríya Vasílevna and her husband mean and contemptible? And your relations with property? Under the pretence that the money is your mother's to make use of wealth which you regard as illegal? And all your empty, foul life. And the crown of it all—your behaviour toward Katyúsha. Scoundrel! Rascal! Let people judge me as they please: I can deceive them, but I shall never be able to deceive myself."

And he suddenly understood that that loathing which he had of late experienced for people—and especially on that very day for the prince, and for Sófya Vasílevna, and for Missy, and for Kornéi—was really a loathing for himself. And, strange to say, in this feeling of confessing his meanness there was something painful and at the same time something pleasurable and soothing.

Several times before Nekhlyúdov had had what he called a "cleansing of his soul." By a cleansing of his soul he understood a condition of his soul such as when he suddenly, sometimes after a long interval of time, recognized the retardation, and sometimes the cessation, of his internal life, and began to clean up all the dirt which had accumulated in his soul, and which was the cause of this retardation.

After such awakenings Nekhlyúdov formed certain rules which he intended to follow henceforth: he kept a diary and began a new life, which he hoped he would never change again—"*turning a new leaf*," as he used to say to himself. But the temptations of the world would press hard on him, and he would fall again, without noticing it, and often lower than before.

Thus he had cleansed himself and had risen several times; thus it had been with him the first time when he had gone to spend the summer with his aunts. That had been the most vivid, the most enthusiastic awakening, and its effects had remained for a considerable time. Then, he had another awakening when he left civil service, and, wishing to sacrifice his life, entered the military service during the war. But here the pollution took place soon after. Then, there was another awakening when he asked for his dismissal from the army and went abroad to study art.

Since then down to this day a long period had passed without any cleansing, and consequently he had never before reached such a pollution and such a discord between what his conscience demanded and the life which he was leading, and he was horror-struck when he saw the distance.

That distance was so great, the pollution so strong, that at first he despaired of being able to cleanse his soul. "I have tried often enough to perfect myself and become better, but nothing has come of it," said in his soul the voice of the tempter, "so what is the use of trying again?" "You are not the only one—everybody's like that—such is life," said this voice. But the free, spiritual being, which alone is true, and powerful, and eternal, was already beginning to waken in Nekhlyúdov. He could not help trusting it. No matter how great the distance was between what he had been and what he wanted to be, everything was possible for the awakened spiritual being.

"I will tear asunder the lie which is binding me at whatever cost and I will profess the truth and I will tell the truth to everybody at all times and will act truthfully," he said to himself aloud, with determination. "I will tell the truth to Missy; I will tell her that I am a libertine and that I cannot marry her, and that I have troubled her for nothing; and I will also tell the truth to Maríya Vasílevna (the wife of the Marshal of Nobility). Still I have nothing to tell her; I will tell her husband that I am a scoundrel, that I have deceived him. I will make such disposition of my inheritance as to be in consonance with the truth. I will tell her, Katyúsha, that I am a rascal, that I am guilty toward her, and I will do everything to alleviate her lot. Yes, I will see her and will ask her to forgive me. Yes, I will ask forgiveness, as children ask it." He stopped. "I will marry her, if that is necessary."

He stopped, crossed his hands over his breast, as he used to do when he was a child, raised his eyes upwards, and uttered these words:

"O Lord, help me, instruct me, come and take Thy abode within me, and cleanse me of all impurity."

He prayed to God to help him, to take up His abode within him, and to purify him, and in the meantime what he asked for had already taken place. God, who was living within him, had awakened in his consciousness. He felt himself to be that new man, and therefore he was conscious not only of freedom, of frankness, and of the joy of life, but also of all the power of goodness. He now felt himself capable of doing everything, the very best that any human being could do.

In his eyes were tears, as he was saying that to himself—both good and bad tears: good tears, because they were tears of joy at the awakening of the spiritual being within him; and bad, because they were tears of pacification with himself, at his own virtue.

He was warm. He went up to the window and opened it. It faced the garden. It was a quiet, fresh moonlight night; in the street some wheels rattled, and then all was quiet. Right under the window could be seen the shadow from the branches of the tall, leafless poplar, which with all its forked boughs lay distinctly outlined on the sand of the cleaned-up open space. On the left was the roof of a barn, which appeared white in the bright moonlight; in front were the intertwined branches of the trees, and behind them could be seen the black shadow of the fence. Nekhlyúdov looked at the moonlit garden and roof and the shadow of the poplar, and he listened, and inhaled the vivifying fresh air.

"How good, how good, O Lord, how good!" he said of what was in his soul.

CHAPTER XXIX

MÁSLOVA'S RETURN TO PRISON

Máslova returned to her cell at six o'clock in the evening, tired and footsore from the unaccustomed fifteen-verst march over the cobblestones, overwhelmed by the unexpectedly severe sentence, and, on top of everything, hungry.

During a recess, the guards beside her had been eating bread and hard-boiled eggs and her mouth had begun to water, and she had felt hungry but had regarded it as humiliating to ask them for anything to eat. When, after that, three hours passed, she no longer felt hungry, but only weak. It was in that condition that she heard the sentence. At first she thought that she had not heard right and was not able to believe what she had heard: she could not think of herself as sentenced to hard labour. But when she saw the quiet, businesslike countenances of the judges and the jury, who received that information as something quite natural, she felt outraged and shouted aloud to the whole court-room that she was not guilty. When she saw that her cry, too, was received as something natural, as something expected and incapable of affecting the case, she burst into tears, feeling that it was necessary to submit to that cruel and amazing injustice which had been committed against her. She was particularly amazed at the fact that she had been so cruelly condemned by men—young men, not old men—who had always looked so favourably upon her. One of them—the assistant prosecuting attorney—she had seen in quite a different mood. While she was sitting in the prisoners' room, waiting for the court to begin, and during the recesses of the session, she had seen those men, pretending to be after something else, pass by the door or walk into the room only in order to take a look at her. And now these same men had for some reason or other sentenced her to hard labour, notwithstanding the fact that she was not guilty of what she had been accused of. She wept, but then grew silent, and in complete stupor sat in the prisoners' room, waiting to be taken back. She wanted only one thing—to smoke. While she was feeling like this, Bóchkova and Kartínkin came in, brought back into the same room after the sentence had been passed. Bóchkova at once began to scold Máslova and to taunt her with the hard labour.

"Well, did you succeed? Did you justify yourself? You could not get off, you slut! You got what you deserved. I bet you give up your fine ways under hard labour."

Máslova sat with her hands stuck into the sleeves of her cloak and, bending her head low, remained motionless, looking two steps ahead of her, at the tracked-up floor, and only said:

"I am not bothering you, so you leave me alone. I am not bothering you," she repeated several times, then grew entirely silent. She revived a little when Bóchkova and Kartínkin were led away, and the janitor came in and brought her three roubles.

"Are you Máslova?" he asked. "Here, take it; a lady has sent it to you," he said, handing her the money.

"What lady?"

"Take it; I should talk to you, too!"

Kitáeva, the madam, had sent the money. Upon leaving the court-room she asked the bailiff whether she could give Máslova some money. The bailiff said she could. Upon receiving this permission, she pulled the three-button chamois glove off her plump white hand, took a fashionable pocketbook out of the back folds of her silk skirt, and selecting from a fairly large heap of coupons, which had been cut from some notes earned by her in her establishment, one for two roubles and fifty kopeks, and having added to this two twenty-kopek pieces and one ten-kopek piece,

handed the sum over to the bailiff. He called the guard and gave him the money in the presence of the donor.

"Please, give it to her in full," Karolína Albértovna said to the guard.

The guard felt insulted by the suspicion, and that was why he was so brusque with Máslova.

Máslova was glad to get the money, because it would furnish her with what she now wanted.

"If I could only get cigarettes, and have a puff at one," she thought, and all her thoughts were centred on this one desire to smoke. She was so anxious for it that she eagerly inhaled the air when there was a whiff of tobacco smoke in it, as it found its way into the corridor from behind the doors of the offices. But she had to wait for quite a while, because the secretary, who had to release her, having forgotten about the defendants, was busy discussing a prohibited article with one of the lawyers. A few men, both young and old, came in to look at her after the trial, whispering something to each other. But now she did not even notice them.

Finally, at about five o'clock, she was permitted to leave, and the two soldiers of the guard—the Nízhni-Nóvgorodian and the Chuvásh—took her away from the court-house by a back door. While in the vestibule of the court-house, she gave them twenty kopeks, asking them to buy her two rolls and cigarettes. The Chuvásh laughed, took the money, and said, "All right, we will buy it for you," and really honestly bought the cigarettes and rolls, and gave her the change. On the way she could not smoke, so that Máslova reached the prison with the same unsatisfied desire to smoke. As she was brought to the door, about one hundred prisoners were being delivered from the railroad train. She fell in with them at the entrance.

The prisoners—bearded, shaven, old, young, Russians and of other nationalities —some of them with half their heads shaven, clanking their leg-fetters, filled the entrance-hall with dust, the noise of their steps, their voices, and the pungent odour of their sweat. Passing by Máslova, the prisoners eagerly looked at her, and some, their faces transformed by lust, went up to her and teased her.

"Oh, a fine wench," said one. "My regards to aunty," said another, blinking with one eye. A swarthy fellow, the back of his head blue and shaven and a moustache on his shaven face, tripping in his fetters and clanking them, rushed up to her and embraced her.

"Did you not recognize your friend? Stop putting on airs!" he cried, grinning and flashing his eyes at her, as she pushed him away.

"You bastard, what are you doing there?" cried the assistant superintendent, coming up to him.

The prisoner crouched and swiftly hopped away. The assistant began to scold Máslova.

"What are you doing here?"

Máslova wanted to tell him that she was brought back from court, but she was too tired to talk.

"From court, your honour," said the elder guard, coming out of the throng of prisoners and putting his hand to his cap.

"Well, transfer her, then, to the warden. What kind of thing is this!"

"Yes, your honour!"

"Sokolóv! Receive her," cried the assistant superintendent.

The warden came up, and, giving Máslova an angry push on the shoulder and indicating the direction to her by a motion of his head, led her to the women's corridor. There she was examined and searched all over, and, as nothing was found (the cigarette box had been stuck into a roll), she was admitted to the same cell which she had left in the morning.

CHAPTER XXX

THE WOMEN'S CELL

The cell in which Máslova was kept was a long room, nine arshíns long and seven wide, with two windows, a protruding, worn-out stove, and sleeping-benches with warped boards, which occupied two thirds of the space. In the middle, opposite the door, was a dark icon with a wax taper stuck to it and with a dusty wreath of immortelles hanging underneath it. Behind the door, and to the left, was a black spot on the floor, and on it stood a stink-vat. The roll had just been called, and the women were locked up for the night.

There were in all fifteen inmates in that cell: twelve women and three children.

It was still quite light, and only two women were lying on the benches: one of them, whose head was covered with her cloak, was a demented woman, who was locked up for having no passport; she was asleep most of the time; and the other—a consumptive woman—was serving a sentence for theft. She was not asleep, but lay with her cloak under her head, her eyes wide open, with difficulty keeping back the tickling and oozing moisture in her throat, in order not to cough. The other women, all of them with bare heads, in nothing but shirts of a coarse texture, were either sitting on the benches and sewing or standing at the window and looking at the prisoners who were passing through the yard. Of the three women who were sewing, one was the same old woman who had seen Máslova off, Koroblyóva by name; she was a sullen, scowling, wrinkled, tall, strong woman, with skin hanging like a loose bag under her chin, a short braid of blond hair that was streaked with gray over her temples, and a hirsute wart on her cheek. The woman had been sentenced to hard labour for having killed her husband with an axe. She had committed that murder because he had been making improper advances to her daughter. Koroblyóva was the head woman of the cell and trafficked in liquor. She was sewing in spectacles and holding the needle in her large working hands in peasant fashion, with three fingers and the point toward her. Next to her sat a snub-nosed, swarthy little woman, with small black eyes, good-hearted and talkative, also sewing canvas bags. She was a flagwoman at a railroad hut, sentenced to three months in jail for having failed to flag a train, a failure by which an accident was caused. The third woman who was sewing was Fedósya—Fénichka her companions called her—a white, red-cheeked, very young, sweet-faced woman, with clear, childish eyes, and two long blond braids circling around a small head, who was imprisoned for an attempt to poison her husband. She tried to poison him soon after her marriage, which had taken place when she was barely sixteen years old. In the eight months which she had been detained awaiting the court's session, she not only made up with her husband, but became so fond of him that the court found the two living in the greatest concord. Notwithstanding the fact that her husband and her father-in-law, and especially the mother-in-law, who had become exceedingly fond of her, tried to exculpate her, she was sentenced to hard labour in Siberia. Good, merry, frequently smiling Fedósya was Máslova's neighbour on the bench, and she not only had become very fond of Máslova, but regarded it as her duty to care for her and look after her. Two other women were sitting on the benches, without any work; one of them, about forty years of age, with a pale, haggard face, had evidently once been very beautiful, but now was pale and lean—she was holding a babe in her arms, and nursing it at her white, long breast. Her crime consisted in this: a recruit was taken away from their village, who, according to the peasants' understanding, had been unlawfully drafted; the people stopped the police-officer and took away the recruit; this woman, the unlawfully seized recruit's aunt, was the first to lay hands on the reins of the horse which was to take away the recruit. The other was a short, wrinkled, good-natured old woman, gray-haired and hunchbacked. This old woman sat on a bench near the stove and pretended to be catching the four-year-old, close-cropped, chubby little boy who was running past her and laughing loudly. He was clad in nothing but a shirt and kept running past and repeating all the time, "See, you did not catch me!" This old woman, who with her son was accused of arson, bore her imprisonment with the greatest good nature, feeling sorry not for herself, but for her son, who was also in jail, and still more for her old husband, who, she was afraid, would be all covered with lice, because the daughter-in-law had left, and there was no one at home to wash him.

In addition to these seven women, four others were standing at one of the open windows, and, holding on to the iron grating, were with signs and shouts conversing with those prisoners with whom Máslova had fallen in at the entrance. One of these women, who was serving for theft, was a large, heavy, flabby, red-haired woman, with a sallow and freckled face, hands, and neck, which stuck out from her untied, open collar. She loudly shouted indecent words in a hoarse voice out the window. Next to her stood a swarthy, ungainly woman, with a long back and very short legs, looking not larger than a ten-year-old girl. Her face was red and all spotted and had widely separated black eyes and short, stout lips, which did not cover up her protruding white teeth. She was laughing with a whine and fitfully at what was going on in the yard. This prisoner, nicknamed Khoroshávka for her foppishness, was under trial for theft and arson. Back of them stood, in a very dirty gray shirt, a miserable-looking, haggard, venous, pregnant woman, with an immense abdomen, who was on trial for receiving stolen goods. This woman was silent, but all the time smiled approvingly and rapturously at what was going on outdoors. The fourth woman at the window, who was serving a sentence for illicit traffic in liquor, was a short, thick-set peasant woman, with very bulging eyes and a good-natured face. This woman, the mother of the boy who was playing with the old woman, and of a seven-year-old girl, both of which children were with her in the prison because she had no one to leave them with, was looking through the window like the rest, but continued to knit a stocking and kept frowning disapprovingly and closing her ears to what the transient prisoners in the yard were saying. Her daughter, the seven-year-old girl, with white, loose hair, was standing in nothing but a shirt near the red-haired woman, and, holding on with her thin little hand to her skirt, was, with big eyes, listening attentively to the vulgar words which the women were exchanging with the prisoners, and repeating them in a whisper, as though to learn them by heart. The twelfth prisoner was the daughter of a sexton, who had drowned her child in a well. She was a tall, stately girl, with tangled hair, which stuck out from her thick short blond braid, and with motionless protruding eyes. She did not pay the least attention to what was going on around her, was barefoot and clad in a dirty gray shirt, and was pacing to and fro in the free space of the cell, abruptly and rapidly turning around whenever she reached the wall.

CHAPTER XXXI

MÁSLOVA'S CELLMATES

When the lock rattled and Máslova was let into the cell, all turned to her. Even the sexton's daughter stopped for a minute and looked at Máslova with uplifted brows, but without saying anything immediately proceeded to walk up and down with her long, determined steps. Koroblyóva stuck her needle into the coarse cloth, and questioningly turned her eyes, through her spectacles, upon Máslova.

"Oh, my. You are back. And I thought you would be acquitted," she said, in her hoarse, deep, almost masculine voice. "Evidently they have sent you up."

She took off her spectacles and put her sewing down on the bench.

"Aunty and I have been talking about you, dear; we thought they would release you at once. Such things do happen. And if you strike it right, you get money, too," began the flagwoman, in her singing voice. "And just the opposite has happened. Evidently our guessing was wrong. The Lord evidently has decided differently, my dear," she chattered without cessation in her kind and melodious voice.

"Have they really sentenced you?" asked Fedósya, with compassionate tenderness, looking at Máslova with her childish, light blue eyes; her whole cheerful, young face was changed, as though she were ready to weep.

Máslova did not make any reply, and silently went up to her place, the second from the end, near Koroblyóva, and sat down on the boards of the bench.

"I suppose you have not had anything to eat," said Fedósya, getting up and walking over to Máslova.

Máslova put the rolls at the head of the bench, without saying a word, and began to undress herself: she took off her dusty cloak, and the kerchief from her curly black hair, and sat down.

The humpbacked old woman who had been playing with the little fellow at the other end of the benches went up and stopped in front of Máslova.

"Tss, tss, tss!" she hissed out, sympathetically shaking her head.

The little boy also came up with the old woman and, opening his eyes wide and pursing his upper lip in one corner, did not take them off the rolls which Máslova had brought. Upon seeing all these sympathetic faces after all that had happened during that day, Máslova felt like weeping, and her lips began to quiver. But she tried to restrain herself and succeeded in doing so until the old woman and little boy came up to her. But when she heard the kindly, compassionate "tss" of the old woman, and especially when her eyes met those of the boy, who had now transferred his serious eyes from the rolls to her, she no longer could hold back. Her whole face trembled, and she sobbed out loud.

"I told you to get the right kind of a counsel," said Koroblyóva. "Well, what is it, exile?" she asked.

Máslova wanted to answer but could not; sobbing, she took out of the roll the box of cigarettes, on which there was a picture of a pink-cheeked woman in a very high head-dress and a low-cut V-necked dress, and handed it to Koroblyóva. Koroblyóva glanced at the picture, disapprovingly shook her head, particularly because

Máslova had spent her money so badly, and, taking out a cigarette, lighted it at the lamp, took herself a puff, and then put it into Máslova's hand. Máslova, without interrupting her weeping, eagerly began to inhale the tobacco smoke in quick puffs.

"Hard labour," she muttered through sobs.

"They are not afraid of God, the spongers and damned bloodsuckers," muttered Koroblyóva. "Sentenced the girl for nothing."

Just then a roar of laughter was heard among the women who were standing at the window. The little girl was laughing, too, and her thin, childish laugh mingled with the hoarse and whining laughter of the grown people. A prisoner on the outside had done something that affected the women who were looking through the window.

"Ah, the shaven dog! See what he is doing," said the red-haired woman, and shaking her whole fat body and pressing her face against the grating, she shouted some senseless and indecent words.

"Go on, you old piece of leather! What are you guffawing about?" said Koroblyóva, shaking her head at the red-haired woman and again turning to Máslova. "How many years?"

"Four," said Máslova, and the tears flowed so copiously from her eyes that one fell on the cigarette.

Máslova angrily crushed it, threw it away, and took another.

The flagwoman, though she did not smoke, immediately picked up the butt and began to straighten it out, speaking all the time.

"I must say, my dear," she said, "truth's gone to the dogs. They now do as they please. And here we had been guessing that you would be released. Matvyéevna said that you would be, and I said, 'No!' says I, 'my heart feels that they will undo her,' and so it is," she said, evidently finding pleasure in listening to the sound of her own voice.

By that time all the prisoners had crossed the yard, and the women who had been conversing with them had left the window and had come over to Máslova. The first to come up was the pop-eyed tavern-keeper with her little girl.

"Well, were they very severe?" she asked, sitting down near Máslova and continuing rapidly to knit at the stocking.

"They were severe because there was no money. If she had had money and had hired a first-class lawyer, I am sure she would have been acquitted," said Koroblyóva. "That fellow, what is his name? That shaggy, big-nosed fellow—he will take a man dry through the water. She ought to have had him."

"That's easily said," retorted Khoroshávka, who had seated herself near them, and was grinning. "He won't as much as spit for less than one thousand."

"Yes, I guess you have an unlucky star," remarked the old woman who was confined for arson. "It is no small matter they have done to me: they have taken the wife away from the young fellow, and have put him where he only breeds lice, and me, too, in my old age." She began for the hundredth time to tell her story. "Guess you can't get way from prison and from begging. It's either begging or prison."

"It seems it is always that way with them," said the tavern-keeper, looking at her daughter's head. She put down the stocking near her, drew the girl between her legs, and began with swift fingers to search through her head. "Then, why do you traffic in liquor?—How are you going to feed your children otherwise?" she said, continuing her customary work.

These words of the tavern-keeper reminded Máslova of liquor.

"Let me have some liquor," she said to Koroblyóva, drying her tears with her shirt-sleeve, and sobbing now and then.

"Any dough? Very well, hand it over," said Koroblyóva.

CHAPTER XXXII

A QUARREL AMONG
THE WOMEN

Máslova took the money out of the roll and gave Koroblyóva the coupon. Koroblyóva took it, looked at it, and, though she could not read herself, trusted Khoroshávka, who knew everything, that the paper was worth two roubles and a half, and so she moved over to the ventilator and from it took out the jar with the liquor, which was concealed there. Seeing this, the women who slept further off went away to their own benches. Máslova, in the meantime, shook the dust out of her cloak and kerchief, climbed on her bench, and began to eat her roll.

"I have kept some tea for you, but I am afraid it is cold now," Fedósya said to her, taking down from the shelf a rag-covered tin pot and a cup.

The drink was quite cold and tasted more of the tin than of the tea, but Máslova filled the cup and drank it with her roll.

"Fináshka, here," she called out, and, breaking off a piece of the roll, gave it to the boy, who was looking straight into her mouth.

Koroblyóva in the meantime handed her the liquor bottle and the cup. Máslova offered some to Koroblyóva and Khoroshávka. These three prisoners formed the aristocracy of the cell, because they had money and shared what they had.

In a few minutes Máslova had brightened up and started to tell about the court, imitating the assistant prosecutor, and about everything which had especially impressed her in the court-room. In the court-room they all looked at her, she said, and all the time they kept filing into the prisoners' room.

Tolstoy
Resurrection
page 102

"The guard kept telling me, 'They come to see you.' Now and then one would come in, pretending to be looking for a paper, or something else, but I saw that he did not want any paper, and only came to devour me with his eyes," she said, smiling and shaking her head as though in surprise. "Real artists."

"That's the way," chimed in the flagwoman, and her singsong speech began at once to ripple. "Like flies on sugar. For other things they are not there, but for this they are always ready. Bread won't do for them—"

"But even here," Máslova interrupted her, "here I had the same trouble. When I was brought in, there was a bunch here from the train. They annoyed me so much that I did not know how to get rid of them. Fortunately, the assistant drove them off. One of them stuck to me so that I had the hardest time to keep him off."

"What kind of a fellow was he?" Khoroshávka asked.

"Swarthy, with a moustache."

"That must be he."

"Who?"

"Shcheglóv. The one that just passed."

"Who is that Shcheglóv?"

"You do not know who Shcheglóv is? Shcheglóv twice ran away from hard labour. They have just caught him, but he will get away again. The wardens even are afraid of him," said Khoroshávka, who carried notes to prisoners and who knew everything that was going on in the prison. "He certainly will get away."

"And if he does, he will not take us with him," said Koroblyóva. "But you better tell me," she addressed Máslova, "what did the lawyer say about the petition? You have to hand it in now."

Máslova said that she did not know anything about that.

Just then the red-haired woman, having put both her freckled hands in her tangled, thick, red hair, and scratching her head with her nails, went up to the drinking aristocrats.

"I will tell you everything, Katerína," she began. "First of all, you must write, 'I am not satisfied with the judgment,' and then you must announce it to the prosecuting attorney."

"What is that to you?" Koroblyóva turned to her, in an angry bass. "You have smelled the liquor, but you need not butt in. Without you we know what is to be done; nobody's asking you."

"I am not talking to you. Don't get so excited!"

"You want some liquor, that's why you have come over."

"Give her some," said Máslova, who always gave away everything she had.

"I will give her such—"

"Come, come," said the red-haired woman, moving up to Koroblyóva. "I am not afraid of you."

"Jailbird!"

"Look who's talking!"

"Flabby tripes!"

"You call me tripes? You convict, you murderer!" cried the red-haired woman.

"Go away, I say," gloomily muttered Koroblyóva.

But the red-haired woman moved up closer, and Koroblyóva struck her in her bare fat breast. That was exactly what the red-haired woman seemed to have been waiting for, and suddenly she, with a swift motion, grabbed Koroblyóva's hair with one hand, and was about to strike her face with the other, but Koroblyóva grasped that hand. Máslova and Khoroshávka caught hold of the red-haired woman's hands, trying to tear her away, but the hand which had hold of the hair would not let go. She let go of the hair for a second, but only to wind it around her wrist. Koroblyóva, with her head bent down, struck with one hand at the red-haired woman's body and tried to bite her hand. The women gathered about the two who were fighting, trying to separate them, and shouting. Even the consumptive woman walked up to them, and, coughing, watched the fight. The children pressed close to each other and wept. At the noise the warden and matron came in. The fighting women were separated, and Koroblyóva unbraided her gray hair, in order to take out the torn tufts, while the red-haired woman held her ripped-up shirt against her yellow chest; both cried, explaining and complaining.

"I know it is all on account of the liquor; I will tell the superintendent to-morrow —and he will deal with you. I can smell it," said the matron. "Take it all away, or else there'll be trouble. I have no time to settle things for you. To your places, and keep quiet!"

But silence did not reign for quite a while. The women continued to quarrel for a long time, telling each other how it had all begun, and who was to blame. Finally the warden and matron went away, and the women slowly quieted down and went to bed. The old woman stood before the icon and began to pray.

"Two convicts have come together," the red-haired woman suddenly said from the other end of the benches, in a hoarse voice, accompanying each word with fantastic curses.

"Look out, or you will catch some more," immediately replied Koroblyóva, joining similar curses to her speech. Both grew silent.

"If they had not interfered, I should have gouged out your eye—" again said the red-haired woman, and again Koroblyóva was not slow with an answer.

Then there was a longer interval of quiet, and again curses. The intervals grew ever longer, and finally everything died down.

All were lying on their benches, and some were already snoring; but the old woman, who always prayed long, was still making her obeisances before the icon, and the sexton's daughter got up the moment the matron left, and once more started pacing up and down in the cell.

Máslova did not sleep, and kept thinking all the time that she was a convict, and that she had been twice called so, once by Bóchkova and the other time by the red-haired woman, and she could not get used to the idea. Koroblyóva, who was lying with her back toward her, turned around.

"I never expected this," softly said Máslova. "Others do terrible things, and they get off, and I am suffering for nothing at all."

"Don't lose courage, girl. There are people in Siberia, too. You will not get lost there," Koroblyóva consoled her.

"I know I won't be lost, but it is disgraceful all the same. I ought to have had a different fate. I am so used to an easy life!"

"You can't go against God," Koroblyóva said, with a sigh. "You can't go against Him."

"I know, aunty, but it is hard."

They were silent for a while.

"Do you hear that blubberer?" said Koroblyóva, directing Máslova's attention to the strange sounds which proceeded from the other end of the benches.

These sounds were the checked sobs of the red-haired woman. She was weeping because she had just been cursed and beaten and had not received any liquor, which she wanted so much. She wept also because all her life she had seen nothing but scoldings, ridicule, affronts, and blows. She wanted to find consolation in thinking of her first love for Fédka Molodyónkov, a factory hand; but upon recalling this love, she also recalled how it ended: Molodyónkov, while drunk, had for a joke smeared some vitriol on her in her most sensitive spot, and then had roared in company with his friends at the sight of her, contorted from pain. She recalled this, and she felt sorry for herself, and, thinking that no one heard her, burst out into tears, and wept, as only children weep—groaning and snuffling and swallowing her salty tears.

"I am sorry for her," said Máslova.

"Of course it is a pity, but she ought not to push in."

CHAPTER XXXIII

NEKHLYÚDOV MAKES
A DECISION

The first sensation which Nekhlyúdov experienced on the following morning upon awakening was the consciousness that something had happened to him, and even before he recalled what it was that had happened to him, he knew that something important and good had taken place. "Katyúsha, the court!" He must stop lying, and tell the whole truth. And, like a remarkable coincidence, that very morning arrived the long-expected letter from Maríya Vasílevna, the marshal's wife, the letter which he now needed so very much. It gave him full liberty, and wished him happiness in his proposed marriage.

"Marriage!" he muttered ironically. "How far I am now from it!"

He recalled his intention of the day before to tell everything to her husband, to humble himself before him, and to be ready for any satisfaction. But on that morning it did not appear so easy to him as it had seemed the evening before. "Besides, why should I make the man unhappy, if he does not know it? If he should ask me, I would tell him. But to go on purpose to him to tell about it? No, that is not necessary."

It seemed to him just as difficult now to tell the whole truth to Missy. Here again, it was impossible to begin telling her—it would simply be an insult. It had unavoidably to remain, as in many affairs of life, untold and merely suspected. There was, however, that morning one thing which he decided he would do: he would not visit them, and would tell them the truth if they asked him.

But there was to be nothing unsaid in his relations with Katyúsha.

"I will go to the prison, will tell her, and will ask her to forgive me. And if it is necessary, yes, if it is necessary, I will marry her," he thought.

The thought that for the sake of a moral satisfaction he would sacrifice everything and would marry her was very soothing to him on that morning.

For a long time he had not greeted a day with such energy. To Agraféna Petróvna, who had come in, he immediately announced, with a decision which he had not expected of himself, that he no longer needed these apartments and her service. It had been established by silent consent that he kept these commodious and expensive quarters in order to get married in them. Consequently, giving up the rooms had a special significance. Agraféna Petróvna looked at him with surprise.

"I am very thankful to you, Agraféna Petróvna, for all the care you have taken of me, but I no longer need such a large apartment and the servants. If you are willing

Book One
Resurrection
page 105

to help me, I shall ask you kindly to look after things and to put them away for the time being, as was done during mamma's lifetime. When Natásha arrives, she will attend to the rest." (Natásha was Nekhlyúdov's sister.)

Agraféna Petróvna shook her head.

"But why put them away? You will need them," she said.

"No, I won't need them, Agraféna Petróvna, I certainly won't need them," said Nekhlyúdov, in reply to what was meant by her shaking her head. "Please tell Kornéi also that I will pay him for two months in advance, but that I no longer need his services."

"You're making a mistake, Dmítri Ivánovich," she said. "Suppose even that you go abroad—you will need the apartment later."

"You are mistaken, Agraféna Petróvna. I won't go abroad; if I leave here it will be for a different place."

He suddenly grew red in his face.

"Yes, I must tell her," he thought. "There is no reason for concealing it. I must tell everything to everybody."

"A very strange and important thing happened to me yesterday. Do you remember Katyúsha at Aunt Maríya Ivánovna's?"

"Of course I do; I taught her how to sew."

"Well, Katyúsha was yesterday tried in court, and I was on the jury."

"O Lord, what a pity!" said Agraféna Petróvna. "What was she tried for?"

"For murder, and it was I who did it all."

"How could you have done it? You are speaking so strangely," said Agraféna Petróvna, and fire flashed in her old eyes.

She knew Katyúsha's history.

"Yes, I am the cause of everything. And it is this which has entirely changed my plans."

"What change can that have caused in you?" said Agraféna Petróvna, keeping back a smile.

"It is this: if it is I who am the cause of her having gone on that path, I must do everything in my power in order to help her."

"Such is your kindness—but there is no particular guilt of yours in that. Such things have happened to others; and if they have the proper understanding, these things are smoothed over and forgotten, and they live on," Agraféna Petróvna said, sternly and seriously, "and there is no reason why you should take it all on yourself. I have heard before that she had departed from the right path: but who is to blame for it?"

"I am. And therefore I wish to mend it."

"Well, this will be hard to mend."

"That is my affair. And if you are thinking of yourself, then that which mamma desired—"

"I am not thinking of myself. Your deceased mother has provided for me so well that I do not want anything. Lizánka wants me to stay with her" (that was her married niece), "and so I will go to her house when I am no longer needed. But there is no reason for your taking it so to heart—such things happen to everybody."

"Well, I think differently about that. And I again repeat my request for you to help me let the apartment and put things away. Don't be angry with me. I am very, very grateful to you for everything."

A strange thing had happened: ever since Nehklyúdov had understood that he was bad and contemptible himself, others ceased being contemptible to him; on the contrary, he had a kind and respectful feeling even for Agraféna Petróvna and for Kornéi. He wanted to confess to Kornéi also, but Kornéi was so impressively respectful that he could not make up his mind to do so.

On his way to the court-house, passing through the same streets and riding in the same cab, Nekhlyúdov was marvelling at himself, to what extent he felt himself an entirely different man today.

His marriage to Missy, which but yesterday had seemed so near, now appeared to him entirely impossible. The day before he had been so sure of his position that there was no doubt but that she would have been very happy to marry him; but now he felt himself not only unworthy of marrying her, but even of being near her. "If she only knew what I am, she would never receive me. How could I have had the courage to reproach her with flirting with that gentleman? Even supposing she married me, how could I be happy, or even satisfied, knowing the other was in the prison and in a day or two would be leaving for Siberia on foot? The woman whom I have ruined will go to hard labour, and I shall be receiving congratulations and making calls with my young wife. Or I shall be with the marshal of the nobility, whom I have so disgracefully deceived in regard to his wife, and counting up with him at the meeting the votes for and against the proposed County Council inspection of the schools, and so forth, and then I shall be making a rendezvous with his wife (how detestable!); or shall I go on with my picture, which obviously will never be finished, because I have no business to occupy myself with such trifles, and anyhow I can't do anything of the kind now," he said to himself, incessantly rejoicing at the internal change which he felt.

"Above everything else," he thought, "I must now see the lawyer and find out his decision, and then—then I must see her in prison, her, yesterday's prisoner, and tell her everything."

When he imagined his meeting with her, how he would tell her everything, confess his sin to her, announce to her that he would do everything he could, even marry her, in order to atone for his guilt—an ecstatic feeling took possession of him, and tears stood in his eyes.

CHAPTER XXXIV

CHAPTER XXXIV

THE SECOND DAY IN COURT

Upon arriving in the court-house, Nekhlyúdov met the bailiff of the day before in the corridor and asked him where the prisoners who had been sentenced by the court were kept, and who it was that would grant permission to see them. The bailiff expained that the prisoners were kept in different places, and that previous to the announcement of the sentence in its final form permission depended on the prosecuting attorney.

"I will tell you, and will take you to him myself after the session. The prosecuting attorney is not yet here. After the session he will be. And now please go to the court-room—it will begin at once."

Nekhlyúdov thanked the bailiff for his kindness, though he seemed to him particularly pitiful now, and went into the jury-room.

As he was approaching it, the jurors were coming out of it to go to the court-room. The merchant was as jolly and had lunched and drunk again as on the previous day, and he met Nekhlyúdov as an old friend. Nor did Pyótr Gerásimovich provoke any disagreeable feeling in Nekhlyúdov by his familiarity and laughter.

Nekhlyúdov felt like telling all the jurors about his relations to yesterday's defendant. "In reality," he thought, "I ought to have got up yesterday and have publicly announced my guilt." But when he came into the court-room with the other jurors, and the procedure of the day before was repeated—again "The Court is coming," again three men on the platform in their collars, again silence, and the sitting down of the jury on the high-backed chairs, the gendarmes, the portrait, the priest—he felt that, although he ought to have done so, he could not have broken this solemnity the previous day.

Resurrection
page 108

The preparations for the trial were the same as the day before (with the exception of the swearing in the jury and the speech of the presiding judge to them).

The case on trial was for burglary. The defendant, guarded by two gendarmes with unsheathed swords, was a haggard, narrow-shouldered, twenty-year-old boy, in a gray cloak, and with a gray, bloodless face. He sat all alone on the defendants' bench and glowered at all who came in. The lad was accused of having, with a companion of his, broken a barn lock and having stolen from the barn old foot-mats worth three roubles and sixty-seven kopeks. It appeared from the indictment that a policeman stopped the boy as he was walking with his companion, who was carrying the mats on his shoulders. The lad and his friend at once confessed, and both were confined in jail. The boy's comrade, a locksmith, had died in prison, and now he was being tried by himself. The old mats lay on the table of the exhibits.

The case was conducted just like the one the day before, with the whole arsenal of proofs, evidence, witnesses, their swearing in, inquests, experts, and cross-examinations. The policeman, who was a witness, to all the questions of the presiding judge, of the prosecutor, and of the prisoner's counsel lifelessly retorted, "Yes, sir," "Don't know, sir," and again, "Yes, sir." Still, in spite of his soldierlike stupidity and mechanicalness, it was evident that he was sorry for the lad and reluctantly told of his arrest.

Another witness, the old man who had suffered the loss, the proprietor of the house and owner of the mats, obviously a bilious man, to the question whether he identified his mats, very reluctantly answered that he did; but when the assistant prosecuting attorney began to ask him to what use he intended to put the mats, and whether he needed them very much, he grew angry and replied: "May these mats go to the devil! I do not need them at all. If I had known how much bother I should have because of them, I should not have tried to find them; on the contrary, I should willingly have given a ten-rouble bill, or two, not to be pestered with these questions. I have spent something like five roubles on cabs alone. And I am not well: I have a hernia and rheumatism."

Thus spoke the witnesses; but the defendant himself accused himself of everything, and, looking senselessly around, like a trapped animal, in a broken voice told all that had happened.

It was a clear case; but the assistant prosecuting attorney kept raising his shoulders as on the day before and putting subtle questions with which to catch the cunning criminal.

In his speech he pointed out that the burglary had been committed in an occupied building; that consequently the lad ought to be subjected to the most severe punishment.

The counsel appointed by the court proved that the theft was not committed in an occupied building, and that therefore, although the crime could not be denied, the criminal was not yet as dangerous to society as the assistant prosecuting attorney had made him out to be.

The presiding judge, just as on the day before, exuding dispassionateness and justice, explained to the jury in detail and impressed upon them what they already knew and could not help knowing. Just as on the previous day, recesses were made; and just so they smoked; and just so the bailiff cried, "The Court is coming!" and just so, trying not to fall asleep, the two gendarmes sat with their unsheathed swords, threatening the prisoner.

The case revealed that the lad had been apprenticed to a tobacco factory while still a boy, and that he had stayed there five years. This last year he had been discharged by his master during some unpleasantness which had taken place between the master and his workmen, and, being without a job, he walked aimlessly through the city, spending his last money on drink. In an inn he fell in with a locksmith who, like him, had lost his place quite a while ago, and who had been drinking heavily. In the night, while under the influence of liquor, they broke open the lock and took the first thing that fell into their hands. They were caught. They confessed everything. They were confined to jail, awaiting trial, and here the locksmith died. Now the lad was being tried as a dangerous creature against whom society must be protected.

"Just as dangerous a creature as the criminal of yesterday," thought Nekhlyúdov, listening to everything that was going on before him. "They are dangerous. And are we not?—I, a libertine, a cheat; and all of us, all those who, knowing me such as I have been, not only did not despise me, but even respected me? But even if that lad is the most dangerous to society of all the people in this court-room, what, indeed, does common sense say should be done, now that he's caught?

"It is obvious that this boy is not a criminal, but a simple man (all see that), and if he has turned out to be what he is, it is due to the conditions which breed such men. And therefore it is obvious that, in order not to have such boys, one must try and do away with the conditions under which such unfortunate creatures are produced.

"But what do we do? We pounce upon this one boy who happens to have fallen into our hands, knowing very well that thousands of others like him remain uncaught and put him in jail where he is either allowed to be completely idle or forced to do useless and unhealthful work in the company of others who, like him, are weak and mixed-up; and then we transport him at public expense, and in the company of these most corrupt men, from Moscow Province to Irkutsk Province.

"And we not only do nothing to wipe out the conditions producing such people, but we even encourage the institutions which produce them. Such institutions are well known: they are plants, shops, and factories, taverns and public houses and houses of prostitution. We not only do not wipe out such institutions, but we encourage and regulate them, considering them essential.

"Thus we breed not one, but millions of such people, and then, having caught one of them, we look upon this as having done something, as having defended ourselves, and that nothing else is to be demanded of us, once we have transported him from Moscow Province to Irkutsk Province," thought Nekhlyúdov with exceptional lucidity as he sat there in his chair next to the colonel listening to the intonations of the voices of the defence counsel, the prosecuting attorney, and the presiding judge, and watching their self-complacent gestures. "But what great and concentrated effort all this pretence costs," Nekhlyúdov went on thinking as he gazed round at the enormous room, at the portraits, lamps, arm-chairs, uniforms, thick walls, windows, the hugeness of the building, and remembering the even greater size of the institution: the whole army of officials, clerks, guards, and messengers not only here but all over Russia, drawing salaries for acting out a completely useless farce. "What would happen if one-hundredth of the effort wasted on this were to be expended on helping those abandoned individuals whom we now look upon as just so many hands and bodies essential to our peace and comfort? If only a man had been found," thought Nekhlyúdov, looking at the lad's sickly, frightened face, "who would have taken pity on him when from want he was taken from the village to the city and would have helped him, or even when in the city, after twelve hours' work in the factory, he went with his older companions to the inn—if a man had been found then who would have said to him, 'Don't go, Ványa, it is no good!' the lad would not have gone, would not have got mixed up, and would not have done anything wrong.

"But such a man, who would have pitied him, was not found, not a single one, when he, like a little animal, was passing his apprenticeship in the city, and, his hair closely cropped in order not to breed lice, ran his masters' errands; on the contrary, everything he heard from the skilled workmen and companions during his sojourn in the city was that the clever fellow is the one who cheats, drinks, curses, hits, and is dissolute.

"And when he, sick and ruined by his unhealthy work, by drunkenness and debauch, in a stupor and bewildered, as though in a dream, walked aimlessly through the city and in his foolishness made his way into a barn and took some absolutely useless mats from there, we all, well-to-do, rich, educated people, did not try to destroy the causes which led this boy to his present condition, but want to improve matters by punishing this boy!—

"Terrible! You can't tell whether there's more cruelty or stupidity in this. But it seems that both have been carried to the ultimate."

Nekhlyúdov thought all that and no longer listened to what was going on before him. And he was horror-struck by what was revealed to him. He was amazed at not having been able to see this before, as others had not been able to.

CHAPTER XXXV

NEKHLYÚDOV ASKS A FAVOUR

Tolstoy

Resurrection

page 112

When the first recess was made, Nekhlyúdov arose and went into the corridor, with the intention of not returning to the court-room. Let them do what they would to him, he could no longer take part in this terrible and disgusting stupidity.

Upon finding out where the prosecuting attorney's office was, Nekhlyúdov went to it. The messenger did not wish to admit him, saying that the prosecuting attorney was busy now; but Nekhlyúdov paid no attention to him, walked through the door, and asked an official whom he met inside to announce to the prosecuting attorney that he was a juror and that he must see him on some very important business. Nekhlyúdov's title and fine apparel helped him. The official announced him to the prosecuting attorney, and Nekhlyúdov was admitted. The prosecuting attorney received him standing, manifestly dissatisfied with Nekhlyúdov's insistence on getting an interview with him.

"What do you wish?" the prosecuting attorney asked him, sternly.

"I am a juror, my name is Nekhlyúdov, and I absolutely must see the defendant Máslova," Nekhlyúdov spoke rapidly and with determination, blushing and feeling that he was doing something that would have a decisive influence on his whole life.

The prosecuting attorney was a small, swarthy man, with short hair streaked with gray, quick, shining eyes, and a thick, clipped beard on a protruding lower jaw.

"Máslova? Yes, I know her. She was accused of poisoning," the prosecuting attorney said, calmly. "Why must you see her?" And then, as though wishing to be less harsh, he added, "I cannot give you permission without knowing why you need it."

"I need it for something which is of great importance to me," Nekhlyúdov said, flushing.

"Very well," said the prosecuting attorney, and, raising his eyes, "Has her case been tried?"

"She was tried yesterday and absolutely unjustly sentenced to four years at hard labour. She is innocent."

"Very well. If she was sentenced only yesterday," said the prosecuting attorney, not paying the slightest attention to Nekhlyúdov's announcement that Máslova was innocent, "she will be kept, until the promulgation of the sentence in its final form, in the house of preliminary detention. Visiting is permitted there only on certain days. I advise you to apply there."

"But I must see her as soon as possible," said Nekhlyúdov, with trembling lower jaw, feeling the approach of the decisive moment.

"But why must you?" asked the prosecuting attorney, raising his eyebrows with some misgiving.

"Because she is innocent and sentenced to hard labour. I am the cause of everything," said Nekhlyúdov, in a quivering voice, feeling all the time that he was saying what he ought not to mention.

"How is that?" asked the prosecuting attorney.

"Because I deceived her and brought her to the condition in which she now is. If she were not what I have made her, she would not have been subjected to such an accusation."

"Still, I do not see what connection that has with your visit."

"This: I wish to follow her—and marry her," Nekhlyúdov said, and, as always when he spoke of this, tears came to his eyes.

"Yes? I say!" remarked the prosecuting attorney. "This is indeed an exceptional case. You are, I think, a voter in the County Council of Krasnópersk District?" asked the prosecuting attorney, recalling the fact that he had heard before about this Nekhlyúdov, who had now announced such a strange decision.

"Pardon me, but I do not think that this can have anything to do with my request," angrily answered Nekhlyúdov, flaming.

"Of course not," said the prosecuting attorney, with a hardly perceptible smile and not in the least embarrassed, "but your wish is so unusual and so transcends all customary forms—"

"Well, may I have the permission?"

"The permission? Yes, I will give you a pass at once. Please be seated."

He went up to the table, sat down, and began to write.

"Please be seated."

Nekhlyúdov remained standing.

Having issued the pass, the prosecuting attorney gave the note to Nekhlyúdov, looking at him with curiosity.

"I must also inform you," said Nekhlyúdov, "that I cannot continue to be present at the session of the court."

"For this, you know, you must present good cause to the court."

"The cause is that I regard every court not only as useless, but even as immoral."

"Very well," said the prosecuting attorney, with the same hardly perceptible smile, as though to say by this smile that he had heard such statements before, and that they belonged to a well-known ridiculous category. "Very well, but you, no doubt, understand that, as the prosecuting attorney of the court, I cannot agree with you; therefore I advise you to announce it to the Court, and the Court will pass on your declaration, and will find it valid or invalid, and in the latter case will impose a fine upon you. Address the Court!"

"I have informed you and won't go elsewhere," Nekhlyúdov replied, angrily.

"Your servant, sir," said the prosecuting attorney, bending his head, evidently wishing to be rid of that strange visitor.

"Who was here?" asked one of the members of the court who came into the prosecuting attorney's office right after Nekhlyúdov had left.

"Nekhlyúdov, you know, who has been making all kinds of strange proposals in the Krasnópersk County Council. Think of it, he is a juror, and among the defendants there was a woman, or girl, who has been sentenced to hard labour, who, he says, was deceived by him, and whom he now wants to marry."

"Impossible!"

"He told me so. He was strangely excited."

"There is a certain abnormality in modern young men."

"But he is not so very young."

"Oh, how your famous Iváshenkov has tired me out. He vanquishes by exhaustion; he talks and talks without end."

"They simply have to be stopped—they are nothing but obstructionists—"

CHAPTER XXXVI

AN UNSUCCESSFUL TRIP

From the prosecuting attorney Nekhlyúdov drove directly to the house of preliminary detention. But it turned out that there was no Máslova there, and the superintendent told Nekhlyúdov that she must be in the old temporary jail. Nekhlyúdov drove there.

Indeed, Ekaterína Máslova was there. The prosecuting attorney had forgotten that some six months ago the gendarmes had stirred up a political affair to the point of exaggeration, and all the places in the house of preliminary detention were filled with students, doctors, workers, girls studying at institutes, and trained nurses.

The distance from the house of preliminary detention to the temporary jail was very great, and Nekhlyúdov reached the prison only toward evening. He started to walk up to the door of the huge, gloomy building, but the sentry did not let him in and only rang a bell. A warden came out in reply to the bell. Nekhlyúdov showed him his pass, but the warden said that he could not let him in without his seeing the superintendent. Nekhlyúdov went to the superintendent's apartment. While ascending the staircase, Nekhlyúdov heard from behind the door the sounds of a complicated, florid piece being played on the piano. When an angry chambermaid, with a bandaged eye, opened the door for him, the sounds seemed to burst from the room and to strike his ears. It was a tiresome rhapsody by Liszt, splendidly played, but only to a certain point. Whenever this point was reached, the same thing was repeated. Nekhlyúdov asked the bandaged chambermaid whether the superintendent was at home.

The chambermaid said he was not.

"Will he soon be here?"

The rhapsody again stopped, and was again repeated brilliantly and noisily up to the enchanted place.

"I will ask."

The chambermaid went out.

The rhapsody again started on its mad rush, but, before reaching the enchanted place, it broke off, and a voice was heard.

"Tell him that he is not here and will not be to-day. He is out visiting—why don't they leave him alone?" said a woman's voice from behind the door, and the rhapsody began again; but it stopped once more, and the sound of a chair's being moved was heard. Evidently the angered pianist wanted to give a piece of her mind to the insistent visitor, who had come at such an untimely hour.

"Papa is not here," angrily said a puny, pale girl, with puffed-up hair and blue rings under her gloomy eyes, upon coming up. But when she saw a young man in a fine overcoat, she relented. "Come in, if you please. What do you wish?"

"I wish to see a prisoner in the jail."

"A political prisoner, I suppose?"

"No, not a political prisoner. I have a pass from the prosecuting attorney."

"I can't help you; papa is away. Please, come in," she again called him away from the small antechamber. "You had better see his assistant, who is in the office, and speak with him. What is your name?"

"Thank you," said Nekhlyúdov, without answering the question, and went out.

The door was hardly closed behind him, when the same brisk, lively tune was heard so badly out of place, considering the surroundings and the face of the miserable-looking girl so persistently trying to learn it by heart. In the yard Nekhlyúdov met a young officer with a stiffly pomaded moustache, dyed black, and asked him for the superintendent's assistant. It was the assistant himself. He took the pass, looked at it, and said that he could not take it upon himself to admit any one with a pass to the house of preliminary detention. Besides, it was late—

"Please come to-morrow. To-morrow at ten o'clock anybody may visit. You come to-morrow, and you will find the superintendent at home. Then you may be in the general visiting-room, or, if the superintendent gives you permission, in the office."

Thus, without having managed a visit, Nekhlyúdov drove home again. Agitated by the thought of seeing her, Nekhlyúdov walked through the streets, thinking not of the court but of his conversations with the prosecuting attorney and the superintendents. His endeavour to get an interview with her and his telling the prosecuting attorney of his intention and his visit to two prisons so excited him that he was not able to compose himself for a long time. Upon arriving at home, he at once took out his long neglected diaries, read a few passages in them, and wrote down the following: "For two years I have not kept my diary, and I thought I should never return to this childish occupation. It was, however, not a childish thing, but a conversation with myself, with that genuine, divine self, which lives in every man. All this time my *I* has been asleep, and I have no one to talk to. It was awakened by an unusual incident on the twenty-eighth of April, in court, while I was on the jury. I saw her on the defendants' bench, her, Katyúsha, seduced by me, in a prison cloak. By a strange misunderstanding, and by my mistake, she has been sentenced to hard labour. I have just come back from the prosecuting attorney and from the jail. I was not permitted to see her, but I have determined to do everything in order to see her, to confess to her, and to atone for my guilt, even by marrying her. Lord, help me! My heart is light and rejoicing."

CHAPTER XXXVII

MÁSLOVA RECOLLECTS

For a long time that night Máslova could not fall asleep; she lay with open eyes, and, looking at the door, which was shaded by the sexton's daughter, who was pacing to and fro, was lost in thought.

She was thinking that she would under no condition marry a convict on the island of Sakhalín, but that she would somehow arrange things differently, with some official, with a scribe, or with a warden, or with some assistant. They were all easy prey. "Only I must not get thin, for then all is lost." And she recalled how the counsel looked at her, and the presiding judge, and all the people in the court-house, who met her or purposely came to see her. She recalled what Bérta, who had visited her in the jail, had told her about the student, whom she had liked while living at Kitáeva's, and who, upon calling there, had asked for her and was sorry for her. She recalled the brawl with the red-haired woman, and she was sorry for her; she recalled the baker, who had sent her out an additional roll. She recalled many persons, but not Nekhlyúdov. She never thought of her childhood and youth, and especially of her love for Nekhlyúdov. That was too painful. Those recollections lay somewhere deep and untouched in her soul. Even in her sleep she had never seen Nekhlyúdov. She had not recognized him that morning at court, not so much because when she had seen him the last time he had been a military man, without a beard, with a moustache, and with short, thick, waving hair, whereas now he was a man of middle age, with a beard, but because she simply never thought of him. She had buried all her recollections of her past with him on that terrible, dark night, when he did not stop over at his aunts' upon his way back from the army.

Up to that night, while she had hoped that he would come to see them, she not only did not feel the burden of the child which she was carrying under her heart, but often with rapturous surprise watched its soft and frequently impetuous motion within her. But with that night everything was changed. The future child from then on was only a hindrance.

The aunts expected Nekhlyúdov and had asked him to stop over, but he telegraphed to them that he could not because he had to be in St. Petersburg at a certain time. When Katyúsha learned this, she determined to go to the station in order to see him. The train was to pass there in the night, at two o'clock. Katyúsha saw the ladies off to bed; she asked the cook's daughter, Máshka, to accompany her, put on some old shoes, covered herself with a kerchief, tucked up her skirt, and ran down to the station.

It was a dark, rainy, windy autumn night. The rain now splashed its large warm drops, now stopped. In the field, the road could not be seen underfoot, and in the forest everything was as dark as in a stove, and Katyúsha, though she knew the road well, lost her way in the woods and reached the small station, where the train stopped only three minutes, not ahead of time, as she had expected to do, but after the second bell. Upon running out on the platform, Katyúsha immediately noticed him in the window of a First Class car. There was a very bright light in that car. Two officers in shirt-sleeves were sitting opposite each other on plush seats and playing cards. On the little table near the window two stout, guttering candles were burning. He was sitting in tightly fitting riding-breeches and white shirt on the arm of the seat, leaning against the back and laughing at something. The moment she recognized him, she knocked at the window with her frosted hand. But just then the third bell rang, and the train began slowly to move—first backwards— then one after another the carriages began to move forwards in jerks. One of the card-players rose with his cards and looked through the window. She knocked a second time and put her face to the pane. Just then the car at which she stood gave a jerk and began to move. She walked along with it, looking through the window. The officer wanted to let the window down but could not do it. Nekhlyúdov rose and, having pushed him aside, started to let down the window. The train was increasing its speed. She was running along, not falling back, but the train went faster and faster still, and just at the moment the window at last was let down, the conductor pushed her aside and jumped into the car. Katyúsha fell behind, but still continued to run over the wet boards of the platform; then the platform came to an end, and Katyúsha had to exert all her strength to keep herself from falling as she ran down the steps to the ground. She was still running, though the car of the First Class was already far ahead of her. Past her raced the cars of the Second Class; and then, faster still, the cars of the Third Class, but she still ran. When the last car with the rear lantern rushed by her, she was already beyond the water-tower, beyond protection, and the wind struck her and carried off the kerchief from her head, and on one side blew her garments against her running feet. The kerchief was borne away by the wind, but she still ran.

"Aunty Mikháylovna!" cried the girl, barely catching up with her, "you have lost your kerchief!"

"He is sitting on a plush seat in a lighted car, laughing and drinking—and I am standing here, in the mud and darkness, in the rain and wind, and weeping," she thought to herself, stopped, and, throwing back her head and clasping it with both her hands, sobbed out aloud.

"He is gone!" she cried.

The girl was frightened and embraced her damp clothes.

"Aunty, let us go home!"

"A train will pass—under the wheels, and the end of it," Katyúsha thought in the meantime, without answering the girl.

She decided she would do that. But just then, as always happens in the first quiet moment after agitation, the child, his child, which was within her, suddenly jerked, and thumped, and then moved more softly, and then again thumped with something thin, tender, and sharp. And suddenly all that which a minute ago had so tormented her, so that it seemed impossible to continue to live, all her anger at him and her desire to have her revenge upon him, even though through death, all that was suddenly removed from her. She calmed down, got up, put on her kerchief, and walked home.

Fatigued, wet, soiled, she returned home, and from that day began that spiritual change, from the consequences of which she became what she now was. From that terrible night she ceased to believe in goodness. Before this she had believed in goodness, and had believed that others believed in it; but from that night on she was convinced that nobody believed in it, and that everything which was said of God and goodness was only to deceive people. He whom she had loved and who had loved her—she knew that—had abandoned her, having enjoyed her and making light of her feelings. And yet he was the best man she had ever known. All the others were worse still. Everything which happened to her confirmed her in her view at every step. His aunts, who were pious old women, sent her away when she was not able to serve them as before. All people with whom she came in contact—women tried to gain money through her, while men, beginning with the old police-officer down to the wardens of the prison, looked upon her as an object of pleasure. Nobody in the world cared for anything else. She was still more confirmed in this by the old author, with whom she lived in the second year of her free life. He told her straight out that in this—he called it poetry and æsthetics—lay all happiness.

Everybody lived only for himself, for his pleasure, and all words about God and goodness were only a deception. If ever questions arose, such as why everything in the world was so bad that everybody harmed everybody else and everybody suffered, one ought not to think of them. If you feel lonely, you smoke a cigarette or take a drink, or, still better, you make love to a man, and it all disappears.

CHAPTER XXXVIII

PREPARING FOR THE SERVICE

On the following day, it being a Sunday, at five o'clock in the morning, when the customary whistle was blown in the women's corridor of the prison, Koroblyóva, who was already awake, awoke Máslova.

"Convict," Máslova thought in terror, rubbing her eyes and involuntarily inhaling the terribly stinking air of the morning; she wanted to fall asleep again, to pass into the realm of unconsciousness, but the habit of fear was stronger than sleep, and she raised herself, drew up her legs, sat up and began to look around. The women were all up; only the children were still asleep. The tavern-keeper with the bulging eyes softly pulled her cloak from underneath the children, so as not to wake them. Near the stove the riotous woman was hanging up some rags that served as diapers, while the baby was yelling in the arms of blue-eyed Fedósya, who was swaying with it and singing to it in her gentle voice. The consumptive woman, holding her chest, and with a bloodshot face, was coughing and, in the intervals, breathing heavily and almost screaming. The red-haired woman lay awake, with her belly upwards and, pulling up her stout legs, in a loud and merry voice told the dream which she had had. The old arsonist again stood before the icon and, continually repeating the same words in an undertone, crossed herself and made low obeisances. The sexton's daughter sat motionless on the bench and gazed in front of her with her sleepy, dull eyes. Khoroshávka was curling her coarse, oily black hair about her finger.

In the corridor were heard steps of flopping prison shoes; the lock rattled, and there entered two convict janitors in blouses and gray trousers that did not reach down to their ankles, and they, with serious, angry looks, raising the stink-vat on a yoke, carried it out of the cell. The women went into the corridor to the faucets to wash themselves. At the water-basin the red-haired woman started a quarrel with a woman who had come out from another, a neighbouring cell. Again curses, shouts, complaints—

"Do you want solitary?" cried the warden, striking the red-haired woman on her fat bare back in such a manner that the blow re-echoed through the corridor. "Don't let me hear your voice again!"

"Say, the old boy is a little wild to-day," said the red-haired woman, looking upon that treatment of her as a special favour.

"Lively there! Get ready for Mass!"

Máslova had not had a chance to comb her hair when the superintendent arrived with his suite.

"Roll-call!" cried the warden.

From the other cell came other prisoners, and they all stationed themselves in two rows along the corridor, the women in the rear placing their hands on the shoulders of those in the front row. They were all counted.

After the roll-call the matron came and led the prisoners to church. Máslova and Fedósya were in the middle of the column, which consisted of more than one hundred women from all the cells. They all wore white kerchiefs, bodices, and skirts, but now and then there was a woman in her own, coloured garments. Those were women with their children, who were following their husbands. The whole staircase was taken up by that procession. There was heard the soft tread of the feet in the prison shoes, conversation, and at times laughter. At the turning, Máslova caught sight of the angry face of her enemy, Bóchkova, who was walking in front, and she pointed her out to Fedósya. On arriving down-stairs, the women grew silent and, making the sign of the cross and bowing, walked through the open door into the empty church, sparkling with its gold. Their places were on the right, and they, crowding and pressing each other, took up their positions. Soon after the women, the men entered in gray cloaks; they were transport convicts, or those who were serving time in the prison, or who were exiled by decree of their communes; they cleared their throats and placed themselves in compact masses on the left and in the middle of the church. Above, in the choir, stood the prisoners who had been brought there before; on one side, with half their heads shaven, the hard-labour convicts, who betrayed their presence by the clanking of their chains; and on the other, unshaven and without fetters, those who were confined pending trial.

The prison church had been newly erected and furnished by a rich merchant, who had spent for this purpose several tens of thousands of roubles, and it was all agleam with bright colours and gold.

For some time silence reigned in the church, and one could hear only the clearing of noses and throats, the cries of infants, and occasionally the clanking of the chains. But now the prisoners who stood in the middle began to move and, pressing against each other, left a path along which the superintendent walked up to the front, where he stationed himself in the middle.

CHAPTER XXXIX

THE MASS

The divine service began.

The divine service consisted in this: the priest, having donned a peculiar, strange, and very inconvenient cloth garment, cut small pieces of bread, which he placed in a vessel, and then into a bowl of wine, all the while pronouncing various names and prayers. In the meantime the sexton, without interruption, first read and then sang, in rotation with the choir of the prisoners, all kinds of Church Slavic songs, which were unintelligible in themselves, but could be grasped even less on account of the rapidity with which they were read and sung. The contents of the prayers consisted mainly in wishing prosperity to the Emperor and his family. The prayers which referred to this were repeated many times, in conjunction with other prayers, or alone, while kneeling. In addition, the sexton read several verses from the Acts of the Apostles in such a strange and tense voice that it was not possible to comprehend a thing; then the priest very distinctly read the passage from the Gospel of St. Mark, where it says how Christ, upon being raised from the dead, and before flying to heaven in order to be seated on the right hand of His Father, appeared first to Mary Magdalene, out of whom he had cast seven devils, and then to his eleven disciples; and how he enjoined them to preach the Gospel to all creatures, proclaiming at the same time that he who would not believe should be damned, but that he who would believe and would be baptized should be saved, and, besides, should cast out devils, heal the sick by the laying on of hands, speak with new tongues, take up serpents, and if they should drink deadly things not die, but remain alive.

The essence of the divine service consisted in the supposition that the pieces cut up by the priest and placed by him in the wine, with certain manipulations and prayers, were changed into the body and blood of God. These manipulations consisted in the priest's evenly raising his hands, although the cloth bag, which he had on, very much interfered with this motion, then holding them in this attitude, kneeling down, and kissing the table and what was on the table. But the chief action was when the priest picked up a napkin with both his hands and evenly and gently waved it over the dish and golden bowl. The supposition was that simultaneously with this the bread and wine were changed into the body and blood; consequently this part of the divine service was surrounded with special solemnity.

"Praise the most holy, most pure, and most blessed Mother of God," thereupon loudly proclaimed the priest behind the partition, and the choir sang out solemnly that it was very good to glorify Her who had borne Christ without impairing Her virginity—the Virgin Mary, who, on that account, deserves greater honour than all the cherubim, and greater glory than all the seraphim. After that the transformation was thought to be complete, and the priest, taking off the napkin from the dish, cut the middle piece into four parts and placed it first in the wine and then in his mouth. The idea was that he had eaten a piece of God's body and had drunk a swallow of His blood. After that the priest drew aside the curtain, opened the middle doors, and, taking the gilt bowl into his hands, went with it through the middle door and invited those who wished also to partake of the body and blood of God, which was contained in the cup.

There were several children who wished to do so.

First asking the children their names, the priest carefully drew out the bread from the cup with a small spoon, then stuck deep down into the mouth of each child a piece of wine-sopped bread; after which the sexton wiped the children's mouths and in a merry voice sang a song about the children's eating God's body and drinking His blood. Then the priest carried the cup behind the partition, and, drinking all the blood left in the bowl and eating all the pieces of God's body, carefully licking his moustache and drying his mouth and the cup, with brisk steps marched out from behind the partition, in the happiest frame of mind and creaking with the thin soles of his calfskin boots.

This ended the main part of the Christian service. But the priest, wishing to console the unfortunate prisoners, added a special service to what had preceded. This special service consisted in the priest's taking up a position before the (black-faced and black-handed) brass and gilt supposed representation of that very God whom he had been eating, a representation illuminated by a dozen or so of wax tapers, and beginning in a strange and false voice to chant the following words: "Sweetest Jesus, glory of the apostles, Jesus, the martyrs' praise, almighty ruler, save me, Jesus my Saviour, Jesus mine, most beautiful, me taking refuge in Thee, Saviour Jesus, have mercy on me, on those who have borne Thee with prayers, on all, O Jesus, on Thy saints, and on all Thy prophets, my Saviour Jesus, and give us the joys of heaven, Jesus, lover of men!"

Tolstoy
Resurrection
page 122

Thereupon he stopped, drew his breath, crossed himself, and made a low obeisance, and all did the same. Obeisances were made by the superintendent, the wardens, the prisoners, and in the balcony the chains clanked very frequently. "Creator of the angels and Lord of hosts," he continued, "Jesus most marvellous, the angels' wonder, Jesus most strong, the ancestors' redemption, Jesus most sweet, the patriarchs' majesty, Jesus most glorious, the kings' support, Jesus most blessed, the prophets' fulfilment, Jesus most wonderful, the martyrs' strength, Jesus most gentle, the monks' joy, Jesus most merciful, the priests' sweetness, Jesus most pitiful, the fasters' restraint, Jesus most suave, the delight of the sainted, Jesus most pure, the virgins' chastity, Jesus from eternity, the sinners' salvation, Jesus, Son of God, have mercy on me," he finally reached a stop, repeating the word Jesus in an ever shriller voice; he held his silk-lined cassock with his hand, and, letting himself down on one knee, bowed to the ground, whereupon the choir sang the last words, "Jesus, Son of God, have mercy on me," and the prisoners fell down and rose again, tossing the hair that was left on the unshaven half and clattering with the fetters which chafed their lean legs.

Thus it lasted for a long time. First came the praises, which ended with the words, "Have mercy on me!" and then came new praises, which ended with the word "Hallelujah." And the prisoners crossed themselves and bowed at every stop; then they began to bow only every second time and even less, and all were happy when the praises were ended, and the priest, heaving a sigh of relief, closed his little book and went back of the partition. There was but one final action left: the priest took a gilt cross with enamelled medallions at its ends, which was lying on the large table, and walked with it into the middle of the church. First the superintendent came up and kissed the cross, then the wardens, then, pressing against each other and cursing in whispers, the prisoners came up to it. The priest, talking all the while with the superintendent, was sticking the cross and his hand into the mouths, and sometimes even into the noses, of the prisoners who were coming up, while the prisoners were anxious to kiss both the cross and the priest's hand. Thus ended the Christian divine service, which was held for the consolation and edification of the erring brethren.

CHAPTER XL

THOUGHTS ABOUT THE MASS

It did not occur to any one present, beginning with the priest and the superintendent and ending with Máslova, that the same Jesus, whose name the priest had repeated an endless number of times in a shrill voice, praising Him with all kinds of outlandish words, had forbidden precisely all that was done there; that He had forbidden not only such a meaningless wordiness and blasphemous mystification of the priestly teachers over the bread and wine, but that He had also in a most emphatic manner forbidden any people to call others their teachers; that He had forbidden prayers in temples, and had commanded each to pray in solitude; that He had forbidden the temples themselves, saying that He came to destroy them, and that one should pray not in temples, but in spirit and in truth; and, above everything else, that He had forbidden not only judging people and imprisoning them, torturing, disgracing, punishing them, as was done here, but even doing any violence to people, saying that He came to set the captives at liberty.

It never occurred to any one present that what was going on here was the greatest blasphemy and mockery upon that very Christ in the name of whom all this was done. It did not occur to any one that the gilt cross, with the enamelled medallions at the ends, which the priest brought out and gave the people to kiss, was nothing else but the representation of the gibbet on which Christ had been executed for prohibiting those very things which were done here in His name. It did not occur to any one that the priests, who imagined that in the form of the bread and wine they were eating the body of Christ and drinking His blood, actually were eating His body and drinking His blood, but not in the pieces of bread and in the wine, but by misleading those "little ones" with whom Christ identified Himself, by depriving them of their greatest good and subjecting them to the severest torments, by concealing from them the very Gospel of salvation which He had brought to them.

The priest did all that he did with the calmest conscience, because from childhood he had been brought up to believe that this was the one true faith which had been believed in by all the holy men of former days and now was believed in by the spiritual and temporal authorities. He did not believe that the bread was changed into the body, that it was good for the soul to pronounce many words, or that he had really devoured a piece of God—it is impossible to believe in such things—but he believed in the necessity of believing in this belief. The main thing that confirmed him in his faith was the fact that for exercising all the functions of his faith he had been receiving an income eighteen years, with which he supported his family, kept his son at a gymnasium and his daughter in a religious school. The sexton believed even more firmly than the priest, because he had entirely forgotten the essence of the dogmas of this faith, and only knew that for the sacramental water, for the mass for the dead, for the Hours, for a simple supplication, and for a supplication with songs—for everything there was a stated price, which good Christians gladly paid, and therefore he called out his "Have mercy, have mercy," and sang and read the established ritual with the same calm confidence in its necessity with which people sell wood, flour, and potatoes. The chief of the prison and the wardens, who had never known and had never tried to find out what the dogmas of the faith consisted in and what all that was going on in the church meant, believed that one must believe in this faith because the higher authorities and the Tsar himself believed in it. Besides, they dimly felt (though they would not have been able to explain why), that this faith justified their cruel duties. If it were not for this faith, it not only would have been harder for them, but, perhaps, even impossible to employ all their powers in order to torment people, as they were now doing with an entirely clear conscience. The superintendent was such a good-hearted man that he would never have been able to live that way if he had not found support in this faith. And, therefore, he stood motionless and straight, zealously made his obeisances and the signs of the cross, and tried to feel contrite as they sang "The Cherubim," and, as they began to give the communion to the children, he stepped forward, and with his own hands lifted up a boy who was receiving the communion, and held him up.

The majority of the prisoners—with the exception of a few who saw through the deception practised on the people of this faith, and who in their hearts laughed at it—the majority believed that in these gilt icons, candles, bowls, vestments, crosses, and repetitions of incomprehensible words, "*Jesus most sweet*," "*Have mercy*," lay a mysterious power by means of which one could obtain great comforts in this life and in the one to come. Although the majority of them had made several efforts to obtain the comforts of life by means of prayers, supplications, and tapers without getting them—their prayers had remained unfulfilled—yet each of them was firmly convinced that this was only an accidental failure and that this institution, approved by learned men and by archbishops, was important and necessary, if not for this life, then for the life to come.

Máslova believed the same way. Like the rest, she experienced a mixed feeling of awe and tedium during the divine service. She was standing at first in the middle of the throng before the partition, and could not see any one but her companions; when the communicants moved forward, she advanced with Fedósya and saw the superintendent, and behind the superintendent and between the wardens she spied a peasant with a white beard and blond hair—Fedósya's husband—who was looking at his wife with motionless eyes. All during the singing Máslova was busy watching him and whispering to Fedósya; she crossed herself and made the obeisances only when the rest did so.

CHAPTER XLI

A SECOND TRIP TO THE PRISON

Nekhlyúdov left the house early. A peasant was still driving along a side street and crying in a strange voice:

"Milk, milk, milk!"

The day before the first warm spring rain had fallen. Wherever there was no pavement the grass had suddenly turned green, the birches in the gardens were covered with a green down, and the bird-cherries and poplars were spreading out their long, fragrant leaves; and in the houses and shops the double windows were being removed and cleaned. In the second-hand market, past which Nekhlyúdov had to ride, a dense throng of people was swarming near the booths, which were built in a row, and tattered people were moving about with boots under their arms and smoothly ironed pantaloons and waistcoats thrown over their shoulders.

Near the inns there were crowds of people who were now free from their factory work: men in clean sleeveless coats and shining boots, and women in brightly coloured silk kerchiefs over their heads and in overcoats with huge glass beads. Policemen, with the yellow cords of their pistols, stood on their beats, watching for some disorder to dispel the boredom which was oppressing them. Along the paths of the boulevards and over the fresh green lawn children and dogs were romping, while the gay nurses were talking to each other, sitting on the benches.

In the streets, still cool and damp on the left hand, in the shade, but dry in the middle, the heavy freight wagons constantly rumbled over the pavement, and light vehicles clattered, and tramways clanged. On all sides the air was shaken by the various sounds and the din of the bells calling the people to attend services similar to the one that was taking place in the prison. The dressed-up people were all going to their parish churches.

The cabman took Nekhlyúdov not to the jail itself but to the turn that led to it.

A number of men and women, mostly with bundles, were standing there, at the turn, about one hundred paces from the prison. On the right were low wooden buildings, and on the left a two-story house, with some kind of a sign. The immense stone structure of the jail was ahead, but the visitors were not admitted there. A sentry with his gun was walking up and down, calling out angrily at those who tried to go around him.

At the gate of the wooden buildings, on the right-hand side, opposite the sentry, a warden, in a uniform with galloons, was sitting on a bench, with a note-book in his hand. Visitors were going up to him and telling him whom they wanted to see, and he was writing this down. Nekhlyúdov also went up to him and gave the name of Ekaterína Máslova. The warden with the galloons wrote down the name.

"Why don't they admit yet?" asked Nekhlyúdov.

"They are holding divine service now. As soon as it is over, you will be admitted."

Nekhlyúdov went up to the throng of the persons waiting. A man in a tattered garment and crushed cap, with torn shoes and no socks, and with red stripes all over his face, pushed himself forward and started toward the jail.

"Where are you headed?" the soldier with the gun shouted to him.

"Don't yell so!" answered the ragged fellow, not in the least intimidated by the sentry's call. He went back. "If you won't let me, I can wait. But don't yell as though you were a general!"

There was an approving laugh in the crowd. The visitors were mostly poorly clad people, some even in tatters, but there were also, to all appearances, decent people, both men and women. Next to Nekhlyúdov stood a well-dressed, clean-shaven, plump, ruddy man, with a bundle, apparently of underwear, in his hand. Nekhlyúdov asked him whether he was there for the first time. The man with the bundle answered that he came every Sunday, and they started a conversation. He was a guard in a bank; he came to see his brother, who was to be tried for forgery. The good-natured man told Nekhlyúdov his whole history and was on the point of asking him for his, when their attention was distracted by a student and a veiled lady, in a light rubber-tired vehicle, drawn by a large, thoroughbred black horse. The student was carrying a large bundle in his hands. He went up to Nekhlyúdov and asked him whether it was permitted to distribute alms—rolls which he had brought with him—and how he was to do it.

"I am doing it at the request of my fiancée. This is my fiancée. Her parents advised us to take it down to the convicts."

"I am here for the first time, and I do not know, but I think you ought to ask that man," said Nekhlyúdov, pointing to the warden with the galloons, who was sitting with his note-book on the right.

Just as Nekhlyúdov was conversing with the student the heavy iron door, with a small window in the middle, was opened, and a uniformed officer emerged from it with a warden, and the warden with the note-book announced that the visitors would now be admitted. The sentry stepped aside, and all the visitors, as though fearing to be late, started with rapid steps toward the door; some of them even rushed forward at a run. At the door stood a warden, who kept counting the visitors as they passed him, saying loudly, "Sixteen, seventeen," and so on. Another warden, inside the building, touched each with his hand and counted them as they passed through the next door, in order that upon leaving the number should tally, and no visitor be left in the prison, and no person confined be allowed to escape. This teller slapped Nekhlyúdov's back, without looking to see who it was that passed by, and this touch of the warden's hand at first offended Nekhlyúdov, but he recalled at once what had brought him here, and he felt ashamed of his feeling of dissatisfaction and affront.

The first place beyond the door was a large room with a vaulted ceiling and iron gratings in tiny windows. In this room, called the assembly-room, Nekhlyúdov quite unexpectedly saw in a niche a large representation of the crucifixion.

"What is this for?" he thought, involuntarily connecting in his imagination the representation of Christ with liberated and not with imprisoned people.

Nekhlyúdov walked slowly, letting the hurrying visitors pass by him, experiencing mixed feelings of terror before the evil-doers who were locked up here, of compassion for those innocent people who, like the boy of yesterday and like Katyúsha, must be confined here, and of timidity and contrition before the meeting which awaited him. Upon leaving this first room, the warden at the other end said something, but Nekhlyúdov was lost in thought and did not pay any attention to it and continued to go in the direction where most visitors were going, that is, to the men's department, and not to the women's, where he was supposed to.

Allowing those who were in a hurry to walk ahead of him, he was the last to enter the hall which was used as the visiting-room. The first thing that struck him when, upon opening the door, he entered the hall, was the deafening roar of hundreds of voices merging into one. Only when he came nearer to the people who, like flies upon sugar, were clinging to the screen that divided the room into two parts, he understood what the matter was. The room, with the windows in the back, was divided into two, not by one, but by two wire screens that ran from the ceiling down to the floor. Between the screens walked the wardens. Beyond the screens were the prisoners, and on this side, the visitors. Between the two parties were the two screens, and about eight feet of space, so that it was not only impossible to transmit any information, but even to recognize a face, especially if one were near-sighted. It was even difficult to speak, for one had to cry at the top of one's voice in order to be heard. On both sides the faces were closely pressed against the screens: here were wives, husbands, fathers, mothers, children, trying to see each other and to say what was necessary. But as each tried to speak in such a way as to be heard by the one he, or she, was talking to, and the neighbours were trying to do the same, their voices interfered with each other, and they had to shout so much the louder. It was this that caused the roar, interrupted by shouts, which had so struck Nekhlyúdov as he entered the room.

There was not the slightest possibility of making out what was said. It was only possible by their faces to guess what they were talking about and what their relations to each other were. Next to Nekhlyúdov was an old woman in a small shawl, who, pressing against the screen, with quivering chin cried something to a pale

Tolstoy

Resurrection

page 128

young man with half of his hair shaven off. The prisoner, raising his eyebrows and frowning, listened attentively to what she was saying. Next to the old woman was a young man in a sleeveless coat, who, shaking his head, was listening to what a prisoner, with an agonized face and grayish beard, who resembled him, was saying. Farther away stood a ragged fellow, who was moving his hands as he spoke, and laughing. Next to him a woman, in a good woollen kerchief, with a babe in her arms, was sitting on the floor, and weeping, evidently for the first time seeing that gray-haired man, who was on the other side, in a prison blouse, and with a shaven head and in fetters. Beyond this woman stood the bank guard, with whom Nekhlyúdov had spoken; he was shouting at the top of his voice to a bald-headed prisoner, with sparkling eyes, on the other side. When Nekhlyúdov understood that he would have to speak under these conditions, there arose within him a feeling of indignation against the people who could have arranged and maintained such a thing. He wondered how it was that such a terrible state of affairs, such a contempt for all human feelings had not offended anybody. The soldiers, the superintendent, the visitors, and the prisoners acted as though they admitted that it could not be otherwise.

Nekhlyúdov remained about five minutes in that room, experiencing a strange feeling of melancholy, a consciousness of his own powerlessness, and of being out of tune with the whole world. A moral sensation of nausea, resembling seasickness, took possession of him.

CHAPTER XLII

THE WOMEN'S VISITORS' HALL

"Still I must do what I have come for," he said, urging himself on. "What must I do now?"

He began to look for somebody in authority, and, upon noticing a short, lean man with a moustache, with officer's shoulder loops, who was walking back of the crowd, he turned to him.

"Can you not tell me, dear sir," he said, with exceedingly strained civility, "where the women are kept, and where one may talk to them?"

"Do you want the women's department?"

"Yes; I should like to see one of the women prisoners," Nekhlyúdov replied, with the same strained civility.

"You ought to have said so when you were in the assembly-room. Whom do you want to see?"

"I want to see Ekaterína Máslova."

"Is she a political prisoner?"

"No, she is simply—"

"Has she been sentenced?"

"Yes, she was two days ago," humbly replied Nekhlyúdov, fearing lest he spoil the disposition of the superintendent, who apparently had taken an interest in him.

"If you wish to go to the women's department, please, this way," said the superintendent, having obviously concluded from Nekhlyúdov's appearance that he deserved consideration. "Sídorov," he addressed a moustachioed non-commissioned officer with medals, "take this gentleman to the women's department."

"Yes, sir."

Just then somebody's heart-rending sobs were heard at the screen.

Everything seemed strange to Nekhlyúdov, but strangest of all was it that he should be thankful and under obligations to the superintendent and chief warden, to people who were doing all the cruel things which were committed in that house.

The warden led Nekhlyúdov out of the men's visiting-room into the corridor, and through the opposite door took him into the women's visitors' hall.

This room, like that of the men, was divided into three parts by the two screens, but it was considerably smaller, and there were fewer visitors and prisoners in it; the noise and din was the same as in the male department. The officer here also walked around between the screens. The officer was the matron, in a uniform with galloons on her sleeves and with blue binding, and a belt similar to the superintendent's. Just as in the men's room, the faces on both sides clung to the screens: on this side, city people in all kinds of attire, and on the other, the prisoners—some in white, others in their own clothes. The whole screen was occupied by people. Some rose on tiptoe in order to be heard above the heads of the others; others sat on the floor, conversing.

Most noticeable of all the prisoners, both by her striking shouts and appearance, was a tattered, haggard gipsy, her kerchief falling down from her curly hair, who was standing in the middle of the room on the other side of the screen, near a post, and with rapid gestures shouting to a gipsy in a blue coat with a tight, low belt. Next to the gipsy, a soldier was sitting on the ground and talking to a prisoner; then stood, clinging to the screen, a young peasant with a light-coloured beard, in bast shoes, with flushed face, obviously with difficulty restraining his tears. He was talking to a sweet-faced blond prisoner, who was gazing at him with her bright, blue eyes. This was Fedósya and her husband. Near them stood a tattered fellow, who was talking to a slatternly, broad-faced woman; then two women, a man, again a woman—and opposite each, a prisoner. Máslova was not among them. But back of the prisoners, on the other side, stood another woman, and Nekhlyúdov at once knew that it was she, and he felt his heart beating more strongly and his breath stopping. The decisive minute was approaching. He went up to the screen and recognized her. She was standing back of blue-eyed Fedósya and, smiling, was listening to what she was saying. She was not in her cloak, as two days ago, but in a white bodice, tightly girded with a belt, and with high full bosom. Her flowing black hair peeped from under the kerchief, just as in the court-room.

"It will be decided right now," he thought. "How am I to call her? Or will she come up herself?"

But she did not come up. She was waiting for Klára and did not suspect that this man had come to see her.

"Whom do you want?" the matron who was walking between the screens asked, coming up to Nekhlyúdov.

"Ekaterína Máslova," Nekhlyúdov said, with difficulty.

"Máslova, you are wanted!" cried the matron.

CHAPTER XLIII

THE MEETING WITH KATYÚSHA

Máslova looked about her and, raising her head and thrusting her bosom forward, with her expression of readiness so familiar to Nekhlyúdov, went up to the screen, pushing her way between two prisoners, and with a questioning glance of surprise gazed at Nekhlyúdov, without recognizing him.

But, seeing by his attire that he was a rich man, she smiled.

"Do you want me?" she said, putting her smiling face, with its squinting eyes, to the screen.

"I wanted to see—" Nekhlyúdov did not know whether to say "thee" or "you," and decided to say "you." He was not speaking louder than usual. "I wanted to see you—I—"

"Don't pull the wool over my eyes," cried the tattered fellow near him. "Did you take it or not?"

"I tell you he is dying—what more?" somebody shouted from the other side.

Máslova could not make out what Nekhlyúdov was saying but the expression of his face, as he was talking, suddenly reminded her of him. But she did not believe her eyes. Still, the smile disappeared from her face, and her brow began to be furrowed in an agonizing way.

"I did not hear what you said," she cried, blinking and frowning more and more.

"I came—"

"Yes, I am doing what I ought to do, and am repenting of my sin," thought Nekhlyúdov.

The moment he thought that, the tears stood in his eyes and choked him; he held on to the screen with his fingers, and grew silent, making an effort to keep from sobbing.

"I say: keep away from where you have no business—" somebody cried on one side.

"Believe me for God's sake, for I tell you I do not know," cried a prisoner on the other side.

Upon noticing his agitation, Máslova recognized him.

"You have changed, but I recognize you," she cried, without looking at him, and her flushed face suddenly looked gloomier still.

"I have come to ask forgiveness of you," he cried in a loud voice, without intonations, like a lesson learned by rote.

Having shouted out these words, he felt ashamed and looked around. But immediately it occurred to him that if he was ashamed, so much the better, because he must bear shame. And he continued in a loud voice:

"Forgive me; I am terribly guilty toward—" he shouted again.

She stood motionless and did not take her squinting eyes off him.

He was unable to proceed and went away from the screen, trying to check the sobs which were agitating his breast.

The superintendent, the one who had directed Nekhlyúdov to the women's department, apparently interested in him, came in and, seeing Nekhlyúdov standing away from the screen, asked him why he did not speak with the person he had asked for. Nekhlyúdov blew his nose and, straightening up and trying to assume an unconcerned look, said:

"I can't speak through the screen—I can't hear a word."

The superintendent thought for a while.

"Well, we will have her brought out for a short time."

"Márya Kárlovna," he turned to the matron. "Bring Máslova out here!"

A minute later Máslova came out of the side door. Walking up with her soft tread close to Nekhlyúdov, she stopped and looked at him with an upward glance. Her black hair, just as two days before, stood out in curling ringlets; her unhealthy, swollen, and white face was sweet and absolutely calm; only the sparkling, black, squinting eyes gleamed with unusual brilliancy from out her swollen lids.

"You may speak here to her," said the superintendent, stepping aside. Nekhlyúdov moved up to the bench which stood against the wall.

Máslova cast a questioning glance at the assistant superintendent, and then, as though shrugging her shoulders in surprise, followed Nekhlyúdov up to the bench and sat down at his side, adjusting her skirt.

"I know it is hard for you to forgive me," began Nekhlyúdov, but again stopped, feeling that his tears impeded him, "but if it is not possible to correct the past, I wish now to do all I can. Say—"

"How did you find me?" she asked, without replying to his question, and hardly glancing at him with her squinting eyes.

"O Lord, help me! Teach me what to do!" Nekhlyúdov kept saying to himself, looking at her changed, bad-looking face.

"Two days ago I was a juror," he said, "when you were tried. Did you not recognize me?"

"No, I did not. I had no time to recognize people. And I did not even look," she said.

"Was there not a child?" he asked, and felt his face flush.

"Thank the Lord, it died at once," she answered curtly and angrily, turning her eyes away.

"How so? What did it die of?"

"I was ill myself and almost died," she said, without raising her eyes.

"How is it my aunts let you go?"

"Who would want to keep a chambermaid with a baby? When they noticed what the matter was, they chased me out. What is the use of mentioning it—I do not remember anything—I have forgotten it. That is all ended."

"No, not ended. I cannot leave it so. I now want to expiate my sin."

"There is nothing to expiate. What has been has been, is a thing of the past," she said, and—a thing he had not expected—she suddenly looked at him and gave him a disagreeable, insinuating, and pitiable smile.

Máslova had not expected to see him, especially then and there, and therefore his appearance at first startled her and made her think of what she had never thought before. In the first moment she dimly recalled that new charming world of feelings and thoughts which had been revealed to her by that attractive young man who loved her and who was loved by her, and then of his incomprehensible cruelty and of the whole series of humiliations and suffering which followed that magic happiness and which was its direct consequence. And she was pained. But not having the strength to analyze it all, she acted as she always did: she dispelled those recollections and tried to shroud them with the special mist of her dissolute life. In the first moment she connected the man who was sitting at her side with the young man whom she had once loved, but upon observing that that caused her pain, she stopped connecting him with that youth. Now this neatly dressed, well-fed gentleman, with the perfumed beard, was for her not that Nekhlyúdov whom she had loved, but only one of those men who, when they needed it, made use of such creatures as she was, and whom a creature like her had to make use of for her own greatest advantage. It was for this reason that she gave him that insinuating smile. She was silent, reflecting in what manner to use him.

"That is all ended," she said. "Now I am sentenced to hard labour." And her lips quivered as she pronounced that terrible word.

"I knew, I was convinced that you were not guilty," said Nekhlyúdov.

"Of course I am not. Am I a thief, a robber?—They say in our cell that everything depends on a lawyer," she continued. "They say that a petition has to be handed in. Only they ask a lot of money for it—"

"Yes, by all means," said Nekhlyúdov. "I have already talked to a lawyer."

"You must not spare money, and get a good one," she said.

"I will do everything in my power."

A silence ensued.

She again smiled in the same way.

"I want to ask you—for some money, if you can let me have it. Not much—ten roubles. That is all I want," she suddenly said.

"Yes, yes," Nekhlyúdov said in confusion, taking out his pocketbook.

She threw a rapid glance at the superintendent, who was walking up and down the room.

"Don't give it to me in his presence, or they will take it away from me."

Nekhlyúdov opened his wallet the moment the superintendent turned away, but before he succeeded in handing her the ten-rouble bill, the superintendent again turned his face to him. He crumpled it in his hand.

"This is a dead woman," Nekhlyúdov thought, looking at her once sweet, now defiled and swollen face, and at the sparkling, evil gleam of her black, squinting eyes, which were watching both the superintendent and his hand with the crumpled bill. A moment of hesitation came over him.

Again the tempter who had been speaking to him in the night spoke up in Nekhlyúdov's soul, as ever trying to lead him away from the question as to what he ought to do to the question of what would result from his actions, questions of what was useful.

"You won't be able to do anything with this woman," that voice said. "You are only hanging a stone around your neck, which will drown you and will keep you from being useful to others. Give her money, all you have; bid her farewell, and make an end of it once and for all!" he thought.

But just then he felt that something exceedingly important was going on in his soul, that his inner life was, as it were, placed on a swaying balance, which by the least effort could be drawn in one or the other direction. He made that effort and acknowledged that God whom he had felt within him the day before; and that God raised His voice in his soul. He decided to tell her everything at once.

"Katyúsha, I have come to ask your forgiveness in everything, but you have not answered me whether you have forgiven me, or whether you will ever forgive me," he said, suddenly passing over to the familiar form of address.

She was not listening to him but only looked at his hand and at the superintendent. The moment the superintendent turned away, she swiftly stretched her hand out to him, grasped the money, and stuck it behind her belt.

"You are saying strange things," she said, smiling contemptuously, as he thought.

Nekhlyúdov felt that there was in her something directly hostile to him, which kept her in her present attitude and which prevented his penetrating into her heart.

Strange to say, this did not repel him, but even attracted him to her with a greater, a special and new force. He felt that he must wake her spiritually, that this was terribly hard—but this very difficulty attracted him. He now experienced a feeling toward her such as he had never before experienced toward her or toward anybody else. There was nothing personal in it: he did not wish anything from her for himself, but wished only that she should cease being what she was, that she awaken and become what she had been before.

"Katyúsha, what makes you talk that way? I know you and remember you such as you were in Pánov—"

"What is the use recalling the past?" she said, dryly.

"I recall it in order to smooth over and expiate my sin, Katyúsha," he began, and was on the point of saying that he wanted to marry her, but he met her glance and read in it something so terrible and coarse and repulsive, that he could not finish his sentence.

Just then the visitors were beginning to leave. The superintendent went up to Nekhlyúdov and told him that the time for the interview was up. Máslova arose, waiting submissively to be dismissed.

"Good-bye! I have to tell you many more things, but you see I cannot now," said Nekhlyúdov, and stretched out his hand. "I shall come again—"

"It seems you have said everything—"

She gave him her hand, but did not press his.

"No. I shall try to see you again where I may have a talk with you, and then I shall tell you something very important, which must be told to you," said Nekhlyúdov.

"Very well, come, then," she said, smiling as she was in the habit of smiling to men whom she wished to please.

"You are nearer to me than a sister," said Nekhlyúdov.

"Strange," she repeated, and went behind the screen, shaking her head.

MÁSLOVA'S VIEW OF HERSELF

Tolstoy
Resurrection
page 136

At his first meeting, Nekhlyúdov expected that the moment Katyúsha would see him and would hear of his intention of serving her and of his repentance, she would rejoice and be contrite, and would be Katyúsha again; to his terror he saw that there was no Katyúsha, but only a Máslova. This surprised and horrified him.

He was particularly surprised to find that Máslova not only was not ashamed of her situation—not as a prisoner (of that she was ashamed) but as a prostitute—but that she seemed to be satisfied with it and even to pride herself on it. However, this could not have been otherwise. Every person, to act, must consider his or her activity to be important and good. Consequently, whatever the position of a man may be, he cannot help but form such a view of human life in general as will make his activity appear important and good.

It is generally supposed that a thief, a murderer, a spy, a prostitute, acknowledging his profession to be bad, must be ashamed of it. But the very opposite happens. People, who by fate and by their own sins—by error—are put in a certain condition, however irregular it may be, form such a view of life in general that their position appears to them good and respectable. In order to support such a view, people instinctively cling to that circle in which the conception which they have formed of life and of their place in it is accepted. We are surprised to find this in the case of thieves bragging of their agility, prostitutes of their debauch, murderers of their cruelty. But we are surprised only because the circle, the atmosphere, of these people, is limited, and, chiefly, because we live outside that circle; but does not the same thing take place in the case of rich men bragging of their wealth, that is, of robbery, of generals bragging of their victories, that is, of murder, and of rulers bragging of their power, that is, of violence? We do not see in these people a corrupted conception of life, of good and evil, in order to justify their position, because the circle of people with such corrupt conceptions is larger, and we ourselves belong to it.

Just such a view of life and of her position in the world had been formed by Máslova. She was a prostitute who was condemned to forced labour, and yet she had formed such a world view that she was able to justify herself and even pride herself on her situation before others.

This world view consisted in the conviction that the chief good of men, of all without exception—of old and young men, of schoolboys, generals, uneducated and educated men—lay in sexual intercourse with attractive women, and for this reason all men, though they pretended to be busy with other affairs, in reality

desired only this. She, an attractive woman, could satisfy or not satisfy their desire—consequently she was an important and necessary person. All her past and present life had been a confirmation of the rightness of this view.

For ten years she had everywhere seen, wherever she had been, beginning with Nekhlyúdov and the old country police-officer, and ending with the wardens of the prisons, that all men needed her; she neither saw nor noticed the men who did not need her. Consequently the whole world presented itself to her as a collection of men swayed by lust, who watched her on all sides, and who with all means, with deception, with violence, purchase, cunning, tried to get possession of her.

Thus Máslova understood life, and, with such a comprehension of the world, she was not only not the least, but even an important, person. Máslova valued this conception of life more than anything else in the world; nor could she help valuing it, because if she had changed this conception of life she would have lost the importance which this conception gave her among men. And in order not to lose her significance in life, she instinctively clung to the circle of people who looked upon life just as she did. Sensing that Nekhlyúdov wished to take her into another world, she set herself against him, for she foresaw that in the world into which he was enticing her she would have to lose that place in life which gave her confidence and self-respect. For this same reason she warded off every recollection of her first youth and of her first relations with Nekhlyúdov. These recollections did not harmonize with her present world view, and so they had been entirely obliterated from her memory, or, to be more correct, they lay somewhere untouched in her memory, but they were shut up and immured as bees immure the nests of the worms which are likely to destroy their whole labour, so that there should be no getting to them. Therefore, the present Nekhlyúdov was for her not the man whom she had once loved with a pure love, but only a rich gentleman who could and must be made use of and with whom she could have the same relations as with all men.

"No, I could not tell her the main thing," thought Nekhlyúdov, walking with the throng to the entrance. "I have not told her that I want to marry her. I have not yet told her, but I will," he thought.

The wardens, standing at the doors, again counted the people twice, as they passed out, lest a superfluous person leave the prison or be left behind. He not only was not offended by the slap on his back, but did not even notice it.

CHAPTER XLV

A NEW WAY OF LIFE?
AN APPEAL

Tolstoy
Resurrection
page 138

Nekhlyúdov wanted to change his external life: to give up his large quarters, send away the servants, and move to a hotel. But Agraféna Petróvna proved to him that there was no sense in making any change in his manner of life before winter; no one would rent his apartment in the summer, and in the meantime one had to live and keep the furniture and things somewhere. Thus, all efforts of Nekhlyúdov to change his external life (he wanted to arrange things simply, like a student) came to naught. Not only was everything left as of old, but intensified activity began in the house: airing the rooms, hanging out and beating all kinds of woollen and fur things, in which the janitor and his assistant, and the cook, and even Kornéi himself took part. First they brought out and hung up on ropes all kinds of uniforms and strange fur things, which were never used by anybody; then they carried out the rugs and furniture, and the janitor and his assistant, rolling their sleeves up over their muscular arms, began to beat these in even measure, and an odour of naphthalene was spread through all the rooms. Walking through the yard and looking out of the window, Nekhlyúdov marvelled at the mass of all these things and how most of them were unquestionably useless. "The only use and purpose of these things," so Nekhlyúdov thought, "was to give Agraféna Petróvna, Kornéi, the janitor, and his assistant a chance for physical exercise."

"It is not worth while to change my way of life now, while Máslova's case has not yet been decided," thought Nekhlyúdov. "Besides, that would be too difficult a matter. Everything will change by itself, when she is released, or exiled, and I will follow her."

On the day appointed by the lawyer Fanárin, Nekhlyúdov drove to his house. Upon entering the magnificent rooms of the lawyer's own house, with immense plants and wonderful curtains in the windows, and, in general, with those expensive furnishings which testify to money earned without labour, such as is found only with people who have suddenly grown rich, Nekhlyúdov met a number of clients in the waiting-room who, as in a physician's office, were waiting for their turns, sitting gloomily around tables with their illustrated magazines, which were to help them while away their time. The lawyer's assistant, who was sitting there, too, at a high desk, upon recognizing Nekhlyúdov, came up to him, greeted him, and told him that he would at once announce him to his chief. But he had barely walked up to the door of the office, when it was opened, and there could be heard the loud, animated conversation of a middle-aged, stocky man, with a red face and thick moustache, in entirely new clothes, and of Fanárin himself. On the faces of both was an expression such as one sees on the faces of people who have transacted a very profitable, but not very clean business.

"It is your own fault, my friend," said Fanárin, smiling.

"I should like to find my way into paradise, but my sins won't let me git there."

"Very well, very well, I know."

And both laughed an unnatural laugh.

"Ah, prince, please come in," said Fanárin, upon noticing Nekhlyúdov, and, nodding once more to the departing merchant, he led Nekhlyúdov into his office, which was furnished in severe style. "Please, have a cigarette," said the lawyer, seating himself opposite Nekhlyúdov and repressing a smile provoked by the success of his previous affair.

"Thank you, I have come to find out about Máslova."

"Yes, yes, in a minute. Oh, what rascals these fat money-bags are!" he said. "You have seen the fellow? He has twelve millions—and yet he says 'git.' But if he can pull a twenty-five-rouble bill out of you, he will pull it out with his teeth."

"He says, 'git,' and you say, 'twenty-five-rouble bill,'" Nekhlyúdov thought in the meantime, feeling an uncontrollable disgust for this glib man, who by his tone wished to show him that he was of the same camp with Nekhlyúdov, but entirely apart from the rest of the clients who were waiting for him, and from all other people.

"He has tired me out dreadfully—he is a real scoundrel. I wanted to have a breathing spell," said the lawyer, as though to justify himself for not talking business. "Well, your affair—I have read it carefully and 'disapprove of the contents thereof,' as Turgénev says; that is, he was a miserable lawyer—he did not establish any basis for appeal."

"So what is your decision?"

"In a minute. Tell him," he turned to the assistant, who had just entered, "that it will be as I told him. If he can, it is all right; if not, he does not have to."

"But he does not agree."

"He does not have to," said the lawyer, and his gay and gracious face suddenly became gloomy and mean.

"And they say that lawyers take money for nothing," he said, the previous suavity overspreading his face. "I saved a bankrupt debtor from an entirely false accusation, and now they all crawl to me. But every such case means an immense amount of labour. As some author has said, we leave a piece of our flesh in the ink-stand. Well, as I said, your case, or the case in which you are interested," he continued, "has been miserably conducted; there is no good basis for appeal; still we shall try, and here is what I have written."

He took a sheet of paper covered with writing, and, rapidly swallowing some formal terms and pronouncing others with particular emphasis, began to read: "To the Criminal Appeal Division, etc., such and such a one, etc., complaining. By the decree of the verdict, etc., of etc., a certain Máslova was declared guilty of having deprived the merchant Smyelkóv of his life by means of poison, and by force of art. 1454 of the Code she has been sentenced to, etc., enforced labour, etc."

He stopped. In spite of being accustomed to it, he evidently listened with pleasure to his own production.

"This sentence is the result of so many important judicial mistakes and errors," he continued, with emphasis, "that it is subject to reversal. In the first place, the reading of the report of the investigation of Smyelkóv's internal organs was, in the very beginning of the trial, interrupted by the presiding judge—that is one."

"But the prosecuting attorney asked for the reading of it," Nekhlyúdov said, in surprise.

"Makes no difference. The defence might have had cause to ask for it."

"But there was no earthly use in it."

"Still, this is a cause. Further: In the second place, Máslova's counsel," he continued to read, "was interrupted during his speech by the presiding judge, just as he, desiring to characterize Máslova's personality, was touching on the internal causes of her fall, on the ground that the counsel's words were not relevant to the case, whereas in criminal cases, as has repeatedly been passed upon by the Senate, the elucidation of the defendant's character and of his moral traits in general are of prime importance, if for nothing else than the correct determination of the question of imputation—that is two," he said, glancing at Nekhlyúdov.

"But he spoke so wretchedly that it was impossible to understand him," said Nekhlyúdov, even more astonished than before.

"The fellow is stupid and, of course, could not say anything sensible," Fanárin said, laughing, "but still it is a cause. Well, next: In the third place, in his final charge, the presiding judge, contrary to the categorical demand of sec. 1, art. 801 of the Code of Crim. Jur., did not explain to the jury of what juridical elements the concept of culpability is composed and did not tell them that they had the right, in assuming as proven the fact that Máslova had administered the poison to Smyelkóv, not to ascribe to her any guilt in the act, if intent of murder was absent, and thus to find her guilty, not of the criminal intent, but of the act, as the result of carelessness, from the consequences of which, contrary to Máslova's intent, ensued the merchant's death. This is the main thing."

"But we ought to have understood that ourselves. It was our error."

"And, finally, in the fourth place," continued the lawyer, "the question of Máslova's guilt was given to the jury in a form which contained a palpable contradiction. Máslova was accused of premeditated murder of Smyelkóv for purely selfish purposes, which appeared as the only motive for the murder; whereas the jury in their answer rejected the purpose of robbery and Máslova's participation in the theft of the valuables—from which it is manifest that it was their intention to refute the defendant's premeditation in the murder, and only by misunderstanding, caused by the incomplete wording in the charge of the presiding judge, did they not express it in proper form in their answer, and therefore such an answer of the jury unconditionally required the application of arts. 816 and 808 of the Code of Crim. Jur., that is, the explanation by the presiding judge of the error which had been committed, and their return for a new consultation in regard to the question of defendant's guilt," read Fanárin.

"Why, then, did the presiding judge not do so?"

"I should myself like to know why," said Fanárin, laughing.

"Then, you think, the Senate will rectify the error?"

"That depends upon which do-gooders are sitting at the given moment."

"What do you mean, do-gooders?"

"Do-gooders from the Do-nothing Office. So. Further I say: Such a verdict did not give the court any right," he continued, in a rapid tone, "to subject Máslova to criminal punishment, and the application in her case of sec. 3, art. 771 of the Code of Crim. Jur. forms a distinct and important violation of the fundamental principles of our criminal procedure. On the basis of the facts herein described I have the honour of petitioning, etc., to set aside, in accordance with arts. 909, 910, sec. 2 of 912, and 928 of the Code of Crim. Jur. etc., and to transfer the case to another division of the same court for retrial.—So, you see, everything has been done that can be done. But I shall be frank with you—there is little probability of any success. However, every-thing depends on the composition of the Department of the Senate. If you have any influence, make a personal appeal."

"I know some people there."

"Do it at once, for they will soon leave to cure their haemorrhoids, and then you will have to wait three months. In case of failure, there still remains an appeal to his Majesty. This also depends on wire-pulling. In that case I am ready to serve you, that is, not in the wire-pulling, but in composing the petition."

"I thank you. And your fee—"

"My assistant will give you a clean copy of the appeal, and he will tell you."

"I wanted to ask you another thing. The prosecuting attorney has given me a pass to see that person in prison; but there I was told that I should need a special permission from the governor, if I wished to see her at any other than the regular time and place. Is that necessary?"

"Yes, I think so. But now the governor is not here, and the vice-governor is performing his duties. He is such an all-around fool that you will scarcely get anything out of him."

"Is it Máslennikov?"

"Yes."

Tolstoy
Resurrection
page 142

"I know him," said Nekhlyúdov, rising, in order to leave.

Just then there glided into the room, with a swift motion, a fearfully homely, snub-nosed, bony, sallow woman—the lawyer's wife, who apparently was not in the least abashed by her ugliness. She was clad in a most original manner—she was rigged up in something velvety, and silky, and bright yellow, and green, and her thin hair was all puffed up; she victoriously sailed into the waiting-room, accompanied by a lank, smiling man with an earthen hue on his face, in a coat with silk lapels and a white tie. It was an author whom Nekhlyúdov knew by sight.

"Anatól," she proclaimed, opening the door. "Come to my apartment. Semyón Ivánovich has promised to read his poem, and you must by all means read about Garshín."

Nekhlyúdov was about to leave, but the lawyer's wife whispered something to her husband and immediately turned to him.

"Please, prince—I know you and consider an introduction superfluous—come to our literary matinée! It will be very interesting. Anatól reads beautifully."

"You see how many different things I have to do," said Anatól, waving his hands, smiling, and pointing to his wife, meaning to say that it was impossible to withstand such an enchantress.

Nekhlyúdov thanked the lawyer's wife, with a sad and stern expression and with the greatest civility, for the honour of the invitation, but excused himself for lack of time and went into the waiting-room.

"What a way to make faces!" the lawyer's wife said of him, when he left.

In the waiting-room, the assistant handed Nekhlyúdov the prepared petition, and, to the question about the fee, he said that Anatóli Petróvich had put it at one thousand roubles, adding that Anatóli Petróvich did not generally take such cases, but he had done so to accommodate him.

"Who must sign the petition?" asked Nekhlyúdov.

"The defendant herself may; but if her signature is difficult to get, Anatóli Petróvich will do so, after getting her power of attorney."

"I will go down myself and get her signature," said Nekhlyúdov, happy to have a chance of seeing her before the appointed day.

A PRISON BIRCHING

At the usual time in the prison the whistles of the wardens were sounded along the corridors; the iron clanking, the doors of the corridors and cells were opened; there was a flopping of bare feet and of the heels of the prison shoes; the janitors passed along the corridors, filling the air with a nauseating stench; the prisoners washed and dressed themselves and came out into the corridors for the roll-call, after which they went for the boiling water to make tea with.

During the tea that day, animated conversations were held in all the cells of the prison in regard to the two prisoners who on that day were to be birched. One of these was an intelligent young man, clerk Vasílev, who had killed his mistress in a fit of jealousy. The fellow prisoners of his cell liked him for his jollity, generosity, and firmness in respect to the authorities. He knew the laws and demanded their execution. For this the prison officials did not like him. Three weeks before, a warden had struck a janitor for having spilled the slop on his new uniform. Vasílev took the janitor's part, saying that there was no law which permitted striking a prisoner. "I will teach you the law," said the warden, and called Vasílev names. Vasílev paid him back in the same coin. The warden was about to strike him, but Vasílev caught hold of his hands, holding them thus for about three minutes, turned him around and kicked him out. The warden entered a complaint, and the superintendent ordered Vasílev to be placed in solitary confinement.

The solitary cells were a series of dark store-rooms, which were locked from the outside by iron bars. In the dark, cold solitary cell there was neither a bed, nor table, nor chair, so that the person confined there had to sit or lie on the dirty floor, where he was overrun by rats, of which there were a large number, which were so bold that it was impossible in the darkness to save the bread. They ate it out of the hands of the prisoners and even attacked them, the moment they ceased to stir. Vasílev said that he would not go to the solitary cell, because he was not guilty of anything. He was taken there by force. He offered resistance, and two prisoners helped him to get away from the wardens. The wardens gathered, and among them Petróv, famous for his strength. The prisoners were subdued and placed in the solitary cells. A report was immediately made to the governor that something like a riot had taken place. A reply was received in which it was decreed that the two instigators, Vasílev and the tramp Nepómnyashchi, should get thirty blows with birch rods.

The flogging was to be administered in the women's visiting-room. All the inmates of the prison had known of this since the previous evening, and the impending flogging formed the subject of animated discussions.

Koroblyóva, Khoroshávka, Fedósya, and Máslova were sitting in their corner, and all of them, red in their faces and agitated, having drunk brandy, of which Máslova now had a constant supply, and to which she liberally treated her companions, were drinking tea and discussing the same thing.

"He has not been riotous," said Koroblyóva of Vasílev, biting off tiny pieces of sugar with all her sound teeth. "He only took his pal's part, because it is against the law now to strike a person."

"They say he is a good fellow," added Fedósya, who, bareheaded, with her long braids was sitting on a log of wood near the bench on which the teapot was standing.

"You ought to tell him, Mikháylovna," the flagwoman addressed Máslova, meaning Nekhlyúdov by "him."

"I will. He will do anything for me," replied Máslova, smiling and tossing her head.

"But who knows when he'll come, and they say they have just gone for them," said Fedósya. "It is terrible," she added, with a sigh.

"I once saw them flogging a peasant in the office of the township. Father-in-law had sent me to the village elder; when I arrived there, lo—" and the flagwoman began a long story.

The flagwoman's story was interrupted by the sound of voices and steps in the upper corridor.

The women grew quiet and listened.

"They have dragged him away, the devils," said Khoroshávka. "They will give him a terrible flogging, for the wardens are terribly angry at him; he gives them no rest."

Everything quieted down up-stairs, and the flagwoman ended her story, how she had been frightened in the township office, as they were flogging a peasant in the barn, and how all her insides had turned. Khoroshávka then told how Shcheglóv had been flogged with whips, and how he had not uttered a sound. Then Fedósya took the tea away, and Koroblyóva and the flagwoman began to sew, while Máslova sat up on the bench, embracing her knees, and pining away from boredom. She was on the point of lying down to take a nap, when the matron called her to the office to see a visitor.

"Do tell him about us," said the old woman Menshóva to her, while Máslova was arranging her kerchief before the mirror, of which half the quicksilver was worn off. "We did not commit the arson, but he himself, the scoundrel, and the labourer saw it; he would not kill a soul. Tell him to call out Mítri. Mítri will make it as plain to him as if it were in the palm of his hand. Here we are locked up, whereas we know nothing about it, while he, the scoundrel, is playing king with another man's wife, and spending all his time in an inn."

"This is against the law," Koroblyóva confirmed her.

"I will tell him, I certainly will," replied Máslova. "Let me have a drink to brace me up," she added, winking with one eye. Koroblyóva filled half a cup for her. Máslova drained it, wiped her lips, and in the happiest frame of mind, repeating the words, "To brace me up," shaking her head, and smiling, followed the matron into the corridor.

CHAPTER XLVII

ANOTHER MEETING
WITH MÁSLOVA

Nekhlyúdov had long been waiting for her in the vestibule. Upon arriving at the prison, he rang the bell at the entrance door, and handed the warden on duty the prosecuting attorney's permit.

"Whom do you want to see?"

"Prisoner Máslova."

"You can't now; the superintendent is busy."

"Is he in the office?" asked Nekhlyúdov.

"No, here in the visitors' room," the warden replied with embarrassment, or so Nekhlyúdov thought.

"Is to-day reception-day?"

"No, there is some special business," he said.

"How, then, can I see him?"

"When he comes out, you may speak to him. Wait awhile."

Just then a sergeant, in sparkling galloons and with a beaming, shining face and a moustache saturated with tobacco smoke, came in through a side door and sternly addressed the warden.

"Why did you let him in here? To the office—"

"I was told that the superintendent was here," Nekhlyúdov said, wondering at the uneasiness which was perceptible in the sergeant, too.

Just then the inner door was opened, and, flushed and perspiring, Petróv came in.

"He will remember this," he said, turning to the sergeant. The sergeant indicated Nekhlyúdov by a glance, and Petróv grew silent, frowned, and passed out through the back door.

"Who will remember? Why do they all feel so awkward? Why did the sergeant make such a sign to him?" thought Nekhlyúdov.

"You cannot wait here. Please, come to the office," the sergeant again addressed Nekhlyúdov, and Nekhlyúdov was about to go, when the superintendent entered through the back door, feeling even more awkward than his subordinates. He was sighing all the time. Upon noticing Nekhlyúdov, he turned to the warden.

"Fedótov, bring Máslova from the women's fifth to the office," he said.

"Please, follow me," he said to Nekhlyúdov. They went over a steep staircase to a small room with one window, a desk, and a few chairs. The superintendent sat down. "Hard, hard duties," he said, returning to Nekhlyúdov and taking out a fat cigarette.

"You are evidently tired," said Nekhlyúdov.

"I am tired of this whole service—the duties are very hard. You try to alleviate their lot, and it turns out worse. All I am thinking of is how to get away. Hard, hard duties."

Nekhlyúdov did not know what was that difficulty of the superintendent's, but on that day he noticed in him a peculiar, gloomy, and hopeless mood, which evoked his sympathy.

"Yes, I suppose it is very hard," he said. "But why do you do this sort of duty?"

"I have no other means, and I have a family."

"But if it is hard for you—"

"Still, I must tell you, I am doing some good, as best I can; I make it as easy as I can. Many a man would do differently in my place. It is not an easy matter to take care of two thousand people, and such people! One must know how to treat them. I pity them. And yet I dare not be too indulgent." The superintendent told of a recent brawl between the prisoners, which had ended in murder.

His story was interrupted by the arrival of Máslova, preceded by a warden.

Nekhlyúdov saw her in the door before she noticed the superintendent. Her face was red. She walked briskly back of the warden and kept smiling and shaking her head. Upon observing the superintendent, she glanced at him with a frightened expression, but immediately regained her composure and boldly and cheerfully addressed Nekhlyúdov.

"Hello," she said, in a singsong voice, smiling; she shook his hand firmly, not as at the previous meeting.

"I have brought you a petition to sign," said Nekhlyúdov, somewhat surprised at the bolder manner with which she now met him. "The lawyer has written this petition, and now you have to sign it before we send it to St. Petersburg."

"Very well, why not. Anything's possible," she said, blinking with one eye and smiling.

Nekhlyúdov drew the folded sheet out of his pocket and went up to the table.

"May she sign it here?" Nekhlyúdov asked the superintendent.

"Come here and sit down," said the superintendent. "Here is a pen. Can you write?"

"I once knew how," she said, and, smiling and adjusting her skirt and the sleeve of her jacket, sat down at the table, awkwardly took up the pen with her small, energetic hand, and, laughing, glanced at Nekhlyúdov.

He showed her where and what to write. Carefully dipping and shaking off the pen, she signed her name.

"Is this all?" she asked, glancing now at Nekhlyúdov, now at the superintendent, and placing the pen now on the inkstand and now on the papers.

"I have something to tell you," said Nekhlyúdov, taking the pen out of her hand.

"Very well, tell it," she said, suddenly becoming serious, as though meditating about something, or wanting to fall asleep.

The superintendent arose and went out, and Nekhlyúdov was left alone with her.

CHAPTER XLVIII

MÁSLOVA REJECTS A PROPOSAL

The warden who had brought Máslova sat down on the window-sill, at a distance from the table. For Nekhlyúdov the decisive moment had arrived. He was continually reproaching himself for not having told her the main thing at their first meeting, namely, that he wished to marry her, and so he now firmly decided to tell her. She was sitting on one side of the table, and Nekhlyúdov sat down opposite her, on the other side. The room was light, and Nekhlyúdov for the first time clearly saw her face, close to him; he saw the wrinkles near her eyes and lips and swollen eyelids, and he felt even more pity for her than before.

Leaning over the table, so as not to be heard by the warden, a man of Jewish type with grayish side-whiskers, who was sitting at the window, he said so that only she could hear:

"If the petition fails, we shall appeal to his Majesty. We shall do all that can be done."

"The main thing would be to have a good lawyer—" she interrupted him. "My counsel was an all-around fool. He did nothing but make me compliments," she said, smiling. "If they had known then that I was acquainted with you, things would have gone differently. But as things are, everybody thinks that I am a thief."

"How strange she is to-day," thought Nekhlyúdov, and was on the point of saying something when she began to speak again.

"This is what I have to say. There is an old woman confined with us, and all, you know, are marvelling at her. Such a fine old woman, and yet she is imprisoned for nothing, and so is her son, and all know that they are not guilty; they are accused of arson. She heard, you know, that I am acquainted with you," said Máslova, turning her head and looking at him, "so she said, 'Tell him about it, so he may call out my son, who will tell him all about it.' Menshóv is their name. Well, will you do it? You know, she is such a charming old woman: anybody can see that she is innocent. Do something for them, now, dear," she said, glancing at him, lowering her eyes, and smiling.

"Very well, I shall find out and do what I can," said Nekhlyúdov, wondering ever more at her familiarity. "But I want to speak to you about my affair. Do you remember what I told you last time?" he said.

"You said many things. What did you say then?" she said, smiling all the time and turning her head now to one side and now to another.

"I said that I came to ask your forgiveness," he said.

"What is the use all the time asking to be forgiven? What good will that do? You had better—"

"That I want to atone for my guilt," continued Nekhlyúdov, "and to atone not in words, but in deeds. I have decided to marry you—"

Her face suddenly expressed fright. Her squinting eyes stood motionless and gazed at him.

"What do you want to do that for?" she said, with a scowl.

"I feel that I ought to do so before God."

"What God have you found there? You are not saying the right thing. God? What God? You ought to have thought of God then—" she said, and, opening her mouth, stopped.

Nekhlyúdov only now smelled her strong breath of liquor, and understood the cause of her agitation.

"Calm yourself," he said.

"There is nothing to calm myself about; you think that I am drunk. So I am, but I know what I am saying!" she spoke rapidly, with a purple blush. "I am a convict, a whore, but you are a gentleman, a prince, and you have no business soiling yourself with me. Go to your princesses; my price is a red bank-note."

"However cruelly you may speak, you cannot say all that I feel," Nekhlyúdov said, softly, all in a tremble. "You cannot imagine to what extent I feel my guilt toward you!"

"Feel my guilt—" she mocked him, with malice. "*Then* you did not feel, but slipped me one hundred roubles. That is your price—"

"I know, I know, but what is to be done now?" said Nekhlyúdov. "I have made up my mind that I will not leave you. I will do what I have told you I would."

"And I say you will not," she cried, laughing out loud.

"Katyúsha!" he began, touching her hand.

"Go away from me. I am a convict, and you are a prince, and you have no business here," she exclaimed, all transformed by her anger, and pulling her hand away from him.

"You want to save yourself through me," she continued, hastening to utter everything that was rising in her soul. "You have enjoyed me in this world, and you want to get your salvation through me in the world to come! I loathe you, and your glasses, and your fat, accursed mug. Go away, go away!" she cried, springing to her feet with an energetic motion.

The warden walked up to them.

"Don't make such a scandal. It will not do—"

"Leave her alone, if you please," said Nekhlyúdov.

"I just wanted her not to forget herself," said the warden.

"No, just wait awhile, if you please," said Nekhlyúdov.

The warden walked back to the window.

Máslova sat down again, lowering her eyes and tightly clasping her small hands with their fingers crossed.

Nekhlyúdov was standing over her, not knowing what to do.

"You do not believe me," he said.

"That you will marry me? That will never happen. I will hang myself rather than marry you! So there."

"Still I will serve you."

"That is your affair. Only I do not need anything from you. I am telling you the truth," she said.

"Why did I not die then?" she added, bursting out into pitiful tears.

Nekhlyúdov could not speak, for her tears were communicated to him.

She raised her head, looked at him, as though in surprise, and with her kerchief began to dry the tears that were coursing down her cheeks.

The warden now came up and reminded them that the time had expired. Máslova got up.

"You are excited now. If I can, I shall be here to-morrow. In the meantime think it over," said Nekhlyúdov.

She did not reply, and, without looking at him, went out with the warden.

"Well, girl, you will have a fine time now," Koroblyóva said to Máslova, when she returned to the cell. "He is evidently stuck on you. Be on the lookout while he comes to see you. He will get you out. Rich people can do everything."

"That's so," said the flagwoman, in her singsong voice. "Let a poor man marry, and it's not so easy; but a rich man—let him make up his mind for anything, and everything will happen as he wishes. My darling, we once had such a respectable gentleman who—"

"Well, did you speak to him about my affair?" the old woman asked.

Máslova did not reply to her companions, but lay down on the bench and, fixing her squinting eyes upon the corner, lay thus until evening. An agonizing work was going on within her. What Nekhlyúdov had told her brought her back to the world in which she had suffered and which she had left, without understanding it, and hating it. She now lost the oblivion in which she had been living, and yet it was too painful to live with a clear memory of what had happened. That evening she bought some more liquor and got drunk with her friends.

CHAPTER XLIX

NEKHLYÚDOV RECEIVES A LETTER

"So this is what it is—" thought Nekhlyúdov, upon coming away from the jail, and now for the first time grasping his whole guilt. If he had not tried to atone, to expiate his act, he would never have felt the extent of his crime; moreover, she would not have become conscious of the whole wrong which had been done her. Only now everything had come to the surface, in all its terror. He now saw for the first time what it was he had done to the soul of that woman, and she saw and comprehended what had been done to her. Before this, Nekhlyúdov had been playing with his sentiment of self-adulation and of repentance, and now he simply felt terribly. To cast her off—that, he felt, he never could do, and yet he could not imagine what would come of his relations with her.

At the entrance, Nekhlyúdov was approached by a warden with crosses and decorations, who, with a disagreeable and insinuating face, mysteriously handed him a note.

"Here is a note to your Excellency from a person—" he said, giving Nekhlyúdov an envelope.

"What person?"

"Read it, and you will see. A political prisoner. I am a warden of that division—so she asked me to give it to you. Although this is not permitted, yet humanity—" the warden said, in an unnatural voice.

Nekhlyúdov was amazed to see a warden of the political division handing him a note, in the prison itself, almost in view of everybody. He did not yet know that this warden was also a spy, but he took the note and read it as he came out of the jail. The note was written with a pencil, in a bold hand, in reformed orthography, and ran as follows:

"Having learned that you are visiting the prison in interest of a criminal prisoner, I wanted to meet you. Ask for a meeting with me. You will get the permission, and I will tell you many important things, both for your protégée and for our group. Ever grateful

"Vyéra Bogodúkhovskaya."

Vyéra Bogodúkhovskaya had been a teacher in the wildernesses of Nóvgorod Province, where Nekhlyúdov had gone bear-hunting with some friends of his. This teacher had turned to him with the request to give her money with which to attend advanced courses. Nekhlyúdov had given her the money and had forgotten all about it. Now it turned out that this lady was a political criminal, and in prison, where, no doubt, she had heard of his affair, and now proposed her services to him. How easy and simple everything had been then. And how hard and complicated everything was now. Nekhlyúdov vividly and with pleasure thought of that time and of his acquaintance with Vyéra Bogodúkhovskaya. That happened before Shrovetide, in the wilderness, about sixty versts from the nearest railroad. The chase had been successful; they had killed two bears, and were at dinner, before their departure, when the proprietor of the cabin in which they were stopping came in and announced that the deacon's daughter had come to see Prince Nekhlyúdov.

"Is she pretty?" somebody asked.

"Please, don't," said Nekhlyúdov, looking serious; he rose from table, wiped his mouth, and wondering what the deacon's daughter could wish of him, went into the landlord's room.

The girl was there. She wore a felt hat and a fur coat; she was venous, and had a thin, homely face, but her eyes, with the brows arching upwards, were beautiful.

"Vyéra Efrémovna, speak with him," said the old hostess; "this is the prince. I will go out."

"What can I do for you?" said Nekhlyúdov.

"I— I— You see, you are rich, you squander money on trifles, on the chase, I know," began the girl, dreadfully embarrassed, "and I want only one thing—I want to be useful to people, and I can't because I know nothing."

Her eyes were sincere and kindly, and the whole expression, both of her determination and timidity, was so pathetic that Nekhlyúdov, as sometimes happened with him, at once put himself in her place and understood and pitied her.

"What can I do for you?"

"I am a teacher, but should like to attend advanced courses. They won't let me. Not exactly they won't let me, but I have no means. Give me the necessary money, and I will pay you back when I am through with my studies. I have been thinking that rich people kill bears and give liquor to peasants—and that all that is bad. Why could they not do some good, too? All I need is eighty roubles. And if you do not wish to do me the favour, well and good," she said, angrily.

"On the contrary, I am very much obliged to you for giving me this opportunity —I shall bring it to you in a minute," said Nekhlyúdov.

He went into the vestibule, and there met his companion, who had heard the whole conversation. Without replying to the jokes of his comrades, he took the money out of his pouch and brought it out for her.

"Please, please, don't thank me for it. It is I who must be thankful."

It now gave Nekhlyúdov pleasure to think of all that; it gave him pleasure to think how he came very near quarrelling with an officer who wanted to make a bad joke about it; and how another friend defended him; and how, on account of that, he became a close friend of his; and how the whole hunt had been successful and happy; and how good he felt as they were returning to the railroad station that night. The procession of two-horse sleighs moved in single file, noiselessly trotting along the narrow road through the forest with its tall trees here and its bushes there and its firs shrouded in thick layers of snow. Somebody, flashing a red fire in the darkness, lighted a pleasant-smelling cigarette. Ósip, the bear driver, ran from sleigh to sleigh, knee-deep in the snow, straightening things out and telling about the elk that now walked over the deep snow, gnawing at the aspen bark, and about the bears that now lay in their hidden dens exhaling their warm breath through the air-holes.

Nekhlyúdov remembered all that, and, above all else, the blissful consciousness of his health and strength and a life free from cares. His lungs, expanding against the fur coat, inhaled the frosty air; snowflakes from the dropped branches touched by the horses' shaft-bows dropped upon his face; he had no cares, no regrets, no fear, no desires. How good it all was! And now? O Lord, how painful and oppressive!

Obviously Vyéra Efrémovna was a revolutionist and now confined in prison for revolutionist affairs. He ought to see her, especially since she promised to advise him how to improve Máslova's situation.

NEKHLYÚDOV SEES MÁSLENNIKOV

Upon awakening the next morning, Nekhlyúdov recalled everything that had happened the day before, and he was terrified.

Still, notwithstanding his terror, he decided, more firmly than ever before, to continue the work which he had begun.

With this feeling of the consciousness of his duty, he left the house and rode to Máslennikov to ask for the permission to visit in the jail, not only Máslova, but also the old woman Menshóva and her son, for whom Máslova had interceded. He also wished to be permitted to see Vyéra Bogodúkhovskaya, who might be useful to Máslova.

Nekhlyúdov used to know Máslennikov in the army. Máslennikov was then the regiment's treasurer. He was a very good-hearted, most obedient officer, who knew nothing and wanted to know nothing but the regiment and the imperial family. Now Nekhlyúdov found him an administrator, who had exchanged the regiment for a province and provincial administration. He was married to a rich and vivacious woman, who had compelled him to leave his military service for a civil appointment.

She made fun of him and petted him like a docile animal. Nekhlyúdov had been at their house once the winter before, but he found the couple so uninteresting that he never called again.

Máslennikov beamed with joy when he saw Nekhlyúdov. He had the same fat, red face and the same corpulence and the same gorgeous attire that distinguished him in the army. There it had been an ever clean uniform which fitted over his shoulders and breast according to the latest demands of fashion, or a fatigue coat. Here it was a civil officer's dress, of the latest fashion, which fitted just as snugly over his well-fed body and displayed a broad chest. He was in his official uniform. Notwithstanding the disparity of their years (Máslennikov was nearly forty), they spoke familiarly to each other.

"Well, I am glad you have come. Let us go to my wife. I have just ten minutes free before the meeting. My chief is away, and so I run the province," he said with a pleasure which he could not conceal.

"I have come to you on business."

"What is it?" Máslennikov said, as though on his guard, in a frightened and somewhat severe tone.

"In the jail there is a person whom I am very much interested in" (at the word "jail" Máslennikov's face looked sterner still), "and I should like to meet that person, not in the general reception-room, but in the office, and not only on stated days, but oftener. I was told that this depended on you."

"Of course, *mon cher*, I am ready to do anything I can for you," said Máslennikov, touching his knees with both hands, as though to mollify his majesty. "I can do that, but, you see, I am caliph only for an hour."

"So you will give me a permit to see her?"

"It is a woman?"

"Yes."

"What is she there for?"

"For poisoning. But she is unjustly condemned."

"So there you have your just court system; *ils n'en font point d'autres,*" he said, for some reason in French. "I know you do not agree with me, but what is to be done? *C'est mon opinion bien arrêtée,*" he added, expressing an opinion which he had for a year been reading in various forms in the reactionary conservative papers. "I know you are a liberal."

"I do not know whether I am a liberal or anything else," Nekhlyúdov said, smiling; he was always surprised to find that he was supposed to belong to some party and was called a liberal because, in judging a man, he used to say that you must hear him out first, that all are equal before the law, that people ought not to be tortured and flogged, especially if they had not been tried. "I do not know whether I am a liberal or not, but I am sure that the courts we now have, whatever their faults may be, are better than those we used to have."

"Who is your lawyer?"

"I went to Fanárin."

"Ah, Fanárin!" said Máslennikov, frowning, recalling how, the year before, that Fanárin had examined him as a witness at court, and how for half an hour he had, with the greatest politeness, subjected him to ridicule.

"I would advise you not to have anything to do with him. Fanárin *est un homme taré.*"

"I also have another request to make of you," Nekhlyúdov said, without answering him. "I used to know a girl, a school-teacher—she is a very pitiable creature, and she also is now in jail and wants to see me. Can you give me a permit to see her, too?"

Máslennikov bent his head a little sidewise and fell to musing.

"Is she a political?"

"So I was told."

"You see, visits to political prisoners are allowed only to relatives, but I will give you a general permit. *Je sais que vous n'abuserez pas*—What is her name? Your protégée—Bogodúkhovskaya? *Elle est jolie?*"

"*Hideuse.*"

Máslennikov shook his head in disapproval, went up to the table, and upon a sheet of paper with a printed heading wrote in a bold hand: "The bearer of this, Prince Dmítri Ivánovich Nekhlyúdov, is herewith permitted to see in the prison office the inmate Máslova, and also the medical assistant Bogodúkhovskaya," he added, and finished with a sweeping flourish.

"You will see what order they keep there. It is very difficult to keep order there, because everything is crowded, especially with transport convicts; but I watch the whole business carefully, and I love it. You will find them all in good condition, and they are satisfied. One must know how to treat them. The other day there was an unpleasant affair—a case of disobedience. Anybody else would have at once declared it to be a conspiracy and would have made it hard for many. But with us everything passed quite well. One must show, on the one hand, great care, and on the other, a firm hand," he said, compressing his white, plump hand, which stuck out from the white, stiff shirt-sleeve with its gold cuff-button, and displaying a turquoise ring, "care and a firm hand."

"I don't know about that," said Nekhlyúdov. "I was there twice, and I felt dreadfully oppressed."

"Do you know what? You ought to meet Countess Pássek," continued talkative Máslennikov; "she has devoted herself entirely to this matter. *Elle fait beaucoup de bien.* Thanks to her, and, perhaps, to me, I may say so without false modesty, it was possible to change everything, and to change it in such a way that the terrible things that were there before have been removed, and that the prisoners are quite comfortable there. You will see for yourself. But now, Fanárin, I do not know him personally, and in my public position our paths diverge—he is positively a bad man, and he takes the liberty of saying such things in court, such things—"

"I thank you," said Nekhlyúdov, taking the paper; without listening to the end of what he had to say, he bade his former friend good-bye.

"Won't you go see my wife?"

"No, you must pardon me, but I am busy now."

"How is that? She will not forgive me," said Máslennikov, accompanying his former companion as far as the first landing of the staircase, just as he did with people not of the first, but of the second importance, such as he considered Nekhlyúdov to be. "Do go in for a minute!"

But Nekhlyúdov remained firm, and just as the lackey and porter rushed up to Nekhlyúdov and, handing him his overcoat and cane, opened the door, outside of which stood a policeman, he said that he could not under any circumstances just now.

"Well, then, come on Thursday, if you please. That is her reception-day. I shall tell her you are coming," Máslennikov cried down the stairs to him.

CHAPTER LI

NEKHLYÚDOV AT THE SUPERINTENDENT'S

Having on that day gone from Máslennikov straight to the prison, Nekhlyúdov directed his steps to the familiar apartment of the superintendent. Again, as before, the sounds of the miserable piano were heard; now it was not the rhapsody that was being played, but Clementi's études, again with unusual power, distinctness, and rapidity. The chambermaid with the bandaged eye, who opened the door, said that the captain was at home, and led Nekhlyúdov into a small drawing-room, with a divan, a table, and a large lamp with a rose-coloured paper shade burnt on one side, which was standing on a crocheted woollen doily. The superintendent, with a care-worn, gloomy face, entered the room.

"What is it, if you please?" he said, buttoning the middle button of his uniform.

"I saw the vice-governor, and here is the permit," said Nekhlyúdov, handing him the paper. "I should like to see Máslova."

"Márkova?" asked the superintendent, not being able to hear well because of the music.

"Máslova."

"Oh, yes! Oh, yes!"

The superintendent arose and walked up to the door, from which were heard Clementi's roulades.

"Marúsya, stop for just a minute," he said, in a voice which showed that the music was the cross of his life, "for I can't hear a word."

The piano was silenced; dissatisfied steps were heard, and somebody peeped through the door.

The superintendent seemed relieved that the music had stopped: he lighted a cigarette of weak tobacco, and offered one to Nekhlyúdov, who declined it.

"So, as I said, I should like to see Máslova."

"It is not convenient to see Máslova to-day," said the superintendent.

"Why?"

"It is your own fault," said the superintendent, with a slight smile. "Prince, don't give her money directly. If you wish, give it to me for her. It all will go to her. But you, no doubt, gave her money yesterday, and she got liquor—it is impossible to root out this evil—and she has been so drunk to-day that she is in a riotous mood."

"Really?"

"Truly. I had even to use severe measures and transfer her to another cell. She is otherwise a peaceful woman, but don't give her any money. They are such a lot—"

Nekhlyúdov vividly recalled yesterday's scene, and he again felt terrified.

"And may I see Vyéra Bogodúkhovskaya, a political prisoner?" asked Nekhlyúdov, after a moment's silence.

"That you may," said the superintendent.

"What are you doing there?" he addressed a little girl of five or six years of age, who had entered the room and was walking toward her father, turning all the time in such a way as not to take her eyes off Nekhlyúdov. "If you don't look out, you will fall," said the superintendent, smiling as he saw the child, who was not looking ahead of her, catch her foot in the rug, and run to him.

"If I may, I should like to go there."

"Yes, you may," said the superintendent, embracing the little girl, who was all the time watching Nekhlyúdov; he rose, and, gently pushing the girl aside, went into the antechamber.

The superintendent had not managed to put on his overcoat, which was handed to him by the servant with the bandaged eye, and get out of the door, when Clementi's clear-cut roulades began to ripple once more.

"She was in the conservatory, but there were disorders there. She has great talent," said the superintendent, descending the staircase. "She wants to appear in concerts."

The superintendent and Nekhlyúdov walked over to the jail. The gate immediately opened at the approach of the superintendent. The wardens, saluting him by putting their hands to their visors, followed him with their eyes. Four men, with heads half-shaven, and carrying some vats with something or other, met them in the anteroom, and they all pressed against the wall when they saw him. One especially crouched and scowled, his black eyes sparkling.

"Of course the talent has to be developed and must not be buried; but in a small house it is pretty hard," the superintendent continued the conversation, not paying the slightest attention to the prisoners; dragging along his weary legs, he passed, accompanied by Nekhlyúdov, into the assembly-room.

"Who is it you wish to see?"

"Bogodúkhovskaya."

"She is in the tower. You will have to wait a little," he turned to Nekhlyúdov.

"And can I not in the meantime see the prisoners Menshóv—mother and son, accused of arson?"

"They're from cell twenty-one. Very well, I shall have them come out."

"May I not see Menshóv in his cell?"

"You will be more comfortable in the assembly-room."

"No, it would be interesting for me."

"How can it interest you?"

Just then the dandyish assistant came out of the side door.

"Please, take the prince to Menshóv's cell. Cell twenty-one," the superintendent said to his assistant, "and then to the office; and I shall have her called out. What is her name?"

"Vyéra Bogodúkhovskaya," said Nekhlyúdov.

The assistant superintendent was a blond young officer, with a blackened moustache, who gave off a smell of eau de Cologne.

"Please, follow me," he turned to Nekhlyúdov with a pleasant smile. "Are you interested in our establishment?"

"Yes; and I am also interested in that man, who, so I was told, is quite innocent."

The assistant shrugged his shoulders.

"Yes, such things happen," he answered calmly, politely letting the visitor pass before him into the stinking corridor. "Sometimes, they lie. If you please!"

The doors of some cells were open, and a few prisoners were in the corridor. Barely nodding to the wardens and looking askance at the prisoners, who hugged the wall and went into their cells or stopped at the door and, holding their arms at their sides, like soldiers followed the officer with their eyes, the assistant took Nekhlyúdov through one corridor, then to another on the left, which was barred by an iron door.

This corridor was narrower, darker and more stinking than the first. Padlocked doors shut off this corridor at both ends. In these doors there were little holes, called "eyelets," about an inch in diameter. There was no one in the corridor but an old warden with a sad, wrinkled face.

"Where is Menshóv?" the assistant asked the warden.

"The eighth on the left."

CHAPTER LII

IN MENSHÓV'S CELL

"May I look?" asked Nekhlyúdov.

"If you please," the assistant said, with a pleasant smile, and turned to the warden to ask him something.

Nekhlyúdov looked into one hole: a tall young man, with a small black beard, wearing nothing but his underclothes, was rapidly walking up and down; upon hearing a rustling sound at the door, he looked up, frowned, and proceeded to walk.

Nekhlyúdov peeped into another hole. His eye met another large frightened eye, which was looking through the hole, and he hurriedly stepped aside. Upon looking through a third hole, he saw a very small man, his head covered by a cloak, all rolled up in a heap and asleep. In a fourth cell sat a broad-faced, pale man, his head low and his elbows resting on his knees. When he heard steps, he raised his head and looked toward the door. His whole face, but especially his large eyes, had an expression of hopeless dejection. Evidently it did not interest him to know who it was peeping into his cell. Whoever it may have been, he did not expect anything good from him. Nekhlyúdov felt terrified; he ceased looking in and went up to cell twenty-one, where Menshóv was confined. The warden turned the key and opened the door. A young man with a long neck, with kindly round eyes and a small beard, was standing near his cot; he hurriedly put on his cloak and, with a frightened face, looked at those who had entered. Nekhlyúdov was particularly struck by his kindly round eyes that glided with an interrogative and frightened glance from him to the warden, to the assistant, and back again.

"This gentleman wants to ask you about your case."

"I thank you most humbly."

"I have been told about your case, "said Nekhlyúdov, walking to the back of the cell and stopping near the dirty, barred window, "and should like to hear about it from you."

Menshóv also walked up to the window and began at once to talk, at first looking timidly at the assistant, but then with ever increasing boldness. When the assistant superintendent left the cell for the corridor, to give some orders there, he regained his courage altogether. To judge from the language and manner, it was the story of a very simple-minded and honest peasant lad, and it seemed especially out of place to Nekhlyúdov to hear it from the mouth of a prisoner in prison garb and in jail. Nekhlyúdov listened to him, and at the same time looked at the low cot with its straw mattress, at the window with the strong iron grating, at the dirty, moist, and daubed walls, at the pitiable face and form of the unfortunate, disfigured peasant in prison shoes and cloak—and he grew sadder and sadder; he tried to make himself believe that what the good-hearted man was telling him was not true—so terrible it seemed to him to think that a man could be seized for being insulted, and clad in prison garb, and be put in such a horrible place. And it was still more terrible to think that this truthful story and the peasant's kindly face should be a deception and a lie. According to the story, the village tavern-keeper had enticed the peasant's wife soon after their marriage. The peasant tried to get justice everywhere. But the tavern-keeper bribed the authorities and was acquitted. Once, the peasant took his wife back by force, but she ran away the following day. Then he came and demanded his wife. The tavern-keeper said that she was not there (he had, however, seen her as he came in), and told him to leave at once. He did not go. The tavern-keeper and his labourer beat him until blood flowed, and on the following day the tavern-keeper's house and outbuildings were burned down. He and his mother were accused of arson but he had been at the house of a neighbour.

"And you really did not commit the arson?"

"I did not even think of it, sir. He, the scoundrel, must have done it himself. They said that he had but lately insured his property. He said that mother and I had threatened him. It is true, I did call him names, for my heart gave way, but I did not set fire to the house. I was not near it when the fire started. He purposely did it on the day after mother and I had been there. He set fire to it for the sake of the insurance, and then he accused us of it."

"Really?"

"I am telling you the truth, before God, sir. I'm talking to you as to my own father!" he wanted to bow to the ground, and Nekhlyúdov with difficulty kept him from doing so. "Get my release, for I am being ruined for no cause whatsoever," he continued. Suddenly his cheeks began to twitch, and he burst into tears; he rolled up the sleeve of his cloak and began to dry his eyes with the sleeve of his dirty shirt.

"Are you through?" asked the assistant superintendent.

"Yes. Don't lose courage. I will do what I can," said Nekhlyúdov and went out.

Menshóv was standing in the door, so that the warden pushed it against him, as he closed it. While the warden was locking the door, he kept looking through the hole.

CHAPTER LIII

FOR HAVING NO PASSPORT

Walking back through the broad corridor (it was dinner-time and all the cells were open), through crowds of men dressed in light yellow cloaks, short, wide trousers, and prison shoes, who were watching him with curiosity, Nekhlyúdov experienced strange feelings of compassion for the people who were confined, and of terror and dismay before those who had placed them there and were keeping them there, and of a certain degree of shame at himself for looking so calmly at them.

In one corridor somebody, flapping his shoes, rushed up to a cell and its inmates rushed out and barred Nekhlyúdov's way, bowing to him.

"Your Honour, I do not know what to call you, please try and get a decision in our case."

"I am not an officer, I know nothing."

"It makes no difference. Tell somebody—the authorities," said he indignantly. "We have committed no crime, and we have been here nearly two months."

"How is that? Why?" asked Nekhlyúdov.

"We have simply been locked up. This is the second month we have been in jail, and we do not know why."

"That is so," said the assistant superintendent. "These people were arrested for not having any passports. They were to be sent to their province, but the prison there was burnt, so the provincial office asked us not to send them. We have despatched all the others to their respective provinces, but we are keeping these."

"Only for this?" said Nekhlyúdov, stopping at the door.

A throng of some forty men, all of them in prison cloaks, surrounded Nekhlyúdov and the assistant. Several voices began to speak at once. The assistant stopped them:

"Let one of you speak."

A tall, respectable-looking peasant of about fifty years of age stood out from the crowd. He explained to Nekhlyúdov that they had all been picked up and confined in prison for having no passports, that is, they had passports, but they were about two weeks overdue. Such oversight happened every year, and they usually were left unmolested; but this year they had been arrested, and this was the second month they had been kept as criminals.

"We are all stone-masons—all of us of the same *artél*.* They say that the provincial prison has burned down, but what have we to do with it? Do us the favour, in the name of God!"

Nekhlyúdov listened, but he hardly understood what the respectable old man was telling him, because all his attention was arrested by a large, dark gray, many-legged louse that was creeping through the hair down the cheek of the respectable stone-mason.

"Is it possible? Only for this?" said Nekhlyúdov, addressing the assistant.

"Yes, the administration bungled; they ought to be sent back and returned to their places of residence," said the assistant.

The assistant had just finished his remark when a small man, also in a prison cloak, pushed himself forward through the crowd and, strangely contorting his mouth, began to say that they were tortured here for nothing.

"Worse than dogs—" he began.

*A partnership of working men.

"Well, you better not talk too much. Keep your mouth shut, or, you know—"

"What have I to know?" retorted the small man, in desperation. "Are we guilty of anything?"

"Shut up!" cried the superior officer, and the small man grew silent.

"What is this, indeed?" Nekhlyúdov said to himself, as he left the cells, driven by hundreds of eyes of prisoners who were looking out of the doors or who passed him in the corridor.

"Is it possible entirely innocent people are kept here?" said Nekhlyúdov, upon coming out of the corridor.

"What is to be done? But, of course, they a lie a great deal. Hearing them, one might think that they were all innocent," said the assistant superintendent.

"But these are not guilty of anything."

"I admit that these are not. But they are all a pretty bad lot. It is impossible to get along with them without severity. There are such desperate people among them, that you dare not put a finger in their mouths. Thus, for example, we were compelled to punish two of them yesterday."

"To punish?" asked Nekhlyúdov.

"They were flogged with birch rods according to instructions—"

"But corporal punishment has been abolished."

"Not for those who are deprived of their rights. They are subject to it."

Nekhlyúdov recalled everything he had seen the day before, and he understood that the punishment had been inflicted just at the time that he had been waiting, and he was overcome with unusual force by that mixed feeling of curiosity, dejection, dismay, and moral nausea, which bordered on the physical and by which he had been overcome on previous occasions, but never so powerfully as now.

Without listening to the assistant superintendent or looking around him, he hastened to leave the corridors and to go to the office. The superintendent was in the corridor, and, being busy with something else, had forgotten to call Bogodúkhovskaya. He did not think of it until Nekhlyúdov entered the office.

"I will send for her at once, while you, please, be seated," he said.

CHAPTER LIV

THE POLITICAL PRISONERS

The office consisted of two rooms. In the first, which had a large, protruding, dilapidated stove and two dirty windows, a black apparatus for the measurement of the prisoners' height stood in one corner, and, in the other, hung the customary appurtenance of a place of torture—a large icon of Christ. In this first room there were several wardens. In the other room, some twenty men and women were sitting along the walls alone and in groups, and talking in an undertone. Near the window stood a desk.

The superintendent sat down at the desk and offered Nekhlyúdov a chair which was near it. Nekhlyúdov sat down and began to watch the people in the room.

The first to attract his attention was a young man in a short jacket, with a pleasant face, who, standing before a middle-aged woman with black eyebrows, was speaking to her excitedly and gesturing with his hands. Near by sat an old man in dark glasses and listened, motionless, to what a young woman in prison garb was telling him, while he held her hand. A boy, a high-school student with an arrested and frightened expression on his face, looked at the old man, without taking his eyes off him. Not far from them, in the corner, sat two lovers: she had short hair and an energetic face—a blonde, sweet-faced, very young girl in a fashionable dress; he, with delicate features and wavy hair, was a beautiful youth in a rubberized jacket. They were seated in the corner, whispering and evidently melting in love. Nearest to the table sat a gray-haired woman, in a black dress—apparently a mother: she had her eyes riveted on a consumptive-looking young man in the same kind of jacket, and wanted to say something to him, but could not speak a word for tears: she began and stopped again. The young man held a piece of paper in his hand, and, evidently not knowing what to do, with an angry face bent it and crumpled it. Near them sat a plump, ruddy, beautiful girl, with very bulging eyes, in a gray dress and cape. She was seated next to the weeping mother and tenderly stroked her shoulder. Everything about that girl was beautiful: her large, white hands, her wavy, short-cut hair, her strong nose and lips; but the chief charm lay in her kindly, truthful, sheep-like, hazel eyes. Her beautiful eyes were deflected from her mother's face just as Nekhlyúdov entered and met his glance. But she immediately turned them away and began to tell her mother something. Not far from the pair of lovers sat a swarthy, shaggy man with a gloomy face, who in an angry voice was saying something to a beardless visitor, who seemed to be one of the Skoptsy. Nekhlyúdov sat down beside the superintendent and looked around him with tense curiosity. His attention was distracted by a close-cropped little boy, who came up to him and in a thin voice asked him:

"Whom are you waiting for?"

Nekhlyúdov was surprised at the question, but upon looking at the child and seeing his serious, thoughtful face, with his attentive, lively eyes, seriously replied to him that he was waiting for a woman he knew.

"Is she your sister?" asked the boy.

"No, not my sister," Nekhlyúdov answered, surprised. "But with whom are you here?" he questioned the boy.

"I am with mamma. She is a political prisoner," said the boy.

"Márya Pávlovna, take Kólya," said the superintendent, apparently finding Nekhlyúdov's conversation with the boy illegal.

Márya Pávlovna, that same beautiful girl with the sheep-like eyes, who had attracted Nekhlyúdov's attention, rose in her full, tall stature, and with a strong, broad, almost manly gait, walked over to Nekhlyúdov and the child.

"Has he been asking you who you are?" she asked Nekhlyúdov, slightly smiling and trustfully looking into his eyes in such a simple manner as though there could be no doubt but that she always had been, now was, and always ought to be in the simplest and kindliest fraternal relations with everybody. "He wants to know everything," she said, smiling in the boy's face with such a kind, sweet smile that both the boy and Nekhlyúdov smiled at her smile.

"Yes, he asked me whom I came to see."

"Márya Pávlovna, it is not allowed to speak with strangers. You know that," said the superintendent.

"All right, all right," she said, and, with her large white hand taking hold of Kólya's tiny hand, while he did not take his eyes off her face, returned to the mother of the consumptive man.

"Whose boy is this?" Nekhlyúdov asked the superintendent.

"The son of a political prisoner. He was born here in the prison," said the superintendent, with a certain satisfaction, as though displaying a rarity of his institution.

"Really?"

"Now he and his mother are leaving for Siberia."

"And this girl?"

"I can't answer you," said the superintendent, shrugging his shoulders. "Here is Bogodúkhovskaya."

CHAPTER LV

VYÉRA EXPLAINS

Short-haired, haggard, sallow little Vyéra Efrémovna, with her immense, kindly eyes, entered with a nervous gait through the back door.

"Thank you for coming," she said, shaking Nekhlyúdov's hand. "You did remember me? Let us sit down."

"I did not expect to find you like this."

"Oh, I feel so happy, so happy, that I do not even wish for anything better," said

Vyéra Efrémovna, as always, looking with her immense, kindly, round eyes at Nekhlyúdov and turning her yellow, dreadfully thin, and venous neck, which stuck out from the miserable-looking, crumpled, and dirty collar of her bodice.

Nekhlyúdov asked her how she had gotten into such a plight. She told him with great animation about her case. Her speech was interlarded with foreign words about propaganda, about disorganization, about groups and sections and sub-sections, of which she was apparently quite sure everybody knew, whereas Nekhlyúdov had never heard of them before.

She spoke to him, evidently fully convinced that it was very interesting and agreeable for him to hear all the secrets of the Narodovólstvo.* But Nekhlyúdov looked at her miserable neck and at her scanty dishevelled hair, and wondered why she was doing all that and telling him about it. He pitied her, but in an entirely different manner from that in which he pitied peasant Menshóv, who was locked up in a stinking prison for no cause whatsoever. He pitied her especially on account of the evident confusion which existed in her mind. She obviously considered herself a heroine, ready to sacrifice her life for the success of her cause, and yet she would have found it hard to explain what her cause consisted in and what its success would be.

The affair of which Vyéra Efrémovna wished to speak to Nekhlyúdov was this: her companion, Shústova, who did not even belong to her sub-group, as she expressed herself, had been arrested five months before at the same time with her and had been confined in the Petropávlovsk Fortress because at her room books and papers, which had been given into her safe-keeping, had been found. Vyéra Efrémovna considered herself partly guilty for Shústova's imprisonment, and so she begged Nekhlyúdov, who had influence, to do everything in his power to obtain her release. The other thing for which she asked him was that he should obtain a permission for Gurkévich, who was confined in the Petropávlovsk Fortress, to see his parents and provide himself with scientific books, which he needed for his scholarly work.

Nekhlyúdov promised he would endeavour to do all in his power, as soon as he should be in St. Petersburg.

Vyéra Efrémovna told her story as follows: upon finishing a course in mid-wifery, she had fallen in with the "People's Will" party, and worked with them. At first everything went well: they wrote proclamations and made propaganda at factories; later, a prominent member was seized; documents were discovered, and they began to arrest everybody.

"I was taken, too, and now we are being deported—" she finished her story. "But that is nothing. I feel in excellent spirits—in Olympian joy," she said, smiling a pitiable smile.

*The "People's Will" movement, a revolutionary movement especially strong in the later nineteenth century.

Book One
Resurrection
page 165

Nekhlyúdov asked about the girl with the sheep-like eyes. Vyéra Efrémovna told him that she was the daughter of a general, that she had long been a member of the revolutionary party, and that she was arrested for having pleaded guilty to shooting a gendarme. She had been living with a group of conspirators in a place where they had a printing press. When they were searched at night, the residents decided to defend themselves, whereupon they put out the lights and began to destroy incriminating material. The police forced an entrance, and one of the conspirators shot and fatally wounded a gendarme. At the inquest she said that she had fired the shot, notwithstanding the fact that she had never held a pistol in her hand and would not have killed a spider. And thus it remained. Now she was being deported to hard labour.

"An altruistic, a good soul," Vyéra Efrémovna said, approvingly.

The third thing that Vyéra Efrémovna wanted to talk about had to do with Máslova. She knew, as everybody else in the prison knew, Máslova's history and Nekhlyúdov's relations with her, and advised him to try to obtain her transfer to the political prisoners, or to a position, at least, as attendant in the hospital, where now a large number of sick people were confined and workers were needed.

Nekhlyúdov thanked her for her advice and told her that he would try and make use of it.

CHAPTER LVI

THE POLITICAL PRISONERS
SAY GOOD-BYE

Their conversation was interrupted by the superintendent, who arose and announced that time was up and that people had to leave. Nekhlyúdov got up, bade Vyéra Efrémovna good-bye, and walked over to the door, where he stopped to see what was happening in front of him.

"Gentlemen, it is time," said the superintendent, now rising, and now sitting down again.

The superintendent's demand only evoked a greater animation in all those who were in the room, both prisoners and visitors, but nobody even thought of leaving. Some rose and went on talking, standing up. Some remained sitting and conversing. Others began to say farewell and to weep. The leave-taking of the mother from her consumptive son was especially touching. The young man kept twisting the piece of paper, and his face grew ever more spiteful, so great was the effort which he was making not to be infected by his mother's feeling. But the mother, hearing that it was time to leave, laid her head on his shoulder and sobbed, snuffling. The girl with the sheep-like eyes—Nekhlyúdov involuntarily kept watching her—stood before the weeping mother and was telling her some consoling words. The old man in the dark glasses was standing and holding his daughter's hand, nodding his head to what she was saying. The young lovers arose and, holding hands, were silently looking into each other's eyes.

"These alone are happy," pointing to the lovers, said the young man in the short jacket, who was standing near Nekhlyúdov and, like him, watching those who were taking leave.

Being conscious of the looks of Nekhlyúdov and of the young man, the lovers—the young man in the rubberized jacket and the blonde sweet-faced girl—extended their linked hands, bent back, and began to circle around, while laughing.

"They will be married this evening, here in the jail, and then she will go to Siberia with him," said the young man.

"Who is he?"

"A hard labour convict. Though they are being gay now, it is too painful to listen," added the young man in the jacket, hearing the sobs of the consumptive man's mother.

"Gentlemen! Please, please. Do not compel me to take severe measures," said the superintendent, repeating one and the same thing several times. "Please, please now," he said, in a feeble and undecided voice. "What's this? Time has long been up. This won't do. I am telling you for the last time," he repeated, reluctantly, now puffing, and now putting out his Maryland cigarette. It was evident that, however artful and old and habitual the proofs were which permitted people to do wrong to others, without feeling themselves responsible for it, the superintendent could not help noticing that he was one of the causes of that sorrow which was manifested in this room; and this obviously weighed heavily upon him.

Finally the prisoners and visitors began to depart: some through the inner, others through the outer door. The men went out: the one in the rubberized jacket, and the consumptive man, and the swarthy, shaggy man went out; and then Márya Pávlovna, with the boy who had been born in the prison.

The visitors, too, began to leave. With heavy tread the old man in the dark glasses went out, and Nekhlyúdov followed him.

"Yes, those are marvellous conditions," said the talkative young man, as though continuing the interrupted conversation, while he descended the staircase with Nekhlyúdov. "Luckily, the captain is a good man, and does not stick to rules. At least they get a chance to talk to each other and ease their souls."

"Aren't there visits like this in other prisons?"

"Oh—oh, not in the least. Only all alone, and with a grating between, besides."

When Nekhlyúdov, conversing with Medýntsev—so the talkative young man introduced himself to him—reached the vestibule, the superintendent, with a wearied look, accosted him.

"If you wish to see Máslova, please come to-morrow," he said, apparently wishing to be kind to Nekhlyúdov.

"Very well," said Nekhlyúdov, hastening to get out.

Terrible, obviously, was the innocent suffering of Menshóv, and not so much the physical suffering as the dismay, the distrust of goodness and of God, which he must experience, seeing the cruelty of men who tormented him without cause; terrible were the disgrace and torments imposed upon the hundreds of people, innocent of crime, simply because their papers were not properly written; terrible were these befogged wardens, who were occupied with torturing their fellow men and were convinced that they were doing good and important work. But more terrible yet was that aging and enfeebled, kind superintendent, who had to separate mother from son, father from daughter—people who were just like him and his children.

"What is this for?" Nekhlyúdov asked himself, experiencing more than ever that sensation of moral nausea, passing into a physical feeling, which always overcame him in prison, and finding no answer.

CHAPTER LVII

NEKHLYÚDOV VISITS THE MÁSLENNIKOVS

On the following day Nekhlyúdov went to the lawyer, to whom he communicated Menshóv's affair, asking him to take the defence. The lawyer listened to him and said that he would look into the case, and if everything was as Nekhlyúdov told him, which was very probable, he would undertake the defence without fee. Nekhlyúdov also told him of the 130 men who were held there by misunderstanding and asked him on whom the matter depended and who was to blame for it. The lawyer was silent for a moment, evidently wishing to give an exact answer.

"Who is to blame? Nobody," he said, with determination. "Ask the prosecuting attorney, and he will tell you that the governor is to blame; ask the governor, and he will tell you that it is the prosecuting attorney. Nobody is to blame."

"I will go at once to Máslennikov and tell him."

"Well, that is useless," the lawyer retorted, smiling, "He is such a—he is not a relative or friend of yours?—such a, with your permission, such a stick and, at the same time, such a cunning beast."

Recalling what Máslennikov had said about the lawyer, he did not reply; bidding him good-bye, he drove to Máslennikov's house.

Nekhlyúdov had to ask Máslennikov for two things: for Máslova's transfer to the hospital, and for the 130 passportless people who were innocently confined in jail. No matter how hard it was for him to ask a favour of a man whom he did not respect, it was the only means of reaching his aim, and he had to employ it.

As he drove up to Máslennikov's house, he saw several carriages at the entrance: there were buggies, calashes and barouches, and he recalled that this was the reception-day of Máslennikov's wife, to which Máslennikov had asked him to come. As Nekhlyúdov approached the house, he saw a barouche at the entrance, and a lackey, in a hat with a cockade and in a cape, helping a lady from the threshold of the porch into it, while she caught the train of her dress in her arm and displayed her black thin ankles in low shoes. Among the other carriages which were standing there, he recognized the covered landau of the Korchágins. The gray-haired, ruddy-faced coachman respectfully and politely took off his hat, as to a well-known gentleman. Nekhlyúdov had not yet finished asking the porter where Mikhaíl Ivánovich (Máslennikov) was, when he himself appeared on the carpeted staircase, seeing off a very distinguished guest, such as he accompanied not merely to the landing, but all the way down. The very distinguished military guest was, as he descended, telling in French about the lottery and ball for the benefit of the orphanages, which were being planned in the city, expressing his opinion that this was a good occupation for women: "They are happy, and money is collected!"

"*Qu'elles s'amusent et que le bon Dieu les bénisse.* Ah, Nekhlyúdov, good day. What makes you so scarce?" he greeted Nekhlyúdov. "*Allez présenter vos devoirs à madame.* The Korchágins are here. *Et Nadine Bukshevden. Toutes les jolies femmes de la ville,*" he said, placing and slightly raising his military shoulders under the overcoat handed him by the lackey with the superb golden galloons. "*Au revoir, mon cher.*" He shook Máslennikov's hand.

"Come up-stairs. How glad I am," Máslennikov spoke excitedly, linking his hand in Nekhlyúdov's arm and, in spite of his corpulence, rapidly drawing him up-stairs.

Máslennikov was in an extremely joyful agitation, the cause of which was the attention which had been bestowed upon him by the distinguished person. One would have supposed that, having served in the Guards, a regiment close to the Tsar's family, he would have become used to meeting royalty. But, clearly, low desires are only whetted by repetition. Every such attention caused Máslennikov the same rapture that is produced in a docile little dog, whenever its master strokes, pats, and scratches it behind its ears. It wags its tail, crouches, winds about, lays down its ears, and insanely runs about in circles. Máslennikov was ready to do the same. He did not notice Nekhlyúdov's serious countenance, did not listen to him, and kept dragging him to the drawing-room, so that there was no possibility of refusing, and Nekhlyúdov went with him.

"Business afterward; I shall do anything you please," said Máslennikov, crossing the parlour with Nekhlyúdov. "Announce to Mrs. General Máslennikov that Prince Nekhlyúdov is here," he said to a lackey, as he went along. The lackey moved forward at a trot and passed them. *"Vous n'avez qu'à ordonner.* But you must by all means see my wife. I caught it last time for not bringing you to her."

The lackey had announced them, when they entered, and Anna Ignátevna, the vice-governor's wife, Mrs. General, as she called herself, turned to Nekhlyúdov, with a beaming smile, from amidst the bonnets and heads of those who surrounded her at the divan. At the other end of the drawing-room, at a table with tea, ladies were sitting, and men, in military and civil attire, were standing, and from there was heard the uninterrupted chatter of masculine and feminine voices.

"Enfin! Have you given us up? Have we offended you in any way?"

With such words, presupposing an intimacy between her and Nekhlyúdov, which had never existed between them, Anna Ignátevna met the newcomer.

"Are you acquainted? Are you? Madame Byelávskaya, Mikhaíl Ivánovich Chernóv. Sit down beside me. Missy, *venez donc à notre table. On vous apportera votre thé*—And you—" she addressed an officer who was talking to Missy, apparently having forgotten his name, "please, come here. Will you have some tea, prince?"

"I shall not admit it for a minute, not for a minute—she simply did not love him," said a feminine voice.

"But she did love tarts."

"Eternally those stupid jokes," laughingly interposed another lady, shining in her silk, gold, and precious stones.

"C'est excellent—these little wafers, and so light. Let me have some more!"

"How soon do you leave?"

"To-day is my last day. It is for this reason that I have come."

"The spring is so charming, and it is so nice now in the country!"

Missy, in a hat and in a dark striped dress, which clasped her slender waist without any folds, as though she had been born in it, was very pretty. She blushed when she saw Nekhlyúdov.

"I thought that you had left," she said to him.

"Almost," said Nekhlyúdov. "I have been kept by business. I have even come here on business."

"Come see mamma. She is very anxious to see you," she said, and, being conscious of telling an untruth, and of his knowing it, she blushed even more.

"I shall hardly have the time," gloomily replied Nekhlyúdov, trying to appear as though he had not noticed her blush.

Missy frowned angrily, shrugged her shoulder, and turned to the elegant officer, who seized the empty cup out of her hand, and, catching his sword in the chairs, gallantly carried it to another table.

"You must contribute something for the orphanage."

"I do not refuse, but want to keep all my liberality until the lottery. There I will show up in all my strength."

"Look out," was heard a voice, accompanied by a manifestly feigned laughter.

The reception-day was brilliant, and Anna Ignátevna was in raptures.

"Míka has told me that you are busy with the prisons. I understand that," she said to Nekhlyúdov. "Míka" (that was her stout husband, Máslennikov) "may have other faults, but you know how good he is. All these unfortunate prisoners are his children. He does not look at them in any other light. *Il est d'une bonté—*"

She stopped, being unable to find words which would have expressed the *bonté* of that husband of hers, by whose order men were flogged; she immediately turned, smiling, to a wrinkled old woman in lilac ribbons, who had just entered.

Having conversed as much as was necessary, and as insipidly as was necessary, in order not to violate the proprieties, Nekhlyúdov arose and walked over to Máslennikov.

"Can you listen to me now?"

"Oh, yes! What is it? Come this way!"

They went into a small Japanese study, and sat down by the window.

CHAPTER LVIII

A BUSINESS TALK
WITH MÁSLENNIKOV

"Well, *je suis à vous*. Do you want to smoke? Only wait—we must make no dirt here," he said, bringing the ash-tray. "Well?"

"I have two things to talk about."

"Indeed?"

Máslennikov's face became gloomy and sad. All the traces of the excitement of the little dog, whom its master has scratched behind its ear, suddenly disappeared. From the drawing-room came voices. A woman's voice said: "*Jamais, jamais je ne croirais,*" and another, from the other end, a man's voice, was telling something, repeating all the time: "*La Comtesse Voronzoff,*" and "*Victor Apraksine.*" From a third side was heard only the rumble of voices and laughter. Máslennikov listened to what was going on in the drawing-room and at the same time to what Nekhlyúdov was saying.

"I have come again about that woman," said Nekhlyúdov.

"Yes, the one who was innocently sentenced. I know, I know."

"I should like to ask you to have her transferred as a servant to the hospital. I was told that that could be done."

Máslennikov compressed his lips and thought a moment.

"Hardly possible," he said. "Still, I will look into it and wire you to-morrow."

"I was told that there were many sick people there and that help is needed."

"All right, all right. I will let you know in any case."

"Please," said Nekhlyúdov.

In the drawing-room was heard a general, and even natural, laugh.

"That is Victor," said Máslennikov. "He is remarkably clever when he is in his proper mood."

"Another thing," said Nekhlyúdov. "There are 130 people in the jail, kept there for more than a month for nothing else but because their passports are overdue."

He told what the cause of their detention was.

"How did you find out about that?" asked Máslennikov, and his face suddenly expressed unrest and dissatisfaction.

"I was on my way to one who is awaiting trial, when I was surrounded in the corridor by these men, who asked me—"

"What prisoner did you go to see?"

"To a peasant who is innocently accused and for whom I have employed counsel. But that is another matter. Is it possible that these people are kept in prison just because their passports are overdue and—"

"That is the prosecuting attorney's affair," Máslennikov angrily interrupted Nekhlyúdov. "You say that trials are speedy and just! It is the duty of the prosecuting attorney's assistant to visit the jail and to find out whether the prisoners are detained there lawfully. But they do nothing but play cards."

"So you can't do anything?" gloomily said Nekhlyúdov, thinking of what the lawyer had said about the governor's throwing it on the prosecuting attorney's shoulders.

"Yes, I will do it. I will institute an investigation at once."

"So much the worse for her. *C'est un souffre-douleur,*" was heard the voice of a woman in the drawing-room, who, apparently, was quite indifferent to what she was saying.

"So much the better. I will take this one," was heard from the other side the playful voice of a man and the playful laughter of a woman, who was refusing something.

"No, no, for nothing in the world," said a feminine voice.

"I will do it all," repeated Máslennikov, putting out his cigarette with his white hand with the turquoise ring. "And now let us go to the ladies."

"Another thing," said Nekhlyúdov, without entering the drawing-room and stopping at the door, "I was told that some men had received corporal punishment in jail yesterday. Is that true?"

Máslennikov grew red in his face.

"Ah, that, too? No, *mon cher*, you really must not be admitted; you meddle with everything. Come, come, Annette is calling us," he said, taking him under his arm, and expressing the same kind of excitement as after the attention of the distinguished person, but this time it was not an excitement of joy, but of trepidation.

Nekhlyúdov tore his arm away from him, and, without bidding any one good-bye or saying a word, with a melancholy expression in his face, crossed the drawing-room and the parlour and went past the officious lackeys, through the vestibule and out into the street.

"What is the matter with him? What have you done to him?" Annette asked her husband.

"This is *à la française*," somebody remarked.

"Not at all *à la française*; it is *à la zoulou*."

"Yes, he has always been like that."

Somebody arose; somebody arrived; and the twittering went on as before: the company used the incident with Nekhlyúdov as a convenient subject for conversation on the present *jour fixe*.

On the day following his visit to Máslennikov's house, Nekhlyúdov received from him, on heavy, smooth paper, with a coat of arms and seals, a letter in a magnificent, firm handwriting, informing him that he had written to the hospital physician about Máslova's transfer, and that, in all likelihood, his wish would be fulfilled. It concluded with "Your loving elder comrade," and below the signature, "Máslennikov," was a wonderfully artistic, large, and firm flourish.

"Fool!" Nekhlyúdov could not restrain himself from saying, especially because in the word "comrade" he felt that Máslennikov condescended to him; that is, he saw that, notwithstanding the fact that he was executing a morally exceedingly dirty and disgraceful function, he considered himself a very important man, and thought, if not to flatter, at least to show that he was not overproud of his majesty, in that he called himself his comrade.

A CHANGE IN RELATIONSHIP
WITH MÁSLOVA

Tolstoy
Resurrection
page 174

It is one of the most deep-rooted and wide-spread superstitions that every man has his well-defined properties, that a man is good or bad, clever or stupid, energetic or apathetic, and so forth. People are not such. We may say of a man that he is more often good than bad, more often clever than stupid, more often energetic than apathetic, and vice versa; but it would be wrong to say of one man that he is good or clever, and of another, that he is bad or stupid. Yet we always classify people in this manner. This is wrong. Men are like rivers: the water is the same in all; but every river is either narrow, or swift, or broad, or still, or clean, or cold, or turbid, or warm. Even thus are men. Each man carries within him the germs of all human qualities, and manifests now some of these, now others, and frequently becomes unlike himself, and yet remains one and the same. With some people these changes are extremely sudden. Nekhlyúdov belonged to this category. Changes took place within him both from physical and spiritual causes. Just such a change had occurred in him now.

That sensation of solemnity and joy of renovation, which he had experienced after the trial and after the first interview with Katyúsha, had completely disappeared and had, after the last meeting, given way to terror, even to disgust for her. He had decided not to leave her, not to change his determination of marrying her, if only she would wish it, but the thought of it was hard and painful to him.

On the day after his visit to Máslennikov's house, he again drove to the prison to see her.

The superintendent granted him an interview, but not in the office, and not in the lawyer's room, but in the women's visiting-hall. Notwithstanding his kind-heartedness, the superintendent was more reserved than before with Nekhlyúdov; obviously his talks with Máslennikov had resulted in an instruction to use greater precaution with that visitor.

"You may see her," he said, "only in regard to the money, please, do as I asked you. As to the transfer to the hospital, as his Excellency had written—that is possible, and the physician is willing. Only she herself does not want to go. She says: 'A lot I need to carry those lousy guys' pots.' Prince, that's what they're like," he added.

Nekhlyúdov did not reply and asked for the interview. The superintendent sent a warden after her, and Nekhlyúdov went with him to the empty visiting-hall of the women.

Máslova was already there. She came out from behind the screen, quiet and timid. She went up close to Nekhlyúdov and, glancing beyond him, said:

"Forgive me, Dmítri Ivánovich! I said many bad things the other day."

"It is not for me to forgive you—" Nekhlyúdov began.

"But still, I beg you, leave me alone," she added, and in the dreadfully squinting eyes with which she looked at him Nekhlyúdov again read a strained and evil expression.

"Why should I leave you?"

"Just do!"

"Why so?"

She again cast the same malicious glance at him, as he thought.

"It is like this," she said. "You leave me— I tell you the truth. I can't. Leave me altogether," she said, with quivering lips, growing silent. "I am telling you the truth. I'd rather hang myself."

Nekhlyúdov felt that in that refusal of hers there was hatred for him, and unforgiven offence, but at the same time something else—something good and significant. This confirmation of her former refusal, made while in a calm state, at once destroyed all doubts in Nekhlyúdov's soul and brought him back to his former serious solemnity and contrite condition.

"Katyúsha, as I have told you before, so I tell you now," he said, with especial seriousness, "I ask you to marry me. But if you do not wish to, and as long as you do not wish to, I will, as before, be where you are, and I will go where you go."

"That is your business, and I won't say anything more about this," she said, and again her lips began to tremble.

He, too, was silent, feeling that he had not the strength to speak.

"I am now going to the country and then to St. Petersburg," he said, at last regaining composure. "There I will look after your—after our affair, and if God grants it, the sentence will be reversed."

"If they do not reverse it, it makes no difference. I deserve it for something else, if not for this," she said, and he saw what a great effort she was making to restrain her tears.

"Well, did you see Menshóv?" she suddenly asked him, in order to conceal her agitation. "Isn't it true they are not guilty?"

"Yes, I think so."

"What a wonderful old woman," she said.

He told her everything he had found out from Menshóv and asked her whether she did not need anything, to which she replied that she did not.

Again they were silent a while.

"Well, about the hospital," she suddenly said, looking at him with her squinting eyes, "if you wish, I will go there, and I will stop drinking—"

Nekhlyúdov looked her silently in the eyes. Her eyes were smiling.

"That is very good," was all he could say and said good-bye.

"Yes, yes, she is an entirely different person!" thought Nekhlyúdov, experiencing, after his previous misgivings, an altogether new, never before experienced feeling of confidence in the invincibleness of love.

Upon returning, after this meeting, to her stinking cell, Máslova took off her cloak and sat down in her place on the benches, putting her hands on her knees. In the cell there were only consumptive Vladímirskaya with her suckling babe, old Menshóva, and the flagwoman with the two children. The sexton's daughter had been declared mentally deranged the day before and taken to the hospital. All the other women were washing clothes. The old woman was lying on the bench and sleeping; the children were in the corridor, the door to which was open.

Vladímirskaya with the babe in her arms and the flagwoman with a stocking, which she kept knitting on all the time with quick fingers, went up to Máslova.

"Well, did you see him?" they asked.

Máslova sat on the high bench, without saying a word, dangling her feet, which did not reach down to the floor.

"Don't mope!" said the flagwoman. "Above everything else, don't lose your courage. Eh, Katyúsha, well?" she said, rapidly moving her fingers.

Máslova made no reply.

"Our women have gone to wash the clothes. They said that to-day there would be great almsgiving. They have brought a lot, they say," said Vladímirskaya.

"Fináshka!" the flagwoman cried through the door. "Where did you go, you little rascal?"

She took out one knitting-needle, and, sticking it into the ball of thread and the stocking, she went into the corridor.

Tolstoy
Resurrection
page 176

Just then was heard the noise of steps and of women's conversation in the corridor, and the inmates of the cell, with their shoes over their bare feet, entered, each of them carrying a roll, and some of them even two. Fedósya at once went up to Máslova.

"What is it? Is something wrong?" asked Fedósya, looking lovingly at Máslova with her clear blue eyes. "Here is something for our tea," and she put the rolls on the shelf.

"Has he given up the idea of marrying you?" said Koroblyóva.

"No, he has not, but I do not want to," said Máslova. "I told him so."

"You are a silly girl!" Koroblyóva said, in her bass voice.

"If you are not to live together, what good would it do you to get married?" said Fedósya.

"But your husband is going along with you," said the flagwoman.

Book One

Resurrection

page 177

"Yes, we are lawfully married," said Fedósya. "But what use is there for him to bind himself lawfully, if he is not going to live with you?"

"What a silly woman! What for? If he married her, he would cover her with gold."

"He told me he would follow me, wherever I might be sent," said Máslova. "If he will go, he will; and if not, I won't beg him. Now he is going to St. Petersburg to look after my case. All the ministers there are his relatives," she continued, "only I have no use for them."

"Of course!" Koroblyóva suddenly agreed, opening up her bag and obviously thinking of something else. "Let's have a drink? All right?"

"I won't," answered Máslova. "Have some yourselves."

RESURRECTION

BOOK TWO

In TWO WEEKS THE CASE WOULD PROBABLY COME
up in the Senate, and by that time Nekhlyúdov intended to be in St. Petersburg,
in order, in case of a failure in the Senate, to petition his Majesty, as the lawyer
who had written the appeal had advised him to do. Should the appeal remain
fruitless—for which, in the lawyer's opinion, he ought to be prepared, as the
grounds for appeal were very weak—the part of the convicts to be deported, of
which Máslova was one, might leave in the first days of June; therefore, in order
to be ready to follow Máslova to Siberia, which was Nekhlyúdov's firm intention,
he had to go down to his villages to arrange his affairs there.

First, Nekhlyúdov went to Kuzmínskoe, his nearest large, black-earth estate,
from which he derived his chief income. He had lived on this estate during his
childhood and youth; then, when he was a grown man, he had been there twice,
and once, at his mother's request, he had taken a German superintendent there, with
whom he had examined the whole property; consequently he had long been
acquainted with the condition of the estate and with the relations of the peasants
to the office, that is, to the landowner. They were such that the peasants were, to

put it politely, wholly dependent on, or, simply, in slavery to, the office. This was not the personal slavery abolished in '61, the slavery of individuals to a master, but the slavery of all landless peasants—or of those with very little land—to the large landowners in general and in the main, but sometimes exclusively to those around whom the peasants lived. Nekhlyúdov knew this, could not help knowing it, so that his household was based on this slavery, and he contributed to the continuation of this economic structure. He knew not only that; he also knew it was unjust and cruel, and he had known it all since his student days, when he had professed and preached Henry George's doctrine and, on account of this doctrine, had distributed the land inherited from his father among the peasants, considering ownership of land in our time as much a sin as owning serfs was fifty years ago. It is true, after his military service, when he became accustomed to spending twenty thousand a year, all this knowledge ceased being obligatory in his life and was forgotten. He not only never questioned his attitude toward property or where the money came from which his mother gave him, but also tried not to think of it. But his mother's death, the inheritance, and the necessity of managing his estate, that is, the land, again gave rise in him to the question of ownership of land. A month before, Nekhlyúdov would have said to himself that he was not able to change the existing order of things, that it was not he who managed the estate—and would have more or less acquiesced, since he was living far away from his property, from which he received the money. But now he decided that, although he was confronted with a journey to Siberia and with complicated and difficult relations with the world of prisons, for which money would be needed, he could not leave affairs in their previous condition, and that he ought to change them, even though he suffer therefrom. He determined not to work the land himself, but to give it to the peasants at a low rental, which would ensure their independence from the landowner. Frequently, upon comparing the condition of the landowner with the owner of serfs, Nekhlyúdov considered the transfer of the land to the peasants, as against the working of it by means of hired labour, as being a parallel case to the action of the serf-owners, when they allowed the peasants to substitute a yearly tax for manorial labour. It was not a solution of the question, but a step in that direction: it was a transition from a coarser to a less coarse form of violence. It was this that he intended to do.

Nekhlyúdov arrived at Kuzmínskoe about midday. Simplifying his life as much as possible, he had not telegraphed about his arrival, but at the station took a two-horse tarantas. The driver was a young fellow in a nankeen sleeveless coat, girded along the folds around the long waist; he sat in driver's fashion, sidewise, on the box, and was only too glad to talk to the gentleman, since, while they were talking, it gave the foundered, limping, white shaft-horse and the lame, weak-kneed off-horse a chance to go at the pace they preferred.

The driver talked about the superintendent at Kuzmínskoe, not knowing he was driving the master. Nekhlyúdov had not told him on purpose.

"A superb German," said the driver, who had lived in the city and read novels. He was sitting half-turned toward the passenger and was playing with the whip-handle, which he caught now from above and now from below, and obviously making a display of his culture. "He has provided himself with a cream-coloured three-span, and when he drives out with his lady, it makes you feel small," he continued. "In winter, at Christmas, there was a Christmas tree in the large house— I took some guests there; it was lighted with an electric spark. You could not find the like of it in the whole province! He has stolen a lot of money! And why not? Everything is in his power. They say he has bought himself a fine estate."

Nekhlyúdov had thought that he was quite indifferent to the way the German was managing and using his estate. But the story of the long-waisted driver was disagreeable to him. He enjoyed the beautiful day, the dense, darkling clouds which now and then shrouded the sun; and the fields of spring grain, over which the peasants were walking behind their ploughs to plough the oats; and the thickly sprouting winter wheat, over which the skylarks hovered; and the forests, which now, with the exception of the late oaks, were covered with fresh foliage; and the meadows, on which the various-coloured herds of cattle and horses could be seen; and the fields, upon which he saw the ploughmen—but no, no, he thought of something unpleasant, and when he asked himself what it was, he recalled the story of the driver about how the German had been managing his Kuzmínskoe estate.

Upon arriving at Kuzmínskoe and setting to work, Nekhlyúdov forgot that feeling.

Examination of the office books and a conversation with the clerk, who naïvely pointed out the advantages of small peasant plots, surrounded by manorial lands, only confirmed Nekhlyúdov in his desire to give up the estate, and transfer all the land to the peasants. From these office books and from his talk with the clerk he discovered that, as before, two-thirds of the best cultivable land was worked by hired labour and improved machinery, while the remaining third was cultivated by the peasants at the rate of five roubles the desyatína; that is, for five roubles a peasant was obliged three times to plough up, three times to harrow, and to sow and mow, to bind, and harvest and deliver to the threshing floor, that is, to perform labour which at the cheapest hired rate would cost ten roubles a desyatína. Similarly the peasants paid the highest price for everything they needed from the office. They worked for the meadows, for the timber, for the potato greens, and nearly all of them were in debt to the office. Thus they paid for the outlying fields, which were let to the peasants, four times as much a desyatína as it possibly could bring by figuring at five per cent interest.

Nekhlyúdov had known all that before; but he now learned it as something new, and he only marvelled how it was that he and all other people in similar conditions could have helped seeing the abnormality of such relations. The proofs which the superintendent adduced that, if he let the peasants have the land, the whole inventory would be ruined, that it would not be possible to sell it at one-fourth its value, after the peasants had exhausted the land, that, in general, Nekhlyúdov would lose a great deal through this transfer—only confirmed him in his belief that he was doing a good act by giving the peasants the land and depriving himself of a great part of his income. He decided to settle the matter at once, during his present stay. The superintendent was to harvest and sell the growing grain, and to sell all the chattels and unnecessary buildings. For the present, he asked the superintendent to call together for the next day the peasants of the three villages, which were surrounded by the estate of Kuzmínskoe, in order to announce his intention to them and to come to an agreement in regard to the land which he was to give them.

With a pleasant consciousness of his firmness in the face of the superintendent's proofs and of his readiness to sacrifice in favour of the peasants, Nekhlyúdov left the office, and, reflecting on the business which was before him, walked around the house, along the flower-beds which now were neglected (there was a well-kept flower-bed opposite the superintendent's house), over the lawn-tennis ground, now overgrown with chicory, and over the avenue of lindens, where he used to go out to smoke his cigar, and where, three years before, he had flirted with pretty Kirímova, who had been visiting them. Having thought out the points of the speech which he intended to make to the peasants on the following day, Nekhlyúdov went over to the superintendent's, and, having considered with him at tea how to liquidate the whole estate, quite calm and satisfied with the good deed which he was about to do to the peasants, he entered the room of the large house, which was always used for the reception of guests, and which now was prepared for him.

In this small, clean room, with its pictures of scenes of Venice and a mirror between two windows, was a clean spring bed and a table with a decanter of water, with matches, and a light-extinguisher. On a large table near the mirror lay his open portmanteau, in which could be seen his toilet-case and a few books which he had taken along: one of these, in Russian, was an essay on the investigation of the laws of criminality; there were also one German and one English book on the same subject. He wanted to read them during his free moments, while travelling from village to village, but it was too late now to-day, and he was getting ready to go to sleep in order to prepare himself early in the morning for the explanation with the peasants.

In the room, in the corner, stood an antique mahogany chair with inlays, and the sight of this chair, which he remembered having seen in his mother's bed-room, suddenly evoked an unexpected feeling in Nekhlyúdov. He suddenly grew sorry for the house, which would now go to ruin, and for the garden, which would become a waste, and for the forests, which would be cut down, and for all those stables, barns, implement sheds, machines, horses, cows; though they had not been got by him, he knew with what labour they had been got together and maintained. Before, it had appeared to him easy to renounce it all, but now he was sorry not only for all this, but also to lose the land and half the income, which might be so useful to him. And at once he was assailed by the reflections that it was not wise or proper to give the land to the peasants and to destroy his estate.

"I must not own land. But if I do not own land, I cannot maintain all this estate. Besides, I am now bound for Siberia, and therefore neither the house nor the estate would be of any use to me," said one voice. "That is so," said another voice, "but in the first place, you are not going to spend all your life in Siberia, and if you marry, there may be children. And you have received the estate in good order and ought to transmit it in the same condition. There are certain obligations to the land. It is very easy to give it up and ruin it, but very difficult to start it anew. But, above everything else, you must well consider what it is you intend to do with your life, and you must take measures in regard to your property in accordance with this decision. And is your determination firm? Then again, are you acting sincerely in conformity with your conscience, or do you do so for the sake of people, in order to boast before them?" Nekhlyúdov asked himself, and could not help confessing that the opinions of people had an influence upon his decision. The longer he thought, the more questions arose before him and the more unsolvable they became. In order to free himself from these thoughts, he lay down on his fresh bed and wanted to fall asleep, in order to solve on the morrow, when his head would be clear, all those questions in which he had become entangled now. But he could not fall asleep for a long time. Through the open windows there poured in, together with the fresh air and moonlight, the croaking of frogs, which was interrupted by the singing and whistling of the nightingales far away in the park, and of one near by, under the window, in a spreading lilac bush. Listening to the sounds of the frogs and nightingales, Nekhlyúdov remembered the music of the superintendent's daughter; he also recalled the superintendent of the prison, and Máslova, whose lips had quivered like the croaking of the frogs, when she said, "Leave me altogether." Then the German superintendent of the estate was going down to the frogs. It was necessary to hold him back, but he not only slipped down, but even became Máslova herself, and began to reproach him, "I am a convict, and you are a prince." "No, I will not submit," thought Nekhlyúdov, awakening, and he asked himself: "Well, am I doing right or wrong? I do not know, and it does not make any difference to me. It makes no difference. But I must sleep." And he himself began to slip down where the superintendent and Máslova had gone, and there everything ended.

NEKHLYÚDOV'S TALK TO THE PEASANTS

On the following day Nekhlyúdov awoke at nine o'clock. The young office clerk, who was attending him, upon hearing him stir, brought him his shoes, which shone as never before, and clear, cold spring water, and announced to him that the peasants had assembled. Nekhlyúdov jumped up from bed, trying to wake up. There was not even a trace left of yesterday's feeling of regret at giving up his land and estate. He now thought of it with surprise. He now was rejoicing in the business ahead, involuntarily proud of it. Through the window of his room he could see the lawn-tennis ground, overgrown with chicory, where the peasants, at the superintendent's request, had gathered. The frogs had not been croaking in vain the night before. The weather was gloomy; a still, windless, warm rain had been drizzling since morning, and it hung in drops on the leaves, branches, and grass. Through the window burst not only the odour of the verdure, but also the odour of the earth crying for moisture. While dressing, Nekhlyúdov several times looked out of the window and watched the peasants coming together in the open space. They walked up one after another, took off their caps, and stood in a circle, leaning over their sticks. The superintendent, a stout, muscular, strong young man, in a short frock coat, with a green standing collar and immense buttons, came to tell Nekhlyúdov that all had come, but that they would wait, while Nekhlyúdov had better drink some tea or coffee, for both were ready.

"No, I prefer to go down to them at once," said Nekhlyúdov, experiencing, quite unexpectedly to himself, a feeling of timidity and shame at the thought of the conversation which he was to have now with the peasants.

He was about to fulfil that wish of the peasants, of which they did not even dare to dream—to give them land at a low price—that is, he was going to do them a kindness, and yet he felt ashamed of something. When Nekhlyúdov approached the peasants gathered there, and the blond, curly, bald, and gray heads were bared, he became so embarrassed that he did not know what to say. The rain continued to drizzle and to settle on the hair, the beards, and the nap of the peasant caftans. The

Tolstoy
Resurrection
page 186

peasants looked at the master and waited for him to say something, while he was so embarrassed that he could not utter a word. This embarrassing silence was broken by the calm, self-confident German superintendent, who regarded himself as a connoisseur of the Russian peasant, and who spoke Russian beautifully and correctly. This strong, overfed man, just like Nekhlyúdov, presented a striking contrast to the lean, wrinkled faces and the thin shoulder-blades of the peasants, which protruded underneath their caftans.

"The prince wants to do you a favour, and to give you land—only you do not deserve it," said the superintendent.

"Why do we not deserve it, Vasíli Kárlych? Have we not worked for you? We are much satisfied with the defunct lady—the kingdom of heaven be hers—and the young prince is not going to abandon us," began a red-haired orator.

"I have called you together in order to give you all the land, if you wish it," said Nekhlyúdov.

The peasants were silent, as though not comprehending, or not believing.

"In what sense do you mean to give the land?" said a middle-aged peasant in a sleeveless coat.

"To let it to you at a low rental, for your own use."

"That is very fine," said an old man.

"If only the price will be within our reach," said another.

"Why should we not take the land?"

"This is our business—to make a living off the land."

"It will easier for you. All you will have to do is to receive the money, and no trouble!" were heard some voices.

"It is you who are causing the trouble," said the German. "If you only worked and kept order."

"It is impossible for us, Vasíli Kárlych," interposed a sharp-nosed, lean old man. "You say, 'Why did you let your horse into the grain,' but who has let him? I work day in, day out, with the scythe, and maybe fall asleep at night, and he is in your oats, and then you flay me alive."

"If you only kept things in order."

"It is easy for you to talk about order, but that is above our strength," retorted a tall, black-haired, bearded, not very old man.

"I have told you to put up fences."

"Well, give us the timber for it," protested an insignificant, small peasant at the rear. "I wanted to fence in last summer, when you stuck me into jail for three months to feed the lice. That's the way I fenced in."

"What is he talking about?" Nekhlyúdov asked his superintendent.

"*Der erste Dieb im Dorfe*," the superintendent said in German. "He has been caught every year in the woods. Learn to respect other people's property," said the superintendent.

"Do we not respect you?" said an old man. "We cannot help respecting you, because we are in your power, and you twist us into ropes."

"Well, my friend, you are not the people to be worsted; it is you who are doing the worsting."

"What do you mean, you do! Last year you smashed my face, and it was left like that. Does no good to try to get justice out of a rich man."

"Do as the law tells you."

Manifestly this was an oratorical bout, in which the participants did not exactly see what they were talking about and to what purpose. On the one side, one could perceive anger restrained by fear, and on the other, the consciousness of superiority and power. Nekhlyúdov was pained by what he heard, and tried to return to the matter in hand—to establish prices and determine the periods of payments.

"How about the land? Do you want it? And what price will you set on it, if it is all given to you?"

"It is your article, so you set a price."

Nekhlyúdov mentioned a price. Although it was much lower than what was paid in the neighbourhood, the peasants, as is always the case, began to haggle and to find the price too high. Nekhlyúdov had expected that his proposition would be accepted with joy, but there was no apparent expression of pleasure. Nekhlyúdov could see that this proposition was advantageous to them, because when the question arose who was going to take the land, whether the whole commune, or by partnership, there began bitter contentions between those peasants who wanted to exclude the feeble and the poor payers from participation in the land, and those who were to be excluded. Finally, thanks to the superintendent, a price and periods of payment were agreed upon, and the peasants, conversing loudly, went down-hill, toward the village, while Nekhlyúdov went to the office to draw up the agreement with the superintendent.

Everything was arranged as Nekhlyúdov had wished and expected: the peasants received their land at thirty per cent less than was asked in the neighbourhood; his income from the land was cut almost in half, but that was more than enough for Nekhlyúdov, especially in conjunction with the sum which he received for the timber which he had sold, and which he was to net from the sale of the implements. Everything seemed to go well, and yet Nekhlyúdov felt all the time ashamed of something. He saw that the peasants, notwithstanding the thanks which some had expressed to him, were dissatisfied and had expected something more. It turned out that he had deprived himself of a great deal, and not done for the peasants what they had expected.

On the following day the contract was signed, and, accompanied by the selected old men, who had come to see him, Nekhlyúdov, with the unpleasant feeling of something unfinished, seated himself in the superintendent's superb "three-span carriage," as the driver from the station had called it. Bidding good-bye to the peasants, who shook their heads in surprise and dissatisfaction, he left for the station. The peasants were dissatisfied. Nekhlyúdov was dissatisfied with himself. What it was he was dissatisfied with he did not know, but for some reason he felt sad and ashamed.

CHAPTER III

NEKHLYÚDOV VISITS
ANOTHER ESTATE

From Kuzmínskoe Nekhlyúdov went to the estate which he had inherited from his aunts, the one where he had become acquainted with Katyúsha. He intended to arrange matters with the land there just as at Kuzmínskoe, and besides, to find out whatever he could about Katyúsha and about her child and his, whether it was true that it died, and how it died. He arrived at Pánovo early in the morning. The first thing he was struck by, as he drove into the courtyard, was the sight of abandonment and decay that was on all the buildings, but especially on the house. The sheet-iron roof, which at one time had been green, not having been painted for a long time, was now red with rust, and several sheets were curled up, apparently by the wind; the boards with which the house was covered had in spots been pulled off by people, wherever the boards came off easily by turning away the rusty nails. Both the front and back porches, especially the memorable back one, had rotted and were broken, and nothing but the cross-beams was left. Some windows were nailed up with boards, and the wing, in which the clerk lived, and the kitchen, and stable—everything was gray and dilapidated. Only the garden did not look forlorn; on the contrary, it had spread out and grown up and was now in full bloom; beyond the fence could be seen, like white clouds, blooming cherry, apple, and plum trees. The clump of lilac bushes was flowering just as it had flowered fourteen years before, when Nekhlyúdov had played the "widow-catch" game with eighteen-year-old Katyúsha, and had fallen and stung himself in the nettles. The larch which had been planted by Sófya Ivánovna near the house, and which then had been not higher than a post, was now a large tree, of the size of building timber, and all covered with yellowish-green, fluffy needles. The river was within its banks and dinned at the mill in the sluices. In the meadow, beyond the river, a mixed many-coloured herd of peasant cattle was grazing. The clerk, a seminarist who had not finished his course, met Nekhlyúdov in the yard, continually smiling; he invited him to the office, and, again smiling, as though promising something special by that smile, went behind the partition. Here there was some whispering, and then all grew silent. The driver, having received a gratuity, drove out of the yard, with tinkling bells, and then everything became completely still. Then a barefoot girl in an embroidered blouse, with fluff-rings in her ears, ran past the window; after the girl ran a peasant, clattering with the hobnails of his heavy boots over the hard path.

Nekhlyúdov sat down near the window, looking at the garden and listening. A fresh spring breeze, bearing the odour of the ploughed-up earth, came in through the small window vent, softly agitating the hair on his perspiring brow, and some notes lying on the window-sill, which was all cut up with a knife. On the river, "tra-pa-tap, tra-pa-tap," interrupting each other, the women's wooden washing bats splashed, and these sounds ran down the millpond shining in the sun; and one could hear the even fall of the water at the mill; and past the ear flew a fly, buzzing frightenedly and loudly.

And suddenly Nekhlyúdov recalled that just in the same way long ago, when he was young and innocent, he had heard here on the river these sounds of the washing bats on the wet clothes, through the even din of the mill; and just in the same way the spring breeze had ruffled the hair on his damp brow and the papers on the cut-up window-sill; and just as frightened a fly had flown past his ear—and he felt himself not the eighteen-year-old youth, which he had been then, but possessed of the same freshness, purity, and a future full of great possibilities, and at the same time, as happens in dreams, he knew that that was no more, and he felt terribly sad.

"When do you wish to eat?" the clerk asked him, smiling.

"Whenever you wish—I am not hungry. I will walk down to the village."

"Would you not like to go into the house? Everything is in good order inside. You will see that if on the outside—"

"No, later. But tell me, if you please, is there a woman here called Matryóna Khárina?"

That was Katyúsha's aunt.

"Certainly. She is in the village. I can't manage her. She has an ale-house. I have upbraided and scolded her for it, but when it comes to writing an accusation, I am sorry for her: she is old, and has grandchildren," said the clerk, with the same smile, which expressed both a desire to be pleasant to the master, and also a conviction that Nekhlyúdov understood matters as well as he.

"Where does she live? I would like to go down to see her."

"At the edge of the village—the third hut from the other end. On the left hand there is a brick cabin, and next to the brick cabin is her hut. I better take you down," said the clerk, with a smile of joy.

"No, thank you. I will find her. In the meantime, please, send word to the peasants to come together: I want to speak to them about the land," said Nekhlyúdov, intending to arrange everything here as at Kuzmínskoe, and, if possible, that same evening.

CHAPTER IV

NEKHLYÚDOV SEES THE PEASANTS' POVERTY

Upon emerging from the gate, Nekhlyúdov met, on the hard-trodden path across the pasture, which was overgrown with dock and plantain, the same peasant girl with rapidly moving, stout, bare feet, in a motley apron, with fluff-rings in her ears. She was now returning. She swung her left hand across in front of her, while with her right she clutched a red rooster. The rooster, with his wavy red crest, seemed to be quiet, and only rolled his eyes, and now stretched and now drew in one of his black legs, catching his claws in the girl's apron. As she was coming nearer to the master, she slowed down and changed her run to a walk; when she came abreast of him, she stopped and, swaying her head back, bowed to him; she moved on with the rooster, when he had passed her. Coming down to a well, Nekhlyúdov met an old woman, who on her stooping shoulders, covered with her dirty, rough blouse, was carrying full, heavy buckets. The old woman carefully let them down and bowed to him with the same back swing of her head.

Beyond the well began the village. It was a clear, hot day, and at ten o'clock it was already scorching, while the gathering clouds now and then veiled the sun. The whole street was filled with the sharp, pungent, and not disagreeable odour of dung, coming from the carts that were climbing up-hill along a shining, smooth road, but more especially from the dug-up manure piles of the yards, past the open gates of which Nekhlyúdov was going. The peasants, who were walking up the hill back of the wagons, were barefooted, and their trousers and shirts were daubed with the manure; they were looking back at the tall, stout gentleman, in a gray hat with a silk band that glistened in the sun who was walking up the village street, at every second step touching the ground with his shining, knotty, bright-knobbed cane. The peasants, who were returning from the field, shaking on the seats of their empty carts, which came down at a gallop, took off their caps and with surprise watched the unusual man who was walking up their street, while the women walked out of the gates or onto the porches and pointed him out to each other, and followed him with their eyes.

At the fourth gate, which Nekhlyúdov happened to pass, he was stopped by a cart that was just coming out with a squeak from the gate; it was packed high with manure and had a mat on top to sit on. A six-year-old boy, excited at the ride which he was going to have, was following the wagon. A young peasant, in bast shoes, making long strides, was driving the horses out of the gate. A long-legged, bluish-gray colt leaped out of the gate, but, becoming frightened at Nekhlyúdov, pressed close to the cart and, bumping its legs against the wheels, jumped ahead of its distressed and slightly neighing mother, that was pulling the heavy wagon. The next horse was being led out by a lean, lively old man, who was also barefoot, in striped trousers and a long, dirty shirt, with protruding shoulder-blades.

When the horses got out on the hard road, which was bestrewn with tufts of manure, gray, as though burnt, the old man turned back to the gate and bowed to Nekhlyúdov.

"Are you the nephew of our ladies?"

"Yes, yes."

"I welcome you on your arrival. Have you come to see us?" said the talkative old man.

"Yes, yes— Well, how are you getting along?" said Nekhlyúdov, not knowing what to say.

"What kind of life we lead? The very worst," the talkative old man said, in a singsong, drawling way, as though it gave him pleasure to tell it.

"Why is it bad?" said Nekhlyúdov, walking into the gate.

"What kind of life is it? The very worst," said the old man, going with Nekhlyúdov to the roofed-over part of the yard which was cleaned out to the ground.

Nekhlyúdov followed him in under the roofing.

"There they are, twelve souls," continued the old man, pointing to two women, who, their kerchiefs slipping off, perspiring, their skirts tucked up, with bare calves soiled half-way up with the manure, were standing with pitch-forks on the platform not yet cleaned out from the dung. "I have to buy six puds every month, and where am I to get it?"

"Haven't you enough of your own?"

"Of my own?" said the old man, with a contemptuous smile. "I have enough land for three souls, and this year I have only harvested eight ricks, so that there was not enough to last until Christmas."

"What do you do, then?"

"We do like this: I have hired out one as a labourer, and have borrowed money from you, gracious sir. I borrowed it before Shrovetide, and the taxes are not yet paid."

"What are your taxes?"

"From my place it's seventeen roubles for four months. God spare us such a life! You don't know where to turn next."

"May I go into your house?" said Nekhlyúdov, moving through the small yard and passing from the cleaned-up place to the untouched, but forked-over, saffron-yellow, strong-smelling layers of manure.

"Why not? Step in," said the old man, and, with rapid strides of his bare feet, that pressed the liquid manure between their toes, running ahead of Nekhlyúdov, he opened the door for him.

The women adjusted the kerchiefs on their heads, let down their skirts, and with terrified curiosity looked at the clean master with the gold cuff-buttons, who was walking into their house.

From the hut rushed out two little girls in shirts. Bending and taking off his hat, Nekhlyúdov went into the entrance and into the dirty, narrow hut, which smelled of some sour food and which was occupied by two looms. Near the oven stood an old woman, her sleeves rolled up, baring her lean, venous, sunburnt arms.

"Here is our master, and he's come calling on us," said the old man.

"You are welcome," kindly said the old woman, rolling down her sleeves.

"I wanted to see how you live," said Nekhlyúdov.

"We live just as you see. The hut is ready to tumble down any time, and it will kill somebody yet. But the old man says that it is good. So we live, and rule over things," said the vivacious old woman, nervously jerking her head. "I am getting dinner ready. I have to feed the workers."

"What are you going to have for dinner?"

"For dinner? We have good food. First course—bread with kvas; the second—kvas with bread," said the old woman, grinning with her half-worn-off teeth.

"No, seriously, show me what you are going to have for dinner to-day."

"What we will eat?" said the old man, laughing. "Our food is not complicated. Show it to him, old woman."

The old woman shook her head.

"So you want to see our peasant food. You are a curious gentleman, I can see that. He wants to know everything. I told you, bread and kvas, and soup made of goutwort, which the women brought yesterday—that's the soup, and then, potatoes."

"And that is all?"

"What else should there be? We wash it down with milk," said the old woman, laughing, and looking at the door.

The door was open, and the entrance was full of people, boys, girls, women with their babies, watching the strange master who was examining the peasant food. The old woman was evidently proud of her ability to converse with the master.

"Yes, sir, it is a bad, bad life we lead," said the old man. "Where are you headed?" he shouted at those who were standing in the door.

"Good-bye," said Nekhlyúdov, experiencing uneasiness and shame, which he could not account for.

"We thank you most humbly for having visited us," said the old man.

In the entrance, the people, pressing against each other, made way for him, and he went into the street and walked up the hill. He was followed by two barefoot boys from the entrance: one of these, the elder, was in a dirty, once white shirt, and the other, in a worthless, faded, pink shirt. Nekhlyúdov looked back at them.

"Where are you going now?" asked the boy in the white shirt.

"To Matryóna Khárina," he said. "Do you know her?"

The little fellow in the pink shirt laughed out for some reason, while the elder seriously asked:

"What Matryóna? An old woman?"

"Yes, an old woman."

"O-oh," he drawled out. "That is Semyón's wife, at the edge of the village. We'll take you there. Come on, Fédya, let us take him there!"

"And the horses?"

"Bet it doesn't matter."

Fédya agreed with him, and all three of them went up the street.

CHAPTER V

NEKHLYÚDOV VISITS KATYÚSHA'S AUNT

Nekhlyúdov was more at ease with the boys than with the grown people, and he talked to them on the way up. The little boy in the pink shirt stopped laughing and spoke as cleverly and clearly as the elder child.

"Who is poorest of you all?" asked Nekhlyúdov.

"Who is poor? Mikháyla is poor, Semyón Makárov, and then Márfa is mighty poor."

"And Anísya—she is poorer still. Anísya has not even a cow, and she has to go begging," said little Fédya.

"She has no cow, but there are only three of them, while there are five in Márfa's house," insisted the elder boy.

"But she is a widow," the pink boy defended Anísya.

"You say Anísya is a widow, but Márfa is as good as a widow," continued the elder boy. "It's all the same; she has no husband."

"Where is her husband?" asked Nekhlyúdov.

"In jail, feeding lice," said the elder boy, using the customary expression.

"Last summer he cut down two little birches in the manorial forest, so he was locked up," the little pink boy hastened to say. "He has been there these six months, and his old woman has to beg, 'cause there are three children and a poor old grandmother," he explained at great length.

"Where does she live?" asked Nekhlyúdov.

"In this house here," said the boy, pointing at a hut in front of which a white-haired little child, barely holding himself up on his crooked legs with turned-out knees, was standing and swaying on the path over which Nekhlyúdov was walking.

"Váska, where are you running, you little scamp?" cried a woman in a dirty gray shirt, which looked as though it were covered with ashes, as she came running out of the hut. She rushed with a frightened face in front of Nekhlyúdov, picked up the child, and carried him into the house, as though she were afraid Nekhlyúdov might harm her child.

That was the woman whose husband was locked up in jail for having taken the birches out of Nekhlyúdov's forest.

"Well, and Matryóna, is she poor?" asked Nekhlyúdov, as they were coming close to Matryóna's hut.

"Not at all poor: she sells liquor," the slim pink boy answered resolutely.

Upon reaching Matryóna's hut Nekhlyúdov dismissed the boys, and went into the entrance, and then into the house. Old Matryóna's cabin was about fifteen feet square, so that on the bed, which was back of the oven, it was not possible for a tall man to stretch. "On this very bed," he thought, "Katyúsha bore the child and then lay ill." Nearly the whole room was occupied by a loom, which the old woman was putting away with her elder granddaughter's assistance, just as Nekhlyúdov, having struck his head against the low door, entered. Two other grandchildren rushed headlong after the master, and stopped in the door, taking hold of the lintel with their hands.

"Whom do you want?" angrily asked the old woman, who was in bad humour on account of the loom that was giving her trouble. Besides, as she secretly sold liquor, she was afraid of all strangers.

"I am the landowner. I would like to talk to you."

Book Two
Resurrection
page 195

The old woman was silent and looked fixedly at him; then she suddenly became transformed.

"Ah, you, dear sir, and I, foolish woman, did not recognize you. I thought it was some transient," she said, in a feignedly kind voice. "Ah, you, my clear-eyed falcon."

"I should like to talk to you without people around," said Nekhlyúdov, looking at the open door where the children stood and, beyond them, a haggard woman with a lean, sickly, pale, continually smiling baby, in a little cap made of rags.

"What are you staring at? I'll show you! Just let me have my crutch," cried the old woman at those who were standing in the door. "Shut the door!"

The children went away, and the woman with the baby closed the door.

"I was wondering, 'Who has come?' And behold! it is the master. My golden one, my precious beauty," said the old woman. "And so you have deigned to come to see me. O you precious one! Sit down here, your Excellency, right here on the bench," she said, wiping off the bench with her apron. "I was wondering what devil it was that was coming here, and behold, it was your Excellency, the good master, the benefactor, our protector."

Nekhlyúdov sat down; the old woman stood in front of him, supported her cheek with her right hand, with her left hand caught hold of the elbow of her right arm, and began to speak in a singsong voice:

"You have grown old, your Excellency; you used to be like a pretty flower, and now? Evidently you, too, have known sorrow!"

"I came to ask you whether you remember Katyúsha Máslova?"

"Katerína! How could I forget her—she is my niece. Of course I remember her; I wept so many tears for her. I know all. Who, my dear, is not sinful before God, and not guilty toward the Tsar? A young thing—she drank tea and coffee—well, the unclean one tempted her, for he is strong, and the sin was committed. What is to be done? If you had abandoned her, but no, you gave her a good reward, a whole hundred roubles. And what did she do? She could not understand it. If she had listened to me, she might have lived well. Though she is my niece, I must say, she is not a sensible girl. I had found such a fine place for her, but she would not submit, and cursed the master. And can we curse our masters? Well, she was dismissed. Then, she might have lived at the house of the forester, but she did not want to."

"I wanted to ask about the child. She gave birth in your house, didn't she? Where is the child?"

"I had, dear sir, well provided for the child. She was very bad off, and I thought she would never get up. I had the little boy baptized, as is proper, and sent him to a foundling house. Really, what was the use of tormenting an angelic little soul, when the mother was dying. Others leave the child without feeding, and it dies;

Tolstoy
Resurrection
page 196

but I thought that it was not right, and so I took the trouble, and sent him to the foundling house. There was some money, and so he was taken there."

"Did he have a number?"

"He did, only he died. She said that he died as soon as he got there."

"Who is she?"

"That woman who used to live at Skoródnoe. That was her business. Malánya was her name—she is dead now. She was a clever woman—and that's the way she did it. If a child was brought to her, she kept it in her house and fed it. And she fed it until time for taking it away. When there were three or four, she took them away. She did it very cleverly: she had a large cradle, in the shape of a double bed, so that the children could be placed either way. And there was a handle attached to it. So she would place four of them with their heads apart, so that they would not bump each other, and with their feet together, and thus she took the four away. She stuck sucking rags into their mouths, so the dear little things were content."

"Well, and then?"

"Well, so she took Katerína's child and kept him for about two weeks. He began to ail in her house."

"Was he a nice child?" asked Nekhlyúdov.

"So nice that you couldn't have found a nicer even if you'd had to. He was just like you," added the old woman, winking her old eye.

"What weakened him so? I suppose he did not get the right food."

"What feeding could there be? Naturally, it was not her child. All she cared for was to get him there alive. She said that he died the moment she reached Moscow with him. She brought a certificate about it, all in proper order. She was a clever woman."

That was all Nekhlyúdov was able to find out about his child.

CHAPTER VI

THE CONSEQUENCES OF OWNING LAND

Having again struck his head against the doors of the house and of the entrance, Nekhlyúdov emerged into the street. The dirty white and the pink boy were waiting for him. A few more had joined them. A few women with their nursing babies were also waiting and among them was the woman who lightly held in her arms the anemic child with the little cap made of rags. This child did not cease smiling strangely with its whole wrinkled face and tensely twirling its large fingers.

Nekhlyúdov knew that this was a smile of suffering. He asked who this woman was.

"This is that Anísya I was telling you about," said the elder boy.

Nekhlyúdov turned to Anísya.

"How do you get along?" he asked. "What do you live on?"

"How do I live? I beg," said Anísya, and burst out weeping.

The wrinkled child melted into a smile, twisting its worm-like little feet.

Nekhlyúdov drew out his pocketbook, and gave the woman ten roubles. He had not taken two steps when he was overtaken by another woman with a child, then by an old woman, and again by another. They all spoke of their poverty, and asked to be helped. Nekhlyúdov distributed the sixty roubles in small bills which he had in his pocketbook, and, with a terrible gnawing in his heart, returned home, that is, to the clerk's wing. The clerk, smiling, met Nekhlyúdov with the news that the peasants would gather in the evening. Nekhlyúdov thanked him, and, without entering the rooms, went to stroll through the garden along the overgrown paths, strewn with the white petals of the apple-blossoms, thinking over everything he had seen.

At first everything near the wing was quiet, but later Nekhlyúdov heard two angry, quarrelsome voices of women, through which now and then came the calm voice of the smiling clerk. Nekhlyúdov listened.

"My strength's gone. Why are you pulling the cross off my neck?" said one furious feminine voice.

"She just got in by mistake," said the other voice. "Give her back to me, I say. Don't torment the cow, and keep the milk away from the children."

"Pay, or work it off," said the calm voice of the clerk.

Nekhlyúdov came out of the garden and went up to the porch, where two dishevelled women were standing, one of them apparently in the last stages of pregnancy. On the steps of the porch stood the clerk, with his hands in the pockets of his linen ulster. Upon noticing the master, the women grew silent and began to fix the kerchiefs which had slipped off their heads, and the clerk took his hands out of his pockets and smiled.

The trouble was, as the clerk explained it, that the peasants purposely let the calves, and even the cows, out on the manorial meadows. Thus two cows belonging to these women had been caught in the meadow and had been driven in. Now the clerk demanded thirty kopeks a cow, or two days' work from each of the women. But the women declared that, in the first place, the cows had just entered there; that, in the second, they had no money; and that, in the third, for the promise to work off the fine, they demanded the immediate return of the cows that had been standing since morning in the hot sun without food and lowing pitifully.

"How often I have asked them in all kindness," said the smiling clerk, looking at

Nekhlyúdov, as though appealing to him as to a witness, "to look after their cattle when they drive them out to pasture!"

"I just ran down to look at my baby, when they ran away."

"Then don't go away, when you are supposed to watch the cattle!"

"And who will feed the baby? You won't give them the breast."

"If she had really cropped the meadow, her belly would not pain her now, but she barely got in," said the other.

"They have grazed off all the meadows," the clerk addressed Nekhlyúdov. "If they are not to be fined there will be no hay at all."

"Oh, don't sin," cried the woman with child. "Mine have never gone there before."

"But they have now, and so pay, or work it off."

"I will work it off, only let the cows go, and don't starve them," she cried, angrily. "As it is, I have no rest, neither by day nor by night. My mother-in-law is sick. My husband is on a spree. I have to attend to everything, and I have no strength. Choke yourself with your working off."

Nekhlyúdov asked the clerk to release the cows, and himself went to the garden to finish his reflections, but there was nothing to think about. Everything was so clear to him that he could not help wondering how it was that people, and he himself included, had not seen long ago what was so manifestly clear.

"The people are slowly dying, and are used to this process of slow death; among them conditions of life, adapted to this slow death, have been formed: the dying off of the children, hard labour for the women which surpasses their strength, insufficiency of food for all, especially for the old people. And thus the people slowly arrive at a state when they no longer see its whole terror and do not complain of it. Therefore we regard this condition as natural and think that that is what it ought to be."

Now it was as clear as day to him that the chief cause of the people's suffering, as perceived and pointed out by the peasants themselves, consisted in the fact that the landowners had taken away the land from which they could provide for their needs. At the same time, it was exceedingly clear that the children and old people died because they had no milk, and they had no milk because there was no land on which to pasture their cows and harvest their grain and hay; it was exceedingly clear that all the poverty of the people, or at least the chief and nearest cause of that poverty, came from the fact that the land which fed them was not in their hands, but in the hands of men who, making use of the right to that land, lived by the labours of the people. And the land, which was so necessary to the peasants that they starved for the lack of it, was worked by these very people, who were reduced to extremity, in order that the grain might be sold abroad, and that the owners of the land might be able to buy themselves hats, canes, carriages, bronzes, and so on. This was now as clear to him as that horses which are shut up in an enclosure where they have eaten all the grass will be lean and starving, unless they be permitted to use the land where they may find food for themselves. And that was terrible, and could not and ought not to be. And means had to be found to do away with this, or at least he himself ought not to take part in it. "I shall certainly find a way," he thought, walking up and down, in the nearest avenue of birches. "In learned societies, governmental institutions, and newspapers we talk about the causes of the people's impoverishment and about the means for improving the people's life, except about the one certain means, which would undoubtedly improve the people's life—that the land which has been taken from them be returned to them." He vividly recalled the fundamental doctrine of Henry George and his former enthusiasm for it, and he wondered how it was he had forgotten it all. "The land cannot be the object of private ownership; it cannot be the object of purchase and sale, any more than water, air, and the sun are. Everybody has the same right to the land and to the privileges which it bestows." And he understood now why he felt so ashamed as he was arranging matters at Kuzmínskoe. He had been deceiving himself. Though he knew that man had no right to the land, he assumed it in his own case, and presented the peasants with a part of that which, in the depth of his soul, he knew he had no right to. He would not do that here, but would change his Kuzmínskoe procedure. He thought out a project, which was that he would give the land to the peasants at a stated rental, which rental was to be the peasants' property and to be used for the payment of taxes and for public needs. This was not the *Single-tax*, but the nearest possible approach to it under present conditions. The chief thing was that he renounced his right of private ownership of land.

When he came back to the house, the clerk, smiling most joyfully, invited him to dine, at the same time expressing his fear lest the food, which had been prepared by his wife with the help of the girl with the fluff-rings in her ears, should be cooked and broiled too much.

The table was covered with a rough cloth; an embroidered towel took the place of a napkin; and on the table stood a *vieux-saxe* soup-bowl, with a broken handle, in which was potato soup with that rooster which had been protruding now one black leg and now another, and which now was cut and even chopped into small pieces, in many places still covered with pin-feathers. After the soup came the same rooster with singed feathers, and cheese dumplings with a large quantity of butter and sugar. Although all that was not very palatable, Nekhlyúdov ate it, without knowing what he was eating, for he was so occupied with his idea, which had at once dispelled the gloom that he had brought with him from the village.

The clerk's wife peeped through the door, while the frightened girl, with the fluff-rings in her ears, was carrying in a dish, and the clerk himself, proud of his wife's art, kept smiling ever more joyfully.

After dinner, Nekhlyúdov with difficulty got the clerk to sit down, and in order to verify his plans to himself and to have somebody to whom to tell what so interested him, he informed him of his project of giving the land to the peasants and asked him for his opinion on the matter. The clerk smiled, trying to look as though he had thought so himself for a long time, and as though he were glad to hear it; in reality, he did not understand a word, apparently not because Nekhlyúdov did not express himself clearly, but because from this project it appeared that Nekhlyúdov was renouncing his advantage for the advantage of others; whereas the truth that every man cared only for his own advantage, to the disadvantage of other people, had taken such firm root in the consciousness of the clerk that he concluded that he had not understood Nekhlyúdov right when he told him that the whole income from the land was to form the common capital of the peasants.

"I see. So you will get a certain per cent from that capital," he said, beaming.

"No, no— You must understand that land can't be the property of individuals."

"Yes, sure."

"And, therefore, everything the land yields belongs to everyone."

"But then you will have no income," said the clerk, no longer smiling.

"No, I won't. I renounce it."

The clerk heaved a heavy sigh, and then once more began to smile. He saw that Nekhlyúdov was not quite sane, and immediately set out to discover in the project of Nekhlyúdov, who was giving up his land, a chance for his own personal advantage; he tried to comprehend that project in the sense of being able himself to make use of the land which was to be given away.

But when he saw that that was not possible, he felt aggrieved and ceased taking any interest in the plan and continued to smile only to please his master. Seeing that the clerk did not understand him, Nekhlyúdov dismissed him and himself sat down at the cut-up and ink-stained table, in order to put his plan down on paper.

The sun had just set behind the newly budded lindens, and the mosquitoes flew into the room in swarms and stung him. When he had ended his note and at the same time heard the lowing of the cattle in the village, the creaking of opened gates, and the conversation of the peasants collecting for the meeting, Nekhlyúdov told the clerk not to call the peasants to the office, but that he himself would go to the village and to the yard where the peasants might be gathered. Having drunk a glass of tea offered him by the clerk, Nekhlyúdov went to the village.

CHAPTER VII

AN ATTEMPT TO SETTLE THE
LAND QUESTION

There was noisy talk near the yard of the elder, but the moment Nekhlyúdov approached, the conversation died down, and all the peasants, just as at Kuzmínskoe, one after another took off their hats. The peasants of this place were much more drab than those at Kuzmínskoe: just as the women and girls wore fluff-rings in their ears, so the men were nearly all of them in bast shoes and caftans. Some were barefoot and in nothing but their shirts, just as they had come from their work.

Nekhlyúdov made an effort and began his speech by saying that he intended to give them the land altogether. The peasants were silent and there was no change in the expression of their faces.

"Because I consider,"said Nekhlyúdov, blushing, "that he who does not work the land has no right to own it and that everybody has a right to make use of the land."

"That is so. That is correct," were heard the voices of the peasants.

Nekhlyúdov continued to speak, telling them that the income from the land ought to be divided up among all, and therefore he proposed that they take the land and pay such rental as they themselves might determine into the common capital, which was to be at their disposal. There were heard words of approval and agreement, but the serious faces of the peasants became ever more serious, and the eyes, which had been looking at the master, were cast down, as though not wanting to shame him with the fact that his cunning had been understood by all, and that he would not deceive anybody.

Nekhlyúdov spoke quite clearly, and the peasants were sensible people, but he was not understood, nor could he ever be, for the same reason that the clerk was unable to comprehend him. They were fully convinced that it was proper for every

Tolstoy
Resurrection
page 202

man to look out for his advantage. But the landowners, they knew by the experience of several generations, always watched their own interests to the disadvantage of the peasants. Consequently, if the landowner called them together and offered them something new, it was manifestly for the purpose of cheating them more cunningly still.

"Well, what rental do you expect to put on the land?" asked Nekhlyúdov.

"What is the use putting a price on it? We cannot do that. The land is yours, and so is the power," was the answer from the crowd.

"But you will be using that money for your own common purposes."

"We cannot do that. The common good is one thing, and this is another."

"Understand," said the smiling clerk, who had come up after Nekhlyúdov, wishing to explain the matter, "that the prince gives the land to you for money, and the money goes back to you as your own capital, for your common good."

"We understand quite well," said an old angry-looking toothless peasant, without raising his eyes. "It is just like in a bank, only we shall have to pay at stated times. We do not wish that, because it is hard for us as it is, and that will ruin us completely."

"It does us no good. Let us live as before," spoke dissatisfied and even insulting voices.

They began to refuse more resolutely when Nekhlyúdov mentioned a contract which he would sign and they would have to sign, too.

"What is the use of signing? As we have worked before, so we shall continue to work. But what good is this? We are ignorant people."

"We can't agree to it, because it is an unusual business. As it has been, so let it be. If only the seeds be changed," were heard some voices.

To change the seeds meant that under present conditions the seeding was done from the peasant grain, whereas they wanted the master to furnish the grain to them.

"So you decline it, and will not take the land?" asked Nekhlyúdov, turning to a middle-aged barefoot peasant with a beaming face, in a torn caftan, who in his bent hand was holding his tattered cap just as soldiers hold theirs when they take them off by command.

"Yes, sir," replied this soldier, who apparently had not yet been freed from the hypnotism of militarism.

"Consequently you have enough land?" said Nekhlyúdov.

"Not at all," said the ex-soldier, with an artificial, happy grin, carefully holding his tattered cap in front of him, as though offering it to anybody who might like to use it.

"Still, you had better consider what I have told you," said Nekhlyúdov, in surprise, and he repeated his proposition.

"We have nothing to think over. As we have said, so it will be," angrily muttered the toothless old man.

"I will be here all day to-morrow. If you have changed your minds, send word to me."

The peasants made no reply.

Nekhlyúdov could not get anything out of them, and went back to the office.

"Let me inform you, prince," said the clerk, upon returning home, "that you will come to no understanding with them: they are stubborn people. The moment they are at a meeting, they become stubborn, and there is no stirring them after that.

They are afraid of everything. And yet, on other occasions these very peasants—take, for example, that gray-haired, or that swarthy man, who did not agree—are clever people. Whenever one of them comes to the office, and I ask him to sit down and drink a glass of tea," said the smiling clerk, "he talks quite freely—and he is a minister as regards his mind—he will judge everything correctly. But at the meeting he is an entirely different man, and he sticks to just one thing."

Tolstoy

Resurrection

page 204

"Can't you send for some of these more intelligent peasants," said Nekhlyúdov. "I should like to explain it to them in detail."

"That can be done," said the smiling clerk.

"Then, please, call them for to-morrow."

"That can be done," said the clerk, smiling even more cheerfully. "I shall call them for to-morrow."

"I declare, he is shrewd!" Swaying on his well-fed mare, the swarthy peasant, with his shaggy, never combed beard, spoke to another old, lean peasant in a tattered caftan, who was riding near him and clanking with the iron hobbles. They were riding to put the horses to pasture for the night on the highway and secretly in the manorial forest. "The idea of his giving away the land if we put down our signatures! They have been fooling us long enough. No, sir, you are joking! Nowadays we understand a thing or two ourselves," he added, and began to call back the straying yearling colt.

"Here, colt," he cried, stopping his horse and looking back, but the colt was not behind, but had gone into the meadow at one side.

"That is where he has gone to, the son of a bitch, into the manorial meadow," said the swarthy peasant with the shaggy beard, as he heard on the dew-covered meadow, fragrant with the swamp, the crashing of the sorrel, over which the straying colt was prancing and whinnying.

"You hear, the meadows are getting full of weeds. On the holiday we shall have to send the women to weed out the meadows," said the slim peasant in the torn caftan. "Else we shall ruin our scythes."

"Put down your signatures, he says," the shaggy peasant continued his judgement of the master's speech. "You sign your name, and he will swallow you alive."

"That is right," answered the old man. And they did not say anything more. There was only the thud of the horses' feet on the rough road.

CHAPTER VIII

A SLEEPLESS NIGHT

Upon returning home, Nekhlyúdov found in the office, which had been prepared for him for the night, a high bed with a feather mattress, two pillows, and a crimson silk, double, coverlet, very stiff, quilted with a small design—evidently from the trousseau of the clerk's wife. The clerk offered Nekhlyúdov what was left of the dinner, but receiving a refusal, he apologized for his meager entertainment and accommodation, and retired, leaving Nekhlyúdov to himself.

The peasants' refusal did not in the least put Nekhlyúdov out. On the contrary, he felt quite composed and happy, although there, at Kuzmínskoe, they had accepted his proposition and kept thanking him all the time, while here they had shown distrust and even hostility. The office was stuffy and dirty. Nekhlyúdov went into the yard and was about to go into the garden, but he recalled that night, the window in the maids' room, and the back porch, and it was unpleasant for him to stroll through places that were fouled by criminal recollections. He sat down on the porch and, inhaling the strong odour of the young birch leaves, which was everywhere in the warm air, he looked at the darkling garden for a long time and listened to the mill, to the nightingales, and to some other kind of bird which was monotonously whistling in a bush near the porch. In the clerk's window the light was extinguished; in the east, back of the barn, crimsoned the glow of the rising moon; heat-lightning even more brightly illuminated the blooming, overgrown garden and the dilapidated house; a distant clap of thunder was heard, and a third of the sky was shrouded by a black cloud. The nightingales and the other bird grew silent. Through the din of the water in the mill was heard the cackling of geese; then the early cocks in the village and in the clerk's yard began to call to each other, as they always crow earlier on hot, stormy nights. There is a saying that cocks crow early on a cheerful night. This was more than a cheerful night for Nekhlyúdov. It was a joyful, a happy night for him. His imagination reconstructed for him his impressions of that happy summer which he had passed here as an innocent youth, and he felt himself now what he had been then and during all his better moments in life. He not only recalled, but even felt himself what he had been, when, fourteen years old, he had prayed to God that He should show him the truth, when, as a child, he wept on his mother's knees, at parting, promising her always to be good and never to give her cause for grief; he felt himself to be what he was when he and Nikólenka Irténev had decided to support each other in a good life and to try to make all people happy.

He now recalled how at Kuzmínskoe he had been tempted, and he had begun to regret the house, the forest, the estate, the land, and he asked himself whether he regretted now. And it even appeared strange to him that he could have regretted. He recalled everything he had seen on that day: the woman with the children and without her husband, who had been locked up in jail for cutting down trees in his, Nekhlyúdov's, forest; and terrible Matryóna, who thought, or, at least, said, that women of their status ought to become gentlemen's mistresses; he recalled her relation to the children, the manner they were carried off to the foundling house, and that unfortunate, smiling child in the little cap, who was slowly dying from lack of food; he recalled that pregnant, feeble woman who was obliged to work for him because, exhausted by labour, she had not watched her hungry cow. And at this point he recalled the prison, the shaven heads, the cells, the loathsome stench, the chains, and, side by side with it, the senseless luxury of his life and of that of every city gentleman. Everything was quite clear and indisputable.

The bright, almost full moon rose from behind the barn, and black shadows fell across the yard, and the sheet iron on the roof of the dilapidated house began to sparkle.

And, as though not wishing to miss the chance of this light, the nightingale again began to pipe and trill in the garden.

Nekhlyúdov recalled how at Kuzmínskoe he had begun to reflect on his life and to solve the questions as to what he should do and how he should do it; and he recalled how he had become entangled in these questions and could not solve them, because there were so many considerations connected with each of them. He now put these questions to himself and was surprised to find how easy they were. They were easy now because he did not think of what would become of him, nor did that interest him, but he thought of what he ought to do. Strange to say, he was absolutely unable to decide what he himself needed, but knew beyond any doubt what was to be done for others. He knew unquestionably that the land must be given to the peasants, because it was wrong to retain it. He knew unquestionably that Katyúsha must not be abandoned; that he must aid her and be ready for everything, in order to expiate his guilt before her. He knew unquestionably that he must study, examine, elucidate to himself, and comprehend all those cases of the courts and the punishments in which he was conscious of sensing something which nobody else saw. He did not know what would come of it all, but he knew unquestionably that this and that had to be done. And this firm conviction gave him joy.

The black cloud had veiled the whole heaven, and not only heat-lightning, but real lightning, which illuminated the whole yard and the dilapidated house with its torn-off porches, was seen, and thunder was heard overhead. All the birds had fallen silent, but the leaves began to rustle, and the wind reached the porch, on which he was sitting, and tossed his hair. One drop fell upon him, then another; then the rain began to drum on the burdock and on the iron sheets of the roof, and the whole air was brilliantly lighted up: everything grew silent, and, before Nekhlyúdov could count three, almost over his head there came a terrible clap of thunder, which then rolled along the sky.

Nekhlyúdov went into the house.

"Yes, yes," he thought, "the work done by our life, all the work, the whole meaning of that work, is incomprehensible and must remain incomprehensible to me. Why were there aunts? Why did Nikólenka Irténev die? and why did I live? Why was there Katyúsha? And my insanity? Why that war? And all my consequent reckless life? It is not in my power to understand all that, all the work of the Master. But it is in my power to do His will as it is written in my conscience, and this I know unquestionably. And when I do it, I am unquestionably calm."

The rain now came down in sheets and ran off the roofs, gurgling into the barrel; the lightning less often lighted up the yard and house. Nekhlyúdov returned to the room, undressed, and lay down in the bed, not without some fear of bed-bugs, the presence of which he suspected from the dirty and torn paper on the walls.

"Yes, to feel yourself not a master, but a servant," he thought and rejoiced at the thought.

His fears came true. The moment he put out the light, the insects began to cling to him and to bite him.

"To give up the land, to journey to Siberia—fleas, bedbugs, dirt. What of it? If I have to bear all that, I shall bear it." But, in spite of his determination, he could not bear it, and so he sat down near the open window, watching the fleeting clouds, and the newly reappearing moon.

CHAPTER IX

A TALK WITH THE PEASANTS

Nekhlyúdov fell asleep only toward morning, and so he awoke late the next day.

At noon seven chosen peasants, who had been invited by the clerk, came to the apple orchard, under an apple tree, where the clerk had made a table and benches over posts driven into the ground. It took quite a while to persuade the peasants to put on their caps and seat themselves on the benches. The ex-soldier, now clad in clean leg-rags and bast shoes, most persistently held his torn cap in front of him, according to regulation, as at funerals. When one of them, a broad-chested old respectable-looking man, with ringlets of a half-gray beard, like Michelangelo's Moses, and with thick gray waving hair over his sunburnt and bared cinammon-coloured brow, put on his large cap and, wrapping himself in his homemade caftan, climbed over the bench and sat down upon it, all the others followed his example.

When all had taken their seats, Nekhlyúdov sat down opposite them and, leaning with his elbows over a paper, which contained a brief of his project, began to expound it to them.

Tolstoy

Resurrection

page 208

Either because there were fewer peasants or because he was occupied not with himself but with work, Nekhlyúdov this time felt no embarrassment. He involuntarily turned chiefly to the broad-chested old man with his beard of white ringlets, awaiting approval or protest from him. But the conception which Nekhlyúdov had formed of him was wrong. Though the respectable old man kept approvingly nodding his handsome, patriarchal head, or tossing it and frowning, whenever the others objected to something, it obviously was hard for him to understand what Nekhlyúdov was saying, and he could understand only when the other peasants had transmitted it to him in their own language. Nekhlyúdov's words were understood much better by a little, almost beardless old man, who was sitting next to the patriarch; he was blind in one eye, and wore a patched, nankeen, sleeveless coat, and old boots, worn down on the sides; he was an oven-builder, as Nekhlyúdov later found out. This man kept moving his eyebrows, in his effort to hear all, and immediately retold in his own way everything Nekhlyúdov said. Of equally quick understanding was a short, stocky old man, with a white beard and gleaming, intelligent eyes, who used every opportunity to make jocular and ironical comments on what Nekhlyúdov said and who obviously was proud of this ability of his. The ex-soldier, too, might have understood, if he had not been made stupid by his military experience and did not get entangled in the habitual, senseless talk of a soldier. Most serious of all in regard to the matter in hand was a tall man, with a long nose and a small beard, who was speaking in a bass voice; he was clad in a clean, home-made garb and new bast shoes. This man comprehended everything and spoke only when it was necessary. The other two old men—one of these, the toothless peasant who on the previous day had shouted a decided refusal to every proposition of Nekhlyúdov at the meeting, and the other, a tall, white, lame old man, with a kind-hearted face, in half-boots, and his lean legs tightly wrapped in leg-rags—were silent nearly all the time, though they listened attentively.

Nekhlyúdov first expounded to them his view of ownership of land.

"The land," he said, "according to my opinion, ought not to be sold or bought, because if it be sold, those who have money will buy it all up, and then they will take from those who have no land as much as they please; they will take money for the right to stand on that land," he added, using Spencer's argument.

"One cure's to tie wings on and fly," said the old man with laughing eyes and the white beard.

"That is correct," said the long-nosed peasant, in a heavy bass.

"Yes, sir," said the ex-soldier.

"The woman picked a handful of grass for her cow—they caught her—to jail with her," said the modest, kind-hearted old man.

"There is some land five versts from here, but it is beyond us to rent it; they have so raised the price that we can't make it pay," said the toothless, angry old man.

"They are twisting us into ropes, according to their will; it is worse than manorial labour," insisted the angry one.

"I think so, too," said Nekhlyúdov, "and I consider it a sin to own land. So I want to give it away."

"That is a good thing," said the old man with the Moses curls, apparently imagining that Nekhlyúdov wanted to let the land.

"That is why I have come here. I do not want to own any land, and now we must consider how I am to get rid of it."

"Give it to the peasants, that is all," said the toothless, angry old man.

Nekhlyúdov was for a moment embarrassed, for he understood these words as doubting the sincerity of his intentions. But he immediately regained his composure, and used this opportunity in order to express his thought.

"I should gladly give it to you," he said, "but to whom shall I give it, and how? To what peasants? Why to you people, and not to the Demínskoe peasants?" (This was a neighbouring village with beggarly parcels of land.)

All were silent. Only the ex-soldier said, "Yes, sir."

"So, tell me," said Nekhlyúdov, "what you would do, if the Tsar told you to take the land from the landowners and give it to the peasants?"

"What we would do? We would divide it all up evenly—peasant and landowner alike," said the oven-builder, rapidly raising and lowering his eyebrows.

"That is right. So much for each man," confirmed the kindhearted, lame peasant in the white leg-rags.

They all agreed to this solution, regarding it as satisfactory.

"What do you mean by each man?" asked Nekhlyúdov. "Are the house servants to get some, too?"

"Not at all," said the ex-soldier, trying to express cheerfulness in his face. But the thoughtful tall peasant did not agree with him.

"If it comes to dividing it up, all ought to get equal shares," he said, in his heavy bass, after a moment's thought.

"That it impossible," said Nekhlyúdov, having prepared his answer in advance. "If all are to get equal shares, those who do not themselves work, who do not plough, the gentry, the servants, the cooks, officials and clerks, everybody over in town, will take their shares and sell them to the rich people. And again the rich will acquire a lot of land. And those who live on their parcels will have an increase in their family, but all the land will have been already distributed. Again the rich men will get into their hands those who need the land."

"Yes, sir," the soldier hastened to add.

"There ought to be a prohibition against selling the land, and let those hold it who themselves plough it," said the oven-builder, angrily interrupting the soldier.

To this Nekhlyúdov replied that it would not be possible to watch whether one was ploughing for himself or for some one else.

Then the tall, thoughtful peasant proposed that they should plough it in partnership, and that it should be divided up among those who did the ploughing. "And those who did not plough should get nothing," he said, in his determined bass.

Against this communistic project Nekhlyúdov had arguments ready; he retorted that for this all the ploughs and horses would have to be the same, and that none should fall behind the others, or that everything, the horses, the ploughs, the threshing-machines, and the whole farm, would have to be commonly owned, and that for such a thing to be possible, everybody would have to be agreed.

"You will never succeed in making our people agree," said the angry old man.

"There will be nothing but brawls," said the old man with the white beard and smiling eyes.

"Then again, how is the land to be divided up according to its quality?" asked Nekhlyúdov. "Why should some get black loam, while others will have clay and sand?"

"Divide it up by parcels, then all will get equal shares," said the oven-builder.

To this Nekhlyúdov replied that it was not only a question of the distribution of the land in one commune, but in various provinces. If the land was to be given away to the peasants, some would have good lots and others bad ones. Everybody would wish to get the good land.

"Yes, sir," said the soldier.

The rest kept silent.

"So, you see, it is not as simple as you imagine," said Nekhlyúdov. "And not only we alone, but other people also are thinking about it. There is an American, George, who has reasoned it out like this, and I agree with him—"

"You are the master, so you give it away if you wish. As you will it," said the angry old man.

This interruption annoyed Nekhlyúdov, but, to his delight, he noticed that the others were also dissatisfied with this interruption.

"Wait, Uncle Semyón, let him tell it," the thoughtful peasant said, in his impressive bass.

This encouraged Nekhlyúdov, and he began to expound to them Henry

George's theory of the Single-tax. "The land is nobody's, it is the Lord's," he began.

"That is so. Yes, sir," several voices interposed.

"All the land is a common possession. Everybody has an equal right to it. But there is better and worse land, and everybody wants to get the good land. What is to be done, in order to equalize things? Let him who owns a good piece of land pay the price of it to those who have none," Nekhlyúdov answered his own question. "And as it is hard to determine who is to pay, and to whom he is to pay, and as money has to be collected for common purposes, it ought to be arranged in such a manner that he who owns a piece of land should pay the value of his land to the Commune for all public purposes. Then all will have equal chances. If you wish to own land, pay more for good land, and less for less good land. And if you do not wish to own any land, you pay nothing; but the taxes for the common needs will be paid by those who own the land."

"That is correct," said the oven-builder, moving his eyebrows. "He who has the better land ought to pay more."

"George had a great head," said the representative old man with the curls.

"If only the price is in our reach," said the tall man with the bass voice, evidently beginning to make out what it all tended to.

"The price ought to be neither too high nor too low. If it is too high, it will not pay, and there will be losses; and if too low, all will begin to buy the land of each other and there will be speculation in land. This system is what I want to establish among you."

"That is correct, that is right. That would be good," said the peasants.

"He had a great head," repeated the broad-chested man with the curls, "that George. He has thought it out well."

"How would it be if I wished to take a piece of land," the clerk said, smiling.

"If there is a free lot, take it and work it," said Nekhlyúdov.

"You do not need it. You have enough to eat as it is," said the old man with the smiling eyes.

This ended the consultation.

Nekhlyúdov again repeated his proposition; he did not ask for an immediate answer, but advised them to talk the matter over with the whole village, and then to come and give him an answer. The peasants promised they would do so, and, bidding him good-bye, went away in an excited mood. Their loud, receding conversation could long be heard on the road. Their voices dinned on until late in the evening and carried along the river from the village.

On the following day the peasants did not work but considered the master's proposition. The village was divided into two parties: one found the master's proposition profitable and harmless; the other saw in it some deception, the significance of which they could not comprehend, and of which they consequently were especially afraid. Two days later they, however, agreed to accept the proposed conditions and came to Nekhlyúdov to announce to him the decision of the Commune. This decision was greatly influenced by the opinion of an old woman, which the old men accepted as putting aside all fear of deception, and which consisted in explaining the master's act as arising from his meditating on his soul and desiring to save it. This explanation was also confirmed by the considerable monetary alms which Nekhlyúdov had distributed during his stay at Pánovo. His contributions of money were due to the fact that here he had for the first time found out the extreme degree of poverty and misery which the peasants had reached, and that, though he knew it to be unwise, he was so struck by that poverty that he could not help giving them money, of which he just then had a large sum, having received some for the forest at Kuzmínskoe, sold a year ago, and also an earnest for the sale of the inventory.

The moment they discovered that the master gave money to those who asked for it, crowds of people, especially women, began to come to him from all the surrounding country, begging for help. He was at a complete loss what to do with them and by what to be guided in solving the question how much to give and to whom. He felt that it was impossible for him not to give to those who asked him and obviously were poor, while he had a great deal of money; at the same time there was no sense in giving haphazardly to those who begged. The only way out of this position was to leave. This he hurried to do.

During the last day of his stay at Pánovo, Nekhlyúdov went into the house and began to sort through the things that were left there. Rummaging through them, he discovered many letters in the lower drawer of his aunts' old big-bellied mahogany chiffonier with bronze rings in lion heads, and among them was a group photograph: Sófya Ivánovna, Márya Ivánovna, himself as a student, and Katyúsha, clean, fresh, cheerful, and full of life. Of all the things that were in the house Nekhlyúdov took only the letters and this picture. Everything else he left for the miller, who, at the intercession of the smiling clerk, bought the house for removal and all the furniture of Pánovo at one-tenth their real value.

Recalling now the feeling of regret at the loss of his property which he had experienced at Kuzmínskoe, Nekhlyúdov wondered how he could have had such a feeling; now he experienced an unceasing joy of liberation and a sensation of novelty, such as a traveller must experience upon discovering new lands.

CHAPTER X

RETURN TO TOWN

The city struck Nekhlyúdov in an extremely strange and novel way on this trip to it. He drove in in the evening, when the lamps were all lighted, from the station to his house. There was still an odour of naphthalene in all the rooms. Agraféna Petróvna and Kornéi both felt worried and dissatisfied, and had even had a quarrel on account of cleaning up things, the use of which seemed to consist only in being hung out, aired, and put away again. Nekhlyúdov's room was not occupied, but not yet tidied; it was hard to move about in it among the many boxes, and it was evident that Nekhlyúdov's arrival interfered with the work, which by a certain strange inertia was going on in this house. After the impressions of the dire want in the village, all this appeared to Nekhlyúdov so disagreeable because of its apparent senselessness, of which he had once himself been guilty, that he decided to move to a hotel the next day, leaving Agraféna Petróvna to fix things according to her wishes until the arrival of his sister, who would make the final dispositions in regard to everything in the house.

Nekhlyúdov left the house early in the morning. In an establishment with modest, somewhat dirty, furnished rooms, which he found in the neighbourhood of the prison, he rented a suite of two rooms, and, having given orders for some things he had set aside in the house to be brought over, he went to see the lawyer.

It was cold outside. After the storms and rains there was a cold spell, as generally happens in spring. It was so chilly and the wind was so penetrating that Nekhlyúdov froze in his light overcoat and kept walking faster and faster, hoping to get warm.

Before his imagination rose the village people, the women, children, and old men, the poverty and exhaustion of whom he now seemed to have noticed for the first time, especially the smiling, wizened baby, twisting its calfless little legs—and he involuntarily compared what was in the city with them. Walking past butcher-shops, fish-markets, and clothing-stores he was startled, as if seeing it for the first time, by the well-fed appearance of such an immense number of clean and fat shopkeepers. There was not one person like this in the whole village. These people were evidently firmly convinced that efforts to cheat people, who knew nothing of their wares, were not only not an idle, but even a useful, occupation. Just as well-fed were the coachmen with their broad backs and buttons on their backs; and so were the porters in their gold-trimmed caps, and the chambermaids in their aprons and curly hair, and more especially the dashing cabmen with their shaven napes, who were sitting jauntily in their cabs, contemptuously and dissolutely watching the passers-by. In all these people he now involuntarily saw the same village people who, deprived of the land, had been driven to the city. Some of these had managed to adapt themselves to the conditions of city life and had become like masters and were satisfied with their situation; others in the city had fallen into conditions even worse than in the village and were even more pitiable. Such miserable creatures seemed to Nekhlyúdov the shoemakers whom Nekhlyúdov saw working in the window of a basement, the haggard, pale, dishevelled laundresses, who, with their lean, bared arms, were ironing at open windows, from which the soap-filled steam was rising in clouds, two house-painters whom Nekhlyúdov met, in aprons, in torn shoes on bare feet, and daubed from head to foot with paint. Their sleeves were rolled up above their elbows, and in their sunburnt, venous, feeble hands they were carrying a bucket of paint and cursing without interruption. Their faces were emaciated and angry. The same expression was to be seen on the dusty, swarthy draymen, shaking on their wagons. The same expression was on the swollen faces of the ragged men and women standing with their children at the street corners and begging alms. The same faces were to be seen in the open windows of the tavern which Nekhlyúdov happened to pass. At the dirty little tables, with bottles and a tea-service upon them and among which waiters in white kept bobbing, perspiring red-faced men sat with stupefied faces, shouting and singing in loud voices. One was sitting near the window, his eyebrows raised and his lips thrust forward, gazing in front of himself, as though trying to remember something.

"Why have they all gathered there?" thought Nekhlyúdov, involuntarily in-haling with the dust, which the chill wind wafted against him, the ubiquitous odour of rancid oil in the fresh paint.

In one of the streets he came across a procession of drays hauling some iron pieces, which made such a terrible noise on the uneven pavement that his ears and head began to ache. He started walking faster to get ahead of the procession, when suddenly he heard his name through the rumble of the iron. He stopped and saw a few steps ahead of him an officer with a sharp-pointed, waxed moustache and a smooth, shining face, who, sitting in a cab, waved his hand to him in a friendly manner, displaying by his smile a row of extremely white teeth.

"Nekhlyúdov, is it you?"

Nekhlyúdov's first sensation was that of pleasure.

"Ah, Shénbok," he said, with delight, but immediately considered that there was no reason whatsoever to be pleased.

It was the same Shénbok who had then come calling at his aunts'. Nekhlyúdov had long ago lost track of him, though he had heard that, despite his debts, having left the regiment and yet staying in the cavalry, he still managed somehow to stay in the world of the rich. His satisfied, cheerful aspect confirmed this.

"I am so glad I have caught you. For there is nobody in town. Well, friend, you have grown older," he said, stepping out of the cab and straightening out his shoulders. "I recognized you by your gait. Well, shall we dine together? Where can one get a good dinner here?"

"I do not know whether I shall have the time," answered Nekhlyúdov, thinking only of how to get rid of his comrade without offending him. "What are you here for?" he asked.

"Business, my friend. A business of guardianship. I am a guardian. I manage Samánov's affairs. You know, the rich man? He is cracked, but he has a hundred fifty thousand acres of land," he said, with especial pride, as though he himself had earned all that land. "His affairs had been dreadfully neglected. The whole land was in the hands of the peasants. They paid nothing, and there were back dues to the amount of eighty thousand roubles. I changed the whole matter in one year, and increased the trust by seventy per cent. Eh?" he asked him proudly.

Nekhlyúdov recalled that he had heard that this Shénbok, for the very reason that he had lost all his property and had unpaid debts, had by some special influence been appointed a guardian over the property of a rich old man, who was squandering his estate. It was evident that he was thriving on his trust.

"How can I get rid of him without offending him?" thought Nekhlyúdov, looking at that sleek, plump face with the pomaded moustache and listening to his goodhearted friendly prattle about where one could get a good dinner, and how he had managed the affairs of his trust.

"So where shall we dine?"

"I have no time," said Nekhlyúdov, looking at his watch.

"I say. There will be races to-night. Will you be there?"

"No, I won't."

"Do come. I no longer have horses of my own, but I bet on Gríshin's. Do you remember him? He has a good stable. So come, and let us have supper together."

"I can't eat supper with you either," Nekhlyúdov said, smiling.

"Now, how come? Where are you going now? If you want to, I will take you there."

"I am on my way to a lawyer. He's just around the corner," said Nekhlyúdov.

"Oh, you are doing something in the prison? Have you become a prison intercessor? The Korchágins were telling me about that," Shénbok, said smiling. "They have left town already. What is it? Tell me."

"Yes, yes, that is all true," replied Nekhlyúdov. "But I can't tell you about it in the street."

"True, true, you have always been odd. So, will you come to the races?"

"No, I cannot, and I do not want to. Please, do not be angry at me."

"Why should I be angry? Where are you staying?" he asked, and suddenly his face became serious, his eyes stood still, and his brows were raised. He was apparently trying to recall the address, and Nekhlyúdov suddenly observed the same dull expression in him that he had noticed in the man with the raised eyebrows and protruding lips which had struck him in the window of the tavern.

"How chilly it is! Eh?"

"Yes, yes!"

"You have the bundles?" Shénbok addressed the cabman.

"Well, good-bye, then. I am very, very glad to have met you," he said, and, firmly pressing Nekhlyúdov's hand, he leaped into the vehicle, waving his broad hand in a new, white, chamois-skin glove in front of his sleek face, and smiling a habitual smile with his unusually white teeth.

"Is it possible I was like him?" thought Nekhlyúdov, continuing on his way to the lawyer. "Yes, if not exactly like him, I had tried to be like him and had thought to pass all my life like that."

CHAPTER XI

THE VISIT TO THE LAWYER

The lawyer received Nekhlyúdov ahead of his turn, and at once proceeded to talk to him about the Menshóv case, which he had read immediately and which had provoked his indignation by its groundless accusation.

"It is a shocking affair," he said. "Very likely the fire was started by the owner himself, in order to get his insurance money, but the worst is that the guilt of the Menshóvs has not at all been proven. There is no evidence at all. This is due to the especial zeal of the examining magistrate and to the negligence of the prosecuting attorney. If the case came up not in the county court, but here, I should guarantee an acquittal and ask for no remuneration. Now, the other affair, the petition of Fedósya Biryukóva to his Majesty is ready. If you go to St. Petersburg, take it with you and hand it in in person, and ask for its consideration. Otherwise an inquiry will be made, and that will be the end of it. You must try and reach the people at the top."

"The sovereign?" asked Nekhlyúdov.

The lawyer laughed.

"That's the very top—the Highest of the High. But the top means the Secretary of the Commission for Appeals, or its chairman. Well, is that all for now?"

"No, I have had a letter from the sectarians," said Nekhlyúdov, taking the sectarians' letter out of his pocket. "It's an amazing case, if what they say is true. I'll try to see them to-day and find out what the story is."

"I see you have become a funnel, a neck of a bottle, through which the complaints are poured out from prison," the lawyer said, smiling. "It is too much; it will be beyond your strength."

"No, but this is a striking case," said Nekhlyúdov, and gave the following brief account: Some peasants gathered in their village to read the Gospels. The authorities came and dispersed them. On the following Sunday they gathered again, and this time a policeman was called who arrested them and took them to Court. The magistrate cross-examined them, the public prosecutor drew up an indictment, and the justices committed them for trial, and they were handed over to the Court. The assistant prosecutor accused them of a crime of which there was material evidence—some Gospels—and they were sentenced to exile. "This is something terrible," said Nekhlyúdov. "Can it be true?"

"What surprises you?"

"Everything. I can see how the policeman, who is under orders, might do it; but the assistant prosecuting attorney, who wrote out the accusation, is an educated man—"

"But this is where the mistake is made: we are accustomed to think that the prosecuting attorneys, the members of the courts in general, are a kind of new, liberal men. That was once true, but now it is quite different. They are officials, who are interested only in the twentieth of each month. They receive their salary, and they need more, and that is the limit of their principles. They will accuse, try, and sentence anybody you please."

"Do there really exist laws which permit them to deport a man for reading the Gospel in company with others?"

"Not only may he be sent to places not so far away, but even to hard labour in Siberia, if it is proved that, while reading the Gospel, he allowed himself to expound it differently from the way he is ordered to do, and that, consequently, he has disapproved of the exposition of the Church. It is considered blasphemy of the Orthodox faith in presence of the people, and, according to Article 196, this means deportation to Siberia for settlement."

"That is impossible."

"I am telling you the truth. I always say to the judicial people," continued the lawyer, "that I cannot help looking gratefully at them, because it is only due to their kindness that I, and you, and all of us, are not in jail. It is the easiest thing imaginable to have us sentenced to the loss of special privileges and have us deported to nearer regions."

"If that is so, and everything depends on the arbitrariness of the prosecuting attorney and of other persons, who may or may not apply a certain law, then what is the court for?"

The lawyer burst out into a merry laugh.

Tolstoy
Resurrection
page 218

"You are propounding fine questions! This, my friend, is philosophy. There is nothing to prevent discussing that. Come on Saturday. You will find at my house scholars, writers, artists. Then we shall discuss these theoretical questions," said the lawyer, pronouncing the words "theoretical questions" with ironical pathos. "You are acquainted with my wife, I think. So come!"

"I shall try to," replied Nekhlyúdov, conscious of telling a lie, and that if there was anything he would try it would be not to be in the evening at the lawyer's in the company of the scholars, writers, and artists, who would gather there. The laughter with which the lawyer had answered Nekhlyúdov's remark that the court had no meaning if the members of the court may or may not apply a law as they are minded to do, and the intonation with which he pronounced the words "philosophy" and "theoretical questions," showed Nekhlyúdov how differently he and the lawyer and, no doubt, the lawyer's friends looked at things, and how, notwithstanding the present gulf between him and his former comrades, such as Shénbok, he felt himself even farther removed from the lawyer and the people of his circle.

CHAPTER XII

A TALK WITH A CABDRIVER

It was far to the prison, and late, so Nekhlyúdov took a cab. In one of the streets the cabman, a man of middle age, with an intelligent and kindly face, turned to Nekhlyúdov and pointed to an immense house which was going up.

"See what an enormous house they are building," he said, as though he had a share in this structure and were proud of it.

Indeed it was a huge building and built in a complicated and unusual style. A solid scaffolding of immense pine timbers, held together by iron clamps, surrounded the structure which was going up, and it was separated from the street by a board fence. Workmen, daubed with mortar, were rushing to and fro, like ants, over the walks of the scaffolding: some were laying stones, others were cutting them into shape, while others carried full hods and barrels up and empty ones down again.

A stout, well-dressed gentleman, apparently the architect, standing near the scaffolding and pointing up, was saying something to a respectfully listening

Vladímir contractor. Through the gate, past the architect and contractor, empty wagons drove out into the street and loaded ones into the yard.

"How sure they all are, both those who work and those who make them work, that it must all be thus, that while their pregnant women work at home beyond their strength, and their children, in little caps, before their imminent death from starvation, smile like old people and twist their little legs, they must build this stupid and useless palace for some stupid and useless man—one of those very men who ruin and rob them," thought Nekhlyúdov, looking at this house.

"Yes, a fool's house," he loudly expressed his thought.

"How a fool's house?" the cabman protested, as though insulted. "It gives people work, and so it is not a fool's house."

"But this is useless work."

"It must be useful, or they would not build it," retorted the cabman, "and the people earn a living."

Nekhlyúdov grew silent, especially since it was not possible to carry on a conversation over the rattle of the wheels. Not far from the prison the cabman left the pavement for a country road, so that it was easy to talk, and he again turned to Nekhlyúdov.

"What a lot of people nowadays rush to the city—it is just terrible," he said, turning on his box and pointing to an artél of village workmen with files, axes, short fur coats, and bundles on their backs, who were coming toward them.

"Are there more of them than in previous years?" asked Nekhlyúdov.

"It is simply terrible the way they are crowding now in all places. The masters fling them around like chips. They are everywhere."

"Why so?"

"They have increased so much. There is no place for them."

"What of it if they have increased? Why don't they stay in the villages?"

"What are they to do in the villages? There is no land there."

Nekhlyúdov experienced a sensation which one has in a bruised spot. One seems eternally to strike it, as though on purpose, though this seems so, actually, merely because only blows on the sore spot are noticeable.

"Is it possible it is the same everywhere?" he thought. He began to inquire of the cabman how much land there was in his village, how much he himself had, and why he was living in the city.

"There are about two and a half acres for each man, sir. There are three of us holding it," the cabman was glad to inform him. "I have a father and a brother at home; another brother is in the army. They manage the farm. But there is nothing to manage, and so my brother wanted to go to Moscow."

"Is it not possible to rent land?"

"Where is one to rent it? The masters have squandered theirs. The merchants have got it all into their hands. You can't buy it from them, for they are working it themselves. There is a Frenchman on our estate. He has bought it from the former master, and he won't let anybody have it, and that is the end of it."

"What Frenchman?"

"Dufar the Frenchman. Maybe you have heard his name. He makes wigs for the actors in the large theatre, and that is a good business in which he has made much money. He has bought our lady's whole estate. Now he rules over us. He rides us as he pleases. Fortunately, he is a good man. Only his wife, who is a Russian, is such a dog that God save us from her. She robs the people. It is just terrible. Well, here is the prison. Where do you wish me to drive you? To the entrance? I think they don't admit now."

CHAPTER XIII

KATYÚSHA IN THE PRISON HOSPITAL

With faint heart and terror at the thought of how he would find Máslova to-day, and with that feeling of mystery which he found in her and in that congeries of people who were in this prison, Nekhlyúdov rang the bell at the main entrance and asked the warden who came out to him about Máslova. The warden made inquiries and informed him that she was in the hospital. A kind-hearted old man, the watch-man of the hospital immediately admitted him, and, upon learning who it was he wanted to see, directed him to the children's division.

A young doctor, all saturated with carbolic acid, came out to Nekhlyúdov in the corridor, and sternly asked him what he wanted. This doctor was very indulgent with the prisoners, and so he continually had unpleasant conflicts with the authorities of the prison, and even with the senior physician. Fearing lest Nekhlyúdov should ask something illegal of him, and, besides, wishing to show that he made no ex-ception for anybody, he pretended to be angry.

"There are no women here; this is the children's department," he said.

"I know; but there is an attendant here who has been transferred from the prison."

"Yes, there are two here. So what do you wish?"

"I am close to one of them, Máslova," said Nekhlyúdov. "I should like to see her: I am going to St. Petersburg to enter an appeal in her case, and I wanted to give her this. It is only a photograph," said Nekhlyúdov, taking out an envelope from his pocket.

"Well, you may do that," said the doctor, softening, and, turning to an old woman in a white apron, he told her to call the attendant, prisoner Máslova.

"Do you not wish to sit down or walk into the waiting-room?"

"Thank you," said Nekhlyúdov, and, making use of the doctor's favourable change, he asked him whether they in the prison were satisfied with Máslova.

"She will pass. She works fairly well, considering the conditions under which she has been," said the doctor. "And here she is."

From one of the doors came the old attendant, and back of her was Máslova. She wore a white apron over a striped garment and a kerchief on her head, which covered all her hair. Upon noticing Nekhlyúdov, her face became flushed, and she stopped as though in indecision; then she frowned, and, lowering her eyes, walked with rapid steps toward him over the corridor strip. As she approached Nekhlyú-dov, she had intended not to give him her hand, but she did extend it to him and blushed even more. Nekhlyúdov had not seen her since the conversation with her when she had excused herself for her excitability, and he expected to find her as she had been then. Now, however, she was quite different, and in the expression of her face there was something new: something restrained, bashful, and, as Nekhlyúdov thought, something hostile toward him. He repeated to her what he had said to the doctor, that he was going to St. Petersburg and handed her the envelope with the photograph, which he had brought with him from Pánovo.

"I found this at Pánovo. It is an old photograph, and may give you pleasure. Take it."

She raised her black eyebrows in surprise, looked at him with her squinting eyes, as though to say, "What is that for?" and silently took the envelope and put it behind her apron.

"I saw your aunt there," said Nekhlyúdov.

"You did?" she said, with indifference.

"Are you well here?" asked Nekhlyúdov.

"Yes, I am," she said.

"Is it not too hard?"

"No, not very. I am not yet used to it."

"I am very happy for your sake. In any case it is better than there."

"Than *where*?" she said, and her face was flushed with a blush.

"There, in the prison," Nekhlyúdov hastened to say.

"What makes it better?" she asked.

"I think the people are better here. There are none of the kind there were there."

"There are many good people there," she said.

"I have taken measures for the Menshóvs, and I hope they will be released," said Nekhlyúdov.

"God grant it. She is such a wonderful old woman," she said, repeating her definition of the old woman, and slightly smiling.

"I shall leave for St. Petersburg to-day. Our case will soon be heard, and I hope the verdict will be set aside."

"Whether it will be or not makes no difference now," she said.

"Why 'now' ?"

"Just does," she said, furtively casting a questioning glance at him.

Nekhlyúdov understood these words and this glance to mean that she wanted to know whether he still stuck to his determination or whether he had accepted her refusal and had accordingly changed it.

"I do not know why it is all the same to you," he said. "But to me it is really quite the same whether you will be acquitted or not. I am ready in any case to do what I said I would," he said, with determination.

She raised her head, and her black, squinting eyes rested on his face and past it, and all her face was beaming with joy. But she spoke something quite different from what her eyes were saying.

"There's no point in your saying this," she said.

"I say it that you may know."

"You have said it all, and there is nothing else to say," she replied, with difficulty restraining a smile.

There was a noise in the hospital room. A child's cry was heard.

"It seems they are calling me," she said, looking restlessly around.

"Well, good-bye, then," he said.

She tried to look as though she had not noticed the extended hand, and, without pressing it, she turned around and, trying to conceal her victory, with rapid strides walked away over the strip of the corridor.

"What is going on within her? What is she thinking about? How does she feel? Does she want to test me, or can she really not forgive me? Can she not, or does she not wish to tell me all she thinks and feels? Is she mollified, or hardened?" Nekhlyúdov asked himself, and could not find any answers. He knew this much, that she had changed, and that an important transformation was taking place in her soul, and this transformation connected him not only with her but also with Him, in whose name this transformation was being accomplished. This connection induced in him a joyously ecstatic and contrite condition.

Upon returning to the room, where eight children's beds were standing, Máslova began, at the nurse's request, to make the beds; in bending too far down with the sheet, she slipped and fell down. A convalescent boy, with a bandage around his neck, who had seen her fall, began to laugh, and Máslova herself could not restrain herself, and sat down on the bed and burst into such a loud and contagious laugh that several children, too, began to laugh, and the nurse scolded her.

"Don't yell like that! You think you are still where you were! Go get the food!"

Máslova grew silent and, taking the dishes, went where she had been ordered, but, upon glancing at the bandaged boy, who was not permitted to laugh, again snorted. Several times during the day, whenever Máslova was left alone, she half pulled the photograph out of the envelope and looked at it; but only in the evening, after her day's work, when left alone in the room, where she slept with another attendant, she drew the photograph entirely out of its envelope, and looked long and fixedly at the faded, yellowed picture, caressing with her eyes every detail of the faces, and dresses, and the steps of the porch, and the bushes, against which as a background his, her, and the aunts' faces had been thrown. She could not get enough of it, especially of herself, her young, beautiful face, with the hair coiling around the forehead. She looked so intently at it that she did not notice her companion coming into the room.

"What is this? Did he give it to you?" asked the stout, kindly attendant, bending over the photograph. "Is it possible it is you?"

"Who else?" said Máslova, smiling, and looking at the face of her companion.

"And who is this? Himself? And is this his mother?"

"An aunt. Would you have recognized me?" asked Máslova.

"No. Not for the world. It is an entirely different face. I suppose ten years have elapsed since then."

"Not years, but a whole life," said Máslova, and suddenly all her animation disappeared. Her face grew gloomy, and a deep wrinkle appeared between her eyebrows.

"I suppose life *there* was easy."

"Yes, easy!" repeated Máslova, closing her eyes and shaking her head. "Worse than hard labour."

"How so?"

"It was that way every night, from eight o'clock in the evening until four in the morning."

"Why, then, don't they give it up?"

"They want to, but they can't. What is the use of talking about it?" said Máslova. She jumped up, flung the photograph into the table drawer, and, with difficulty repressing her angry tears, ran out into the corridor, slamming the door after her. As she had been looking at the photograph, she had felt herself to be such as she was pictured there, and had dreamed of how happy she had then been and could be with him even now. The words of her companion reminded her of what she now was and had been there, reminded her of all the horror of that life, which she then had felt but dimly and had not permitted herself to become conscious of. Only now did she recall all those terrible nights, and especially one during Shrovetide, when she had been waiting for a student, who had promised to buy her out. She recalled how she was clad in a décolleté, wine-stained, red silk dress, with a red ribbon in her tangled hair; how, being tired out and weakened and drunk, she saw some guests off at two o'clock in the night; and how, during an interval between the dances, she seated herself near the lean, bony, pimpled woman who accompanied the fiddler, and complained to her of her hard life, and how that woman herself told her that she was tired of her occupation and wished to change it, and how Klára came up to them, and all three of them suddenly decided to quit this life. They thought that the night was ended and were on the point of retiring, when suddenly some drunken guests made a stir in the antechamber. The fiddler started a ritournelle, and the woman began to strike off an accompaniment to a hilarious Russian song in the first figure of a quadrille; suddenly a small, drunken, wine-sopped, and hiccoughing man, in a white tie and dress coat, which he later, in the second figure, took off, seized her, while another, a stout fellow, with a beard, also in a dress coat (they had just arrived from some ball), grasped Klára, and for a long time they whirled, danced, shouted, drank — And thus it went one year, two, three years. How can one help changing! He was the cause of it all. And within her rose her former fury against him, and she wanted to scold and upbraid him. She was sorry she had missed an opportunity to-day of telling him again that she knew him, and that she would not submit to him, that she would not permit him to use her spiritually as he had used her physically, that she would not permit him to make her an object of his magnanimity. In order in some measure to drown that tormenting feeling of regret at herself and of uselessly reproaching him, she wanted some liquor. And she would not have kept her word and would have drunk it, if she had been in the prison. But here it was not possible to get the liquor except from the surgeon's assistant, and she was afraid of the assistant, because he importuned her with his attentions. All relations with men were distasteful to her. Having sat awhile on a bench in the corridor, she returned to the cell, and, without replying to her companion's question, long wept over her ruined life.

CHAPTER XIV

NEKHLYÚDOV'S TRIP
TO ST. PETERSBURG

In St. Petersburg, Nekhlyúdov had three things to attend to: Máslova's appeal to the Senate for annulment, Fedósya Biryukóva's case in the Commission for Appeals, and, at Vyéra Bogodúkhovskaya's request, the affair in the Office of the Gendarmery, or the Third Division, for the liberation of Shústova, and for obtaining permission for a mother to see her son, who was kept in the fortress, as mentioned in Vyéra Bogodúkhovskaya's note. The last two cases he regarded as his third affair. Then there was a fourth matter, that of the sectarians, who were to be sent from their families to the Caucasus for reading and expounding the Gospel. He had promised, not so much to them as to himself, to do everything in his power in order to clear up this business.

Since his last visit to Máslennikov's house, especially after his journey to the country, Nekhlyúdov not so much decided to disregard, as with his whole being felt a disgust for, that circle in which he had lived until then—for that circle from which the suffering that is borne by millions of people in order to secure comforts and pleasures to a small number is so carefully concealed that the people belonging to that circle do not see, nor ever can see, this suffering and the consequent cruelty and criminality of their own lives. Nekhlyúdov could not now, without awkwardness and reproaching himself, converse with people of that circle. And still, the habits of all his former life drew him to that circle; and he was drawn to it by his family connections and by his friends; but, above everything else, in order to do what now interested him, in order to help Máslova and all those sufferers whom he wished to help, he had to invoke the help and services of the people of that circle whom he not only did not respect, but who frequently roused his indignation and contempt.

Upon arriving in St. Petersburg, he stopped with his maternal aunt, Countess Chárskaya, the wife of a former minister, and thus at once plunged into the very midst of that aristocratic society from which he had become estranged. This was unpleasant for him, but he could not act otherwise. If he had stopped at a hotel and not with his aunt, she would have been offended, whereas his aunt had influential connections and could be extremely useful to him in all the affairs to which he wished to devote himself.

"What do I hear about you? Marvellous things," Countess Ekaterína Ivánovna said to him, serving him coffee soon after his arrival. "*Vous posez pour un Howard!* You are helping criminals. You travel about prisons. You are mending things."

"No, I do not think so."

"Well, that is good. There must be some romance connected with it. Tell me about it."

Nekhlyúdov told her about his relations with Máslova exactly as they were.

"I remember, I remember. Poor Hélène told me something about it at the time when you were living with those old ladies. I think they wanted to marry you to that ward of theirs." (The Countess Ekaterína Ivánovna had always despised those paternal aunts of Nekhlyúdov's.) "So it's she. *Elle est encore jolie?*"

Aunt Ekaterína Ivánovna was a woman of sixty, healthy, gay, energetic, and talkative. She was tall and plump, and on her upper lip a black moustache was discernible. Nekhlyúdov liked her and ever since his childhood was easily infected by her energy and cheerfulness.

"No, *ma tante,* all that is ended. I only want to help her, because, in the first place, she has been unjustly sentenced, and I am to blame for it, as I am to blame for her whole fate. I feel myself under obligation to do all I can for her."

"But I have been told that you want to marry her?"

"Yes, I wanted to, but she does not consent."

Ekaterína Ivánovna, smoothing out her brow and lowering her pupils, looked at her nephew in surprise and silence. Suddenly her countenance was changed, and pleasure was expressed upon it.

"Well, she has more sense than you have. Oh, what a fool you are! And you would have married her?"

"By all means."

"After what she has been?"

"So much the more. I am to blame for it."

"No, you are simply a dummy," his aunt said, repressing a smile. "A terrible dummy, but I love you for being such a terrible dummy," she repeated, evidently taking a liking to this word, which, in her opinion, precisely rendered the mental and moral condition of her nephew. "You know this is very opportune," she continued. "Aline has a remarkable home for Magdalens. I was there once. They are horrid, and I did nothing but wash myself afterward. But Aline is *corps et âme* in it. So we shall send that woman of yours to her. If anybody is to mend her ways, it must be Aline."

"But she is sentenced to hard labour. I have come here to appeal from the verdict. This is the first business I have with you."

"Indeed? Where does that case of hers go to?"

"To the Senate."

"To the Senate? Yes, my dear cousin Lyóvushka is in the Senate. However, he is in the department of fools—heraldry. I do not know any of the real Senators. They are all God knows who, or Germans: G, F, D, *tout l'alphabet,* or all kinds of Ivánovs, Semyónovs, Nikítins, or Ivanénkos, Simonénkos, Nikiténkos, *pour varier. Des gens de l'autre monde.* Still, I shall tell my husband. He knows them. He knows all kinds of people. I shall tell him, but you had better explain matters to him, for he never understands me. Whatever I say, he says he does not understand. *C'est un parti pris.* Everybody else understands, but he does not."

Just then a lackey in knee-breeches brought a letter on a silver tray.

"Just from Aline. You will hear Kiesewetter there."

"Who is Kiesewetter?"

"Kiesewetter? You come today, and you will find out who he is. He speaks so eloquently that the most inveterate criminals kneel down and weep and repent."

Countess Ekaterína Ivánovna, however strange this may seem, and however little it comported with her character, was a fervent adherent of the doctrine according to which the essence of Christianity consisted in belief in redemption. She attended meetings where this then fashionable doctrine was preached, and gathered these devotees about her. Notwithstanding the fact that according to this doctrine all ceremonies, icons, and even mysteries were denounced, Countess Ekaterína Ivánovna had icons not only in all the rooms, but even over her bed, and continued to comply with all the demands of the Church, seeing no contradiction in all that.

"Your Magdalen ought to hear him; she would become converted," said the countess. "Stay home tonight. You will hear him. He is a remarkable man."

"That does not interest me, *ma tante.*"

"But I tell you, it is interesting. And you be sure and come. Tell me what else you want of me? *Videz votre sac.*"

"I have some business in the fortress."

"In the fortress? Well, I can give you a note to Baron Kriegsmut. *C'est un très brave homme.* You yourself know him. He was a friend of your father's. *Il donne dans le spiritisme.* Well, that is not so bad. He is a good fellow. What do you want there?"

"I want to ask permission for a mother to see her son who is confined there. But I have been told that this does not depend on Kriegsmut, but on Chervyánski."

"I do not like Chervyánski, but he is Mariette's husband. I can ask her. She will do it for my sake. *Elle est très gentille.*"

"I want also to ask about a woman. She has been in the fortress for several months, and nobody knows why."

"Don't tell me that. She certainly knows why. They all know. It serves them right, those short-haired ones."

"We do not know whether right or not. In the meantime they suffer. You are a Christian and believe in the Gospel, and yet you are so pitiless."

"That has nothing to do with it. The Gospel is one thing, and what we despise is another. It would be worse if I should pretend to love nihilists, and especially short-haired nihilists, when, in reality, I hate them."

"Why do you hate them?"

"Do you ask me why after March first?"*

"But not all of them have taken part in the affair of March first."

"It makes no difference: let them keep out of what does not concern them. That is not a woman's business."

"But Mariette, you think, may attend to business," said Nekhlyúdov.

"Mariette? Mariette is Mariette. And that other one is God knows who—some Khaltyúpkina who wants to instruct everybody."

"They do not want to instruct but to help the people."

"We know without them who is to be helped and who not."

"But the people are suffering. I've just come back from the country. Is it right that the peasants should work as hard as they can without getting enough to eat, while we live in extreme luxury?" said Nekhlyúdov, involuntarily drawn on by his aunt's good-heartedness to tell her all he was thinking.

"Do you want me to work and eat nothing?"

"No, I do not want you to starve," Nekhlyúdov replied, with an involunatry smile. "All I want is that we should all work and all have enough to eat."

His aunt again looked askance, staring at him with curiosity.

"*Mon cher, vous finirez mal*," she said.

"But why?"

Just then a tall, broad-shouldered general entered the room. That was the husband of Countess Chárskaya, an ex-minister.

"Ah, Dmítri, hello," he said, offering him his freshly shaven cheek. "When did you arrive?"

He silently kissed his wife's forehead.

"*Non, il est impayable*," Countess Ekaterína Ivánovna turned to her husband. "He tells me to go down to the river to wash the linen, and to eat nothing but potatoes. He is a terrible fool, but still you do for him what he asks you. He is a terrible dummy," she corrected herself. "Have you heard, they say Kámenskaya is in such despair that they are afraid for her life," she addressed her husband. "You had better call on her."

"That is terrible," said her husband.

"You go and have a talk with him, for I must write some letters."

Nekhlyúdov had just gone into the room next to the drawing-room, when she called out to him:

"Shall I write to Mariette?"

* Alexander II was assassinated March 1, 1881 (Old Style).

"If you please, *ma tante*."

"So I shall leave *en blanc* what you wish to say about that short-haired one, and she will tell her husband. And he will do it. Don't think that I am a malicious woman. They are all very, very horrid, those protégées of yours, but *je ne leur veux pas de mal*. Pay no attention to them. Well, go on! By all means be at home in the evening, and you will hear Kiesewetter. And we shall pray. If only you won't resist it, *ça vous fera beaucoup de bien*. I know both Hélène and all of you are way behind in this. So, good-bye."

CHAPTER XV

COUNT CHÁRSKI. NEKHLYÚDOV CALLS ON MARIETTE

Count Iván Mikhályovich was an ex-minister and a man of very firm convictions.

The convictions of Count Iván Mikháylovich had from his earliest youth consisted in this: just as it is proper for a bird to feed on worms, to be clad in feathers and down, and to fly through the air, so it was proper for him to feed on costly dishes, prepared by expensive cooks, to be clad in the most comfortable and expensive garments, to travel with the best and the fastest horses, and to expect everything to be ready for him. Besides this, Count Iván Mikháylovich considered that the more kinds of various amounts he received from the treasury, and the more decorations, inclusive of all kinds of diamond tokens, he should have, and the more often he met and spoke with distinguished personages, the better things were. Everything else, in comparison with these fundamental dogmas, Count Iván Mikháylovich regarded as uninteresting and insignificant. Everything else might be as it was, or the reverse, for all he was concerned. Iván Mikháylovich lived and acted in St. Petersburg for forty years in conformity with this belief, until at last he reached the post of minister.

The chief qualities of Count Iván Mikháylovich, by means of which he attained this post, consisted, in the first place, in his ability to comprehend the meaning of documents and laws and to compose comprehensible, if not entirely grammatical documents, without any spelling mistakes; in the second place, he was very much a representative, and, wherever it was necessary, he was able to give an impression not only of haughtiness, but also of inaccessibility and majesty, and, on the other hand, wherever this was necessary, to be servile to the point of self-effacement and baseness; in the third place, he had no general principles or rules, either of personal or of state morality, so that he could agree with everybody, if this was necessary, or equally well disagree with everybody, if that was necessary. In proceeding in this manner, he was concerned only about preserving his tone and not manifesting any palpable contradiction to himself; but he was quite indifferent as to whether his acts were in themselves moral or immoral, or whether from them any great good or great evil would accrue to the Russian Empire or to the rest of Europe.

When he became minister, not only those who depended upon him (and there were very many people and close friends who depended upon him), but even all outsiders, and he himself, were convinced that he was a very wise statesman. But when some time passed and he had done nothing, had shown nothing, and when, by the law of the struggle for existence, just such men as he, who had learned how to write and comprehend documents, and who were representative and unprincipled officials, had pushed him out, and he was compelled to ask for his discharge, it became clear to everybody that he was not only not a very intelligent man, but even a man of very limited capacities and of little culture, though a self-confident man, whose views barely reached the level of the lead articles in the most vulgar conservative papers. It turned out that there was nothing in him which distinguished him from other little-educated, self-confident officials, who had pushed him out, and he himself came to see that, but this did not in the least shake his convictions that he must every year receive a large sum of government money and new decorations for his parade uniform. This conviction was so strong in him that nobody dared to refuse them to him, and each year he received, partly in the form of a pension, and partly in the form of remuneration for his membership in a higher state institution, and for presiding over various commissions and committees, several tens of thousands of roubles, and, besides, each year new rights highly esteemed by him to sew new galloons on his shoulders or pantaloons, and to attach new ribbons and enamelled stars to his dress coat. In consequence of this Count Iván Mikháylovich had great connections.

Count Iván Mikháylovich listened to Nekhlyúdov just as he used to listen to the report of his secretary, and having heard all he had to say, told him that he would give him two notes, one to Senator Wolff, in the Department of Cassation.

"They say all kinds of things about him, but *dans tous les cas c'est un homme très comme il faut*," he said. "He is under obligation to me, and he will do what he can."

The other note Iván Mikháylovich gave him was to an influential person in the Commission for Appeals. The case of Fedósya Biryukóva, as Nekhlyúdov told it to him, interested him very much. When Nekhlyúdov told him that he wanted to write a letter to the Empress, he said that it really was a very pathetic case, and that he would tell it there, whenever an opportunity should offer itself. But he could not promise to do so. He had better send in the petition any way. But if there should be a chance, he said, if they should call him to a *petit comité* on Thursday, he would probably tell it.

Having received the two notes from the count, and the note to Mariette from his aunt, Nekhlyúdov at once went to all those places.

First of all he went to Mariette. He used to know her as a young girl; he knew that she was the daughter of a poor, aristocratic family, and that she had married a man who had made a career and of whom he had heard some very bad things, chiefly that he showed not the least clemency for the hundreds and thousands of political prisoners whom it was his official duty to torture. Nekhlyúdov, as always, found it unbearable that, in order to aid the oppressed, he had to stand on the side of the oppressors, seeming to sanction their activities through the mere act of applying to them with a request that they slightly modify their cruelty, at least in respect to certain individuals—a cruelty which had become habitual with them and which they themselves were probably unaware of. In such cases he always felt an internal discord, a dissatisfaction with himself, and a wavering, whether he should ask or not, and he always decided that he should. The thing was that he would feel awkward, ashamed, uneasy at Mariette's and her husband's; but perhaps, on the other hand, an unhappy woman, tormented by solitary confinement, would be released and would stop suffering, she and her family. Besides being conscious of the unnaturalness of his position as a petitioner among people whom he did not regard as his own, but who considered him as theirs, in that society he felt that he was entering his former habitual routine and that he involuntarily succumbed to the frivolous and immoral tone which reigned in that circle. He had experienced this even at the house of his aunt Ekaterína Ivánovna. He had that very morning fallen into a jocular tone, as he had been talking to her about the most serious things.

St. Petersburg in general, where he had not been for a long time, produced upon him its usual physically bracing and morally dulling effect. Everything was so clean, so comfortable, and so well-arranged, but, above everything else, people were morally so little exacting that life seemed to be easy there.

A beautiful, clean, polite cabman took him past beautiful, polite, and clean policemen, over a beautiful, smooth pavement, past beautiful, clean houses, to the one in which Mariette lived.

At the entrance stood a span of English horses in blinders; and an English-looking coachman, with side-whiskers up to the middle of his cheeks, and in livery, sat on the box, holding a whip and gazing around.

A porter in an uncommonly clean uniform opened the door to the vestibule, where stood, in still cleaner livery with galloons, a carriage lackey with superbly combed side-whiskers and an orderly in a new, clean uniform.

"The general is not receiving. Nor is the lady. She is going out in a minute."

Nekhlyúdov handed him the letter from Countess Ekaterína Ivánovna, and, taking out a visiting-card, went up to a small table on which lay a book for the registry of visitors, and began to write that he was very sorry not to find her at home, when the lackey moved up to the staircase, the porter went out to the entrance, and the orderly straightened himself up, with his hands down his legs, in a motionless attitude, meeting and following with his eyes a small, lean lady, who was walking down the staircase with a rapid gait, which did not comport with her dignity.

Mariette wore a large hat with a feather, a black gown, a black mantle, and new, black gloves; her face was covered with a veil.

Upon noticing Nekhlyúdov, she raised her veil, displayed a very sweet face with gleaming eyes, and looked at him interrogatively.

"Ah, Prince Dmítri Ivánovich," she exclaimed, in a merry, pleasant voice. "I should have recognized—"

"What, you even remember my name?"

"Certainly. My sister and I were even in love with you," she said, in French. "But how you have changed! What a pity I am driving out. However, let us go back," she said, stopping in indecision.

She looked at the clock.

"No, it is impossible. I must go to Kámenskaya's for a mass for the dead. She is terribly cast down."

"Who is Kámenskaya?"

"Have you not heard? Her son was killed in a duel. He fought with Pózen. An only son. Terrible. The mother is so very much cast down."

"Yes, I have heard."

"No, I had better go, and you come to-morrow, or this evening," she said, walking through the entrance door with rapid, light steps.

"I cannot come this evening," he answered, walking out on the front steps with her. "I have some business with you," he said, looking at the span of bay horses, which drove up to the steps.

"What is it?"

"Here is a note from my aunt about it," said Nekhlyúdov, handing her a narrow envelope with a large monogram. "You will see from this what it is."

"I know, Countess Ekaterína Ivánovna thinks that I have some influence on my husband in business matters. She is wrong. I cannot and will not interfere. But, of course, for the countess and for you I shall depart from my rules. What is it?" she said, in vain trying to find her pocket with her small hand in the black glove.

"There is a girl who is confined in the fortress; she is ill, and not guilty."

"What is her name?"

"Shústova. Lídiya Shústova. You will find it in the note."

"Very well, I shall try to do it," she said, lightly stepping into the softly cushioned carriage which glistened in the sun with the lacquer of its wings. She opened her parasol. The lackey sat down on the box, and gave the coachman a sign to drive on. The carriage started, but the same minute she touched the coachman's back with her parasol, and the slender-legged, handsome, short-tailed mares stopped, compressing their reined-in beautiful heads, and stamping with their slender feet.

"Do come, but, if you please, disinterestedly," she said, smiling a smile, the power of which she knew very well. The performance, so to say, being over, she drew down the curtain—let down her veil. "Well, let's go," and she again touched the coachman with the parasol.

Nekhlyúdov raised his hat. The thoroughbred bay mares, snorting, struck their hoofs against the pavement, and the carriage rolled off swiftly, now and then softly bouncing with its new tires over the unevennesses of the road.

CHAPTER XVI

NEKHLYÚDOV VISITS SENATOR WOLFF

Recalling the smile which he had exchanged with Mariette, Nekhlyúdov shook his head at himself:

"Before you even look around, you're again drawn into that life," he thought, experiencing that internal dissension and those doubts awakened in him by the necessity of invoking the help of people whom he did not respect. He considered where he should go first, where later, so as not to recross his way, and started off to the Senate. Upon arriving there, he was led into the chancery, where, in a magnificent room, he saw an immense number of exceedingly polite and clean officials.

Máslova's petition had been received and submitted for consideration and report to that same Senator Wolff, to whom he had a letter from his uncle, so the officials told Nekhlyúdov.

"There will be a meeting of the Senate this week, but Máslova's case will hardly come up then. But if it should be requested, there is hope that it might come up this week, on Wednesday," said one.

In the chancery of the Senate, while waiting for the information, Nekhlyúdov again heard a conversation about the duel and a detailed account of how Kámenski had been killed. Here he for the first time heard all the details of the story which interested all St. Petersburg. Some officers had been eating oysters in a shop, and, as usual, drinking a great deal. Someone said something uncomplimentary about the regiment in which Kámenski was serving: Kámenski called him a liar. The other struck Kámenski. The following day they duelled, and Kámenski was hit by a bullet in the abdomen, and died from it in two hours. The murderer and the seconds were arrested, but it was said, although they were now confined in the guard-house, they would be released in two weeks.

From the chancery of the Senate, Nekhlyúdov drove to the Commission for Appeals to see there an influential official, Baron Vorobyóv, who occupied superb quarters in a government house. The porter and the lackey sternly informed Nekhlyúdov that the baron could not be seen on any but reception-days, that he now was at the Emperor's palace, and that on the next day he would have to report there again. Nekhlyúdov left his letter, and went to Senator Wolff.

Wolff, who had just breakfasted, and, as usual, was encouraging his digestion by smoking a cigar and walking up and down in his room, received Nekhlyúdov. Vladímir Vasílevich Wolff was, indeed, *un homme très comme il faut*, and this quality he placed higher than anything else. From this height he looked at all other people, nor could he help highly valuing this quality, since, thanks only to this, he had made a brilliant career, such as he had wished to make: that is, by his marriage he had acquired property giving him an income of eighteen thousand roubles, and by his own labours he had risen to the rank of a Senator. He not only regarded himself *un homme très comme il faut*, but also a man of chivalrous honesty. By honesty he understood his rule not to take secret bribes from private individuals. But he did not consider it dishonest to extort from the government all kinds of travelling expenses, post moneys, and rentals, in return for which he servilely executed what even the government did not demand of him. To ruin and destroy, to be the cause of the deportation and incarceration of hundreds of innocent people, for their attachment to the people and to the religion of their fathers, as he had done while a governor of one of the provinces of the Kingdom of Poland, he not only did not consider dishonest, but even an act of noble-mindedness, courage, and patriotism. Nor did he regard it as dishonest to fleece his wife, who was enamoured of him, and his sister-in-law. On the contrary, he looked upon this as a wise arrangement of his domestic life.

Vladímir Vasílevich's family consisted of his impersonal wife, her sister, whose property he had also taken into his hands, and whose estate he had sold, depositing the money in his own name, and a meek, timid, homely daughter, who was leading a hard, isolated life, from which she of late found distraction in evangelism, in the meetings at Aline's and at Countess Ekaterína Ivánovna's. Vladímir Vasílevich's son, a good-hearted fellow, who had had a beard at fifteen and had been drinking and leading a dissolute life since then, continuing to live thus to his twentieth year, had been driven out of the house for not having graduated from anywhere and for compromising his father by moving in bad society and making debts. His father had once paid 230 roubles for him, and another time 600 roubles, when he informed him that this was the last time, that if he did not improve he would drive him out of the house and would break off all connections with him. His son not only did not improve, but even made another debt of 1,000 roubles, and, besides, took the liberty of telling his father that it was a torment for him to live in his house. Then Vladímir Vasílevich informed his son that he could go where he pleased, that he was not a son to him. Since then Vladímir Vasílevich pretended that he had no son, and no one in the house ever dared to talk to him about his son, and Vladímir Vasílevich was absolutely convinced that his family life was arranged in the best manner possible.

Wolff stopped in the middle of his promenade in the room, with a gracious and somewhat ironical smile (that was his mannerism, the involuntary expression of his consciousness of his *comme il faut* superiority above the majority of men) greeted Nekhlyúdov, and read the note.

"Please be seated, and pardon me. I shall continue to walk, if you will permit it," he said, placing his hands in the pockets of his jacket, and treading with soft, light steps along the diagonal of the cabinet, which was appointed in severe style. "I am very happy to make your acquaintance and, of course, to be able to do Count Iván Mikháylovich a favour," he said, emitting a fragrant bluish puff of smoke and cautiously removing the cigar from his mouth, in order not to drop the ashes.

"I should like to ask you to consider the case as early as possible, so that the prisoner may go to Siberia as soon as possible, if she has to go at all," said Nekhlyúdov.

"Yes, yes, by the first steamers from Nízhni-Nóvgorod—I know," said Wolff, with his condescending smile, knowing always in advance what people were going to tell him. "What is the prisoner's name?"

"Máslova—"

Wolff went up to the table and looked at a paper which was lying on a box with documents.

"Yes, yes, Máslova. Very well. I shall ask my associates about it. We shall take the case under advisement on Wednesday."

"May I wire the lawyer that?"

"You have a lawyer? What is that for? If you wish, you may."

"The causes for appeal may be insufficient," said Nekhlyúdov, "but it may be seen from the case that the verdict was due to a misunderstanding."

"Yes, yes, that may be so, but the Senate does not consider the case on its essential merit," sternly said Vladímir Vasílevich, looking at the ashes. "The Senate is concerned only about the correct application and exposition of the laws."

"This seems to me to be an exceptional case."

"I know, I know. All cases are exceptional. We shall do all we can. That is all." The ashes still held on, but had a crack and were in imminent peril. "But you're seldom in Petersburg?" said Wolff, holding his cigar in such a way that the ashes could not fall down. But the ashes trembled, and Wolff cautiously carried his cigar to the ash-tray, into which they dropped.

"What a terrible incident that was with Kámenski," he said. "A fine young man. An only son. Especially his mother's condition," he said, repeating almost the identical words that all St. Petersburg was at that time saying about Kámenski. Having said something about Countess Ekaterína Ivánovna and her infatuation for the new religious movement, which Vladímir Vasílevich neither condemned nor approved of, and which was manifestly superfluous to him in his *comme il faut* state, he rang a bell.

Nekhlyúdov bowed himself out.

"If it is convenient to you, come to dinner," Wolff said, giving him his hand, "say, on Wednesday. I shall then give you a decisive answer."

It was late, and Nekhlyúdov drove home, that is, to his aunt's.

CHAPTER XVII

DINNER AT THE CHÁRSKIS'

Dinner was served at Ekaterína Ivánovna's at half-past seven in a new fashion, which Nekhlyúdov had not seen before. The dishes were placed on the table, and the lackeys went out at once, so that the diners helped themselves to the food. The gentlemen did not permit the ladies to exert themselves by superfluous movements, and, being the strong sex, bravely attended to the labour of filling the ladies' and their own plates with food, and filling their glasses with drinks. When one course was consumed, the countess pressed the button of an electric bell on the table, and the lackeys entered noiselessly, rapidly, cleaned off the table, changed the dishes, and brought the next course. The dinner was excellent, and so were the wines. In the large, well-lighted kitchen a French chef was busy with two assistants in white. There were six persons at the table: the count and the countess, their son, a gloomy officer of the Guards, who put his elbows on the table, Nekhlyúdov, a French companion, and the count's manager, who had come up from the country.

The conversation here, too, turned upon the duel. They discussed the Emperor's view of the affair. It was known that the Emperor was very much grieved for the mother, and all were grieved for the mother. But, as it was also known that, although the Emperor sympathized with her, he did not wish to be severe on the murderer, who had defended the honour of his uniform, all were condescending to the murderer, who had defended the honour of his uniform. Countess Ekaterína Ivánovna alone, with her frivolous free ideas, condemned him.

"I would not forgive them for anything in the world for carousing and killing innocent young men," she said.

"I cannot understand that," said the count.

"I know that you never understand what I say," said the countess, turning to Nekhlyúdov. "Everybody understands except my husband. I say that I am sorry for the mother, and that I do not want them to kill and to be content."

Then the son, who had been silent until now, defended the murderer and attacked his mother, proving to her in a rather coarse manner that the officer could not have acted differently, that if he had he would have been expelled from the regiment by a court of officers. Nekhlyúdov listened, without taking part in the conversation; having been an officer, he understood, though he did not approve, the proofs which young Chárski adduced; at the same time he involuntarily compared the officer who had killed another with the prisoner, the fine-looking young fellow, whom he had seen in prison, and who had been sentenced to hard labour for killing a man in a brawl. Both became murderers through drinking. The peasant had killed in a moment of excitement, and he was separated from his wife, his family, his relatives, was chained in fetters, and with a shaven head was on his way to hard labour, while the officer was sitting in a beautiful room at the guard-house, eating good dinners, drinking good wine, and reading books, and in a few days he would be let out, continuing his previous life, only having become a more interesting person for his deed.

He said what he thought about the matter. At first Countess Ekaterína Ivánovna agreed with her nephew, but later she was silent.

Nekhlyúdov felt, like the rest, that with his story he had, as it were, committed an impropriety.

In the evening, after dinner, chairs with high carved backs were placed in the parlour, as though for a lecture, in rows, and in front of the table was put a chair with a small table, with a decanter of water for the preacher, and people began to congregate, to listen to the sermon of the newly arrived Kiesewetter.

Near the entrance stood expensive carriages. In the luxuriously furnished parlour sat ladies in silk, velvet, and laces, with false hair and tightly laced or padded waists. Between the women sat gentlemen, military persons and private citizens, and five men from the lower classes: two janitors, a shopkeeper, a lackey, and a coachman.

Kiesewetter, a strongly built, gray-haired man, spoke in English, and a lean young lady, with eye-glasses, translated rapidly and well.

He said that our sins were so great, and the punishment for these was so great and unavoidable, that it was impossible to live in expectation of this punishment.

"Let us only think, dear sisters and brethren, of ourselves, of our lives, of what we are doing, how we are living, how we anger long-suffering God, how we cause Christ to suffer, and we shall see that there is no forgiveness for us, no issue, no salvation—that we are all doomed to perdition. A terrible doom, eternal torments await us," he said, in a weepy, trembling voice. "How are we to be saved, brethren, how are we to be saved from this terrible conflagration? It has already seized the house, and there is no issue from it!"

He grew silent, and real tears flowed down his cheeks. He had been delivering this speech for eight years, without any errors, and whenever he reached that passage of the sermon he himself liked so much he was seized by convulsions in his throat, and tickling in his nose, and tears began to flow from his eyes.

And these tears touched him still more. Sobs were heard in the room. Countess Ekaterína Ivánovna sat near a mosaic table, leaning her head on both her arms, and her fat shoulders shook convulsively. The coachman looked in surprise and fear at the foreigner, as though he had driven right into him with the shaft, and he did not budge. The majority sat in poses similar to that of Countess Ekaterína Ivánovna. Wolff's daughter, who looked like him, in a fashionable garment, was on her knees, covering her face with her hands.

The orator suddenly revealed his face and smiled that strikingly real-looking smile by which actors express joy, and began to speak in a sweet and tender voice:

"There is a salvation. Here it is: it is easy and blissful. This salvation is the blood of the only begotten Son of God, who has allowed Himself to be tormented for our sakes. His suffering, His blood saves us. Sisters and brethren," he again said, with tears in his eyes, "let us praise the Lord who has given His only begotten Son for the redemption of the human race. His holy blood—"

Nekhlyúdov was overcome by such a painful feeling of nausea that he softly rose and, frowning and repressing a groan of shame, walked out on tiptoe and went to his room.

CHAPTER XVIII

MARIETTE'S NOTE.
BARON VOROBYÓV

On the following day, just as Nekhlyúdov had finished dressing and was on the point of going down-stairs, a lackey brought him the visiting-card of the Moscow lawyer. The lawyer had arrived to look after his affairs and, at the same time, to be present at the discussion of Máslova's case in the Senate, if it was to be heard soon. The telegram which Nekhlyúdov had sent him had missed him. Upon hearing from Nekhlyúdov when Máslova's case was to come up and who the Senators were, he smiled.

"There you have all three types of Senators," he said: "Wolff is a Petersburg official; Skovoródnikov is a learned jurist; and B is a practical jurist, consequently the liveliest of them all," said the lawyer. "There is most hope in him. And how is it about the Commission for Appeals?"

"I am going down to see Baron Vorobyóv today. I could not see him yesterday."

"Do you know how Vorobyóv comes to be a baron?" said the lawyer, replying to the somewhat comical intonation with which Nekhlyúdov had pronounced this foreign title in connection with such a Russian name. "It was Paul rewarded his grandfather, a lackey of the chamber, I think, for some great favour of his, as much as to say: 'Have a baronetcy, and don't interfere with my pleasure!' That's how the race of Barons Vorobyóv got started. He is very proud of it. And he is an old fox."

"I am on my way to see him," said Nekhlyúdov.

"Very well, let us go together. I will take you down to his house."

Nekhlyúdov was already in the antechamber, being on the point of leaving, when he was met by a lackey with a note from Mariette:

"Pour vous faire plaisir, j'ai agi tout à fait contre mes principes, et j'ai intercédé auprès de mon mari pour votre protégée. Il se trouve que cette personne peut être relâchée immédiate-ment. Mon mari a écrit au commandant. Venez donc disinterestedly. *Je vous attends.* м."

"What's this?" Nekhlyúdov said to the lawyer. "This is simply terrible. The woman whom he has been keeping for seven months in solitary confinement proves to be innocent, and, in order to release her, it was only necessary to say the word."

"It is always that way. At least, you have got what you wanted."

"Yes, but this success grieves me. Just think what must be going on there! What were they keeping her for?"

"Well, it would be better not to try to get to the bottom of that. So let me take you down," said the lawyer, as they came out to the front steps, and a fine carriage, which the lawyer had hired, drove up to the entrance.

"You want to go to Baron Vorobyóv?"

The lawyer told the coachman where to drive, and the good horses soon brought Nekhlyúdov to the house which the baron occupied. The baron was at home. In the first room were two young ladies and a young official in uniform, with an exceedingly long neck and a bulging Adam's apple, and an extremely light gait.

"Your name?" the young official with the bulging Adam's apple asked, passing with an extremely light and graceful gait from the ladies to Nekhlyúdov.

Nekhlyúdov told him his name.

"The baron has mentioned you. Directly !"

The young official went through the closed door and escorted out of the room a lady in mourning, who was in tears. The lady with her bony fingers adjusted the tangled veil, in order to conceal her tears.

"Please," the young official turned to Nekhlyúdov, walking with a light step over to the door, opening it, and stopping.

Upon entering the study, Nekhlyúdov found himself in front of a middle-sized, stocky, short-haired man in half-uniform, who was sitting in an armchair at a large desk and cheerfully looking in front of him. His good-natured face, which stood out quite prominently with its ruddy blush from the white moustache and beard, formed itself into a gracious smile at the sight of Nekhlyúdov.

"Very glad to see you. Your mother and I were old friends. I used to see you when you were a boy, and later as an officer. Sit down and tell me what I can do for you. Yes, yes," he said, shaking his close-cropped gray head as Nekhlyúdov was telling him Fedósya's history. "Go on, go on, I have understood it all. Yes, yes, this is touching indeed. Well, have you entered a petition?"

"I have prepared a petition," said Nekhlyúdov, taking it out of his pocket. "I wanted to ask you to give it your especial attention, and I hope you may."

"You have done well. I shall by all means make the report myself," said the baron, awkwardly expressing compassion in his merry face. "It is very touching. She was apparently a child, and the husband treated her rudely; this made him repulsive to her, and later came a time when they began to love each other— Yes, I shall report it."

"Count Iván Mikháylovich said that he wanted to ask the Empress."

Before Nekhlyúdov even finished his phrase, the baron's face was suddenly changed.

"You had better hand in the petition at the chancery, and I shall do what I can," he said to Nekhlyúdov.

Just then the young official, apparently proud of his gait, entered the room.

"The lady asks to be permitted to say two words more."

"Well, call her in. Ah, *mon cher*, what a lot of tears one sees here; if one only could dry them all! I do what I can."

The lady entered.

"I forgot to ask you not to let him give up the daughter, or else—"

"I told you I would do it."

"Baron, for God's sake! You will save a mother."

She seized his hand and began to kiss it.

"Everything will be done."

When the lady left, Nekhlyúdov, too, rose to say good-bye.

"We shall do what we can. We shall consult the minister of justice. He will give us his view, and then we shall do what we can."

Nekhlyúdov went out and walked into the chancery. Again, as in the Senate, he found in a superb apartment superb officials, who were clean, polite, correct in their dress and speech, precise, and severe.

"How many there are of them, how very many, and how well fed they are! What clean shirts and hands they have! How well their shoes are polished! And who does it all? And how well they are off in comparison not only with the prisoners, but even with the peasants," Nekhlyúdov again involuntarily thought.

CHAPTER XIX

THE COMMANDER OF
THE FORTRESS

The man on whom depended the alleviation of the lot of those who were confined in St. Petersburg had decorations enough to cover him, but, with the exception of a white cross in the buttonhole, he did not wear them; he was a superannuated old general, in his dotage, as they said, and was of German baronial origin. He had served in the Caucasus, where he had received this extremely flattering cross because under his command Russian peasants, with their hair cropped and clad in uniforms and armed with guns and bayonets, had killed more than a thousand people who were defending their liberty, their homes, and their families. Then he had served in Poland, where he again compelled Russian peasants to commit all kinds of crimes, for which he received new decorations and embellishments on his uniform. Then he had served somewhere else, and, being an enfeebled old man, had obtained the position which he now was occupying and which supplied him with good apartments and support, and gave him honours. He severely executed all orders from above and was exceedingly proud of this execution; to these orders from above he ascribed a special meaning and thought that everything in the world might be changed, except these orders from above. His duty consisted in keeping political prisoners in barracks, in solitary confinement, and keeping them there in such a way that half of them perished in the course of ten years, some becoming insane, some dying from consumption, and some committing suicide: some by starving themselves, others by cutting their veins open with pieces of glass, others by hanging, others by burning themselves to death.

The old general knew all this; all this took place under his eyes, but all these cases did not touch his conscience any more than his conscience was touched by accidents arising from storms, floods, and so on. These accidents happened on account of his executing orders from above, in the name of the Emperor. These orders had to be carried out without questioning, and therefore it was quite useless to think of the consequences resulting from these orders. The old general did not let himself even think of such affairs, considering it his patriotic duty as a soldier not to think, in order not to weaken in the execution of these, as he thought, extremely important duties of his.

Once a week the old general regarded it his duty to visit all the barracks and to ask the prisoners whether they had any requests to make. The prisoners generally had requests to make of him. He listened to them calmly and in impenetrable silence, and never granted them because they were all contrary to the regulations of the law.

As Nekhlyúdov was approaching the residence of the old general, the soft chimes of the tower played "Praise ye the Lord," and the clock struck two. Listening to the chimes, Nekhlyúdov involuntarily recalled having read in the memoirs of the Decembrists what an effect this sweet music, repeated every hour, had on the souls of those who were confined for life. As Nekhlyúdov drove up to the entrance of his lodgings, the general was sitting in a dark drawing-room at an inlaid table and, together with a young man, an artist, a brother of one of his subordinates, was twirling a small dish on a sheet of paper. The thin, moist, feeble fingers of the artist were linked with the rough, wrinkled fingers of the general, which were stiff in their joints, and these linked hands were jerking about, together with the inverted saucer, over the sheet of paper upon which were written all the letters of the alphabet. The saucer was answering the question put by the general as to how spirits would recognize each other after death.

Just as one of the orderlies, who was acting as valet, entered with Nekhlyúdov's card, Joan of Arc's spirit was communicating with them by means of the saucer.

Joan of Arc's spirit had already spelled out, "They will recognize each other after their," and this had been noted down. Just as the orderly had entered, the saucer, which had first stopped at "l," was jerking about in all directions just after it had reached the letter "i." It was wavering because the next letter, according to the general's opinion, was to have been "b," that is, Joan of Arc, in his opinion, was to have said that the spirits would recognize each other after their liberation from all earthly dross, or something to that effect, and the next letter, therefore, had to be "b"; but the artist thought that the next letter would be "g," that the spirit was going to say that the souls would recognize each other after their lights, which would emanate from their ethereal bodies. The general, gloomily arching his thick gray eyebrows, was looking fixedly at the hands, and, imagining that the saucer was moving of its own accord, was pulling it in the direction of letter "b." But the young, anemic artist, with his scant hair combed behind his ears, was looking with his lifeless blue eyes into the dark corner of the drawing-room, and, nervously twitching his lips, was pulling the saucer in the direction of "g." The general scowled at the interruption of his occupation, and, after a moment's silence, took the card, put on his eyeglasses, and, groaning from a pain in the small of his back, arose to his full tall stature, rubbing his stiffened joints.

"Take him to the study."

"Permit me, your Excellency, I shall finish it myself," said the artist, getting up. "I feel the presence."

"Very well, finish it," the general said, in a resolute and severe voice, while with a resolute and even gait he headed toward his study with long strides, his feet held parallel.

"Glad to see you." The general said these gracious words to Nekhlyúdov in a coarse voice, pointing to a chair at the desk. "Have you been in Petersburg long?"

Nekhlyúdov told him that he had arrived recently.

"Is the princess, your mother, well?"

"Mother is dead."

"Pardon me, I am very sorry. My son told me that he had met you."

The general's son was making the same career as his father. After leaving the military academy, he served in the detective bureau, and was very proud of the business which there was entrusted to him. His occupation consisted in supervising the spies.

"Yes, I have served with your father. We were friends and comrades. Well, are you serving?"

"No."

The general shook his head disapprovingly.

"I have a request to make of you, general," said Nekhlyúdov.

"Oh, oh, I am very glad. What can I do for you?"

"If my request is improper, you will forgive me, I hope. But I must communicate it to you."

"What is it?"

"There is a certain Gurkévich confined in the fortress. His mother wishes to see him, or, at least, to let him have certain books."

The general expressed neither joy nor displeasure at Nekhlyúdov's question; he bent his head sidewise and closed his eyes, as though lost in thought. He really was not thinking of anything and was not even interested in Nekhlyúdov's question, knowing very well that he would answer him in accordance with the laws. He was simply taking a mental rest, thinking of nothing.

"This, you see, does not depend on me," he said, after a moment's rest. "In regard to interviews there is a regulation confirmed by his Majesty, and whatever is decreed is carried out. As to the books, we have a library, and they get such books as are permitted to them."

"But he needs scholarly books. He wants to work."

"Don't believe that." The general was silent for a while. "That is not for work. Nothing but unrest."

"But they have to do something to pass the time in their difficult situation," said Nekhlyúdov.

"They always complain," said the general. "We know them." He spoke of them in general as of some especially bad species of men. "They are furnished such comforts here as one will rarely find in prisons," continued the general.

And, as though to justify himself, he began to tell in detail of all the comforts which the prisoners had, as though the chief aim of this institution consisted in providing pleasant quarters for its inmates.

"Formerly, it is true, it was very hard, but now they are kept nicely. They eat three courses, and one of these is meat, either meatballs or chops. On Sundays they get a fourth course—something sweet. God grant that every Russian have such meals!"

The general, like all old people, having once come to a subject which he knew by rote, kept saying what he had repeated so often before to prove the prisoners' excessive demands and ingratitude.

"They get books, both of a religious character, and old periodicals. We have a library with the proper books. But they read only rarely. At first they seem to be interested, but afterward the new books remain half uncut, while the pages of the old ones are not turned over. We have tried them," said the baron, with a distant resemblance to a smile, "by putting pieces of paper in. The papers remain untouched. Nor are they kept from writing," continued the general. "They get slates and pencils, so that they may write for their amusement. They may rub off what they have written, and write over again. But they don't write. No, they very soon become very quiet. Only in the beginning they are restless; and later they grow fat, and become very quiet," said the general, without suspecting what terrible meaning his words had.

Nekhlyúdov listened to his hoarse old voice; he looked at his stiffened joints, at his dimmed eyes beneath his gray brows, at his shaven, overhanging, old cheeks, supported by a military collar, at the white cross, which this man prided himself on, especially since he had received it for an extraordinarily cruel and wholesale murder — and he understood that it was useless for him to explain to him the meaning of his words. But, nevertheless, with an effort, he asked about another affair, about prisoner Shústova, about whom he had that day learned that she would be released.

"Shústova? Shústova— I do not remember them all by name. There are so many of them," he said, apparently reproaching them for overcrowding. He rang a bell and sent for his secretary.

While they went to fetch his secretary, he tried to persuade Nekhlyúdov that he should serve, saying that honest and noble-minded people, including himself, were especially useful to the Tsar—"and the country," he added, apparently as an adornment of speech.

"I am old, but I am serving so far as my strength permits."

The secretary, a dried-up, lean man, with restless, clever eyes, arrived and informed them that Shústova was kept in some strange fortified place, and that no document in reference to her had been received.

"We shall send her away the day we get the papers. We do not keep them, and we do not particularly value their visits," said the general, again with an attempt at a playful smile, which only contorted his old face.

Nekhlyúdov arose, trying to repress an expression of a mixed feeling of disgust and pity, which he experienced in regard to this terrible old man. The old man, on his side, thought that he ought not to be too severe with a frivolous and, obviously, erring son of his friend, and ought not to let him go away without giving him some instruction.

"Good-bye, my dear. Don't be angry with me for what I am going to tell you. I tell you this because I like you. Don't keep company with the people who are confined here. There are no innocents. They are all a very immoral lot. We know them," he said, in a tone which did not admit the possibility of a doubt. He really did not doubt, not because it was actually so, but because, if it were not so, he could not regard himself as a respected hero who was finishing a good life in a worthy manner, but as a villain who had been selling, and in his old age still continued to sell, his conscience. "Best of all, serve," he continued. "The Tsar needs honest men

—and so does the country," he added. "If I and all the others refused to serve, as you do, who would be left? We condemn the order of things, and yet do not ourselves wish to help the government."

Nekhlyúdov drew a deep breath, made a low bow, condescendingly pressed the large, bony hand stretched out to him, and left the room.

Tolstoy
Resurrection
page 246

The general shook his head in disapproval, and, rubbing the small of his back, again entered the drawing-room, where the artist was awaiting him, with the answer from the spirit of Joan of Arc all written out. The general put on his *pince-nez* and read: "They will recognize each other after their lights, which will emanate from their ethereal bodies."

"Ah," the general said approvingly, closing his eyes, "but how are you going to tell if the light is the same with all?" he asked and again sat down at the table, linking his fingers with those of the artist.

Nekhlyúdov's cabman came out of the gate.

"It is dull here, sir," he said, turning to Nekhlyúdov, "and I was about to leave, without waiting for you."

"Yes, it is dull," Nekhlyúdov agreed with him, inhaling the air with full lungs and restfully gazing at the smoky clouds that were scudding along the sky, and at the sparkling waves of the Nevá, rippling from the boats and steamers that were moving on it.

CHAPTER XX

NEKHLYÚDOV AT THE SENATE

On the following day Máslova's case was to be heard, and Nekhlyúdov went to the Senate. The lawyer met him at the grand entrance of the Senate building, where several carriages were already standing. Mounting the magnificent main staircase to the second story, the lawyer, who knew all the corridors, turned to the left to a door on which was written the year of the introduction of the code of laws governing the courts. Having taken off his overcoat in the first long room and having learned from the porter that the Senators had all arrived and the last had just entered, Fanárin, now remaining in his dress coat and his white tie over his white shirt front, passed into the next room with cheerful self-confidence. Here there were, on the right, a large cupboard and then a table, and, on the left, a winding staircase, down which now came an elegant-looking official in uniform with a portfolio under his arm. In this room attention was attracted by a patriarchal old man, with long white hair, in a jacket and gray trousers, near whom stood two assistants in a respectful attitude.

The old man with the white hair went into the cupboard and shut himself in. Just then Fanárin, having spied a friend of his, a lawyer in a white tie and a dress coat, immediately entered into an animated conversation with him. In the meantime Nekhlyúdov watched those who were in the room. In all there were about fifteen persons present, among them two ladies. One of these wore *pince-nez*, and the other was a gray-haired old woman. The case which was to be heard today dealt with a libel of the press, and therefore a more than usual number of people had assembled—nearly all people belonging to the newspaper world.

The bailiff, a ruddy-faced, handsome man, in a magnificent uniform, with a note in his hand, walked over to Fanárin to ask him what his case was and, having heard that it was the Máslova case, made a note of something and went away. Just then the door of the cupboard was opened, and the patriarchal old man emerged from it, no longer in his jacket, but in a galloon-embroidered garment, with metal plates on his breast, which made him look like a bird.

This ridiculous costume apparently embarrassed the old man himself, and he walked more rapidly than was his custom through the door opposite the entrance.

"That is B, a most respectable man," Fanárin said to Nekhlyúdov, and, introducing him to his colleague, told him of the extremely interesting case, as he thought, which was to be heard now.

The case soon began, and Nekhlyúdov, with the rest of the audience, went into the hall on the left. All of them, Fanárin included, went behind a railing, to seats intended for the public. Only the St. Petersburg lawyer stepped out beyond the railing to a desk.

The hall of the meetings of the Senate was smaller than the one of the District Court, simpler in its appointments, and differed from it only in that the table, at which the Senators were sitting, was not covered with green cloth, but with crimson velvet, embroidered with gold lace; all the other attributes of the execution of justice were the same: there was the mirror,* the icon, and the portrait of the emperor. The bailiff announced in the same solemn voice, "The Court is coming." All rose in the same manner; the Senators, in their uniforms, walked in in the same way, sat down in the same way in the chairs with the high backs, and in the same way leaned over the table, trying to look natural.

There were four Senators: the presiding officer, Nikítin, a clean-shaven man with a narrow face and steel eyes; Wolff, with compressed lips and white little hands, with which he fingered some sheets of paper; then Skovoródnikov, a fat, massive, pockmarked man—a learned jurist; and the fourth, B, that patriarchal old man who had been the last to arrive. With the Senators came out the secretary-

*A triangular prism with certain laws promulgated by Peter the Great printed upon it, to be found in every court.

general and the associate prosecuting attorney-general, a middle-sized, spare, clean-shaven young man, with a very dark skin and black, melancholy eyes. In spite of his strange uniform, and although six years had passed since Nekhlyúdov had last seen him, he at once recognized him as one of his closest friends in his student days.

Tolstoy

Resurrection

page 248

"Is that Associate Prosecuting Attorney-General Selénin?"

"Yes. Why?"

"I know him well. He is a fine man—"

"And an excellent associate prosecuting attorney-general, knows his business. You ought to have gone to him," said Fanárin.

"He will, in any case, be conscientious," said Nekhlyúdov, recalling his close relations and friendship with Selénin, and his gentle qualities of purity, honesty, and decency, in the best sense of the word.

"It is too late now," Fanárin whispered to him, giving his attention to the report of the case.

The case was an appeal from the verdict of the Superior Court which had left unchanged the judgement of the District Court.

Nekhlyúdov listened and tried to understand the meaning of what was going on before him, but, just as in the District Court, the chief impediment to comprehension was that they were not considering what naturally seemed to be the main point, but a side issue. The case under consideration involved an article in a newspaper, in which a swindle by a presiding officer of a certain stock company had been brought to light. It would seem that the only important question was whether really the president of the stock company was stealing from his creditors, and what means were to be taken to stop him from stealing. But that was not at all considered. The only question they discussed was whether the publisher had a legal right to print the article or not, and what crime he had committed by printing it: whether it was a defamation or libel, and how defamation includes libel, or libel, defamation, and other points unintelligible for ordinary people about various articles and decrees of some general department.

There was one thing which Nekhlyúdov understood and that was that, notwithstanding the fact that Wolff, who made the report on the case, and who on the previous day had so sternly informed him that the Senate could not consider the essence of a case, in this particular affair reported with an obvious bias in favour of annulment of the verdict of the Superior Court, and that Selénin, quite out of keeping with his characteristic reserve, suddenly hotly expressed an opposite opinion. The impassionedness of the ever reserved Selénin, which surprised Nekhlyúdov, was based on the fact that he knew the president of the stock company as unreliable in business matters, and that he had accidentally found out that Wolff had almost on the eve of the hearing of this case been present at a luxurious dinner given by this suspicious business man. When Wolff now reported in an obviously biassed, even though very cautious, manner on the case, Selénin became excited and expressed his opinion with greater vigour than was necessary for such a usual matter. His speech evidently offended Wolff: he blushed, twitched, made silent gestures of surprise, and with a very dignified and offended look retired with the other Senators to the consultation-room.

"What is your case?" the bailiff again asked Fanárin, the moment the Senators had retired.

"I have told you before that I am here to hear Máslova's case," said Fanárin.

"That is so. The case will come up to-day. But—"

"What is it?" asked the lawyer.

"You see, it has been put down without discussion, and the Senators will hardly come out after the announcement of their decision. But I shall inform them—"

"What do you mean?"

"I shall inform them," and the bailiff made a note of something on the paper.

The Senators actually intended, after announcing their decision in the libel-suit, to finish all the other business, including Máslova's case, at tea and cigarettes, without leaving the consultation-room.

CHAPTER XXI

DENIAL OF MÁSLOVA'S APPEAL

The moment the Senators sat down at the table of the consultation-room, Wolff began in a very animated manner to adduce the reasons why the case ought to be annulled.

The presiding Senator, who was as a rule not well disposed, happened to be in an unusually bad humour. Listening to the case during the session, he had formed his opinion, and so he now sat lost in thought, without paying any attention to what Wolff was saying. His thought was centred on consideration of what he had written the day before in his memoirs in regard to Vilyánov's appointment, instead of him, to that important post which he had long wished to get. Presiding Senator Nikítin was very firmly convinced that his reflections on the officials of the highest two ranks with whom he came in contact during the time of his service formed very important historical material. Having on the previous day written a chapter in which he gave some hard knocks to some officials of the first two classes for having prevented him, as he formulated it, from saving Russia from the destruction into which the present rulers were drawing it—but in reality for having kept him from getting a larger salary than he now was receiving—he now was meditating on the fact that this circumstance would have an entirely new light thrown upon it for the use of posterity.

Tolstoy
Resurrection
page 250

"Yes, of course," he replied to Wolff's words which he had addressed to him, but which he had not heard.

With a sad expression B listened to what Wolff was saying, drawing garlands on the paper which was lying before him. B was a liberal of the purest water. He sacredly preserved the traditions of the sixties, and if he ever departed from his severe impartiality it was always in favour of liberalism. Thus, in the present case, apart from the fact that the stock speculator, who had brought the accusation of libel, was a questionable individual, B was for denying the appeal because this accusation of libel against a writer was a restraint upon the freedom of the press. When Wolff had finished his proofs, B, without having finished drawing a garland, with sadness—he was aggrieved that he had to prove such truisms—in a soft, pleasant voice, gently, simply, and convincingly proved the groundlessness of the complaint, and, lowering his head with its white hair, continued to draw the garland.

Skovoródnikov, who was sitting opposite Wolff, and who was all the time pulling his beard and moustache into his mouth with his fat fingers, the moment B ceased talking, stopped chewing his beard, and in a loud, creaking voice said that, notwithstanding the fact that the president of the stock company was a great scoundrel, he would be for the annulment of the verdict if there were legal reasons for it, but as such were lacking, he seconded the opinion expressed by Iván Semyónovich (B), he said, enjoying the sting which he had thus given to Wolff. The presiding Senator sided with Skovoródnikov, and the case was decided in the negative.

Wolff was dissatisfied, expecially since he was, so to say, accused of dishonest partiality. However, he pretended to be indifferent and opened the next case to be reported upon, that of Máslova, and buried himself in it. In the meantime the Senators rang the bell and asked for tea; they began to discuss an affair, which together with Kámenski's duel, then interested all Petersburg.

It was the case of a director of a department who had been caught and convicted of a crime provided for in Article 995.

"What baseness," B said, in disgust.

"What evil do you see in it? I shall show you in our literature a plan of a German writer who proposes point-blank that this should not be regarded as a crime, and that marriage between two men be permitted," said Skovoródnikov, eagerly sucking in the smoke from a crushed cigarette which he was holding at the roots of his fingers, near the palm of his hand, and bursting out into a loud laugh.

"Impossible," said B.

"I will show it to you," said Skovoródnikov, quoting the full title of the work, and even the year and place of publication.

"They say he is to be appointed governor in some Siberian city," said Nikítin.

"That is fine. The bishop will come out to meet him with the cross. They ought to have a bishop of the same kind. I could recommend a bishop to them," said Skovoródnikov, and, throwing the stump of the cigarette into the ash-tray, he took into his mouth as much as he could of his beard and moustache, and began to chew at them.

Just then the bailiff, who had entered, informed them of the lawyer's and Nekhlyúdov's desire to be present at the discussion of Máslova's case.

"Now this case," said Wolff, "is a whole romance," and he told all he knew about Nekhlyúdov's relations with Máslova. After having talked of this, and having finished smoking their cigarettes and drinking their tea, the Senators returned to the hearing-room, announced their decision in the previous case, and took up Máslova's.

Wolff in his thin voice reported in a very detailed manner on Máslova's appeal for annulment, and again spoke not entirely without impartiality, but with the manifest desire to have the judgement of the court annulled.

"Have you anything to add?" the presiding Senator addressed Fanárin. Fanárin arose, and, expanding his broad white chest, began, by points, and with remarkable impressiveness and precision, to prove the departure of the court in six points from the exact meaning of the law, and, besides, took the liberty of touching, though briefly, on the merits of the case itself, and on the crying injustice of the verdict. The tone of Fanárin's short but strong speech was to the effect that he begged the Senate's indulgence for insisting on something which the Senators, in their sagacity and judicial wisdom, saw and understood better than he, saying that he did so only because his duty demanded it. After Fanárin's speech, there seemed to be not the least doubt but that the Senate would reverse the decision of the court. Having finished his speech, Fanárin smiled a victorious smile. Looking at his lawyer and seeing this smile, Nekhlyúdov was convinced that the case was won. But when he glanced at the Senators, he noticed that Fanárin was the only one who was smiling and triumphing. The Senators and the associate prosecuting attorney-general neither smiled nor triumphed, but had the look of people who felt bored and who were saying, "We have heard a lot of your kind of people, and it all leads to nothing." They were all, apparently, glad only when the lawyer got through and stopped delaying them. Immediately after the end of the lawyer's speech, the presiding officer turned to the associate prosecuting attorney-general. Selénin clearly and precisely expressed himself in a few words against the reversal of the judgement, finding the grounds for annulment insufficient. Thereupon the Senators arose and went away to hold their consultation. In the consultation-room the votes were divided. Wolff was for annulment. B, having grasped the whole matter, also very warmly sided with the annulment, vividly presenting to his associates a picture of the court and the misunderstanding of the jury, just as he had comprehended it very correctly. Nikítin, who always stood for severity in general and for severe formality, was against it. The whole affair depended on Skovoródnikov's vote. He cast it against a reversal chiefly because Nekhlyúdov's determination to marry this girl in the name of moral demands was in the highest degree distasteful to him.

Skovoródnikov was a materialist and a Darwinist, and considered all manifestations of abstract morality, or, still worse, of religiousness not only a contemptible madness, but a personal affront to him. All this interest in the prostitute, and the presence in the Senate of a famous lawyer, who was defending her, and of Nekhlyúdov himself, was extremely distasteful to him. And thus, he stuck his beard into his mouth and, making a grimace, pretended not to know anything about the affair except that the causes for annulment were insufficient, and that, therefore, he agreed with the president in denying the appeal.

The appeal was denied.

CHAPTER XXII

NEKHLYÚDOV TALKS TO SELÉNIN

"Terrible!" said Nekhlyúdov, walking into the waiting-room with the lawyer, who was putting his papers away in his briefcase. "In the most obvious case they stickle for form, and refuse it. Terrible!"

"The case was spoilt in court," said the lawyer.

"And Selénin is for denial! Terrible, terrible!" Nekhlyúdov continued to repeat. "What is to be done now?"

"Let us appeal to his Majesty. Hand in the petition while you are here. I will write it out for you."

Just then little Wolff, with his stars and uniform, came into the waiting-room and walked over to Nekhlyúdov.

"What is to be done, dear prince? There wasn't sufficient cause," he said, shrugging his narrow shoulders and closing his eyes. He passed on.

After Wolff came Selénin, having learned from the Senators that Nekhlyúdov, his former friend, was there.

"I did not expect to find you here," he said, going up to Nekhlyúdov, smiling with his lips, while his eyes remained sad. "I did not know you were in St. Petersburg."

"And I did not know that you were prosecuting attorney-general—"

"Associate," Selénin corrected him. "What are you doing in the Senate?" he asked, looking sadly and gloomily at his friend. "I heard that you were in St. Petersburg. But what brings you here?"

"Here? I came here, hoping to find justice and to save an innocent condemned woman."

"What woman?"

"The one whose case has just been decided."

"Oh, the Máslova case," Selénin said, recalling it. "An entirely unfounded appeal."

"It's not a question of the appeal, but of the woman, who is not guilty and yet condemned."

Selénin heaved a sigh: "Very likely, but—"

"Not very likely, but absolutely—"

"How do you know?"

"Because I was one of the jury. I know where we made a mistake."

Selénin fell to musing. "You ought to have announced it then and there," he said.

"I did."

"You ought to have written it down in the protocol. If that had been in the appeal for annulment—"

Selénin, who was always busy at home and never went out in society, had apparently heard nothing of Nekhlyúdov's romance; and Nekhlyúdov, being aware of this, decided that it was not necessary for him to speak of his relations with Máslova.

"But it is obvious now that the verdict was senseless."

"The Senate has no right to say so. If the Senate should take the liberty of annulling the judgments of the courts on the basis of their own views of their justice, not only would the Senate lose every point of support and be in danger of violating justice rather than establishing it," Selénin said, recalling the previous case, "but the verdicts of the juries would also lose their meaning."

"I know only this much: the woman is absolutely innocent, and the last hope to save her from an unmerited punishment is gone. The highest court has confirmed a case of absolute illegality."

"It has not confirmed it, because it has not considered, and it cannot consider, the merits of the case itself," said Selénin, blinking. "You, no doubt, are staying at your aunt's," he added, evidently wishing to change the subject. "I heard from her yesterday that you were here. The countess invited me to be with you at the meeting of the visiting preacher," said Selénin, smiling with his lips only.

"Yes, I was there, but went away in disgust," angrily said Nekhlyúdov, provoked at Selénin for changing the subject.

"But why in disgust? It is, nevertheless, a manifestation of religious feeling, even though one-sided and sectarian," said Selénin.

"It is nothing but some wild nonsense," said Nekhlyúdov.

"Not at all. The only strange thing about it is that we know so little the teachings of our own church that we receive our fundamental dogmas as a kind of new revelation," said Selénin, as though hastening to express his views, which were new to his old friend.

Nekhlyúdov looked at Selénin with surprised attention. Selénin did not lower his eyes, in which there was an expression not only of sadness, but of animosity as well.

"Do you believe in the dogmas of the church?" Nekhlyúdov asked.

"Of course I do," Selénin replied, gazing with a straight and dead stare at Nekhlyúdov.

Nekhlyúdov sighed.

"Remarkable," he said.

"However, we shall speak of it later," said Selénin. "I am coming," he turned to the bailiff, who had walked up to him with a respectful gait. "We must by all means see each other," he added, with a sigh. "But shall I find you at home? You will always find me at home at seven o'clock, at dinner. Nadézhdinskaya," and he gave the number of the house. "Much water has flowed under the bridge since then," he added, walking away, and again smiling only with his lips.

"I will come if I can," said Nekhlyúdov, feeling that Selénin, who had once been a close and favourite friend of his, had suddenly become, in consequence of this short conversation, strange, distant, and unintelligible, if not hostile.

CHAPTER XXIII

A DESCRIPTION OF SELÉNIN

When Nekhlyúdov knew Selénin as a student, he was a good son, a faithful friend, and, for his years, a cultivated man of the world, with much tact, always elegant and handsome, and, at the same time, of extraordinary truthfulness and honesty. He studied beautifully without any effort and without a sign of pedantry, receiving gold medals for his themes.

Not only in words, but in deeds, he made serving people the aim of his young life. This service he never presented to himself in any other form than as government service, and therefore, the moment he graduated, he systematically reviewed all the activities to which he might devote his energy, and decided that he would be most useful in the second division of the Privy Chancery, which has charge of making laws, and so he entered there. But, in spite of the most precise and conscientious execution of everything demanded of him, he did not find satisfaction in this service of his desire to be useful and could not appease his conscience with the thought that he was doing the right thing. This discontent was so strengthened by his conflicts with the petty and vainglorious superior immediately above him that he left the second division and transferred to the Senate. Here he was more at ease, but the feeling of discontent pursued him still.

He did not cease feeling that it was completely different from what he had expected and from what it ought to be. While he was in the Senate, an appointment as Gentleman of the Bedchamber was obtained for him by a relative, and he was obliged to drive around in a carriage, wearing an embroidered uniform and a white linen apron, to thank all kinds of people for having promoted him to the dignity of a lackey. However much he tried, he could not discover a sensible explanation for this office. And he felt even more than in the service that it was "not it"; at the same time he could not refuse this appointment, on the one hand, in order not to offend those who were convinced that they had given him a great pleasure, while, on the other, the appointment flattered the lower qualities of his nature, and it gave him pleasure to see himself in the mirror in an embroidered gold lace uniform, and to enjoy that respect which his appointment elicited from certain people.

The same thing happened with him in regard to his marriage. They arranged a very brilliant marriage for him, from the standpoint of society. And he married, mainly because by refusing to he would have offended and pained the bride, who was very anxious to marry him, and those who had arranged the marriage for him; and also, because his marrying a young, sweet, aristocratic maiden flattered his vanity and gave him pleasure. But the marriage soon proved to be "not it" in a far greater way than the service and his court duties. After the first baby was born, his wife did not want to have any more children, and began to lead a luxurious society life, in which he was compelled to take part against his will. She was not particularly beautiful, was faithful to him, and, although she poisoned her husband's life by it and herself gained nothing from it but an expenditure of terrible strength, and weariness, she zealously continued to lead such a life. All his attemps to change this existence were wrecked, as against a stone wall, against her conviction that it had to be so, in which opinion she was supported by her relatives and acquaintances.

The child, a girl with long golden locks and bare legs, was entirely estranged from her father, more especially because she was brought up differently from the way he wished her to be. Between husband and wife naturally arose misunderstandings and even an absence of any desire to understand each other, and a quiet, silent struggle, concealed from outsiders and moderated by proprieties, which made life for him at home exceedingly hard. Thus even more than his service and his court appointment his domestic life proved to be "not it."

His relation to religion was, however, most "not it." Like all people of his circle and time, he had, without the least effort, by his mental growth, broken those fetters of religious superstitions in which he had been brought up, and he himself did not know when that liberation had taken place. Being a serious and honest man, he did not conceal this freedom from the superstitions of the official religion while he was still young, during his student days and his friendship with Nekhlyúdov. But with advancing years and his rise in service, especially during the conservative reaction which in the meantime had taken possession of society, this spiritual freedom stood in his way. Not to mention domestic pressures, especially at the death of his father, at the masses for his soul, and because his mother desired him to prepare himself for the sacrament, and public opinion partly demanded this—but the service required he be continually present at prayers, dedications, thanksgivings, and other similar services: hardly a day passed without his coming in contact with some external forms of religion, which it was impossible to avoid. Being present at these services, one of two things had to be done: either he had to pretend (which, with his truthful character he never could do) that he believed in what he did not believe in, or, admitting that all these external forms were a lie, so arrange his life as not to be compelled to take part in what he considered a lie. But, in order to do what seemed so unimportant, much had to be done: it was necessary to take up an unending struggle with all his close friends; it was necessary to change his position, to give up his service, and to sacrifice all his usefulness, which he now was convinced he brought people by his service and hoped even to increase in the future. And in order to do this, it was necessary to be convinced of the justice of his views. Of this he was as firmly convinced as every cultivated man of our time must be of the justice of his sound reason, if he knows anything of history, and if he knows anything of the origin of religion in general, and of the origin and decay of the Christian Church in particular. He could not help knowing that he was right in refusing to acknowledge the truth of the Church teachings.

But, under the pressure of the conditions of life, he, a truthful man, permitted himself a small lie, which consisted in saying to himself that, in order to assert that the senselessness is senseless, it is necessary first to study that senselessness. This was a small lie, but it led him to that great lie, in which he now was stuck fast.

In putting the question to himself whether that Orthodoxy in which he had

been born and brought up, which was demanded of him by all those who surrounded him and without which he could not continue his useful activity among
men, was right, he had already prejudged it. Therefore, in order to elucidate this
question, he did not take Voltaire, Schopenhauer, Spencer, Comte, but the philoso-
phical works of Hegel, and the religious books of Vinet and Khomyakóv, and he
naturally found in them what he wanted: a semblance of acquiescence and justification of that religious teaching in which he had been educated, which his reason
had long rejected, but without which all his life was filled with annoyances, and by
the acceptance of which all these annoyances would at once be removed. He
appropriated all those customary sophisms that a separate human mind cannot
comprehend truth, that truth is revealed only to the aggregate of mankind, that the
only means for knowing it is revelation, that revelation is in the keeping of the
Church, and so forth. Since then he could calmly, without being conscious of
the lie, be present at prayers and masses, take the sacrament, and cross himself before
the icons, and he could continue in his post, which gave him the consciousness
of his utility and a consolation in his cheerless domestic life. He thought that he believed, and yet he was conscious with all his being, even more than in anything
else, that this faith was absolutely "not it."

And it was this that made his eyes look so melancholy. And it was this which
caused him, at the sight of Nekhlyúdov, whom he used to know when these lies
had not taken possession of him, to recall the time when he was still different;
especially after he had hastened to hint to him about his religious views, he felt more
than ever that all this was "not it," and he was overcome by painful melancholy.
The same sensation took possession of Nekhlyúdov, after the first impression of joy
in seeing his old friend had passed.

It was for this reason that, although they had promised to see each other, neither
of them sought the meeting, and they never again met during Nekhlyúdov's stay
in St. Petersburg.

CHAPTER XXIV

NEKHLYÚDOV AND MARIETTE

Upon leaving the Senate, Nekhlyúdov walked down the sidewalk with the lawyer.
The lawyer ordered his carriage to follow him and began to tell Nekhlyúdov the
history of that director of a department of whose conviction the Senators had been
talking, and who, instead of being condemned to hard labour, was to be appointed
governor in Siberia. He told him the whole story and all its nastiness, and also
expatiated with special pleasure on the story of the high-ranking persons who had

stolen the money which had been collected for the construction of the unfinished monument past which they had driven that morning; and of how the mistress of a certain man had made millions on the Exchange; and of how one man had sold and another had bought a wife; then he began his narrative about the swindles and all kinds of crimes of higher government officials, who were not confined in jails, but occupied president's chairs in various institutions. These stories, of which the supply seemed inexhaustible, gave the lawyer much pleasure, since they gave evident proof of the fact that the means which he, the lawyer, employed to make money were quite lawful and innocent in comparison with the means employed for the same purpose by the highest functionaries at St. Petersburg. Therefore, the lawyer was very much surprised when Nekhlyúdov did not wait for the end of the last story about the crimes of the officials, but said good-bye, took a cab, and drove home to the quai.

Nekhlyúdov felt very sad. He was sad especially because the Senate's refusal confirmed the senseless torture of innocent Máslova, and because this refusal made more difficult his unchangeable determination to unite his fate with hers. This melancholy was increased by those terrible stories of the reigning evil, which the lawyer had been telling him about with such delight; in addition to this, he continually thought of the grim, cold, repelling look of Selénin, whom he had known as a gentle, frank, and noble-minded man.

When Nekhlyúdov returned home, the porter, with a somewhat contemptuous look, handed him a note which a certain woman, as he put it, had written in the the porter's lodge. It was a note from Shústova's mother. She wrote that she had come to thank the benefactor and saviour of her daughter, and, besides, to beg and implore him to call at their house, on Vasílevsky Island, Fifth Line, Number so and so. This was very necessary for Vyéra Efrémovna's sake. She said he need not be afraid of being annoyed by expressions of gratitude, that this would not even be mentioned, but that they would be very happy to see him. If he could, he should come the next morning.

There was also another note from his former fellow-officer, Aide-de-camp Bogatyryóv, whom Nekhlyúdov had asked to hand personally to the emperor the petition in the name of the sectarians. Bogatyryóv wrote in his large, firm hand that he would hand the petition to the emperor, as he had promised, but that it had suddenly occurred to him that it might be better for Nekhlyúdov to go and see the person on whom the matter depended and to ask him to use his influence.

After the impressions of the last few days in St. Petersburg, Nekhlyúdov was in a state of complete hopelessness as regards the success of anything. His plans, which he had formed in Moscow, appeared to him like those youthful dreams, in which people are invariably disenchanted when they enter life. Still, while he was in St.

Petersburg, he regarded it as his duty to do everything he had set out to do, and so he resolved that to-morrow, after having seen Bogatyryóv, he would go and see the person on whom the affair of the sectarians depended.

He drew the petition of the sectarians out of his briefcase and began to read it, when the lackey of Countess Ekaterína Ivánovna knocked at the door and entered, inviting him up-stairs to tea.

Nekhlyúdov said he would be there at once. Having put away his papers, he went to his aunt's rooms. On his way up, he looked through the window into the street and saw the span of Mariette's bays, and he suddenly felt unexpectedly happy, and wished to smile.

Mariette, in a hat, but in a bright-coloured, many-coloured dress, not in a black one, was sitting near the countess's armchair with a cup in her hand and was chattering, beaming with her beautiful, smiling eyes. As Nekhlyúdov entered the room, Mariette had just finished telling something funny, something indecently funny— this Nekhlyúdov saw from the character of the laughter—so that the good-natured, mustachioed Countess Ekaterína Ivánovna shook with her stout body, rolling from laughter, while Mariette, with a peculiarly mischievous expression, twisting her smiling mouth a little and turning her energetic and merry face to one side, looked silently at her friend.

Nekhlyúdov understood from the few words which he heard that they had been speaking about the second latest St. Petersburg news—the episode of the Siberian governor, and that it was in this region Mariette had said something so funny that the countess could not control herself for a long time.

"You're killing me," she said, coughing.

Nekhlyúdov greeted them and sat down near them. He was on the point of condemning Mariette for her frivolity, when she, noticing the serious and slightly dissatisfied expression of his face, immediately changed, not only her expression, but also her whole mood, in order that she might please him—and this she had wanted to do ever since she had met him. She suddenly grew serious, discontented with her life, seeking something, and striving for something. She did not exactly simulate the mood Nekhlyúdov was in, but actually appropriated it to herself, although she would not have been able to express in words what it was.

She asked him how he had succeeded in his affairs. He told her about his failure in the Senate and about his meeting with Selénin.

"Ah, what a pure soul! Now this is really a *chevalier sans peur et sans reproche*. A pure soul," both ladies used the invariable epithet under which Selénin was known in society.

"What kind of a woman is his wife?" Nekhlyúdov asked.

"She? Well, I am not going to criticize her. But she does not understand him."

"Is it possible he, too, was for denying the appeal?" she asked, with sincere sympathy. "That is terrible, and I am very sorry for her!" she added, with a sigh.

He frowned, and, wishing to change the subject, began to speak of Shústova, who had been confined in the prison and now was released by her intercession. He thanked her for her appeal to her husband and wanted to tell her how terrible it was to think that that woman and her whole family suffered only because nobody thought of them, but before he had a chance to finish saying what he wanted to say, she herself expressed her indignation.

"Don't tell me," she said. "The moment my husband told me that she could be released, I was struck by that very idea. Why was she kept, if she is innocent?" she said, expressing Nekhlyúdov's thought. "It is shocking, shocking!"

Countess Ekaterína Ivánovna saw that Mariette was flirting with her nephew, and this amused her.

"Do you know what?" she said, when they grew silent, "come to Aline's to-morrow evening: Kiesewetter will be there. And you too," she turned to Mariette.

"*Il vous a remarqué*," she said to her nephew. "He told me that everything you said—I told him about it—was a good sign, and that you will certainly come to Christ. Be there to-morrow by all means. Tell him to come, Mariette, and come yourself."

"Countess, in the first place, I have no right to advise the prince," said Mariette, looking at Nekhlyúdov, and, by this glance, establishing between him and herself full agreement in regard to what the countess said and to evangelism in general, "and in the second place, I am not very fond, you know—"

"You always do everything topsy-turvy and in your own way."

"What do you mean, in my own way? I believe, like the commonest kind of a woman—" she said smiling. "And, in the third place," she continued, "I am going to the French Theatre to-morrow."

"Ah! Have you seen that—oh, what is her name?" said Countess Ekaterína Ivánovna.

Mariette helped her out with the name of a famous French actress.

"Go there by all means, it's remarkable."

"Whom am I to see first, *ma tante*, the actress or the preacher?" said Nekhlyúdov, smiling.

"Please, don't catch me at words."

"I think, first the preacher and then the French actress, otherwise I will lose all interest in the sermon," said Nekhlyúdov.

"No, you had better begin with the French Theatre and then repent of your sins," said Mariette.

"Now, don't you try to make fun of me. The preacher is one thing, and the theatre another. In order to be saved it is not necessary to make a face a yard long and weep all the time. One must believe, and then you are happy."

"*Ma tante*, you preach better than any preacher."

"Do you know what," said Mariette, thoughtfully, "come to-morrow to my opera-box."

"I am afraid I won't be able—"

The conversation was interrupted by the lackey's announcement of a visitor. It was the secretary of a charitable institution, of which the countess was the president.

"He is a dreadfully tiresome man. I had better receive him in there. And then I shall come out here again. Give him tea to drink, Mariette," said the countess, walking to the parlour with her rapid, waddling gait.

Mariette took off her glove and bared an energetic, rather flat hand, its fourth finger covered with rings.

"Will you have a cup?" she said, taking hold of the silver teapot over the spirit-lamp, and strangely spreading out her little finger.

Her face became serious and sad.

"It is always terrible, terrible and painful, for me to think that people, whose opinion I value, should confound me with the situation in which I am placed."

She looked as though ready to weep, as she was saying these words. Although, upon analysis, these words had either no sense at all, or only a very indefinite meaning, they seemed to Nekhlyúdov to be of unusual depth, sincerity, and goodness— for he was attracted by the glance of those sparkling eyes, which accompanied the words of the young, beautiful, and well-dressed woman.

Nekhlyúdov looked at her in silence, and could not take his eyes off her face.

"You think that I do not understand you and everything that is going on inside you. Everybody knows what you have done. *C'est le secret de polichinelle*. And I rejoice in it and approve of it."

"Really, there is nothing to rejoice in; I have done so little as yet."

"That makes no difference. I understand your feeling, and I understand her. Well, well, I won't speak of it," she interrupted herself, noticing an expression of dissatisfaction on his face. "I also understand that, having seen all the suffering and all the horrors of the prisons," said Mariette, who had but the one wish to attract him, with her feminine instinct guessing all that might be important and dear to him, "you wish to succour all those people who suffer and suffer so terribly, so terribly from men, from indifference, from cruelty—I comprehend how one may give his life for it, and I myself should give up mine. But everybody has his own fate—"

"Are you dissatisfied with yours?"

"I?" she asked, as though startled by such a question. "I *have* to be satisfied, and I am. But there is a worm which awakens—"

"You must not let it fall asleep again. You must trust this voice," said Nekhlyúdov, submitting completely to her wiles.

Afterward Nekhlyúdov often thought with shame of his whole conversation with her; he thought of her words, which were not so much false as imitative of his own, and of her face, feigning humble attention, as she listened to his recital of the horrors of the prison and of his impressions of the country.

When the countess returned, they were conversing, not only as old, but as intimate friends, like those who understand each other in a throng which does not understand them.

They spoke of the injustice of authority, of the sufferings of the unfortunate, of the poverty of the masses, but in reality their eyes, which watched each other through the sounds of the conversation, kept asking, "Can you love me?" and answered, "I can," and the sexual feeling, assuming the most unexpected and joyous aspect, drew them to each other.

As she was leaving, she told him that she was always ready to serve him to the best of her ability and asked him to be sure and come to see her in the theatre on the following evening, at least for a moment, as she had to talk to him about an important matter.

"When shall I see you again?" she added, with a sigh, carefully putting the glove on her ring-bedecked hand. "Say that you will come."

Nekhlyúdov promised he would.

That night, Nekhlyúdov, being all alone in his room, lay down on his bed and put out the light. He could not sleep for a long time. Thinking of Máslova, of the decree of the Senate, and of his determination still to follow her, of his renunciation of his rights to the land, there appeared suddenly before him, as though in reply to his questions, Mariette's face, her sigh, and her glance, when she said, "When shall I see you again?" and her smile; she appeared before him as clearly as though she were actually standing before him, and he smiled. "Am I doing well to go to Siberia? And will I be doing well in giving up my wealth?" he asked himself.

The answers to these questions on that clear St. Petersburg night, which streamed in through the half-drawn blinds, were indistinct. Everything was mixed up in his head. He called back his former mood and thought of his former ideas, but they no longer had their former convincing power.

"But what if I have imagined all this and won't have the strength to live it, I'll be sorry I acted rightly," he said to himself, and, not being able to answer these questions, he experienced a feeling of melancholy and despair such as he had not experienced for a long time. Unable to find his way through the maze of these questions, he fell into that heavy sleep which used to come over him after some great loss at cards.

CHAPTER XXV

NEKHLYÚDOV AT SHÚSTOVA'S

Upon awakening on the next morning, Nekhlyúdov's first feeling was that he had done something foul the day before.

He began to reflect: there was nothing foul, no bad act, but there were thoughts, bad thoughts, which were that all his present intentions—marrying Katyúsha and giving the land away to the peasants—that all this was an unrealizable dream, that he would not carry it to its conclusion, that it was all artificial, unnatural, and that he ought to live as he had been living.

There was no bad act, but there was something much worse than a bad act: there were those thoughts from which spring all bad deeds. A bad act may not be repeated, and one may repent of it; but evil thoughts generate all evil deeds.

A bad act only smooths out the path for other bad acts; bad thoughts irresistibly drag one down that path.

Having recalled in his imagination all the thoughts of the previous evening, Nekhlyúdov marvelled how it was he could have believed in them even for a moment. However new and difficult all that he intended to do was, he knew that it was the only possible life for him, and that, however easy and natural it was for him to return to his former life, that would be his death. The temptation of the previous day now appeared to him analogous to the feeling of a man who has had a good sleep and still wishes not to sleep, but to stay awhile in his bed, although he knows full well that it is time to get up in order to attend to an important and joyful matter.

On that day, the last of his sojourn in St. Petersburg, he went to the Shústovs on Vasílevsky Island early in the morning.

The Shústovs' apartment was on the second floor. Nekhlyúdov, following the janitor's directions, got to the back stairs, and mounted a straight, steep staircase, and walked straight into a hot, close kitchen, smelling of cooking. An elderly woman with rolled-up sleeves, in an apron, and in glasses, was standing at the stove and mixing something in a steaming pan.

"Whom do you wish?" she asked, sternly, looking at the stranger over her glasses.

Nekhlyúdov had barely mentioned his name, when the woman's face assumed a frightened and joyful expression.

"Oh, prince!" cried the woman, drying her hands on her apron.

"But why did you come by the back staircase? You are our benefactor. I am her mother. They had entirely ruined the girl. You are our saviour," she said, grasping Nekhlyúdov's hand and trying to kiss it. "I was at your house yesterday. My sister especially asked me to go. She is here. This way, this way, please follow me," said Shústova's mother leading Nekhlyúdov through a narrow door and a dark little corridor, and on her way adjusting her tucked-up dress and her hair. "My sister is Kornílova, you certainly have heard her name," she added, in a whisper, stopping before the door. "She has been mixed up in political affairs. A very clever woman."

Having opened a door in the corridor, Shústova's mother led Nekhlyúdov into a small room, where, in front of a table, on a small sofa, sat a short, plump girl in a striped chintz blouse, with waving blond hair, which framed her round and very pale face that resembled her mother's. Opposite to her sat a young man with a black moustache and beard, wearing a national Russian shirt with embroidered collar, and hunched up in an arm-chair. They both were evidently so absorbed in their conversation that they turned around only after Nekhlyúdov had entered through the door.

"Lída, Prince Nekhlyúdov, the same one—"

The pale girl sprang up nervously, putting back a lock of hair which had strayed from behind her ear, and timidly fixed her large gray eyes on the stranger.

"So you are that dangerous woman for whom Vyéra Efrémovna has interceded," said Nekhlyúdov, smiling, and extending his hand to her.

"Yes, that's me," said Lídiya, and, opening wide her mouth and displaying a row of beautiful white teeth, she smiled a kindly, childish smile. "It is my aunt who was so anxious to see you. Aunt!" she called out through the door, in a sweet, tender voice.

"Vyéra Efrémovna was very much grieved at your arrest," said Nekhlyúdov.

"Sit down here, or better still, here," said Lídiya, pointing to the soft broken chair from which the young man had just arisen. "My cousin, Zakhárov," she said, noticing the glance which Nekhlyúdov cast upon the young man.

The young man, smiling as kindly a smile as Lídiya, greeted the guest, and, when Nekhlyúdov sat down in his seat, took a chair from the window and sat down near him. From another door came a blond schoolboy, about sixteen years old, who silently sat down on the window-sill.

"Vyéra Efrémovna is a great friend of my aunt's, but I hardly know her," said Lídiya.

Just then a woman with a very sweet, intelligent face, in a white blouse, girded by a leather belt, came out from the adjoining room,

"How do you do? Thank you for having come," she began, the moment she had seated herself on the sofa near Lídiya. "Well, how is Vyéra? Have you seen her? How does she stand her situation?"

"She does not complain," said Nekhlyúdov. "She says that she feels like an Olympian."

"Ah, Vyéra, I recognize her," said the aunt, smiling, and shaking her head. "One must know her. She is a splendid person. Everything for others, nothing for herself."

"Yes, she did not want anything for herself but was concerned only about your niece. She was tormented, chiefly because your niece had been arrested without cause."

"That's true," said the aunt, "it is something terrible! She has suffered, really, in my stead."

"Not at all, aunt," said Lídiya. "I would have taken the papers even without you."

"Let me say I know you better," continued the aunt. "You see," she continued, turning to Nekhlyúdov, "everything began with a certain person's request that I keep his papers for awhile, and I, having no apartment, took them to her. They searched her that night and took both the papers and her and kept her all this time, and wanted her to tell from whom she had received them."

"But I did not tell," Lídiya said rapidly, nervously twirling a lock of hair which was not at all in her way.

"I do not say you did," her aunt retorted.

"If they did take Mítin, it was not through me," said Lídiya, blushing, and restlessly looking about her.

"Don't talk about it, Lídochka," said her mother.

"Why not, I want to," said Lídiya, no longer smiling, but blushing, and no longer adjusting her lock but curling it about her finger, and all the time looking about her.

"You know what happened yesterday when you began to talk of it."

"Not at all—let me alone, mamma. I did not say anything, but only kept silent. When he questioned me twice about my aunt and about Mítin, I said nothing, and told him that I never would answer his questions. Then that—Petróv—"

"Petróv is a spy, a gendarme, and a great scoundrel," interposed the aunt, explaining her niece's words to Nekhlyúdov.

"Then he," continued Lídiya, in an agitated and hurried manner, "began to persuade me. 'All you tell me,' he said, 'will hurt nobody; on the contrary, by telling the truth, you will only free some innocent people whom we are, perhaps, tormenting for nothing.' I still said that I would not tell. Then he said: 'Very well, say nothing, only do not deny what I am going to say.' And he mentioned Mítin."

"Don't talk," said her aunt.

"Oh, aunt, don't interrupt me—" and she kept pulling her lock and looking all around her, "and suddenly, imagine, on the following day I found out—by knockings on the wall—that Mítin had been arrested. Well, I thought I betrayed him. And that began to torment me, to torment me so that I almost went insane."

"And then it turned out that it was not at all through you that he was arrested," said the aunt.

"But I did not know it. I thought I had betrayed him. I kept walking from wall to to wall, and I could not keep from thinking. I thought I had betrayed him. I lay down, covered myself, and I heard somebody whispering into my ear, 'You have betrayed, you have betrayed Mítin, you have betrayed him.' I knew it was a hallucination, but I could not keep from listening. I wanted to fall asleep, and I could not. I wanted to keep from thinking, and I could not. It was so terrible!" said Lídiya, becoming more and more agitated, winding her lock around her finger, again unwinding it, and looking all around her.

"Lídochka, calm down," repeated her mother, putting her hand on her shoulder.

But Lídiya could not stop now.

"It is terrible because—" she began to say, but she burst into sobs, without finishing, jumped up from the sofa, and, having caught her dress in the arm-chair, ran out of the room. Her mother started out after her.

"These scoundrels ought to be hanged," said the schoolboy, who was sitting on the window.

"What did you say?" asked the mother.

"Oh, nothing— I was just talking," replied the schoolboy, picking up a cigarette, which was lying on the table, and lighting it.

CHAPTER XXVI

SHÚSTOVA'S AUNT

"Yes, for young people this solitary confinement is terrible," said the aunt, shaking her head and also lighting a cigarette.

"I think, for everybody," said Nekhlyúdov.

"No, not for all," replied the aunt. "For real revolutionists, so I was told, it is a rest, a relief. These illegal people live in eternal turmoil and material want and fear for themselves, for others, and for the cause; and when, at last, they are arrested and everything is finished, they are relieved of all responsibility: all they have to do is to sit and rest. I have been told that they really experience joy when they are arrested. But for young innocent people—they always take innocent people, like Lídochka, first—for these the first shock is terrible. Not because you are deprived of liberty, treated rudely, fed badly, and the air is bad—in general, all the privations are nothing. If even there were three times as many privations, they could all be borne easily, if it were not for that moral shock which you get when arrested for the first time."

"Have you experienced it?"

"Me? I have been in twice," said the aunt, smiling a sad, pleasant smile. "When I was arrested the first time—and it was for no cause whatsoever," continued she— "I was twenty-two years old. I had a baby, and I was pregnant. However hard my loss of liberty was, and my separation from my child and my husband, all that was nothing in comparison with what I felt when I saw that I had ceased to be human, and had become a thing. I wanted to bid my child good-bye—I was told to hurry to take my seat in a cab. I asked where I was being taken—I was told I would find out when I got there. I asked what I was accused of. I received no reply. When I was undressed after the inquest and a prison garb with a number was put on me, and I was taken to a vaulted room and a door was opened and I was pushed in and the door was locked after me, and they went away, and only a sentry with a gun was left, walking silently up and down and once in a while peeping in through the crack in my door—a terribly oppressive feeling overcame me. I was particularly struck at the inquest by the fact that the officer of the gendarmes offered me a cigarette. That meant he knew that people like to smoke, consequently knew that people like liberty and light, knew that mothers loved their children, and children, their mothers. How, then, could they have pitilessly torn me away from everything which was dear to me and have me locked up like a wild beast? One cannot go through this unharmed. If one has believed in God and men, and that people love each other, after that he will cease believing. I have stopped believing in men ever since that time and have become bitter," she concluded, and smiled.

The mother came in the door through which Lídiya had left, and announced that Lídiya would not come in, as she was all unnerved.

"And what has this young life been ruined for?" said the aunt. "It pains me especially since I was the involuntary cause of it."

"With God's aid she will improve in the country," said the mother. "We will send her out to her father."

"Yes, if it had not been for you, she would have been entirely ruined," said the aunt. "Thank you. But I wanted to see you to ask you to give a letter to Vyéra Efrémovna," she said, drawing a letter out of her pocket. "The letter is not sealed. You may read it and tear it up, or give it to her, whichever you find more in line with your convictions," she said. "There is nothing compromising in the letter."

Nekhlyúdov took the letter, and, promising to give it to her, rose, and, having said good-bye, went out into the street.

He sealed the letter without reading it and decided to deliver it to its destination.

CHAPTER XXVII

THE CHURCH AND
THE PEOPLE

The last business which kept Nekhlyúdov in St. Petersburg was the case of the sectarians, whose petition he intended to hand to the Tsar through his fellow-officer in the army, Aide-de-camp Bogatyryóv. He went to see him in the morning and found him at home at breakfast, though on the point of leaving. Bogatyryóv was short and stocky, endowed with unusual physical strength—he could bend horseshoes—a kindly, honest, straightforward, and even liberal man. In spite of these qualities, he was an intimate at court, and loved the Tsar and his family, and, in some astonishing way, knew, while living in that highest circle, how to see only its good side and not to take part in anything bad and dishonest. He never criticized either people or measures, but either kept silent or said whatever he had to say in a bold, loud voice, as though shouting, frequently bursting into laughter just as loud. He did this, not to be diplomatic, but because such was his character.

"Now it is wonderful that you have come. Do you not want to have breakfast with me? Sit down. Superb beefsteak! I always begin and end with substantial things. Ha, ha, ha! Come, have a glass of wine. I have been thinking of you. I will hand in the petition. I will put it into his hands; only, it has occurred to me that it would be better for you first to see Toporóv."

Nekhlyúdov frowned at the mention of Toporóv.

"Everything depends on him. They will ask his opinion in any case. And maybe he himself will satisfy you."

"If you so advise, I will go to see him."

"Splendid. Well, how does St. Pete affect you?" shouted Bogatyryóv. "Tell me, eh?"

"I feel I am becoming hypnotized," said Nekhlyúdov.

"You are becoming hypnotized?" repeated Bogatyryóv, laughing out loud. "If you don't want to, all right." He wiped his mouth with a napkin. "So, you will go to see him? Ah? If he won't do it for you, let me have it, and I will hand it in to-morrow," he exclaimed, rising from the table. He crossed himself with a broad sign of the cross, apparently as unconsciously as he had wiped his mouth, and began to gird on his sword. "Now good-bye, I must be off."

"Let's go out together," said Nekhlyúdov, delighted to press Bogatyryóv's strong, broad hand, and parting from him at the steps of his house with, as always, a pleasant feeling of something healthy, unconscious, fresh.

Although he did not expect anything good to come from his visit, he took

Tolstoy

Resurrection

page 268

Bogatyryóv's advice and went to see Toporóv, the person on whom the case of the sectarians depended.

The post which Toporóv held, by its very constitution, was a self-contradiction to which only a man who was stupid and deprived of all moral sense could be blind. Toporóv possessed both these negative qualities. The contradiction in the post he held lay in the fact that its purpose was to maintain and defend by external means, not excluding violence, that church, which by its own definition, had been established by God Himself and could not be shaken either by the fiends of hell or by any human efforts. This divine and imperturbable godly institution had to be supported and defended by the human institution over which Toporóv and his officials presided. Toporóv did not see this contradiction, or did not wish to see it, and therefore he was seriously concerned lest some Roman Catholic priest, or pastor, or sectarian destroy the Church which the gates of hell could not vanquish. Toporóv, like all people deprived of a fundamental religious sense and of the consciousness of the equality and brotherhood of men, was firmly convinced that the people were creatures quite different from himself, and that the people were in dire need of what he himself could very well do without. In the depth of his soul, he himself believed in nothing, and he found such a condition very convenient and agreeable, but he was in fear lest the people come to the same state and considered it his sacred duty, as he said, to save the people from this.

Just as it says in a certain cook-book that lobsters like to be boiled alive, so he was firmly convinced, by no means in a figurative sense, as was meant in the cook-book, but in a literal sense—and so he expressed himself—that the people like to be superstitious.

He stood in the same relation to the religion which he was supporting as the poultry-keeper stands in relation to the carrion which he feeds his chickens: the carrion is a very disagreeable business, but the chickens like to eat it, and so they must be fed on it.

Of course, all these miracle-working icons of Íver, Kazán, and Smolénsk are a very crude idolatry, but the people believe in it and like it, and so these superstitions must be maintained. Thus thought Toporóv, forgetting to reflect that the reason he thought the people liked the superstitions was because there have always been such cruel men as he, Toporóv, who, having themselves become enlightened, used their light not for what they ought to use it—to succour the people emerging from the darkness of ignorance—but only to confirm them in it still more.

As Nekhlyúdov entered the waiting-room, Toporóv was conversing in his study with an abbess, a lively aristocrat, who was spreading and supporting Orthodoxy in the western country among the Uniates, who had been by force driven into the folds of the Orthodox Church.

An official on special missions, who was in the waiting-room, asked Nekhlyúdov about his business, and, having discovered that Nekhlyúdov had made up his mind to hand in the petition of the sectarians to the emperor, asked him whether he could not let him have the petition to look it over. Nekhlyúdov gave it to him, and the official went into the study with it. The abbess, in cowl, wavy veil, and trailing black skirt, having folded her white hands with their clean nails, in which she held a topaz rosary, came out of the study and headed for the entrance. Nekhlyúdov still was not asked in yet. Toporóv was reading the petition and shaking his head. He was unpleasantly surprised, as he read the clearly and strongly formulated petition.

"If it gets into the hands of the emperor, it might give rise to unpleasant questions and misunderstandings," he thought, as he finished the petition, and, putting it down on the desk, rang and ordered Nekhlyúdov shown in.

He remembered these sectarians' case; he had already had a petition from them. The trouble was that the Christians who had departed from Orthodoxy had been reprimanded and then tried before a court of justice, but the court had acquitted them. Then the bishop and the governor had decided, on account of the illegality of their marriages, to deport the men, women, and children to different places. What these fathers and wives asked was that they should not be separated. Toporóv thought of the first time the case had come to his notice. He had then wavered whether he had better not quash the case. But there could be no harm in confirming the decree of scattering the various members of peasant families; their sojourn in the same places might have bad consequences on the rest of the population in the sense of their defection from Orthodoxy; besides, it showed the zeal of the bishop; and so he let the case take the course which had been given to it.

But now, with such a defender as Nekhlyúdov, who had connections in St. Petersburg, the affair might be brought to the emperor's *particular* attention, as something cruel, or it might get into the foreign newspapers, and so he at once took an extraordinary stand.

"Good morning," he said, with the look of a very busy man, meeting Nekhlyúdov while standing, and immediately passing to the case.

"I know this case. The moment I looked at the names, I recalled this unfortunate matter," he said, taking the petition into his hands and showing it to Nekhlyúdov. "I am very grateful to you for reminding me of it. The governmental authorities have been a little too zealous—"

Nekhlyúdov was silent, looking with an evil feeling at the motionless mask of the pale face.

"I will order this measure withdrawn, and these people restored to their places of residence."

"So I do not need to press the petition any farther?" asked Nekhlyúdov.

"Certainly not. *I* promise you this," he said, with special emphasis on the word "I," being evidently quite convinced that *his* honesty, *his* word, were the best guarantee. "I shall write at once. Please be seated."

He went up to the table and began to write. Nekhlyúdov, without sitting down, looked down on that narrow, bald skull, and upon his hand with its large blue veins, which was rapidly moving the pen, and wondered why he was doing it, and why a man, who seemed to be so indifferent to everything, did this thing with so much apparent anxiety. Why—?

"So here it is," said Toporóv, sealing the envelope. "You may inform your *clients* of it," he added, compressing his lips into a semblance of a smile.

"For what, then, have those people been suffering?" Nekhlyúdov said, taking the envelope.

Toporóv raised his head and smiled, as though Nekhlyúdov's question afforded him pleasure.

"That I am unable to tell you. I can only tell you that the interests of the people, over which we watch, are so important that superfluous zeal in matters of faith are not so terrible and dangerous as the superflous indifference to them, which is now spreading."

"But how, in the name of religion, are the first demands of goodness violated, and families broken up?"

Toporóv was still smiling in the same condescending way, as though finding Nekhlyúdov's remarks very charming. Whatever Nekhlyúdov might have said, Toporóv would have found it charming and one-sided from the height of that broad government position which, he thought, he maintained.

"From the standpoint of a private individual that may seem so," he said, "but from the point of view of the government it appears somewhat different. My regards to you," said Toporóv, bending his head and extending his hand.

Nekhlyúdov shook it, and silently and hurriedly went away, regretting the fact that he had shaken his hand.

"The interests of the people," he repeated Toporóv's words. "Your interests, only yours," he thought, upon leaving Toporóv.

He mentally ran down the list of persons against whom the activity of the institutions that reëstablish justice, support faith, and educate the people was exercised— the woman who was punished for the illegal sale of liquor, and the young fellow for stealing, and the tramp for being a tramp, and the arsonist for arson, and the banker for fraud, and also unfortunate Lídiya, simply because it might have been possible to obtain the necessary information from her, and the sectarians for violating Orthodoxy, and Gurkévich for wishing a constitution—and Nekhlyúdov was suddenly struck with unusual force by the thought that all these people had been arrested, confined, and deported, not because they had all violated justice, or committed lawlessness, but only because they interfered with the officials and rich people in their possession of the wealth which they were amassing from the people.

They were interfered with equally by the woman who was trafficking without a license, and by the thief who was tramping through the city, and by Lídiya with her proclamations, and by the sectarians who were breaking down superstition, and by Gurkévich with his constitution. And therefore it seemed quite clear to Nekhlyúdov that all these officials—beginning with his aunt's husband, the Senators, and Toporóv, down to all those petty, clean, and correct gentlemen who were sitting at the tables in the various ministries—were not in the least concerned about the suffering of innocent people under such an order of things, but about the removal of all the dangerous elements.

So that not only was the rule neglected which enjoins that ten guilty men be pardoned lest one innocent man suffer, but, on the contrary, just as it is necessary to cut out the healthy part together with the decay, in order to remove the latter, so they removed ten innocent people by means of punishment in order to get rid of one genuinely guilty person.

Such an explanation of all that was taking place seemed so very simple and clear to Nekhlyúdov, but it was this same simplicity and clearness which made him hesitate in accepting it. It seemed hardly possible that such a complicated phenomenon should have such a simple and terrible explanation; it could not be that all these words about justice, goodness, laws, faith, God, and so on, should be nothing but words, and should conceal the coarsest selfishness and cruelty.

CHAPTER XXVIII

WITH MARIETTE AT THE THEATRE

Nekhlyúdov would have left that very evening, but he had promised Mariette to meet her in the theatre, and, although he knew that he ought not to do it, he nevertheless compromised his soul and went, considering himself bound by his word.

"Can I withstand this temptation?" he thought, not quite sincerely. "I shall see for the last time."

Having put on his dress coat, he arrived during the second act of the eternal *Dame aux camélias*, in which the visiting actress showed a new way for consumptive women to die.

The theatre was filled. Mariette's box was at once pointed out to Nekhlyúdov with due respect.

A liveried lackey stood in the corridor, bowed to him as to an acquaintance, and opened the door.

All the rows of the boxes opposite, with the figures sitting there and standing behind them, and the near-by backs and the gray, half-gray, bald, and pomaded, fixed-up heads of those who were sitting in the orchestra circle—all the spectators centred their attention on the lean, bony actress who, dressed up in silk and laces, was contorting herself and declaiming a monologue in an unnatural voice. Somebody hissed as the door was opened, and two streams of warm and cold air passed over Nekhlyúdov's face.

In the box were Mariette and a strange lady in a red wrap and a large, massive coiffure, and two men: a general, Mariette's husband, a handsome, tall man, with a severe, impenetrable, hook-nosed face and a broad, military chest, padded with cotton and starched linen, and a light-complexioned, bald man, with a clean-shaven, dimpled chin between majestic side-whiskers. Mariette, graceful, slender, elegant, décolletée, with her strong muscular shoulders, slanting from the neck, at the juncture of which there was a black birthmark, immediately turned around, and, indicating a seat behind her to Nekhlyúdov with her fan, smiled to him approvingly, gratefully, and, as he thought, meaningfully. Her husband calmly looked at Nekhlyúdov, as he always did, and nodded his head. One could see in him, in the glance which he exchanged with his wife, the master and owner of a beautiful wife.

When the monologue was finished, the theatre shook with applause. Mariette arose and, holding her rustling silk skirt, went to the back of the box and introduced her husband to Nekhlyúdov.

The general kept smiling with his eyes, and, saying that he was very glad, grew impenetrably silent.

"I must leave to-day, but I promised you," said Nekhlyúdov, turning to Mariette.

"If you do not wish to see me, you will see a remarkable actress," said Mariette, replying to the meaning of his words. "Was she not fine in the last scene?" she addressed her husband.

Her husband nodded his head.

"This does not touch me," said Nekhlyúdov. "I have seen so many real miseries to-day that—"

"Sit down and tell me about them."

Her husband listened and ironically smiled more and more with his eyes.

"I called on the woman who has been released, and who had been confined so long: she is a crushed being."

"That is the woman I told you about," Mariette said to her husband.

"I was very glad that it was possible to release her," he said, calmly, shaking his head and smiling quite ironically under his moustache, so Nekhlyúdov thought. "I will go out and have a smoke."

Nekhlyúdov sat in expectation that Mariette would tell him that important something of which she had spoken, but she said nothing and did not even try to say anything, but only jested and talked about the play which, so she thought, ought to interest him very much.

Nekhlyúdov saw that she had nothing to tell him, but that she only wished to appear before him in all the splendour of her evening toilet, with her shoulders and birthmark, and he felt both pleased and repulsed.

All that covering of charm, which lay over everything before, was now, as far as Nekhlyúdov was concerned, taken away, and he also saw what there was beneath that covering. He admired Mariette as he looked at her, but he knew that she was a liar, who was living with a man who was making his career by the tears and lives of hundreds and hundreds of people, while all this was a matter of indifference to her, and that everything she had said the day before was an untruth, and that she wanted, he did not know why, nor did she, to make him fall in love with her. He was both attracted and repelled by her. He made several attempts to leave, and picked up his hat, and again remained. But finally, when her husband returned to the box, with the odour of tobacco on his thick moustache, and cast a condescendingly contemptuous look at Nekhlyúdov, as though not recognizing him, Nekhlyúdov left for the corridor, before even the door was closed, and, having found his overcoat, left the theatre.

On his way home along the Nevski Prospect, he involuntarily noticed in front of him a tall, very well built, and provokingly dressed woman, who was slowly walking over the asphalt of the broad sidewalk; both in her face and in her whole figure could be seen the consciousness of her evil power. All the people who met her or came abreast of her looked her over. Nekhlyúdov was walking faster than she and, also, involuntarily looked at her face. Her face, no doubt painted, was handsome, and the woman smiled at Nekhlyúdov, flashed her eyes at him. Strange to say, Nekhlyúdov at once thought of Mariette, because he experienced the same sensation of attraction and repulsion which he had experienced in the theatre. Walking hurriedly past her, Nekhlyúdov turned into Morskáya Street, and upon reaching the quai, began, to the surprise of a policeman, to stroll up and down.

Tolstoy

Resurrection

page 274

"Just so she smiled at me in the theatre, as I entered," he thought, "and there was the same meaning in that smile as in this. The only difference is that this one says simply and directly, 'If you need me, take me! If not, pass on.' While the other pretends not to be thinking of it, but to live by some higher, refined sentiments, whereas in fact there is no difference. This one, at least, is telling the truth; the other one lies.

More than that: this one is driven to her condition by necessity; while the other one plays and dallies with that beautiful, repulsive, terrible passion. This street-walker is stinking, dirty water which is offered to those whose thirst is greater than their disgust; the one in the theatre is poison which imperceptibly poisons that into which it falls." Nekhlyúdov thought of his connection with the marshal's wife, and disgraceful memories burst upon him. "Disgusting is the animality of the beast in man," he thought, "but when that beast in man is in its pure form, you survey it from the height of your spiritual life and despise it; whether you have fallen or not, you remain what you have been; but when this animal is concealed beneath a pseudo-æsthetic, poetical film and demands worship, then you become all rapt in it, and, worshipping the animal, no longer distinguish right from wrong. Then it is terrible."

Nekhlyúdov saw this now as clearly as he saw the palaces, the sentries, the fortress, the river, the boats, the Exchange.

And as there was no soothing, restful darkness on earth that night, but an indistinct, cheerless, unnatural light without source, even thus there was no longer a restful darkness of ignorance in Nekhlyúdov's soul. Everything was clear. It was clear that what is considered important and good is bad and detestable, and that all that luxury and splendour conceal old, habitual crimes, which not only go without being punished, but are triumphant and adorned with all the charm which people are able to invent.

Nekhlyúdov wanted to forget this, not to see it, but he no longer could keep from seeing it. Although he did not see the source of the light which revealed all this to him, as he did not see the source of the light which lay over Petersburg, and although this light appeared to him indistinct, cheerless, and unnatural, he could not help seeing what was revealed to him in this light, and he had a simultaneously joyous and anxious feeling.

CHAPTER XXIX

MOSCOW, AND A VISIT TO KATYÚSHA

Upon arriving at Moscow, Nekhlyúdov first of all drove to the prison hospital to give Máslova the sad news of the Senate's confirmation of the verdict of the court, and to tell her that she must prepare herself for the journey to Siberia. He had little hope in the appeal to his Majesty, which the lawyer had drawn up for him and which he now took to the prison to have signed by Máslova. Strange to say, he did not desire success now. He had become used to the thought of going to Siberia and of living among deported and hard-labour criminals, and he found it hard to imagine how he would arrange his life and that of Máslova, if she were acquitted. He recalled the words of the American author, Thoreau, who had said, at the time when there was slavery in America, that the only place which was proper for an honest man in a country where slavery is legalized and protected was jail. Nekhlyúdov thought the same, particularly after his visit to St. Petersburg, and after all he had learned there.

Tolstoy
Resurrection
page 276

"Yes, the only proper place for an honest man in Russia at the present time is jail!" he thought. He felt this personally, as he now approached the prison and entered within its walls.

The porter in the hospital, recognizing Nekhlyúdov at once, informed him that Máslova no longer was there.

"Where is she, then?"

"Again in the prison."

"Why has she been transferred?" asked Nekhlyúdov.

"They are such a lot, your Excellency," said the porter, smiling contemptuously. "She started playing games with the assistant, so the senior doctor sent her back."

Nekhlyúdov had not thought that Máslova and her spiritual condition were so close to him. The news stunned him. He experienced a sensation akin to the feeling which overcomes one when suddenly informed of some great misfortune. He felt a severe pain. The first sensation which he experienced upon hearing the news was that of shame. First of all, he appeared ridiculous to himself with his joyful expectation of her changing spiritual condition. All those words about not wishing to receive his sacrifice, and the reproaches, and tears—all this, he thought, was only the cunning of a corrupt woman wishing to make the best possible use of him. It now seemed to him that at his last visit he had noticed the symptoms of that incorrigibility which had now become apparent. All that flashed through his mind as he instinctively put on his hat and left the hospital.

"But what am I to do now?" he asked himself. "Am I bound to her? Am I not freed by her having done exactly this?" he asked himself.

The moment he put this question to himself, he immediately saw that, considering himself free and abandoning her, he would not be punishing her, as he wished to do, but himself, and he felt terrified.

"No, what has happened cannot change, it can only confirm me in, my decision. Let her do what results from her spiritual condition—even her games with the assistant are her own affair. My business is to do that which my conscience demands of me," he said to himself. "My conscience demands the sacrifice of my liberty for the expiation of my sin, and my decision to marry her, even though in fictitious marriage, and to follow her wherever she may be sent, remains unchanged," he said to himself, with angry stubbornness. Upon leaving the hospital, he went determinedly toward the large gate of the prison.

At the gate he asked the warden on duty to tell the superintendent that he wished to see Máslova. The warden on duty knew Nekhlyúdov, and, being an acquaintance, he informed him of an important piece of prison news. The captain had been discharged, and in his place there was now another, severe chief.

"They are terribly severe here now," said the warden. "He is here now, they'll let him know at once."

Indeed, the superintendent was in the prison and soon came out to Nekhlyúdov. The new superintendent was a tall, bony man with protruding cheekbones, very slow in his movements, and gloomy.

"Interviews are granted only on stated days in the visiting-room," he said, without looking at Nekhlyúdov.

"But I have to give her a petition to his Majesty to sign."

"You can give it to me."

"I have to see the prisoner myself. I have always been granted permission before."

"That was before," said the superintendent, looking cursorily at Nekhlyúdov.

"I have a pass from the governor," Nekhlyúdov insisted, taking out his wallet.

"Let me see it," the superintendent went on without looking Nekhlyúdov in the eye. He took the paper which Nekhlyúdov handed to him with his long, dry, white fingers, with a gold ring on the index-finger, and read it slowly. "Please step into the office," he said.

This time there was nobody in the office. The superintendent sat down at the table, rummaging through the papers that were lying on it, apparently intending to be present at the interview.

When Nekhlyúdov asked him whether he could not see the political prisoner, Bogodúkhovskaya, the superintendent curtly replied that it was impossible.

"No interviews are granted with political prisoners," he said, again burying himself in the reading of the papers.

Having a letter to Bogodúkhovskaya in his pocket, Nekhlyúdov felt himself in the position of a guilty person whose plans have been discovered and destroyed.

When Máslova entered the office, the superintendent lifted his head and, without looking at either Máslova or Nekhlyúdov, said, "You may!" and continued to busy himself with his documents.

Máslova was dressed as before, in a white jacket, skirt, and kerchief. Upon approaching Nekhlyúdov and seeing his cold, unfriendly face, she grew red in the face and, fingering the edge of her jacket, lowered her eyes. Her embarrassment was to Nekhlyúdov a confirmation of the words of the hospital porter.

Nekhlyúdov wanted to address her as at the previous meeting, but he *could not*, however much he wished it, give her his hand, because she was so repulsive to him.

"I have brought you bad news," he said, in an even voice, without looking at her or giving her his hand. "The Senate has refused the appeal."

"I knew it," she said, in a strange voice, as though choking.

At any previous time Nekhlyúdov would have asked how she knew, but now he only glanced at her. Her eyes were full of tears.

But this did not appease him; on the contrary, it only irritated him still more.

The superintendent arose and began to walk up and down the room.

In spite of the disgust which Nekhlyúdov now felt for Máslova, he felt that he must express his regret to her for the Senate's refusal.

"Do not lose your courage," he said, "the petition to his Majesty may be successful, and I hope that—"

"I don't mean that," she said, pitifully looking at him with her moist and squinting eyes.

"What, then?"

"You were in the hospital, and, no doubt, they told you—"

"That is your affair," coldly said Nekhlyúdov, frowning.

The dormant cruel feeling of offended pride arose in him with renewed vigour the moment she mentioned the hospital.

"He, a man of the world, whom any girl of the highest circle would consider herself lucky to marry, had proposed to this woman to become her husband, and she could not wait, but had to start playing games with the assistant," he thought, looking hatefully at her.

"You sign this petition," he said, and, getting a large envelope out of his pocket, he laid it out on the table. She wiped her tears with the end of her kerchief and sat down at the table, asking him where and what to write.

He showed her where and what to write, and she sat down, adjusting the sleeve of her right arm with her left hand; he stood over her and silently looked at her bending back, which now and then shook from repressed sobs, and in his soul struggled feelings of evil and of good: of offended pride and of pity for her suffering, and the latter feeling was victorious.

He did not remember what happened first, whether his heart felt pity for her, or whether he first thought of himself, his sins, his own vileness, of which he accused her. But he suddenly became conscious both of his guilt and of his pity for her.

Having signed the petition and wiped her stained finger on her skirt, she arose and looked at him.

"Whatever may be the issue of this, nothing will change my decision," said Nekhlyúdov.

The thought of his forgiving her intensified the feeling of pity and tenderness in him, and he wished to console her. "I will do what I have told you I would. I will be with you, wherever you may be."

"What for?" she interrupted him, and beamed with joy.

"Think of what you need for the journey."

"I think, nothing special. Thank you."

The superintendent walked over to them, but Nekhlyúdov did not wait for him to make any remarks and bade her good-bye. He went out, experiencing an entirely new sensation of quiet joy, calm, and love for all men. Nekhlyúdov was rejoiced to find himself elevated to such an unaccustomed height where no acts of Máslova's could change his love for her. Let her play games with the assistant—that was her business; he loved her not for his own sake, but for hers and God's.

The games with the assistant, for which Máslova had been expelled from the hospital, and in the existence of which Nekhlyúdov believed, consisted in this: at the request of the female assistant, she went to the dispensary, which was at the end of the corridor, to get some pectoral tea; there she found an assistant, Ustínov by name, a tall fellow with a blistered face, who had long been annoying her with his attentions; in trying to escape from him, she pushed him so hard that he knocked against a shelf, from which two bottles fell down and broke.

The senior doctor, who happened to be passing along the corridor just then, heard the sound of broken glass and called out angrily at Máslova, who was running out, with her face all red.

"Girl, if you are going to start playing games here, I'll have you taken away. What is it?" he turned to the assistant, looking severely at him over his glasses.

The assistant smiled and began to justify himself. The doctor did not listen to all he had to say, but, raising his head in such a way that he began to look through his glasses, went to the hospital rooms; he told the superintendent that very day to send him another attendant in Máslova's place, one that would be more reliable. That was all there was to Máslova's games with the assistant. This expulsion from the hospital, under the pretext of her having started playing around with men, was particularly painful to Máslova, since after her meeting with Nekhlyúdov, all relations with men, distasteful as they had been, had become unusually repulsive to her. She was especially offended to see everybody, and among them the assistant with the blistered face, judge her by her past and present position, considering it proper to insult her and wondering at her refusal; this provoked her pity for herself and tears. As she had come out to see Nekhlyúdov now, she had intended to explain away the unjust accusation which, no doubt, he must have heard. But, as she began to justify herself, she saw that he did not believe her and that her vindication only confirmed his suspicion, and the tears rose in her throat, and she grew silent.

Tolstoy
Resurrection
page 280

Máslova was still under the impression, and she continued to assure herself of it, that she had not forgiven him and that she hated him, as she had expressed it to him at their second meeting, but in reality she loved him, and loved him so much that she involuntarily did everything he wished: she stopped drinking and smoking, gave up flirting, and had entered the hospital as an attendant. She had done it all because she knew he wished it. The reason she so firmly refused to accept his sacrifice of marrying her, every time he spoke of it, was because she wanted to repeat the proud words which she had once uttered to him, but chiefly because she knew that his marrying her could only make him unhappy. She had firmly decided not to accept his sacrifice, and yet she was pained to think that he despised her, that he thought that she continued to be what she had been, and that he did not see the change which had taken place in her. She was more pained by the fact that he was convinced she had done something wrong in the hospital than by the news that she had finally been condemned to hard labour.

CHAPTER XXX

THOUGHTS ON CRIMINALITY

Máslova might be sent away with the first deportation party, and therefore Nekhlyúdov was getting ready for the journey. He had so many things to attend to that he felt that, no matter how much free time he should have, he would never finish them. Everything was different from what it had been before. Formerly he had to think of what to do, and the centre of interest was always the same Dmítri Ivánovich Nekhlyúdov; and yet, notwithstanding the fact that all the interests of life focused on that Dmítri Ivánovich, all these matters were uninteresting to him. Now, all his business referred to people other than Dmítri Ivánovich, and they were all interesting and attractive, and there was no end to them.

More than that—all the previous occupations and affairs of Dmítri Ivánovich had always provoked annoyance and petulance, but these affairs of other people generally put him in a happy mood.

The affairs which at that time occupied Nekhlyúdov divided into three categories; he himself, with his customary pedantry, divided them in that manner, arranging them, in accordance with that division, in three briefcases.

The first affair dealt with Máslova and the effort to bring influence to bear on the petition to his Majesty which he had sent in, and in making preparations for the journey to Siberia.

The second affair dealt with his estates. In Pánovo the land had been given to the peasants, on condition that the rental thereof was to be used for the common needs of the village. But, in order to confirm them in their rights, he had to write out and sign the conditions and the deed. In Kuzmínskoe matters were still left as he had arranged them; that is, he was to receive money for the land; so, he had still to determine the periods of payment and how much of that money he was to take for his own use, and how much was to be left for the benefit of the peasants. As he did not know what expenses he would have in the proposed journey to Siberia, he could not decide to give up this income, which was already cut down by half.

The third affair dealt with helping the prisoners, who kept turning to him ever more frequently.

When he first came in contact with the prisoners, who turned to him for help, he immediately set out to intercede for them, trying to alleviate their fate; but later there was such a large number of petitioners that he felt his inability to help each of them, and so he was involuntarily led to a fourth affair, which of late occupied him more than any other.

This fourth affair involved solution of the question: what was that remarkable institution called the criminal court, the result of which was that prison, the inmates of which he had partly become acquainted with, as well as all those places of confinement, from the Petropávlovskaya Fortress to Sakhalín, where there languished hundreds and thousands of victims of what was for him an astonishing criminal law? What did it exist for? Where had it come from?

From his personal relations with the prisoners, from his questions to the lawyer, the prison priest, the superintendent, and from the lists of those confined, Nekhlyúdov came to the conclusion that the prisoners, the so-called criminals, could be divided into five categories.

The first of these consisted of entirely innocent people, victims of judicial error, like the suspected arsonist Menshóv, like Máslova, and others. There were not very many of that category—according to the priest's observation, about seven per cent, but the position of these people evoked special interest.

The second category consisted of people who were condemned for crimes committed under exceptional circumstances, such as rage, jealousy, drunkenness, and so on, that is, crimes which would be, no doubt, committed by those who judged and punished them if subjected to the same conditions. This category, according to Nekhlyúdov's observations, accounted for more than one-half of all the criminals.

The third was composed of people who were punished for doing what, in their opinion, constituted very common and even good acts, which, in the opinion of the strangers who had written the laws, were crimes. To this category belonged people who secretly trafficked in liquor, who smuggled, and who cut grass and picked up wood in the large proprietary and government forests. To this same category also belonged the thieving mountaineers and the infidels who robbed churches.

The fourth category was formed by people who were considered criminals only because they stood morally above the level of society. Such were the sectarians, the Poles, the Circassians, who rebelled for their freedom; such were also the political prisoners, socialists and strikers, who were condemned for opposing the authorities. The percentage of such people, the very best of society, was, according to Nekhlyúdov's observation, very large.

Finally, the fifth category was composed of people before whom society was much more guilty than they were before society. Those were the outcasts who were dulled by constant oppressions and temptations like the boy with the foot-mats and hundreds of other people, whom Nekhlyúdov had seen in prison and outside prison, whom the conditions of life systematically lead to the unavoidable act which is called a crime. To such people belonged, according to Nekhlyúdov's observation, very many thieves and murderers, with some of whom he had come in contact during this time. To this category he, having closely examined the matter, assigned also all those corrupt and debauched men whom the new school calls a criminal type and whose presence in society is regarded as the chief proof of the necessity for criminal law and punishment. These so-called corrupt, criminal, abnormal types were, in Nekhlyúdov's opinion, nothing other than those people against whom society had sinned more than they had sinned against society but toward whom society was not guilty directly, but against whose parents and ancestors society had sinned long ago.

Of all those in this group, Nekhlyúdov was particularly struck by the habitual criminal, Okhótin the thief, the illegitimate son of a prostitute, the product of a night lodging-house, who apparently, up to his thirtieth year, had never met men of higher morality than policemen, who had early joined a gang of thieves, and who, at the same time, was endowed with an unusual comic talent, by which he attracted people to himself. He asked Nekhlyúdov to intercede for him, all the while scoffing at himself, at the judges, at the prison, and at all the laws, not only criminal, but also divine. Another was handsome Fyódorov, who, with a gang of which he was the leader, had killed and robbed an old official. He was a peasant whose father had been completely illegally deprived of his house, and who later served in the army, where he suffered for falling in love with the mistress of an officer. He had an attractive, impassioned nature and was a man who wished to enjoy himself at any cost, who had never seen any people who in any way restrained themselves in their enjoyments,

and who had never heard that there was any aim in life other than enjoyment. It was evident to Nekhlyúdov that both were men, richly endowed by nature, who had been neglected and deformed like discarded plants. He also saw a tramp and a woman who repelled him by their stupidity and seeming cruelty, but he could not bring himself to see them as that criminal type of which the Italian school speaks, but saw them only as people who were personally repulsive to him, just as were those whom he had seen outside prison in dress coats, epaulets, and laces.

So the fourth business which interested Nekhlyúdov at that time was the investigation of the question why these many different people were imprisoned, while others, just such people as these, were not only at liberty but sitting in judgment over them.

At first, Nekhlyúdov had hoped to find an answer to this question in books, and so he bought everything that touched on this subject. He bought the books of Lombroso, and Garofalo, and Ferri, and Liszt, and Maudsley, and Tarde, and carefully read these books. But the more he read, the more he was disappointed in them. What always happens to people who turn to science, not in order to play a role in science, to write, to discuss, to teach, but to get answers to straight, simple, living questions, happened to him: science gave him answers to thousands of various, extremely clever, and wise questions, which stood in some relation to criminology, but not to the question for which he was trying to find an answer. He propounded a very simple question: Why and by what right does one class of people confine, deport, flog, and kill another, when they themselves are no better than those whom they torture, flog, and kill? To which he received replies in the shape of reflections like these: Does man have free will or not? Can a man be declared a criminal from cranial measurements, and so forth, or not? What part does heredity play in crime? Is there innate immorality? What is morality? What is insanity? What is degeneration? What is temperament? What influence on crime have climate, food, ignorance, suggestion, hypnotism, the passions? What is society? What are its duties? and so forth.

These reflections reminded Nekhlyúdov of an answer he had once received from a small boy who was returning from school. Nekhlyúdov asked the boy whether he had learned to spell. "I have," replied the boy. "Well, spell 'paw.'" "What kind of a paw, a dog's?" the boy answered, with a cunning face. In the scientific books Nekhlyúdov found, in response to his basic question, just such answers framed as questions themselves.

There was much in them which was clever, learned, and interesting, but there was no answer to the chief question: By what right do they punish others? Not only was there no answer to it, but all discussions took place in order to explain and justify punishment, the necessity for which was assumed as an axiom. Nekhlyúdov read a great deal, but in snatches, and he ascribed the absence of an answer to this superficial reading, hoping later to find a reply, and so he did not permit himself to believe the correctness of that answer which recently had presented itself to him ever more frequently.

CHAPTER XXXI

NEKHLYÚDOV'S SISTER

The party with which Máslova was to be deported was to start on July 5th. Nekhlyúdov was getting ready to leave on the same day. On the day before his departure, Nekhlyúdov's sister and her husband came to town to see him.

Nekhlyúdov's sister, Natálya Ivánovna Ragózhinskaya, was ten years older than her brother. He had grown up partly under her influence. She had loved him very much as a boy, and later, just before her marriage, when she was twenty-five years old and he fifteen, they met almost as equals. She was then in love with his now dead friend, Nikólenka Irténev. Both of them loved Nikólenka, loving in him and in themselves what was good, what unites all people.

Since then they had both become corrupted: he by his military service, and she by her marrying a man whom she loved in a sensual way, but who not only did not love everything which had been most sacred and dear to her and Dmítri, but who did not even understand what it was and ascribed all her striving for moral perfection and for serving people, which had formed the basis of her life then, to vanity and a desire to excel among people, the only sentiment he understood.

Ragózhinski was a man without a name or fortune, but a very sly official, who had made a comparatively brilliant judicial career by artfully steering between liberalism and conservatism, making use of the one or the other of the two tendencies which at a given moment and in a given case gave him the best results for his life, and, chiefly, by something special in him pleasing to the ladies. He was a man already past his youth when he met the Nekhlyúdovs abroad; he made Natálya, who, also, was not a very young girl then, fall in love with him, and married her, almost against her mother's will, who saw a *mésalliance* in this marriage. Nekhlyúdov, however much he concealed his feeling from himself and struggled against it, hated his brother-in-law. He loathed him for the vulgarity of his sentiments, his self-confident narrowness, and, chiefly, because of his sister, who was able to love this barren creature so passionately, selfishly, and sensually, and, to please him, to choke everything good that had been in her. It was always anguishing for Nekhlyúdov to think that Natálya was the wife of that bearded, self-confident man, with the shining bald spot on his head. He even could not repress a feeling of disgust for their children. Every time he heard she was about to become a mother, he experienced a feeling akin to regret that she had once again become infected with something bad from this man, alien to them all.

The Ragózhinskis arrived without their children (they had two, a boy and a girl), and stayed in the best room of the best hotel. Natálya Ivánovna at once went to her mother's old place, but not finding her brother there and learning from Agraféna Petróvna that he had taken furnished rooms, went there. A dirty servant, who met her in the dark, oppressive-smelling corridor, which had to be lighted in the daytime, told her that the prince was out.

Natálya Ivánovna wanted to go to her brother's room in order to leave him a note. The servant took her there.

Upon entering his two small rooms, Natálya Ivánovna carefully looked them over. She saw the familiar order and cleanliness in everything but was struck by the simplicity of the furnishings, completely new for him. On the desk she saw the familiar paperweight with the bronze dog; equally familiar to her were the properly placed briefcases and papers, and the writing materials, and the volumes of criminal jurisprudence, and an English book by Henry George, and a French book by Tarde, with a familiar large, crooked ivory paper-knife between its leaves.

She sat down at the table and wrote a note to him, asking him to be sure to come see them that very day; shaking her head in surprise at what she saw, she returned to her hotel.

Two questions now interested Natálya Ivánovna in reference to her brother: his marriage to Katyúsha, which she had heard about in her town, since everybody was talking about it, and his distribution of land among the peasants, which was also known to everybody and which seemed to many political and dangerous. On the one hand, marriage to Katyúsha pleased Natálya Ivánovna. She admired this determination, in it recognized both him and herself as they had been in those good days before her marriage, but at the same time she was horrified at the thought that her brother was going to marry such a terrible woman. The latter feeling was the stronger, and she decided to use all her influence to keep him from it, although she knew that this would be difficult.

The other matter, his distribution of the land to the peasants, was not so near to her heart, but her husband was incensed by it, and demanded she use her influence with her brother. Ignáti Nikíforovich said that such an act was the acme of inconsistency, frivolity, and pride, that this act could only be explained—if there was any possibility at all of explaining it—as a desire to show off, and brag, and make people talk about him.

"What sense is there in giving land to peasants with the rental to revert to them?"

he said. "If he wanted to do it, he could have sold it through the peasants' bank. There would have been some sense in that. Taken altogether, this act verges on abnormality," said Ignáti Nikíforovich, with an eye to the guardianship, insisting that his wife have a serious talk with her brother about this strange intention of his.

CHAPTER XXXII

NEKHLYÚDOV SEES HIS SISTER. AN ARGUMENT

When Nekhlyúdov returned home and found the note from his sister on his table, he immediately went to see her. It was evening. Ignáti Nikíforovich was resting in another room, and Natálya Ivánovna met her brother alone. She was dressed in a black silk close-fitting dress, with a red ribbon on her bosom, and her black hair was puffed up and combed according to the latest fashion. She evidently tried to appear as young as possible for her husband, who was her age. When she saw her brother, she jumped up from the divan and rapidly walked up to him, producing a rustling sound with her silk skirt. They kissed and looked at each other with smiles. There took place that mysterious, inexpressible, meaningful exchange of looks, in which everything was truth, and there began an exchange of words, which lacked that truth. They had not seen each other since the death of their mother.

"You have grown stouter and younger," he said.

Her lips puckered with delight.

"And you have grown thinner."

"How is Ignáti Nikíforovich?" asked Nekhlyúdov.

"He is resting. He did not sleep last night."

There was much to be said, but the words said nothing, while the glances said that much which ought to have been said had been left unsaid.

"I was at your room."

Tolstoy
Resurrection
page 286

"Yes, I know. I have left the house. It is too large for me, and lonely, and dull. I need none of those things, so you had better take them, the furniture, and all that."

"Yes, Agraféna Petróvna told me. I was there. I am very grateful to you, but—"

Just then the hotel waiter brought a silver tea service.

They kept silent as long as the waiter was busy about the service. Natálya Ivánovna walked over to a chair near a small table and silently poured the tea. Nekhlyúdov was silent, too.

"Dmítri, I know it all," Natálya said, looking at him with determination.

"I am very glad you do."

"Can you hope to correct her after such a life?" Natálya Ivánovna said.

He was sitting straight, not leaning on his elbows, on a small chair, and attentively listened to her, trying to catch all her meaning and to answer her carefully. The mood evoked in him by his last meeting with Máslova continued to fill his soul with calm joy and good-will to all men.

"I am not trying to correct her, but myself," he answered.

Natálya Ivánovna heaved a sigh.

"There are other means than marriage."

"I think this is the best; and, besides, it takes me into that world where I can be useful."

"I do not think," said Natálya Ivánovna, "that you can be happy there."

"It is not a question of my happiness."

"Of course. But she, if she has a heart, cannot be happy, and cannot even wish it."

"She does not wish it—"

"I understand, but life—"

"What about life?"

"Demands something else."

"It demands nothing but that we do what is necessary," said Nekhlyúdov, looking at her face, which was still beautiful, though already covered with small wrinkles near the eyes and mouth.

"I do not understand," she said, with a sigh.

"Poor, dear sister. How could she have changed so?" Nekhlyúdov thought, remembering Natálya as she was before her marriage, and drawn to her by a tender feeling made up of endless childish memories.

At this time Ignáti Nikíforovich, bearing his head high, as always, expanding his broad chest, stepping softly and lightly, sparkling with his spectacles, his bald spot, and his black beard, entered the room, smiling.

"How do you do, how do you do," he said, emphasizing his words in an unnatural and conscious manner.

(At first, after the marriage they had tried hard to say "thou" to each other, but they had not succeeded.)

They shook hands, and Ignáti Nikíforovich sank lightly into an arm-chair.

"I am not interfering with your conversation?"

"No, I don't hide from anybody the things I say and do."

The moment Nekhlyúdov saw this face, these hirsute hands, and heard this condescending, self-confident voice, his meek spirit fled from him.

"We were speaking of his intention," said Natálya Ivánovna. "Do you want some?" she added, taking hold of the teapot.

"Yes, please. What intention?"

"To go to Siberia with the party of prisoners which includes the woman toward whom I consider myself guilty," said Nekhlyúdov.

"I have heard that you intend not only to go with them, but to do something more."

"Yes, to marry her, if she wishes it."

"Really! If it is not unpleasant to you, explain your motives to me. I do not understand them."

"The motives are that this woman—that her first step on the path of immorality—" Nekhlyúdov was angry at himself for not being able to find the proper expression. "The motives are that I am guilty, and she is punished."

"If she is punished, she, no doubt, is not guiltless."

"She is absolutely innocent."

Nekhlyúdov told of the whole affair with unnecessary agitation.

"Yes, it is an omission of the presiding judge and, consequently, carelessness in the reply of the jury. But there is a Senate for such a thing."

"The Senate has refused the appeal."

"If it has refused it, there could not have been sufficient ground for annulment," said Ignáti Nikíforovich, apparently sharing the well-known opinion that truth is a product of a judicial verdict. "The Senate cannot enter into the merits of the case. But if there really is an error of the court, his Majesty ought to be appealed to."

"That has been done, but there is no probability of success. They will inquire of the ministry, the ministry will refer it to the Senate, the Senate will repeat its verdict, and, as ever, the innocent person will be punished."

"In the first place, the ministry will not ask the Senate," Ignáti Nikíforovich said, with a smile of condescension, "but will ask the court for the proceedings in the case, and, if an error is discovered, they will report accordingly; and, secondly, innocent people are never punished, or, at least, only in exceptional cases. Only guilty people are punished," said Ignáti Nikíforovich, leisurely, with a self-satisfied smile.

"I have become convinced of the opposite," said Nekhlyúdov, with a feeling of ill-will toward his brother-in-law. "I am convinced that the greater part of those who are condemned by courts are innocent."

"How is that?"

"They are innocent in the literal sense of the word, just as this woman is innocent of poisoning, as a peasant, whose acquaintance I have just made, is innocent of murder, which he has not committed; as a mother and her son, who came very near being convicted, are innocent of the arson caused by the owner of the property."

"Of course, there always have been and always will be judicial errors. A human institution cannot be perfect."

"And then, an immense number are innocent because, having been brought up in a certain circle, they do not regard their acts as crimes."

"I'm sorry, this is wrong. Every thief knows that stealing is not good," Ignáti Nikíforovich said, with the same calm, self-confident, and slightly contemptuous smile, which irritated Nekhlyúdov.

"No, he does not. You tell him, 'Don't steal!' and he sees that the owners of factories steal his labour, retaining his wages, that the government, with all its officials, does not stop robbing him, by means of taxes."

"This is anarchism," Ignáti Nikíforovich quietly defined the meaning of the words of his brother-in-law.

"I do not know what it is; I only tell you what actually takes place," continued Nekhlyúdov. "He knows that the government robs him; he knows that we, the landowners, robbed him long ago by taking away his land, which ought to be a common possession; and then, when he gathers twigs on that land in order to make a fire in his stove with them, we put him in jail and want to convince him that he is a thief. He knows that the thief is not himself but the man who has taken the land from him, and that every restitution of what has been stolen is a duty he has to his family."

"I do not understand, or if I do, I do not agree. The land cannot help being somebody's property. If you were to divide it up," began Ignáti Nikíforovich, with the full and calm conviction that Nekhlyúdov was a socialist, and that the theory of socialism consisted in the demand that the land be divided up in equal parts, and that such a division was very foolish and he could easily prove its inconsistencies, "if you were to divide it up to-day in equal parts, they will to-morrow pass back into the hands of the most industrious and able men."

"Nobody intends to divide the land up equally. The land ought to be nobody's property; it ought not to be the subject of purchase and sale, or of mortgaging."

"The right of property is inborn in man. Without property rights there will be no interest in working the land. Take away the right of ownership, and we return to the savage state," Ignáti Nikíforovich said, authoritatively, repeating the customary argument in favour of ownership of land, which is considered incontestable, and which consists in the assumption that the greed for ownership of land is a sign of its necessity.

"On the contrary. The land will not lie idle, as it does now when the proprietors, like dogs in the manger, do not allow those who can to make use of it, and themselves do not know how to."

"Listen, Dmítri Ivánovich! This is absolutely senseless! Is it possible in our day to do away with the ownership of land? I know this is your old hobby. But let me tell you straight—" Ignáti Nikíforovich grew pale, and his voice trembled: this question evidently touched him closely. "I should advise you to consider this subject carefully, before you enter on its practical solution."

"Are you speaking of my own personal affairs?"

"Yes. I assume that all of us, placed in a certain position, must carry out the duties which issue from this position, that we must maintain the conditions of existence under which we were born, which we have inherited from our ancestors, and which we must transmit to our posterity."

"I consider my duty to be—"

"Excuse me," Ignáti Nikíforovich continued, not allowing himself to be interrupted. "I am not speaking for myself, nor for my children, who are securely provided for; I am earning enough to live comfortably, and I suppose my children will not have to suffer; therefore my protest against your ill-advised actions, let me say, originates not in my personal interests, but because I cannot agree with you on principle. I should advise you to think about them a little more carefully, and to read—"

"Please let me attend to my own business, and decide for myself what I am to read and what not," said Nekhlyúdov, growing pale. He felt his hands becoming cold and that he was losing control of himself, so he grew silent and began to drink tea.

CHAPTER XXXIII

THE ARGUMENT IS CONTINUED

"Well, how are the children?" Nekhlyúdov asked his sister, after he had somewhat composed himself.

She told him that they had been left with their grandmother, her husband's mother. Happy to see that the argument with her husband had come to an end, she began to tell him how her children played travelling, just as he once had done with his dolls—one a Negro, and the other called the French lady.

"Do you remember that?" said Nekhlyúdov, smiling.

"Just think of it, they are playing exactly the same way."

The disagreeable conversation was over. Natálya calmed herself, but in the presence of her husband she did not wish to talk about what her brother alone could understand; in order to introduce a general subject, she mentioned the St. Petersburg news that had just reached them in reference to the sorrow of Kámenski's mother at having lost her only son in a duel. Ignáti Nikíforovich expressed disapproval of the order of things which excluded murder in a duel from ordinary crimes.

This remark provoked a retort from Nekhlyúdov, and there again an argument flared up on the same theme, in which everything was only half said, and both men did not express their full views, but persisted in their mutually condemnatory convictions.

Ignáti Nikíforovich felt that Nekhlyúdov criticized him and despised all his activity, and he was anxious to show him the whole injustice of his judgements. Nekhlyúdov, independently of the annoyance he experienced at his brother-in-law's interference in his land affairs (in the depth of his soul he felt that his brother-in-law and his sister and their children, as his heirs, had a right to do it), fretted because this narrow-minded man continued, with the greatest confidence and composure, to regard as regular and legal what to Nekhlyúdov now seemed unquestionably senseless and criminal. This self-confidence irritated Nekhlyúdov.

"What would a court have done?" asked Nekhlyúdov.

"It would have convicted one of the two duellists as a common murderer and would have sent him to hard labour."

Nekhlyúdov's hands again grew cold, and he said, excitedly:

"What would that have amounted to?"

"Justice would have been done."

"As though justice formed the aim of a court's activity," said Nekhlyúdov.

"What else, if not that?"

"The maintenance of class interests. The courts, in my opinion, are only an administrative tool for the maintenance of the existing order of things, which is advantageous for our class."

"This is an entirely novel view," Ignáti Nikíforovich said, with a calm smile. "A somewhat different meaning is commonly ascribed to the courts."

"Theoretically, and not practically, as I have had occasion to see. The purpose of the courts is the maintenance of society in its present condition, and so they prosecute and punish equally those who stand higher than the common average and who wish to lift it up, the so-called political criminals, and those who stand below it, the so-called criminal types."

"I cannot agree with you, first, that all so-called political prisoners are punished for standing higher than the common average. They are chiefly social outcasts, just as corrupt, although somewhat differently, as those criminal types, whom you consider to be below the average."

"I know many people who stand incomparably higher than their judges; all the sectarians are moral, steadfast people—"

But Ignáti Nikíforovich, with the habit of a man who is never interrupted when speaking, was not listening to Nekhlyúdov, and continued to speak at the same time as Nekhlyúdov, which especially irritated him.

"Nor can I agree with your statement that the purpose of the courts is the maintenance of the existing order. The courts pursue their aims, which are the correction—"

"It's a fine correction you get in jail," interposed Nekhlyúdov.

"Or the removal," stubbornly proceeded Ignáti Nikíforovich, "of those corrupt and beastly people who threaten the existence of society."

"The point is it does neither the one nor the other. Society has no means for doing it."

"What do you mean? I do not understand," said Ignáti Nikíforovich, with a forced smile.

"I mean to say that there are only two really sensible punishments, those that were in vogue in ancient days, corporal and capital punishments, which, on account of the refinement of manners, are falling more and more out of use," said Nekhlyúdov.

"This is new, and rather remarkable from you."

"There is some sense in causing a man bodily pain, so that he will abstain in future from doing what he has been beaten for, and there is good reason to chop off the head of a dangerous and harmful member of society. Both these punishments have a sensible purpose. But what sense is there in locking up a man, who is corrupt through indolence and bad example, subjecting him to conditions of secure and obligatory indolence, in company with the most corrupt people? Or in transporting him at government expense—each costs more than five hundred roubles—from Túla Province to Irkútsk, or from Kursk—"

"But people are afraid of this journey at government expense, and if it were not for these journeys and prisons, we should not be sitting here as securely as we are."

"These prisons cannot ensure our security, because these people do not stay there all the time, but are let out again. On the contrary, in these institutions these people become acquainted with the highest degree of vice and corruption, that is, the danger is only increased."

"You mean to say that the penitentiary system ought to be improved."

"It cannot be improved. The improved prisons would cost more than what is spent on popular education and would impose a new burden on the people."

"But the imperfections of the penitentiary system by no means invalidate the courts," Ignáti Nikíforovich continued his speech, paying no attention to his brother-in-law.

"These imperfections cannot be corrected," Nekhlyúdov said, raising his voice.

"So, according to you, we shall have to kill? Or, as a statesman has proposed, we ought to put out their eyes," said Ignáti Nikíforovich, with a victorious smile.

"This would be cruel, but to the point. What is being done now is not only not

Tolstoy
Resurrection
page 292

to the point, but so stupid that it is impossible to understand how mentally healthy people can take part in so stupid and cruel a business as a criminal court."

"I am taking part in it," Ignáti Nikíforovich said, growing pale.

"That is your business. But I do not understand it."

"I think there are many things which you do not understand," Ignáti Nikíforovich said, in a trembling voice.

"I saw the associate prosecutor bend all his efforts in court to convict an unfortunate boy, who in any uncorrupted man would have provoked nothing but compassion. I know how another prosecutor examined a sectarian and made out that the reading of the Gospel is a criminal offence. The whole activity of the courts consists in such senseless and cruel acts."

"I would not serve if I thought so," said Ignáti Nikíforovich, rising.

Nekhlyúdov noticed a peculiar sparkle under the spectacles of his brother-in-law. "Can it be tears?" thought Nekhlyúdov. Indeed, those were tears of affront. Ignáti Nikíforovich went up to the window, took out his handkerchief, and, clearing his throat, began to clean his glasses, which he had taken off, at the same time wiping his eyes. Upon returning to the sofa, Ignáti Nikíforovich lighted a cigar, and never said another word. Nekhlyúdov was ashamed and pained at having grieved his brother-in-law and his sister to such an extent, especially since he was to leave the next day and would not see them again. In embarrassment, he bade them farewell and went home.

"It may be that what I said was true, at least he has not successfully answered me; but I ought not to have spoken to him in such a manner. I have changed little enough, if I can allow myself to be so carried away by ill-will, and so insult him and grieve poor Natálya," thought he.

CHAPTER XXXIV

NEKHLYÚDOV GETS READY FOR THE TRIP

The group which included Máslova was to start from the station at three o'clock, and therefore, in order to see them depart from the prison and to reach the station with them, Nekhlyúdov intended to arrive at the prison before noon.

As Nekhlyúdov was putting away his things and his papers, he came across his diary and began to read some passages in it and what he had last written down. The last thing he had noted down before his departure for St. Petersburg ran as follows:

"Katyúsha does not wish my sacrifice, but her own. She has conquered, and so have I. I rejoice in that internal change which I think—I hardly dare believe it—is taking place within her. I hardly dare believe it, but it seems to me she is coming alive again." Immediately after it was written: "I have had a very oppressive and a very joyful experience. I have learned that she did not behave well in the hospital. It suddenly hurt me very much. I hadn't expected such pain. I spoke to her in disgust and hatred, and then I suddenly thought of myself and of how often I have been, even now, in thought, guilty before her of the very thing for which I hated her, and immediately I both loathed myself and pitied her, and I was happy. How much better we should be if we succeeded in seeing the beam in our own eye in time." On this last day he had written: "Saw Natásha, and this time my contentment made me unkind and cross, and an oppressive feeling was left behind. What is to be done? A new life begins to-morrow. Good-bye to the old for ever! There is an accumulation of many impressions, but I cannot yet harmonize them."

Tolstoy
Resurrection
page 294

Upon awakening on the following morning, Nekhlyúdov's first feeling was regret at what had happened between him and his brother-in-law.

"I cannot leave thus," he thought. "I must go to see them and smooth it over."

But when he looked at his watch, he saw that it was too late and that he had to hurry, in order not to miss the departure of the group. He quickly collected all his things and sent them by the porter and by Tarás, Fedósya's husband, who was travelling with him, straight to the station; then he took the first cab he could get and drove to the prison.

The prisoners' train left two hours ahead of the mail-train on which Nekhlyúdov was to travel, and he therefore settled his bill at the hotel, not intending to come back again.

It was an oppressive July day. The stones of the streets and houses, and the iron sheets of the roofs, which had not cooled off after the sultry night, reflected their heat into the close, immovable air. There was no wind; whenever a breeze started, it wafted a hot and stinking air, saturated with dust and the stench of oil-paint. There were but few people in the streets, and those that were out tried to walk in the shade of the houses. Only the tawny, sunburnt peasant street-pavers in their bast shoes were sitting in the middle of the street and striking their hammers on the cobblestones that were placed in the hot sand; gloomy policemen, in unbleached blouses and with the orange ribbons of their revolvers, stood in the middle of the streets, sullenly changing places; and the tram-cars, shaded by blinds on the sunny side, and drawn by horses in white capotes, with their ears sticking through the openings in the cloth, ran, tinkling, up and down the streets.

When Nekhlyúdov reached the prison, the convoy of prisoners had not yet started, and inside the jail the transfer of the prisoners to be taken away, which had begun at four o'clock in the morning, was still causing busy work. There were 623 men and 64 women in the group. They had all to be checked off on the lists; the ailing and feeble had to be segregated and handed over to the soldiers of the guard. The new superintendent, two assistants of his, the doctor with his assistant, the officer of the guard, and the clerk were seated at a table, placed in the yard in the shade of a wall; on it were lying papers and appurtenances of the chancery. They called out, examined, and noted down one prisoner after another as they walked up to the table.

The sun was now falling over half the table. It was growing hot and extremely sultry, both from the absence of breeze and from the exhalations of the throng of prisoners who were standing there.

"Will there ever be an end to it?" said the tall, stout, red-faced officer of the guard, with his raised shoulders and short arms, who never stopped puffing the smoke of his cigarette through his moustache, which covered his mouth. "They are tiring me out. Where did you get such a lot of them? Are there many more?"

The clerk looked it up.

"Twenty-four more men and the women."

"Don't stand there, but walk up here!" cried the officer to the prisoners who had not yet been checked off, and who were crowding each other.

They had been standing for three hours in rows, not in the shade, but in the sun, waiting their turns.

This was the work which was going on within the precincts of the prison; outside at the gate stood a sentry with a gun, as always, and about twenty drays for the belongings of the prisoners and for the feeble, and at the corner there was a throng of relatives and friends, who were waiting for the prisoners to come out, in order to see them, and, if possible, to say a few words and give them something for their journey. Nekhlyúdov joined this crowd.

He stood there about an hour. At the end of that time the clanking of chains was heard within the gate, the sound of steps, the voices of the officers, clearing of throats, and the subdued conversation of a large throng. This lasted about five minutes, during which the wardens walked in and out through a small door. Finally a command was given.

The gate opened with a crash, the clanking of the chains became louder, and the soldiers of the guard, in white blouses and with their guns, came out and, apparently executing a familiar and habitual manœuvre, took up position in a large semicircle around the gate. When they had taken their stand, another command was heard, and the prisoners began to come out in pairs: they wore pancake-shaped caps on their shaven heads, and carried bags on their backs; they dragged their fettered legs, swung their one free arm, and with the other held the bags over their shoulders. First came the male prisoners, who were to be deported to hard labour—all of them wearing the same gray trousers and cloaks, with black marks on their backs. All of them—whether they were young, old, lean, stout, pale, red, black, bearded, mustachioed, beardless, Russians, Tartars, or Jews—came out rattling their chains and briskly swinging their arms, as though going out for a long walk, but after making about ten steps they stopped and docilely arranged themselves in rows of four, one behind the other. After these, without interruption, there poured forth from the gate just such shaven prisoners, without their leg-fetters, but chained to each other by handcuffs, and wearing the same kind of garb. These were the prisoners to be deported for settlement. They walked out just as briskly, stopped, and also arranged themselves in rows of four. Then came those deported by the Communes. Then the women, also in successive order: first the hard-labour convicts, in gray prison caftans and kerchiefs, then the deportation convicts, and those who voluntarily followed their husbands, in their city and peasant attires. A few of the women carried nursing babies in the folds of their gray caftans.

With the women walked their children, boys and girls. These children pressed close to the women prisoners, like colts in a herd of horses. The men stood silent, now and then clearing their throats, or making abrupt remarks. But the women chattered incessantly. Nekhlyúdov thought he had recognized Máslova as she came out of the gate, but later she was lost in the large throng of the women who were placed back of the men, and he saw only a crowd of gray beings, which seemed to have lost all human, especially all feminine, qualities, with their children and their sacks.

Notwithstanding the fact that all the prisoners had been counted inside the walls of the prison, the soldiers of the guard began to count them again, in order to see whether they tallied with the previous count. This recounting lasted a long time, especially since some of the prisoners kept moving about and confusing the counts of the soldiers. The soldiers cursed and pushed the submissive, but angry prisoners, and began to count anew. After all had been counted, the officer of the guard gave a command, and then there was a disturbance in the crowd. Feeble men, women, and children, trying to outrun each other, hurried to the wagons, where they deposited their bags, and themselves climbed in. The women with the crying babes, the cheerful children, who were contending for seats, and grim, gloomy prisoners also climbed into them.

A few prisoners doffed their caps and walked over to the officer of the guard, to ask him for something. Nekhlyúdov later learned that they were asking to be allowed to ride in the wagons. Nekhlyúdov saw the officer calmly puff at his cigarette, without looking at the speaker, and then suddenly lift his short arm, as though to strike the prisoner, and the latter, ducking his head, in expectation of a blow, jump away from him.

"I will make such a nobleman of you that you will remember me! You will get there on foot!" cried the officer.

The officer let only one tottering tall old man, in leg-fetters, take a seat in a wagon, and Nekhlyúdov saw this old man take off his pancake-shaped cap and make the sign of the cross, as he was walking toward the wagon. He had a hard time getting in, as the chains made it hard for him to lift his weak, fettered legs, and a woman, who was already seated in the wagon, helped him, by pulling him up by his arms.

When all the wagons were filled with the bags, and those who were permitted had taken their seats in them, the officer of the guard took off his cap, wiped his forehead, his bald pate, and his stout red neck with his handkerchief, and made the sign of the cross.

"Group, march!" he commanded.

The soldiers clattered their guns; the prisoners took off their caps, some doing so with their left hands, and began to cross themselves; the friends who were seeing them off called out something; the prisoners cried something in reply; among the women weeping was heard—and the group, surrounded by soldiers in white blouses, started, raising dust with their fettered legs. In front were soldiers; behind them, clanking with their chains, were the fettered men, four in a row; then came the settlement convicts, then the communal prisoners, handcuffed by twos; and then the women. After these followed the wagons with the bags and the feeble prisoners. On one of these, on a high load, sat a woman, who was all wrapped up, and who did not stop wailing and sobbing.

CHAPTER XXXV

THE PRISONERS PROCEED
THROUGH TOWN

The procession was so long that the wagons began to move only when the men in front had disappeared from view. When these started, Nekhlyúdov seated himself in the cab, which was waiting for him, and ordered the driver to drive past the party, in order to see whether there were no men among them whom he knew, and then, to find Máslova among the women and to ask her whether she had received the things which he had sent her.

It was very hot. There was no breeze, and the dust raised by a thousand feet hovered all the time above the prisoners who were walking in the middle of the street. They marched rapidly, and the slow-moving horse of the cab in which Nekhlyúdov was riding took a long time in getting ahead of the procession. There were rows and rows of unfamiliar creatures of strange and terrible aspect, moving their similarly clad legs in even measure in time to their step, and swinging their free arms, as though to give themselves courage. There were so many of them, and they so resembled each other, and were placed in such exceptional and strange conditions, that it seemed to Nekhlyúdov that they were not men but some peculiar, terrible beings. This impression was shattered by his espying, in the throng of the hard-labour convicts, murderer Fyódorov and, among the deportation convicts, his acquaintance, the comedian Okhótin, and another, a tramp, who had asked for his help.

Nearly all the prisoners turned around, eyeing the vehicle which was driving past them, and the gentleman in it, who was looking closely at them. Fyódorov gave an upward shake of the head in token of his having recognized Nekhlyúdov; Okhótin only winked. Neither the one nor the other bowed, considering this to be against the regulation. Upon coming abreast of the women, Nekhlyúdov at once recognized Máslova. She was walking in the second row of women. On the outside walked a red-faced, short-legged, black-eyed, ugly woman; it was Khoroshavka. Then followed a pregnant woman, who with difficulty dragged her legs along; the third was Máslova. She was carrying a bag over her shoulder and was looking straight ahead of her. Her face was calm and determined. The fourth one in the same row was a young, handsome woman, in a short cloak and with her kerchief tied in peasant fashion, stepping briskly—that was Fedósya. Nekhlyúdov got down from the vehicle and walked over to the moving women, wishing to ask Máslova whether she had received the things, and how she felt; but the under-officer of the guard, who was walking on the same side of the group, having at once noticed him, ran up to him.

"It is not permitted, sir, to walk up to the group—it is against the law," he cried, as he was coming up.

Having come close, and recognizing Nekhlyúdov (everybody in the prison knew him), the under-officer put his fingers to his cap, and, stopping near Nekhlyúdov, said, "Here it is not permitted. At the station you may, but here it is against the law. Don't stop! March!" he cried to the prisoners, and, trying to appear dashing, in spite of the heat, galloped off to his place in his new foppish boots.

Nekhlyúdov walked back to the sidewalk, and, ordering the vehicle to follow him, kept in sight of the group. Wherever the procession passed, it attracted attention, mingled with compassion and terror. People in their carriages put out their heads and followed the prisoners with their eyes. Pedestrians stopped and looked in amazement and fear at this terrible spectacle. Some walked up and offered alms. The soldiers of the guard received these gifts. Some followed in the wake of the procession, as though hypnotized, and then they stopped and, shaking their heads, accompanied the party with their eyes only. People rushed out from the front steps and gates, calling to each other, or hung out of the windows, and immovably and silently watched the terrible procession. At a cross street the group held up an elegant carriage. On the box sat a broad-backed coachman, with a shining face and a row of buttons on his back; in the carriage, on the back seat, sat a man with his wife; the wife was thin and pale, in a bright hat, with a coloured parasol, and her husband wore a silk hat and a tight foppish overcoat. In front, opposite them, sat their children: a little girl, dressed up and shining like a flower, with loosely hanging blond hair, also with a bright-coloured parasol, and an eight-year-old boy with a long, thin neck and protruding shoulder-bones; he wore a sailor hat, adorned with long ribbons. The father angrily upbraided the coachman for not having passed in time ahead of the procession, while the mother finically blinked and frowned, shielding herself against the sun and dust with her silk parasol, which she put close to her face. The broad-backed coachman scowled angrily, listening to the unjust accusation of his master, who had himself ordered that they take that street, and with difficulty restrained the glossy black stallions, lathered at their bits and necks, that were eager to start.

A policeman was very anxious to serve the owner of the elegant carriage and to let him pass by stopping the prisoners, but he felt that in this procession there was a gloomy solemnity, which could not be violated even for that rich gentleman. He only saluted, in sign of his respect for wealth, and sternly looked at the prisoners, as though promising under all conditions to protect the persons in the carriage from them. Thus, the carriage was compelled to wait for the passing of the whole procession, and it went on only when the last dray with the bags and prisoners upon it had gone by; the hysterical woman, who was sitting on the wagon, and who had quieted down, at the sight of the elegant carriage again burst out into screaming and wailing. Only then, the coachman lightly touched his reins, and the black chargers, clattering their hoofs on the pavement, whisked off the softly swaying carriage with its rubber tires into the country, where the gentleman, and his wife, his girl, and the boy with the thin neck and protruding shoulder-bones were driving for an outing.

Neither the father nor the mother gave their children an explanation of what they saw; thus the children were compelled to solve for themselves the question what this spectacle meant.

The girl, taking into consideration the expression of her parents' faces, came to the conclusion that these were very different people from what her parents and their acquaintances were; that they were bad people, and that, consequently, they had to be treated as they were. Therefore the girl felt terrible, and was glad when they had disappeared from sight.

But the boy with the long, thin neck, who did not take his eyes off the prisoners, as long as the procession went by, found a different answer to this question. He knew firmly and beyond any doubt, having learned it directly from God, that they were just such people as he himself and all other people were, and that, consequently, something very bad had been done to them, something that ought not to have been done to them, and he was sorry for them and experienced terror both before the people who were fettered and shaven, and before those who had fettered and shaved them. And so the boy's lips kept swelling more and more, and he made great efforts to keep from crying, assuming that it was shameful to weep under such circumstances.

CHAPTER XXXVI

NEKHLYÚDOV IN THE TAVERN

Nekhlyúdov walked with as rapid a gait as the prisoners, but even though he was lightly clad, as the weather demanded, he felt dreadfully hot and oppressed by the dust and motionless sultry air in the streets. Having walked about a quarter of a verst, he seated himself in the cab and drove ahead, but in the middle of the street, in the cab, he felt even hotter. He tried to recall his thoughts about his last conversation with his brother-in-law, but now they no longer agitated him as they had in the morning. They were overshadowed by the impressions of the start from the prison and the procession of the prisoners. Above everything else, it was oppressively hot. At a fence, in the shade of trees, two school students were standing with their caps off before a squatting ice-cream seller. One of the boys was already enjoying the feast, licking off the bone spoon, while the other was waiting for the glass to be filled to the top with something yellow.

"I wonder where I can get a drink here?" Nekhlyúdov asked the cabman, being overcome by irrepressible thirst.

"There is a good inn not far from here!" said the driver, and, turning the corner, he took Nekhlyúdov to a building with a large sign.

A puffy clerk in a shirt, who was standing back of the counter, and waiters, who had once looked clean and white and who were now sitting at the tables, since there were no guests present, looked with curiosity at the unusual guest and offered their services to him. Nekhlyúdov asked for seltzer water and sat down away from the window at a small table with a dirty cloth. Two men were sitting at a table, on which stood a tea service and a bottle of white glass. They kept wiping off the perspiration from their brows, and figuring at something in a peaceable manner. One of these was swarthy and baldheaded, with just such a border of black hair on the back of his head as Ignáti Nikíforovich had. This impression again reminded Nekhlyúdov of his conversation with his brother-in-law on the previous day, and of his desire to see him and his sister before his departure. "I shall hardly have enough time before the train leaves," he thought. "I had better write her a letter." He asked for paper and an envelope, and a stamp, and, sipping the fresh, effervescent water, was thinking what to write. But his thoughts were distracted, and he was unable to compose the letter.

"Dearest Natásha—I cannot leave under the heavy impression of yesterday's conversation with Ignáti Nikíforovich," he began. "What next? Shall I ask forgiveness for what I said yesterday? But I said what I thought. And he will imagine that I recant. Besides, his interference in my personal affairs— No, I cannot—" and, feeling again a rising hatred for this, to him, strange, self-confident man, who did not understand him, Nekhlyúdov put the unfinished letter in his pocket and, paying his check, went out into the street and set off to catch up with the group.

The heat had become even more intense. The walls and stones seemed to exhale hot air. Feet burnt on the heated pavement, and Nekhlyúdov felt as though he burnt his hand when he put it to the lacquered fender of the vehicle.

The horse dragged himself along the streets in an indifferent amble, evenly striking the dusty and uneven pavement with his hoofs; the cabman kept dozing off; Nekhlyúdov sat, thinking of nothing in particular and looking indifferently in front of him. At a slope of the street, opposite the gate of a large house, stood a throng of people and a soldier of the guard with his gun.

Nekhlyúdov stopped the cab.

"What is it?" he asked a janitor.

"Something the matter with a prisoner."

Nekhlyúdov left the vehicle and walked up to the crowd. On the uneven stones of the inclined pavement, near the sidewalk, lay a broad-shouldered, middle-aged prisoner, with a red beard, red face, and flat nose, in a gray cloak and gray trousers, his head lower than his feet. He lay on his back, stretching out his freckled hands, with their palms down, and at long intervals evenly heaved his broad, high chest and sobbed, looking at the sky with his staring, bloodshot eyes. Over him stood a frowning policeman, a peddler, a letter-carrier, a clerk, an old woman with a parasol, and a short-haired boy with an empty basket.

"He has grown weak sitting in jail, quite feeble—and they take him through a very hell," the clerk condemned somebody, turning to Nekhlyúdov, who had stepped up.

"He will, no doubt, die," said the woman with the parasol, in a tearful voice.

"You ought to untie his shirt," said the letter-carrier.

The policeman began with trembling, stout fingers awkwardly to loosen the tape on his venous, red neck. He was apparently agitated and embarrassed, but, nevertheless, he deemed it necessary to address the crowd.

"Why have you gathered there? It is hot enough even without you. You are cutting off the breeze."

"The doctor ought to inspect the weak and keep them back. Instead, they have taken a man who is half-dead," said the clerk, evidently displaying his knowledge of the law. Having untied the tape of the shirt, the policeman straightened himself up and looked about him.

"Step aside, I say. It is none of your business. What is there to be seen here?" he said, turning with a glance of compassion to Nekhlyúdov, but not getting any sympathy from him, he looked at the soldier of the guard. But the soldier was standing to one side, and, examining the worn-off heel of his boot, was quite indifferent to the trouble the policeman was in.

"People who know better don't take the proper trouble. Is it right to kill a man that way?"

"A prisoner is a prisoner, but still he is a man," somebody remarked in the crowd.

"Put his head higher, and give him some water," said Nekhlyúdov.

"They have gone to bring some," said the policeman, and, taking the prisoner under his arms, with difficulty raised his body.

"What is this gathering for?" suddenly was heard a commanding voice, and to the crowd, collected around the prisoner, a sergeant of police strode with rapid steps in an exceedingly clean and shining blouse and even more shining long boots.

"Move on! You have no business standing here!" he cried to the crowd, before he knew what they were doing there. When he came close and saw the dying prisoner, he nodded his head approvingly as though he had expected that very thing, and turned to the policeman.

"What is the matter?"

The policeman informed him that a group of prisoners had walked past, and he had fallen down, and the officer of the guard left him there.

"Well, take him to the station. Get a cab!"

"A janitor has run to fetch one," said the policeman, saluting.

The clerk began to say something about the heat.

"That is not your business, is it? Walk along," exclaimed the sergeant, looking so sternly at the clerk that he grew silent.

"You ought to give him some water to drink," said Nekhlyúdov.

The sergeant looked as sternly at Nekhlyúdov, without saying anything. When a janitor brought some water in a cup, he ordered the policeman to give it to the prisoner. The policeman raised the man's listless head and tried to pour the water into his mouth, but the prisoner would not take it; the water streamed down his beard, wetting the blouse and the dusty hempen shirt on his chest.

"Pour it on his head!" commanded the sergeant, and the policeman took off his pancake-shaped cap, and poured out the water on his red curly hair and bare skull.

The prisoner's eyes opened wide, as though frightened, but the position of his body did not change. Down his face trickled dirty streams, but the same sobs escaped from his mouth, and his body kept jerking convulsively.

"What about this one? Take it," the sergeant addressed the policeman, pointing to Nekhlyúdov's cab. "Ho there, come along!"

"I am hired," gloomily said the driver, without raising his eyes.

"This is my cab," said Nekhlyúdov, "but you may take it. I shall pay for it," he added, turning to the driver.

"Don't stand here!" cried the sergeant. "Get a move on!"

The policeman, some janitors, and the soldier raised the dying man, carried him to the vehicle, and placed him on the seat. He could not hold himself; his head fell back, and his body slipped off the seat.

"Lay him down," commanded the sergeant.

"Never mind, your Honour. I will take him down," said the policeman, firmly seating himself at the side of the dying man and putting his strong right hand under his arm.

The soldier lifted his feet, which were clad in prison shoes without leg-rags, and straightened them out under the box.

The sergeant looked around, and, noticing on the pavement the prisoner's pancake-shaped cap, lifted it and put it on his dirty, flabbily hanging head. "March!" he commanded.

The cabman looked back angrily, shook his head, and, accompanied by the soldier, slowly moved toward the police station. The policeman, who was sitting with the prisoner, kept adjusting the slipping body, with its head shaking in all directions. The soldier, who was walking near by, stuck the feet back under the box. Nekhlyúdov walked behind him.

CHAPTER XXXVII

ANOTHER PRISONER DIES

Passing by a sentry of the fire-brigade, the cab with the prisoner drove into the yard of the police station and stopped before a building.

In the yard, firemen, with rolled-up sleeves, were conversing loudly and laughing, while washing a wagon. The moment the cab stopped, several policemen surrounded it, took the lifeless body of the prisoner under his arms and by his legs, and raised him from the squeaking vehicle.

The policeman who had brought him jumped down from the cab, waved his stiffened arm, doffed his cap, and made the sign of the cross. The dead man was carried through the door up-stairs. Nekhlyúdov followed them. In the small dirty room to which the body was carried there were four cots. Two sick men in cloaks were sitting on two of them—one, a wry-mouthed fellow with his neck wrapped up, and the other, a consumptive man. Two cots were unoccupied. The prisoner was placed on one of these. A small man, with sparkling eyes and continually moving brows, in nothing but his underwear and stockings, walked over to the prisoner with soft, rapid steps, looked at him, then at Nekhlyúdov, and burst out laughing. This was an insane person who was kept in the waiting-room.

"They want to frighten me," he said. "Only, they won't succeed."

Soon after the policemen, who had brought in the body, came the sergeant and a surgeon's assistant.

The assistant walked up to the prisoner, touched the cold, yellow, freckled, still soft, but deathly pale hand of the man, held it awhile, and then dropped it. It fell lifelessly upon the dead man's abdomen.

"He is done with," said the assistant, shaking his head, but, apparently to comply with the rules, he pushed aside the wet, coarse shirt of the dead man, and, brushing his curly hair away from his ear, leaned over the prisoner's yellowish, immovable, high breast. Everybody was silent. The assistant arose, again shook his head, and put his finger, now on one, now on the other lid of the open and staring blue eyes.

"You won't frighten me, you won't frighten me," said the insane man, all the time spitting in the direction of the assistant.

"Well?" asked the sergeant.

"Well?" repeated the assistant. "He ought to be taken to the morgue."

"Careful! Are you sure?" said the sergeant.

"It is time I knew," said the assistant, for some reason covering the dead man's open breast. "I will send for Matvyéy Iványch, and let him take a look. —Petróv, go get him," said the assistant, walking away from the body.

"Carry him to the morgue," said the sergeant. "You come to the chancery, and sign a receipt," he added to the soldier of the guard, who all this time stuck closely to the prisoner.

"Yes, sir," replied the soldier.

The policemen lifted the dead man and carried him down-stairs. Nekhlyúdov wanted to follow them, but the insane person stopped him.

"You are not in the conspiracy, so give me a cigarette," he said. Nekhlyúdov took out his cigarette-case, and gave him one. The insane man, moving his eye-brows, began to speak rapidly and to tell him that they tortured him with sugges-tions.

"They are all against me, and they torment me through their mediums—"

"Excuse me," said Nekhlyúdov, and, without waiting to hear what he had to say, went out. He wanted to know where they would take the body.

The policemen had already crossed the yard with their burden, and were about to walk down into a basement. Nekhlyúdov wanted to walk up to them, but the sergeant stopped him.

"What do you want?"

"Nothing," said Nekhlyúdov.

"If nothing, step aside."

Nekhlyúdov obeyed and went back to his cab. The driver was dozing. Nekh-lyúdov woke him, and again started for the railway station.

He had not gone a hundred steps when he came to a dray accompanied by a soldier with his gun, on which another prisoner, apparently dead, was lying. The prisoner was on his back, and his shaven head with its black beard, covered by the pancake-shaped cap, which had slipped down to his nose, shook and tossed at every jolt of the wagon. A drayman in stout boots guided the horse, walking at its side. Back of the wagon walked a policeman. Nekhlyúdov touched his driver's shoulder.

"Terrible things they are doing!" said the driver, stopping his horse.

Nekhlyúdov climbed down from his vehicle and followed the dray, again past the sentry of the fire-brigade, to the yard of the police station. The firemen had finished washing the wagon, and in their place stood a tall, bony fire-captain, in a visorless cap. He stuck his hands in his pockets and was sternly looking at a fat, stout-necked dun stallion, which a fireman was leading up and down before him. The stallion was lame in his fore leg, and the fire-captain was angrily saying some-thing to a veterinary standing near him.

The sergeant of police was there, too. Upon noticing another dead man, he walked over to the dray.

"Where did you pick him up?" he asked, disapprovingly shaking his head.

"On Old Gorbátovskaya," answered the policeman.

"A prisoner?" asked the fire-captain.

"Yes, sir."

"This is the second to-day," said the sergeant of police.

"A fine thing! And the heat!" said the fire-captain, and, turning to the fireman, who was leading the lame dun stallion away, he cried: "Put him in the corner stall! I will teach you, you son of a bitch, how to maim horses that are worth more than you are, you rascal!"

The policemen lifted the body, just as they had the one before, and carried it to the waiting-room. Nekhlyúdov followed them, as though hypnotized.

"What do you want?" one of the policemen asked him.

He went, without answering, to the place where they were carrying the dead man.

The insane man, sitting on a cot, was eagerly smoking the cigarette Nekhlyúdov had given him.

"Ah, you have come back," he said, laughing out loud. Upon seeing the dead man, he scowled. "Again," he said. "I am tired of them. I am not a boy, am I?" he turned to Nekhlyúdov, with a questioning smile.

In the meantime, Nekhlyúdov was looking at the dead man, whom nobody was standing around, and whose face, covered by the cap before, was now plainly visible. The first prisoner had been ugly; this one was unusually handsome in body and face. He was a man in the full bloom of his strength. In spite of the disfigured, half-shaven head, the low, abrupt forehead with its arches over the black, now lifeless eyes was very beautiful, and so was the small, slightly curved nose above the thin black moustache. The livid lips were drawn back into a smile; a small beard fringed only the lower part of the face, and on the shaven side of the skull could be seen a small, firm, and handsome ear. The face had a calm, severe, and good expression. Not to mention the fact that it was evident from his face what possibilities of spiritual life had been lost in this man, one could see, by the lanky bones of his arms and fettered legs and by the strong muscles of his well-proportioned limbs, what a handsome, strong, agile human animal he had been—in its way a much more perfect animal than that dun stallion, whose lameness so angered the fire-captain. And yet, he died, and no one pitied him, either as a man, or even as a pointlessly ruined beast of burden. The only feeling which had been evoked in people by his death was a feeling of annoyance at the trouble of disposing of this rapidly decaying body.

The doctor, the assistant, and a captain of police entered the waiting-room. The doctor was a thick-set, stocky man, in a pongee silk coat, and narrow trousers of the same material, that fitted closely over his muscular thighs. The captain was a stout little man, with a globe-shaped red face, which grew rounder still from his habit of filling his cheeks with air and slowly emitting it. The doctor sat down on the cot on which the dead man lay, and, just as the assistant had done, touched the hands, listened for the heart-beat, and arose, adjusting his trousers.

"They are never deader," he said.

The captain filled his cheeks with air and slowly let it out.

"From what prison?" he turned to the soldier.

The soldier answered him and reminded him of the fetters, which were on the dead man.

"I will order them to be taken off. Thank the Lord there are blacksmiths," said the captain, and, again puffing up his cheeks, he went to the door, slowly letting out the air.

"Why is this so?" Nekhlyúdov turned to the doctor.

The doctor looked at him over his spectacles.

"Why is what so? Why do they die from sunstroke? It is like this: they are locked up all winter, without motion or light, and suddenly they are let out in the sun, and on such a day as this; then they walk in such crowds, where there is no breeze. And the result of it is sunstroke."

"Why, then, do they send them out?"

"You ask them! But who are you, anyway?"

"A passer-by."

"Ah!—My regards to you, I am busy," said the doctor, and, angrily pulling his trousers down, he walked over to the cots of the patients.

"Well, how goes it with you?" he turned to the wry-mouthed, pale man with bandaged neck.

The insane man, in the meantime, was sitting on his cot and spitting in the direction of the doctor, after he got through with his cigarette.

Nekhlyúdov went down out into the yard and past the fire-brigade's horses and chickens and the sentry in a brass helmet, walked through the gate, where he seated himself in his cab, the driver of which was again asleep, and had himself driven to the railway station.

CHAPTER XXXVIII

AT THE RAILWAY STATION

When Nekhlyúdov reached the station, the prisoners were already sitting in cars, behind grated windows. On the platform stood a number of people who were seeing off the prisoners: the soldiers of the guard did not let them walk up to the cars. The guards were very much disturbed. On the way to the station three men had died from sunstroke, besides the two which Nekhlyúdov had seen: one of these had been taken to the nearest police station, like the other two, while two more fell at the station.* The officers of the guard were not concerned about the five men whom they had lost and who might have lived. This did not interest them. They were interested only in executing all that the law demanded of them under these circumstances: to deliver the dead persons and their papers and things where it was

*In the beginning of the eighties five prisoners died in one day from sunstroke, while being taken from Butýrski Prison to the Nízhni-Nóvgorod Railroad Station.—*Author's Note.*

necessary, and to subtract them from the count of those who were to be taken to Nízhni-Nóvgorod—and this was quite troublesome, especially in such hot weather.

It was this which gave the men of the guard so much trouble, and it was for this reason that neither Nekhlyúdov nor the others were permitted to go up to the cars. Nekhlyúdov, however, was permitted to go up, because he bribed an under-officer of the guard. The under-officer let Nekhlyúdov pass, and only asked him to say what he wished to and go away as soon as possible, so that the superior officer should not see him. There were eighteen cars in all, and all of them, except the car of the officers, were jammed with prisoners. Passing by the windows of the cars, Nekhlyúdov listened to what was going on inside. In all of them could be heard the clanking of chains, bustle, and conversation, mixed with senseless profanity, but nowhere was a word said about the sunstruck companions, which was what Nekhlyúdov had expected to hear. They were talking mainly about their bags, about water to drink, and about the choice of a seat. Upon looking through one window, Nekhlyúdov saw, in the middle of the car, in the passageway, some soldiers who were taking the handcuffs off the prisoners. The prisoners extended their hands, and a soldier opened the manacles with a key, and took them off. Another gathered them up. Having walked past all the men's cars, Nekhlyúdov came to the women's. In the second one of these, he heard the measured groans of a woman, interrupted by exclamations, "Oh, oh, oh! Help me! Oh, oh, oh! Help me!"

Nekhlyúdov went past it, and, following a guard's directions, went up to the third car. As Nekhlyúdov put his head against the window, he was stifled by a hot breath, saturated with the heavy smell of human sweat, and he could clearly hear squeaking feminine voices. Perspiring women, red in their faces, were sitting on all the benches, dressed in cloaks and jackets, and chattering away. Nekhlyúdov's face at the grated window attracted their attention. Those that were nearest grew silent and moved up to him. Máslova, in her jacket only and without a kerchief, was seated at the opposite window. Nearest him sat white, smiling Fedósya. Upon recognizing Nekhlyúdov, she nudged Máslova and indicated the window to her. Máslova arose hurriedly, threw the kerchief over her black hair, and with an animated, red, perspiring, smiling face went up to the window and grabbed the iron bars.

"It is hot," she said, with a gay smile.

"Did you get the things?"

"I did, thank you."

"Do you need anything?" asked Nekhlyúdov, feeling as though the car were heated inside like a bathroom oven.

"Thank you, nothing."

"If we could only get a drink," said Fedósya.

"Yes, a drink," repeated Máslova.

"Have you no water there?"

"They put in some, but it has all been used up."

"Just a minute," said Nekhlyúdov, "I will ask a soldier. We won't see each other before Nízhni-Nóvgorod."

"Are you going there?" said Máslova, as though not knowing it and casting a joyful glance at Nekhlyúdov.

"I go on the next train."

Máslova said nothing; only a few seconds later she sighed deeply.

"Tell me, sir, is it true that they killed off twelve prisoners?" said an old, harsh woman, in a coarse man's voice.

This was Koroblyóva.

"I have not heard of twelve. I saw two," said Nekhlyúdov.

"They say, twelve. Won't they be punished for it? They are devils."

"Did none of the women get ill?" asked Nekhlyúdov.

"The women are tougher," said another, a small prisoner, smiling. "Only there's one has taken it into her head to have a baby. There she's moaning," she said, pointing to the next car from which the groans were still coming.

"You ask me if I need something?" said Máslova, trying to keep her lips from smiling with joy. "Can't this woman be kept here? She is suffering so much. Can't you tell the authorities?"

"Yes, I will."

"Another thing. Could she not see Tarás, her husband?" she added, indicating with her eyes smiling Fedósya. "He is travelling with you, isn't he?"

"Mister, no talking allowed," was heard the voice of a sergeant of the guard. This was not the one who had given Nekhlyúdov permission.

Nekhlyúdov stepped aside and went to find the officer, in order to intercede for the woman in childbirth and for Tarás, but he could not find him for a long time, nor could he get any answer out of the guards. They were in great turmoil: some were taking a prisoner somewhere; others were running to buy provisions for themselves or placing their things in the cars; others, again, were attending to a lady who was travelling with the officer of the guard. They all answered Nekhlyúdov's questions reluctantly.

Nekhlyúdov saw the guard officer after the second bell. The officer, wiping the moustache which concealed his mouth with his stubby hand, and raising his shoulder, was reproaching the sergeant for something.

"What do you want?" he asked Nekhlyúdov.

"There is a woman in labour in the car, so I thought she ought to—"

"Let her be. We'll see later," said the officer, walking to his car and briskly swinging his short arms.

Just then the conductor, with the whistle in his hand, passed by. The last bell was rung, the whistle blown, and among those who were waiting on the platform and in the women's car were heard weeping and lamentations. Nekhlyúdov was standing with Tarás on the platform, and watching the cars with the grated windows and the shaven heads of men behind them, pass one after another. Then the first woman's car came abreast of them, and in the window were seen the heads of women with kerchiefs and without; then the second car, in which Máslova was. She was standing at the window with others and looking at Nekhlyúdov, a pitiable smile on her face.

CHAPTER XXXIX

BROTHER AND SISTER

There were two hours left before the departure of the passenger train on which Nekhlyúdov was to travel. At first he had intended to drive down to his sister's in the interval, but now, under the impressions of the morning, he felt so agitated and crushed that, upon sitting down on a sofa in the first-class waiting-room, he was suddenly so overcome by sleepiness that he turned on his side, put his hand under his cheek, and immediately fell asleep.

He was awakened by a waiter in a dress coat, holding a napkin.

"Mister, mister, you wouldn't be Prince Nekhlyúdov? A lady is looking for you."

Nekhlyúdov jumped up, and, rubbing his eyes, recalled where he was and all that had happened that morning.

In his memory were the procession of the prisoners, the dead men, the cars with the grated windows, and the women shut up inside, of whom one was in the agony of labour without receiving any help and another pitiably smiled from behind the iron bars. In reality there was something entirely different in front of him: a table, covered with bottles, vases, candelabra, and dishes, and agile waiters bustling near it. In the back of the hall, in front of a cupboard and behind some vases filled with fruit and behind bottles, were the buffet-keeper and the backs of travellers at the counter.

Just as Nekhlyúdov was changing his lying position for a sitting one and slowly coming to, he noticed that those who were in the room were looking with curiosity at something that was taking place at the door. He looked in that direction and saw a procession of people carrying a lady in a chair, her head loosely covered with a gauze veil. The front bearer was a lackey and seemed familiar to Nekhlyúdov. The one in the back was also a familiar porter, with galloons on his cap. Back of the chair walked an elegant chambermaid, in apron and curls, carrying a bundle, a round object in a leather case, and umbrellas. Farther behind walked Prince Korchágin in a travelling-cap, displaying his thick lips and apoplectic neck, and expanding his chest; after him walked Missy, Mísha, a cousin, and a diplomat Ósten, whom Nekhlyúdov knew, with his long neck and prominent Adam's apple and an ever-cheeful expression on his face. As he walked along, he was proving some point to smiling Missy impressively and, obviously, jocularly. Behind them came the doctor, angrily puffing his cigarette.

The Korchágins were moving from their suburban estate to the estate of the prince's sister, which was down on the Nízhni-Nóvgorod line.

The procession of the bearers, of the chambermaid, and the doctor proceeded to the ladies' waiting-room, evoking the onlookers' curiosity and respect. The old prince sat down at the table, immediately called a waiter, and began to order something to eat and drink. Missy and Ósten also stopped in the dining-room and were on the point of sitting down when they noticed a lady they knew in the door and went up to meet her. This lady was Natálya Ivánovna.

Natálya Ivánovna, accompanied by Agraféna Petróvna, looked all around her as she entered the dining-room. She noticed Missy and her brother about the same time. She first went up to Missy, nodding her head to Nekhlyúdov. But having kissed Missy, she at once went up to her brother.

"At last I have found you," she said.

Nekhlyúdov arose, greeted Missy, Mísha, and Ósten, and stopped to talk to them. Missy told him of the fire on their estate which compelled them to go to her aunt's. Ósten used this opportunity to tell a funny anecdote about the fire.

Nekhlyúdov was not listening to Ósten, but turned to his sister: "How glad I am that you have come," he said.

"I have been here quite awhile," she said. "Agraféna Petróvna is with me." She pointed to Agraféna Petróvna, who wore a hat and a mackintosh and with gracious dignity was bowing confusedly to Nekhlyúdov from a distance, not wishing to be in his way. "We have been looking for you everywhere."

"I fell asleep in here. How glad I am you have come," repeated Nekhlyúdov. "I had begun to write a letter to you," he said.

"Really?" she said, frightened. "About what?"

Missy and the gentlemen, noticing that an intimate conversation had begun between brother and sister, walked aside. Nekhlyúdov and his sister sat down near the window, on a velvet divan, near somebody's things—a plaid and paper boxes.

"Yesterday, after I left you, I wanted to come back and express my regrets, but I did not know how he would take it," said Nekhlyúdov. "I did not treat your husband right, and this worried me," he added.

"I knew, I was convinced," said his sister, "that you did not mean to. You know yourself," and tears stood in her eyes, and she touched his arm. The phrase was not clear, but he understood her quite well, and was touched by what she meant by it. These words meant that in addition to her love, which possessed her—her love for her husband—her love for him, her brother, was important and dear to her, and that every misunderstanding with him was a source of great suffering to her.

"Thank, thank you. Ah, what I have seen to-day!" he said, suddenly recalling the second dead prisoner. "Two prisoners were killed."

"How do you mean killed?"

"I tell you, killed. They were taken out through this heat. Two of them died from sunstroke."

"Impossible! What? Today? A little while ago?"

"Yes, a little while ago. I saw their dead bodies."

"But why did they kill them? Who killed them?" said Natálya Ivánovna.

"Those who took them by force," Nekhlyúdov said with irritation, feeling that she looked even at this through her husband's eyes.

"Ah, my God!" said Agraféna Petróvna, coming up to them.

"Yes, we have not the slightest idea of what is done to these unfortunates, and yet it ought to be known," added Nekhlyúdov, looking at the old prince, who, having tied a napkin around his neck, was sitting at the table with a glass of punch and at that moment glanced at Nekhlyúdov.

"Nekhlyúdov!" he cried. "Do you want to cool yourself off? It is good for the journey!"

Nekhlyúdov declined and turned away.

"What are you going to do?" proceeded Natálya Ivánovna.

"Whatever I can. I do not know, but I feel that I must do something. And I will do what I can."

"Yes, yes, I understand that. Well, and with these," she said, smiling and indicating the Korchágins with her eyes, "is it all absolutely ended?"

"Absolutely, and I think that there are no regrets on either side."

"A pity. I am sorry. I like her. Well, let's say that's it. But what do you want to get yourself involved for?" she added, timidly. "Why are you going?"

"I am going because I must," Nekhlyúdov said, dryly and seriously, as though wishing to end the conversation.

But he at once felt ashamed of his coldness to his sister. "Why can't I tell her everything I think?" he thought. "Let Agraféna Petróvna hear it, too," he said to himself, looking at the old chambermaid. Agraféna Petróvna's presence urged him on to repeat his decision to his sister.

"Are you speaking of my intention to marry Katyúsha? You see, I decided to do that, but she has definitely and firmly refused me," he said, and his voice trembled, as it always did whenever he thought of it. "She does not want my sacrifice, and herself sacrifices very much for one in her situation, but I cannot accept that sacrifice, if that is but a whim. And so I am following her and will be where she is, and will do all in my power to help her and to alleviate her lot."

Natálya Ivánovna said nothing. Agraféna Petróvna looked questioningly at Natálya Ivánovna and shook her head. Just then the procession started again from the waiting-room. The same handsome lackey, Filípp, and the porter were carrying the princess. She stopped the bearers, beckoned to Nekhlyúdov to come up to her, and, with an expression of pity and pining, gave him her white, ring-bedecked hand, in terror expecting a strong handshake.

"*Epouvantable!*" she said about the heat, "I can't stand it. *Ce climat me tue.*" Having talked awhile about the terrors of the Russian climate and having invited him to visit them, she gave a sign to the bearers. "Be sure and come," she added, turning her long face to him while being carried away.

Nekhlyúdov went out on the platform. The procession of the princess turned to the right, to the first-class cars. Nekhlyúdov with the porter, who was carrying his things, and Tarás, with his bag, went to the left.

"This is my companion," Nekhlyúdov said to his sister, pointing to Tarás, whose history he had told her before.

"You don't mean to say you will travel third class," said Natálya Ivánovna, when Nekhlyúdov stopped in front of a car of the third class, and the porter with the things and Tarás entered it.

"It is more comfortable for me, and Tarás and I will be together," he said. "By the way," he added, "I have not yet given the Kuzmínskoe land to the peasants, so, in case of my death, your children will inherit it."

"Dmítri, stop," said Natálya Ivánovna.

"And if I give it to them, I must tell you that everything else will be theirs, because there is little chance of my marrying, and if I should, there will be no children—so that—"

"Dmítri, please don't say that," said Natálya Ivánovna, but Nekhlyúdov saw that she was glad to hear what he told her.

Ahead, in front of the first class, stood a small throng of people still looking at the car into which Princess Korchágin had been carried. All the other people had already taken their seats. Belated passengers, hurrying, clattered on the boards of the platform; the conductors slammed the doors and asked the passengers to be seated and their friends to leave.

Nekhlyúdov walked into a sunny, hot, and stinking car, and immediately stepped out on the brake platform. Natálya Ivánovna stood opposite the car, in her fashionable hat and wrap, by the side of Agraféna Petróvna, and apparently was trying to find a subject for conversation but was unable to discover any. It was not even possible to say *"Écrivez,"* because her brother and she had long made fun of this habitual phrase of people parting. That short conversation about money matters and inheritance had at once destroyed all their tender relations of brother and sister—they now felt estranged from each other. Consequently, Natálya Ivánovna was glad when the train started, and it was possible only to nod and with a sad and kindly face to say, "Good-bye, Dmítri, good-bye!" The moment the car had left, she began to think how to tell her husband of her conversation with her brother, and her face looked solemn and troubled.

Although Nekhlyúdov had none but the very kindest feelings for his sister and never concealed anything from her, he now felt awkward and oppressed in her presence and wished to get away from her as soon as possible. He felt that there was nothing left of that Natálya who once had been so near to him, but only the slave of a strange and disagreeable, swarthy, and hirsute man. He saw this clearly because her face lit up with especial animation only when he said something which interested her husband—that is, when he spoke about giving away the land to the peasants and about the inheritance—and that pained him.

C H A P T E R   X L

THOUGHTS ON THE TRAIN PLATFORM

The heat in the large third-class car, baked by the sun all day long and now filled with people, was so stifling that Nekhlyúdov did not enter the car, but remained on the brake platform. Even here it was not possible to breathe, and Nekhlyúdov drew a deep breath only when the cars came out of the rows of houses, and a fresh breeze began to blow. "Yes, they killed them," he repeated the words he had said to his sister. In his imagination arose, through all the impressions of that day, with especial vividness, the handsome face of the second dead prisoner with the smiling expression of his lips, the severe aspect of his forehead, and the small, firm ear beneath the shaven, livid skull. "The most terrible thing of all this is that he has been killed, and nobody knows who killed him. There is no doubt about his having been killed. He was led, like all the prisoners, by order of Máslennikov. Máslennikov, no doubt, sent out his habitual order, with his stupid flourish signed a paper with a printed heading, and, of course, in no way will consider himself guilty. Still less can the prison doctor who examined the prisoners consider himself guilty. He accurately executed his duty, segregated the weak, and in no way could foresee this terrible heat, nor that they would be taken away so late and in such a mob. The superintendent?—but the superintendent only executed the order to send out on such and such a day so many forced-labour and deportation convicts, men and women. Nor can the officer of the guard be guilty, whose duty consisted in receiving a certain number of prisoners and delivering the same to such and such a place. He led the party according to the regulation, and he could not foresee that such strong men as those two whom Nekhlyúdov had seen would not hold out and would die. Nobody is guilty—but the people have been killed, and they have been killed by these very men who are innocent of their deaths.

"All this was done," thought Nekhlyúdov, "because all these people, governors, superintendents, sergeants, policemen, think that there are situations in the world in which man-to-man relations are not obligatory. If all these people—Máslennikov, the superintendent, the officer of the guard—were not governors, superintendents, and officers, they would have considered twenty times whether they ought to take the prisoners out in such a heat and in such a mob; they would have stopped twenty times during the march in order to take out such men as were weakening and falling ill; they would have taken them into the shade, would have given them water to drink, would have allowed them to rest, and, if something unfortunate had happened, would have expressed their compassion. They have not done it, and have even interfered with others who would have done it, because they saw before them not men and their obligations to them, but their own service and its demands, which they placed higher than the demands of human relations. That is where the trouble is," thought Nekhlyúdov. "If it is possible to acknowledge that anything is more important than the feeling of humanity, even for one hour and in any one exceptional case, then any crime may be committed against men without a feeling of guilt."

Nekhlyúdov became so lost in thought that he did not notice how the weather had changed: the sun had disappeared behind a low, tattered, advance cloud, and from the western horizon moved a solid, light gray cloud, which somewhere far away was already pouring forth its slanting, abundant rain over fields and woods. A damp, rain-fed breeze was wafted from the storm-cloud. Now and then lightning crossed the cloud, and the rumble of thunder ever more frequently mingled with the rumble of the car-wheels. The cloud came nearer and nearer, and slanting drops of rain, driven by the wind, began to wet the brake platform and Nekhlyúdov's overcoat. He went over to the other side, and, inhaling the moist air and the odour of growing corn from the thirsty earth, looked at the passing gardens, forests, yellowing fields of rye, the still green strips of oats and the black furrows of the dark green, flowering potato-beds. Everything looked as though covered with lacquer; what was green became greener, what was yellow grew yellower, and what was black, blacker.

"More, more," said Nekhlyúdov, rejoicing at the sight of fields, gardens and orchards, which were reviving under the influence of the beneficent rain.

The heavy rain did not come down long. The storm-cloud was partly exhausted and partly carried beyond, and only the last, straight, abundant, and tiny drops fell on the damp earth. The sun again peeped out; everything sparkled, and in the west there arched above the horizon a low but bright rainbow, with prominent violet hue, discontinuous at one end only.

"What was it I was thinking about?" Nekhlyúdov asked himself, when all these changes in nature had taken place and the train was running through a cutting with steep, sloping sides.

"Yes, I was thinking that all these people—the superintendent, the soldiers of the guard—that all these officials—most of them meek, kind people—have become bad only because they're officials."

He recalled Máslennikov's indifference, when he was telling him about what went on in the prisons, the severity of the superintendent, the cruelty of the officer of the guard when he did not permit the men to get into the drays and when he paid no attention to the woman who was in labour in the car. "All these people were apparently immune and impervious to the simplest sense of compassion only because they were officials. They, as officials, were impervious to the feeling of humanity, as this paved earth is to rain," thought Nekhlyúdov, looking at the incline of the embankment paved with many-coloured stones, over which the rain-water flowed down in runlets without soaking into the earth. "Maybe it's necessary to pave embankments with stones, but it is sad to see the earth deprived of vegetation, whereas it could have brought forth grain, grass, shrubs, trees, like the land above the ravine. It is the same with men," thought Nekhlyúdov. "Maybe these governors, superintendents, policemen, are necessary, but it is terrible to see people deprived of their chief human quality—of love and pity for each other.

"The whole thing is," thought Nekhlyúdov, "that these men accept as law what is not law, and do not acknowledge as law what is eternal, unchangeable, inalienable law, written by God Himself in the hearts of men. It is this which makes it so hard for me to be with these men," thought Nekhlyúdov. "I am simply afraid of them. Indeed, they are terrifying people—more terrifying than robbers. A robber may have pity—these never can; they are inured against pity, as these stones are against vegetation. It is this which makes them so terrible. They say Pugachóv and Rázin were terrifying. These are a thousand times more so!" he continued thinking. "If a psychological problem were given—what is to be done so that people of our time, humane Christians, simple, good people, should commit the most atrocious deeds without feeling themselves guilty?—only one solution would present itself: it is necessary to do what actually is being done; it is necessary for these people to be governors, superintendents, officers, policemen, that is, they must, in the first place, be convinced that there is a thing called government service, by which one may treat people as objects, without any human, fraternal relation to them, and, secondly, that the people of this government service must be so interrelated that the responsibility for their treatment of people falls on no one separately. Outside of these conditions, it is impossible nowadays to commit such atrocities as those I saw to-day. The thing is that people think there are conditions under which one may treat men without love, whereas there are no such conditions. Things may be treated without love: one may chop wood, make bricks, forge iron, without love; but people cannot be treated without love, just as one cannot handle bees without care. Such is the nature of bees. If they are carelessly handled by a person, they hurt both themselves and him. Just so it is with people. This cannot be otherwise, because mutual love between men is the fundamental law of human existence. It is true, a man cannot make himself love as he can make himself work, but from this it does not follow that people may be treated without love, especially if something is demanded from them. If you feel no love for men—keep your peace," Nekhlyúdov thought, addressing himself. "Busy yourself with yourself, with things, only not with men. Just as one can eat without harm and profitably only when one is hungry, so one may profitably and harmlessly make use of men only as long as one loves them. Permit yourself to treat people without love, just as you yesterday treated your brother-in-law, and there is no limit to cruelty and bestiality in regard to other people, as I saw to-day, and there is no limit to suffering, as I have discovered in my own life. Yes, yes, that is so," thought Nekhlyúdov. "It is good, it is good!" he repeated to himself, experiencing the double pleasure of coolness after the sweltering heat and of having become conscious of the highest degree of clearness in regard to a question which had concerned him for a long time.

CHAPTER XLI

TARÁS'S GRIEF

The car in which Nekhlyúdov's seat was, was half-filled with people. There were servants, artisans, factory hands, butchers, Jews, clerks, women, wives of labourers, and a soldier, and two ladies—one young, the other of middle age, with bracelets on her bare wrist—and a stern-looking gentleman with a cockade in his black cap. All these people, having settled themselves in their seats, were sitting in orderly fashion, some of them cracking sunflower seeds, some smoking cigarettes, while others were carrying on animated conversations with their neighbours.

Tarás, with a happy expression, was sitting to the right of the aisle keeping a place for Nekhlyúdov and was chatting away with a muscular man in an unbuttoned, sleeveless, cloth coat, sitting opposite him; Nekhlyúdov later learned that he was a gardener travelling to a job. Without going up to Tarás, Nekhlyúdov stopped in the aisle near a respectable-looking old man with a white beard, in a nankeen coat, who was conversing with a young woman in peasant clothes. At the woman's side sat a seven-year-old girl, in a new sleeveless coat, with a braid of almost white hair. Her feet dangled way above the floor, and she cracked seeds all the time. Upon noticing Nekhlyúdov, the old man pulled in the fold of his coat from the shiny bench, on which he was sitting, and said, in a kind voice:

"Please be seated."

Nekhlyúdov thanked him and took the indicated seat. As soon as he had, the woman continued her interrupted story. She was telling how her husband, from whom she was now returning, had received her in the city.

"I was there at Shrovetide, and now God has granted that I be there again," she said. "And now, if God grant it, I'll see him again at Christmas."

"That is good," said the old man, looking at Nekhlyúdov. "You must watch him, or else a young man, living in the city, will soon get spoiled."

"No, grandpa, mine is not that kind. He not only does not do anything foolish, he is like a young girl. He sends all his money home, to the last kopek. And he was so glad to see the girl—I can hardly tell you how happy he was," said the woman, smiling.

The little girl, who was spitting out the shells and listening to her mother, looked with quiet, intelligent eyes at the faces of the old man and of Nekhlyúdov.

"If he is clever, so much the better," said the old man. "He doesn't do that, does he?" he added, with his eyes indicating a pair, man and wife, apparently factory hands, who were sitting on the other side of the aisle.

The man had raised a vodka bottle to his mouth, and, throwing his head back, was taking some swallows from it, while his wife was holding a bag in her hand, from which the bottle had been taken, and looking fixedly at her husband.

"No, mine neither drinks nor smokes," said the woman, using the opportunity to praise her husband once more. "The earth brings forth few such men as he. That's the kind of a man he is," she said, turning to Nekhlyúdov.

"Nothing better," repeated the old man, who was watching the drinking factory workman. The workman, having had his fill, handed the bottle to his wife. She took it and, smiling and shaking her head, raised it to her mouth. Upon noticing Nekhlyúdov's and the old man's glances, the workman turned to them.

"Ah, sir, you are wondering why we are drinking? When we work, no one sees us, but when we drink, everybody watches us. When I earn money, I drink and treat my wife and nobody else."

"Yes, yes," said Nekhlyúdov, not knowing what to answer.

"Right, sir? My wife is a steady woman! I am satisfied with my wife, because she knows how to think of me. Right, Mávra?"

"Take it; I do not want any more," said his wife, giving him the bottle. "Don't prattle senselessly," she added.

"That's it," continued the workman, "she is all right, but she squeaks like an ungreased wagon. Mávra, right?"

Mávra, laughing, with a drunken gesture waved her hand.

"There he goes—"

"That's it, she is all right, as long as she is all right, but when the reins get under her tail, she carries on awfully—I am telling the truth. You must excuse me, sir. I have had a few drinks—well, what is to be done?" said the workman. He put his head into his wife's lap and was getting ready to sleep.

Nekhlyúdov sat awhile with the old man, who told him about himself. He said that he was a stove-builder, that he had worked for fifty-three years, putting up an endless number of stoves in his lifetime, and that he was now trying to take a rest, but could not get the time for it. He had been in the city, where he had put the boys to work, and now he was on his way to the village, to see how his people were getting on. After having listened to the old man's story, Nekhlyúdov arose and went over to the place which Tarás had reserved for him.

"Well, sir, take a seat. We'll put the sack over here," kindly remarked the gardener who was sitting opposite Tarás, looking up at Nekhlyúdov's face.

"Pretty crowded, but nice," Tarás said with a smile, in a sing-song voice, lifting his seventy-five-pound bag up as if it were a feather and carrying it over to the window. "There is plenty of room here, and we can stand, or go down under the bench. It is quiet there. What nonsense I am saying!" he said, beaming with good nature and kindness.

Tarás said of himself that when he did not drink he could not find words, but that liquor gave him good words, and he could express himself well. Indeed, when sober, Tarás was generally silent; but when he had had something to drink, which happened rarely and only on special occasions, he became unusually communicative. He then spoke a great deal, and he spoke well, with great simplicity, truthfulness, and, above everything else, with gentleness, which shone in his kindly blue eyes, and with a pleasing smile, which did not leave his lips.

He was in such a state now. Nekhlyúdov's arrival for a moment stopped his narrative. But, having found a place for his bag, he sat down in his old place, and putting his strong working hands on his knees and looking straight into the gardener's eyes, continued his story. He was telling his new acquaintance all the details of his wife's story, why she was being deported, and why he was following her to Siberia.

Nekhlyúdov had never heard all the details of this story, and so he listened with interest. The story had reached the point where the poisoning had been done and the family found out that Fedósya had done it.

"I am telling about my sorrow," said Tarás, turning to Nekhlyúdov, with an expression of friendly intimacy. "I have fallen in with a nice man, and so I am telling him my story."

"Yes, yes," said Nekhlyúdov.

"So, my friend, the affair was discovered like this. Mother took that very cake and said, 'I am going to the officer.'—My father, who is a wise old man, said, 'Wait, old woman! She is a mere child; she does not know herself what she has done, and you ought to pity her. She may regret her deed.'—No, she would not listen to his words.—'While we are keeping her, she will destroy us like cockroaches.'—So she went to the policeman. He immediately made for our house, and brought the constables with him."

"And what about you?" asked the gardener.

"My friend, I was tossing about, with a pain in my belly, and vomiting. It turned all my inside out—it was worse than I can tell you. Father at once hitched the horses to the wagon, put Fedósya in it, and took her to the village office, and from there to the magistrate. And just as she had at first confessed her guilt, so she now told the magistrate everything—where she got the arsenic, and how she had made the cake.—'Why,' says he, 'did you do it?'—'Because,' says she, 'I am tired of him. In Siberia,' says she, 'I'll be better off than with him'—that's me, you see," Tarás said, smiling.—"She confessed everything. Of course, she was sent to jail. Father came back alone. And then came working time, and all the women we had was mother, and she was not strong. We wondered whether we could not get her out on bail. Father went to see some officer, but nothing came of it; then father went to see another. He saw five men that way, but all in vain. He had just about given up trying, when he fell in with a clerk. He was sly—a rare man—'Give me,' says he, 'a five, and I will get her out.'—They made a bargain at three roubles. My friend, I had to pawn her linen to get the money. And so he wrote a document," Tarás stretched out his arm, as though he were speaking of a shot, "and it came off at once. By that time I was already up from bed, and I myself went to town for her.

"And so, my friend, I came to town. I left my mare at a hostelry, took my document, and went to the prison.—'What do you want?'—'So and so,' says I, 'my wife is locked up here.'—'Have you a document?' says he.—I gave it to him. He looked at it. 'Wait,' says he. I sat down on a bench. The sun was past noon. Comes in the chief. 'Are you,' says he, 'Vargushóv?'—'I am.'—'Take her,' says he.—They opened the gate. They brought her out in her garb, as is proper.—'Come, let us go.'—'Are you on foot?'—'No, I brought the horse with me.'—We went to the hostelry; I paid my bill, harnessed the mare, and put what hay there was left under the mat. She took her seat, wrapped herself in her kerchief, and off we went. She was silent, and so was I. As we were getting near the house, she said: 'Is mother alive?'—'She is.'— 'Is father alive?'—'He is.'—'Forgive me, Tarás, my stupidity. I did not know my-self what I was doing.'—But I said: 'Whatever you say won't make any change, because I have forgiven you long ago.'—She did not say another word. When we came home, she fell down at mother's feet. Says mother: 'God'll forgive you.'—And father greeted her, saying, 'What is the use recalling the past? Do the best you can. Now,' says he, 'there is no time—we have to reap the field. Back of Skoródnoe,' says he, 'on the manured plot, God has given us such a crop of rye that you can't get at it with a hook; it is all tangled up and lying flat. It has to be reaped. So you go there with Tarás to-morrow, and reap it.'—And so she went and began to work. It was a sight to see her work. We had then seven rented acres, and God had given us a rare crop of rye and oats. I would cut with the sickle, and she would bind, or we would both cut with the scythe. I am a good hand at work, but she is better still at whatever she does. She is a quick worker and young. And she grew so industrious that I had to hold her back. When we came to the house, our fingers would be swollen and our hands would smart, so that we ought to have taken a rest, but she would run to the barn, without eating supper, in order to get the sheaf-cords ready for the morrow. How things had changed!"

"And had she become kind to you?" asked the gardener.

"You would not believe me how she stuck to me—she just became one soul with me. I would barely think of something when she would understand me. Even my mother, who is a cross woman, used to say: 'Fedósya acts as though she were some-body else—she is a different woman.'—Once we were both going for sheaves, and we were sitting both together. So I said to her: 'What made you do it, Fedósya?'—'I just did it,' says she, 'because I did not want to live with you. I would rather die, I thought, than live with you.'—'Well, and now?' says I.—'And now,' says she, 'you are deep in my heart.'" Tarás stopped and, smiling joyfully, shook his head in surprise. "We had returned from the field, and I had gone to soak some hemp; just as I came home," he said, after a moment's silence, "behold, a summons: the trial was on. And we had forgotten what the trial was all about."

"This must have been the devil did it," said the gardener. "No man would have thought of ruining a soul. There was once a man in our village—" and the gar-dener started telling a story, but the train began to slow down.

"Here is a station," he said, "I want to go get a drink."

The conversation ended, and Nekhlyúdov followed the gardener out of the car onto the wet planks of the platform.

CHAPTER XLII

A STATION STOP.
THE KORCHÁGINS

Even before coming out of the car, Nekhlyúdov had noticed several elegant carriages, drawn by sets of three and four well-fed horses tinkling with their bells. When he came out on the wet platform, which looked black from the rain, he saw a gathering of people in front of the first-class car. Among them stood out a tall, stout lady in a mackintosh with a hat of expensive feathers and a lank young man with thin legs, in a cycling outfit with an immense well-fed dog with an expensive collar. Back of them stood lackeys with wraps and umbrellas, and a coachman, who had come to meet the train. On all that crowd, from the stout lady to the coachman, who with one hand was supporting the skirts of his long caftan, lay the seal of quiet self-confidence and superabundance. Around this group soon formed a circle of curious people, servilely admiring wealth: they were the chief of the station, a gendarme, a haggard maid in a native costume with glass beads, always present in the summer at the arrival of trains, the despatcher, and passengers, men and women.

Nekhlyúdov recognized the young man with the dog as the schoolboy, young Korchágin. The stout lady was the princess's sister, to whose estate the Korchágins were going. The chief conductor, in shining galloons and boots, opened the door of the car and held the door, in token of respect, while Filípp and a labourer in a white apron carefully carried out the long-faced princess in her folding chair. The sisters greeted each other; there were French phrases about whether the princess would travel in a carriage or in a barouche; and the procession, rounded out by the chambermaid with the curls, carrying the umbrellas and the box, moved to the door of the station.

Nekhlyúdov, who did not wish to meet them because he did not wish to bid them farewell again, stopped, not walking up as far as the door, waiting for the whole procession to pass. The princess and her son, Missy, the doctor, and the chambermaid went first, while the prince stopped to talk to his sister-in-law, and Nekhlyúdov, who did not walk up close, caught only broken sentences of their conversation, which was in French. One of these phrases, spoken by the prince, for some reason impressed itself deeply, as often happens, in Nekhlyúdov's memory, with all its intonations and sounds.

"Oh, il est du vrai grand monde, du vrai grand monde," the prince was saying about someone in his loud, self-confident voice. With his sister-in-law he passed through the station door, accompanied by the respectful conductors and porters.

Just then a throng of workingmen in bast shoes and short fur coats with bags over their shoulders appeared on the platform from somewhere around the corner of the station. The workingmen with firm, soft steps walked up to the first car and started to enter but were driven off by the conductor. They did not stop, but, hastening and stepping on each other's feet, went to the next car, and, catching their bags on the corners and doors of the car, were starting to go in when a conductor standing in the door of the station noticed their intention and angrily called out to them. The workingmen hastily retreated and with the same soft steps went on to the next car, the one Nekhlyúdov was in. Again a conductor stopped them. They were about to stop, intending to move on, but Nekhlyúdov told them that there were unoccupied seats in the car and for them to come in. They did what he said, and Nekhlyúdov went in after them. The workingmen were on the point of sitting down, but the gentleman with the cockade and the two ladies, taking their attempt to seat themselves in this car as a personal affront, resolutely opposed them and began to drive them out. The workingmen—there were about twenty of them—both old and young men, with tired, sunburnt, lean faces, their bags catching against the benches, walls, and doors, apparently feeling themselves completely at fault, passed on through the car, evidently ready to walk to the end of the world, and to sit down anywhere they were told to, even on nails.

"Where are you going, you devils? Sit down here," cried another conductor, who came from the opposite direction.

"Voilà encore des nouvelles," said the younger of the two ladies, quite convinced that she would attract Nekhlyúdov's attention with her good French.

The lady with the bracelets kept sniffing and frowning, saying something about the pleasure of sitting in the same car with stinking peasants.

The workingmen, experiencing joy and peace, such as people experience who have passed a great peril, stopped and began to seat themselves, with a jerk of their shoulders throwing down the heavy bags from their shoulders and pushing them under the benches.

The gardener who had been speaking with Tarás went back to his seat, which was not the one he had occupied, and so, near Tarás and opposite him, three places were free. Three workingmen sat down on these seats, but when Nekhlyúdov came up to them, the sight of his fine clothes so confused them that they got up;

Nekhlyúdov asked them to keep their seats, and himself sat down on the arm of the bench, near the aisle.

One of two workingmen, a man of about fifty, in dismay and even fright looked at the younger man. They were very much surprised and baffled to see a gentleman give up his seat to them, instead of calling them names and driving them away, as gentlemen generally do. They were even afraid lest something bad should come from it. Seeing, however, that there was no trickery in it, and that Nekhlyúdov was talking to Tarás very simply, they quieted down, told the youngster to sit down on a bag, and insisted on Nekhlyúdov's taking the seat. At first the elderly working-man, who was seated opposite Nekhlyúdov, pressed himself in the corner, and carefully drew back his feet, which were clad in bast shoes, in order not to push the gentleman, but later he entered into such a friendly chat with Nekhlyúdov and Tarás that he even struck Nekhlyúdov's knee with the back of his hand, whenever he wished to attract his attention to some particular point in his story. He was telling about all his affairs and about his work in the peat-bogs, from which they were now returning, having worked there for two months and a half. They were taking home about ten roubles each, as part of the wages had been given them when they were hired. Their work, as he told it, was done in water which stood knee-deep, and lasted from dawn until dark with two hours out for dinner.

"Those who are not used to it naturally find it hard," he said, "but if you are used to it, it is not bad. If only the grub were good. At first it was bad. But the men objected, and then the grub was better, and it was easier to work."

Then he told how he had been working out for twenty-eight years, and how he gave his earnings, first to his father, then to his elder brother, and now to his nephew, who was in charge of the farm, while he himself spent, out of the fifty or sixty roubles which he earned a year, two or three roubles on foolishness—on tobacco and matches.

"I'm a sinner, sometimes take a drink of vodka, when I'm tired," he added, smiling a guilty smile.

Tolstoy
Resurrection
page 324
He also told how the women looked after things for them at home; how the contractor had treated them before their journey to half a bucket; how one had died; and how they were taking one sick man home. The sick man, of whom he spoke, was sitting in the same car in a corner. He was a young boy, grayish pale in his face, with blue lips. He was apparently suffering from ague. Nekhlyúdov went up to him, but the boy looked at him with such a stern, suffering glance, that Nekhlyúdov did not bother him with questions, but only advised the elder man to buy quinine and wrote out the name of the medicine on a piece of paper for him. He wanted to give him money, but the old workingman said that it was not necessary, that he would give his.

"As much as I have travelled, I have not seen such gentlemen. He not only did not kick me, but even gave me his seat. Apparently there are all kinds of gentlemen," he concluded, addressing Tarás.

"Yes, it is a new, a different and new, world," thought Nekhlyúdov, looking at these drawn, muscular limbs, these coarse, home-made garments, and these sunburnt, kind, and exhausted faces, and feeling himself surrounded on all sides by entirely new men, with their serious interests, joys, and sufferings of a real, busy, and human life.

"Here it is, *le vrai grand monde*," thought Nekhlyúdov, recalling the phrase which had been used by Prince Korchágin and all that empty, luxurious world of the Korchágins, with their petty, miserable interests. And he experienced the sensation of a traveller who has discovered a new, unknown, and beautiful world.

RESURRECTION

BOOK THREE

Tʜᴇ ɢʀᴏᴜᴘ ᴡʜɪᴄʜ Máslova ᴡᴇɴᴛ ᴡɪᴛʜ ᴛʀᴀᴠᴇʟʟᴇᴅ about five thousand versts. As far as Perm, Máslova travelled by rail and water with the criminals; but here Nekhlyúdov succeeded in getting her transferred to the politicals, as Vyéra Bogodúkhovskaya, who was in the group, had advised him to do.

The journey to Perm was very hard for Máslova, both physically and morally. Physically, on account of the close quarters, the dirtiness and the disgusting vermin, which gave her no rest; and morally, on account of the no less disgusting men who, just like the vermin, though they changed at every stopping-place, were always equally persistent and annoying, and gave her no rest. Among the prisoners, the warders, and the guards, the habit of a cynical debauch was so firmly established that every woman, especially if she was young, had to be eternally on the lookout, if she did not wish to make use of her position as a woman. This continuous condition of fear and struggle was very hard to bear. Máslova was more especially subject to these attacks on account of the attractiveness of her looks and her well-known past. The positive opposition to the men who annoyed her with their attentions presented itself to them as a personal affront, and provoked, in addition, their malice toward her. Her position in this respect was alleviated by her closeness to Fedósya and Tarás, who, having heard of the attacks to which his wife was subjected, had himself arrested, in order to protect her, and travelled from Nízhni-Nóvgorod as a prisoner with the convicts.

The transfer to the division of the politicals improved Máslova's condition in every respect. Not only were the politicals better housed and fed and subject to less brutality, but also, by transfer to the politicals, Máslova's condition was further improved because all the persecution by men at once stopped, and she was able to live without being reminded every moment of her past, which she was trying to forget. The chief advantage of this transfer, however, lay in the fact that she became acquainted with some people who had a most decided and beneficent influence upon her.

At the halting-places, Máslova was permitted to be housed with the politicals, but, being a strong woman, she had to travel with the criminals. Thus she walked all the way from Tomsk. With her went, also on foot, two politicals: Márya Pávlovna Shchetínina, that pretty girl with the sheep eyes who had so impressed Nekhlyúdov during his interview with Vyéra Bogodúkhovskaya, and a certain Simonsón, who was being deported to the Yakútsk Territory—that swarthy, shaggy man with deep-set eyes, whom Nekhlyúdov had noticed during the same visit. Márya Pávlovna went on foot because she had given up her place on the cart to a pregnant criminal; Simonsón did so because he regarded it unjust to make use of his class privilege. All the other politicals left later in the day on carts, but these three started early in the morning with the criminals. This was how things were also on the last march, before reaching a large town, where a new officer of the guard took charge of the prisoners.

It was an early stormy September morning. It both snowed and rained, with gusts of a chill wind. All the prisoners of the group—four hundred men and about fifty women—were already in the yard of the halting-place; some of them were crowding around the commissary of the guard, who was distributing provision money among the foremen for two days; others were buying food from the hawking women, who had been admitted in the courtyard of the halting-place. One could hear the din of the prisoners' voices counting money and buying provisions and the squeaky voices of the hucksters.

Katyúsha and Márya Pávlovna—both in long boots and short fur coats and wrapped in kerchiefs—came out from the building of the stopping-place and walked toward the hucksters, who, sitting along the north wall of the yard to protect themselves against the wind, were vying with each other in offering their wares: fresh white bread, pies, fish, noodles, grits, liver, beef, eggs, milk; one of them had even a roast pig.

Simonsón, in a rubber jacket and overshoes, tied over his woollen stockings by means of twine (he was a vegetarian and did not use the skin of dead animals), was also in the yard, waiting for the group to start. He was standing near the porch and noting down in his diary a thought which had occurred to him. His thought was this: "If a bacterium were to observe and investigate a man's nail, it would come to the conclusion that it was inorganic matter. Similarly we, who have observed the rind of the earth, have declared the terrestrial globe to be inorganic matter. This is not correct."

Having purchased some eggs, pretzels, fish, and fresh wheat bread, Máslova put all these things into her bag, and Márya Pávlovna was paying the hucksters, when the prisoners suddenly started moving. Everything grew silent, and the prisoners began to line up. The officer came out and gave his final orders before the start.

Everything went as usual: the prisoners were counted; the fetters were examined; and the pairs that walked together were handcuffed. But suddenly were heard the imperious and angry voice of the officer, blows on a body, and the cries of a child. Everything grew silent for a moment, and then a dull murmur ran through the throng. Máslova and Márya Pávlovna moved up to the place from where the noise came.

CHAPTER II

THE OFFICER PUNISHES A PRISONER

Upon reaching the spot, Márya Pávlovna and Katyúsha saw this: the officer, a stout man with a long, blond moustache, was frowning and with his left hand rubbing the palm of his right, which he had hurt by striking a prisoner's face. He did not stop uttering coarse, indecent curses. In front of him stood a lean, haggard prisoner, in a short cloak and still shorter trousers, one-half of whose head was shaven. With one hand he was rubbing his mauled and bleeding face, while with the other he held a little girl who was wrapped in a kerchief and whined piercingly.

"I will teach you" (an indecent curse) "to talk!" (Again a curse.) "Give her to the women!" cried the officer. "Put them on!"

The officer demanded that the prisoner, exiled by his commune, be handcuffed. He was being deported and all the way had been carrying a little girl left him by his wife, who had died of typhus at Tomsk. The prisoner's remark that he could not carry his girl while handcuffed had angered the officer, who was out of sorts, whereupon he hit the prisoner, who had not submitted at once.*

In front of the beaten prisoner stood a soldier of the guard and a thick-set, black-bearded prisoner with a handcuff on one hand, gloomily looking up, now at the officer, and now at the beaten prisoner and the girl. The officer repeated his command to the soldier to take the girl away. Among the prisoners the murmuring became ever more audible.

"He had no handcuffs on him all the way from Tomsk," was heard a hoarse voice in the back ranks.

"It is not a pup, but a child."

"What is he to do with the girl?"

"This is against the law," said somebody else.

"Who said that?" the officer shouted, as though stung, rushing at the prisoners. "I will show you the law. Who said it? You? You?"

"All say it, because—" said a broad-shouldered, stocky man.

He did not finish his sentence. The officer began to strike his face with both hands.

"You mean to riot? I will teach you how to riot! I will shoot you down like dogs, and the authorities will only thank me for it. Take the girl!"

The throng grew silent. A soldier tore away the desperately crying girl; another began to manacle the prisoner, who submissively offered his hand.

"Take her to the women," the officer cried, adjusting his sword-belt.

The little girl tried to free her hands from the kerchief and, with flushed face, screamed without let-up. Márya Pávlovna stepped out from the crowd and walked over to the solder.

"Mr. Officer, let me carry the girl!"

The soldier with the girl stopped.

"Who are you?" asked the officer.

"I am a political."

Apparently, Márya Pávlovna's pretty face, with her beautiful bulging eyes (he had noticed her before, when receiving the prisoners), had an effect upon the officer. He looked in silence at her, as though considering something.

"It makes no difference to me. Carry her, if you want to. It is easy enough for you to pity him; but who's responsible, if he runs away?"

"How can he run away with the girl?" said Márya Pávlovna.

"I have no time to talk to you. Take her, if you want to."

"May I give the child to her?" asked the soldier.

"Yes."

*This fact is described in D. A. Línev's work, *The Long March.—Author's Note.*

"Come to me," said Márya Pávlovna, trying to win the girl over.

But the girl, who, in the soldier's arms, stretched her hands toward her father, continued to scream and did not want to go to Márya Pávlovna.

"Wait, Márya Pávlovna! She will come to me," said Máslova, taking a pretzel out of her bag.

The girl knew Máslova, and, seeing her face and the pretzel, readily went to her.

Everything grew quiet. The gate was opened and the party walked out and drew up in rows; the soldiers counted them once more; the bags were tied up and put away, and the feeble were put on the carts. Máslova, with the girl in her arms, stood with the women, at Fedósya's side. Simonsón, who had all the time watched the proceeding, with large determined steps went up to the officer, who had made all the arrangements and was seating himself in his tarantas.

"You have acted badly, Mr. Officer," said Simonsón.

"Go back to your place! It is none of your business!"

"It is my business to tell you that you have done wrong," said Simonsón, fixedly looking up at the officer through his thick eyebrows.

"Ready? March!" cried the officer, paying no attention to Simonsón and helping himself into the tarantas by taking hold of the shoulder of the soldier coachman. The group started, and, spreading out, walked into the muddy, rutted road, which was ditched on both sides and ran through a dense forest.

CHAPTER III

KATYÚSHA AND THE POLITICAL PRISONERS

After the debauched, luxurious, and effeminate life of the last six years in the city, and after the two months in prison with the criminals, the life with the politicals, notwithstanding all the difficult conditions under which they were living, seemed very pleasant to Katyúsha. Marches of from twenty to thirty versts a day, with good food, and a day's rest after every two days on the road, physically braced her; while her dealings with her new companions opened up new interests for her, such as she had never known before. She had never known and could not even have imagined such *wonderful* people, as she put it, as those with whom she was now marching.

"How I wept at being sentenced!" she said. "But I ought to thank God: I have learned things I would never have found out otherwise."

She very easily and without effort understood the motives which guided these people, and, herself one of the people, she fully sympathized with them. She understood that they were behind the people against the masters; and what particularly made her esteem them and admire them was the fact that they themselves belonged to the better classes and yet sacrificed their privileges, their liberty, and their lives for the people.

She was delighted with all her new companions; but more than all she admired Márya Pávlovna. She not only admired her, but loved her with a special, respectful, and rapturous love. She was surprised to see this beautiful girl, the daughter of a rich general, who could speak three languages, behaving like the simplest working woman, giving away everything which her rich brother sent her, and dressing herself not only simply, but even poorly, paying not the least attention to her looks. This trait—the complete absence of coquetry—particularly impressed and enchanted Máslova. Máslova saw that Márya Pávlovna knew, and that it even was pleasant for her to know, that she was beautiful, and yet that she did not in the least enjoy the impression which her looks produced on men, but that she was afraid of it and had a loathing and dread of falling in love. Her male companions, knowing this, if they felt attracted to her, did not let themselves show it and treated her as an equal; but strangers were frequently after her, and from these, she said, she was saved by her great physical strength, of which she was especially proud. "Once," she laughingly told Katyúsha, "a certain gentleman annoyed me in the street and would not go away. I then gave him such a shaking that he was frightened and ran away."

She became a revolutionist, she said, because ever since her childhood she had taken a dislike to the life the masters led and liked that of the simple people, being always scolded for preferring the maids' rooms, the kitchen, the stable, to the drawing-room.

"I always felt happy with the cooks and coachmen, but bored with our gentlemen and ladies," she said. "Later, when I began to understand things, I saw that our life was very bad. I had no mother, I did not like my father, and when I was nineteen years old I went away from home with a friend of mine and became a factory girl."

After working in the factory she lived in the country; then she came to the city and lived in lodgings where there was a secret printing office, and there she was arrested and sentenced to hard labour. Márya Pávlovna never told this herself, but Katyúsha found out from others that she was sentenced to hard labour for claiming to have fired a shot, which had, in reality, been fired by a revolutionist in the dark during a search.

Ever since Katyúsha knew her, she saw that wherever she was, and under whatever circumstances, she never thought of herself, but was concerned about serving and helping others, in large and in small things. One of her present companions, Novodvórov by name, jestingly remarked of her that she was addicted to the sport of doing good. And that was the truth. Just as the hunter is bent on finding game, so all the interests of her life consisted in finding an occasion to do some one a good turn. This sport became a habit with her and the business of her life. She did all this so naturally that those who knew her no longer valued it, but demanded it as a matter of course.

When Máslova joined them, Márya Pávlovna experienced a disgust and loathing for her. Katyúsha noticed it; but she also saw later that Márya Pávlovna made an effort to overcome her feelings and began to treat her with exceeding kindness. The kindness from so unusual a being so touched Máslova that she surrendered herself to her with all her soul, unconsciously adopting Márya Pávlovna's views and involuntarily imitating her in everything. This devotion of Katyúsha touched Márya Pávlovna, and she, in her turn, began to love Katyúsha.

These two women were also drawn to each other by that loathing which both had for sexual love. One of them despised this love because she had experienced all its horrors; the other, who had not experienced it—because she looked upon it as something incomprehensible and at the same time disgusting and insulting to human dignity.

CHAPTER IV

SIMONSÓN'S INFLUENCE

Márya Pávlovna's influence was one of the influences on Máslova. It was due to the fact that Máslova loved Márya Pávlovna. There was also Simonsón's influence on her. This was due to the fact that Simonsón loved Máslova.

All people live and act partly according to their own ideas, and partly according to the ideas of others. One of the chief distinctions among people is the degree to which they live according to their own ideas or according to those of others: some people, in the majority of cases, make use of their own thoughts as a mental toy and treat their reason as a flywheel from which the driving-belt has been taken off, while in their acts they submit to thoughts of others—to custom, tradition, law; others, regarding their own ideas as the prime movers of all their activities, nearly always listen to the promptings of their own reason and submit to it, only in exceptional cases—and only after due critical consideration—following the decisions of others. Simonsón was such a man. He weighed and tested everything by reason, and what he decided he did.

Having decided, while a student at the gymnasium, that the property acquired by his father, an ex-quartermaster officer, had been dishonestly obtained, he informed his father that he ought to give his wealth to the people. When his father not only did not do it but even cursed him, he left home and stopped availing himself of his father's means. Having decided that all existing evil was due to the ignorance of the people, he, upon leaving the university, fell in with the Narodniks, became a teacher in a village, and boldly preached to his pupils and to the peasants what he thought right and denied what he considered false.

He was arrested and tried.

During his trial, he decided that the judges had no right to judge him, and he so told the judges. When they did not agree with him and continued the trial, he decided not to answer any questions and remained silent all the time. He was deported to Arkhángelsk Province. There he formulated a religious doctrine for himself, and this formed the basis of his whole activity. According to this doctrine everything in the world is alive; there is nothing inert, but all the objects which we regard as dead and inorganic are only parts of an enormous organic body which we cannot comprehend, and therefore the problem of man, as a particle of this huge organism, consists in sustaining the life of this organism and all its living parts. Therefore he considered it a crime to destroy animal life: he was opposed to war, capital punishment, and all kinds of murder, not only of men, but of animals as well. He had also a theory of his own in regard to marriage, which was to the effect that the increase of the human race was only a lower function, and that a higher function consisted in serving all existing life. He found a confirmation of this idea in the presence of the phagocytes in the blood. Unmarried people, according to his theory, were just such phagocytes, whose purpose was to aid the weak and ailing parts of the organism. From the moment he had decided this, he began to live accordingly, though in his early youth he had been dissipated. He regarded himself, and Márya Pávlovna, too, as human phagocytes.

His love for Katyúsha did not impair this theory, since he loved her platonically, assuming that such a love not only did not interfere with his phagocyte activity of social help, but even spurred him on to it.

He decided not only moral questions in his own way, but also a great number of practical questions. He had his own theories for all practical affairs. He had his rules about the number of hours he had to work, to rest, to eat, to dress, how to make a fire in the stove, and how to light a lamp.

At the same time, Simonsón was exceedingly shy with people and modest. But when he made up his mind about something, nothing could keep him back.

It was this man who had a decisive influence on Máslova by dint of his love for her. Máslova, with her feminine sense, soon became aware of it, and the consciousness of being able to provoke love in so unusual a man raised her in her own estimation. Nekhlyúdov proposed to marry her as an act of magnanimity and on account of what had happened; but Simonsón loved her for what she was, and loved her just because he did. Besides, she felt that Simonsón considered her an unusual woman, different from all the rest and having certain special, high moral qualities. She did not exactly know what qualities he ascribed to her, but, in order not to deceive him, she tried to rouse in herself all the best qualities of which she could think. This caused her to endeavour to become as good as she was capable of being.

This had begun even in the prison, when, on one general visiting-day which included the politicals, she had noticed the peculiarly stubborn look of his innocent, kindly, dark blue eyes underneath his overhanging forehead and eyebrows. She had noticed, even, that he was a peculiar man and that he looked at her in a peculiar way; she had remarked the strange and striking combination in one face of severity, produced by his towering hair and frowning eyebrows, and of the childlike kindness and innocence of his look. In Tomsk she was transferred to the politicals, and she saw him again. Although not a word had been said between them, there was in the look which they exchanged, an acknowledgment of their remembering each other and of their mutual importance. There never was any long conversation between them even after that, but Máslova felt that whenever he spoke in her presence, his speech was meant for her, and that he was speaking in such a way as to be as intelligible as possible to her. Their special, closer friendship began when he marched with the criminals.

CHAPTER V

A CHANGE IN KATYÚSHA

From Nízhni-Nóvgorod to Perm, Nekhlyúdov succeeded in seeing Katyúsha only twice: once in Nízhni-Nóvgorod, before the prisoners were placed on a caged-in barge, and the next time in Perm, in the prison office. At both meetings he found her secretive and hostile. To his question whether she was comfortable and whether she did not need anything, she replied evasively, in an embarrassed and what to him seemed hostile, reproachful way which he had noticed in her before. This gloomy mood, which actually resulted from the molestations of the men, to which she was subjected at that time, tormented Nekhlyúdov. He was afraid that under the influence of the heavy and demoralizing conditions under which she lived during her transportation, she might again fall into her old discontentment and despair, when she was provoked against him and smoked heavily and drank in order to forget herself. He was quite unable to assist her because he had no chance, during this first part of her journey, of seeing her. Only after she was transferred to the politicals, he not only convinced himself of the groundlessness of his fears, but, on the contrary, at every meeting with her noticed the ever more clearly defined internal change, which he had been so anxious to see in her. At their first meeting in Tomsk, she was again what she had been before her departure. She did not pout or become embarrassed upon seeing him, but, on the contrary, met him joyfully and simply, and thanked him for what he had done for her, especially for having brought her in contact with the people with whom she now was.

After two months' marching, the change which had taken place in her was also manifested in her looks. She had grown thinner and sunburnt, and looked aged; on her temples and around her mouth wrinkles appeared; she did not let her hair hang over her brow, but covered it with her kerchief, and neither in her dress, nor in the way she did her hair, nor in her manners were there any of the previous signs of coquetry. This change which had taken place and was still in progress constantly made Nekhlyúdov extremely happy.

He now experienced toward her a feeling that he had never experienced before. It had nothing in common with his first poetical rapture, and still less with that sensual love which he had experienced later, nor even with that consciousness of a duty performed, united with egotism, which had led him, after the trial, to decide to marry her. This feeling was the simplest sensation of pity and contrition, which had come over him for the first time during his visit to her in prison, and later, with renewed strength, after the hospital, when he, curbing his disgust, forgave her for the supposed incident with the assistant (an injustice which was later cleared up); it was the same feeling, but with the difference that then it had been temporary, now it had become permanent. Whatever he now thought or did, his general mood was a feeling of pity and tenderness, not only in respect to her, but to all people.

This feeling seemed to have revealed in Nekhlyúdov's soul a stream of love, which formerly had had no outlet, but now was directed toward all men with whom he came in contact.

Nekhlyúdov was during his whole journey conscious of that agitated condition when he involuntarily became affable and attentive to all people with whom he had any business, from the driver and soldier of the guard up to the chief of the prison and the governor.

During this time, Nekhlyúdov, because of Máslova's transfer to the politicals, had occasion to become acquainted with many politicals, at first in Ekaterinbúrg, where they enjoyed great liberty, being all kept together in a large hall, and later on the road, with the five men and four women, to whom Máslova was attached.

Nekhlyúdov's acquaintance with the deported politicals entirely changed his view of them.

From the very beginning of the revolutionary movement in Russia, but especially after March 1st, Nekhlyúdov was animated by a hostile and contemptuous feeling for the revolutionists. Above everything else he had been repelled by the cruelty and secrecy of the means they used in their struggle with the government, especially by the cruelty of the murders committed by them; then again, their common characteristic of self-importance was disgusting to him. But, upon seeing them at close range and discovering that they frequently suffered innocently from the government, he perceived that they could not be anything else than what they were.

No matter how dreadfully senseless were the torments to which the so-called criminals were subjected, a certain semblance of lawful procedure was observed toward them, even after their judicial sentence; but for the politicals there was not even that semblance, as Nekhlyúdov had noticed in Shústova's case and, later, in the cases of very many of his new acquaintances. These people were treated as fish are when caught with a net: the whole catch is thrown out on the shore; then all the large fish that can be used are picked out, and the small fry are left to die and dry up on the land. Just so, hundreds of men who, apparently, were not only innocent, but who could in no way be dangerous to the government, were arrested and frequently held for years in prisons, where they contracted consumption, or grew insane, or committed suicide. They were kept in these prisons only because there was no special reason for releasing them, and, by keeping them in jail, they might be of use in clearing up questions at an inquest. The fate of all these people, who frequently were innocent even from the government's standpoint, depended on the arbitrariness, leisure, and mood of the officer of gendarmery or police, of the spy, prosecutor, examining magistrate, governor, minister. If such an official got tired or wanted to distinguish himself, he made arrests and held the people in prison or released them, according to the mood he or the authorities happened to be in. The higher official again, according to whether he must distinguish himself, or in what relations he was with the minister, sent them to the end of the world, or kept them in solitary confinement, or sentenced them to deportation, hard labour, or capital punishment, or released them, if a lady asked him to do so.

They were treated as men are in war, and they, naturally, employed the same means which were used against them. And just as the military always live in an atmosphere of public opinion which not only conceals the criminality of the deeds committed by them, but even represents them as heroic—so there existed for the politicals a favourable atmosphere of public opinion in their own circle, by dint of which the cruel acts committed by them, at the risk of losing liberty, life, and all that is dear to man, presented themselves to them not as bad deeds but as acts of bravery. For Nekhlyúdov this explained the remarkable phenomenon that the meekest people, who were not able to cause a living being any pain or even to look at it, calmly prepared themselves to kill people, and that nearly all of them considered murder in certain cases a means of self-defence and of obtaining the highest degree of public good, both lawful and just. The high esteem in which they held their work and, consequently, themselves naturally flowed from the importance which the government ascribed to them and from the cruelty of the punishments to which they were subjected. They had to have a high opinion of themselves in order to be able to bear all they had to bear.

Upon knowing them better, Nekhlyúdov became convinced that they were neither the complete villains which they seemed to some, nor the complete heroes which others held them to be, but ordinary people, among whom there were, as everywhere else, good and bad and mediocre individuals. Among them there were some who had become revolutionaries because they honestly felt duty-bound to struggle against the existing evil; there were others who had selected this activity from selfish, vainglorious motives; but the majority were attracted to revolution by a desire for danger, risk, and enjoyment of playing with their own lives—feelings which are common to all energetic youth and which were familiar to Nekhlyúdov from his military life. They differed from other people, and that, too, was in their favour, in that their requirements of morality were higher than those current among ordinary people. They regarded as obligatory not only moderation and asceticism, truthfulness and unselfishness, but also readiness to sacrifice everything, even their lives, for the common good. Therefore those of them who were above their average stood very high above it and represented rare examples of moral excellence; those who were below the average stood much lower, representing a class of people that were untruthful, hypocritical, and, at the same time, self-confident and haughty. Consequently Nekhlyúdov not only respected, but even loved, some of his new acquaintances, while to others he remained more than indifferent.

CHAPTER VI

KRYLTSÓV'S STORY

Nekhlyúdov took a special liking to a consumptive young man, Kryltsóv, who was being deported to hard labour and was travelling with the group that Katyúsha had joined. Nekhlyúdov had met him for the first time at Ekaterinbúrg, and later he had seen him several times on the road and had conversed with him. Once, in the summer, when they halted for a day, Nekhlyúdov spent nearly all that day with him, and Kryltsóv, becoming communicative, told him his whole story, how he had become a revolutionary. His story previous to imprisonment was very simple. His father, a rich landowner of the southern provinces, had died while he was still a child. He was an only son, and his mother brought him up. He learned easily both at school and in the university and graduated at the head of the class in the mathematics department. He was offered a place at the university and was to receive a travelling fellowship. He hesitated. There was a girl whom he loved and he was considering marriage and working in local country affairs. He wanted everything and could not make up his mind on anything in particular. Just then his university friends asked him for a contribution to the common cause. He knew that this common cause meant the revolutionary party, in which he was not at all interested at the time, but he gave them money from a feeling of comradeship and pride, lest they think he was afraid. Those who had collected the money were caught; a note was found, by which it was discovered that the money had been contributed by Kryltsóv. He was arrested and confined, at first in the police jail, and then in prison.

"In the prison, where I was locked up," Kryltsóv told Nekhlyúdov (he was sitting with his sunken chest on a high sleeping-bench, leaning on his knees, and only now and then looked at Nekhlyúdov with his sparkling, feverish, beautiful, intelligent, and kind eyes), "there was no especial severity. We not only conversed with each other by knocking, but met in the corridors, talked to each other, shared our provisions and tobacco, and at evening even sang together. I had a good voice. Yes. If it had not been for my mother—she pined away for me—I would have been satisfied in prison—everything was pleasant and very interesting. Here I became acquainted, among others, with the famous Petróv (he later cut his throat with a piece of glass in the fortress) and with others. I was not a revolutionary. I also became acquainted with two neighbours to my cell. They were caught in the same affair, with some Polish proclamations, and were under trial for having tried to escape from the guard as they were being led to the railroad station. One of them was a Pole, Lozínski, and the other a Jew, Rozóvski by name. Yes. Rozóvski was just a boy. He said he was seventeen, but he did not look more than fifteen. He was small and lean, with sparkling eyes, lively, and, like all Jews, very musical. His voice still broke, but he sang beautifully. Yes. They were led off to court while I was in prison. They left in the morning. In the evening they returned and said that they had been condemned to death. Nobody had expected it. Their case was so unimportant: they had merely tried to get away from the guard and had not hurt anybody. And then it seemed so unnatural to execute such a boy as Rozóvski. All of us in the prison decided that this was only to frighten them, but that the decree would never be confirmed. At first we all were stirred up, but later quieted down, and life went on as of old. Yes. One evening an attendant came to my door and mysteriously informed me that the carpenters had come to put up the gallows. At first I did not understand what he meant, what gallows he was talking about. But the old attendant was so agitated that when I looked at him I understood that it was for our two men. I wanted to converse by taps with my companions, but was afraid that they might hear it. My companions were silent, too. Apparently everybody knew of it. There was a dead silence in the corridor and in the cells all the evening. We did not tap or sing. At about nine o'clock the attendant again came up to my door and told me that the hangman had been brought down from Moscow. He said this and went away. I began to call to him to come back. Suddenly I heard Rozóvski call to me across the corridor from his cell: 'What is the matter? Why do you call him?' I told him that he had brought me some tobacco, but he seemed to guess what it was, and continued asking me why we did not sing, and why we did not tap. I do not remember what I told him; I went away as soon as I could, so as not to talk to him. Yes. It was a terrible night. I listened all night long to every sound. Suddenly, toward morning, I heard them open the door of the corridor, and a number of people walking in. I stood at the window of my door. A lamp was burning in the corridor. First came the superintendent. He was a stout man, and seemed self-confident and determined. He was out of countenance: he looked pale and gloomy, as though frightened. After him came his assistant, scowling, with a determined look; then followed the guards. They passed by my door and stopped at the one next to me. I heard the assistant calling out in a strange voice: 'Lozínski, get up and put on clean clothes!' Yes. Then I heard the door creak, and they went in. Then I heard Lozínski's steps, and he went over on the other side of the corridor. I could see only the superintendent. He stood pale, and was buttoning and unbuttoning his coat, and shrugging his shoulders. Yes. Suddenly he acted as though something had frightened him. It was Lozínski, who went past him and stopped at my door. He was a fine-looking youth, of that fine Polish type: broad-chested, a straight forehead with a head of blond, wavy, fine hair, and beautiful blue eyes. He was such a blooming, healthy, vigorous young man. He stood in front of my door so that I could see his whole face. It was a terribly drawn, gray face. 'Kryltsóv, have you a cigarette?' I wanted to give him some, but the assistant, as though fearing to be late, took out his cigarette-case and offered him one. He took a cigarette, and the assistant lighted a match for him. He began to smoke and seemed to be musing. Then he looked as though he had recalled something, and he began to speak: 'It is cruel and unjust. I have committed no crime. I—' Something quivered in his youthful, white throat, from which I could not tear my eyes away, and he stopped. Yes. Just then I heard Rozóvski calling out something in the corridor in his thin, Jewish voice. Lozínski threw away the butt of his cigarette and went away from the door. Then Rozóvski could be seen through

Tolstoy
Resurrection
page 342

the window. His childish face, with its moist, black eyes, was red and sweaty. He, too, had on clean clothes, and his trousers were too wide for him, and he kept pulling them up with both his hands, and was trembling all over. He put his pitiful face to my window: 'Anatóli Petróvich, isn't it true? The doctor ordered me to drink pectoral tea. I am not well, and I will drink some.' Nobody answered him, and he looked questioningly now at me, and now at the inspector. I did not understand what he meant by his words. Yes. Suddenly the assistant looked stern, and again he called out, in a wheezy voice: 'No joking now! Come!' Rozóvski was apparently unable to understand what was awaiting him, and went hurriedly along the corridor, ahead of them all, almost on a run. But later he balked, and I heard his piercing voice and weeping. There was a scuffle and a thud of steps was heard. He was crying and shrieking piercingly. Then farther and farther away—the door of the corridor rang shut, and all was quiet. Yes. They hanged them. Choked the lives out of them with ropes. Another attendant saw the hanging, and he told me that Lozínski offered no resistance, but that Rozóvski struggled for a long while, so that he had to be dragged to the gallows and his head had to be stuck through the noose. Yes. That attendant was a stupid fellow. 'I was told, sir, that it was terrible. But it is not. When they were hanged, they moved their shoulders only twice'— he showed me how the shoulders were raised convulsively and fell. 'Then the hangman jerked the rope so that the noose should lie more tightly on their necks, and that was all: they did not stir again.' It is not at all terrible," Kryltsóv repeated the attendant's words, and tried to smile, but instead burst into sobs.

He was for a long time silent after this, breathing heavily and swallowing the sobs that rose in his throat.

"Since then I have been a revolutionary. Yes," he said, calming down, and then he finished his story in a few words.

He belonged to the People's Will party and was the head of a disorganizing group, whose purpose was to terrorize the government, so that it might itself abdicate its power and call the people to assume it. For this purpose he travelled, now to St. Petersburg, now abroad, or to Kíev, to Odéssa, and he was everywhere successful. A man on whom he fully relied betrayed him. He was arrested, tried, kept two years in prison, and sentenced to death, which was commuted to hard labour for life.

In prison he developed consumption, and now, under the conditions of his life, he had evidently but a few months left to live. He knew this, and did not regret what he had done, but said that if he had a life to live over he would use it for the same purpose—for the destruction of the order of things which made possible what he had seen.

This man's history and the companionship with him made many things intelligible to Nekhlyúdov which he had not understood before.

CHAPTER VII

AT THE GATES OF A
MID-WAY POINT

On the day when, at the start from the halting-place, the conflict over the child had taken place between the officer of the guard and the prisoners, Nekhlyúdov, who had spent the night at an inn, awoke late, and for a long time wrote letters, which he was getting ready to mail from the provincial capital; he consequently left the inn later than usual and did not catch up with the marching group on the road, as he had done on previous days, but arrived at twilight at the village near which the mid-way stop was made. Having changed his wet clothing at the inn, which was kept by an elderly widow with a white neck of extraordinary size, Nekhlyúdov drank tea in the clean guest-room, which was adorned by a large number of icons and pictures, and hastened to the halting-place to ask the officer's permission for a visit.

At the six preceding halting-places the officers of the guard, although several changes had been made, all without exception had refused Nekhlyúdov's admission to the prison enclosure, so that he had not seen Katyúsha for more than a week. This severity was caused by an expected visit from an important prison chief. Now the chief had passed, without as much as looking at the halting-place, and Nekhlyúdov hoped that the officer who had taken charge of the group in the morning would, like former officers, permit him to see the prisoners.

The hostess offered Nekhlyúdov a tarantas to take him to the halting-place, which was at the other end of the village, but Nekhlyúdov preferred to walk. A young, broad-chested, powerful-looking lad, in immense boots freshly smeared with tar, offered himself to take him there. It was misting, and it was so dark that whenever the lad got three steps from him in places where the light did not fall through the windows, Nekhlyúdov could not see him, but only heard the smacking of the boots in the deep, sticky mud.

After passing the square in front of the church and a long street with brightly illumined windows, Nekhlyúdov followed his guide into complete darkness, at the edge of the village. Soon, however, they saw, melting in the fog, beams of light from the lamps which were burning near the halting-place. The reddish spots of light became larger and brighter; they could see the posts of the enclosure, the black figure of a sentry moving about, the striped pole, and the sentry booth. The sentinel met the approaching men with his usual "Who goes there?" and, finding that they did not belong, became so stern that he would not allow them to wait near the enclosure. But Nekhlyúdov's guide was not disconcerted by the severity of the sentry.

"What an angry fellow you are!" he said to him. "You call the sergeant and we will wait."

The sentry did not answer, but called out something through the small gate, and stopped to watch the broad-shouldered lad intently as in the lamplight he cleaned off with a chip the mud that was sticking to Nekhlyúdov's boots. Beyond the posts of the enclosure was heard the din of men's and women's voices. About three minutes later there was a clanking of iron, the door of the gate was opened, and out of the darkness a sergeant emerged into the lamplight, wearing his overcoat over his shoulders. He asked them what they wanted. Nekhlyúdov handed him the card he had prepared, with a note asking to be admitted on a private matter, and begged him to take it to the officer. The sergeant was less severe than the sentry, but more inquisitive. He insisted upon knowing what business Nekhlyúdov had with the officer, and who he was, apparently scenting a tip, and not wishing to miss it. Nekhlyúdov said that it was special business and asked him to take the note to the officer. The sergeant took it and, shaking his head, went away. A little while after his disappearance the door clanked again, and there came out women with baskets, with birch-bark boxes, clay vessels, and bags. They stepped across the threshold of the door, sonorously babbling in their peculiar Siberian dialect. They were all dressed not in village but in city fashion, wearing jackets and fur coats; their skirts were tucked high, and their heads were wrapped in kerchiefs. With curiosity they eyed Nekhlyúdov and his guide, who were standing in the lamplight. One of these women, obviously happy to meet the broad-shouldered lad, immediately began to banter him with Siberian curses.

"You fiend, plague take you, what are you here for?" she turned to him.

"I brought a stranger here," replied the lad. "What have you been carrying here?"

"Milk stuff—and they want me to come back in the morning."

"Did they not let you stay there overnight?" asked the lad.

"Go to hell, you liar," she cried, laughing. "Won't you take us all back to the village?"

The guide said something else to her, which made not only the women laugh, but also the sentry, and turned to Nekhlyúdov.

"Well, can you find your way back by yourself? Won't you lose your way?"

"I'll find it, I will."

"Beyond the church, the second house after the two-storied one. Here, you have a staff," he said, giving Nekhlyúdov a long stick, which was taller than he, and which he had been carrying and, splashing with his immense boots, disappeared in the darkness with the women.

His voice, interrupted by that of the women, could be heard through the mist, when the door clanked again, and the sergeant came out, inviting Nekhlyúdov to follow him to the officer.

CHAPTER VIII

NEKHLYÚDOV AT THE OFFICER'S

The mid-way point was situated like all the other mid-way points and full halts along the Siberian road: in the yard, surrounded by pointed pales, there were three one-story buildings. In one of these, the largest, with latticed windows, the prisoners were placed; in another, the guards; and in the third, the commander and the office. In all three houses now fires were going, which, as always, especially here, illusively promised something good and cosy within the lighted walls. In front of the entrance steps of the houses lamps were burning, and there were five other lamps along the wall, illuminating the yard. The sergeant took Nekhlyúdov over a board walk to the steps of the smallest building. Having mounted three steps, he let him pass in front of him into an antechamber which was lighted by a small lamp emitting smoky fumes. At the stove stood a soldier, in a coarse shirt and tie and black trousers; he had on only one boot, with a yellow bootleg, and, bending over, was fanning the samovár with the other boot. Upon seeing Nekhlyúdov, the soldier went away from the samovár, took off Nekhlyúdov's leather coat, and went into the inner room.

"He has arrived, your Honour!"

"Well, call him in," was heard an angry voice.

"Go through the door," said the soldier, and immediately began to busy himself about the samovár.

In the next room, which was lighted by a hanging lamp, an officer, with long blond moustache and a very red face, dressed in an Austrian jacket, which closely fitted over his broad chest and shoulders, was sitting at a table covered with remnants of a dinner and two bottles. The warm room smelled not only of tobacco smoke but also of some strong, vile perfume. Upon noticing Nekhlyúdov, the officer half-raised himself and almost scornfully and suspiciously fixed his eyes upon the stranger.

"What do you wish?" he said, and, without awaiting a reply, called through the door: "Bérnov, will you ever get the samovár ready?"

"Right away!"

"I will give you such a right away that you will remember me," cried the officer, his eyes sparkling.

"I am bringing it!" cried the soldier, and entered with the samovár.

Nekhlyúdov waited until the soldier had put down the samovár (the officer followed him with his small, mean eyes, as though choosing a spot on which to hit him). When the samovár had been put down, the officer began to steep the tea, then he took out of a lunch-basket a square decanter of brandy and Albert biscuits. After he had placed everything on the table, he again addressed Nekhlyúdov.

"So what can I do for you?"

"I should like to visit a lady prisoner," said Nekhlyúdov, still standing.

"A political? That is prohibited by law, "said the officer.

"She is not a political," said Nekhlyúdov.

"But please be seated," said the officer.

Nekhlyúdov sat down.

"She is not a political," he repeated, "but at my request she has been permitted by the higher authorities to go with the politicals—"

"Ah, I know," the officer interrupted him. "A small brunette? Yes, you may. Won't you have a cigarette?"

He handed Nekhlyúdov a box with cigarettes, and, carefully filling two glasses of tea, pushed one over to Nekhlyúdov.

"If you please," he said.

"I thank you. I should like to see—"

"The night is long. You will have plenty of time. I will have her called out."

"Could I not be admitted to their room, without calling her out?" said Nekhlyúdov.

"To the politicals? That is against the law."

"I have been admitted several times. If there is any fear that I might transmit something to them—then you must not forget that I could do so even through her."

"No, not at all. She will be searched," said the officer, with an unpleasant laugh.

"Well, then search me."

"Oh, we will get along without that," said the officer, raising the uncorked decanter to Nekhlyúdov's glass. "May I pour some? Well, as you please. One feels so happy to meet an educated man here in Siberia. Our fate, you know yourself, is a very sad one. It is hard when a man is used to something else. There is an opinion abroad that an officer of the guard must be a coarse man, without any education. They never consider that a man may have been born for something quite different."

The red face of this officer, his perfume, his ring, but more especially his disagreeable laugh, were quite repulsive to Nekhlyúdov; but on that day, as during his whole journey, he was in that attentive and serious mood when he did not allow himself to treat any person frivolously or contemptuously, and when he considered it necessary to "let himself loose," as he defined this relation of his to other people. Having listened to the officer's words and having understood his state of mind as being wearied by compassion for the suffering of the people subject to him, he remarked seriously:

"I think that in your occupation you can find consolation by alleviating the suffering of the people," he said.

"What suffering? They are a terrible lot."

"Not at all terrible," said Nekhlyúdov. "They are just like the rest. There are even some innocent people among them."

"Of course, there are all kinds. Of course, I pity them. Others would not be less rigorous for anything, but I try to make it easier for them whenever I can. I prefer to suffer in their places. Others will invoke the law on every occasion, and are even ready to shoot them, but I pity them. Will you have another glass? Please," he said, filling his glass with tea again. "What kind of a woman is the one you want to see?" he asked.

"An unfortunate woman who found her way into a house of prostitution, and there she was accused of poisoning—but she is a good woman," said Nekhlyúdov.

The officer shook his head.

"Yes, these things happen. In Kazán, let me tell you, there was one—they called her Emma. She was a Hungarian by birth, but her eyes looked like those of a Persian woman," he continued, unable to repress a smile at the recollection. "She was as elegant as any countess—"

Nekhlyúdov interrupted the officer and returned to his former conversation:

"I think you can alleviate the condition of these people while they are in your power. I am sure that if you did so, you would experience great joy," said Nekhlyúdov, trying to speak as distinctly as possible, just as one speaks to a stranger or a child.

The officer looked at Nekhlyúdov with sparkling eyes, and apparently was impatiently waiting for him to get through, so as to give him a chance to continue his story about the Hungarian woman with the Persian eyes, who, evidently, stood out vividly before his imagination and absorbed his whole attention.

"Yes, that is so, I will admit," he said. "I am sorry for them; but let me finish my story about this Emma. So this is what she did—"

"This does not interest me," said Nekhlyúdov, "and let me tell you outright that, although I myself formerly was different, I now despise such relations with women."

The officer looked in a terrified way at Nekhlyúdov.

"Won't you have another glass of tea?" he said.

"No, thank you."

"Bérnov!" cried the officer, "take the gentleman to Bakúlov and tell him to admit him to the special room of the politicals; the gentleman may stay there until roll-call."

CHAPTER IX

THE PRISON AT THE MID-WAY HALT

Accompanied by the orderly, Nekhlyúdov again went out into the dark yard which was dimly lighted by the red-burning lamps.

"Where are you going?" a guard, whom they met, asked the one who was guiding Nekhlyúdov.

"To the special room—Number 5."

"You can't go through here: it is locked. You will have to go across that porch."

"Why is it locked?"

"The sergeant locked it, and himself went down to the village."

"Well, then, let's go this way!"

The soldier took Nekhlyúdov to the other porch, and crossed a board walk to another entrance. Even from the yard one could hear the din of voices and the motion within, such as one hears in a good beehive which is getting ready to swarm, but when Nekhlyúdov came nearer and the door was opened, this din was increased and passed into a noise of scolding, cursing, laughing voices. There was the metallic sound of the chains, and the familiar oppressive odour of excrement and tar.

These two impressions—the din of the voices combined with the clanking of the chains, and that terrible odour—always united in Nekhlyúdov in one agonizing feeling of moral nausea passing into physical nausea. Both impressions mingled and intensified each other.

Upon entering the vestibule of the mid-way halt, where stood an immense stink-vat, Nekhlyúdov noticed a woman sitting on the edge of this vat; opposite her stood a man, with his pancake-shaped cap poised sidewise on his shaven head. They were talking about something. When the prisoner noticed Nekhlyúdov, he winked and said:

"Even the Tsar can't hold his water."

The woman pulled down the skirt of her cloak and looked abashed.

From the vestibule ran a corridor, into which the doors of cells opened. The first was the family cell; then followed a large cell for unmarried persons, and at the end of the corridor, two small rooms were reserved for the politicals. The interior of the halting-place, which, although intended for 150 prisoners, held 450, was so crowded that, not being able to find places in the cells, the prisoners filled the corridor. Some sat or lay on the floor, while others moved up and down, carrying full or empty teapots. Among the latter was Tarás. He ran up to Nekhlyúdov and exchanged a pleasant greeting with him. Tarás's kind face was disfigured by purple bruises on his nose and under his eyes.

"What is the matter with you?" asked Nekhlyúdov.

"We had a fight," said Tarás, smiling.

"They are fighting all the time," the guard said, contemptuously.

"On account of the woman," added a prisoner, who was walking behind them. "He had a set-to with Fédka the blind."

"How is Fedósya?" asked Nekhlyúdov.

"All right. She is well. I am taking this boiling water to her for tea," said Tarás, entering the family cell.

Nekhlyúdov looked into the door. The whole cell was full of women and men, both on the sleeping-benches and underneath them. The room was filled with the evaporations of wet clothes getting dry, and there was heard the incessant squeak of female voices. The next door led into the cell of the single persons. This room was even more crowded, and even in the door and out in the doorway stood a noisy crowd of prisoners in wet clothes, dividing or deciding something. The guard explained to Nekhlyúdov that the foreman was paying out to a gambler the provision money which had been lost or won before by means of small tickets made out of playing-cards. Upon noticing the sergeant and the gentleman, those nearest grew silent, hostilely eyeing them. Among those who were dividing up, Nekhlyúdov noticed Fyódorov, the hard-labour convict of his acquaintance, who always kept at his side a miserable-looking, pale, bloated lad with arching eyebrows, and a repulsive, pockmarked, noseless tramp, of whom it was said that during an escape into the taiga he had killed his companion and eaten his flesh. The tramp stood in the corridor, with his wet cloak thrown over one shoulder, and scornfully and boldly looked at Nekhlyúdov, without getting out of his way. Nekhlyúdov went around him.

Although this spectacle was not new to Nekhlyúdov, although he had, in the last three months, frequently seen these four hundred criminal prisoners in all kinds of situations—in heat, in the cloud of dust which they raised with their feet dragging the chains, on the stops along the road, in the yards of the halting-places during warm weather, where appalling scenes of open immorality took place—he experienced an agonizing feeling of shame and a consciousness of guilt before them every time he went in among them and felt their attention directed to himself. Most oppressive for him was the fact that an unsurmountable feeling of loathing and

terror mingled with this sensation of shame and guilt. He knew that, under the conditions in which they were placed, they could not be anything else than what they were, and yet he could not suppress his feeling of loathing for them.

"They have an easy time, these hangers-on," Nekhlyúdov heard, as he approached the door of the politicals. "What're they doing, these bastards?—they don't get no bellyache," a hoarse voice said, adding an indecent curse.

There was hostile, scornful laughter.

CHAPTER X

MAKÁR DYÉVKIN'S REQUEST

As they passed the cell of the unmarried prisoners, the sergeant, who accompanied Nekhlyúdov, said to him that he would come for him before the roll-call and went back. The sergeant had barely left when a prisoner, holding up his chains, rapidly walked up close to Nekhlyúdov, wafting an oppressive and acid smell of sweat upon him, and said to him, in a mysterious whisper:

"Sir, please help! They have messed the lad up by making him drunk. He called himself Karmánov to-day at roll-call. Please help, for I can't—I'll be killed," said the prisoner, looking restlessly about and immediately walking away from Nekhlyúdov.

What this man informed Nekhlyúdov of was that prisoner Karmánov had persuaded a lad who resembled him and who was being deported for settlement in Siberia to exchange places with him, so that the one who was to go to hard labour was to be deported, while the lad would go to hard labour.

Nekhlyúdov knew of this affair, since this very prisoner had informed him of the exchange a week before. Nekhlyúdov nodded to indicate he had understood and that he was willing to do what he could, and, without looking around, passed on.

Nekhlyúdov had known this prisoner all the way from Ekaterinbúrg, where he had asked him to get permission for his wife to follow him, and the prisoner's act surprised him. He, the prisoner, was of medium height, about thirty years of age, and in no way differed from an ordinary peasant. He was being deported to hard labour for attempted robbery and murder. His name was Makár Dyévkin. His crime was a very strange one. He told Nekhlyúdov that the crime was not his, Makár's, but *his*, the devil's. He said that a traveller stopped at his father's, from whom he hired a sleigh for two roubles to take him to a village forty versts distant. His father told him to take the traveller there. Makár harnessed the horse, dressed himself, and drank tea with the traveller. The traveller told him at tea that he was on his way to get married and that he had with him five hundred roubles, which he had earned in Moscow. When Makár heard this, he went into the yard and put his axe in the straw of the sleigh.

Tolstoy
Resurrection
page 352

"I do not know myself why I took the axe along," he told Nekhlyúdov. "Something told me to take the axe with me, and so I did. We seated ourselves, and off we went. I entirely forgot about the axe. There were about six versts left to the village. From the cross-road to the highway the road went up-hill. I climbed down and walked back of the sleigh, but *he* kept whispering to me: 'What is the matter with you? When you get onto the highway, there will be people, and then comes the village. He will get away with the money. If anything is to be done, it must be done now.' I bent down to the sleigh, as though to fix the straw, and the axe handle seemed to jump into my hand. He looked around. 'What do you mean?' says he. I swung my axe and wanted to bang at him, but he was quick, and so he jumped down from the sleigh and caught me by the hand. 'What are you doing, you villain?' He threw me down on the snow, and I did not even struggle, but gave myself up. He tied my arms with the belt and threw me into the sleigh. He took me straight to the rural office. I was locked in jail and tried. The Commune testified to my good record, and that nothing bad had been noticed in me. The people with whom I was living said the same. I had no money to hire a lawyer," said Makár, "and so I was sentenced to four years."

It was this man who was trying to save his countryman, although he knew full well that he was risking his life in the attempt. If the prisoners had found out that he had given away the secret to Nekhlyúdov, they would certainly have strangled him.

CHAPTER XI

AMONG THE
POLITICAL PRISONERS

The quarters of the politicals consisted of two small cells, the doors of which opened into a barred-off part of the corridor. Upon entering this part of the corridor, the first person noticed by Nekhlyúdov was Simonsón, dressed in his jacket and squatting with a pine log in front of the quivering stove door drawn in by the current in the brightly burning stove.

Upon seeing Nekhlyúdov, he looked up through his overhanging eyebrows, without rising from his squatting position, and gave him his hand.

"I am glad you have come. I have something to tell you," he said, with a significant look, gazing straight at Nekhlyúdov.

"What is it?" asked Nekhlyúdov.

"Later. Now I am busy."

Simonsón again began to attend to the stove, which he fired according to his own theory of the minimum waste of heat energy.

Nekhlyúdov was about to go into the first door, when Máslova came out of the other, bending down and holding a broom in her hand, with it pushing a large pile of dirt and dust toward the stove. She had on a white jacket, a tucked-up skirt, and stockings. Her head was wrapped against the dust with a white kerchief, which reached down to her brows. Upon noticing Nekhlyúdov, she straightened up, and, all red and agitated, put down the broom and, wiping off her hands on her skirt, stopped right in front of him.

"Are you fixing up your apartment?" Nekhlyúdov asked, giving her his hand.

"Yes, my old occupation," she said, smiling. "There is incredible dirt in there. We have been doing nothing but cleaning."

"Well, is your plaid dry?" she turned to Simonsón.

"Almost," said Simonsón, looking at her with a special glance, which surprised Nekhlyúdov.

"Then I will come for it and bring out the furs to dry. Our people are all in there," she said to Nekhlyúdov, going into the farther door and pointing to the nearer.

Nekhlyúdov opened the door and went into a small cell which was dimly lighted up by a metallic lamp standing low on a sleeping-bench. The room was cold and smelled of unsettled dust, dampness, and tobacco. The tin lamp brightly illuminated those who were around it, but the benches were in the dark, and wavering shadows were on the walls.

All were in the small room, with the exception of two men who were in charge of the provisions and who had gone off to fetch boiling water and food. Here was Nekhlyúdov's old acquaintance, Vyéra Efrémovna, grown more thin and yellow, with her immense frightened eyes and the swollen vein on her forehead, dressed in a gray jacket, and with short hair. She was sitting over a piece of newspaper with tobacco on it, and, with a jerky motion, was filling cigarette papers.

Here also was Emíliya Rántseva, who, so Nekhlyúdov thought, was one of the most pleasant politicals. She had charge of the housekeeping, to which she managed to give a feminine cosiness and charm, even under the most trying circumstances. She was seated near the lamp and, her sleeves rolled up over her sunburnt beautiful arms, with agile hands was cleaning cups and saucers and placing them on a towel which was spread on a bench. Rántseva was a plain-looking woman with an intelligent and gentle expression on her face, which possessed the property of suddenly, during a smile, transforming itself and becoming merry, lively, and enchanting; she now greeted Nekhlyúdov with such a smile.

"We thought you had gone back to Russia," she said.

Here also, in the shadows of a far corner, was Márya Pávlovna, who was doing something to the flaxen-haired little girl who kept lisping in her sweet childish voice.

"How good of you to have come! Have you seen Kátya?" she asked Nekhlyúdov. "See what a guest we have!" She showed him the girl.

Here was Anatóli Kryltsóv, too. Haggard and pale, with his legs wrapped in felt boots bent under him, he sat, stooping and trembling, in a far corner of the sleeping-benches, and, putting his hands in the sleeves of his short fur coat, he looked at Nekhlyúdov with feverish eyes. Nekhlyúdov wanted to go up to him, but on the right of the door sat a curly-headed, red-haired man in spectacles and a rubber jacket, conversing with pretty, smiling Grabéts. This was the famous revolutionary Novodvórov, and Nekhlyúdov hastened to exchange greetings with him. He was particularly in a hurry to do this because of all the politicals of this party this one man was disagreeable to him. Novodvórov flashed his blue eyes through his glasses at Nekhlyúdov and, frowning, gave him his thin hand.

"Well, are you having a pleasant journey?" he said obviously ironically.

"Yes, there are many interesting things," replied Nekhlyúdov, pretending he did not see the irony, but accepting it as politeness, and went up to Kryltsóv.

Nekhlyúdov's appearance expressed indifference, but in his heart he was far from being indifferent to Novodvórov. These words of Novodvórov, his obvious desire to say and do something unpleasant, disturbed the good-natured mood in which Nekhlyúdov was. He became gloomy and sad.

"Well, how is your health?" he said, shaking Kryltsóv's cold and trembling hand.

"So-so. Only I can't get warm—I got so wet," said Kryltsóv, hastening to hide his hand in the sleeve of the short fur coat. "It is god-damned cold here. The windows are broken." He pointed to broken windows in two places behind the iron bars. "What was the matter with you? Why did you not come?"

"They would not admit me—the authorities were so strict. Only the officer today proved to be obliging."

"Well, he is obliging!" said Kryltsóv. "Ask Másha what he did this morning."

Márya Pávlovna, without rising from her place, told what had happened to the little girl in the morning at the departure from the halting-place.

"In my opinion, it is necessary to make a collective protest," Vyéra Efrémovna said, in a determined voice, looking now at one person, now at another, with an undecided and frightened look. "Vladímir has made a protest, but that is not enough."

"What protest?" Kryltsóv muttered, with an angry scowl. Apparently the lack of simplicity, the artificiality of the tone, and the nervousness of Vyéra Efrémovna had long been irritating him. "Are you looking for Katyúsha?" he turned to Nekhlyúdov. "She has been working—cleaning up. They have been cleaning out this room—ours, the men's; now they are working in the women's room. But they won't get rid of the fleas: they will eat us alive.—What is Márya doing there?" he asked, with his head indicating the corner in which Márya Pávlovna was.

"She is combing her adopted daughter," said Emíliya Rántseva.

"And won't she let loose her vermin on us?" asked Kryltsóv.

"No, no, I am careful. She is clean now," said Márya Pávlovna. "Take her," she turned to Emíliya Rántseva. "I'll go and help Kátya. And I'll bring him the plaid."

Emíliya Rántseva took the girl, and, with maternal tenderness pressing to herself the bare, plump little hands of the child, placed her on her knees and gave her a piece of sugar.

Márya Pávlovna went out, and, immediately after, two men entered the room with boiling water and food.

CHAPTER XII

TWO REVOLUTIONARIES

One of those who entered was a short, lean young man in a cloth-covered short fur coat and tall boots. He walked with a light, rapid gait, carrying two large steaming teapots with boiling water and holding bread wrapped in a cloth under his arm.

"Here our prince has come," he said, placing a teapot amidst the cups and giving the bread to Máslova. "We have bought some fine things," he said, throwing off his fur coat and flinging it over the heads to the corner of the benches. "Markél has bought milk and eggs; we will have a party this evening. Kiríllovna, I see, is again busy with her æsthetic cleanliness," he said, looking with a smile at Rántseva. "Now, let's have tea," he turned to her.

The whole exterior of this man, his movements, the sound of his voice, his look, breathed vivacity and merriment. The other of the new arrivals—also a short, bony man, with an ashen-gray face that had very protruding cheek-bones and puffed-up cheeks, with beautiful, greenish, widely placed eyes and thin lips—was, on the contrary, gloomy and melancholy. He wore an old wadded coat and boots with overshoes. He was carrying two pots and two birch-bark boxes. Having placed his burden in front of Emíliya Rántseva, he bowed with his neck to Nekhlyúdov in such a way that he kept his eyes on him all the time. Then, unwillingly giving him his clammy hand, he slowly began unloading the provisions from the basket.

These two political prisoners were men of the people: the first was the peasant Nabátov, the other was the factory workman, Markél Kondrátev. Markél had found his way among the revolutionaries at the advanced age of thirty-five, while Nabátov had joined them at eighteen. Having, through his conspicuous ability, made his way from the village school to the higher school, Nabátov supported himself all the while by giving lessons. He graduated with a gold medal, but did not proceed to the university, because he had decided, while in the seventh form, to go among the people from whom he had come, in order to educate his neglected brethren. And thus he did: at first he accepted a position as a clerk in a large village, but he was soon arrested for reading books to the peasants and forming among them a Consumers' Coöperative League. The first time he was kept in prison eight months, after which he was released and placed under secret surveillance. After his liberation, he immediately went to another village, in another province, and there established himself as a teacher, continuing his old activity. He was again arrested, and this time he was kept a year and two months in prison, and there he was only strengthened in his convictions.

After his second imprisonment, he was sent to the province of Perm. He ran away from there. He was again arrested, and, having been imprisoned for seven months, was sent to the province of Arkhángelsk. From there he ran away again, and was again caught; he was sentenced to deportation to the Yakútsk Territory; thus he had passed half of his adult life in prison and in exile. All these adventures did not in the least sour him; nor did they weaken his energy—on the contrary, they only fanned it. He was a mobile man, with an excellent digestion, always equally active, cheerful, and vivacious. He never regretted anything, and never looked far into the future, but with all the powers of his mind, of his agility, and of his practical good sense worked only in the present. When he was at liberty, he worked for the goal which he had set for himself, namely, the enlightenment and organization of the working classes, especially of the peasants; but when he was imprisoned, he just as energetically and practically worked for contact with the outside world, and for the arrangement of the best possible life under the given conditions, not only for himself, but for his circle. Above everything else he was a communist. It seemed to him that he did not need anything for himself personally, and he was satisfied with anything, but for his group of comrades he was exacting; and for them he could do all kinds of physical and mental work, day and night, without sleeping or eating. As a peasant, he was industrious, quick to understand, agile in his work, naturally temperate, polite without effort, and respectful not only to the feelings, but also to the opinions of others. His old mother, an illiterate widow, full of superstitions, was alive, and Nabátov helped her, and, whenever he was at liberty, went to see her. During his stays at home he entered into the details of her life, helped her in her work, and did not break his relations with his old friends, the peasant lads: he smoked cheap cigarettes with them bent in the shape of a dog's leg, boxed around with them, and pointed out to them how they were all deceived, and how they must free themselves from the deceptions in which they were held. Whenever he thought and spoke of what the revolution would give to the masses, he always imagined the same people from which he had issued, only with land and without masters and officers. The revolution was, according to him, not to change the fundamental forms of the people's life—in this he differed from Novodvórov and Novodvórov's follower, Markél Kondrátev—the revolution, in his opinion, was not to tear down the whole structure, but was only to change the arrangement of the apartments of this beautiful, solid, immense, old building which he loved so fervently.

In respect to religion, he was also a typical peasant: he never thought of metaphysical problems of the beginning of all things, of life after death. God was for him, as He had been for Arago, a hypothesis, the need of which he did not feel as yet. He was not in the least concerned about the origin of the world, whether it had its beginning according to Moses or to Darwin, and Darwinism, which seemed to be of such importance to his comrades, was for him just such a play of imagination as the creation of the world in six days.

He was not interested in the question of how the world was formed, because the question how to live best in this world was paramount to him. Nor did he ever think of the future life, bearing in the depth of his soul that firm and quiet conviction, common to all toilers of the soil, which he had also inherited from his ancestors, that, as in the world of animals and plants nothing ever comes to an end, but is eternally transformed from one shape into another—manure into grain, grain into a chicken, the tadpole into a frog, the caterpillar into a butterfly, the acorn into an oak—so man is not destroyed, but only changed into something else. This he believed, and therefore he boldly and even cheerfully looked death in the eye and courageously bore all suffering which led to it, but did not like and did not know how to speak of it. He liked to work and was always occupied with practical labours and urged his comrades on to practical labours.

The other political prisoner in this group, who came from the people, Markél Kondrátev, was a man of a different type. He started to work at fifteen and began smoking and drinking in order to drown his dim consciousness of wrong. He had become conscious of this wrong for the first time when he, with other boys, was called in to look at a Christmas tree, which had been fixed up by the manufacturer's wife, and received as a present a penny-whistle, an apple, a gilt walnut, and a fig, while the manufacturer's children received toys which to him appeared as fairy gifts, and which, as he later found out, cost more than fifty roubles. He was twenty years old when a famous revolutionary woman began to work in the factory. She noticed Kondrátev's marked ability, began to give him books and pamphlets, and to speak with him, explaining to him his position and its causes, and the means for improving it. When the possibility of freeing himself and others from his position of oppression was clearly presented to him, the injustice of this position seemed even more cruel and terrible than before, and he not only passionately wished for his liberation, but also for the punishment of those who had arranged and sustained this cruel injustice. This possibility, so he was told, could be got through knowledge, and so Kondrátev devoted himself ardently to the acquisition of knowledge. It was not clear to him how the realization of the socialistic ideal was to come about through knowledge, but he believed that, as knowledge had manifested to him the injustice of his position, so it would also remedy this injustice. Besides, knowledge raised him in his opinion above other people. Therefore he quit smoking and drinking and used all his spare time, of which he had now more, having been made a stock-clerk, to study.

The revolutionary lady taught him, and marvelled at the wonderful ability with which he eagerly devoured all kinds of knowledge. In two years he had learned algebra, geometry, and history, of which he was especially fond, and had read all the fiction and criticism and especially all socialistic works.

The revolutionary was arrested, and Kondrátev with her, for keeping forbidden books in his room. He was put in prison, and later deported to the province of Vológda. There he became acquainted with Novodvórov, read many more revolutionary books, memorized everything, and was even more confirmed in his socialistic views. After his exile he became the leader of a large strike, which ended in the storming of the factory and the death of its director. He was arrested and sentenced to loss of his civil rights and exile.

He assumed the same negative attitude toward religion as toward the existing economic order of things. Having become convinced of the insipidity of the faith in which he had been brought up, and having with delight freed himself from it, at first experiencing terror and later transport in this liberation, he, in retribution for the deception which had been practised upon him and his ancestors, never ceased venomously and maliciously to ridicule the priests and religious dogmas.

He was by habit an ascetic; he was satisfied with the smallest allowance, and, like all people who are early used to work and who have well-developed muscles, could easily and well perform all kinds of physical labour; but he esteemed leisure more than anything, because it gave him, in prisons and at the halting-places, a chance to continue his studies. He now pored over the first volume of Marx, a book he kept in his bag with great care, like a very precious thing. He treated all his companions with reserve and indifference, except Novodvórov, to whom he was particularly devoted and whose opinions in regard to all subjects he accepted as incontrovertible truths.

For women, on whom he looked as a hindrance in all important matters, he had an unconquerable contempt. However, he pitied Máslova and was kind to her, seeing in her an example of the exploitation of the lower classes by the upper. For the same reason he did not like Nekhlyúdov, was incommunicative with him, and did not shake his hand, but only offered his to be shaken whenever Nekhlyúdov exchanged greetings with him.

CHAPTER XIII

LOVE AMONG THE POLITICALS

The stove burnt brightly and warmed up the room; the tea was steeped and poured out in the glasses and cups, and whitened with milk; pretzels, fresh rye and wheat bread, hard-boiled eggs, butter, and a head and legs of veal were spread out. All moved up to the place on the benches which was used as a table and ate, and drank, and conversed. Rántseva sat on a box, pouring out the tea. All the others stood around her in a crowd, except Kryltsóv, who had taken off his short fur coat and, wrapping himself in the dry plaid, was lying in his place on the benches and talking with Nekhlyúdov.

After the cold and dampness during the march, after the dirt and disorder which they had found here, after all the labours they had had to expend to get things into shape, after having had food and hot tea—all were in a very happy and cheerful frame of mind.

The feeling of comfort was increased by the very fact that beyond the wall were heard the thumping, the cries, and the curses of the criminals, as though to remind them of their surroundings. Just as on an island in the sea, these people for a time did not feel themselves overwhelmed by all the humiliations and all the suffering which surrounded them, and so they found themselves in an elated and animated mood. They spoke of everything except of their situation and of what awaited them. Besides, as is always the case with young men and women, especially when they are forcibly brought together, as were those collected there, there had arisen among them all kinds of agreed-on and not agreed-on and variously interwoven attractions to each other. They were nearly all of them in love. Novodvórov was in love with pretty, smiling Grabéts. Grabéts was a young student of the Courses for Women, who was not very intelligent and who was quite indifferent to problems of the revolution; but she submitted to the influence of the times, in some way was compromised, and thus deported. At liberty, the chief interests of her life consisted in having success with men; she kept up the same interest at the inquest, in prison, in exile. Now, during the journey, she found consolation in Novodvórov's infatuation with her, and herself fell in love with him. Vyéra Efrémovna, who was prone to fall in love but did not incite others to love her, though she always hoped for reciprocation, was in love now with Nabátov, now with Novodvórov. There was something like love in what Kryltsóv felt for Márya Pávlovna. He loved her as men love women, but, knowing her attitude toward love, he artfully concealed his feeling under the cloak of friendship and gratitude for the tender care which she bestowed upon him. Nabátov and Rántseva were united by very complex love relations. As Márya Pávlovna was an absolutely chaste girl, so Rántseva was an absolutely chaste wife.

Sixteen years old, while still in school, she fell in love with Rántsev, a student of St. Petersburg University, and, when nineteen years old, she married him, while he was still attending the university. In his last year he was mixed up in some university affair, for which he was expelled from St. Petersburg, and became a revolutionary. She left her medical courses, which she was attending, followed him, and herself became a revolutionary. If her husband had not been the man he was—she considered him the best and cleverest of everyone in the world—she would not have fallen in love with him, and, not loving him, she would not have married him. But having once fallen in love with and having married the best and cleverest man in the world, as she thought, she naturally understood life and its aims precisely as they were understood by the best and cleverest man in the world. At first he conceived life to be for study, and so she understood life in the same sense. He became a revolutionary, and so she became one. She could prove very well that the existing order was impossible, and that it was the duty of every man to struggle with this order and to endeavour to establish that political and economic structure in which personality could develop freely, and so forth. She thought that those were actually her ideas and feelings, but in reality she only thought that everything which her husband thought was the real truth, and she sought only for a complete concord, a merging with the soul of her husband, which alone gave her moral satisfaction.

Her parting from her husband and from her child, whom her mother took, was hard for her. But she bore this separation bravely and calmly, knowing that she bore it all for her husband and for the cause which was unquestionably the true one, because he served it. She was always with her husband mentally, and, as she had before been unable to love anybody, so she now was unable to love any one but her husband. But Nabátov's pure and devoted love touched and disturbed her. He, a moral and firm man, the friend of her husband, tried to treat her as a sister, but in his relations with her there appeared something more, and this something more frightened them both and, at the same time, beautified their hard life.

Thus, the only ones who were completely free from any infatuation were Márya Pávlovna and Kondrátev.

CHAPTER XIV

AN ARGUMENT ABOUT THE PEOPLE

Counting on a separate conversation with Katyúsha, such as he had had on previous occasions after the common tea and supper, Nekhlyúdov sat near Kryltsóv and talked with him. Among other things, he told him of Makár's request and of the story of his crime. Kryltsóv listened attentively, fixing his beaming eyes on Nekhlyúdov's face.

"Yes," he suddenly said, "I have frequently been thinking that we are going with them, side by side with them—with what 'them'? with the same people for whom we are going into exile. And yet, we not only do not know them, but even do not wish to know them. And they are even worse: they hate us and regard us as their enemies. This is terrible."

"There is nothing terrible in this," said Novodvórov, who was listening to the conversation. "The masses always worship power," he said, in his clattering voice. "The government is in power—and they worship it and hate us; to-morrow we'll be in power—and they will worship us—"

Just then an outburst of curses was heard beyond the wall, and the thud of people hurled against the wall, the clanking of chains, screaming, and shouts. Somebody was being beaten, and somebody cried "Help!"

"There they are, the beasts! What contact can there be between them and us?" quietly remarked Novodvórov.

"You say beasts? And here Nekhlyúdov has just told me of an act," Kryltsóv said, irritated, and told the story of how Makár had risked his life in order to save a countryman of his. "This is not bestiality, but a heroic deed."

"Sentimentality!" said Novodvórov scornfully. "It is hard for us to understand the emotions of these people and the motives of their acts. You see magnanimity in it, whereas it may only be envy for that convict."

"You never want to see anything good in others," Márya Pávlovna suddenly remarked in excitement. (She was on familiar *thou* terms with everyone.)

"It is impossible to see what is not there."

"How can you say, not there, when a man risks a terrible death?"

"I think," said Novodvórov, "that if we want to do our work, the first condition for it is" (Kondrátev put down the book which he was reading by the lamp and attentively listened to his teacher) "not to be given to fancies, but to look at things as they are. Everything is to be done for the masses, and nothing is to be expected from them. The masses are the object of our activity, but they cannot be our co-labourers, as long as they are inert," he began, as though giving a lecture. "Therefore it is quite illusory to expect aid from them before the process of development has taken place—that process of development for which we are preparing them."

"What process of development?" Kryltsóv exclaimed, growing red in his face. "We say we're against arbitrariness and despotism, but isn't this the most appalling despotism?"

"There is no despotism about it," Novodvórov calmly replied. "All I say is that I know the path over which the people must travel, and I can show them this road."

"But why are you convinced that the path which you show is the true one? Is this not despotism, from which the Inquisition and the executions of the great Revolution resulted? They, too, scientifically knew the only true path."

"The fact that they were mistaken does not prove that I am, too. Besides, there is a great difference between the raving of ideologists and the data of positive economic science."

Novodvórov's voice filled the cell. He alone was speaking, and everybody else was silent.

"They're always arguing," said Márya Pávlovna, when he grew silent for a moment.

"What do you yourself think about it?" Nekhlyúdov asked Márya Pávlovna.

"I think Anatóli is right, that we mustn't impose our views on the people."

"Well, and you, Katyúsha?" Nekhlyúdov asked, smiling, timidly waiting for her answer, with misgivings lest she say something wrong.

"I think that the common people are maltreated," she said, flaming up; "they are dreadfully maltreated."

"Correct, Mikháylovna, correct," cried Nabátov. "The people are dreadfully maltreated. They must not be, and it is our business to see that they are not."

"A strange conception about the problems of the revolution," said Novodvórov, growing silent and angrily smoking a cigarette.

"I cannot talk to him," Kryltsóv said, in a whisper, and grew silent.

"It is much better not to," said Nekhlyúdov.

CHAPTER XV

NOVODVÓROV

Although Novodvórov was very much respected by all the revolutionaries and though he was very learned and considered very clever, Nekhlyúdov counted him among those revolutionaries who by their moral qualities stood below the average, were very much below it. The mental powers of this man—his numerator—were very great; but his own opinion about himself—his denominator—was unbounded and had long ago outgrown his mental powers.

He was a man of a diametrically different spiritual nature from Simonsón. Simonsón was one of those men, of a preëminently masculine turn, whose acts flow from the activity of their minds and are determined by them. But Novodvórov belonged to the category of men, of a preëminently feminine turn, whose activity of mind is directed partly to the realization of aims posited by their feelings and partly to the justification of deeds evoked by their feelings.

Novodvórov's whole revolutionary activity, in spite of his ability eloquently to explain it by persuasive arguments, seemed to Nekhlyúdov based only on vanity, on a desire to be a leader among men. Thanks to his ability to appropriate the ideas of others and accurately to transmit them, he was at first a leader, during the period of his studies, among his teachers and fellow students, where this ability is highly valued—at school, in the university, and while working for his master's degree—and he was satisfied. But when he received his diploma and stopped studying, and this leadership came to an end, he suddenly completely changed his views, Nekhlyúdov learned from Kryltsóv, who did not like Novodvórov, and from a progressive liberal became a rabid adherent of the People's Will party. Thanks to the absence of moral and æsthetic qualities in his character, which call forth doubts and wavering, he soon became a leader of the party, a position in the revolutionary world which satisfied his egotism.

Having once and for all chosen his direction, he never doubted nor wavered, and therefore he was convinced that he was never in error. Everything seemed unusually simple, clear, incontrovertible. And, in reality, with the narrowness and one-sidedness of his views, everything was simple and clear, and all that was necessary, as he said, was to be logical. His self-confidence was so great that it could only repel people or subdue them. And as his activity occurred among very young people who interpreted his boundless self-confidence as depth of thought and wisdom, he had a great success in revolutionary circles. His activity consisted in preparing for an uprising when he would take the government in his hand and call a popular parliament. This parliament was to receive a programme which he had composed.

He was absolutely convinced that this programme exhausted all the questions, and that it was impossible not to carry it out.

His companions respected him for his boldness and determination but did not love him. He himself did not love anybody and looked upon all prominent people as his rivals; he would gladly have treated them as old male monkeys treat the young ones, if he could have. He would have torn out all the brains, all the ability from other people, so that they would not interfere with the manifestation of his own ability. He was on good terms only with people who bowed down before him. This was how he bore himself, on the road, toward the workman Kondrátev, who had been won over to propaganda-work by him, and toward Vyéra Efrémovna and pretty Grabéts, both of whom were in love with him. Though by principle he was for the women's movement, yet, in the depth of his soul, he regarded all women as stupid and insignificant, with the exception of those with whom he frequently was sentimentally in love, as now with Grabéts, and in that case he considered them unusual women, whose worth he alone was capable of appreciating.

The question about the relation of the sexes, like all other questions, seemed very simple and clear to him, and was fully solved by free love.

He had one fictitious and one real wife; he had separated from the latter, having become convinced that there was no real love between them, and now he intended to enter into a new free marriage with Grabéts.

He despised Nekhlyúdov for being "finical" with Máslova, as he called it, and especially for allowing himself to think about the faults of the existing order and about the means for its improvement, not only not word for word as he himself, Novodvórov, did, but even in a special, princely, that is, stupid, manner. Nekhlyúdov knew that Novodvórov had this feeling toward him, and, to his own sorrow, he felt that, in spite of the benevolent mood in which he was during his journey, he paid him with the same coin, and he was quite unable to suppress his strong antipathy for this man.

CHAPTER XVI

SIMONSÓN TELLS ABOUT HIS INTENTION

From the neighbouring cell came the voices of the authorities. Everything grew quiet, and immediately afterward the sergeant entered with two guards. This was the roll-call. The sergeant counted everyone, pointing his finger at each person. When it came to Nekhlyúdov's turn, he said, with good-hearted familiarity:

"Now, prince, after the roll-call you can't remain here any longer. You must leave."

Nekhlyúdov knew what this meant, and so he went up to him and put three roubles, which he had held ready, into his hand.

"Well, what can I do with you? Stay awhile longer!" The sergeant was about to leave, when another sergeant entered, and behind him a tall, lean prisoner with a black eye and scant beard.

"I come to see about the girl," said the prisoner.

"Here is daddy," a melodious child's voice was suddenly heard, and a blond-haired little head rose back of Rántseva, who, with Márya Pávlovna and Katyúsha, was sewing a new dress for the child from a skirt which she herself had offered for the purpose.

"Me, daughter, it's me," tenderly said Buzóvkin.

"She is comfortable here," said Márya Pávlovna, compassionately looking into Buzóvkin's mauled face. "Leave her here with us!"

"The ladies are sewing new clothes for me," said the girl, showing her father Rántseva's work. "It's nice—a red one," she lisped.

"Do you want to stay overnight with us?" asked Rántseva, stroking the girl.

"Yes. And daddy, too."

Rántseva beamed with a smile.

"Daddy can't," she said. "So leave her here," she turned to her father.

"All right, leave her," said the roll-call sergeant, pausing in the door and going away with the other sergeant.

The moment the guards left, Nabátov went up to Buzóvkin and, touching his shoulder, said: "Say, friend, is it true that Karmánov wants to change places?"

Buzóvkin's good-natured, kind face suddenly became sad, and his eyes filmed over.

"We have not heard. Hardly," he said, and, without losing the films over his eyes, he added: "Well, Aksyútka, have a good time with the ladies," and hurried out.

"He knows everything, and it is true that they have exchanged," said Nabátov. "What are you going to do about it?"

"I will tell the authorities in town. I know them both by sight," said Nekhlyúdov.

Everybody was silent, apparently fearing the renewal of the quarrel.

Simonsón, who had all the time been lying in silence in a corner of the benches, with his arms thrown back of his head, rose with determination and, carefully walking around those who were sitting up, went up to Nekhlyúdov.

"Can you listen to me now?"

"Of course," said Nekhlyúdov, getting up in order to follow him.

Looking at Nekhlyúdov, as he was getting up, and her eyes meeting his, Katyúsha grew red in the face and shook her head, as though in doubt.

"This is what I have to say," began Simonsón, when he had reached the corridor with Nekhlyúdov. In the corridor the din and the explosions of the criminals' voices were quite audible. Nekhlyúdov frowned but Simonsón was evidently not disturbed by this.

"Knowing of your relations with Katerína Mikháylovna," he began, looking straight into Nekhlyúdov's face with his kind eyes, "I consider it my duty," he continued, but was compelled to stop, because near the door two voices were quarrelling about something, shouting both together.

"I am telling you, dummy, they're not mine," cried one voice.

"Choke yourself, you bastard," the other shouted, hoarsely.

Just then Márya Pávlovna came out into the corridor.

"How can you talk here?" she said. "Go in here. There is no one but Vyéra there." And she walked ahead into the adjoining door of a tiny single cell, which had now been turned over to the use of the political women. On the benches, covering up her head, lay Vyéra Efrémovna.

"She has a terrible headache. She is asleep and can't hear anything; and I will go out," said Márya Pávlovna.

"On the contrary, you may stay," said Simonsón. "I have no secrets from anybody, least of all from you."

"All right," said Márya Pávlovna, and in childish fashion moving her whole body from side to side, and with this motion receding farther and farther back on the benches, she got ready to listen, looking with her beautiful sheep eyes somewhere into the distance.

"So this is what I have to say," repeated Simonsón. "Knowing your relations with Katerína Mikháylovna, I consider it my duty to inform you of my relations with her."

"Well, what is it?" asked Nekhlyúdov, involuntarily admiring the simplicity and truthfulness with which Simonsón spoke to him.

"I would like to marry Katerína Mikháylovna—"

"Amazing," said Márya Pávlovna, fixing her eyes upon Simonsón.

"—and I have decided to ask her about it—to become my wife," continued Simonsón.

"What can I do? It depends on her," said Nekhlyúdov.

"Yes, but she won't decide this question without you."

"Why?"

"Because, as long as the question of your relations with her is not definitely solved, she cannot choose anything."

"As far as I'm concerned the question is definitely solved. I wished to do what I regarded my duty, and, besides, I wanted to alleviate her condition, but under no circumstances do I wish to restrict her."

"Yes, but she does not wish your sacrifice."

"There is no sacrifice whatsoever."

"But I know that this decision of hers is unshakable."

"Why, then, speak to me?" said Nekhlyúdov.

"She must be sure that you share her view."

"How can I say that I must not do what I consider it my duty to do? All I can say is that I am not free to do as I please, but she is."

Simonsón was silent for awhile, lost in thought.

"Very well, I will tell her that. Don't imagine that I am in love with her," he continued. "I love her as a beautiful, rare person who has suffered much. I want nothing from her, but I am very anxious to help her, to alleviate her con—"

Nekhlyúdov was surprised to hear Simonsón's voice quiver.

"—to alleviate her condition," continued Simonsón. "If she does not want to accept your help, let her accept mine. If she consented to it, I should petition to be sent into exile with her. Four years are not an eternity. I would be living near her, and might be able to ease her fate—" He again stopped from agitation.

"What can I say?" said Nekhlyúdov. "I am glad she found such a protector as you—"

"That is what I wanted to find out," continued Simonsón. "I wanted to know whether, in loving her and wishing her good, you would regard her marrying me as good?"

"Why, yes," Nekhlyúdov said, with determination.

"I am concerned only about her. I want to see this suffering soul at rest," said Simonsón, looking at Nekhlyúdov with childish tenderness such as could hardly have been expected from a man of such gloomy aspect.

Simonsón arose and, taking Nekhlyúdov by the hand, drew his face toward him, smiled shyly, and kissed him.

"I will tell her that," he said, going out.

CHAPTER XVII

THE IMPRESSION PRODUCED
BY SIMONSÓN

"Well, what do you know," said Márya Pávlovna. "He is in love, just in love. I should never have expected Vladímir Simonsón to fall in love in such a stupid and boyish way. Amazing! And to tell you the truth, it annoys me," she concluded, with a sigh.

"How about her, Kátya? How do you think she looks at it?" asked Nekhlyúdov.

"She?" Márya Pávlovna stopped, apparently wishing to reply to the question as precisely as possible. "She? You see, notwithstanding her past, she is by nature one of the most moral persons—and she is so sensitive. She loves you, really likes you, and is happy to be able to do you at least the negative good of not getting you entangled with herself. For her, marrying you would be a terrible fall, worse than her former fall, and so she will never consent to it. At the same time your presence agitates her."

"Well, then I had better disappear?" said Nekhlyúdov.

Márya Pávlovna smiled her sweet, childlike smile.

"Yes, partly."

"How can I disappear partly?"

"I'm talking nonsense. But I wanted to tell you about her that she probably sees the absurdity of his so-called ecstatic love (he has not told her anything), and she is flattered and afraid of it. You know, I am not competent in these matters, but it seems to me that on his side it is nothing but the common male sentiment, even though it be masked. He says that this love increases his energy, and that it is a platonic love. But I know this much, that if it is an exceptional love, at the base of it lies the same nastiness—as with Novodvórov and Lyúbochka."

Márya Pávlovna was departing from the question, having struck her favourite theme.

Tolstoy
Resurrection
page 368

"But what am I to do?" asked Nekhlyúdov.

"I think you ought to tell her. It is always better to have everything clear. Talk with her! I will call her. Do you want me to?" said Márya Pávlovna.

"If you please," said Nekhlyúdov, and Márya Pávlovna went out.

A strange feeling came over Nekhlyúdov when he was left alone in the small cell, listening to the quiet breathing of Vyéra Efrémovna, now and then interrupted by groans, and to the din of the criminals, coming uninterruptedly from behind two doors.

What Simonsón had told him freed him from the obligation which he had assumed and which, in moments of weakness, had appeared hard and strange to him, and yet he not only had an unpleasant, but even a painful, sensation. This feeling was united with another, which reminded him that Simonsón's proposition destroyed the singularity of his deed and diminished in his own eyes and in those of others the value of the sacrifice which he was offering: if a man, such a good man, who was not bound to her by any ties, wished to unite his fate with hers, his sacrifice was not so important, after all. There was also, no doubt, the simple feeling of jealousy: he was so used to her love for him that he could not admit the possibility of her loving anybody else. There was also the destruction of the plan which he had formed—to live by her side as long as she had to suffer punishment. If she was to marry Simonsón, his presence would become superfluous, and he would have to form a new plan for his life. He had not yet succeeded in disentangling all his feelings, when through the opened door burst the intensified din of the criminals (there was something special going on there), and Katyúsha entered the cell.

She walked over to him with rapid steps.

"Márya Pávlovna sent me," she said, stopping close to him.

"Yes, I must talk to you. Sit down! Vladímir Ivánovich has been speaking with me."

She sat down, folding her hands on her knees, and seemed to be calm, but the moment Nekhlyúdov pronounced Simonsón's name, she flushed crimson.

"What did he tell you?" she asked.

"He told me that he wanted to marry you."

Her face suddenly became wrinkled, expressing suffering. She said nothing, and only lowered her eyes.

"He asks for my consent or advice. I told him that everything depended upon you—that you must decide."

"Ah, what is this? What for?" she muttered, looking into Nekhlyúdov's eyes with that strange, squinting glance, which had a peculiar, strong effect upon him. They looked into each other's eyes in silence for a few seconds. This glance said much to both of them.

"You must decide," repeated Nekhlyúdov.

"What am I to decide?" she said. "Everything has been decided long ago."

"No, you must decide whether you accept Vladímir Ivánovich's proposal," said Nekhlyúdov.

"What kind of a wife can I, a convict, make? Why should I ruin Vladímir Ivánovich's life, also?" she said, frowning.

"But, suppose you should be pardoned?" said Nekhlyúdov.

"Oh, leave me in peace! There is nothing more to be said," she said, and, rising, went out of the room.

CHAPTER XVIII

THE FATE OF PÉTLIN
AND NEVYÉROV

When, after Katyúsha, Nekhlyúdov returned to the male cell, all were in great
agitation. Nabátov, who got about everywhere, who knew everybody, who saw
everything, had just brought a piece of news which astounded them all. This was
that he had found a note on the wall, written by revolutionary Pétlin, who had
been sentenced to hard labour. Everybody had supposed that Pétlin had long ago
been at the Kára, and now it suddenly turned out that he had but lately passed over
this road, alone among criminal prisoners.

"On August 17th," so ran the note, "I was sent out all alone with the criminals.
Nevyérov was with me, but he hanged himself at Kazán, in the insane asylum. I am
well and in good spirits, and hope for the best." Everybody discussed Pétlin's condition and the causes of Nevyérov's suicide. Kryltsóv, however, kept silent, with a
concentrated look, staring ahead of him with his arrested, sparkling eyes.

"My husband told me that Nevyérov had had visions while locked up in Petropávlovsk," said Rántseva.

"Yes, a poet, a visionary—such people cannot stand solitary confinement," said
Novodvórov. "Whenever I was kept in solitary confinement, I did not allow my
imagination to work, but arranged my time in the most systematic manner. On
account of this I always bore it well."

"Why not bear it? I used to be so happy when I was locked up," said Nabátov,
with vivacity, apparently wishing to dispel the gloomy mood. "You're afraid of
everything: that you'll get caught yourself, and get others implicated, and ruin the
whole thing, but once you're locked up—that's the end of responsibility, you can
relax. You can sit back and have a smoke."

"Did you know him well?" asked Márya Pávlovna, looking restlessly at the
suddenly changed, drawn face of Kryltsóv.

Tolstoy
Resurrection
page 370

"Nevyérov a visionary?" suddenly said Kryltsóv, panting, as though he had
been shouting or singing long. "Nevyérov was a man *such as the earth bears few of,*
as our porter used to say. Yes. He was a man of crystal—you could see through him.
Yes. He could not lie; he could not feign. He was more than thin-skinned: he was
all lacerated, so to speak, and his nerves were bare. Yes. A complex, a rich nature,
not like—Well, what is the use of talking?" He was silent for a moment. "We
debate about what's better," he said, with a scowl, "first to educate the people and
then change the forms of life, or first to change the forms of life, and then how to
carry on the struggle, whether by peaceful propaganda or by terrorism. We argue,

sure. But *they* don't debate. They know their business. For them it's all the same whether dozens and hundreds of men perish. And what men! Yes, Herzen said that when the Decembrists were removed from circulation, the level of society was lowered. How could they help lowering it! Then they took Herzen and his contemporaries out of circulation. And now the Nevyérovs—"

"They won't destroy them all," said Nabátov, in his bold voice. "There will be enough left to keep the breed going."

"No, there will not be, if we pity *them*," said Kryltsóv, raising his voice and not allowing himself to be interrupted. "Give me a cigarette!"

"It is not good for you, Anatóli," said Márya Pávlovna. "Please, don't smoke!"

"Oh, leave me alone," he said, angrily, lighting a cigarette. He soon began to cough, and he looked as though he were going to vomit. He spat out and continued: "We haven't been doing the right thing. We oughtn't to have been debating, but banding together to destroy them."

"But they are men, too," said Nekhlyúdov.

"No, they aren't men—people who can do what they are doing. They say they have invented bombs and balloons. We ought to rise in the air in these balloons and scatter bombs on them like bedbugs until not one of them is left. Yes. Because—" he began, but he grew red in his face and coughed even more than before, and blood rushed out of his mouth.

Nabátov ran out for some snow. Márya Pávlovna took out some valerian drops and offered them to him, but he, with closed eyes, pushed her away with his white, lean hand, and breathed heavily and rapidly. When the snow and cold water had given him some relief, and he was put to bed for the night, Nekhlyúdov bade everybody good-bye and went toward the door with the sergeant, who had come for him and had been waiting for him quite awhile.

The criminals were now quieted down, and most of them were asleep. Although the people in the cells were lying on the benches and beneath the benches and in the aisles, they could not all find a place, and some of them lay on the floor of the corridor, having placed their bags under their heads and their damp cloaks over them.

Through the doors of the cells and in the corridor could be heard snoring, groans, and sleepy conversation. Everywhere could be seen masses of human figures, covered with their cloaks. A few men in the unmarried criminals' cell were not asleep: they were seated around a candle-end, which they extinguished when they saw the soldier. In the corridor, under the lamp, an old man was sitting up, naked, and picking the vermin off his shirt. The foul air of the quarters of the politicals seemed fresh in comparison with the stinking closeness here. The smoking lamp shimmered as though through fog, and it was hard to breathe. In order to make one's way along the corridor, without stepping on any of the sleepers or tripping up, it was necessary first to find a clear spot ahead and, having placed the foot there, to find a similar spot for the next step. Three people, who apparently had been unable to find a place even in the corridor, had settled down in the vestibule near the stink-vat, where the foul water moistened their very clothing. One of these was an old idiot, whom Nekhlyúdov had frequently seen on the marches; another was a ten-year-old boy: he lay between the two prisoners, and, putting his hand under his chin, was sleeping over the leg of one of them.

Upon coming out of the gate, Nekhlyúdov stopped and, expanding his chest to the full capacity of his lungs, for a long time intensely inhaled the frosty air.

CHAPTER XIX

NEKHLYÚDOV SUMS UP
WHAT HE HAS SEEN

The stars had come out. Having returned to his inn over the frozen mud, only in spots broken through, Nekhlyúdov knocked at a dark window, and the broad-shouldered servant in his bare feet opened the door for him and let him into the vestibule. On the right hand of the vestibule one could hear the snoring of the drivers in the servant-room; in front, beyond the door, one could hear a large number of horses in the yard chewing oats. On the left, a door led to the clean guest-room. The clean guest-room smelled of wormwood and sweat, and beyond a partition was heard the even sucking snore of some mighty lungs, and an icon-lamp in a red glass cup was burning in front of the icons. Nekhlyúdov undressed, spread his plaid on the oil-cloth sofa, adjusted his leather pillow, and lay down, mentally running over all he had heard and seen that day. Of everything he had seen, the most terrible appeared to him the sight of the boy sleeping in the foul puddle running out of the stink-vat, placing his head on the leg of the prisoner.

In spite of the unexpectedness and importance of his evening conversation with Simonsón and Katyúsha, he did not dwell on that event: his relation to it was too complex and, besides, too indefinite, and therefore he kept all thought of it away from himself. But so much the more vividly he remembered the sight of these unfortunate creatures choking to death in the foul atmosphere and slopping in the liquid which oozed out from the stink-vat, and, especially, of the boy with the innocent face, who was sleeping on the prisoner's leg and whom he could not get out of his mind.

To know that somewhere far away one set of people are torturing another, subjecting them to all kinds of debauches, inhuman humiliations, and suffering, is quite a different thing from continually seeing that debauch and that torture practised by one class of people on another. Nekhlyúdov was experiencing this. During these three months he had asked himself more than once: "Am I insane because I see what others do not, or are those insane who bring about what I see?" But the people (and there were so many of them) brought about what so bewildered and terrified him, with such quiet conviction that it had to be so, and that what they were doing was important and useful, that it was hard to pronounce all these people insane; nor could he pronounce himself insane, because he was conscious of the clearness of his thoughts. Consequently he was in continuous doubt.

What Nekhlyúdov had seen during these three months presented itself to him in this form: from all those who are free, the most nervous, ardent, excitable, gifted, and strong individuals, who are less cunning and cautious than the rest, are selected by means of the courts and the administration, and these people, not more guilty or more dangerous to society than those who are at liberty, are locked up in prisons, halting-places, and hard-labour camps, where they are kept for months and years in complete idleness and material security, and removed from Nature, family, and labour, that is, they are forced outside all the conditions of a natural and moral human existence. So much in the first place. In the second place, in these establishments these people are subjected to all kinds of unnecessary humiliation—to chains, shaven heads, and disgracing attire, that is, they are deprived of what is, for weak people, the chief impulse to a good life—of the regard of human opinion, of shame, of the consciousness of human dignity. In the third place, being continually subject to the perils of life—not to mention the exceptional cases of sunstroke, drowning, fires, of the ever-present contagious diseases in the places of confinement, of exhaustion and of beatings—these people are all the time under the condition when the best and most moral man, from a feeling of self-preservation, commits and condones the most terrible and cruel acts. In the fourth place, these people are forced to deal exclusively with dissolute people who have been corrupted by life, and especially by these very institutions—with murderers and villains, who, like leavening on dough, act on all the others who have not yet been completely corrupted by the means employed against them. And, lastly, in the fifth place, all the people who are subjected to these influences are, in the most persuasive manner, encouraged, by means of all kinds of inhuman acts committed against themselves—by means of the torture of children, women, and old men, of beating and flogging with rods and straps, of offering rewards to those who will give up a fugitive alive or dead, of separating men from their wives and connecting for cohabitation strange men with strange women, of shooting and hanging—they are encouraged in the most persuasive manner to believe that all kinds of violence, cruelty, bestiality, are not only not forbidden but even permitted by the government, when it derives any advantage from them, and that therefore they are especially permissible to those who are under duress, in misery and want.

All these institutions seemed to him to have been specially invented in order to produce the most concentrated possible debauch and vice, such as could not be attained under any other conditions, with the further purpose in view later to disseminate these concentrated debauches and vices as broadly as possible among the people. "It looks as though a problem had been put how to corrupt the largest possible number in the best and surest manner," thought Nekhlyúdov, as he tried to get at the essence of jails and prisons. Hundreds of thousands of people were every year brought to the highest degree of corruption, and when they were thus completely debauched, they were let loose to carry the corruption, which they had acquired in prison, among the masses.

Nekhlyúdov saw how this aim, which society had in view, was successfully reached in the prisons of Tyúmen, Ekaterinbúrg, and Tomsk, and at the halting-places. People, simple, common people, brought up in the tenets of Russian social, Christian, peasant morality, abandoned these concepts and acquired new prison ideas, which consisted mainly in the conviction that every outrage and violation of the human personality, every destruction of the same, was permissible whenever it was advantageous. People, who had lived in the prisons, with all their being came to see that, to judge from what was being done to them, all the moral laws of respect and compassion for man, which had been preached by religious and moral teachers, had, in reality, been set aside, and that, therefore, there was no need for holding on to them. Nekhlyúdov saw this process in all the prisoners whom he knew: in Fyódorov, in Makár, and even in Tarás, who, having passed two months with the convicts, impressed Nekhlyúdov by the immorality of his judgments. On his way, Nekhlyúdov learned that tramps, who run away to the taiga, persuade their comrades to run with them, and then kill them and feed on their flesh. He saw a living man who was accused of it, and who admitted it to be true. Most terrible was the fact that these were not isolated cases, but of common occurrence.

Only by a special cultivation of vice, such as is carried on in these institutions, could a Russian be brought to that condition to which the tramps are brought, who have anticipated Nietzsche's doctrine and consider nothing forbidden, and who spread this doctrine, at first among the prisoners, and later among the people at large.

The only explanation of all that was going on was that it was intended as an abatement of evil, as a threat, correction, and legal retribution, as the books said. But, in reality, there was not a semblance of any of these things. Instead of abatement, there was only dissemination of crimes. Instead of threat, there was only encouragement of criminals, many of whom, as, for example, the tramps, voluntarily entered the prisons. Instead of correction, there was systematic spreading of all the vices, while the need of retribution was not only not lessened by governmental punishment, but was even nurtured among the masses, where it did not exist before.

"Why, then, do they do all these things?" Nekhlyúdov asked himself, and found no answer.

What surprised him most was that all this was not done haphazardly, by mistake, incidentally, but continuously, in the course of centuries, with this distinction only, that in former days they had their noses slit and their ears cut off, then, later, they were branded and beaten with rods, and now they were manacled and transported by steam, instead of on carts.

The reflection that what provoked him originated, as those serving in these institutions told him, in the imperfection of the arrangements in the prisons and deportation places, and that all this could be remedied, did not satisfy Nekhlyúdov, because he felt that what provoked him had nothing to do with more or less perfect arrangements in the prisons. He had read about perfected prisons with electric bells, of electrocutions, recommended by Tarde, and this perfected violence offended him only more.

What provoked Nekhlyúdov was, mainly, that there were people in the courts and ministries, who received large salaries, collected from the masses, for consulting books written by just such officials, with just such aims, for classifying the acts of men who had violated the laws which were written by them, according to certain articles, and for sending these people, in accordance with these articles, to places where they would never see them again, and where these people, under full control of cruel, hardened superintendents, wardens, and guards, perished mentally and bodily by the million.

Having become closely acquainted with the prisons and halting-places, Nekhlyúdov noticed that all the vices which are developed among the prisoners, drunkenness, gambling, cruelty, and all those terrible crimes which are committed by the inmates of the prisons, and even cannibalism itself, are not accidents or phenomena of degeneration, criminalism, and cretinism, as dull scholars explain it, playing into the hands of the government, but the inevitable result of the incredible error that people may punish others. Nekhlyúdov saw that the cannibalism did not begin in the taiga, but in the ministries, committees, and departments, and was only accomplished in the taiga; that his brother-in-law, for example, and all the court members and officials, beginning with the captain of police and ending with the minister, were not in the least concerned about justice or the people's weal, of which they spoke; and that they all wanted only those roubles which they were paid for doing that from which this corruption and suffering came. That was quite evident.

"Is it possible all this has been done only by misunderstanding? Could there not be invented a means for securing a salary for these officials, and even offering them a premium, provided that they should abstain from doing all that they are doing?" thought Nekhlyúdov. With this thought, after the second cock-crow, he fell into a heavy sleep, in spite of the fleas which spirted around him as from a fountain, every time he stirred.

CHAPTER XX

NEKHLYÚDOV OVERTAKES THE PRISONERS

When Nekhlyúdov awoke, the drivers had left long ago, the hostess had had her tea, and, wiping her stout, sweaty neck with her kerchief, she came to inform him that a soldier from the halting-place had brought him a note. The note was from Márya Pávlovna. She wrote that Kryltsóv's attack was more serious than they had thought. "At one time we wanted to leave him and stay with him, but we were not allowed to do that, and so we will take him along, but we fear the worst. Try to arrange it so in the city that, if he is to be left behind, one of us may stay with him. If, in order to accomplish this, it is necessary for me to marry him, I am, of course, ready to do so."

Nekhlyúdov sent the lad to the station for the horses and at once began to pack. He had not finished his second glass of tea, when the stage troika, tinkling with its little bells and rattling with its wheels on the frozen mud as on a pavement, drove up to the steps. Nekhlyúdov paid his bill to the stout-necked hostess. He hastened to go out, and, seating himself in the wicker body of the cart, ordered the driver to go as fast as possible, in order to catch up with the group. Not far from the gate of the herding enclosure he fell in with the carts which were loaded with bags and sick people, and which rattled over the tufty, frozen mud. (The officer was not there—he had driven ahead.) The soldiers, who had evidently been drinking, were chatting merrily, walking behind and on the sides of the road. There were many carts. In each of the front carts sat, closely huddled together, some six feeble criminals; in the back vehicles rode the politicals, three in each. In the very last sat Novodvórov, Grabéts, and Kondrátev; in the one before it, Rántseva, Nabátov, and that weak, rheumatic woman to whom Márya Pávlovna had given up her place; in front of this was the vehicle in which Kryltsóv lay on hay and pillows. Márya Pávlovna sat on a box, near him. Nekhlyúdov stopped his driver near Kryltsóv's vehicle, and went up to him. An intoxicated guard waved his hand to him, but Nekhlyúdov paid no attention to him. He walked over to the cart, and, holding on to a round, walked alongside. Kryltsóv, in sheepskin coat and a lamb-fur cap, his mouth covered by a kerchief, looked even more haggard and pale than the day before. His beautiful eyes seemed to be particularly large and sparkling. Swaying feebly from the jolts of the cart, he did not take his eyes off Nekhlyúdov, and, in response to his question about his health, he only closed his eyes and angrily shook his head. His whole energy apparently went in bearing the jolts. Márya Pávlovna was sitting at the other side of the cart. She and Nekhlyúdov glanced meaningfully at each other, a glance which expressed all her anxiety about Kryltsóv's condition, and then she said in a cheerful voice:

"Evidently the officer was ashamed," she shouted, so that Nekhlyúdov might hear her over the rumble of the wheels. "They have taken off Buzóvkin's handcuffs. He is carrying the girl himself, and Katyúsha and Simonsón, and instead of me Vyéra, are going along with them."

Kryltsóv said something which could not be heard, pointing to Márya Pávlovna, and, frowning, in an effort to repress a cough, shook his head. Then Kryltsóv raised the handkerchief from his mouth and whispered:

"Now I am much better. If only I don't catch cold!"

Nekhlyúdov nodded his head affirmatively and exchanged glances with Márya Pávlovna.

"Well, how is the problem of the three bodies?" Kryltsóv whispered and smiled a heavy, painful smile. "Is the solution hard?"

Nekhlyúdov did not understand, but Márya Pávlovna explained to him that it was a famous mathematical problem about the determination of the relation of three bodies, of the sun, moon, and earth, and that Kryltsóv had jestingly applied this comparison in relation to Nekhlyúdov, Katyúsha, and Simonsón. Kryltsóv nodded to indicate Márya Pávlovna had explained his jest correctly.

"It is not for me to solve it," said Nekhlyúdov.

"Did you get my note? Will you do it?" Márya Pávlovna asked.

"Certainly," said Nekhlyúdov, and, noticing dissatisfaction in Kryltsóv's face, he went back to his vehicle, climbed into its sunken wicker body, and, holding on to the sides of the cart, which jolted him over the clumps of the uneven road, he drove fast ahead along the column of prisoners in gray cloaks and of chained and manacled men in short fur coats, which stretched out for a whole verst. On the opposite side of the road he recognized Katyúsha's blue kerchief, Vyéra Efrémovna's black wrap, and Simonsón's jacket and knit cap, his white woollen stockings, which were tied up by bands like those of sandals. He was walking by the women's side and talking about something excitedly.

Upon noticing Nekhlyúdov, the women bowed to him, and Simonsón solemnly raised his cap. Nekhlyúdov did not have anything to say to them, so he did not stop his driver, but drove past them. When the driver came out on the smooth road again, he went even faster, but he was all the time compelled to get off the road in order to avoid the loaded wagons which were going along on both sides of the highway.

The road, which was all cut up by deep ruts, ran through a dark pine forest, which on both sides was interspersed with the bright sand-yellow autumn leafage of birches and larches. About half-way between the stations the forest came to an end, and there appeared fields and the crosses and cupolas of a monastery. Day was now out in all its glory; the clouds were dispersed; the sun had risen above the forest; and the damp leaves, and the puddles, and the cupolas, and the crosses of the church shone brightly in the sun. In front and toward the right, grayish-blue mountains could be seen in the far distance. The troika drove into a large suburban village. The street was full of people, both Russians and natives in their strange caps and cloaks. Drunken and sober men and women swarmed and chattered near the shops, inns, taverns, and wagons. One could feel the nearness of the city.

Giving the right horse the whip and pulling in the rein, the driver sat down sidewise on his box, so that the reins were on his right, and, apparently trying to appear dashing, flew down the wide street, and, without checking in his horses, drove down to the river's bank, which was to be crossed by means of a ferry. The ferry was in the middle of the swift river and was coming toward them. On this side about twenty wagons were waiting for it. Nekhlyúdov did not have to wait long. The ferry, which had gone far upstream against the current, soon landed near the boards of the landing-place, carried down by the water. The tall, broad-chested, muscular, and silent ferrymen, in short fur coats and Siberian boots, threw the ropes up and fastened them to posts and, opening the bars, let out the wagons which were standing on the ferry, and again began to load the ferry with the wagons on the shore, putting them close together, and beside them the horses, which shied from the water. The swift and broad river washed the sides of the ferry-boat, straining the ropes. When the ferry was full and Nekhlyúdov's vehicle, with its horses detached, pressed in on all sides, stood at one end, the ferrymen put up the bars, paying no attention to those who had failed to find a place on the ferry, took off the ropes, and started across. On the ferry everything was quiet, except for the thud of the ferrymen's steps and the tramp of the hoofs of the horses on the boards, as they changed their position.

CHAPTER XXI

A CONVERSATION ON THE FERRY

Nekhlyúdov stood at the edge of the ferry, looking at the broad, rapid river. Two pictures rose in his imagination, one after another: the shaking head of angry, dying Kryltsóv, and Katyúsha's figure briskly walking along the edge of the road with Simonsón. The one impression—that of the dying Kryltsóv, who was unprepared for death—was oppressive and sad. The other impression—that of vivacious Katyúsha, who had found the love of such a man as Simonsón, and who now was standing on the firm and secure path of goodness—ought to have been cheerful, but to Nekhlyúdov it, too, was oppressive, and he was not able to overcome this oppressive feeling.

The din and metallic tremor of a large brass church-bell was borne from the city over the water. The driver, who was standing near Nekhlyúdov, and all the other drivers one after another took off their caps and made the sign of the cross. But a shaggy-haired old man, who was standing nearest to the balustrade, and whom Nekhlyúdov had not noticed before, did not cross himself, but, raising his head, stared at Nekhlyúdov. This old man was clad in a long patched coat, cloth trousers, and worn-out patched boots. On his back was a small knapsack and on his head a tall, worn-out fur cap.

"Old man, why don't you pray?" said Nekhlyúdov's driver, putting on and adjusting his cap. "Aren't you a Christian?"

"To whom shall I pray?" said the shaggy-haired old man, in a firm, challenging voice, rapidly pronouncing one syllable after another.

"Of course, God!" the driver retorted, ironically.

"You show me where He is! I mean, God!"

There was something serious and firm in the expression of the old man, so that the driver, who felt that he was dealing with a strong man, was a little confused; however, he did not show it, and, trying not to be silenced and shamed before the public present, he quickly answered:

"Where? Of course, in heaven!"

"Have you been there?"

"No, I have not, but everybody knows that we must pray to God."

"Nobody has ever seen God. The only begotten Son, who is in His Father's lap, He has appeared," said the old man, with a stern frown and speaking just as fast.

"It's clear you aren't a Christian, and you pray to a hole in the ground," said the driver, sticking the whip-handle in his belt and fixing the off-horse's crupper.

Somebody laughed out.

"Old man, what is your faith?" asked a middle-aged man, who was standing with a wagon at the edge of the ferry.

"I have no faith whatever. I do not believe in anybody but myself," the old man answered just as fast and with the same determination.

"How can you believe in yourself?" said Nekhlyúdov, entering into the conversation. "You might make a mistake."

"Not on my life," the old man replied, with determination, shaking his head.

"Why, then, are there different religions?" asked Nekhlyúdov.

"There are different religions, because people believe others, but not themselves. I used to believe others, and I was wandering, as in the taiga; I got so entangled that I never thought to get out from it. There are Old-believers and New-believers, Judaizers, and Khlysty, and Popovtsy, and Bezpopovtsy, and Avrstriaks, and Molokans, and Skoptsy. Every faith praises itself up. And so they have all crawled apart like blind pups. There are many faiths, but the spirit is one—in you, in me, and in him. Consequently, let everybody believe in his spirit, and all will be connected! Let each be for himself, and all will be united!"

The old man spoke loud and looked around all the time, obviously wishing to be heard by as many people as possible.

"Well, have you believed this for a long time?" Nekhlyúdov asked him.

"Me? For a long time. They have been persecuting me these twenty-three years."

"What do you mean, persecuting?"

"As they persecuted Christ, so they persecute me. They grab me, and take me to courts and to priests—they take me to the scribes and to the Pharisees. They have had me in the insane asylum. But they can't do anything with me, and so I am free.— 'What is your name?' they say. They think that I will give some name, but I do not. I have renounced everything: I have neither name, nor place, nor country—I have nothing. I am myself. 'What are you called?' Man.—'How old are you?—I do not count my years, I say, because it is impossible to count them: I have always been, and I shall always be.—'Who are your father and mother?'—No, I say, I have no father, nor mother, except God and earth. God is my father, and the earth my mother.—'And do you acknowledge the Tsar?'—Why not? He is a tsar, and so am I.—'What's the point of talking to you?' they say. And I answer: I do not even ask you to talk with me. And so they torture me."

"Where are you going now?" asked Nekhlyúdov.

"Wherever God takes me. I work, and when I have no work, I beg," ended the old man, noticing that the ferry was approaching the other side. He cast a victorious glance upon all those who had been listening to him.

The ferry landed at the other shore. Nekhlyúdov took out his purse and offered the old man some money. The old man refused it.

"I do not take this. I take bread," he said.

"Well, forgive me."

"There is nothing to forgive. You have not offended me. It is impossible to offend me," said the old man, shouldering the knapsack, which he had taken off. In the meantime the stage troika was taken ashore and hitched up again.

"What good, sir, does it do you to talk to him?" said the driver, when Nekhlyúdov, having paid the powerful ferrymen, climbed into the cart. "He is a worthless tramp."

CHAPTER XXII

NEKHLYÚDOV SEES THE REGIONAL COMMANDER

Upon arriving at the summit of a hill, the driver turned back.

"To what hotel shall I take you?"

"Which is the best?"

"Nothing better than the Siberia. It is nice at Dyúkov's too."

"Whichever you please."

The driver again sat down sidewise and gave the horses the reins. The town was like all towns: the same houses with attic windows and green roofs; the same cathedral, the same small and large shops, and even the same policemen. The only difference was that nearly all the houses were frame buildings, and the streets not paved. In one of the busiest streets the driver stopped in front of a hotel. There were no rooms to be had in that hotel, and so he had to drive to another. In this one there was an unoccupied room, and Nekhlyúdov, for the first time in two months, found himself in customary conditions of comparative cleanliness and comfort. The room which was given to Nekhlyúdov was not very luxurious, but he experienced a great relief after the stage troika, the inns, and the halting-places. Above everything else, he had to clean himself from the lice, of which he never could completely rid himself after his visits at the halting-places. He unpacked his things and went at once to the Russian bath; then, having donned his city clothes, a starched shirt, creased trousers, a black coat, and an overcoat, he made for the regional commander. The porter of the hotel called a cab, and the clattering carriage, pulled by a large, well-fed Kirghiz horse, took Nekhlyúdov to a large, beautiful building, before which stood sentries and a policeman. In front of the building and in back of it was a garden, in which, amidst bared aspens and birches with their towering branches, could be seen the thick, dark green foliage of pines, firs, and spruces.

The general was not well and not receiving. Nekhlyúdov, nevertheless, asked the lackey to take in his card, and the lackey returned with a favourable answer.

"Please come in!"

The antechamber, the lackey, the orderly, the staircase, the parlour with the shining, waxed parquet—it all was like St. Petersburg, only more dirty and majestic. Nekhlyúdov was taken to the study.

The general, a puffed-up man, with a potato-shaped nose, protruding bumps on his forehead, closely shaved skull, and bags under his eyes, a man of a sanguine temperament, was sitting in a silk Tartar morning-gown, and, with a cigarette in his hand, was drinking tea from a glass in a silver holder.

"Good morning, sir! Excuse me for receiving you in my morning-gown. It is certainly better than not to receive you at all," he said, covering with his gown the stout, wrinkled nape of his neck. "I am not very well, and do not go out. What has brought you here, to our out-of-the-way realm?"

"I have been accompanying a group of prisoners, in which there is a person near to me," said Nekhlyúdov, "and I have come to ask your Excellency something, partly in respect to this person, and partly in another matter."

The general puffed at his cigarette, sipped some tea, put out the cigarette in a malachite ash-tray, and, without taking his narrow, swimming, sparkling eyes off Nekhlyúdov, listened to what he had to say. He interrupted him only to ask him whether he did not want to smoke.

The general belonged to the type of learned military men who regarded liberalism and humanitarianism as compatible with their calling. But, being by nature an intelligent and good man, he soon convinced himself of the impossiblity of such a union, and, in order not to see his own internal contradiction, in which he continually was, he more and more became addicted to the habit of drinking, so widespread among military men, and grew to be such a victim of this habit that, after thirty-five years of service, he was what physicians denominate an alcoholic. He was saturated with liquor. It was enough for him to drink any liquid in order to feel intoxicated. Drinking had become such a necessity with him that he could not live without it; in the evening he was almost always quite drunk, but he had become so used to this condition that he did not stagger or speak foolishly. Or, if he did, he occupied such an important and leading position that, whatever insipidity he might utter, it was taken for wisdom. Only in the morning, precisely at the time when Nekhlyúdov met him, he seemed a sensible man and was able to understand what was said to him and more or less successfully to verify the problem, which he was fond of repeating: "Drunk and clever—two advantages ever." The higher authorities knew that he was a drunkard, but he was more educated than the rest—although his education had stopped where drunkenness overtook him—that he was bold, agile, representative, that he could carry himself tactfully even though drunk, and so he was appointed to and kept that prominent and responsible position which he now held.

Nekhlyúdov told him that the person who interested him was a woman, that she was unjustly condemned, and that the emperor had been appealed to.

"Yes, sir. Well, sir?" said the general.

"In St. Petersburg I was promised that the information about this woman's fate would reach me in a month, at latest, and in this place—"

Without taking his eyes off Nekhlyúdov, the general extended his short-fingered hand, rang the bell, and continued to listen in silence, puffing at the cigarette, and coughing quite loudly.

"So I should like to ask you, if possible, to keep this woman here until an answer is received to my petition."

A lackey, dressed in military attire and serving as orderly, entered.

"Go and ask whether Anna Vasílevna is up," the general said to the orderly, "and bring me some more tea.—And the other thing?" the general again turned to Nekhlyúdov.

"My other request," continued Nekhlyúdov, "is in regard to a political prisoner, who is travelling with this group."

"Indeed!" said the general, significantly shaking his head.

"He is very sick—he is a dying man. No doubt, he will be left here in the hospital. One of the political women would like to remain with him."

"Is she a stranger to him?"

"Yes, but she is willing to marry him, if this would give her a chance of staying with him."

The general looked fixedly at him with his beaming eyes and kept silent, listening and smoking. Apparently he wished to embarrass him by his glance.

When Nekhlyúdov had finished, he took a book from the table, and, rapidly thumbing it, as he turned the leaves, found the article on marriage and read it.

"What is she sentenced to?" he asked, raising his head from his book.

"To hard labour."

"Well, then the situation of the sick man cannot be improved by such a marriage."

"But—"

"Excuse me! Even if a free man were to marry her, she would have to serve out her punishment. The question is who pays the greater penalty, he or she."

"They are both condemned to hard labour."

"Well, they are quits, then," said the general, with a smile. "She gets what he does.

He can be left here, if he is sick," he continued, "and, of course, everything will be done to alleviate his condition; but she, even if she married him, could not stay here—"

"Her Excellency is drinking coffee," the lackey announced.

The general nodded his head and continued:

"However, I will think it over. What are their names? Write them down, here!"

Nekhlyúdov wrote them down.

"Nor can I do this," the general said to Nekhlyúdov, in reply to his request to be admitted to the sick man. "Of course, I do not suspect you," he said, "but you are interested in him and in others, and you have money. Here, with us, everything hinges on money. I am told to uproot bribery. But how am I to abolish it, when all are bribe-takers? The lower in rank, the worse. How can I watch them five thousand versts away? There he is just such a little tsar as I am here," and he smiled. "You have, no doubt, seen the politicals—you have given them money, and you have been admitted?" he said, smiling. "Am I right?"

"Yes, it is so."

"I know that you must act like that. You want to see a political, and you are sorry for him. The superintendent or a guard will accept a bribe, because he gets about forty kopeks' wages, and he has a family, and cannot help accepting the bribe. In your place or in his, I would do just like you or him. But in my place, I do not let myself deviate from the strictest letter of the law, for the very reason that I am a man and might be moved by compassion. I am an executor. I have been given a trust under certain conditions, and I must justify this trust. Well, this question is settled. Now, tell me what is going on there, in the metropolis."

The general began to ask questions and to tell things, obviously wishing simultaneously to hear the news and to show his importance and humanity.

CHAPTER XXIII

THE PETITION IS ANSWERED

"Well, so where are you staying? At Dyúkov's? Well, it is not particularly good there, either. You come to dinner," said the general, seeing Nekhlyúdov off, "at five o'clock. Do you speak English?"

"Yes, I do."

"That is splendid. There is an English traveller here. He is making a study of deportation and prisons in Siberia. He will be at dinner to-day, and you come, too. We dine at five, and my wife demands promptness. I will give you an answer then as to what can be done with that woman, and about the sick man. Maybe it will be possible to leave somebody with him."

Bowing to the general, Nekhlyúdov went out, and, feeling energetic, drove to the post-office.

The post-office was a low, vaulted building. Back of the counter sat some officials, who were handing out letters to a crowd of people. One official, bending his head toward one side, kept stamping envelopes, which he handled with great facility. Nekhlyúdov was not made to wait long. Upon hearing his name, they handed out a rather large amount of mail. Here was money, a few letters and books, and the latest issue of the *Notes of the Fatherland*. Having received his letters, Nekhlyúdov went over to a wooden bench, on which a soldier, holding a small book, was sitting and waiting for something, and sat down near him to look over his letters. Among them was a registered letter, a beautiful envelope with a clean imprint on the bright red sealing-wax. He opened the envelope, and, upon seeing a letter from Selénin, together with an official document, he felt the blood rush to his face and his heart compress. It was the decree in Katyúsha's case. What was this decree? Could it possibly be a refusal? Nekhlyúdov hurriedly ran over the letter, which was written in a small, illegible, firm, abrupt hand, and he gave a sigh of relief. The decree was favourable.

"Dear friend!" wrote Selénin. "Our last conversation has left a deep impression on me. You were right about Máslova. I carefully looked through the case, and I saw that a shocking injustice had been done her. The only place where this could be remedied was the Commission for Appeals, where you had handed in your appeal. I was fortunate enough to influence the decision in the case, and I send you a copy of the pardon to the address given me by Countess Ekaterína Ivánovna. The original was sent to the place of her confinement during her trial, and, no doubt, will soon be transmitted to the Siberian Central Office. I hasten to inform you of this pleasant news. Warmest regards. Yours, Selénin."

The contents of the document itself ran as follows: "The Chancery of His Imperial Majesty for the Reception of Petitions Directed to the Sovereign. Such and such a case. Such and such a division. Such and such a date and year. By order of the Chief of the Chancery of His Imperial Majesty for the Reception of Petitions Directed to the Sovereign, the lower-middle-class woman Ekaterína Máslova is hereby informed that his Imperial Majesty, in conformity with her most humble petition to him, condescending to Máslova's prayer, has deigned to order the commutation of her hard-labour sentence to deportation to less remote regions of Siberia."

The information was cheerful and important: everything Nekhlyúdov could have expected for Katyúsha and for himself had happened. True, this change in her condition presented new complications in respect to her. As long as she remained a convict, the marriage which he had proposed to her could be only fictitious and might serve merely to alleviate her position. Now, nothing interfered with their living together. For this Nekhlyúdov had not prepared himself. Besides, there were her relations with Simonsón. What did her words of the day before mean? And if she should agree to be united to Simonsón, would it be good or bad? He was completely unable to straighten out his thoughts, and so stopped thinking of the matter entirely. "All this will clear itself up later," he thought, "now I must see her as soon as possible and inform her of the joyful news and free her." He thought that the copy which he had in his hands was sufficient for that. Upon leaving the post-office, he ordered the driver to take him to the prison.

Although the general had not given him permission to visit the prison in the morning, Nekhlyúdov knew from experience that frequently it was possible to obtain from the lower authorities that which it was impossible to get from the higher, and so he decided to try to get into the prison in order to announce the joyful news to Katyúsha, and, if possible, to liberate her, and at the same time to find out about Kryltsóv's health and to tell him and Márya Pávlovna what the general had said.

The superintendent of the prison was a very tall and stout, majestic-looking man, with a moustache and side-whiskers bending toward the edge of his mouth. He received Nekhlyúdov with great severity, and at once informed him that he could not admit strangers for interviews without a pass from the commander. To Nekhlyúdov's remark that he had been admitted even in the capitals, the superintendent answered:

"Very likely so, only I won't admit you." His tone seemed to say: "You gentlemen from the capital think that you will puzzle us the moment you see us: but we, in Eastern Siberia, are firmly grounded in the regulations, and we can teach you a thing or two."

The copy of the document from the Private Chancery of His Imperial Majesty had no effect on the superintendent. He absolutely refused to let Nekhlyúdov inside the walls of the prison. To Nekhlyúdov's naïve supposition that Máslova might be set free on presentation of this copy, he only smiled contemptuously, remarking that in order to set any one free he had to have the order from his immediate superior. All he promised to do was to announce to Máslova that she was pardoned, and that he would not keep her a single hour after the moment he had received the papers from his superior.

He also refused to give him any information about Kryltsóv's health, saying that he could not even tell him whether there was any such prisoner. Thus, without having obtained anything, Nekhlyúdov got into his cab and went back to his hotel.

The severity of the superintendent was mainly due to the fact that in the prison, which was crowded to double its capacity, there was an epidemic of typhus. The cabman who was driving Nekhlyúdov told him on the way that "in the prison the people are dying awfully. Some kind of plague has fallen on them. They bury about twenty people a day."

CHAPTER XXIV

NEKHLYÚDOV A GUEST AT THE COMMANDER'S

Notwithstanding his failure at the prison, Nekhlyúdov, still in the same cheerful, energetic frame of mind, drove to the governor's office to find out whether the document about Máslova's pardon had been received. There was no such document, and so Nekhlyúdov, immediately upon his return to the hotel, hastened to write to Selénin and to the lawyer about it. Having finished his letters, he looked at his watch and saw that it was time to drive to the general's for dinner.

On his way, he was again troubled by the thought how Katyúsha would receive her pardon. Where would they deport her? How would he live with her? What would Simonsón do? What was her relation to him? He recalled the change which had taken place in her. And, with this, he recalled her past.

"That must be forgotten, wiped out," he thought, hastening to drive away all thoughts of her. "It will all be clear later," he said to himself, and began to think of what he ought to say to the general.

The dinner at the general's, surrounded by all the luxury of rich people and important officials such as Nekhlyúdov had been used to, was especially agreeable to him after the long privation not only of luxury, but even of the most primitive comforts.

The hostess was a St. Petersburg *grande dame* of the old school, a former maid of honour at the court of Nicholas, who spoke French naturally and Russian unnaturally. She held herself remarkably straight and, in moving her hands, did not take her elbows away from her waist. She was calm and somewhat sadly respectful to her husband, and exceedingly gracious to her guests, though with different shades of attention, according to the persons. She received Nekhlyúdov like one of her own, with that peculiar, refined, imperceptible flattery, which brought back to Nekhlyúdov the consciousness of all his worth and gave him a pleasurable satisfaction. She made him feel that she knew his honest, though odd, act which had brought him to Siberia, and that she regarded him as an exceptional man. This subtle flattery and all the artistically luxurious appointments in the house of the general had the effect of making Nekhlyúdov surrender himself to the pleasure of the beautiful surroundings and the appetizing food and to the ease and charm of relations with well-brought-up people of his familiar circle, as though everything, amidst which he had lived heretofore, had been a dream, from which he had awakened to the present reality.

Tolstoy
Resurrection
page 388

At dinner there were, besides the family—the general's daughter with her husband, and the adjutant—an Englishman, a rich gold dealer, and the governor of a distant Siberian city. All these people were pleasant to Nekhlyúdov.

The Englishman, a healthy, ruddy man, who spoke French very poorly but English with remarkable fluency and oratorical impressiveness, had seen a great deal, and was very interesting with his stories of America, India, Japan, and Siberia.

The young gold dealer, the son of a peasant, in evening dress which had been made in London and diamond cuff-buttons, who had a large library, gave much to charities, and held European-type liberal views, was agreeable and interesting to Nekhlyúdov because to him he represented an entirely new and good type of an educated graft of European culture on healthy peasant stock.

The governor of the remote Siberian city was that same director of a department of whom there was so much talk when Nekhlyúdov was in St. Petersburg. He was a puffed-up man with scanty curling hair, tender blue eyes, large around his waist, with well-kept white, ring-bedecked hands, and a pleasant smile. The host esteemed this governor because, among bribe-takers, he was the only one who did not receive bribes. The hostess, a great lover of music and herself a very good pianist, esteemed him because he was a good musician and played duets with her. Nekhlyúdov was in such a benevolent frame of mind that even this man was not disagreeable to him to-day.

The merry, energetic adjutant, with his grayish blue chin, who offered his services to everybody, was pleasing for his good nature.

Most agreeable to Nekhlyúdov was the charming couple—the general's daughter and her husband. She was a homely, simple-hearted woman, all absorbed in her first two children; her husband, whom she had married for love, after a long struggle with her parents, a graduate of Moscow University and a liberal, a modest and intelligent man, served in the department of statistics, busying himself particularly with the native tribes, whom he studied and loved, and whom he tried to save from extinction.

Not only were they all kind and gracious to Nekhlyúdov, but they were obviously glad to see him, as a new and interesting person. The general, who came out to the dinner in his military coat, with a white cross on his neck, greeted Nekhlyúdov as an old acquaintance, and immediately invited him over to the appetizers and vodka. To the general's question of what Nekhlyúdov had been doing since he left him, Nekhlyúdov told him that he had gone to the post-office, where he learned of the pardon granted to the person of whom they had been speaking in the morning, and he now again asked permission to visit the prison.

The general, apparently dissatisfied to hear him speak of business at dinner, frowned and did not say anything.

"Do you wish some vodka?" he said in French to the Englishman, who had come up to them. The Englishman drank the vodka and said that he had visited the cathedral and factory to-day, but that he would still like to see the large prison for transients.

"Now, this is excellent," said the general, turning to Nekhlyúdov—"you can go together. Give them a permit," he said to the adjutant.

"When do you want to go there?" Nekhlyúdov asked the Englishman.

"I prefer to visit prisons in the evening," said the Englishman. "They are all at home, no preparations are made, and everything is natural."

"Ah, he wants to see it in all its glory? Let him. When I wrote, they paid no attention to me, so let them hear about it from the foreign press," said the general, going up to the table, where the hostess pointed out the places to the guests.

Nekhlyúdov sat between the hostess and the Englishman. Opposite him sat the general's daughter and the ex-director of the department.

At table the conversation went on by fits, now about India, of which the Englishman told something, now of the Tonkin expedition, which the general criticized severely, and now of universal Siberian rascality and bribery. None of these conversations interested Nekhlyúdov very much.

But after dinner, when they were at coffee in the drawing-room, a very interesting conversation was started between the Englishman and the hostess in regard to Gladstone, during which Nekhlyúdov thought he had made many a clever remark, and that this had been noticed by the others. Nekhlyúdov felt more and more comfortable, after the good dinner and wine, at coffee, seated in a soft arm-chair, amidst kind and well-brought-up people. And when the hostess, in reply to the Englishman's request, sat down at the piano with the ex-director of the department, and played Beethoven's Fifth Symphony, which they had well practised together, Nekhlyúdov became conscious of a spiritual condition of complete self-contentment, such as he had not experienced for a long time, as though he had now for the first time discovered what a good man he was.

The piano was an excellent grand, and the performance of the symphony was good. At least, Nekhlyúdov thought so, and he loved and knew that symphony. When he heard the beautiful andante, he felt a tickling in his nose, being touched by the contemplation of himself and all his virtues.

Thanking the hostess for a pleasure he had so long not enjoyed, Nekhlyúdov was on the point of saying good-bye and leaving when the daughter of the hostess walked over to him with a determined look and, blushing, said:

"You have been asking about my children. Would you like to see them?"

"She thinks that everybody is interested in seeing her children," said the mother, smiling at the sweet tactlessness of her daughter. "The prince is not at all interested in this."

"On the contrary, I am very, very much interested," said Nekhlyúdov, touched by this happy, ebullient maternal feeling. "Please, do show them to me!"

"She is taking the prince to see her young brood," the general shouted, laughing, from the card-table, where he was sitting with his son-in-law, the gold dealer, and the adjutant. "Go do your duty!"

In the meantime the young woman, apparently agitated because her children would soon be subject to criticism, rapidly walked ahead of Nekhlyúdov to the inner apartments. In a third high room, papered white and lighted by a small lamp with a dark shade, stood, side by side, two little beds, and between them, in a white cape, sat a Siberian nurse with a good-natured face and high cheek-bones. The nurse got up and bowed. The mother bent down to the first bed, in which, with her mouth open, a two-year-old girl with long, wavy hair, dishevelled by the pillow, was softly sleeping.

"This is Kátya," said the mother, adjusting the blue-striped quilt coverlet, from underneath which peeped out a tiny white foot. "Isn't she pretty? She is only two years old."

"Charming!"

"And this is Vasyúk, as his grandfather calls him. An entirely different type. He is a Siberian—don't you think so?"

"A beautiful boy," said Nekhlyúdov, looking at the chubby little boy, sleeping on his stomach.

"Really?" said the mother, with a significant smile.

Nekhlyúdov recalled the chains, the shaven heads, the brawls, the debauch, dying Kryltsóv, Katyúsha with all her past—and he became envious and wished happiness for himself just as refined and pure as this now seemed to him to be.

Having praised the children several times, and thus having partly satisfied the mother, who eagerly drank up all these praises, he followed her back to the drawing-room, where the Englishman was waiting for him, in order, as they had agreed, to go to the prison together. Nekhlyúdov bade the old and the young hosts good-bye and with the Englishman went out on the porch of the general's house.

The weather had changed. A heavy snow was falling in large flakes and had already covered the road, and the roof, and the trees of the garden, and the driveway, and the top of the carriage, and the horse's back. The Englishman had his own carriage, and Nekhlyúdov, having told the Englishman's coachman to drive to the prison, seated himself in his own cab and, with a heavy sensation of performing an unpleasant duty, followed him in his own carriage, which rolled softly but with difficulty over the snow.

CHAPTER XXV

A DECISIVE TALK WITH KATYÚSHA

The gloomy prison building, with the sentry and lamp near the gate, in spite of the pure, white shroud which now covered everything—the driveway, the roof, and the walls—produced by the lighted windows of its façade an even more melancholy impression than in the morning.

The majestic superintendent came out to the gate, and, reading by the light of the lamp the pass which had been given to Nekhlyúdov and the Englishman, shrugged his mighty shoulders in perplexity, but obeyed orders and invited the visitors to follow him. He first led them into the yard, then through a door on the right and up the stairs to the office. He asked them to be seated, and wanted to know what he could do for them. Upon learning that Nekhlyúdov wished to see Máslova he sent a warden for her and got ready to answer the questions which the Englishman began to put through Nekhlyúdov.

"For how many persons is the prison intended?" asked the Englishman. "How many inmates are there now? How many men? How many women and children? How many hard-labour convicts, deportation prisoners, and followers? How many sick?"

Nekhlyúdov translated the words of the Englishman and of the superintendent without entering into their meaning, as he was, quite unexpectedly to himself, agitated by the impending meeting. When, in the middle of a sentence which he was translating to the Englishman, he heard approaching steps and the door of the office was opened and, as had happened often before, the warden entered, and, after him, Katyúsha, in a prisoner's bodice and wrapped in a kerchief—upon seeing her, he was overcome by an oppressive sensation.

"I want to live; I want a family, children; I want a human existence," flashed through his mind just as she walked into the room with rapid steps, without raising her eyes.

He arose and took a few steps toward her. Her face seemed stern and disagreeable to him. She was the same as she had been when she had reproached him. She blushed and turned pale; her fingers convulsively twirled the edge of her jacket; sometimes she looked into his face, sometimes, again, looked down.

"Do you know that the pardon came through?" said Nekhlyúdov.

"Yes, the warden told me."

"So, as soon as the papers are received, you may leave and settle where you please—We will think it over—"

She hastened to interrupt him:

"What have I to think about? I will go wherever Vladímir Ivánovich will be."

Notwithstanding her agitation, her eyes raised to Nekhlyúdov's, she said this rapidly and clearly, as though she had prepared it all in advance.

"Indeed!" said Nekhlyúdov.

"Why not, Dmítri Ivánovich? If he wants me to live with him—" She stopped, frightened, and corrected herself, "to be with him. What can there be better for me? I must regard it as my good fortune. What else can I do?"

"One of two things is the case: either she loves Simonsón and does not care for the sacrifice which I imagined I was bringing her, or she still loves me and for my own good renounces me and burns her ships by uniting her fate with that of Simonsón," thought Nekhlyúdov, and he felt ashamed. He was conscious of blushing.

"If you love him—" he said.

"It is not a question of love. I have given that up long ago. Besides, Vladímir Ivánovich is quite a different man."

"Yes, of course," began Nekhlyúdov. "He is a fine man, and I think—"

She again interrupted him, as though fearing lest he should say too much, or she, not enough.

"Dmítri Ivánovich, you must forgive me for not doing what you want," she said, looking into his eyes with her mysterious, squinting glance. "Obviously this is how it must be. You, too, have to live."

She told him exactly what he had just been saying to himself. But now he was no longer thinking of this; he was thinking and feeling something quite different. He was not only ashamed, but sorry for everything he was losing in her.

"I did not expect this," he said.

"Why should you live here and torture yourself? You have suffered enough."

"I have not suffered; I was happy here, and I should like to serve you more, if I could."

"We," she said, "*we*," and she looked at Nekhlyúdov, "do not need anything. You have done enough for me as it is. If it were not for you—" she wanted to say something but her voice quivered.

"You have nothing to thank me for," said Nekhlyúdov.

"What is the use trying to add it up? God will do that for us," she muttered, and her black eyes glistened with tears that had appeared there.

"What a good woman you are!" he said.

"I good?" she said through tears, a pitiful smile lighting up her face.

"*Are you ready?*" the Englishman asked, in the meantime.

"*Directly,*" Nekhlyúdov answered, and asked her about Kryltsóv.

She overcame her agitation, and quietly told him what she knew: Kryltsóv had become very feeble on the road, and immediately after their arrival had been placed in the hospital. Márya Pávlovna was very much disturbed about him and asked to be transferred to the hospital as a nurse, but they would not have her.

"I had better go," she said, noticing that the Englishman was waiting for him.

"I do not say good-bye—I will see you again," said Nekhlyúdov, giving her his hand.

"Forgive me," she said, almost inaudibly. Their eyes met, and in the strange, squinting glance and pitiful smile, with which she said "forgive me," instead of "good-bye," Nekhlyúdov read that of the two propositions as to the cause of her decision the second was the correct one—that she loved him and thought that, by uniting herself with him, she would ruin his life, but that, by going away with Simonsón, she freed him, and now was glad to accomplish what she wished and, at the same time, suffered in parting from him.

She pressed his hand, swiftly turned around, and walked out.

Nekhlyúdov looked back at the Englishman, ready to go with him, but the Englishman was writing something down in his note-book. Nekhlyúdov did not disturb him, but sat down on a wooden bench which was standing near the wall, and suddenly experienced a terrible fatigue. He was not tired from a sleepless night, nor from the journey, nor from agitation; he simply felt that his whole life had made him dreadfully tired. He leaned against the back of the bench on which he was sitting and immediately fell into a deep, heavy sleep.

"Well, would you like to visit the cells now?" asked the superintendent.

Nekhlyúdov awoke and wondered where he was. The Englishman had finished his notes and wished to see the cells. Nekhlyúdov followed them, tired and listless.

CHAPTER XXVI

THE ENGLISHMAN DISTRIBUTES
THE GOSPELS

Having passed through the vestibule and the nauseating corridor, where, to their surprise, they found two prisoners urinating straight on the floor, the superintendent, the Englishman, and Nekhlyúdov, accompanied by wardens, entered the first cell of the convicts. In this cell, with benches in the middle, all the prisoners were already lying down. There were seventy of them. They lay head to head and side to side. At the appearance of the visitors, all jumped up, rattling their chains, and stood up near the benches, glistening with their half-shaven heads. Only two were left lying. One was a young man, who was red in his face and apparently in a fever; the other was an old man, who did not stop groaning.

The Englishman asked how long the young prisoner had been ill. The superintendent said that he had been ill since morning, while the old man had long been suffering from pains in his stomach, but that there was no other place for him because the hospital was overcrowded. The Englishman shook his head in disapproval and said that he should like to say a few words to these men and asked Nekhlyúdov to translate what he would say to them. It turned out that the Englishman, in addition to the one purpose of his journey—the description of the places of deportation and confinement in Siberia, had also another aim, and that was to preach salvation by faith and redemption.

"Tell them that Christ pitied and loved them," he said, "and died for them. They will be saved if they believe this." While he was saying this, all the prisoners stood in silence near the benches, with their hands hanging down at their sides. "In this book, tell them," he concluded, "it tells all about it. Are there any among them who can read?"

It turned out that there more than twenty who could read. The Englishman took a few bound copies of the New Testament out of a hand-bag, and the muscular hands, with strong, black nails, were stretched out toward him, pushing each other away. He left two Gospels in this cell and went to the next.

In the next cell it was the same. There was the same closeness and stench. Just as in the other, an icon was hanging in front between two windows, and to the left of the door stood the stink-vat, and all lay in the same way, close together and side by side, and they all jumped up and arrayed themselves in the same manner, and, similarly, three persons remained lying down. Two of these raised themselves and sat up, but one remained lying and did not even look at the visitors: these were the sick. The Englishman repeated his speech and again distributed two Gospels.

Noise and cries came from the third room. The superintendent pounded on the door and cried, "Silence!" When the door was opened the visitors again found the prisoners standing erect beside their benches, with the exception of a few who were ill and two who were fighting; the faces of these two were distorted with anger and they were clutching each other—one by the hair, the other by the beard. Only when the superintendent ran over to them did they let go. One of them who had been given a blow on the nose was dripping blood, snot, and saliva, which he wiped on the sleeve of his kaftan. The other was picking up the hair that had been wrenched out of his beard.

"Monitor!" shouted the superintendent severely.

A strong and handsome man stepped forward.

"I couldn't tear them apart, your Honour," he said with a lively twinkle in his eyes.

"I'll show them!" said the superintendent, frowning.

"*What did they fight for?*" asked the Englishman.

Nekhlyúdov asked the monitor.

"One of them stole the other's rags," said the monitor, still smiling. "This one pushed him, and the other paid him back."

Nekhlyúdov translated to the Englishman.

"I'd like to say a few words to them," said the Englishman to the superintendent.

Nekhlyúdov translated. "You may," said the superintendent and the Englishman took out a Testament with a leather binding.

"Please translate this," he said to Nekhlyúdov: "You have had an argument and come to blows, but Christ, who died for us, has given us another means of settling our disputes. Ask them if they know, according to Christ's precepts, how we are to deal with those who do us wrong?"

Nekhlyúdov translated the Englishman's words and question.

"Complain to the chief; he'll settle things, is that it?" asked one of the belligerents, casting a sidelong glance at the superintendent's imposing figure.

"Give him a sock in the jaw, then he'll leave you alone the next time," said the other.

A titter of approval passed through the room.

Nekhlyúdov translated their answers.

"Tell them that, according to Christ's precepts, they ought to behave in just the opposite way; if you receive a slap on one cheek, turn the other," said the Englishman, demonstrating by turning his cheek.

Nekhlyúdov translated.

"Let him try it himself," came a voice.

"And what if it's not your cheek he slaps? What are you to turn then?" asked one of the sick prisoners.

"Then he'll bang you up from top to toe."

"Let him try it!" said someone with a loud guffaw. The entire room was caught up in a burst of laughter; even the man with the bloody nose laughed through the blood and the snot, and the sick prisoners joined in.

Tolstoy
Resurrection
page 396

But the Englishman was not abashed. He asked Nekhlyúdov to tell them that the doing of things which seem impossible becomes possible and a pleasure for those who are true believers.

"Ask them if they drink," he said.

"Don't they, just!" came a voice that was followed by snorts and another burst of laughter.

In the third cell there were four sick people. To the Englishman's question why it was that the sick were not put together in one room, the superintendent answered that they did not wish it themselves. These patients, he said, were not suffering from infectious diseases, and the medical assistant was watching them and looking after them.

"He has not shown up for two weeks," said a voice.

The superintendent did not answer and led them to the next room. The door was again unlocked, and again all arose and grew silent, and again the Englishman distributed Gospels; the same took place in the fifth and sixth cells, on the right and left, on both sides.

From the hard-labour convicts they went over to the exiled prisoners, and from the exiled prisoners to the prisoners from the communes and to those who followed voluntarily. It was the same everywhere. Everywhere the same cold, hungry, idle, diseased, humiliated, confined people looked like wild beasts.

Having distributed a set number of Gospels, the Englishman did not give away any more, and did not even make his speech. The oppressive spectacle and, chiefly, the stifling atmosphere apparently undermined even his energy, and he went from cell to cell, saying only, "*All right*," to all the remarks of the superintendent about the prisoners of each cell. Nekhlyúdov walked around as if in a dream, having no strength to excuse himself and go away, and experiencing all the time the same fatigue and hopelessness.

CHAPTER XXVII

KRYLTSÓV AT REST

In one of the cells of the exiles, Nekhlyúdov, to his surprise, saw the strange old man whom he had seen on the ferry in the morning. This old man, all wrinkled and with shaggy hair, dressed in nothing but a dirty ash-coloured shirt with holes at the shoulder and trousers of the same description, was sitting barefooted on the floor near the benches and casting a stern, interrogative glance at the strangers. His emaciated body, which could be seen through the holes in his shirt, looked wretched and weak, but his face looked even more earnestly concentrated and animated than on the ferry. All the prisoners jumped up, as in the other cells, and stood erect at the sight of the entering officers; but the old man remained sitting. His eyes sparkled, and his eyebrows frowned in anger.

"Get up!" the superintendent cried to him.

The old man did not stir and only smiled contemptuously.

"Your servants are standing before you, but I am not your servant. You have the seal—" muttered the old man, pointing to the superintendent's forehead.

"What?" the superintendent cried threateningly, moving toward him.

"I know this man," Nekhlyúdov hastened to say. "What has he been arrested for?"

"The police sent him up for having no passport. We ask them not to send them, but they continue doing so," the superintendent said, angrily looking askance at the old man.

"You, I see, are also of the legion of the Antichrist," the old man turned to Nekhlyúdov.

"No, I am a visitor," said Nekhlyúdov.

"Well, have you come to see how the Antichrist tortures people? All right, look! He has taken up a lot of people and has shut a whole army up in a cage. People ought to eat their bread in the sweat of their brows, and he has shut them up like pigs and feeds them without work so as to make beasts of them."

"What does he say?" asked the Englishman.

Nekhlyúdov told him that the old man condemned the superintendent for keeping people under restraint.

"What, then, ask him, is to be done with those who transgress the law?" asked the Englishman.

Nekhlyúdov translated the question.

The old man laughed out strangely, displaying two full rows of teeth.

"The law!" he repeated, contemptuously. "First he has robbed everybody, the whole earth, has taken away the riches of all the people, has turned it to his own uses, has beaten all such as went out against him, and then he wrote a law not to rob and kill. He ought to have written that law before."

Nekhlyúdov translated. The Englishman smiled.

"Still, ask him what is to be done now with thieves and murderers? Ask him!"

Nekhlyúdov again translated the question. The old man frowned austerely.

"Tell him to take the seal of the Antichrist away from him, then there will be no thieves and murderers. Tell him so!"

"*He is crazy!*" said the Englishman, when Nekhlyúdov had translated for him the words of the old man, and, shrugging his shoulders, he went out of the cell.

"You do your duty, and leave them alone! Everybody for himself. God knows whom to punish and whom to pardon, but we do not," said the old man. "Be your own master, then there will be no need of masters. Go, go," he added, scowling and flashing his eyes at Nekhlyúdov, who was lagging behind in the cell. "You have seen how the servants of the Antichrist feed lice on human beings. Go, go!"

When Nekhlyúdov came out into the corridor, the Englishman and the superintendent were standing at the open door of an empty cell, the Englishman asking the meaning of that cell. The superintendent explained to him that it was the dead-house.

"Oh," said the Englishman, when Nekhlyúdov had translated it to him, and expressed his desire to walk in.

The dead-house was an ordinary, small cell. A small lamp was burning on the wall; it dimly lighted up some bags and wood lying in a corner and four dead bodies lying on benches, to the right. The first body, in a hempen shirt and trousers, was that of a tall man with a small, pointed beard and half of his head shaven. The body had already become stiff; the ash-gray hands had apparently been placed over the breast, but they had fallen apart; the feet, too, had fallen apart and had their soles turned in different directions. Next to him lay a barefooted, bareheaded old woman, in a white skirt and jacket, with a short braid of scanty hair, a small, wrinkled, yellow face, and a sharp nose. Then, beyond the old woman, there was another male body in something lilac-coloured. This colour reminded Nekhlyúdov of something.

He walked over closer and began to look at it.

A small, sharp, upturned little beard; a strong, handsome nose; a white, tall forehead; scanty, wavy hair. He recognized the familiar features and did not believe his own eyes. Yesterday he had seen that face agitated, provoked, suffering. Now it was quiet, motionless, and terribly beautiful.

Yes, it was Kryltsóv, or, at least, that vestige which his material existence had left behind.

"Why did he suffer? Why did he live? Does he understand it now?" thought Nekhlyúdov, and it seemed to him that there was no answer, that there was nothing but death, and he felt ill.

Without bidding the Englishman good-bye, Nekhlyúdov asked the warden to take him out into the courtyard, and, feeling the necessity of being left alone, in order to think over everything which he had experienced that evening, he drove back to the hotel.

CHAPTER XXVIII

NEKHLYÚDOV ON THE
THRESHOLD OF A NEW LIFE

Nekhlyúdov did not go to bed, but for a long time paced up and down in the room. His affair with Katyúsha was over. He was of no use to her, and this made him sad and ashamed. But it was not this that now tormented him. His other affair was not only not over but tormented him more than ever before and demanded his activity.

All that terrible evil which he had seen and experienced during all that time, but especially on this day in this horrible prison, all that evil which had killed kind Kryltsóv too, triumphed and lorded it, and he could see no possibility of subduing it, not even of understanding how to subdue it.

In his imagination arose those incarcerated in the foul air, those hundreds and thousands of degraded people, who were confined by indifferent generals, prosecutors, and superintendents; he recalled the strange, free old man, who had attacked the authorities and who was declared a lunatic, and, among the corpses, the beautiful, wax-like, angry face of dead Kryltsóv. And his previous question—whether he, Nekhlyúdov, was insane, or those people who considered themselves wise and who did all those things were insane—arose before him with renewed force and demanded an answer.

He grew tired of walking up and down and of thinking. He sat down on the sofa before the lamp and mechanically opened the Gospel which the Englishman had given him as a souvenir and which, when looking for something in his pockets, he had thrown out on the table. "They say that here is the solution of everything," he thought, and, opening the Gospel, he began to read at the place where he had opened the book. Matthew, chapter 18:

1. At the same time came the disciples unto Jesus, saying, Who is the greatest in the kingdom of heaven?

2. And Jesus called a little child unto him, and set him in the midst of them,

3. And said, Verily I say unto you, Except ye be converted, and become as little children, ye shall not enter into the kingdom of heaven.

4. Whosoever therefore shall humble himself as this little child, the same is greatest in the kingdom of heaven.

Book Three

Resurrection

page 399

"Yes, yes, that is so," he thought, recalling how he had experienced calm and the joy of life only in measure as he had humbled himself.

5. And whoso shall receive one such little child in my name, receiveth me.

6. But whoso shall offend one of these little ones which believe in me, it were better for him that a millstone were hanged about his neck, and that he were drowned in the depth of the sea.

Tolstoy

Resurrection

page 400

"Why does it say here, *Whoso shall receive*? and where will he receive? and what means, *In my name*?" he asked himself, feeling that these words did not mean anything to him. "And why a millstone about the neck, and the depth of the sea? No, that is not quite right: it is not exact, not clear," he thought, recalling how he had several times tried to read the Gospel, and how the indefiniteness of such passages had repelled him. He read the seventh, eighth, ninth, and tenth verses about the offences, and how they must come, of the punishment by being cast into hell fire, and of the angels of children, who in heaven behold the face of the Father. "What a pity that this is all so incoherent," he thought, "while one feels that there is something good in it!" He continued to read:

11. For the Son of man is come to save that which was lost.

12. How think ye? if a man have an hundred sheep, and one of them be gone astray, doth he not leave the ninety and nine, and goeth into the mountains and seeketh that which is gone astray?

13. And if so be that he find it, verily I say unto you, he rejoiceth more of that sheep, than of the ninety and nine which went not astray.

14. Even so it is not the will of your Father which is in heaven, that one of these little ones should perish.

"Yes, it was not the will of the Father that they should perish, but there they are, perishing by the hundreds and thousands. And there is no means of saving them," he thought.

21. Then came Peter to him, and said, Lord, how oft shall my brother sin against me, and I forgive him? till seven times?

22. Jesus saith unto him, I say not unto thee, Until seven times; but, Until seventy times seven.

23. Therefore is the kingdom of heaven likened unto a certain king, which would take account of his servants.

24. And when he had begun to reckon, one was brought unto him, which owed him ten thousand talents:

25. But forasmuch as he had not to pay, his lord commanded him to be sold, and his wife, and children, and all that he had, and payment to be made.

26. The servant therefore fell down, and worshipped him, saying, Lord, have patience with me, and I will pay thee all.

27. Then the lord of that servant was moved with compassion, and loosed him, and forgave him the debt.

28. But the same servant went out, and found one of his fellow-servants which owed him an hundred pence; and he laid hands on him, and took him by the throat, saying, Pay me that thou owest.

29. And his fellow-servant fell down at his feet, and besought him, saying, Have patience with me, and I will pay thee all.

30. And he would not; but went and cast him into prison, till he should pay the debt.

31. So when his fellow-servants saw what was done, they were very sorry, and came and told unto their lord all that was done.

32. Then his lord, after that he had called him, said unto him, O thou wicked servant, I forgave thee all that debt, because thou desiredst me:

33. Shouldst not thou also have had compassion on thy fellow-servant, even as I had pity on thee?

"And only this?" Nekhlyúdov suddenly exclaimed aloud, as he read these words. And the inner voice of his whole being said: "Only this."

And there happened with Nekhlyúdov what often happens with people who live a spiritual life, namely, the thought which at first had appeared to him as strange and paradoxical, even as jocular, having ever more frequently found confirmation in life, suddenly arose before him as the simplest, incontrovertible truth. Thus, the thought became clear to him that the only sure means of saving people from that terrible evil from which they were suffering was for people to acknowledge themselves guilty before God and therefore incapable of punishing or correcting others. It now became clear to him that all that terrible evil which he had witnessed in jails and prisons, and the calm self-confidence of those who committed this evil, originated in the fact that people tried to do the impossible: being evil, to correct evil. Vicious people tried to correct vicious people, and they thought they could do so by mechanical means. All that came of it was that needy and selfish men, having made a profession of this supposed punishment and correction of people, have themselves become corrupted to the last degree and were not stopping corrupting those whom they tormented. Now it became clear to him what was the cause of all the horrors which he had seen and what was to be done in order to destroy them. The answer, which he had been unable to find, was the same that Christ had given to Peter: it consisted in the injunction to forgive always, everybody, an endless number of times, because there were no people who were guiltless themselves and who therefore could punish or correct.

"It just cannot be so simple," Nekhlyúdov said to himself, and yet he saw beyond any doubt that—however strange it had seemed to him in the beginning, being used to the opposite—it was unquestionably not only a theoretical, but also the most practical solution of the question. The customary retort about what was to be done with evil-doers, whether they were to be left unpunished, no longer disturbed him.

This retort would have meaning if it could be proved that punishment diminishes crime and corrects the transgressors; but when the very opposite is the fact, and when it is seen that it is not in the power of one set of men to correct another, then the only sensible thing to do is to stop doing what is not only useless but also harmful, and, in addition, immoral and cruel. For several centuries you have been executing people you term criminals. Well, have they been abolished? They have not only not been abolished, but their numbers have increased, by those transgressors who are corrupted by punishment, and by those transgressing judges, prosecutors, examining magistrates, jailers, who sit in judgment over people and punish them. Nekhlyúdov now understood that society and order in general existed not because there are these legalized transgressors, who judge and punish people, but because, in spite of such corruption, people do not cease pitying and loving each other.

Hoping to find confirmation of this thought in this Gospel, Nekhlyúdov began to read it from the beginning. Having read the Sermon on the Mount, which had always touched him, he for the first time now saw in this sermon not abstract beautiful thoughts, presenting for the most part exaggerated and unrealizable demands, but simple, clear, and practical injunctions, which, in case of their fulfillment (which was quite possible), would establish a wonderful new order of human society in which all the violence which made Nekhlyúdov so irritated was not only eliminated, but also the greatest possible human good was obtained—the kingdom of God on earth.

There were five such injunctions.

First injunction (Matt. v. 21–26). This was that one must not only not kill his brother, but not even be angry with him; he must not regard any one as insignificant, "Raca"; and that if he quarrelled with any one, he must be reconciled before offering a gift to God, that is, before praying.

Second injunction (Matt. v. 27–32). This was that man must not only not commit adultery, but must also avoid the enjoyment of a woman's beauty, and having once come together with a woman, he must not be false to her.

Third injunction (Matt. v. 33–37). This was that man must not promise anything with oaths.

Fourth injunction (Matt. v. 38–42). This was that man must not only not demand an eye for an eye, but must also turn the other cheek when smitten on one; that he must forgive offences and in humility bear them, and never refuse people that which they ask of him.

Fifth injunction (Matt. v. 43–48). This was that man must not only not hate his enemies and not fight with them, but he must love, help, and serve them.

Nekhlyúdov stared at the light of the burning lamp and stood as though petrified. Recalling the ugliness of our life, he vividly imagined what this life might be if people were brought up under these rules, and a long-forgotten transport took possession of his soul, as though, after long pining and suffering, he had suddenly found peace and freedom.

He did not sleep all night, and, as happens with many many people who read the Gospel, he for the first time understood now, in all their significance, the words which had been read many a time without leaving any impression. As a sponge sucks in water, so he imbibed everything necessary, important, and joyful, which was revealed to him in this book. And everything which he read seemed familiar to him, seemed to confirm and bring into consciousness what he had known long ago but did not completely become conscious of or believe. Now he both knew and believed.

But he not only knew and believed that, by executing these injunctions, people would attain the highest possible good; he also knew and believed that a man had nothing else to do than to carry out these injunctions, that in this lay the only sensible meaning of human life, and that every deviation from it was a mistake which immediately brought punishment in its wake. This flowed from the whole teaching and was, with special clearness, expressed in the parable of the vineyards. The husbandmen imagined that the vineyard, where they had been sent to work for their master, was their property; that everything in the vineyard was made for them, and all that they had to do was to enjoy themselves in this vineyard, forgetting their master, and killing those who reminded them of their master and of their obligations to him.

"Just so we act," thought Nekhlyúdov, "living in the insipid conviction that we are ourselves the masters of our life, and that it was given us for our enjoyment. This is obviously foolish. If we have been sent here, this was done by somebody's will and for a certain purpose. We, however, have decided that we are living for our own joy, and apparently we are suffering for it, as will the husbandman who is not doing the will of his master. But the master's will is expressed in these injunctions. Let the people execute these injunctions, and there will be on earth the kingdom of God, and people will attain the highest good, which is within their reach."

But seek ye first the kingdom of God, and his righteousness; and all these things shall be added unto you. We are seeking "all these things" and obviously do not find them.

"So this is the work of my life. One thing has ended, and another has begun."

With that night there began for Nekhlyúdov an entirely new life, not so much because he entered it under new conditions, as because everything which happened to him after that assumed an entirely new meaning. The future will show how this new period of his life will end.